just friends

Camilla is an engineer turned writer after she quit her job to follow her husband on an adventure abroad.

She's a cat lover, coffee addict, and shoe hoarder. Besides writing, she loves reading—duh!—cooking, watching bad TV, and going to the movies—popcorn, please. She's a bit of a foodie, nothing too serious. A keen traveler, Camilla knows mosquitoes play a role in the ecosystem, and she doesn't want to starve all those frog princes out there, but she could really live without them.

You can find out more about her here: www.camillaisley.com and by following her on Twitter.

@camillaisley

www.facebook.com/camillaisley

Also by Camilla Isley

<u>Romantic Comedies</u>

Stand Alones

I Wish for You
A Sudden Crush

First Comes Love Series

Love Connection
I Have Never
A Christmas Date
To the Stars and Back

<u>New Adult College Romance</u>

Just Friends Series

Let's Be Just Friends
Friend Zone
My Best Friend's Boyfriend
I Don't Want To Be Friends

just

friends

(A FRIENDS TO LOVERS BOX SET)

THE COMPLETE SERIES

BY CAMILLA ISLEY

This is a work of fiction. Names, characters, businesses, places, events and incidents either are products of the author's imagination or are used fictitiously. Any resemblance to actual events or locales or persons, living or dead, is entirely coincidental.

Copyright © 2018 Pink Bloom Press

All rights reserved.

ISBN-13: 978- 8887269222

LET'S BE JUST FRIENDS

JUST FRIENDS BOOK 1

CAMILLA ISLEY

Rose

Something woke Rose with a start. She tried to pinpoint the source of the noise, but it stopped before she could. A quick peek at the alarm clock sitting in silence on her bedside table told Rose it was only 9:00 a.m. *Good. At least two more hours to sleep.*

The noise started again just as Rose was beginning to drift off. Already half-awake, she managed to identify the sound clearly this time. It was Tyler's phone ringing in the distance. *But, where?* Not in the adjoining room where Rose assumed he was sleeping. No, the sound seemed to be coming from farther away, somewhere on the lower floor of Tyler's townhouse.

Curled under her soft covers, Rose waited for the sound of his quick footsteps down the stairs, but it never came. He must've been fast asleep, in which case she doubted the faint noise of his ringtone would be enough to wake him. Tyler was a heavy sleeper ordinarily, and he'd been out all night, or at least until three this morning when she'd gotten in. She guessed he wouldn't wake up until at least noon.

Rose waited for the phone to stop ringing so she could go back to sleep. But Tyler's vintage MC Hammer ringtone started playing again almost immediately. *Can't touch this...*

Throwing the blankets away from her, Rose sat up and swung her legs off the side of the bed. What the hell! Who was so eager to talk to Tyler this early on a Saturday morning?

Georgiana! The name popped into Rose's mind. She was the only person who'd obsessively binge-call him on a Saturday morning and not get the message people wanted to sleep. Even Tyler's mom would've given up after two missed calls. Why was Georgiana so desperate to talk to him? Did they have a huge fight? Did he finally ditch her? No, that would be too good to be true; they probably just had some kind of argument.

Rose sat on the edge of her bed, tense, listening. The phone had gone quiet again. She waited to hear if it was going to ring again and began twisting her long brown hair into a side braid. Sure enough, after a few seconds, she heard the same familiar tune. *Can't touch this...*

Irritated, she hopped off her bed, threw open her door, and stepped out onto the landing.

Tyler's door was shut. Rose pressed her right ear to the wooden panels. She heard the faint, regular breathing of someone sleeping. Listening more closely, she tried to make out the sound of a second person breathing, but she could only hear Tyler. It seemed he was alone.

Rose stepped away from the door, disappointed. So the argument had not been about Tyler cheating on Georgiana with some other girl. Rose was surprised—and a little annoyed—that Tyler had been faithful to Georgiana for as long as he had. Not that she supported the cheating, but she was eager for Georgiana to be out of their lives, and Tyler *had* cheated on every girl he'd ever been with. It was maddening that the one girl he'd decided to be faithful to was an obnoxious Regina George type.

The house fell silent again. Standing there in the hall in nothing but a turquoise tank top with a frilly trim and matching shorts, Rose shivered. Boston always seemed too cold compared to Texas, no matter the season. She would've preferred to wear an oversized sweater to bed, but last night she'd had no other choices. Busy with her Summer Academic Fellowship for Harvard Law, she hadn't bothered to do laundry in weeks. Her Victoria's Secret PINK set was the only clean thing left at the bottom of the sleepwear drawer. It was either that or two drops of Chanel number five.

Rose massaged her arms with her hands to warm herself up as she turned around, away from Tyler's door and toward the bathroom. *Might as well, since I'm already up.* She finished her business and was about to exit the bathroom when she caught herself in the mirror. Her mini-pajama fit her well. Yes, not bad at all. Pity she turned into a popsicle when she wore them.

Rose moved her gaze up to her face. Her eyes were such a dark brown as to be almost black, and her skin tone made her look constantly tanned. Not like Georgiana with her impossibly white skin, long licorice-black hair, and startling blue eyes. Did Tyler prefer blue eyes? Over the years, he hadn't shown any particular trend in his women. Tall, short, curvy, androgynous, brunette, blonde, redhead—it didn't matter to him. As long as they were attractive.

Tyler's phone began ringing again downstairs. Like an angry cat, Rose hissed at the mirror. How was she supposed to sleep if that damn thing was going to go off every five minutes? She exited the bathroom and ran down the stairs, the carpet muffling her steps.

After a quick scan of the living room—no phones in sight—she eventually located the phone in the kitchen: a shiny rectangle lying innocently on the table—lifeless. Rose looked at its black screen accusingly just as it started ringing again. Georgiana's smiling face greeted her. So it *was* her calling. Rose grabbed the phone, turned it to silent, and put it back down, relieved. Georgiana's face remained lit for a few more seconds and then disappeared.

With the phone neutralized, she could go back to her peaceful sleep-in day. But as she turned to leave, a speech bubble popped up on the screen. The temptation was too strong; Rose snatched up the phone and read it.

I'm sorry, ok? Can you please pick up?

So they definitely had an argument. And it looked like it was Georgiana's fault. What could she have done? Nothing too bad, Rose was sure. Georgiana was all sweetness with Tyler. She acted nasty only when he wasn't around, during the rare times when Georgiana and Rose were alone together.

Georgiana was jealous of her. That was the only explanation. The sentiment was strong and reciprocated, too. Georgiana didn't like the idea of her boyfriend living with his attractive female best friend. As for Rose, she didn't appreciate Georgiana's intrusion into their friendship— or the intrusion of any of Tyler's girlfriends, for that matter.

And Georgiana was more annoying than most of the girls he dated. She went to Harvard Law with them, meaning she imposed not only on their free time, but on their school time as well. In class, she sat with them—Rose on one side, Georgiana on the other, and Tyler sandwiched in the middle. At lunch, she ate with them. When they were studying, she followed them to the library. And she was at the house so often that Rose wondered if she was trying to move in without Tyler noticing. Georgiana being beautiful and rich didn't help. Nor the fact that she was the daughter of one of the most powerful and recognized lawyers in Boston, Bradley Smithson.

This was the first time since high school that Tyler had dated someone who was in school with them. Rose had forgotten how hard it was to have a daily reminder of him being with someone else. Not to mention the unwelcome novelty of being in the next room when Georgiana spent the night. Contractors should make thicker walls. It was almost like Georgiana was being a loud lover on purpose, to make sure Rose knew just how well Tyler satisfied her in bed. *Her*. Not Rose. Never Rose.

When Tyler had first started going out with Georgiana, it hadn't been so hard. Not while Rose had been with her boyfriend Marcus, her longest relationship to date. She suspected the two years she'd spent with Marcus had been Tyler's first experience with jealousy. She remembered being glad when he'd started dating Georgiana so she could finally stop feeling guilty for spending all her time with her boyfriend. Rose also hadn't told Tyler she was moving in with Marcus and hadn't been sure how he would take the news. Then everything had collapsed. Marcus had been offered a huge promotion in LA. And in less than a month, he'd left Rose heartbroken, with a canceled lease and nowhere to live. Of course, Tyler had stepped in immediately and invited Rose to stay in his spare bedroom. She'd accepted, grateful to have her best friend near her 24/7. Georgiana hadn't been happy about it.

Rose sat in a chair at the kitchen table and rolled Tyler's phone in her hands, tempted to snoop. She didn't know why, but it seemed important she found out why Tyler and Georgiana had argued. But if Tyler discovered her at it, he'd flay her. He'd always been protective of his things, especially his phone, at least with his girls, and usually with a good reason. Although lately, he'd been growing increasingly private with her, too. Rose felt left out, and she couldn't help but blame Georgiana.

Georgiana, who was sorry for something she'd done. *What was it?* She contemplated the black screen, trying to make up her mind. *To spy or not to spy?*

"What are you doing?"

Tyler's voice put a sharp end to her dilemma. He was standing at the foot of the stairs, wearing only a pair of gray sweat pants.

"Oh, you're awake, good!" Rose said, faking anger to cover her embarrassment at nearly being caught in the act. "Next time if you leave your phone lying around, do me a favor and put it on silent so it doesn't wake me up."

"Rose." There was an edge to his voice. "Why were you looking into my phone?"

"I wasn't looking into your phone." She dropped the phone on the table. "This thing has been ringing nonstop for almost an hour. I couldn't sleep, and it didn't seem like you were getting up anytime soon, so I came downstairs to silence it."

"If you were just putting the phone on silent, why were you sitting on a chair with it in your hands?"

Always the lawyer.

"I was trying to decide if your cuckoo girlfriend had ruined my sleep-in," Rose said, getting up. Her chair scraped loudly on the kitchen floor. "Or if I could go back to bed."

Rose stared him down; attack was the best defense. But would he believe her?

Tyler

Rose's aggressive tone was familiar. It was the one she used when she got caught doing something she shouldn't and wanted to steer the attention away from herself. She was *so* busted. Tyler didn't really care if she'd tried to hack his phone. Try as she might, his password was an alphanumeric nightmare, and he was sure not even the CIA would be able to crack it. One bad experience with an above-average tech savvy girlfriend had been enough to force Tyler to up his security.

Still, what business did Rose have nosing around his things? Usually, it was hysterical girlfriends who tried to hack him, not his best friend. He kept no secrets with Rose. Well, except maybe his constant arguments about her with Georgiana. Rose had never been BFF with any of his previous girlfriends, but with Georgiana, it had been hate at first sight. On both sides. Had Rose sensed she'd been the reason for their argument? But if she wanted to know, all she had to do was ask.

Tyler was planning a way to make her confess when she stood up, and he saw what she was wearing—or rather how much she wasn't. His eyes widened and his mouth dropped open. He was used to seeing his best friend in faded loose T-shirts three or four sizes too big for her. Not in mini shorts. Definitely not in mini shorts.

Rose must have noticed his staring because she blushed bright red. Yet, she didn't lower her gaze or rush off. *Weird.* Regular Rose was so shy and reserved. So much so that in the six months they'd been living together, she'd never shown more skin than that on her ankles. When she showered, she brought her clothes in the bathroom and came out already changed. He'd never even seen her in a towel. Even when she did the wash, she planted herself outside of the tiny laundry room like a watchdog. She said she didn't want him to see her underwear because it embarrassed her. So her standing there half-naked and bold was seriously freaking him out.

Frozen, Tyler watched her walk toward him.

"Anyway, Georgiana says she's sorry," Rose said, brushing past him as she continued toward the stairs. "And before you ask, no—I didn't spy. The message popped up on the screen."

Tyler followed her, not quite able to tear his eyes from her derrière as she climbed the stairs. He was shocked into silence. Seeing her like this was like being slapped in the face. He hadn't tried to sleep with her, sober or drunk, for how long now? *Two years.* Not since she'd been with Marcus, not since her last fierce refusal of his advances. That night he'd been drunk and came on to her hard. Her "no" had been equally strong, worse than an ice shower. Sobered up by her rejection, he'd never been tempted to try again. Call it a strong reality check. To him, it had become clear she wasn't interested. So Tyler had set his mind on being her friend, *just* a friend.

His reaction to her lack of clothes was a dead giveaway that he'd been kidding himself. He collapsed onto the living room couch, taking a few minutes to steady himself and reboot his brain. He'd always thought Rose was beautiful, but he'd never considered her sexy. Yet today, her outfit combined with her defiant attitude made her irresistible. He needed to know what was going on to make her act so strangely. As if pulled by an invisible rope, Tyler got to his feet and followed Rose up the stairs.

His phone remained forgotten and lonely on the kitchen table, Georgiana's face surfacing on the screen yet again.

***

At the top of the stairs, Tyler looked toward Rose's room. She'd left the door half-open. Was it an invitation?

He approached, padding quietly across the carpet, and peeked inside. Rose was lying on the bed, propped on a mound of pillows with her legs

6

stretched out and crossed at the ankles. She was playing with her phone. To his delight, she hadn't changed, or put on a sweater. His Rose, after being caught in mini shorts, would be covered head-to-toe by now. Something was definitely up with her.

Tyler knocked on the door and stepped inside without waiting for permission.

"Oh," she said, surprised. "I thought you'd be downstairs making peace with Georgiana."

"What's up with the shorts?" he asked.

She looked down at herself. "I was behind with my laundry, and this was the only clean set left."

"Weren't you against Victoria's Secret and their objectification of women?" Tyler retorted.

"I didn't buy them." Rose shrugged. "They were a present from Marcus."

She said it casually, but he knew her well. He could detect the lingering sadness hidden behind that simple response. As a loyal friend, he ought to feel sorry for the abrupt way her relationship with Marcus had ended. Instead, Tyler couldn't help but be relieved that Marcus had moved to LA and out of their lives for good. But now a new emotion had entered the mix—a fierce jealousy he'd never experienced before. He was jealous that Rose would wear something so not like herself for Marcus.

Tyler sat on the bed next to her. He took her right foot into his left hand, placed it in his lap, and started massaging her ankle. *Time to switch on the charm and make Rose talk.*

Rose

Rose was extremely aware of Tyler's thumb swirling around her ankle. How long had it been since he'd tried to sleep with her? Tyler had been "well-behaved" since that stupid night two years ago when she'd refused him in no uncertain terms. She almost flinched at the memory. At the time, she'd been so taken with Marcus that she'd been harsh with her best friend, treating him with contempt—and not in their usual playful way. Rose hoped Tyler had been drunk enough not to remember how badly she'd turned him down. But given that he hadn't tried anything ever since, not even after her breakup, some of it must've sunk in. Before that night, his cute, double-meaning jokes and her constant turning him down had let Rose believe she and Tyler weren't together by her choice. That if she only wanted, she could be his girlfriend. That he'd be different for her. But not anymore.

A tingle rose up her legs from where Tyler touched her with the tips of his fingers. It had been easier to say no to Tyler when he was hitting on her once a week. But now she was out of practice and vulnerable. Especially when he was standing in her room looking impossibly hot in sweatpants and nothing else. Rose's gaze traveled over his naked chest and down to his sculpted stomach before she forced herself to adopt a neck-and-above only view policy. Not that staring at his face helped. With messy light brown hair, gray eyes, and lips to die for, Tyler was gorgeous. And he knew it.

"So what's up with Georgiana?" Rose put her phone down and looked at Tyler expectantly.

"Oh, nothing," he replied.

"It must've been something if she felt the need to call you ten times on a Saturday morning."

"I've already told you it was nothing."

"So why was she sorry about nothing?"

"Why do you have to always insist so much when it comes to Georgiana?"

"And why are you so adamant about not telling me? You used to tell me everything!"

"I still do."

"No, you don't."

Tyler's shoulder tensed and his grip on her feet tightened. "I can't stand the two of you bickering anymore. I'm always caught in the middle."

"I've never said anything bad about Georgiana," Rose said, feeling her cheeks warm up. "But apparently she doesn't have a problem talking behind my back."

Tyler held her gaze for a few seconds before looking at the floor, embarrassed.

Comprehension dawned. "The argument, it *was* about me, wasn't it?" Rose said, leaning forward. She folded her legs, her ankle slipping away from Tyler's grip. "Why does she hate me so much?"

"Don't be melodramatic. She's just jealous, that's all."

"Why am I the only friend she's jealous about? Especially when I'm the only one you haven't slept with."

"Well, you're the only friend who lives with me. And Georgiana has this theory: the fact we haven't slept together is more meaningful than if we had. She actually said she wished we'd done it before I met her and got over it!"

"And what exactly makes Georgiana think sleeping with me would make you get over us?"

"Would it?" Tyler asked with a hint of flirtation. He raised one eyebrow and smirked, making one of his cutest, mischievous faces.

"It doesn't matter. We're not going to test it." Rose kept her sulky frown. "So, what was she going on about this time?"

Tyler released a breath. "Georgiana asked me when you were planning on moving out."

Rose shot out of the bed as if it were made of burning coals. "I didn't know I'd overstayed my welcome," she spat. It was just like Georgiana to stick her posh nose into Rose's life, where it didn't belong.

True, Rose was living in Tyler's swanky apartment without paying any rent. But only because Tyler didn't let her pay her share. To compensate, Rose did what she could. She bought most of the groceries and paid all the bills. Even though she and Tyler had never spoken about it, she thought he was fine with their arrangement. Georgiana had already made a snarky comment once to her: "How nice it must be to live rent-free in such a nice neighborhood." Rose could only imagine what other things along that line she was telling Tyler. The thought made her livid.

"I can start packing immediately." Rose moved to grab some discarded clothes from a chair.

"Rose, will you calm down?" Tyler said, grabbing her wrist and pulling her onto his lap. "I've told Georgiana to piss off."

"You know I feel guilty about not paying rent," she protested, trying to ignore the fact that she was sitting on top of him and they were both half-naked.

"And you know I don't want you to pay anything. You already sneak around and pay all the bills before I even have a chance to open them. It's more than enough."

He put his hands around her waist, making her stomach drop.

"Are you sure?" Rose asked. She needed more than just a physical assurance.

"Rose, my life has improved since you moved in with me. The fridge used to look like a war zone, but now you make sure I eat all my vegetables," he joked.

"I bet she just wants me out so *she* can move in," Rose couldn't help saying.

"As if." Tyler snorted, and the goofy sound made Rose happier than she'd been all morning.

She beamed at him, looking him straight in the eyes. Tyler stared back with a strange intensity, and suddenly, Rose's smile disappeared. He leaned in closer, slowly, and her breath caught in her throat in anticipation

Georgiana

A few miles away, in another posh neighborhood of Boston, Georgiana paced around her living room. As she circled the couch, she was seething with hatred for Rose, anger for Tyler, and resentment for Marcus. Whom she didn't exactly know, but who she was positively sure had ruined her life by moving to LA.

She tried Tyler's number again. When he didn't pick up, she threw her phone across the room and let out a growl. The phone hit an armchair and bounced off its soft cushions, landing on the carpeted floor.

This wasn't going to work. Another woman living with Tyler wasn't right. How could he not see it? What was his house, a stupid co-ed? A charity? Georgiana didn't know for sure, but since Rose and Tyler came from the same rich neighborhood in Dallas, she doubted Rose had money problems. She was just a parasite. Tyler's best friend was poison ivy, and she was sprouting roots in his house.

Why wasn't he picking up his damn phone?

Georgiana checked the time on her Rolex: 9:45 already. She'd been calling him for almost an hour now. Bracing her arms on the back of the couch, Georgiana stared out of her floor-to-ceiling windows without focusing on anything in particular. Maybe his phone was switched to silent and he hadn't heard it ring. What if Tyler was still asleep? It wasn't unusual for him to sleep late on weekends, and they'd been arguing until the small hours last night. Tyler had left her apartment at—three, four a.m.? By the time he'd gotten home and to bed, it must've been late.

That was it, she decided, Tyler was still sleeping. Nothing to worry about. Yeah, they had a row, and he'd taken Rose's side, *again,* but it would pass. It always did.

Georgiana's nervous fingers tightened their grip on the soft cushions fabric. *Men*! They could sleep through everything. Unlike her. She'd barely slept and had been forced to use all of her willpower not to call him before nine—Georgiana didn't want to come off as the hysterical girlfriend.

Anyway, Tyler asleep or not, the problem remained. Georgiana needed to weed the poisonous bitch out of her boyfriend's place. The sneaky little ho was after her man. She'd probably been since puberty. Why did Marcus have to dump Rose and give her the perfect excuse to move in with Tyler? To feed off his generosity and good nature?

If Tyler and Rose stayed under the same roof much longer, something was bound to happen. Tyler's relationship with Rose wasn't strictly brotherly—no matter how many times Tyler swore it was. Georgiana didn't believe in male-female friendships. And their body language sent a clear message: there was tension between them. The fact they hadn't done the deed yet wasn't an assurance it would not happen in the future. It was even worse, in a way. It built pressure, making Rose—the one girl Tyler had never had—too big of a temptation for him to resist.

Why did everything have to go down this way? And why now?

Georgiana felt as if a cosmic conspiracy was in place to undermine her relationship with Tyler. But she wasn't a "live and let live" kind of girl. She was used to taking action and gaining control over things. She'd even tried to convince her brother to provide a distraction for Rose as soon as she'd moved in with Tyler six months ago. Ethan, five years their senior, was drop dead gorgeous and a womanizer. But he'd refused without even meeting Rose. And now was dating one of Georgiana's best friends, Alice, so his charms were out of the picture. To hell with him, too. Georgiana needed a different plan, something final that would keep Tyler and Rose apart for good.

Georgiana turned away from the window and started pacing the apartment again in search of inspiration. It took her a few laps of the room before an idea began forming in her mind. At first, she couldn't quite grasp it. Georgiana was sure she'd overlooked something, but couldn't put her finger on what. Then, out of the blue, a possibility came to her. She needed to talk to her dad and see if he could help her.

Georgiana sprang into action. She grabbed her bag and car keys from the coffee table and hurried toward the door. Halfway there, she paused and turned around to go get her phone. She picked it up from the floor and checked the screen, only half-hoping to see if Tyler had called her back. He hadn't.

Never mind, he could wait. Right now, she had bigger fish to fry. Filled with purpose, Georgiana plonked the phone into her bag and exited her apartment. She felt strangely calm and regenerated. It was good to finally have a plan.

It'd be complicated to achieve, and she'd have to pull a lot of strings to make it work. Hard, but not impossible. And, *oh*, Rose wouldn't even know what had hit her. Georgiana opened her car and sat behind the wheel. She paused a second with her finger on the ignition button. She closed her eyes, imagining the face her rival would make when she found out. It'd be priceless. But now wasn't the time to celebrate, it was the time to set her plan in motion. To pull it off, she had to act quickly. Georgiana revved the engine and backed out of her parking spot, speeding away on the almost empty street.

Tyler

Tyler watched the smile disappear from Rose's face, dazed by her beauty. Her dark eyes sent a clear message. It wasn't his best friend staring at him, but a woman who wanted him. After all this time, would she finally give in? Today, of all days, when he'd least expect it, and when he hadn't tried one of his many stunts to seduce her?

His pulse picked up, and his skin started to burn around his neck where Rose laced her hands. Suddenly, Tyler realized where they were. In her room, on the bed, already half-naked and on top of each other.

Rose's face was only inches away from his own—one breath away. Tyler leaned in closer as if to kiss her and felt her body stiffen on his legs, but she didn't move away. Nor did she make any motion to get up. Rose's eyes widened, and she inhaled sharply, but she didn't retreat.

Tyler didn't need any more hints. This was his opportunity; he would not waste this chance and give Rose time to think about what was happening or to change her mind. He bent her backward and pressed his lips to hers.

***

Afterward, Tyler lay in Rose's bed. He was staring at the ceiling mesmerized by what had just happened, and cherishing the weight of her body on his chest as she slept. Tyler trailed a finger down her neck, to her shoulder, and down her arm. Rose shivered without waking up, and then her breathing relaxed again.

Tyler was stunned by what had just happened between them. Finally, he understood what making love meant as opposed to having sex. Everything happened spontaneously with no inhibitions. Even if it was their first time together, they knew each other too well to be shy. At least in the passion of the moment. And making love to Rose had been unique, explosive, and urgent, like taking that first breath of air after being underwater for a long time. Why had they waited so long? The last ten years seemed like a total waste of time now. But that was over. Everything would change now.

Guilt tightened his chest, the same sensation that ripped through Tyler whenever he cheated on any of his girlfriends. With Georgiana, he'd honestly thought things would be different. His girlfriend was cool, never too clingy, and—except for the subject of Rose staying with him— they never argued about anything. And now Tyler could see Georgiana had been right all along. She'd picked up on something he'd been blind to.

He'd have to break up with her at once. Tyler wasn't looking forward to that "friendly" chat. He was sure Georgiana would not make it easy for him. But there was no space left in his life for her, not now that his friendship with Rose had transformed into something new, something better…

Could it be possible he'd been in love with his best friend all these years without ever realizing it? Was this why he'd cheated in all his previous relationships? Because he'd never loved any of the girls he'd dated?

Tyler had always been attracted to Rose. But he'd always assumed it was a natural I-am-a-boy-you-are-a-girl kind of attraction. Nothing more. Today, he was no longer sure about anything. All the air had left his lungs and his heart wouldn't stop racing. Whenever he had a flashback of the past hour, his stomach contracted as if plunging down a steep rollercoaster ride. Was this what being in love felt like?

The L-word sent a thrill of fear down his spine. This was Rose in his arms; he couldn't screw this one up. He had to be cautious and take it slow, one day at a time. He looked down at her. Rose was snuggled against him, her head resting on his chest, her eyes closed. He brushed the hair away from her face to have a clear view of her beautiful, serene features as she slept.

Yep, he was in trouble.

Rose

Rose kept her eyes tightly shut, pretending she was still asleep, despite Tyler trailing a finger down her arm. She was sure the loud thuds of her heart would soon give her away, but she didn't know what to do next. After what just happened between them, was her friendship with Tyler ruined forever?

Rose was mad at herself for being so weak. Today, she hadn't been able to resist. Not with Georgiana being a bitch. Not with Marcus dumping her and leaving her as insecure as ever. And not with Tyler being Tyler.

Oh, Tyler! He was a lost cause. A romantic relationship between them was impossible. Hope for a future with Tyler had died a long time ago. Rose spent years waiting for him to change, not dating anyone, sticking around for when he'd be mature enough or for the girl of the moment to be dumped. Until she'd finally accepted he would never change.

Unbidden, her mind began a mental recap of all the girls Tyler had dated over the years. He had sex for the first time during sophomore year in high school with Amanda Lockwood, a junior. Amanda was a popular girl, and after his conquest, Tyler became the hero of the school. Despite girls finding him irresistible, he remained faithful to Amanda for a whole year; after all, she was his first. They were happy together until summer break when Amanda's nemesis, Charlotte Pierce, seduced him during summer break. With Amanda gone for a month, teenage Tyler was easy prey for Charlotte.

When Amanda found out, drama ensued. Amanda and Charlotte became the first entries on a long list of girls who would end up hating Tyler for cheating on and dumping them. By twelfth grade, Tyler was the most popular guy in school, basking in the glory of fooling around with a never-ending stream of girls.

Rose had hoped college would steady him. Instead, it sent him on an even wilder spree. In their freshman year at Harvard, Tyler slept with a different girl almost every night. Rose told herself it was only their first year; once he got it out of his system, he would be ready for something serious. Across their sophomore and junior year, hope returned briefly as Tyler stayed in a serious relationship with Jessica, an English major he'd met at the library. Tyler and Jessica were together for nine months before Tyler cheated on her, making Rose officially give up on him. If he couldn't stay true to Jessica, the closest thing he'd ever had to a long-term girlfriend, then how could Rose trust him with her own heart?

After Jessica, it had been the same story with every new girlfriend. He cheated on all of them, and they each ended up loathing him. Rose didn't want to end up loathing her best friend; he was the most important person in her life besides her parents. He was family. And she knew a romantic relationship would lead exactly to that. In the end, he'd cheat on her—if not in a year, in five, or ten. It was a given. Tyler simply wasn't a monogamist. Rose would end up bitter, with her heart shattered. Today had been a mistake, a big one. But they could fix it. They had to.

Rose stirred as if just now waking up. She looked at Tyler shyly, blushing.

"What?" she asked, self-consciously pulling the sheets around her body.

Tyler flashed her a mischievous grin. "I find it funny you choose to blush now."

"I didn't choose to, and don't look at me like that."

"Like what?"

His wolfish smile was making it impossible to keep a steady mind.

"As if you want to eat me."

"Maybe I do." Tyler bit her hand affectionately.

"Pff." Rose's face burned red, so she buried it in his chest to cover up her uneasiness. Shame attacked as she replayed the past hour in her head in an all-consuming vortex of emotions. *Oh*, the things Tyler had done to her, and the way she'd responded! It wasn't just sex—Tyler had made love to her. Or had it all been a dream?

Unable to meet his gaze yet, Rose burrowed her face deeper.

"Don't play shy, Rosalynn," Tyler said, using her full name. He planted a soft kiss on her collarbone. *No, definitely not a dream.* "After today, I won't buy it."

After today. That's the problem.

She shifted position so that he couldn't kiss her. "So…" she began.

"I know that expression, Rosalynn Atwood. It's your serious-talk one."

"Tyler. This is serious."

"What's serious?"

"Me, you, naked in bed."

"Relax, Rose. It's not the end of the world."

"No, but it could be the end of our friendship. Doesn't that scare you?"

"What do you mean?" he asked, frowning.

Tears welled in Rose's eyes. Emotions were running high, and her throat closed, making it difficult to get the words out. "I think it was a mistake."

"Why?"

"All your exes hate you."

"What's that supposed to mean?"

"You cheated on all of them."

"That's not true."

"Name one you haven't."

Tyler scrunched his face for a while and then said, "I haven't cheated on Georgiana."

"Oh, right, your girlfriend!" Hearing him say her name sent Rose into a frenzy. "The one you *just cheated on*!"

"But it was with you, so it doesn't count."

"I don't think Georgiana would agree."

Tyler shrugged, unconcerned. "I can dump her if that's what's bothering you."

"How nice of you," she replied with an edge. "Please, don't dump her on my account."

"Rose, I wouldn't cheat on you."

"How do you know?" She narrowed her eyes at him. "Do you really expect me to trust you'd be fine sleeping with me, and only with me, for the rest of your life?"

"Yes. No. What the hell do I know! I haven't even had breakfast and you're already talking marriage. Why don't we choose the name of our kids already and be done with it?"

"It's not like we can date and see how it goes, right?" Rose bit back.

"Why not? What's wrong with that?"

"Everything's wrong with that."

"Nothing's wrong with that."

"Tyler, please stop talking. You're making it worse."

"I don't get you, Rose. What do you want me to say?"

"Nothing. You've already said enough."

"Why do you girls have to go cuckoo the moment the sex is over?"

"See, Tyler, that's the problem. I'm not one of your girls, and I'll never be." Rose sat up, leaning away from him. "This was a big mistake. I wasn't thinking."

"I preferred you when you weren't."

"Well, I am now. This," she added, flipping a finger between them, "shouldn't have happened. It won't happen again." Rose gathered the bed linens around her, transforming into a human cocoon to shield her naked body from him, and further retreated to her side of the bed.

"Don't worry, Rose," Tyler said, grabbing his pants and pulling them on. "I'll get out of your way."

He jumped off the bed and was out of the room in three quick strides. He slammed the door behind him, making her chest jolt. The knot in her throat worsened.

The moment Tyler left, Rose felt dead inside. She reached out her hand to his side of the bed where the sheets were still warm from his body heat. Tears pricked her eyes again. She wasn't ready to let him go, not yet.

Still wrapped in the sheets, Rose followed him out of the room. In the hall, she paused to listen. The shower was running. Rose tried the bathroom door. *Unlocked.* Turning the knob, she pushed the door open and tiptoed into the room. As expected, Tyler was in the shower. She tapped on the glass, the sound barely audible over the water noise.

He flung the glass door open and stared at her in shock. With a pounding heart, Rose let the bed sheet drop to the floor and stepped into the shower with him. Tyler raised his eyebrows. He probably thought she was crazy. She'd just said sleeping together had been a mistake. Yet, here she was, jumping him in the shower not two minutes later.

"Today doesn't count," Rose said curtly, answering his unspoken question. She stood on tiptoes and pulled him toward her in a wet kiss.

***

The next day ended up not counting as well. And the next. And the next.

Rose and Tyler fell into a weird routine of having sex (making love?) wherever, whenever, without ever talking about it. Afterward, they pretended nothing had happened. Rose knew she was playing a dangerous game, one impossible to win. She knew Tyler wasn't ready for a serious relationship with her, but she couldn't help herself. Even if having an affair with Tyler was so wrong, for so many reasons.

For one, it put their friendship, the most important thing in her life, at stake. Then there was the obvious moral issue: Tyler still had a girlfriend. He hadn't broken up with Georgiana. And even if he didn't bring her to the house anymore, he was still with her. Was he sleeping with her too? On the odd nights when he didn't come home and stayed at her place, Rose cried herself to sleep in her room. For the next few days, she would pout and ignore Tyler, but eventually, she'd break. Then she would jump right back into his arms, and their unhealthy routine started all over.

Another week like this—another day—and she'd go crazy. The right thing to do would be to stop. But Rose didn't know how to be strong, not anymore. She'd wanted Tyler for too long to be able to keep saying no. Rose told herself she preferred to be the one he was cheating *with*, instead of the one he was cheating *on*. After a month, however, even this excuse was running thin.

True, Rose had told him he didn't have to leave Georgiana for her, but that had been ages ago! After a month of sleeping together, everything was different. How could Tyler not see it? She refused to beg him—what if he said no? What if he said *yes*? They'd get together, and then he'd cheat on her. Nothing terrified Rose more. On one hand, she wanted Tyler to leave Georgiana and be with her officially. On the other, it scared her to death. Unsure of everything else, the only thing Rose knew for a fact was that her life couldn't keep going like this.

Something had to change, soon, but Rose didn't know what, or how.

Tyler

For the first time in his life, Tyler didn't understand his best friend. How to read her, how to translate what she said as opposed to what went on inside her head. Rose had been adamant they shouldn't be together. Not unless he proposed right then and there, and he wasn't ready for that kind of commitment. At twenty-four and still in school, who the hell would be? He didn't want to be tied down already. But Rose had become a drug for him. He couldn't go back to being just her friend, and he couldn't be with her, either—not in the way she wanted.

Screwed, he was so screwed.

Georgiana was driving him mad, too. His girlfriend wasn't stupid, and she must have sensed his emotional distance. The few nights she forced him to stay at her apartment, he pretended to be tired to avoid sleeping with her, and he never invited her to the house anymore. They were arguing more often than not, and he was getting tired. And school hadn't even started yet. His love life was proving more stressful than Harvard Law. To survive one was hard, but the two combined? *Impossible*. How would he handle the pressure in less than a month when the academic year started? What would happen when he'd have to spend all his days in class squeezed between the two women in his life? It would be a disaster, no doubt. He should dump Georgiana, but the idea scared him. If he became single, what would happen with Rose? Wedding bells? And what would happen if he kept a girlfriend on the side to avoid commitment?

If he didn't do something, the situation with Rose and Georgiana was going to explode in his face. But what could he do? Tyler was stuck, strangled in a situation of his own making, with no escape in sight. He wished girls came with an instruction manual. The only thing he knew was that his life couldn't keep going like this.

Something had to change, soon, but Tyler didn't know what, or how.

Georgiana

Something was up with Tyler. No sex since the night of their fight about Rose moving out of his apartment. That was a month ago. *A month.* Whenever Georgiana tried initiating, Tyler mumbled some lame excuse about being tired. Usually, he couldn't keep his hands off her, and now nothing for a month. *Thirty. Freaking. Days.* He also made it clear she wasn't welcome at his apartment anymore. Why? What did he have to hide?

If not with her, he was sleeping with someone else. Rose? It must be that bitch. Why keep his girlfriend away from the house otherwise?

Georgiana was almost certain something had happened between them. When she finally admitted to herself that her boyfriend was cheating on her, Georgiana went to a dark place. She shut herself in her apartment without eating and without getting out of bed for two days. Tyler didn't check on her once. His conspicuous absence and indifference transformed the numbing pain in a rampaging fury. The blind rage manifested in a strong desire to burn Tyler's expensive car to the ground. She'd also been tempted to dump him without ever looking back. But then her pride took over. She discovered she didn't care if he'd cheated on her—she was in love with Tyler. He was hers, and she was ready to fight for him. She wasn't going to let that ho snatch him away from her. No matter what it took, Georgiana was determined to keep Tyler. But their relationship couldn't keep going like this.

Something had to change, soon, and Georgiana knew exactly what, and how.

Rose

"Rose, can you please pass me the ketchup bottle?" Georgiana asked, her tone so viciously polite, she might as well have said, "I know what you did."

Rose lowered her gaze. Georgiana's razor sharp blue eyes were too much for her now. "Sure." She took the red plastic bottle and handed it to Tyler's girlfriend.

Two weeks later, and not only had her "situation" with Tyler not resolved—or improved, or changed at all—now she was also having lunch with the happy couple in a cafeteria on campus. The fall semester hadn't started yet, but it was orientation period, and the campus was already buzzing with students. How in hell did this lunch happen? The three of them eating burgers together was too weird.

Tyler's text, "lunch 2gether," had been innocent enough; it didn't say, "Georgiana the Ice Queen will attend too," anywhere, not even a hint. Since their affair, Tyler had avoided any unnecessary contact between *mistress* and *girlfriend*. Rose suspected Georgiana must've orchestrated the lunch trapping them here.

But, why? Did she know? That had to be it. Georgiana knew about her and Tyler, and now she would slowly torture them until they confessed. No matter how many fake smiles Georgiana shot Rose, they never reached her cold, calculating eyes. That freezing blue gaze sent Rose a clear message, "I hate you."

Rose studied Georgiana as she sat possessively next to Tyler, eating all his fries. Did she know Rose loved eating his fries? Was her dominion over his French fries a metaphor for their love triangle? Rose hated that out in the open Tyler belonged to Georgiana, and that she, *the other woman*, was powerless about it.

"Rose," Georgiana said, still all sweetness, "do you have any plans for this coming Friday?"

"No, nothing in particular," Rose said cautiously.

This had to be an ambush or some kind of plot—Georgiana never asked about her "plans." Not to mention she was still being uncharacteristically nice. Had Tyler's girlfriend decided to kill her with kindness? Rose wasn't a fan of this sudden change; it was easier to sneak around with Tyler behind her back when Georgiana was being a bitch to her. If she considered Georgiana a nice, normal girl, then Rose's guilt would overwhelm her. The Ice Queen almost certainly had an ulterior motive.

"Oh, that's perfect!" Georgiana exclaimed. "I'm having a dinner with some friends for my birthday. I want you to be there. Will you come?"

Rose couldn't think of a polite way to say no. "Um… yeah, sure. Where?"

"Great." Georgiana's lips parted in a cruel grin. "I haven't decided yet. But you can come with Tyler straight from your house. I'll meet you there."

"Okay."

Even more peculiar. Georgiana not bugging Tyler to pick her up and instead suggesting he chauffeured Rose. Something was definitely up.

Tyler

Tyler followed the exchange, at a loss for words. He pushed his plate away, his stomach churning. What was Georgiana planning? She'd already thrown him a curve ball impossible to catch. He was trapped; what else did she need?

He should've left her when he had the chance. He should've known Georgiana wouldn't stand idly by while he was having his way with Rose. That his conniving girlfriend would fight. And she had. She'd fought and won, at least the first battle: make sure Tyler and Rose didn't share a roof. Heck, make sure they didn't live in the same continent!

Tyler smiled a bitter smile. He had to give it to Georgiana. She was resourceful. Even without proof, he was sure she had orchestrated everything. Scholarships abroad did not reopen out of the blue. Georgiana's doing or not, the damage was done, and Tyler was left with no other choice other than when to tell Rose. No turning back time at this point.

He looked at his best friend with longing. He'd have to talk to her soon, but Tyler couldn't bear the thought of losing her. And after talking to her, he'd consider himself lucky if she ever spoke two words to him again.

***

Friday night, on the way to the restaurant, Tyler still hadn't spoken to Rose. He'd vowed to do it tonight after they got back home, but maybe it had been a mistake to wait a week. It'd only make Rose angrier. And the prospect of Rose and Georgiana in the same room for a whole dinner made him nervous. An ominous feeling about the party crept up his back and settled heavily on his shoulders.

Rose sat in silence beside him, staring out the window. She was holding a tiny gift-wrapped package in her hands. He'd told her it wasn't necessary to buy Georgiana a present, but Rose had insisted. Thinking about it, he had no clue what was in the box. Something poisonous? Tyler could only hope.

At home, Rose had stunned him again. She'd emerged from her room dressed in a tight black jumpsuit with cutouts around the waist, and an almost bare back. She was also wearing black heels and a furry-leathery jacket thingy. The outfit looked like a Catwoman costume. Rose was only missing the ears, whiskers, and tail. Again, he'd never seen these clothes before. He was discovering an entirely new side of her she'd kept secret all this time. And even if it was great to see Rose in a different light, sometimes Tyler wished he were still oblivious. His life would be much simpler without the temptation.

This sort of gear must've been reserved for Marcus. Jealousy made Tyler swallow hard. He still hated Rose's ex with all his guts, but tonight the sexiness was for him, or to compete with Georgiana. To be honest, he didn't know which one.

Tyler's skittish mood worsened as they entered the restaurant. Georgiana and some of her guests were already there, sitting at a long, rectangular table laid for at least twenty people. Georgiana sat at the head of the table with an empty space on her left, followed by a couple of nicely dressed girls. On her right sat a rather plain guy followed by two other girls and another arrogant-looking dude who seemed older than everyone else. Fifteen or so empty places were left at the table.

The older guy fixated his gaze on Rose the moment she entered the door. Noticing the competition, Tyler felt an immediate, irrational surge of hatred for the stranger. For no other reason than the way he was looking at Rose, Tyler wanted to punch the dude's face.

Rose

Walking inside the restaurant, Rose watched Georgiana rise to her feet to greet them. Tyler's girlfriend looked resplendent in a short dress made of lace flowers, white from the waist up and pale pink on the skirt.

"You've made it!" she said. "Here, come meet the others." She did a quick round of introduction, starting counterclockwise and working around the whole table.

Rose stood there awkwardly, looking around at half a dozen strangers. In particular, the guy sitting at the edge of the group, who Georgiana introduced as Ethan, made her self-conscious with all his staring. Rose met his gaze shyly. He had bright, unsettling light blue eyes that looked somewhat familiar. Short black hair, high cheekbones, and a square jaw made the dude good-looking in that arrogant vampire-flick-villain kind of way.

Embarrassed by all the attention, Rose delivered her gift to Georgiana—a noncommittal makeup palette—who thanked her without opening the present. With nothing left to do, Rose wanted to shrink away and play invisible for the rest of the evening. Sitting down was the first camouflaging step. A quick scan of the table told Rose where she stood in the food chain. The seat beside Her Birthday Majesty was obviously intended for Tyler, and the ones nearest for her court. Rose didn't want to be anywhere near the couple, anyway, so she backtracked to the opposite end of the table. Georgiana protested with no real conviction that she shouldn't sit so far away, but Rose assured her majesty she'd be fine, and Georgiana didn't insist further.

Rose had a hunch about the night ending badly for her. She'd never seen Georgiana look so radiant, so smug. At this very moment, Georgiana was watching Rose with an expression in-between triumph and pity. Why? Something was happening, and Rose felt like the only clueless party present. Tyler had been behaving strangely all week, and she couldn't tell what had changed. Combining that with the evil stare above Georgiana's smiles only increased her anxiety about this party. What on earth had made her agree to come?

The moment Rose sat down, Ethan got up and whispered something in Georgiana's ear. He took his half-empty cocktail with him and moved toward Rose. The dude was tall, although maybe an inch or two shorter than Tyler. Speaking of the devil, she stole a glance at Tyler for just a second. He wore an expression of contempt on his face as he followed Ethan's movements. *Good. Serves him right to be the jealous one for a change.*

Rose looked around at the other guests and spotted another hostile gaze, only this one was targeting *her*. The blonde girl who'd been sitting next to Ethan didn't appear at all happy with his move. *Don't glare at me, lady. I didn't ask your guy to come talk to me. Is he even your guy?*

"Hello," Ethan said as he took the seat next to her. "It didn't seem right to have you sit here all alone. I'm Ethan, Georgiana's brother."

Ah, that explains why the eyes looked familiar.

"And you're Rose, right?" he continued.

"Right." She smiled at him, blushing under his piercing gaze despite herself. Was this what Tyler felt whenever Georgiana looked at him? Rose's heart sank into her chest.

Ethan

Ethan was intrigued by the faint blush that appeared on Rose's cheeks as he spoke to her. In fact, he was intrigued by everything about Rose. When his sister had begged him to seduce her boyfriend's new roommate, she'd described Rose as austere-looking, but pretty. The woman seated next to him was neither austere nor pretty. To call Rose pretty would be the understatement of the millennium. She was a dark beauty with her long brown hair, olive skin, and almost-black eyes. And to think he'd wanted to stay at the office tonight.

"So, how do you know my sister?" he asked, feigning cluelessness.

"We're at Harvard Law together, and she's dating my best friend Tyler," Rose said.

"You came here together?"

"Yeah, I'm crashing at his place until I can find one of my own. I had a lease mishap."

"What kind of mishap?" Ethan asked. Georgiana had already filled him in on the drama with the ex-boyfriend, but he wanted to see if Rose would volunteer the information.

She did. "Oh, nothing serious. My ex-boyfriend dumped me a month before we were supposed to move in together, and I'd already canceled my lease on my old place." Rose shrugged, smiling awkwardly.

Ethan realized he liked her even more after her straightforward answer.

"So, being Georgiana's brother, can I safely assume you're a lawyer?" Rose asked.

"I am afraid you can't," he said with a naughty smile.

"You didn't go to Harvard Law? I thought every offspring of the

Smithson family went to Harvard."

"I did go to Harvard Law, as did all my siblings and cousins before and after me," Ethan replied, amused by the way she'd wrinkled her nose in confusion.

"And after all that pain, you didn't become a lawyer?"

"Actually, I did."

"I don't understand," Rose said. "What happened?"

"I tried the big studio with the big cases and the long hours for a year and hated it, so I quit."

"And your father let you?"

"He had little a choice. I'm over eighteen, you know."

"You stood up to Bradley Smithson. I'm impressed."

Ethan roared with laughter. "To me, he's just Dad."

"So he didn't make a fuss?" she asked.

"Of course he did. But in the end, when he saw my mind was set, all he could do was make me pay him back my tuitions."

"For law school?"

"And college, too."

"Ouch." Rose winced. "And you managed?"

"Just about. I'm still paying. Having him as a creditor makes me regret not taking out student loans."

"So what do you do now?"

"I'm in real estate." Ethan scrutinized her face for a reaction. Was she going to give him the downright sorrowful look of contempt other lawyers reserved for him when he told them his new occupation?

She didn't.

"My father is in real estate," Rose said. "What do you do, exactly?"

"I buy places that need refurbishing and restore them. When I'm done, I re-sell them or rent them out."

"If you have some nice studio apartments to rent, you could show them to me," she said and then looked away as if she immediately regretted her words.

"So you're looking to move out?" Ethan said, his eyes never leaving her face.

He saw her throw a furtive, guilty glance at Tyler, who was looking back at her pointedly. "I mean, not that I have much of a budget," she backtracked.

"I'll see what I can do," he promised. "If something interesting pops up, you'll be the first one I call."

Ethan meant the words. For once, he found himself united with his sister and her wishing for Tyler and Rose not to live under the same roof. From what he'd gathered from Georgiana on their way here, he didn't think it'd be a problem for much longer. Still, Ethan wanted Rose out of Tyler's house as soon as possible. Why? He wasn't sure yet. He just recognized it as a fact.

Rose

Once all the guests had arrived, menus were distributed and Rose picked one up as an excuse to conclude the conversation with Ethan.

She stared at the pages, not really reading them. Instead, she felt guilty for lying about her need for an apartment, or for it to be on a budget. Well, not exactly lied. Her dad was in real estate; she'd just omitted that his company owned half of Dallas, where she and Tyler were from. Rose wasn't as comfortable as Tyler when it came to displaying her family's wealth. Yes, she asked her dad to help with money. But only to cover her tuition and limited living expenses. So it was sort of true she was on a budget for her rent, even if the budget was self-imposed.

What wasn't true was that she was looking for a house. She had no intention of moving out of Tyler's home.

Rose focused on the menu, for real this time, but didn't understand what she was supposed to order. What were a nigiri, a maki, or a miso? There were no pictures to provide context, as the restaurant was definitely too classy for those. Yeah, everyone was supposed to eat sushi and speak foodie-Japanese these days, and it was unsophisticated of her not to, but she couldn't digest the idea of eating raw fish. The concept made her slightly nauseous.

"Pssst," she whispered with her face hidden behind the leather menu.

"Are you talking to me?" Ethan asked, cocking his head toward her.

"Mm-hmm. Are you a sushi connoisseur?"

"I've had my fair share. Why?" He spoke with his whole head hidden behind the black menu and his face turned toward hers.

"I don't have the faintest idea what any of this is. Can you help me out?"

"You've never had sushi?" Ethan seemed shocked.

"I'm from Texas where eating something that hasn't been barbequed, or at least grilled, is considered a state offense."

"You're from Texas! But you don't have a southern accent."

"My mom is from Chicago. But we moved here ages ago for college."

"Your mom and you?" Ethan asked.

"Oh. No, I meant Tyler and me." Rose shifted uncomfortably in her seat, not sure she wanted to talk about Tyler with Ethan. "We've known each other since preschool. He's like family."

"Family, huh?" Ethan appeared skeptical. Was she such an open book?

She deliberately changed the subject. "Will you order for me?"

He laughed. "Sure."

"I want something like a beginner set of the less gross things."

"By 'gross,' I'll assume you're referring to the raw fish. In case you didn't know, they also have cooked stuff here—you want me to get you one of those?"

"You know what? I don't think I'll give sushi another try any time soon, so I might as well go all in with the uncooked bits."

"Mmm, you're the adventurous type." Ethan winked one of those daring blue eyes at her, causing her stomach to do a little involuntary flip. "I like it."

When their food arrived, Rose found herself in another predicament—she did not grasp the use of chopsticks.

"Ethan?" she murmured. It was the first time she said his name, and she liked the sound of it.

"How can I be of assistance?"

"Do you think they'd flay me if I asked for a fork and a knife?"

He chuckled. "You're helpless, aren't you?"

"I'd like to see you fight a full rack of greasy barbequed pork ribs with your bare hands in your neat white shirt," she joked. "Then it'd be my turn to laugh."

Ethan chuckled again. "Japanese actually eat sushi with their hands. It's supposed to be eaten that way, at least for real hardcore sushi diners. Chopsticks are for sissies. If you do it, you'll impress everyone at the table."

"Will you do it with me?" she asked.

His blue eyes hardened. Rose got the impression he wasn't one to back down from a challenge.

"Sure, why not?" he said, and set his chopsticks back on the table.

Rose hesitated to use her fingers. But when Ethan picked up a roll, she was finally certain he wasn't joking. She followed his lead, raising one of her rolls halfway to her mouth.

"Cheers!" she said, bumping her California Maki into his before bravely putting the whole thing into her mouth.

"Cheers!" he responded, smiling.

After she'd tried a bite of everything he'd ordered for her, he said, "So, what's the verdict?"

Rose swallowed the last mouthful of the piece she was chewing. "To be honest, I've had better food…"

"Like a barbequed rack of greasy pork ribs?" he teased.

"Exactly. But I thought this would be a lot worse."

"So I haven't managed to bring you over to the raw side."

"I'm afraid not. Hey, I've been meaning to ask—what's this?" Rose pointed at a lime-green ball that looked like Play-Doh.

"That's wasabi."

"What's it for?"

"It adds a spicy flavor to the rolls."

"Oh, I like spicy food." She grabbed the ball.

"Don't," he warned. "It's really spicy."

She considered him for a second, the tiny ball still held between her thumb and index finger. *Okay, let's see…* Rose placed the tiny ball back on the wooden tablet acting as a plate and used one of her discarded chopsticks to split the wasabi into two identical halves.

"Is this better?" she asked.

He shook his head. "Not really, it's still too much."

"I can handle it."

Ethan was clearly trying and failing to suppress a grin as she raised the wasabi to her mouth. His expression said, *If you want to find out for yourself, I won't stop you.*

So it was a dare. Rose put the half ball in her mouth decided to win the challenge. But after gnawing for just a few seconds, her eyes started to water and her cheeks burned. Her nostrils flared wide as she tried to chew off the offending substance. She was sure she must look like a dragon breathing fire. To her credit, she managed to keep an almost straight face throughout the whole ordeal. When she finally managed to swallow the whole thing, she grabbed her diet Coke, shoved the straw aside, and downed the whole glass.

"Don't say anything," she hissed at Ethan once she could breathe again.

Rose needn't have admonished him as Ethan didn't seem able to talk. He was too busy laughing his head off.

When the dessert menu arrived, Rose disappeared behind it once again.

"Pssst," she whispered at Ethan a few moments later.

"You need help with the dessert?"

"No, thanks. I can figure out 'Green Tea Ice-Cream' all on my own. I wanted to ask you if there's something going on between you and that blonde chick." Rose jerked her chin toward the other end of the table. "The one sitting two seats down from Georgiana. She's been giving me a death stare all night."

"Ah, yes," Ethan admitted reluctantly. "That'd be Alice. We hooked up a couple of times, and now she probably thinks she's my girlfriend."

"Bah." Rose made a sarcastic swatting gesture with her hand. "How old-fashioned of her to think so."

So Ethan was a player, just like Tyler. But just how big of one? She quickly dismissed the train of thought; what did she care, anyway? Tonight had been a nice evening, sure—way more fun than she expected—but it wasn't as if they would see each other again after the dinner was over. So, player or not, it really made no difference to her.

Clink. Clink. Clink. Clink. Clink.

Georgiana was on her feet, looking down at all her guests, and batting a chopstick against her glass. The chatter quieted down, and twenty sets of eyes fixated on Georgiana. It was clear she loved being the center of attention. What was the big announcement, Rose wondered—a new Prada bag? A new Mercedes from Daddy?

"I wanted to thank you all for being here tonight for this special day…"

Oh, no. Her Birthday Majesty was really going to make a speech. Rose was about to roll her eyes at Ethan when she remembered he was

Georgiana's brother and caught herself just in time.

"Tonight is special," Georgiana continued. "Not only because it's my birthday, but also because, as most of you already know"—Georgiana looked pointedly at Rose—"I won't be seeing you all for a few months, as I'm leaving in two weeks for France."

Did she say leaving? In two weeks? Going to *France*? *For months?*

Rose couldn't believe her luck. Georgiana out of the way meant one less complication for her and Tyler. She looked over at him, filled with hope and trepidation. But he'd gone very pale—he looked almost ill as he stared fixedly at the tablecloth. At that moment, as if sensing Rose's eyes on him, he lifted his head and looked at her from across the table. Rose knew that expression: guilt. Why? Georgiana moving to Europe was Christmas in August. So why the guilty face?

Rose's question was answered by the end of Georgiana's speech. "I couldn't believe my luck when Professor Hendricks told me there'd been a reshuffling in the semester abroad scholarship, and that Tyler and I would be able to join the program in the upcoming fall term! We're going to spend the next six months in Paris together! How exciting is that?" Georgiana addressed her question directly to Rose. As the table erupted in cheers and applause, Georgiana kept her gaze fixated on Rose, her lips twisted in a smug smile. Rose could practically feel the triumph wafting off her.

Despite the knife slicing deep into her heart, Rose didn't give Georgiana the satisfaction of crumbling right before her eyes. She managed to maintain an impassive expression on the outside—but inside?

Rose's brain whirled with thoughts. Her heart was pounding so fast she was afraid it'd escape her chest. Tyler was moving to Paris with his girlfriend, and he hadn't even bothered to tell her. A year ago, when he had applied for the program and lost the scholarship, Rose had been genuinely sorry. But now… she didn't want him to go. Rose hadn't bought Georgiana's explanation of a "reshuffling" in Hendricks's exchange program. He was one of the sternest, most revered professors at Harvard and didn't play favorites. Rose could only imagine what strings Georgiana's father must have pulled to get Tyler and his daughter in.

Whatever he'd done, it had worked. Tyler was leaving her. Rose felt the beginning of a sob forming in her throat, and choked it into her glass, pretending it was a hiccup.

Ethan

Ethan watched Rose closely during Georgiana's speech. To the casual observer, she might have appeared unaffected by the news. But his scrutiny did not miss the flicker of hope on her face when Georgiana announced she was moving to France. In that moment, Rose's forehead lost all its creases, her eyes sparkled, and her mouth relaxed in a contented smile. It was only after Georgiana added that Tyler would be going with her that Rose's cheeks lost all their color and her expression soured, resembling the one she'd sported earlier while trying to swallow wasabi.

To her credit, Rose wasn't falling apart. At least not on the outside. She was sitting on her chair, staring ahead with a composed mask. Her fingers tapping on the table in a nervous tempo provided the only clue to her fury.

Interesting. So, Georgiana's she's-trying-to-steal-my-boyfriend theory wasn't paranoia. Something stronger than friendship linked Tyler to his attractive roommate. But from the pout of suppressed rage on Rose's lips, Ethan was sure Gigi's move would crush their blossoming romance.

The icy stare Rose gave Tyler at the end of Georgiana's speech surprised Ethan. How quickly Rose's warm eyes could turn into a frosty wall of black steel when she was angry. He prayed he'd never be at the end of that stare. He felt almost sorry for Tyler. But, most of all, Ethan felt happy for himself. For once, Georgiana's scheming would prove quite useful. Rose fascinated him. It wasn't often these days that Ethan Smithson found a girl interesting. If he thought about it, it hadn't happened since Sabrina, and that had been a long time ago.

Georgiana

Outside the restaurant, Georgiana fidgeted with the fabric of her clutch, her jittery fingers picking a thread out of the floral embroidery. All the guests had left except for Tyler, Ethan, and Rose, who stood in the parking lot facing one another in an awkward circle.

Georgiana studied Rose's face for any sign of emotion. *Nothing.* She was just standing there looking annoyingly beautiful in her unusual clothes. In class, Rose wore a uniform of buttoned-to-the-neck shirts, pullovers, jeans, and flat boots. But tonight with her high heels and sexy jumpsuit, she was dressed to impress. Georgiana was sure Rose had dressed up to look good for her boyfriend.

The evening hadn't turned out as well as Georgiana had hoped. The stone-cold bitch had remained impassive throughout her speech. Had Tyler already told her about Paris? Georgiana couldn't be sure, one way or the other. Sometimes Rose was inscrutable. And her announcement tonight had not produced the powerful effect Georgiana anticipated, longed for. Rose crumbling in front of everybody or leaving the restaurant in a sobbing fit would've been the icing on her birthday cake. But it didn't really matter. In two weeks, Georgiana would be gone with Tyler, and Rose would no longer be a problem.

"Baby," Georgiana said to Tyler, linking arms with him. "Do you want to stay over at my place tonight?"

"Actually, I came here with Rose," Tyler said. "I should probably drive her home."

"Oh, I can do that," Ethan offered, stepping forward.

"I think it's better if I drive her home," Tyler said.

His possessive attitude irritated Georgiana. The day they left for France couldn't come fast enough.

"I'm sure Ethan is a proficient enough driver to see me home safely," Rose said, putting an end to the discussion. Her cold stare dared Tyler to add something.

Mmm. Well, well, well, look at that. Just when Georgiana thought her fun was spoiled, her moment of triumph had finally arrived. Rose was angry—*very* angry. Tyler hadn't told her about Paris after all. Georgiana made an evil laugh inside her head. *Muahahah, mission accomplished.*

"It's all set, then," Georgiana chirped, moving toward Tyler's car.

It was annoying for her brother to pay attention to Rose tonight since he didn't have to anymore. Not to say mortifying for the way he'd ignored her sorority little sister, Alice. From what Alice had told her, she and her brother were in a committed relationship. So why flirt with another girl all night and offer to take her home? Especially now that Georgiana didn't need him involved with Rose. Anyway, if her brother wanted to toy with Rose, whatever. The more water under the bridge of Rose and Tyler, the better. But poor Alice.

"I'm this way," Ethan said, steering Rose away with a hand on the small of her back.

Georgiana pulled Tyler toward his car and tried to ignore the fact that her boyfriend appeared jealous of her brother.

Rose

Ethan drove a black Mercedes SL—a sports car that fitted his character like a glove. Rose was glad it was *him* driving her home tonight. The thought of being stuck in a confined space with Tyler was unbearable just now. She didn't even care that he was staying over at Georgiana's. She was too angry for that.

They didn't speak much on the way to Tyler's house, except for Rose offering the occasional direction. All the playfulness of the night had evaporated, and with too much on her mind to make small talk, Rose kept quiet. Ethan didn't seem to mind the silence, though.

When they pulled up in front of Tyler's building, Ethan was jumping out of the car before Rose even had a chance to thank him for driving her home. He circled it to reach her side and opened the car door for her. A tiny smile escaped her lips; this guy was full of surprises.

"How gentlemanly of you," she said, taking his outstretched hand.

"I'm no gentlemen," he said, his eyes suddenly dark in the cold night. "I only wanted to do this."

Ethan pulled her up and out of the car toward him. Moving his free hand to the small of her back and forcing their bodies closer together, he kissed her.

At first, she turned rigid in his arms. Rose hadn't expected the kiss, but after the initial surprise, she found herself responding. Her body took control, and she pressed herself against him. As suddenly as she'd let herself go, though, Rose regained control and pulled away from him.

She threw him a quick glance, blushing. Rose's eyes traveled low, fixating on the curb for a while before she was steady enough to look at him again.

Leaning with her back against his car, she said, "I guess that was good night, then."

"I guess it was."

"Good night, Ethan." Rose stepped toward him.

"Good night, Rose." He cupped her face in his hands and planted a soft kiss on her lips.

Rose could sense his stare on her back as she walked away, and couldn't resist glancing back at him one last time. Ethan had taken her place against his car, watching her go, his gaze smoldering. Rose ran the last few steps toward the door and disappeared inside the house, feeling out of breath.

The moment she closed the door, however, the brief elation Ethan's kiss had given her vanished. As she collapsed to the floor, a strong pain constricted her lungs. Rose rested her head on her knees and let the tears she'd been holding back for the past hour run freely.

Tyler

In Georgiana's apartment, in her bed, Tyler lay awake, restless. Georgiana was sleeping naked beside him, snoring faintly. He'd had sex with her tonight, more out of frustration than anything else. Tyler hadn't enjoyed it; he'd been thinking about Rose the entire time. Even when she wasn't here, she was all he could think about. He'd been livid with her all night for the way she'd openly flirted with Georgiana's brother. And now, white-hot jealousy was coursing through his veins like venom.

Tyler couldn't get the image of her going home with Ethan out of his mind. Had she really gone home, or had she gone back to his apartment? Was she having sex with him now? The thought of Rose, naked, with somebody else was unbearable. Unthinkable. The image was enough to send him shooting out of the bed. Tyler needed to know, *now*. He had to know if she was at home, waiting for him or not.

The sudden movement woke Georgiana. She stirred and looked at him. The room was in half-darkness; the only light came from the street lamps outside. Tyler doubted she could see much more of him than his dark silhouette.

"What's up, baby?" she asked.

"I can't sleep. I need my bed."

"You never had a problem with my bed before."

"I do tonight," he said harshly. Then, realizing it'd be easier to be nice to Georgiana rather than start an argument, he leaned toward her to kiss her forehead. "I'll call you tomorrow when I wake up, okay? Now, go back to sleep."

Apparently soothed by his sweet tone, Georgiana didn't protest further, her eyelids fluttering shut.

The journey home seemed infinite to Tyler, even though the streets were deserted this late at night. Every red light seemed to linger for an eternity. He sat in his car nervously drumming his fingers on the wheel, coils of anxiety twisting his stomach into knots. Rose was home, she had to be home. Tyler needed to explain Paris to her, and then she'd forgive him. Rose always did. Six months was nothing. They'd known each other for all their lives; six months in France didn't matter.

When he finally pulled over in front of his house, Tyler parked the car in a hurry and ran up the alleyway. Once inside, he paused briefly in the entrance hall, listening for any sound. Nothing. All was silent. He took off his shoes and jacket without turning on any lights and ran up the stairs, trying not to make too much noise.

Rose's door was closed. He stopped in front of it for a moment, undecided. But he had to know. He turned the knob slowly, again careful not to produce a sound.

Tyler peered into the room, filled with trepidation. The lights were all off, and the curtains closed. But his eyes were already used to the semi-darkness, and he could distinguish the slim outline of a body lying on the bed, curled up under the covers.

Rose was home. Of course, she was home. Relief washed over him. How stupid had he been to think she would've gone home with that dude? Rose loved him. She'd be angry with him in the morning, sure, and would probably yell at him, but she'd always be there for him. Tyler went to bed, the most relaxed he'd been the entire week. Everything would be fine.

Rose

Rose cried herself to sleep and woke up the next morning feeling miserable. A few groggy seconds passed before Rose remembered why she was in such a terrible mood. *Tyler was moving to France with Georgiana.* At the thought, her stomach churned and Rose pressed her lips together trying not to gag. What now? She'd have to move out at once. The realization made her even angrier; in one swift move, Georgiana was going to get everything she wanted. Rose hated her like she'd never hated anyone in her entire life.

Her loathing of Georgiana was interrupted by the sound of the toilet being flushed. Tyler was home. Rose's heart skipped a beat. When had he returned? What was the time? 7:45. What was Tyler doing home so early? Rose couldn't talk to him, not a mere few hours after learning the truth of where she stood with him. In fact, her plan was to sneak out of the house before he got back from Georgiana's place and return long after his bedtime. What was she going to do now? Rose wasn't ready to face him. She didn't want to see him at all.

Her heart felt like it stopped altogether when a faint knock sounded on her door. *Shoot! What now?* Rose didn't move. She didn't breathe.

The knock came again, louder this time. A shiver ran down Rose's spine and she lifted the covers higher over her head as if they could shield her from Tyler.

"Rose?" Tyler's voice came tentatively from the other side. "Rose, I know you're in there."

How did he know?

"Rose, we need to talk."

Oh, so now he wants to talk.

"Go away!" she shouted, jerking out of bed. No chance of being embarrassed as she was wearing a baggy T-shirt and long pajama pants.

"Rose, I'm coming in."

Tyler came into the room, dressed in a white T-shirt and gray sweat pants.

"I don't want to talk to you," she said.

They faced each other, standing on opposite sides of her bed.

"Rose, please, I had no choice."

She'd expected this excuse and was ready for it. "Oh, really?" Rose snapped. "And what exactly stopped you from telling me you were moving to France with your girlfriend?"

"That's not what I meant."

"Why didn't you tell me? *Why?*" Rose yelled, hysterical. "Oh, yeah! Because you wanted to keep screwing me until you left. You're a jerk."

"Rose, please, it's not like that and you know it. I wasn't expecting any of this to happen. Professor Hendricks summoned me into his office last Monday to tell me Montgomery had backed out of the French scholarship and that, if I wanted it, the spot was mine. But since the program started in three weeks, I had to give him an answer right then—and you know how much I wanted that scholarship. So, I said yes. I didn't even know Georgiana was also going until I'd already accepted."

"That witch made this happen, didn't she? *How?*" Rose could hear the venom in her voice, but she didn't care.

"I don't know. Both Montgomery and Brown withdrew from the exchange program at the last second. Georgiana must've had her father involved—I'm guessing he offered them something to give up their spots."

"Did you sleep with her?" Rose hissed.

"What?" Tyler seemed thrown off balance by the fury of her question.

"Last night. Did. You. Have. Sex. With. *Her?*"

It was the first time Rose asked him, and she had a hunch it was also the wrong time to ask.

Tyler looked at her with a desperate expression.

"You bastard…" Rose started to sob.

"Rose, please, it didn't mean anything. I was thinking about you the entire time."

How many times had she heard that same plea? Every time he'd cheated on one of his girlfriends and had been caught…

Oh, no. She'd become one of his girls. The thing she'd feared the most had become true.

"Get out," she commanded. "I don't want to talk to you. I don't even want to see you."

"Rose, please…"

"Get out."

"Rose…"

"I said GET OUT!" she screamed.

Tyler

Tyler had never seen Rose this mad, and to be honest, she was scaring him a little. So he did as she asked and gave her space, resolving to talk to her later, once she calmed down.

He never got the chance. In the next few days, Rose became a ghost. She left the house at dawn and always came back after midnight. When he waited up for her, Rose ran from the entrance door to her room, ignoring his calls as she locked herself inside. One night he camped outside her bedroom, determined to catch her before she left the next morning. But he fell asleep on the floor as he kept vigil. When Tyler awoke the next morning, Rose was gone. She must've stepped over his sleeping body and left without waking him. Even outside the house, he couldn't find a chance to talk to her—Georgiana shadowed him everywhere, and he was never alone long enough to seek Rose out.

During his last week in the States, Rose disappeared altogether, only to reappear two days before he was to leave for Paris. Tyler suspected she'd gone home to Dallas to visit her family without telling him.

The night before his departure, Tyler was in his room, finishing packing, when he heard the front door slam shut. Rose was home; no one else had a key. For a moment, he was tempted to go out and try to talk to her again. But given how badly every previous attempt had gone, he decided it was better to wait until he was back from France. When Tyler returned, he'd get rid of Georgiana, and then Rose would forgive him.

Rose

Rose hid in her room, feeling dead inside. Tyler was leaving tomorrow; he wouldn't just be in a different city, he'd be on a different continent entirely. She'd done her best to avoid him after their fight. Rose didn't want to hear his excuses; she'd heard all of them before. The same words uttered a thousand times to as many girls. When she'd found him sleeping outside her door, she'd almost given in, but somehow she'd managed to stay strong.

But tonight was different. It was their last night.

Rose changed into one of the longish T-shirts she liked to use to sleep and lay on the bed, but she couldn't stand still. On impulse, she got up, crossed the hall, and burst Tyler's door open. He was already in bed, his hand halfway to the table lamp, ready to turn it off.

Tyler looked up at Rose, surprised. "Oh, so now you're talking to me?" he asked.

"No," she said, removing her T-shirt in one swift movement. "Not talking."

***

Afterward, Rose spent the night awake on the bed, staring at the black ceiling and listening to Tyler's deep breathing as he slept beside her. When she got scared he might wake up, she snuck out of the bed. Outside his window, the first light of dawn was approaching, and the night fled before it. Just like Rose was fleeing from Tyler.

She collected her discarded T-shirt from the floor and tiptoed toward the safety of her room. Once inside, Rose locked the door. Tyler wouldn't try to wake her the next morning; he had to leave early for the airport. She didn't want to say goodbye. She couldn't.

***

Over the next few weeks, the memory of that night haunted Rose, no matter how much she tried to push it out of her mind. She needed to forget Tyler. He was in Paris with Georgiana. What were they doing? No, no, no. She had to stop torturing herself obsessing over what Tyler was or wasn't doing and move on.

A six-month break would do the trick. It had to. If she wanted things to go back to the way they'd been, she only needed time to forgive and forget. It wasn't too late for them to be friends again. But she needed to move out before he came back; this house was too full of him, too full of them.

Right, *move*. It was a Saturday morning, three weeks after Tyler and Georgiana had left. Rose was at the kitchen table scrolling through Craigslist, looking for rental houses. She'd already found a few options within her price range, but the pictures were so revolting that the search was doing nothing to improve her mood.

As she looked at one ugly house picture after another, her phone started ringing. An unknown number beginning with the Boston area code appeared on-screen.

"Hello?" she greeted, perplexed. It wasn't often she received phone calls from unknown numbers.

"Rose?"

It was a male voice, one she didn't recognize.

"Yes? Who is this?"

"You have no idea who I am. Ouch, I'm hurt."

He was funny, and she liked his voice, but she kept quiet.

"It's Ethan."

Her stomach did a little flip.

"Georgiana's brother," he added for good measure.

Georgiana. Tyler. France. Her stomach landed from the flip with an almighty crash.

"Oh, hi," she said, trying to keep an even tone. It wasn't easy; she felt like she might start sobbing at any moment.

"Hi." He sounded put-off by her subdued reply—which, somehow, uplifted her.

She resumed in a much cheerier tone. "Just when I thought you'd forgotten all about me." She had a hunch it wasn't by chance he'd waited until Tyler was out of the country before calling her.

"Well, I had to make sure I could present a winner before calling you."

"A winner?" Rose asked, both puzzled and captivated.

"I have a wager to propose."

"This early on a Saturday morning? Shouldn't we wait until at least, I don't know, late afternoon before we start gambling?"

"Normally I'd say yes, but since I have a better chance of winning in broad daylight, you'll have to make an exception."

"Would I want you to win?" she asked, surprised by her own coquettishness.

"I think it'll be a win-win, so yeah…"

"Mmm, I'm intrigued. Tell me everything."

An hour later, as she walked up the steps of a fancy new building just a few blocks away from Harvard, she knew she'd lost the bet. As Ethan had predicted, she was not at all sorry about her defeat.

Ethan had called to show her an apartment he thought she might like on the condition that if she were to take it, she'd have to go out to dinner with him. Rose vaguely remembered telling him about her search for an apartment the night of Georgiana's party. It hadn't been true back then, and she hadn't foreseen her lie becoming the truth quite so abruptly. But now she was glad for it. She welcomed the distraction; it was the first positive thing that had happened to her in a while.

Ethan had picked her up in his black Mercedes thirty minutes after calling her. She'd barely had time to take a quick shower and get dressed before he'd arrived.

"Are you sure this is within my budget?" she asked, eying the luxurious building.

"The owner's a good friend of mine, and he's agreed to lower the price for a reliable, tidy tenant who won't trash the place," Ethan explained shrugging. "A lot of rich, spoiled frat boys want to live here, but they're trying to keep them out of the building and make it more of an adult community."

"How do you know I'm not a crazy party girl?"

"Are you?" Ethan called her bluff.

"No," she admitted, unsettled by the x-raying of his light blue eyes.

"Shall we?" he asked, holding the door open for her.

The apartment was perfect, just perfect. It was a spacious one-bedroom with one wall made entirely of floor-to-ceiling windows. The kitchen was ultra-modern, brand new, and had a huge island that overlooked the dining table and part of the living room. The bedroom was bigger than the one Rose was occupying now and had a walk-in closet. Even the bathroom was cozy with all-new counters and sinks, and furnished in a minimal style that suited the place. Both the furniture and walls were painted white with splashes of warm gray and wood accents.

Compared to what was on Craigslist, this place was a palace. Rose could hardly believe her luck.

"Do I take it we have a date?" Ethan asked when she was finished examining every inch of the apartment.

"When can I move in?" she asked, beaming.

"Next weekend. I'll have you sign some papers, and it's a done deal."

"You don't need to check with the owner?"

"Nah, I had you pre-approved."

"Confident, are we?"

He smiled dashingly.

"When do you want to go out?" Ethan asked once the paperwork was taken care of.

"You're the winner, you call the shots."

"Next Friday?"

Something dangerous fluttered in Rose's belly. "Next Friday it is," she said.

***

In the following days, Rose changed her mind about how she felt about going out with Ethan every other hour. At first, she'd be happy for the distraction. Then she'd get worried about getting into even bigger trouble. Ethan was another bad boy, possibly even worse than Tyler. Why couldn't she find one of the good ones?

Because you find them boring as hell, a nasty little voice replied in Rose's head.

When she was done worrying about how much Ethan might hurt her, guilt towards Tyler crept in, even though she knew she shouldn't feel anything but anger about the situation. After all, Tyler was in Paris with his girlfriend. But her heart was stupid, and it kept telling Rose she was being disloyal. Once the guilt trip was over, Rose switched almost immediately to vindictiveness—of all the guys she could have gone out with, Ethan would definitely annoy Tyler the most.

Not that he'd find out considering they barely talked these days. She'd emailed him once to say she was moving out, and that she'd check on his house every now and then, and pay the bills while he was in France. But Tyler hadn't emailed her back, probably because he almost never checked his non-Harvard email account. And she was perfectly happy with him not knowing, at least for a while, until she had enough time to settle into her new place—and life, hopefully.

Ethan was due to pick her up at 7:00 pm. It was 6:30, and Rose was already dressed. She had chosen her clothes for tonight well in advance as everything else was packed away in two huge suitcases for her big move tomorrow. She'd opted for a casual-chic style: a white neoprene quilted sweater over lightly faded ultra-skinny jeans and a pair of high-heeled nude pumps. In front of the mirror, Rose let her hair down and styled it in soft waves. As for makeup, she kept it simple: foundation, bronze blush, a double coat of mascara, and lip balm. Rose didn't like to wear lipstick or lip-gloss at restaurants. She didn't see the point when it would just end up on a napkin by the end of the night.

At 6:55, the doorbell rang. Rose unhooked her black fur jacket from its hanger and hurried out of the house to meet Ethan.

He drove to a fancy steak house for their first official date—he'd remembered meat was her favorite. She added one point for him in her mental scoreboard.

"I wish I'd given in to Georgiana sooner," Ethan said after they'd drunk their first glass of wine.

"Meaning?" Rose asked, uneasy at the mention of Georgiana. She tried to store the notion of her being Ethan's sister in a remote corner of her brain.

"She's been bugging me to go out with you for ages," Ethan explained.

"How nice of her to worry about me," Rose said, unable to keep the sarcasm out of her voice. Anger at Georgiana's scheming resurfaced immediately.

"I don't think she was being utterly altruistic," Ethan said. He was direct; Rose liked it. "I guess she was jealous of you and Tyler living together."

Tyler's name made Rose blush. She hoped the reaction wasn't too obvious, even if Ethan's attentive stare told her otherwise.

"So what made you change your mind?" Rose asked, steering the conversation away from Tyler. She didn't want to think about him tonight.

"I met you," Ethan said simply, holding her gaze.

He meant it to be a charming statement, but suspicion flared in Rose's chest at once. "So what is this?" She wiggled a finger between them. "A favor you're doing your sister?"

"Ah, no. Miss Atwood, your accusations wound me."

"Please be square with me." Rose broke the courting act. She was tired of guys playing games. "Are you here only because Georgiana asked you?"

Ethan's ever-present lopsided smile disappeared. "I would never do that," he said. "I'm here because I want to be. I'm here because the night I met you was the first night I'd had fun in forever. And because I hope that by the end of the night you'll let me kiss you again."

"Okay." Rose swallowed. When Ethan Smithson switched on the charm, he was impossible to resist. Maybe she really was jumping head first into bigger trouble. "Let's not talk about other people then."

Ethan nodded just as the server was arriving to take their orders.

The rest of the night passed in a blur of general getting-to-know-you talk. Rose found she was able to relax with Ethan; he had an easy way about things, quite the opposite of his snotty sister, and he made her laugh—a lot! He didn't mention Tyler again during the dinner, much to Rose's relief. Besides her asking, Rose suspected Ethan was avoiding the topic so as not to spoil their first date. Deep down, Rose feared the moment she'd have to come clean about her relationship with Tyler. If she wanted to keep seeing Ethan, she'd have to tell him the ugly truth eventually. How would Ethan react? Would he hate her for hurting his sister? Think of her as the other woman?

When Ethan pulled up in front of Tyler's house, Rose was surprised to see the clock of his car read 1:00 a.m.

"Do you need any help with the big move tomorrow?" Ethan asked.

"Yeah, sure, I'll stick my humongous luggage in your spacious trunk," she joked, wondering if his sports car even had a trunk.

"I'll have you know I'm also equipped with a pickup, Miss Atwood. It should be more than capable of hauling your humongous luggage."

She'd planned to call a cab, but the possibility of Ethan helping her was far more enticing.

"Okay then. But only if you'll let me buy you breakfast afterwards."

"Deal," he said.

"Should we shake on it?"

"I have a better idea," he said, and leaned in to kiss her.

***

"You seem undecided," Ethan said.

They'd just finished moving Rose's luggage into her new apartment, and Rose was famished.

"Well," Rose said, shifting her gaze between the two sides of the road. "I love Starbucks' coffee, but I prefer donuts from Dunkin' Donuts."

All night she'd thought about Ethan. About their date the night before, the conversations they'd had, the occasional fluttering in her belly, and the kiss! Yesterday had been the first night Tyler had not haunted her dreams.

"You get the coffee, and I'll get the donuts," Ethan proposed.

"But breakfast was supposed to be on me!" Rose protested.

He laughed. "So pay me back the two dollars the donuts will cost."

Rose smiled and gave in. "Okay. Let's meet back here and we can eat in my new kitchen."

***

"Do you ever miss Texas?" Ethan asked her as they ate breakfast seated at Rose's new table next to the wall-wide windows. Sunlight filtered through the glass, making her new apartment appear even brighter than when she'd seen it the first time.

"Sometimes, but we moved here seven years ago, so now Boston feels like home too," Rose said.

"You keep saying *we*."

"Ah," Rose said, embarrassed. "Bad habit."

"Any other bad habits I should know of?"

Ethan's question was vague enough, but the is-there-something-going-on-between-you-and-Tyler subtext was all too clear.

"Who am I talking to?" Rose asked. "Georgiana's brother or just Ethan?"

"Just Ethan," he replied, and somehow Rose trusted him.

"Tyler is my best friend; we managed to stay *just* friends for a long time."

"Past tense?"

"Past tense," she confirmed.

Ethan didn't press her; he waited for her to tell him more, or not tell him anything. This made her even more confident she could open up to him, and she did. Rose told him everything; she started with Marcus and ended with the disaster the last couple of months had been.

"…and now you probably hate me because Georgiana is your sister and I've been horrible to her."

"I don't hate you," Ethan said, though he'd gone rigid in his chair. "I know my sister's not an angel, but she doesn't deserve to be cheated on. Still, I'm not angry at you—how could I be? You weren't the one cheating on Georgiana. Tyler's the bastard who was playing both of you like that. He's lucky he's on another continent!"

Rose's cheeks were beyond red at this point. "Do you think she knows?" she asked, not daring to look him in the eye.

"From what Gigi told me, she's almost certain."

"And she doesn't care?"

"My sister's peculiar like that," Ethan said noncommittally. "Georgiana has decided she wants to be with Tyler, and as long as she gets what she wants, she doesn't seem to care if he wants to be with her or not."

"So you don't hate me for hurting her? Are you sure?"

"As I said, you aren't the one who's in the wrong here. That Tyler dude, though—him, I hate. I could snap his neck. Do you love him?"

"I do," Rose said sincerely. "But I'm not sure if I'm *in* love with him. Our relationship is too complicated to trace a line where the friendship ends and the love starts. But what we did was a huge mistake, and I hope we can find our way back to being just friends. What about you? Anyone I should know about?"

"Not really…"

"What about that blonde girl at Georgiana's birthday?" *The one glaring at me*, Rose silently added. "What was her name?"

"Alice."

"Alice, right. Are you still seeing her?"

Ethan shrugged.

Meaning, yes.

"The night we met, did you go see her after you dropped me off?" Rose pressed.

Ethan's eyebrows flew upward; he was clearly taken aback by the question. "I did," he admitted.

"Did you sleep together?"

Ethan replied with a curt nod, his jaw tense.

"And after that?"

Another small nod.

"When was the last time?"

"Two nights before our date."

"Will there be a next?" Rose asked, not sure she wanted to know.

"I don't know," Ethan answered honestly.

"Listen." Rose took a sip of her coffee, which had gone cold. "I genuinely like you…"

"I sense a 'but' coming," Ethan said with a skeptical smile.

"But… I don't want to be mixed up in another love triangle. My life is already too complicated as is. I don't want to fool around. And let's not kid ourselves—you're Georgiana's brother. That's not irrelevant."

"You're right," Ethan said. He stood up and pulled on his black leather jacket. "I should sort myself out first." He moved toward the door.

"If you ever do, well, you know where I live." Rose followed him to the door and held it open for him.

"Goodbye, Miss Atwood." Ethan kissed her on the forehead.

Rose liked that he acted like a gentleman out of a Jane Austen novel whenever he was flirting. "Goodbye, Mr. Smithson," she said, playing along.

She watched Ethan go and closed the door behind him, leaning her forehead against the cold metal. Rose was already feeling a pang of regret. Had she done the right thing? If so, then why the disappointment?

Because doing the right thing sucked, she answered herself. But she'd done enough wrong for a while, and she wanted her next relationship to start out clean. No secrets, no sneaking around, and most definitely no other women. If the bare mention of an exclusive relationship sent Ethan running for the hills, it'd be even clearer she'd made the right choice.

***

Once she was settled into her new home, Rose started settling into her new, independent life as well. Being out of Tyler's house helped more than she'd expected. Not having to see him or Georgiana was the icing on her recovery cake. Six months was a long break. By the time Tyler came back, her heart would be healed, and she'd be in control of her feelings once again. Really, France was the perfect solution, and the only way to salvage her friendship with Tyler.

This forced break was the longest they'd ever been apart, but Rose didn't have time to feel alone. Harvard Law was more than enough to keep her mind busy, and without distractions her grades had become even better than usual. Rose was concentrating on herself and on her studies. She was alone, independent, in control of her life… and it felt good.

***

Rose stretched in bed, half asleep. It was Saturday morning and even if she had to study, she hadn't set the alarm clock. Unexpectedly, the doorbell rang, cutting her morning treat short.

Rose stared at the ceiling, confused for a few seconds. It must be the mailman delivering her latest textbook order. She reluctantly shuffled out of bed, adjusted her hair in a messy bun, and went to open the door wearing only her pale gray just-above-the-knee nightdress and a pair of socks. She had a paper to write anyway, so the delivery was as good a wake-up call as any.

But there wasn't a mailman waiting for her on her landing. Rather, it was Ethan, holding a tray of coffee cups and a box of donuts.

"Trick or treat?" he asked.

"Aren't you supposed to wear a costume for that?" Rose said groggily, her voice still thick with sleep. She'd forgotten it was Halloween.

"Not a morning person, huh?" Ethan said with a wicked smile.

"Guilty."

"Don't you even want to know the plea bargain first?"

"You have donuts in one hand and coffee in the other. I'm good." Rose smiled. "Come on in. Let me go put something on."

"No, please, it's the first time I've seen your legs. They look too good to be covered up."

"Well, sorry, but I'm not comfortable being the only one in the room not wearing pants."

"In that case…" In a swift move, Ethan dropped everything on the kitchen table and kicked away his shoes. He was already unbuttoning his pants before Rose realized what he was doing.

"That's not what I meant!" she protested, covering her face with her hands. But he was already folding his pants neatly in two. Ethan laid the pants on the back of a chair on which he sat afterwards. Rose had no choice left other than to sit opposite him and try to ignore the fact that there was a half-naked, very attractive guy sitting in her kitchen.

"So what brings you to this part of town?" Rose sipped her coffee, pleased to notice he'd remembered she loved cappuccinos.

"Oh, I like to check on tenants I've helped find a place for from time to time."

"You mean you bring coffee and donuts to all of them?"

"No, donuts are a special perk I reserve for you."

"I'm honored." She took a bite to show her appreciation.

"You've been all right, then? You have all you need?"

Rose knew his question wasn't a casual one, but she gave him a casual answer all the same. "I'm missing something red."

"Red?"

"Yeah, I like the minimalist style, but I need a pop of color."

"Don't tell me you have an artistic side! So un-lawyer-like of you. How's everything else been?"

"Same old. You know, I'm having fun with Constitutional Law." Rose knew she was avoiding his questions, but she wasn't sure what he was doing here yet. "How about you?"

"I've pretty much been a lone wolf for the last month."

He looked a bit like a wolf—one with piercing blue eyes.

"Not on my account, I hope?" Rose hid her face behind her coffee cup.

"To be honest, Miss Atwood, it has been on your account."

Rose smiled. She really liked when he acted the gentleman. "You want more coffee?"

"Sure."

She moved into the kitchen and Ethan sprawled out on the couch. Rose had almost forgotten he was pants-less. Watching Ethan Smithson wander around her living room in boxer shorts was weird and thrilling at the same time.

"Just coffee, or do you want a cappuccino?" she asked from behind the kitchen island.

"You make cappuccinos at home?"

"Yeah, I have a frothing machine."

"Then a cappuccino."

Rose brought two huge mugs to the couch and sat opposite Ethan, draping her calves on his lap. For a horrible moment, Rose feared she'd forgotten to shave her legs, before remembering she'd done it last night. *Phew.*

"Is this what your typical Saturday morning looks like?"

"Nah, I'm usually caught up in boring stuff like accounting or supervising some remodeling project. Running a company is a 24/7 job. And being a grownup isn't fun."

"I wouldn't know about that. I'm still in grad-school limbo. And I have at least another year before I have to grow up."

"Lucky you."

"So what were you like as a kid, before you went over to the grownups side?"

"I was a little terror…"

Rose chuckled. "I can imagine that."

"I drove my mom and sisters crazy, but they adored me all the same."

"Sisters, plural?"

"Yeah, Georgiana is the youngest. Victoria—Vicky—is the middle kid, and I'm the oldest."

"I didn't know you had another sister. Georgiana never mentioned her, and she wasn't at her birthday."

"That's weird because they're tight as hell. I'm sure Vicky didn't make it to Gigi's party because she was stuck in an office with a big case to work on. Ever since I quit the practice, Vicky's career has been my father's consolation. She puts eighty to ninety hours a week into the family business, and she's even engaged to another pedigreed lawyer. They're getting married next year, and I'm sure they'll breed another generation of perfect little lawyers. She's a daughterly dream come true. Despite that, I love her. Vick manages to remain human even after going over to the Dark Side."

"You really can't stand lawyers. Should I remind you I'm going to be one pretty soon?"

"I won't hold it against you, I promise."

"So you never liked law?"

Ethan shrugged. "In school, I didn't mind it per se. It was more the fact of not having a choice that didn't sit well with me. To do it just because I was supposed to, expected to. And yes, I hated staying all those hours in the office, but running a company isn't that different. I have to be on the job just as much, but since it's my choice, I'm happy about it. Does that make any sense?"

"It makes a lot of sense."

"And being a lawyer still has its perks. I don't need anyone to draft my contracts, which saves me a lot of money. What about you? Have you always wanted to be a lawyer?"

"Yeah, my dad passed it on to me. He wanted to be a lawyer, but couldn't."

"Couldn't?"

"My grandparents both died in a car accident right after he graduated from college. He'd already been accepted to Harvard Law, but couldn't go. His brother and sister were still young—my uncle, Adam, was in high school and Aunt Debra was even younger. My dad had to go back home to take care of them."

"I'm sorry."

"Thank you, but it's okay. It was a long time ago. Anyway, when my dad moved back to Dallas, he took over the family business and provided for his brother and sister. He was already engaged to my mom, so dad became their stepfather and mom their stepmother, sort of. By the time my aunt and uncle were old enough to take care of themselves, I was already three and the company was doing well. With a daughter and a wife to care for, my dad didn't want to leave a secure position to follow his dream, but he kept studying on his own. He'd discuss cases and sentences with me when I became old enough. We always watched crime shows together, judging the cases they presented. And we loved playing court or just discussing this or that sentence."

"No dolls and fairy tales for you?"

Rose chuckled. "No, only vicious crimes. Anyway, Dad was so passionate about it that he passed on his love of the law to me, and I absorbed it like a sponge. It's what I wrote in my admission paper to Harvard Law; in fact, I think it was one of the main reasons I was accepted into the program. So yeah, I've always wanted to be a lawyer."

"I should introduce you to my dad. He'd probably want to adopt you right away," Ethan commented with a dashing smile.

He really is a terror, Rose thought. *A dangerously attractive one.* She tried to speak with an even tone when she asked her next question, the one she'd been burning to ask since he'd arrived. "So you've gone solitary just for me, huh? May I ask why?"

"You've piqued my interest, Miss Atwood."

"How so?"

"For one, you look adorable with a foam mustache." Ethan leaned in to wipe it away with his thumb. *Uh-oh, too close*, she thought. And then he was kissing her.

Rose let herself melt into the kiss, even knowing she shouldn't trust Ethan. She'd done some asking around in Georgiana's inner circle of friends, and they'd all confirmed he was a big player. But even against her better judgment, she felt secure in his arms. So she let him drop their mugs on her coffee table, and she let herself go without thinking, without being in control… and it felt even better.

Ethan

"You look worried," Ethan said, watching Rose dress herself self-consciously hiding behind the couch. He couldn't help thinking she was even more adorable when she frowned.

"I was just wondering if you were going to give me the speech now."

"Meaning?"

Ethan snatched his pants, pulled them on, and started buttoning up his shirt.

"I ran a background check on you, Mr. Smithson," Rose said. "You have quite a reputation."

"Ah, Miss Atwood, you don't do me justice." He flashed Rose his most dashing grin. "What falsehoods have you heard?"

"That you pretty much run away from relationships the minute they become serious."

Ethan's smile evaporated. "I don't like to waste anyone's time."

"Is that so?" Rose's face darkened.

Ethan sat at the kitchen table, undecided on what to say. True, he hadn't had a serious relationship in forever, not since… *Sabrina.* In part, because he had yet to meet someone who really interested him. In part, it had been his fault. Ethan had bolted from a number of relationships because they were becoming too serious, just like Rose said. It had been too soon after Sabrina. But now? Was he finally ready to move on? Could he open up with Rose? Bare his heart to her? He'd never told anyone about what had really happened with Sabrina. The official version for everyone—relatives, including Ethan's parents, and friends—had been cold feet. And even if Ethan's mom suspected the truth, only his sisters knew the story firsthand.

Rose followed him into the kitchen and braced her hands on the back of a chair. "Come on," she prompted. "I don't judge. Plus, you're obliged to tell me."

"And why is that?"

"Because I've already confessed my darkest secrets to you. And if you tell me about those closet skeletons, I'll feed you."

"Feed me what?" Ethan said.

Rose opened a cupboard and studied its insides. "How does boxed mac and cheese sound?"

"Perfect." Despite himself, Ethan smiled again. Rose was so un-domestic it was endearing. "If you throw in a beer, we have a deal."

Rose put the pasta on the stove to cook and sat in front of him, placing two bottles of Coors Light on the table. No glasses—Ethan liked her style. He liked it even more when she laid the head of the bottle on the edge of the table and punched the cap loose.

Ethan chuckled. "That's a handy skill."

"Dorm-earned skills," Rose joked.

"I don't want to know." Ethan really didn't; thinking of Rose in a college dorm made him jealous. He was already becoming territorial and didn't like just how much.

Rose smiled, passed him the opened bottle, and repeated the procedure with the other. Once done, she lifted the second bottle in a "cheers" gesture, and said, "Mr. Smithson, you owe me a story."

"Would you rather have the short or long version?"

Rose studied him, took a sip of beer, and said, "Short, please."

"Her name was Sabrina, and we were engaged. Not a distant future thing, we had the whole marriage shenanigans going. Booked venue, sent invitations, she had a dress..." Ethan winced at the memory. "Anyway, one sorry evening three months before the wedding, I came home early and found her in bed with the best man. Bit cliché, I know." Ethan hid his pain behind sarcasm. "Now they're married. They moved to New York about two years ago."

"I'm sorry," Rose whispered.

"No need to be. It was a long time ago. But now it takes me a little longer to commit to anything or anyone. When a girl starts talking rings after three dates, I tell her I'm not marriage material and we usually part ways."

"That's so cynical."

"More fair."

"So where does this leave us?"

"Not sure what you're asking." Ethan shrugged. "Where do you want it to leave us?"

"Here's what I think." Rose scrunched her face, trying to order her thoughts. "I'm tired of investing in relationships and people who walk out on me. I'm not saying we should define anything today. I only want to know that if we start going out, and if things get serious, you won't bolt just because. Do you think you can keep an open mind?"

"I think your mac and cheese is burning."

Rose threw herself at the pot to salvage whatever was left of the pasta. Not much from the smell of it.

"It's ruined." She sighed, turning towards him.

Ethan stood up and wrapped his arms around her waist. "How about I take you out to lunch?"

Rose tilted her face upward and her beautiful dark eyes met his. "And where would you take me?"

Her question had nothing to do with food. Neither did his answer. "You can trust me."

Four Months Later

Tyler

Tyler was nervous, edgy as he walked up the steps of Rose's new building. He hadn't called her to tell her he'd stop by—heck, she probably didn't even know he was back from France. He'd deliberately chosen not to give her warning. What if Rose refused to see him? Tyler couldn't wait a minute longer. One night home without her had been enough.

When his plane landed, he had to use all his self-control not to go to Rose in the middle of the night the moment he set foot in the US. Instead, Tyler had settled for leaving home super early the next morning. As he reached the building entrance, a chill wind blew on him from behind, the air even crisper than usual for January in Boston.

Tyler warmed his clenched fists by puffing hot air into them and opened the heavy door. He searched the hall for the elevators. Rose should be on the second floor, apartment 2B. His heart wouldn't stop beating hard in his chest. Six months away from Rose had seemed to last forever—he didn't want to spend a minute longer away from her, and today he'd tell her. Tyler would fix things between them.

After reading the move-out email two months after Rose sent it, Tyler had panicked. Rose was leaving him. He'd almost jumped on the first plane for Boston to tell her to stop punishing him and come back home. Given the way she'd chosen to say goodbye to him, Tyler knew Rose wanted him as much as he wanted her. That last night together had been the only thing keeping him sane during all these months apart. Still, he'd decided to let her cool down while he was away. Once he got back, he was certain he could charm her into forgiving him.

Now the moment had finally arrived.

More than receiving Rose's forgiveness, Tyler simply wanted to be with her. No one, not one girl, had ever made him feel anything close to the passion he had for Rose. She was his best, and oldest friend; Rose was kind, smart, and smoking hot. All his fears of a serious commitment, however important they'd felt before, seemed irrelevant now. Rose mattered more. Being away from her had made Tyler realize just how much he needed her, how lost he was without her. *So much wasted time.*

Tyler pursed his lips. Yesterday had been the last lost day. Today he'd tell her he was in love with her, and everything would be fine.

He took a deep breath and rang Rose's doorbell. Quick, excited steps preceded the door opening.

"You're early," Rose said with a big smile. Then her eyes met his, and the smile disappeared, replaced by shock. A gasp escaped her. "Tyler."

"Surprise," he said uncertainly. Rose's dark eyes were different: they held a coldness Tyler wasn't used to. Well, he deserved it. He'd pulled a number on her, but he was sure he could make her forgive him. Especially with what he'd come to say. "Expecting someone else?"

"I didn't expect to find you on my doorstep," Rose said noncommittally. "Come on in. When did you get back?" She was still awkward, guarded.

"Last night."

"How was Paris? I was making coffee, you want some?"

Rose was nervous; she always busied her hands with something when she needed to calm.

"Coffee would be great, thanks," Tyler said. "Nice new place."

"Yeah, I was really lucky to find it." Rose avoided meeting his gaze as she spoke.

"I've brought you a housewarming gift and some upscale chocolate." Tyler handed her a gift-wrapped package and a Fauchon tin box.

"Fauchon, wow. Fancy." Rose set down the chocolate and unwrapped her present. "Thank you," she said, beaming. Her fond tone told Tyler he'd scored a point. "I've been looking for something red since I moved in," she added, still smiling as she admired the bright lacquered apple he'd bought in a Parisian design shop. "This house needed a splash of color."

Rose studied some options and finally positioned the apple in a corner of the kitchen island where it'd be visible from both the kitchen and living room.

"Wow, it looks perfect." Rose stared at him with a renewed light in her eyes. "Thank you."

This was his moment.

"Listen, Rose, I'm sorry." Tyler took her hands into his. "I've been an idiot and messed up badly. But everything happened so suddenly, so unexpectedly. I didn't know what to do, then there was France, and there wasn't much I could've done about that. Rose, I'm sorry. I've been a jerk, and you didn't deserve it. Can you forgive me?"

"Tyler, I forgave you a long time ago." Rose shook her head, sighing. "We made a mess. I wasn't such a straight arrow either, but that is all gone now. We're fine."

Tyler couldn't believe his luck. The reconciliation had been even easier than he'd expected. "I couldn't wait to see you, to say how sorry I am."

"Come on, cheer up. We're fine."

"I've missed you so much."

"It's okay now."

Rose leaned in for a hug, and Tyler shifted sideways to kiss her.

"Whoa!" Rose pushed him back, planting both of her hands on his chest. "I said we're fine, not 'let's make out.'"

"If we're fine, why can't we make out?" Tyler asked, leaning in again.

Rose wiggled away, putting space—and the kitchen island—between them. "You just said you were sorry, and the minute I say it's okay, you try to jump me?"

"What's wrong with jumping you? I want to be with you, Rose." Tyler tried to come around to her side of the island, but she made a stay-there gesture. Okay, he deserved some grief. But now he needed to make her see how much he cared about her. "These months away from you have been a nightmare. I was stupid before and scared about getting serious with you, but I had time to think, a lot of time, and I'm sure now. We can make it work. Please give me another chance."

"Tyler, no. We both know it won't work. We're great as friends, and that's it. Look at the mess we made last time. Let's be *just* friends. Please. I want my best friend back."

"And I'm here. But I want more. So what if it was messy last time? I've said I'm sorry. Why can't we try again?"

"Listen, Tyler." Rose braced her hands on the countertop. "I'm not saying it was all your fault because it wasn't. The mess was as much me as it was you. But now we've had enough time to cool off and we can go back to how things were before, like it never happened."

"But I can't pretend, and I don't want to. Rose, I've spent the last six months thinking about you, and only you. I don't want to be friends with you. I want everything—the whole package. I've never felt like this about anyone else."

"That's because you're my best friend, and we've known each other forever. Tyler, listen, please. We can't be anything more than friends, we just can't. It'd never work."

"I'd make it work. I can't go back..." Tyler paused. "Rose, I love you. I'm in love with you."

Rose

Rose stared at Tyler, shell-shocked. She'd dreamt of hearing those exact words for over a decade now. Tyler, in love with her. A dream come true. Only reality didn't feel as right as the dreams. Thinking about it, she hadn't daydreamed about being with Tyler for some time, her heart had been somewhere else. A flash of blue eyes invaded her mind. Ethan's eyes. Georgiana's eyes. Rose sobered up at once.

"How did Georgiana take the news?" Rose asked, crossing her arms over her chest.

"Georgiana?" Tyler seemed dumbfounded. "What does Georgiana have to do with any of this?"

"I'm just curious. After all the strings she pulled to organize your romantic gateway in France, she must've been pretty stone-faced when you dumped her."

Tyler stared back at her in confusion.

"You *did* dump her, didn't you?" Rose pressed.

The dark shadow that passed over his face was enough of an answer.

"This is exactly why it'll never work," Rose said, turning away.

"Rose, if this is about Georgiana, don't worry. I can break up with her in a second."

"So why haven't you already?"

"Rose, it would've been awkward. We were in Paris, living in the same house—"

"And did you sleep with her while you were in Paris, living in the same house?"

Again, she could read the answer on his face.

"It didn't m—"

"Don't say it didn't mean anything."

Tyler stood silent, petrified in the middle of the living room.

"But Rose, I didn't cheat on you. It's not like we were together. If you give me a chance, I would—"

"It doesn't matter if we were together or not, don't you see?" Rose could hardly keep it together. Tyler's declaration of love had thrown her off, and now he was making her so angry. Rose didn't like how worked up she was getting. "You say you're in love with me. You say you've spent six months thinking about me nonstop. But that didn't stop you from sleeping with your girlfriend, and that's the problem."

"But we weren't together," Tyler protested.

"It's irrelevant. Love should be enough for you not to want to fool around with whoever else is available." Rose's voice trembled. "You shouldn't want to sleep with other people if you're in love with me.

Period."

"You're not being fair. Why can't you give me another chance?"

"Because if you blew it, then we'd be over for good, and I don't want that. Plus…" Rose hesitated just for a moment. "I'm kind of seeing someone else."

"Who?" Tyler was suddenly cold.

"Ethan."

The name took a moment to register, and Rose witnessed the shock in Tyler's eyes when it did.

"Georgiana's brother?" Tyler hissed. "Are you kidding me? He's a bigger player than I am."

"He's not, at least not with me."

Tyler snorted. "Why does he get a chance and I don't?" His tone was bitter.

"Because if I break up with him, it's just that: a breakup. If we broke up, I'd lose my best friend too, and I don't want that to happen. Ever."

"It's not fair." Tyler pouted. "I would never hurt you, Rose, you have to believe that."

"Tyler." Rose moved closer to him. "I do. I know you wouldn't hurt me on purpose. And I know you think you can behave, but the fact remains… you probably wouldn't. There's too much at stake, and I care about you too much. Tyler, if you cheated on me, I would never recover from that. *Never*. And I'm not willing to take that risk. Plus, I'm happy with Ethan. Really happy."

At that, Tyler moved away and started pacing around the living room like a caged lion. "Bullshit, Rose. You care about me too much! If I tell you I can do something, it means I can. It's all about that dude, isn't it? Georgiana's brother was all over you from the moment he set eyes on you." Tyler sagged on the couch like an empty sack. "Do you love him?"

The question made Rose's legs unsteady. Did she love Ethan? She wasn't sure, but if it wasn't love, her emotions were something close enough. Rose sat next to Tyler, staring hypnotized at his legs twitching up and down. "Tyler… I honestly don't know."

He looked at her with sadness in his eyes. "I always thought we'd end up together at some point. I never thought I'd blow it so big time, or that I'd be too late."

Rose didn't know what to say to that. She'd felt the same for a long time. Even when she was with Marcus, somehow she'd sensed the relationship wouldn't last forever. But something had changed between her and Tyler. Rose had had a taste of what her love life with him could turn into. The paranoia, the jealousy, the second-guessing. She hadn't liked it, and it had made her not like Tyler that much either. Rose didn't want to not like Tyler; she loved him too much. But Rose didn't know if she was in love with him anymore, or if she'd ever been truly.

A long silence lingered between them.

Tyler spoke first. "Am I?"

"What?"

"Too late?"

Rose closed her eyes to search within herself and decide where she stood. She'd imagined Tyler saying all the things he'd just said to her a million times before. But in all her fantasies she'd been elated, giddy, out-of-this-world happy, and never… *empty.*

"Tyler, it wasn't meant to be between us. Not romantically. Even if I was willing to risk our friendship and give it a shot—which I'm not— the truth is I don't want to. I'm with Ethan, and I want to be with him. Can we go back to being just friends?" As she asked the question, she felt a bit hypocritical. If she had to be honest, they'd never been just friends. There'd always been something deeper between them—a deeper bond that the sex had ruined. She hoped with all her heart they could find a way back to each other, but she was no longer sure it was possible.

Tyler stood up from the couch without saying a word. He moved toward the door, opened it, and paused, his back to her. After a few seconds, Tyler stepped outside, slamming the door behind him, not once turning around.

Ethan

Ethan drummed his fingers on the leather wheel of his black Mercedes as he waited for the light to turn green. Another red light, and Ethan swore he'd speed through it. The drive through town toward Rose's apartment was taking ages. Georgiana had just called him to say she was back, that she'd left France two weeks early to be with Vicky, and help her with her final wedding preparations. As happy as Ethan was to have Gigi back home, he was more scared of the three-hundred pound gorilla she'd brought along—Tyler Bronfman.

Boston felt too small for the two of them, and Ethan didn't like the idea of Tyler anywhere near Rose. After four months with her, Ethan was in a good place. But now the d-bag was back and Tyler and Rose would see each other every day at school, and possibly outside of it, too.

The notion irked Ethan in a way he wasn't prepared to handle. He'd known he was in trouble the night he and Rose met. Rose stirred something in him; she held a power over him that not even Sabrina had had. Ethan wasn't the jealous type, but with Rose, he'd become possessive in a way he was ready to admit wasn't normal. And Tyler's return spiked this urge to new heights.

Finally, Ethan parked outside Rose's building and jogged inside, not stopping until he was standing in front of her door. When Rose answered, she had puffy eyes.

"Have you been crying?" Ethan asked, entering the apartment. "What happened?"

At once, he noticed a vivid red apple on the kitchen island. He didn't like the new addition. The thing was too red, too in-your-face, offensive almost. Ethan liked it even less than Rose's miserable expression, although he wasn't sure why. Not until he noticed the Fauchon chocolate box next to the apple.

"Nothing, I'm okay," Rose said.

"Found your red thingy?" Ethan asked, aware of the edge in his voice.

"Mmm, yeah, it's a present," Rose replied warily.

"From Paris?"

Rose nodded.

"How did Tyler know you were looking for something red?" Ethan asked between gritted teeth. "I thought you two weren't talking."

"We weren't, but Tyler knows me."

That was an even worse explanation, and Ethan lashed out. "Not twenty-four hours in the country and he's already been here? What did he want?"

"Ethan, please don't get jealous. I've had a bad enough morning already."

"Why? What happened?" Ethan's hands curled into fists and his knuckles went white. But he was mostly able to stay in control, and he resisted the desire to punch the wall as he listened to Rose's tale.

Rose

Ethan didn't look good. Rose had wanted to tell him everything, but looking at the cold fury mounting on her boyfriend's face right now, she wasn't sure she'd made the right choice. His jaw was set tight and twitching, while his hands were turned into fists, clenched so hard the knuckles were turning stark white.

"So let me get this straight," Ethan hissed. "The only reason you're not with Tyler is because you're too scared he'd break your heart. Otherwise, you would've already run off into the sunset together."

"Ethan, that's not what I said." Panic flared in Rose's chest.

"I must've gone deaf, then, because that's exactly what I heard."

Ethan and Rose glared at each other from opposite sides of the room, neither able to talk. Both were panting as if they'd just run a marathon.

"Ethan, please." Rose broke first. "Can you calm down? I don't want to argue with you. I'm just trying to be honest. Can we talk about it without shouting or getting mad?"

Rose watched him struggle to keep cool—Ethan was clearly beyond mad at this point. He flared his nostrils, paced around the room a couple of times, and finally settled on a stool at the kitchen bar. Rose was actually surprised by how quickly he'd calmed down—for the first time, she appreciated what it meant to be with someone older, more mature. Ethan might be mad, but he wasn't out of control.

"I'm listening," he said. "But I hate the power Tyler still has over you."

"Ethan, it's impossible not to be affected. If Sabrina walked through that door right now, you'd be upset even if you haven't seen her in five years. We're humans, not robots."

"I'm not in love with Sabrina," Ethan said pointedly.

"And I'm not in love with Tyler."

"Are you sure about that?"

"Listen, I care about him, and I always will. But no, I'm not in love with Tyler. I'm not sure I ever was."

Ethan's shoulders relaxed.

"The nerve of that dude," he grumbled. "He still hasn't broken up with my sister, and he came here to get all over you. Makes me want to punch him."

"Please don't. I'm happy with you, and I don't need anyone else. But Tyler is still a big part of my life."

Ethan shrugged, annoyed.

"I know you don't like our friendship," Rose pressed, "but can you accept it?"

Ethan was silent for a few tension-charged minutes, making Rose wonder what was going on inside his head. Finally, he looked up and pinned her with a hard stare.

"Talk to me," Rose whispered.

"I've been in this situation before." Ethan shook his head. "With Sabrina, I'd noticed one stare too many between her and Max, but I didn't trust my instincts. I couldn't believe what was right before my eyes. I didn't want to. And I ended up being made the fool. I won't make the same mistake twice.

"Rose, I trust you, so I'll ask you one last time: Are you sure Tyler is just a friend to you? After everything that happened? And please, be honest. I couldn't stand walking in on you and him together. So if you're not one hundred percent sure, if you need time to think things through, just say so. I'd much rather we end things now, clean. If you say there's nothing between you two, you have to mean it."

Ethan's speech was so full of passion it made Rose's tingle all over. Her body practically sang with warmth.

"Ethan, I do mean it," she said. Rose closed the distance between them and cupped his face in her hands. She didn't need to think about it, she was sure. "I want to be with you. Only you." Rose leaned in and kissed him.

He tugged her into a bone-crushing hug that told Rose how scared he'd been over possibly losing her. She smiled.

"I prefer you when you smile," Ethan said.

"I prefer you when you're kissing me."

"Ah, Miss Atwood, I must oblige you then." He kissed her again. And after breaking the kiss, he added, "What do you say we make it official?"

"How?"

"My sister, Vicky, is getting married in two months. She's been pestering me to know if I'm going alone or with a date. Would you like to be my plus one?"

"Whoa! And meet the entire Smithson clan, are you sure?"

"As I'll ever be. I promise they don't bite."

Rose hesitated, and Ethan stiffened in her arms.

"I mean, if you don't want to, I completely understand. You don't have to come. I can go alone."

"No, I want to… but…"

Ethan raised his brows.

"Will Georgiana be okay with me coming? I mean, I don't want to create an awkward situation at your sister's wedding. Everyone in your family should be relaxed and able to enjoy the day, Georgiana included. If she still hates me…"

"As long as she's with Tyler, I don't see why she should have a problem."

"You think Georgiana will go with Tyler?"

"She already told Vicky she would."

"And don't you think that's going to be even more awkward?"

"To be honest, I don't care. Georgiana is my sister, and you are you. If we stay together, you girls will have to learn how to talk to each other while keeping your claws sheathed. And I want you to meet my family."

"I don't have claws," Rose protested.

"You sure?"

"Mm-hmm."

"So you're coming?"

"I guess so. I mean, it's only a day. How bad can it be?"

"Oh. I should've said the wedding is on Martha's Vineyard… for the entire spring break."

"You bastard."

"I'm sure you can survive."

"Isn't the middle of March too early to go to Martha's Vineyard?"

"What can I say, my family is weird. And Vicky loves the island at the end of winter."

"How can a wedding last for *a week*?"

"I've no idea." Ethan tucked her in closer to him, and Rose felt reassured that with him by her side, she could endure an entire week of Georgiana. And maybe after France, Georgiana didn't hate her so much. Rose could only hope.

Georgiana

Georgiana pulled on a hairband to keep her hair out of her face. "Can I use your concealer?" she asked Vicky.

They were doing their makeup in Vicky's hotel room on Martha's Vineyard. The same way they used to when they were younger and both lived with their parents. A giant mirror lined the upper half of a wall with a cozy shelf underneath that now resembled a beauty booth. Downlights in the ceiling completed the setup, making it better than a professional dressing room.

"Use this one," Vicky said, passing her a stick with a built-in brush. "It's the best."

Georgiana and her sister shared the same pale complexion, dark hair, and sparkly blue eyes. Same as Ethan, same as their father when he was younger, before stress and age turned his hair to white.

Georgiana flicked the brush all around her eyes and while she waited for her skin to absorb the liquid concealer, she turned in her chair to look at Vicky.

"What do you think of the stray?" she asked.

On their second night on the island, after a day of studying Rose and Tyler interact, Georgiana wanted a second opinion.

"Come on, Gigi," Victoria said. "Rose isn't a stray. She seems perfectly nice to me."

"She's a sneaky little ho. I can't believe Ethan brought her here, and that he dumped Alice for that bitch."

"Who's Alice?"

"One of my best friends and my sorority little sister," Georgiana explained. "You met at Christmas, the year before last. Madison's friend who came to the house?"

"Yeah, I remember her."

"Anyway, Alice was dating Ethan when Rose stole him. That's what she does."

"I don't know. What if Ethan was over your friend? After Sabrina, he's gone through so many girlfriends."

"Exactly. So why stick to the stray? He must be out of his mind."

"He seems a little out of his mind," Victoria agreed. "But in a

Sabrina-out-of-his-mind way."

Georgiana lowered the sponge she was using to apply foundation and threw her sister an evil glare through the mirror. "You think he's in love with her?"

"Gigi, you're blind if you haven't noticed."

"I hoped he wouldn't be so stupid."

"Why? I haven't seen Ethan this cheerful in years. You should be happy for him."

"I would be if it was anyone *but her*."

"Didn't you ask him to go out with her a while ago?"

"Yeah, but only because he usually chews girls up and spits them out in the blink of an eye. I never thought he'd be so dumb as to actually fall for her. And that was before he was dating Alice, anyway."

Before her sister could reply, there was a knock at the door. Only one eye done, Vicky closed the mascara stick she was using and went to answer.

"Hi," Madison, their younger cousin, said.

"What are you doing here?" Georgiana asked.

"I invited her." Vicky gave her a pointed, be-good stare in the mirror.

Madison blushed. "If you were talking, I can come back later."

Geez. Her cousin was such a pushover Georgiana almost didn't enjoy teasing her. It was too easy.

"Actually, yeah," Georgiana said. "We were having a private conversation. So if you don't mind…" She made a shoo gesture.

Madison was already turning toward the door when Vicky stopped her. "Don't be silly, Madison." Victoria took Madison's hand and made her sit in front of the giant mirror. "We were only discussing Ethan's new girlfriend."

"Rose? She seems really nice."

"Of course you'd think that," Georgiana snapped.

Madison blushed again and lowered her gaze. While their cousin wasn't watching, Vicky slapped the back of Georgiana's head and mouthed, "Stop it," in the mirror. Aloud, she added, "I like her too."

Madison lifted her head and gave a weak smile. "I preferred Alice, though."

Vicky's eyes widened, making the lack of mascara in one even more obvious. "What's so special about this Alice?" she asked Madison.

"She's my roommate and best friend," Madison confirmed. "It would've been super cool if she'd joined the family. Anyway, she has a new boyfriend now, so all's well that ends well…"

Georgiana rolled her eyes. "Quoting Shakespeare, Madison? Seriously?" She wondered how Alice could live with her cousin without shooting herself in the head. Madison was so boring. "Here." Georgiana passed Madison the liquid concealer. "Start with those awful circles under your eyes. You spend too much time locked inside, reading poems."

Madison made a grimace in the mirror but did as she was told.

Georgiana finished smudging eye shadow on her lids before she said, "Anyway, you're both wrong. Rose is a horrible person."

Vicky sighed, exasperated. "What is it you have against her?"

"For one, as soon as her ex dumped her, she was all over Tyler. Even though he was with me, she moved into his house right away and who knows what else she tried to do."

"Rose and Tyler seem pretty cold towards each other," Vicky said, finally applying a thick coat of mascara on the missing lashes.

"That's true," Madison said. "They barely spoke last night at dinner."

"Which only proves my point," Georgiana continued. "Why did they argue? Probably because he's with me and not with her."

"I don't know." Vicky shook her head. "To be honest, I don't like the way Tyler glowers at our brother every time they cross paths."

"What are you saying?"

"Just be careful," Victoria said. "I don't want you to get hurt."

"So you think the stray is still after Tyler?"

"*Enough.*" Vicky banged a hand on the shelf, making the makeup items bounce. "Stop calling her that. Or, at least, don't let Ethan catch you."

"All right, I'll call her by her full name, then, *Rosalynn*." Georgiana smirked. "How quaint."

Vicky rolled her eyes. "Anyway, to answer your question: no. From the way she looks at our brother, she's not after Tyler. Are you sure it's not Tyler who's after her?"

Georgiana positively glowered at Vicky and noticed Madison shrink in her chair.

"Excuse me," Georgiana hissed. "You're talking about my boyfriend.

Tyler wouldn't be with me if he was into her. We're perfect for each other, and who knows? Maybe in a year's time, it will be me getting ready for my rehearsal dinner."

Or sooner, if her new plan worked. France had not been the success she'd hoped for. They had had a lovely time in Paris, with no arguments or troubles. But their relationship lately could be summed up as lukewarm. Tyler was slipping away from her. And even if she'd never admit it aloud, she suspected Tyler still wasn't out of reach from Rose's claws. So, at least for now, she tolerated Ethan's relationship with her, as it provided a sort of safeguard. But with a bit of luck, soon there'd be no doubts about whom Tyler belonged to. And Georgiana was confident Ethan would grow tired of Rose sooner or later. She couldn't wait for the time she'd be rid of the stray for good.

Rose

Rose shuffled around the dining hall of the hotel, hating that Ethan was not by her side for this social apéritif. But her boyfriend had a lot of friends on the island who he hadn't seen in months, and Rose couldn't demand he babysit her every second of the week. Still, she found it hard to socialize with so many unknown people. Not to mention she was on edge trying to avoid both Tyler and Georgiana. The wedding party was a certified minefield.

On cue, Tyler walked into the room, and Rose navigated the other guests to disappear into the adjoining hall. Too busy with her escape to pay attention to other people, Rose bumped into someone.

"Oh, I'm sorry," she said.

"Please don't be. You must be the famous Rose," a distinguished man with trimmed white hair said. "I'm Ethan's father, Bradley Smithson. Nice to meet you."

"Rosalynn Atwood. Very pleased to meet you, sir."

"The pleasure is all mine. It isn't often that our boy brings home a girl. Ethan tells me you're in your second year at Harvard Law. Have you already decided what branch of the law you want to follow?"

"I'd like to work in litigation in the area of criminal law, sir."

"Oh, interesting." Mr. Smithson chuckled. "I have a soft spot for criminal law myself. Many interesting cases. In fact, a couple of years ago we had this case on our hands…"

Mr. Smithson started outlining the grounds of the case, and Rose listened attentively. Was he putting her to the test? He must be. Why else would he discuss legal matters with her five seconds after introducing himself? Ethan's dad finished his speech and stared expectantly. "What's your legal opinion?" he asked.

Yes, definitely a test.

Rose collected her thoughts. In the particular case he'd outlined, textbook solutions would only get the defendant into deeper trouble, which was probably why he'd selected it. So what would a shrewd lawyer do? Was there a way out? Some aspect was escaping her. She concentrated, trying to get a firmer grasp on the solution. After closing her eyes for a second, inspiration hit. *Jurisdiction!* It was a jurisdiction issue. The crime had been committed on a federal enclave and it did not fall within the jurisdiction of the state where it was being tried. Her dad had told her about a similar case ages ago.

Rose smiled and offered her response.

Mr. Smithson smiled back, a new respect twinkling in his eyes. "Do they teach that to second year students these days?"

"No, I don't think so. But my dad has always been passionate about the law. As a child, he read me supreme court sentences instead of fairy tales."

"Hi Dad," Ethan said, coming up from behind them. He stepped up next to Rose and slid an arm around her waist in a protective gesture.

"Son," Mr. Smithson said, acknowledging Ethan with a nod. Then he returned his focus to Rose. "Your father is a lawyer? I'm not aware of any Atwood law firms in the Boston area."

"Oh, no. He couldn't pursue a career. When my grandparents died in a car accident, he'd barely finished college before he had to go back to Dallas to take care of his younger brother and sister."

"Dallas? What does your father do back in Texas?"

"He's in real estate."

Ethan tightened his grip on her waist, he clearly tensed at the mention of his profession in front of his father, even if they were discussing her dad's work and not Ethan's.

"Atwood, Atwood," Mr. Smithson repeated. "Are you by any chance related to David Atwood?"

"Yes… he's my dad," Rose replied, embarrassed.

Mr. Smithson's eyes bulged for a brief second before he caught himself.

"Well, I'll let you young kids enjoy the party," he said. "It was a real pleasure meeting you, Rose." He smiled fleetingly, then turned on his heel and was gone.

Ethan

Ethan followed the exchange between Rose and his father with unease. Since he'd started his own business, his relationship with his dad had been hard, to put it nicely. To say his dad could barely stand to look at him would be more accurate. Smithson and Smithson was the number one law firm in Boston. And for one of "the heirs" to abandon it was a slight too serious for his father to ever forgive.

Ethan wouldn't have put it past him to make a sour remark to Rose, making her uncomfortable just to get at him. Even if, so far, they seemed to get along well. Yet when Rose mentioned her father was in real estate, Ethan was ready to go on the offensive if his dad dared say something insulting about that particular line of work.

Instead, his dad had stunned him by recognizing Rose's father by name and winking at him just before he'd left. Bradley Smithson— *winking*! Dad had shown no comradeship toward him since, well, since he'd abandoned the law. What was up with him? Ethan looked at Rose, perplexed, and was even more confused when he found her blushing tomato red.

"What was that about?" he asked.

"Not now." She looked mortified. "I'll explain later."

"Rose, is something wrong? Did my dad say something to you?"

"No, Ethan." Rose shook her head. "Your dad was perfectly nice."

"What then? Why did my dad know your father by name?"

"Can we do this later? I need a drink." She skipped forward, away from him and toward the bar.

Ethan followed, curiosity building. He wasn't going to let this go. He'd ask her later, in private, when he had better ways of mollifying her.

Tyler

Tyler paced around his room, he was hiding from Georgiana and still hadn't managed to speak to Rose. How had things come to this? He was trapped in a relationship he didn't want, but somehow needed. The only reason he remained with Georgiana, ironically, was to be closer to Rose. Like this weeklong wedding—he'd agreed to come only because Rose would be here. Tyler had hoped he'd be able to talk to Rose, but Ethan stuck to her like a shadow. At least everyone was staying in separate rooms. Georgiana's parents were old-fashioned like that.

He picked up the room's phone and dialed nine.

"Reception, how may I help you?"

"Hi, hello, I'm here with the Smithson wedding party. May I have the room number of a guest?"

"Sure, sir. What's the guest's name?"

"Rosalynn Atwood."

"Miss Atwood is staying in room 2405. You want me to connect you, sir?"

"No, that's all, thank you." Tyler hung up.

Damn. Room 2405 was on the same floor as Georgiana's room, but he had to try. Tyler ruffled his hair in the mirror—yeah, the bad boy look suited him—and walked out of his room.

After waiting for what felt like hours for the elevator to arrive, Tyler hopped in and pushed the second floor button. To his relief, there wasn't a soul in the hallway on the next floor. So why the anxiety? He wasn't doing anything wrong. And if someone caught him… ah hell, America was still a free country, wasn't it?

2401, 2403… there, room 2405. The door had a bell, but Tyler decided to knock since he didn't want to risk someone from an adjoining room hearing the bell ringing. When no one answered after a minute or so, Tyler knocked again. Was Rose not in her room? Was she still downstairs in the dining hall? That wasn't likely—when he'd left the party, Tyler had searched for her. Rose wasn't downstairs. Rage seared his veins. Was she in Ethan's room? Tyler knocked once more, louder this time, so that if Rose was inside, it would be impossible not to hear.

"I think you have the wrong room," a deep voice said from behind, making Tyler jump. "My sister is two doors down the hall."

Tyler turned around to meet a stare of manly hate. Ethan had a black expression that told Tyler the dude was more than ready to fight. He wouldn't mind knocking out the old guy, but instincts suggested the move wouldn't score him any points with Rose. The two men stared at each other aggressively for a few seconds, until Tyler finally broke eye contact and moved down the hall without saying anything.

He paused at Georgiana's door and looked back before knocking. Tyler watched Ethan go through the door that had remained shut for him, and a wave of resentment took over. He rapped his knuckles on Georgiana's door in a loud, vindictive knock. Not that Rose cared about anything—or anyone—he did anymore.

The knowledge made him livid.

Rose

When Rose heard the first knock, she assumed it was Ethan. Only her innate sixth sense prompted her to have a look through the peephole before throwing the door open. Seeing Tyler standing in the hall outside froze her cold. What did he want? Rose couldn't go through another conversation like the one they'd had in January. Not here, not now. Even if they'd hardly spoken in a month and a half, it was too soon. Their friendship was still bleeding from a thousand wounds, and they couldn't afford to add more fresh cuts. Plus, Ethan was going to be here at any minute, and the three of them standing in a confined space together was a hell-no situation.

Even through the glass's distortion, she could see Tyler's pained expression, and it killed her. She backed away from the door. Rose couldn't bear to see Tyler suffering like this. But what could she do? Nothing Rose could say right now would improve the situation—it'd only make it worse. The easiest thing was to pretend she wasn't in her room. If she didn't open the door, Tyler would go away, and they'd talk another time. Yes, this was the only sensible thing to do. But as another knock came, and then another, her heart churned. Rose willed Tyler to leave because it wasn't in her nature to shove him away, over and over.

"I think you have the wrong room."

Ethan's voice sent a chill down her spine, and Rose glued her eye to the peephole.

Ethan and Tyler were glaring at each other like angry beasts ready to attack.

"My sister is two doors down the hall," Ethan added, his tone as cold and hard as metal.

Tyler's expression was murderous—not that Ethan's was all hearts and clouds. If Rose could magically dematerialize right now, she would. Her heart beat faster as the two stood there, glowering at each other. After what seemed like forever, Tyler finally left.

A soft knock came immediately after, and she opened the door to let Ethan in. His stare was a wall of ice.

"What did he want?" Ethan hissed.

"I don't know."

"I don't like it, Rose. I don't like it one bit." Ethan nervously paced around the room. "I don't care if he's a big part of your life or your best friend; if he keeps this shit going, I'm going to whack the bastard."

"Ethan, calm down. Everyone's going to hear you if you—"

"I don't give a shit if everybody hears."

"But your sister—"

"It'd be about time she opened her eyes. Listen, Rose, I have to tell her. I can't stand that he's all over you while he's still dating her."

"Tell her what, exactly?" Rose said icily.

"About you and Tyler. Your history together. I have to tell her. It's the only way she'll be able to move on."

"Ethan, you can't tell her that. When I told you, you said I wasn't talking to Georgiana's brother."

"But she's obsessed with him, how else can I make her see the truth?"

"Not by telling her about me and Tyler. You promised."

"I know, I know. But it's killing me to see the way he's hurting her. And I can't stand him anywhere near you." Ethan's shoulders relaxed for the first time since he came into the room.

"Come here." Rose grabbed his hand and pulled him toward the bed, where they cozied into each other's arms. "I know it's hard," she said, stroking his hair. "But I'm sure everything is going to be all right. Tyler and Georgiana will break up on their own. If Tyler doesn't love her, he'll break up with her. To be honest, I'm surprised he hasn't done it yet."

"What if he doesn't?"

"Ethan, I don't think he's going to propose to your sister, so they'll break up sooner or later. And when it comes to me… look, he's been spoiled his whole life. He's not used to hearing no. This is just a tantrum. It'll pass. He needs some time. That's all."

"I still don't like it."

"I know, and I'm sorry."

"Don't be. It's not your fault." Ethan kissed her forehead. "But don't think you're so easy to forget."

Rose scrunched her face.

"You're adorable." Ethan showered her face and neck with tender kisses. "You even impressed my dad. I told you he'd want to adopt you."

"Oh, come on. He was just being polite."

"No, he wasn't. Rose, he winked at me! You must've done something to really impress him. And why did he know your father?"

"About that." Rose flushed red. "Remember when I said my dad was in real estate?"

"Mm-hmm."

"I may have understated that a little. I mean…" Ethan looked at her questioningly. Rose hoped he wouldn't see her differently after she told him. "Let's just say his company is just shy of a Fortune 500…"

Ethan stared at her. "What, you're saying your dad's a real estate mogul, and you're a billionaire?"

"Pretty much." Rose's cheeks flared hot. She was sure her face was about to melt.

"That would explain my father's approval. If I'd known you were an heiress, I wouldn't have rented your place to you at half price."

"You said the owner didn't want to have it go to frat boys!"

"More the owner wanted to get in your pants."

"It's your apartment, isn't it? You sneak!"

"Me, sneak? What about all that 'I have a low budget' crap you pulled, Miss Heiress?"

"I prefer Miss Atwood. And my reasonable-rent need was true, I don't like to flaunt my dad's money around. I prefer to live on a reasonable budget until I can make a living of my own. And I don't like people knowing about my dad, because no matter what they say, they look at you differently once they find out."

"I know the feeling. It was the same in school for me. Once my surname was public knowledge, I had a whole lot of new *friends*. I hated it."

"So you get it?"

"I do."

"Are you mad I didn't tell you?"

"No." Ethan leaned in and kissed her.

"You must've really liked me to pull that rent stunt," Rose said with a mischievous smile. "How much did you lose?"

"I do a little more than like you. And I didn't lose anything. I gained you. Rose…" Ethan paused. He almost never used her first name, and it gave Rose goose bumps all over. "I love you."

Rose's heart skipped a beat. "I love you, too," she replied, one hundred percent sure of her feelings.

Tyler was forgotten. The man standing next to her consumed everything in Rose's world. Ethan, the man Rose loved and who loved her back. He kissed her and Rose sighed, forgetting everything, even her name.

***

"Tyler?" Rose said into her phone. She'd heard nothing from him since the wedding two months back, and now he was calling her out of the blue.

"I-I need to talk to you." Tyler sounded agitated. "Can you meet me?"

"Right now?"

"Yeah, right now."

Rose looked at her watch. In forty-five minutes, she had a meeting for a group project that was due in less than a week. "I have a group meeting in forty-five minutes, but we can meet on campus and talk there before I head to the library to meet the others."

"Rose, to hell with classes and finals and group projects!" There was a hint of desperation in his words. "I need to talk to you, and it's going to take a lot longer than forty-five minutes."

"Tyler, did something happen? What is it?"

"Not over the phone. I'll pick you up at your house in fifteen."

The line went dead. Tyler had hung up without leaving her room to reply.

Exactly fifteen minutes later, her doorbell rang. Rose picked up her bag and hurried to meet Tyler downstairs at his car.

"Hey," she greeted him, opening the passenger door and climbing in. "What's up?"

Tyler turned toward her, and Rose gasped. With his ghastly pale skin, bloodshot eyes, disheveled hair, and dark, five-o'clock shadow, her best friend looked a mess. Thinner than she'd ever seen him, and ten years older.

"Tyler, what's going on?" Rose asked, alarmed.

"Later." He put the car into gear and started driving, gripping the wheel so tightly his knuckles turned stark white.

After ten minutes of driving in silence with no radio and no talking, Rose began to feel uneasy. She had no idea where they were going. They might be heading north, but that was the extent of Rose's sense of orientation.

"Tyler, can you at least give me a hint here?"

He shook his head. "I can't talk about it in the car… I can't…"

"Can I at least ask where we're going?"

"Salem."

Salem? Was this a witch-hunt? But when they kept going on I-93 North instead of turning onto I-95, Rose realized they were going to Salem, New Hampshire, not Salem, Massachusetts. The "why" remained a mystery. She kept quiet for the rest of the ride until they stopped in the parking lot of what looked like an amusement park.

Why would Tyler want to drive forty-five minutes on a random Saturday to go to an amusement park? And on a day like this? At the end of April, the weather was still chilly and windy, and the park looked like a ghost town. Rose had so many questions she wanted to ask him, but once again, she didn't. Certain he wouldn't answer anyway, she decided to wait, even if Tyler looked more wretched with every passing minute.

She followed him to the ticket booth where he bought two daily passes. Tyler took a free map of the park and started walking down a paved path. Rose walked behind him, a million scenarios playing in her head. Was this about them, their friendship? Their love quadrangle? They hadn't talked properly after the wedding. When they bumped into each other on campus, there were always other people around to provide a buffer. The unspoken arrangement had suited both of them. Somehow, though, Rose knew this mysterious trip was about something else. Tensions lingered between them, but nothing strong enough to turn Tyler into the mess he appeared to be right now.

Rose was so absorbed in her thoughts, she didn't see Tyler stop, and when he did, she bumped into his back.

"We're here," he said.

Rose followed his gaze upwards and saw they'd stopped in front of a Ferris wheel. Her heart jumped in her throat. So it was something bad, really bad. Ferris wheels were their special place. The most important turning points of their life and friendship had been discussed while on a wheel ride. Mostly the one back at home, the Texas Star, but others worked in a pinch, too.

Rose thought back to some of the things they'd said and done inside a Ferris car. They'd promised each other they would be friends forever, piercing their index fingers with a needle and mixing their blood to seal the pact.

When they were twelve, they'd shared their first kiss—just because they'd decided they should practice the technique together before they did it for real with someone else. At least, that had been Rose's excuse. She'd wanted Tyler to be the first boy she kissed. It had also been on a Ferris wheel that Tyler had told Rose about losing his virginity. Years later, Rose had done the same.

On one dreadful ride, they'd tried their first beer out of a flask Tyler had stolen from his dad and hidden under his football jacket. The beer had been warm and disgusting, and Rose had ended up getting sick, earning them one of the harshest groundings in their teenage history.

They'd opened their Harvard admission letters together in a car much like the ones currently rotating high above her. After high school, they'd gone less often, but Rose had cried over Marcus for the first time while on a ride. They'd kept the tradition of going at least once whenever they were at home in Dallas.

Everything important had been said on a Ferris wheel, and now here they were in front of one. Tyler had something so big to tell her that it called for a wheel ride. What was it?

A cold shiver crawled up Rose's spine. She was scared.

"I know it's no Texas Star," Tyler said with a forced smile, "but it was the best I could find up here."

There was no line, and as they entered the first available car, an eerie silence lingered between them. As soon as the ride started, Tyler dropped his head into his hands, and Rose realized with horror that he was crying. She'd never seen Tyler cry. *Never.* Rose wanted to comfort him, but she didn't understand why he needed comforting. Asking didn't seem like an option, so she just sat beside him in sympathetic silence.

After the wheel did a full circle, the attendant on the ground moved forward as if to help them dismount, but Rose signaled they were taking another ride. The park was empty. No one was in line, and after their second go-round, the attendant left them alone and kept the ride spinning.

Cold air blew on them, especially when they passed the upper part of the wheel. Still, Rose buttoned her jacket to the neck and waited patiently for Tyler to be ready to talk, ignoring both the wind and the cold.

"My life is over," Tyler said once they reached the top for the third time. "I feel so sick I want to throw up."

"You're ill?" Rose's voice cracked.

Tyler shook his head.

"Tyler, what is it? Tell me." Rose felt ready to explode from anxiety.

"She… she's…" Tyler shook his head again. "She trapped me."

"Who? Who trapped you? What do you mean?"

"Georgiana."

Another chill raced down Rose's spine. "What did she do this time?" There were no more semesters abroad to force on him. "Is it school again?"

"No." Tyler kept shaking his head in his hands. "I'm done. No way out."

"Tyler, what did she do?" Rose whispered.

"She lied. S-she tricked me. She did it on purpose. She says she didn't, but I know she did."

"What? What did she do?"

Tyler let out a desperate cry. "She's pregnant."

After his confession, Tyler cracked and collapsed into Rose's arms, crying like a baby. Rose hugged him close to her chest, whispering soothing words, all the while boiling inside with rage. Tyler was one hundred percent right. Georgiana had done it on purpose. Probably telling Tyler some lame excuse about the pill not always working or some other false crap. Rose didn't need to hear the details. When her phone started vibrating in her bag, she shifted in the booth to turn it off without looking at the caller ID.

"Pick up if you need to," Tyler half-sobbed.

"No. Whatever it is can wait." Rose let Tyler have a few more minutes. When he seemed a little calmer, she asked, "Have you... mmm... discussed options?"

"There's nothing to discuss. Georgiana says she wants to keep the baby."

Well, of course, after all the trouble the bitch went through to engineer the pregnancy in the first place. Rose felt homicidal. "And what do *you* want?"

"It doesn't matter what I want, I can't have it." Tyler sighed. "Rose, I want my life back. I want you back. But, most of all, I want our friendship back!"

"Tyler, I'm here, and we're friends. No matter what happens, we'll always be friends. I'm so sorry Georgiana did this to you, but we'll get through this pregnancy like everything else. What are you going to do?"

"No clue." Tyler shook his head. "What *can* I do?"

"Well, Georgiana didn't leave you much choice..."

"She didn't leave me *any* choice. Even if she was open to discussing options, you know my views on abortion, and she knows them, too."

"How come?"

"She knows I'm adopted and against abortion, as I wouldn't be here if my biological mom had one."

"You told her you're adopted?" Rose was shocked; Tyler never told anyone.

"Yeah."

"When?"

"Ages ago. I don't remember when. The topic just came up somehow..."

"Oh, Tyler, look at me, please."

"What?"

"You'll be an amazing father for this baby, no matter what."

"Rose, please. I'm the most irresponsible person in the world. I can't take care of myself. How will I care for a helpless child?"

"That's crap and you know it. Tyler, you're a good guy, and you'll be a great dad."

"Stop saying that word. I want to throw up."

"And who said morning sickness was just for the girls?" Rose attempted a joke.

Tyler looked grim. "I'm going to be someone's father."

"It appears so."

Tyler and Rose sat in silence for another half-turn of the wheel, both staring at the view, lost in thought. Until Rose finally spoke. "I feel a bit guilty about this whole situation."

"Guilty, you? Why would *you* feel guilty?"

"Do you think Georgiana would've gone to these extremes if I hadn't moved in with you? It made her go cuckoo jealous."

"I don't care if Georgiana was jealous—she didn't have the right to do this to me. When she told me…" Tyler growled. "All I can say for myself is that I didn't strangle her—and not because I didn't want to."

"Ethan says she's obsessed with you—"

"Don't bring *him* into this discussion," Tyler hissed. "I don't want to remember he even exists right now. And please don't tell me again I should've dumped Georgiana a long time ago. I don't need an 'I told you so' speech. I'm already aware of the mistakes I've made. Don't you think I regret every day not leaving Georgiana right after we… Anyway, I think about it every day. If I had, we'd be together now, and you wouldn't be dating the devil's brother, and I wouldn't be having a baby *with* the devil!"

"Don't go there. This is not your fault."

"But it is, Rose, it's all my fault. If I hadn't been so damn scared, right now we'd be happy together. I've been an idiot, Rose. I wanted to be with you so bad, but I was scared because I knew with you, it would've been the real deal. And so I did what I do best: I ran. I ruined everything. Georgiana got all scheme-y because I left her suspicions room to grow. I shouldn't have stayed with her, I shouldn't have gone to France, and I should've used a condom even if Georgiana swore she was on the pill. I mean, how many idiots have been in my position before?"

"Listen—I'm not condoning what Georgiana did because it's so wrong on so many levels. But it shows you how much she cares about you…"

Tyler snorted.

"In her own perverse way, I think Georgiana really loves you. Look at all she's done to be with you. And it's not like she's after money or anything." In the past, Rose had suspected more than a few of Tyler's girlfriends of finding his wallet more attractive than the person. Georgiana wasn't one of them. "The Smithsons are well off, so all Georgiana has to gain from this mess is you, and I'm not saying you should forgive her—"

"Are you sure? Because that sounded a lot as if you were making excuses for her."

"No, there's no excuse for her behavior. But I am stating a fact: Georgiana loves you. A lot."

"Love?" Tyler scoffed bitterly. "You don't trap the people you love."

"True. Let's say her love leans a little toward the selfish side—okay, a lot toward the selfish side—but you can't deny it's there. What about you? How do you feel about her?"

"I hate her, Rose. I *hate* her." Tyler stared ahead at empty space. "Don't even make me think about her…"

"Tyler…"

"I don't like that tone."

"Can I ask you something?"

"I have a feeling you're going to ask anyway."

"How did you feel about Georgiana—I mean, really—before all this happened? Before… me?" Rose gripped the security metal bar. "Were you in love with her? Because if I have to be completely honest with you, she used to scare me more than any of your other girlfriends. And that's why maybe… er…"

Tyler turned toward her with a confused frown. "What are you saying, Rose?"

"I'm saying that before I messed things up, you seemed really happy with Georgiana. I'm saying that partially—*subconsciously*—things may have happened between us when they did because I felt threatened by Georgiana. Yeah, I was sad about Marcus, but I was also jealous of you and Georgiana." Rose released a breath. "Oh, Tyler. I've been selfish and stupid and petty. I couldn't stand her, and I was scared she would take you away from me for good. That's part of the reason we—I mean… did… you know… when we did."

"If you felt that way, why did you turn me down when I came home begging to be with you?"

"When you moved to France I had time to clear my head. I know I love you, and I thought I was in love with you for most of my life… but then all that shit happened, and you moved to Paris, and then… I met Ethan, and…"

"Please don't tell me how much you're in love with him because I couldn't stand to hear it right now."

"That's not… My point is this: I idealized you for more than a decade, and you probably did the same with me. In my head, I'd always pictured us ending up married after you straightened up a bit and had seen enough women naked to be good for life…"

"Yeah, I had that same idea. But what's your point?"

"My point is that maybe this fantasy we've both been having was just that—a fantasy. What I'm saying is, in all the years I've known you, I've never seen you as emotionally involved as you were with Georgiana. I mean, before I spoiled everything by jumping into bed with you because I wanted to ruin your relationship. Because if I'm being honest, that's what I wanted. I couldn't stand that you hadn't cheated on her. I couldn't stand that you were no longer making a go at me, so I had to go ahead and screw your love life."

Tyler smirked. "Quite literally."

Rose blushed but smiled. This was the first glimmer that made her recognize the Tyler she loved under the broken man, under all his sadness and worries. If Tyler could make jokes on a day like this, there was still hope.

"To be honest," Rose continued. "I've been the worst friend—person, even. Worse than Julia Roberts in My Best Friend's Wedding. I am the fungus growing on pond scum."

"No, you're just the scum," Tyler said with the tiniest hint of a smile. "We both are. But Georgiana… she's the fungus feeding on scum."

"She's a bit of a fungus or the mucus of the fungus… But the fact remains that despite everything—despite me, and France—you didn't break up with her. It has to mean something."

"I came to that stupid wedding only because I wanted to see you."

"Okay, but you had a million other opportunities to dump her, and you never did."

"I've already told you, I'm aware of all the mistakes I've made. I don't need you to rub my face in them."

"What if it wasn't a mistake? You've never been faithful to someone for as long as Georgiana. Before I ruined everything, I mean. Not even with Jessica. So, are you sure you can't find that love again, that there's no way you could ever forgive Georgiana and be happy with her? Even if she's a bit… mmm—"

"Of a conniving bitch?"

"I was going to say *pushy*. I know you're mad right now—"

"Mad doesn't begin to cover it."

"Okay, but the only choice you can make right now is how to fit into this baby's life."

"Meaning?"

"Meaning: are you going to be a single dad, or are you and Georgiana going to be a family?"

Ethan

Ethan had been pacing up and down Rose's lobby for an hour now, and his patience was running thin. Why wasn't she picking up the phone? She was with him, wasn't she? The notion only served to fuel his anger. He had the keys to Rose's apartment, being the owner, but it didn't feel right to let himself in when Rose wasn't there. She hadn't given him a key, and anyway, waiting inside the apartment would hardly be better. At least down here he'd see Rose the minute she came home.

Half an hour later, Ethan watched a black car pull up in front of Rose's building. *Tyler's car.* So he'd been right, they were together!

The lights of the car went dark, and everything stood still. If Rose didn't come out of that damn car at once, Ethan would not feel responsible for his actions. He wanted to snap Tyler's neck so badly, and his being in the same car with Rose did nothing to calm the urge.

Luckily, just when Ethan was about to spring into action, the car lights came back on and Rose climbed out. As she trotted up the few steps to the front door, the car sped away.

Rose's eyes widened as she entered the lobby and spotted him. "Ethan?"

"Why didn't you pick up your phone?" Ethan accused, not even bothering with a hello.

Rose fired a question back instead. "Did you talk to Georgiana?"

Ethan nodded.

"So do you really need to ask why I wasn't picking up the phone?" Ethan was about to come out with some petty retort, but Rose cut him off. "Listen, it's been a long day. Why don't we go upstairs to talk?"

He followed her to the elevator, and as it climbed to her floor, both kept quiet. The metallic ding announcing they'd reached Rose's floor sounded deafening after their silent ride.

"I want pizza, a giant one," Rose said, unlocking the door and taking off her jacket.

"Pizza? How can you think about pizza right now?"

"I skipped lunch, I'm hungry, and I could use some comfort food. Are you mad at me for some reason?"

"You were with him all day, don't deny it. And you didn't pick up your phone!"

"If you're up to date on the 'good' news, I don't really need to explain why I spent the day with Tyler. He's still my best friend, and I'm his. Tyler needed to talk to someone. Do you want just cheese or pepperoni?"

"Just cheese," Ethan said, pouting.

Rose dialed the delivery number. "Um, hello. Yes, one cheese pizza and one pepperoni, please... Rose Atwood... correct, that's me... okay, perfect. Bye." She hung up and opened the fridge. "Beer?"

"Yeah, I need one before I go strangle that bastard." Ethan flopped onto the couch.

Rose handed Ethan his beer and sat rigidly next to him. "Excuse me?"

"You heard me."

"Yes, I did, but honestly, this whole situation is hardly Tyler's fault."

"Last time I checked, it took two to make a baby."

"Yes, it does take two, but if one of the two says she's on the pill when, in fact, she's not... all it takes is one lying b—"

"Watch it," Ethan threatened. "You're talking about my sister."

"I don't care if she's your sister. You're not on Georgiana's side on this, are you?"

"I'm not even sure what her side would be. Her side would be Georgiana not being pregnant with that bastard's baby, and her never seeing Tyler again."

"Well, that'd be Tyler's side, too, but it's too late for that."

"And whose fault is that?" Ethan looked at Rose pointedly.

"Are you saying it's my fault? How is any of this my fault?"

"If you'd let me talk to her, tell Gigi the truth, she would've never done it."

Rose glowered at him, eyes black with anger. "Don't you even dare go there," she hissed. "There's no way it's my fault if your psycho of a sister decided to get herself pregnant. *No. Way.* So don't even try to put this on me. Why are *you* mad, anyway? The only person with any right to be angry here is Tyler."

"Of course you'd be on darling Tyler's side."

"You're being petty on purpose. Are you mad because I spent the day with him? Is this only a jealousy tantrum?"

"Rose, I can't stand him. And you spent the entire day with him not picking up your phone."

"Because we were talking. There weren't any romantic implications in the conversation. Tyler is destroyed… I've never seen him this bad."

"He's a cheating, lying—"

"And what does that make your sister?" Rose continued to glare at him. "Georgiana schemed and lied just as bad."

"At least Gigi did it for love. Why did he do it? Why did he stay with her if he doesn't love her? Only to be closer to you, or to make you jealous, and now my sister will pay the consequences for life."

"Only because she got herself pregnant against Tyler's will. And please don't act as if you were a beacon of moral behavior. None of us have been."

"Meaning?"

"How many casual hook ups did you have after Sabrina?"

"Don't try to turn the focus away from that bastard—"

"Really? Georgiana traps him and Tyler is the bastard?" Rose was close to screaming.

"Calm down," Ethan said.

"No, you calm down." Rose shot up from the couch. "You haven't answered me."

"What was the question?"

"How many girls have you screwed without being in love?"

Ethan shrugged. "A few," he said casually, seeking to hurt Rose, to infuriate her.

It worked. Her nostrils flared in anger, and Rose struggled to keep her voice steady as she spoke. "Tell me, Ethan. How would you have felt if one of those girls had trapped you by deliberately lying about taking the pill? Think about it." Rose gave him a minute to, before continuing. "What if Alice had played the same trick on you? Would you be rooting for her, saying how, after all, you were the bastard for not loving her? I don't think so."

Touché. He was no saint, and neither was Georgiana. Ethan began to calm down. Rose was right; he was being over-protective of his sister, and over-jealous of Rose's relationship with Tyler.

"I know you love your sister," Rose continued, "and that you're worried about her. But for once, this mess was not Tyler's fault, or mine. It was all Georgiana. One hundred percent her. She's far from stupid or naïve, and she knew all the risks and consequences when she decided to go through with her little scheme. So it's all on her."

"But she doesn't know about you and Tyler. Maybe if she'd known, she wouldn't have done it."

"Didn't you say Georgiana suspected us? Do you really think it would've stopped her, even if she knew for sure? Seems like the opposite to me. It would've made her even more desperate to cling onto Tyler, instead of stopping her altogether."

"Maybe you're right, but what if you're wrong? I need to tell her. Please, let me tell her."

"Why? What good would it do now?"

"She could reconsider and…" Ethan didn't like what he was about to say, but he saw no other solution. "Not have the baby."

"Tyler would never let her do that."

"Why not? It'd be the perfect way out for him."

The doorbell rang in the background.

"Pizza's here."

Rose buzzed the delivery guy in. A few minutes later, she was back on the couch with two huge cardboard boxes and two more beers. They ate the first half of the pizza in silence. Ethan didn't want to be mad at Rose, but he was. He was convinced that if she'd let him talk with Georgiana, none of this would've happened.

"Why do you think Tyler wouldn't let her end the pregnancy?" Ethan asked.

"Because..." She looked unsure and wiped her mouth on a napkin to cover. "Well, you'll find out anyway sooner or later. Tyler is adopted and against abortion."

"Really?"

"Mm-hmm."

"Does Georgiana know?"

"She does, has for a long time."

Ethan snorted. His sister really was a piece of work.

"Do you think that's part of the reason she did it? Because she knew Tyler would want to keep the baby?"

"I'm pretty sure she took everything into account."

"Dooming herself for life."

"And bringing Tyler along for the ride."

"What is he going to do?" Ethan wasn't able to keep the animosity from his voice.

"What would you do in his place, since you seem to have all the right answers today, Mr. Self-righteous?" Rose sounded hurt more than angry.

Her vulnerability made him feel ashamed. He'd been yelling at her all night for no reason. Ethan had wanted someone to blame, but he shouldn't target Rose.

"Come here," Ethan said, grabbing her by the waist and pulling her onto his lap.

"Oh, so I'm back to hugging privileges?"

"And kissing privileges, too..." It felt good having her close, kissing her. Ethan relaxed. "It's just that my sister is crazy, and I can't stand him. But I'm sorry I took it out on you."

"Well, you'd better get used to Tyler being around; he might become your brother-in-law soon."

"Ugh, don't say that."

"Why?"

"Do you really think he'll propose?"

"They'll either split up for good and be single parents, or they'll get married and give it a shot at being a family. And, despite what you think, Tyler has a pretty big sense of responsibility, especially when it comes to family."

"Has he already decided?"

"No, but I think he'll try. At least if he can start looking at Georgiana again without wanting to kill her on the spot. It'll take time... but eventually, once he has come to terms with the situation and the idea of becoming a father..."

"But is that the best option?" The prospect of Georgiana marrying Tyler made Ethan sick. "Will he keep being a cheating loser if they get married?"

"I don't have a crystal ball. I've no idea what's best or how it will turn out. All I know is that Tyler will love this baby with all he has. He'll be a wonderful dad; I'm not so sure about a great husband. It's hard for anyone to start a family and have kids, but if you're forced into it, especially if you're Tyler..." Rose shook her head.

"So my sister basically dug her own grave."

"It's not necessarily going to be a fairy tale wedding, but there's a part of Tyler that cares about your sister. If he can forgive her, they could make it work."

"At least Mom will be ecstatic if she has another daughter married before the end of the year. And my dad too, with all these lawyer genes getting mixed up. He'll have a lawyer empire with all these grandkids."

"Mmm... but with us, babies could end up with mixed real estate genes..." Rose blushed all of a sudden. "Not that... I mean... I wasn't saying we should have kids or anything, it was just... you know..."

"You're so cute when you blush."

"And you're so annoying when you look that smug."

"That's not true; you adore me all the same." Ethan smirked. "So much so that you want to have my babies."

"I-I said it just for the sake of talking."

Ethan pressed one hand to his chest mockingly. "Now you're hurting me."

"Oh, stop it."

She silenced him with a kiss, and he wasn't about to complain.

"I have to study," Rose said after a short make-up cuddle. "Finals are in ten days, and I haven't done any homework today. Plus, I have a bunch of angry emails from my group project members who I blew off at the library that I need to read and reply to. Do you mind spending a cozy night in while I study?"

"I couldn't imagine a better way of spending the night than cozied in with you, and I always have work to do."

"I love you," Rose said out of the blue. "Never doubt that."

"I love you too, Miss Atwood." Guilt still gnawed at him, though. He'd been too harsh with her today. Rose didn't deserve to be treated this way. "Sorry again for today. I know it's not your fault. I was as worried for my sister as I was mad you spent the day with Tyler."

"You know," she said, and kissed Ethan, "the feminist movement will shoot me for saying this, but I sort of like it when you get crazy jealous. You're annoying as hell but way too adorable."

"I won't tell, I promise."

Rose got her books from her room and sat at the dining table. Ethan sat next to her, took out his iPad, and they began working and studying, respectively. Despite all that was happening, Ethan found himself happier than ever. A simple night in, doing ordinary, boring stuff, and Ethan was in heaven because he had Rose by his side.

Rose

"Woo–hoo! Finals are over!" Rose tilted her face up, enjoying the first warm day of May.

"You mind taking a walk with me?" Tyler asked seriously.

"Is Georgiana around?" Rose checked behind them.

Since the pregnancy announcement, Georgiana had become even more clingy and possessive of Tyler. Which usually resulted in escalating nasty behaviors toward Rose.

"Nah, she had an exam right"—Tyler checked his watch—"about now. We should be good for at least two hours."

"Okay then."

They walked in silence until Tyler stopped in front of a sunlit bench. He sat on the backrest and Rose sat on the bench next to him, her head level with his knees.

"So, I might've decided what to do with Georgiana and the baby," Tyler announced. "But I need to talk to you first."

"Okay…" Rose's heart started beating faster.

"I'll ask her to marry me and try to make it work. But before I do, I need to know you mean it when you say there isn't a future for us. That you see me as just a friend."

Air left Rose's lungs. So this was the moment when she'd have to say goodbye to Tyler forever. The day had been coming—fast—but somehow in all the scenarios Rose had imagined, being on a bench in the sun on campus had not been one of them.

Rose's voice failed her, the words caught in her throat. She paused and tried again. "Tyler, I don't see you just as a friend. You're so much more than that. You're my best friend, my oldest friend… you're family, and I love you."

"But you're not in love with me anymore."

Rose shook her head.

"'Cause you love him."

Rose nodded. Funny how Tyler and Ethan kept avoiding saying each other's names and just kept calling each other *him.*

"I hate his guts, you know."

"If it's any consolation, Ethan hates yours, too."

Tyler snorted. "Excuse me if I don't feel sorry for him."

Rose tried to keep her emotions in check. Her relationship—um, friendship?—with Tyler wouldn't be the same after today. For years, they'd flirted with the possibility of romance, of a distant future together. But today they were putting a stop to that for good. Rose hoped she'd manage to finish this conversation without bursting into tears.

"Okay, then. I'll be a married man soon!"

"You already guessed what I would say?"

"Pretty much."

"How?"

"From the way you look at him; you've never looked at me that way. Rose, you've never looked at anyone that way."

"Can I get a hug?" Rose was about to break down.

"Course you can. Come here."

Tyler jumped down from the bench backrest and pulled Rose into a tight embrace. A new sadness overcame her, and hugging Tyler provided little in the way of comfort. This newfound melancholy would take a long time to shake off. But, at least for the first time in forever, there wasn't tension between them.

"Promise me we will stay best friends no matter what happens," Rose whispered.

"Hey, I know I've gone soft, but I'm not Paris Hilton BFF material yet." Tyler smiled. "And who knows? You could become my sister-in-law very soon. One day, we'll be one big, happy family!" he added sarcastically.

"Aw, come on." Rose pushed him away and sat back on the bench. "It's not like I'm going to marry Ethan anytime soon."

"If he's not stupid, he'll ask you. Plus, he's such an old guy; he'd better get a move on."

Rose beamed at Tyler. It was good that he was making jokes again.

"So, when are you going to propose?" she asked.

"This weekend," Tyler said, sitting next to her. "Just before the term ends. Knowing Georgiana, she'll want to get married straight away before her bump shows."

"You've already picked a ring?"

"I have one on hold…"

"You seem calm enough."

"No. I'm freaking out, Rose. My guts are screaming at me to hop on a plane, go get lost somewhere in Asia, and not come back for years. But, like you said, I'll become a father no matter what, so I want to at least try to be a decent one."

"You'll be a great dad, Tyler. I'm sure of it."

"I have another question for you…"

"Is this one easier?"

"Pretty straightforward. Will you be my best man?"

"Of course I will, Tyler!"

"Thank you. It means a lot to have you there by my side."

"Will Georgiana… mmm… be okay with me being your best man?"

"Why? You think she has you lined up for the maid of honor role?"

"Ha, ha. I'd be surprised if she let me inside the church at all."

"Between me and the old guy, I'm sure she won't have much of a choice."

"He's not old!"

"He so is. So, will you be there by my side?"

"Always!" Rose squeezed his hand. They'd been on a long journey that had seen them together and apart, but, finally, Rose had her best friend back.

***

A mere three weeks later, Rose examined Tyler's appearance in his

92

wedding suit. They were in the chapel's side room reserved for the groom, and the ceremony was supposed to start in one hour. After Tyler's proposal, Georgiana had not wasted a second. The Bronfman-Smithson wedding had been organized in record time.

"You look like a ghost," Rose said.

"And you look like a boy."

"I was under strict orders to dress in a tux and comb my hair in a low chignon. Your wife-to-be was worried I'd ruin the visual equilibrium of the ceremony if I were to stay by your side dressed like a girl."

"What?"

"Interpreting Georgiana's thoughts with some liberty, I think she wanted me to look as ugly as possible."

"You're never ugly, not even when you dress like a boy."

"Well, I wasn't forbidden from wearing makeup at least. How are you doing?"

"I want to throw up."

"That good, huh?"

"Yep. Where did you leave the old guy?"

"Ethan's outside helping his father welcome the guests. Your parents are doing the same. It's a funny mix… You can spot the Texans from a mile away, even if they can't wear hats inside the church!"

"Bet you can." Tyler chuckled. "How was the big dinner last night?"

"I suspect my mom has a crush on Ethan. As for my dad, he couldn't understand how someone could not want to be a lawyer, but he and Ethan had plenty of topics to discuss, and they hit it off pretty well…"

"Uh-huh."

"You asked," Rose said, straightening his bowtie.

"I'm a masochist, didn't you know? Why else would I be doing this right now?"

"Because you're a good man, because it's the right thing to do, and because despite what you might think, deep down you care about Georgiana. A lot. And, I had a little peek at the bride; she's going to take your breath away," Rose said, smiling.

She was trying her best, but seeing Tyler marrying someone else wasn't the piece of cake she'd expected. Seeing Georgiana resplendent in her white gown hadn't helped, either.

There was a knock on the door. Ethan came in.

"How's everything going? Gigi wanted me to check that everything was in order… You're a little on the pale side," Ethan added, looking at Tyler.

A gasp caught in Rose's throat. Ethan in a tux was something else. She was melancholic about Tyler and everything, they had a lot of history that was hard to let go of, but *Ethan* was her future. Of this, Rose was certain.

"You try the 'getting married' thing, and then we'll see how you look," Tyler retorted.

The two men still didn't like each other. But they were coming to terms with the fact that, for better or for worse—literally—they were about to become family.

"You sound like my mother now! Anyway, I come bearing gifts." Ethan removed a flash and three plastic shot glasses from his jacket. "Here," he said, filling each with a transparent liquid and then passing them out. "To the bride and groom—cheers!"

The three of them raised the glasses, tilted their head backwards, and downed the shot in one swig. Rose wrinkled her nose—blech, vodka. A little too strong for the a.m. hours, yet Tyler looked far happier than he had a minute ago. There was even some color returning to his cheeks.

"If we're all set, I'll go tell the priest we can start," Ethan said, tucking the flask and glasses back into his jacket. "You should come out in a few minutes and wait for the bride at the altar."

Tyler nodded bravely.

When Ethan was gone, Tyler turned to Rose. "The old guy… he's not too bad."

"I know." Rose was close to tears again. Vodka was a great idea for a guy with a bad case of cold feet, but probably not the best for an overemotional friend.

"Come here," Tyler said.

Rose went over to him and they hugged tightly. This felt like the last private moment they would ever share.

"Nothing will change between us," he whispered in her ear.

"Nothing," she said, repeating the lie.

Tyler let go of her. "Let's go do this," he said. He straightened his jacket and then marched out of the room.

Rose watched him go, knowing that in many ways she was letting go of him, forever. When she came out of the small room, she was just Rose—there was no more Tyler and Rose.

***

"I'm not sure if the fact that I find you hot while you're dressed like a boy should scare me or not," Ethan teased as he and Rose waltzed across the dance floor—a platform that had been set up in the middle of the Smithson's family home garden.

"I'm about to cut into your dilemma," Rose said. "Do you think the style-gestapo will flay me if I let my hair loose? This chignon is killing me. And the bow tie is strangling! How do you guys wear these around your neck every day?" She started pulling some pins out of her hair.

"Here, let me help…" Ethan pulled her to the edge of the garden and started working his fingers into her hair.

When the last pin came loose, Rose shook her head and let her hair cascade down onto her shoulders. Ethan was already undoing the bow tie.

"I have to stop now, or I'll end up undressing you completely. It wouldn't be very proper."

"No, it wouldn't, especially not with your mother staring at us. She's been watching us like a hawk all day. What's up with her?"

"Ah, my dear." Ethan grinned. "I'm afraid that with my sister's nuptials, I remain the sole Smithson sibling yet to be matched. I'm pretty sure my mother has designs on you."

"Aren't two weddings in six months enough for her?"

"Is the thought of joining yourself to me in holy matrimony so unappealing to you, Miss Atwood?"

"What? No, I-I mean…" Rose was stuttering, her face searing red. "Are you serious?"

"Why not?"

His stare was like burning ice.

"I thought you w-were against getting married."

"I'm against girls shopping for rings after one date; I'm not against getting married to the woman I love."

"Are you proposing?" Rose's heart was beating way too fast.

"Now, don't go getting a big head, Miss Atwood…"

She swatted him playfully. "Jerk."

He grabbed her hand and pulled her into a kiss.

95

"I love you," Ethan whispered. "One day, I want you to be my wife. What do you say?"

"One day." Rose couldn't help but smile like an idiot. "I love you too."

"Now that my noble intentions are in the open, can I bring you to my room?"

Ethan and Rose discreetly disappeared behind a bush and ran across the lawn toward the house, holding hands and laughing like a pair of kids. Never, not even in her wildest dreams, could Rose have imagined the day Tyler married another woman would end up being the happiest of her life. But life held many happy surprises in store, and running free on the grass holding the hand of the man she loved, Rose felt exactly that. The happiest she'd ever been.

End of Book 1

FRIEND ZONE

JUST FRIENDS BOOK 2

CAMILLA ISLEY

Now

Rose

Inside the Smithson's country house, Rose followed Ethan up the stairs and down a corridor with too many white doors to count. He stopped in front of one toward the end, pausing with his hand on the handle. "You're about to have a glimpse into my teenage lifestyle," he said, and flung open the door.

Sprawled on Ethan's bed was a bulging middle-aged man, fast asleep and snoring.

"Rose, meet Uncle Frank." Ethan sighed. "He must've decided my room was as good a place as any to fall asleep."

Rose giggled, taking in what she could of Ethan's room before he closed the door. As it clicked shut, they tiptoed away, careful not to wake the sleeping man.

"We'll have to take one of the guest rooms." Ethan turned on his heel and headed back toward the beginning of the hall.

He opened a random door. Before Rose could peek inside, Ethan roared and rushed into the room. Rose made to follow him but stopped dead on the threshold. She raised a hand to cover her mouth as she stared at the scene before her eyes in shocked silence…

99

Seven Months Ago

Alice

Jack had beaten her to the library. He was waiting inside the small reading room, head bent over his laptop, and a cute frown on his face. He hadn't spotted her yet, so Alice paused and studied him through the glass door.

Even seated, it was easy to tell Jack was tall; all basketball players had to be. Not to mention playing varsity sports gave him a lean, flat-muscled body all too visible under his tight t-shirt and faded jeans. Dark eyes and hair, high cheekbones, and a straight nose made her best friend dangerously gorgeous. And his mouth… it was made to keep girls awake at night, which unfortunately it did—*too often.*

As Alice leaned closer to the glass, a dark lock slipped out from behind her ear, startling her. She still wasn't used to being a brunette. What would Jack say? Would he like it? Only one way to find out. Alice grasped the door handle and her chest tightened. He would reject her. Telling Jack the truth now was a bad idea; she should wait. *Yeah, definitely wait.* Today was a regular work-on-your-group-project-and-not-tell-Jack-you-love-him kind of day.

Alice pushed the door open. "Hey," she greeted Jack.

"Hey, Ice." Jack looked up from behind his laptop. "Whoa!" His dark eyes widened in shock, and his gaze made Alice's stomach flip. "What's up with the hair?"

"Change of style." She dropped her messenger bag on the floor and sat in the chair next to him. "Ethan dumped me." Alice pretended the news was trivial as she set up her laptop on the table.

"So you dyed your hair black?" Jack tousled his fringe, perplexed.

It was a habit of his, one that made Alice want to run a hand through his soft curls every time he messed them around. The gesture exposed more of his biceps, too, making Alice wonder what kissing him would feel like if she were free to lock one hand in Jack's hair, pull his lips to hers, and wrap the other hand around the marble-like smoothness of his arm.

She mentally slapped away her hands, and said, "I was tired of the fake blonde. Like it?" Alice hoped the makeover would stir something in Jack, but he ignored her question point blank.

"What happened with the dude? You've been dating him for what… three, four months now?"

"Remember when I told you about the night of Georgiana's birthday party?"

"Your former sorority big sister?"

"A big sister is for life, even if she graduates and moves on to grad school. But, yes, her."

"She's hot." Jack smirked. "You should introduce me."

"Can't do. She's in Paris with her boyfriend until next semester." Alice rolled her eyes, and Jack laughed.

"So? What does Georgiana have to do with Ethan dumping you?"

"Well, he's her brother, for one—"

"Seriously?" Jack made a mind-blown gesture.

"Yeah. We were at that hip sushi restaurant downtown for Georgiana's birthday and Ethan ditched me at the table to go flirt with this other girl. But then he showed up at my place later and apologized, and I thought we were okay. It was business as usual—and then he ghosted me for a month straight."

"That's awful."

Jack was clearly trying and failing to keep his lips from twitching. Ghosting was his favorite breakup strategy.

Alice ignored his distracting lips, and said, "The radio silence was driving me mad, so last night I confronted him. He didn't even try to deny it."

"The ghosting part, or that he's seeing someone else?"

"Either. Both," Alice admitted. "At least he was honest."

"Do we know the other woman?"

"No, but she's a grad student, too."

"Hot?"

"Yeah, she's hot." Alice swatted him playfully. "You're not helping…"

Jack waggled his eyebrows. "Want me to seduce her for you?"

Yeah. Just what I need. "I doubt she's into college juniors."

"You never know," Jack said, focusing on his laptop screen. With a few clicks of the mouse, he opened the 3D model of a complex molecule they had to design for their Organic Chemistry group assignment. Jack started to rotate the model but stopped to regard Alice with a suspicious air. "Wait, is this girl… What's her name?"

"Rose."

"How sweet," Jack said. "Is she a brunette?"

Alice's cheeks burned. "Yep."

"Hence the hair change?"

"No. Ethan made it clear I got a one-way ticket to the dumpster. Dark brown is actually my natural hair color. I've decided I want to be truer to myself from now on. Starting with my hair, I guess." *And my feelings for you.*

"If it's any consolation"—Jack knocked twice on the table—"Lori and I are over, too."

Alice shifted in her chair as a slow melting sensation started in her stomach. Jack's low voice did weird things to her. Especially when he was saying he was single. Alice had feared Lori would become a long-term problem. And now, *poof,* she was gone. Was it a sign she should talk to Jack today? And say what, I love you? *Nah.* Maybe a physical approach would be better with Jack. She should just grab his face and kiss that mouth. *How would he react if I did?* The thought made her cheeks flame red, and Alice decided to take it slow. She didn't have to kiss him right now. Better to hear about the breakup first.

Alice pursed her lips, schooling her face to appear concerned instead of elated as she spoke. "Why? I thought your bio concentration was a keeper, what with all her talk of med school and her short skirts."

Jack snorted. "Until she went from super fun to a clingy nightmare in the space of five dates."

"I wasn't the only one who had a bad night, huh?" Alice suppressed a satisfied smile. Her plan to make a move on Jack had just become much simpler.

"Mine was horrible, trust me."

"Worse than mine? At least you did the dumping." Jack hated confrontations, in particular with the girls he dated. Hence the ghosting. "What happened? Lori a crier?"

Jack scowled at her. "It's not funny. She's a kidnapper. Batshit crazy."

"A kidnapper?" That was a new one. "What did she do?" Alice was genuinely curious at this point.

"She picked me up after school because we had a date." Jack abandoned the 3D model and turned toward Alice. "So I naively got into her car."

"Wait—to dump her?"

"Yeah, my plan was to tell her and leave."

"Wow, no ghosting?"

"Nah." He shook his head. "I'd run into her too often to pull that off. She's taking pre-med Chemistry, remember?"

"No, I'd forgotten," Alice lied, and gestured for him to keep talking.

"So I got into her car and she drove away. I asked her if we could go talk somewhere quiet, and she told me I'd just read her mind."

"She was expecting the 'Sayonara' speech?"

"No way. This is where my tale gets interesting." Jack grimaced as if in pain. "I noticed she was heading out of town toward the middle of nowhere, so I asked her where we were going. 'A special place,' she told me."

"Oh gosh." Alice put a hand to her head. "This story is about to get dreadful, isn't it?"

"In a second. The best part is coming." Jack winced. "I tried to tell her I didn't have much time, and that we needed to talk. She ignored me and kept driving, insisting I had to see this place, no matter how many times I asked her to pull over."

"But couldn't you have made it clear you didn't want to go?"

"Believe me, I did. At that point, I had two options: either keep sitting in the car or grab the wheel and make her pull over by force." Jack frowned at the memory. "Lori literally kidnapped me."

"How long were you in the car?"

"Close to an hour?"

Alice let out a low whistle. "Where to?"

"Here's the best part." Jack groaned. "She took me to this scenic viewpoint on top of a hill and timed it so we would get there at sunset."

Alice almost felt sorry for Lori, except that her total fiasco served Alice's cause too well.

"My day is improving," she said. "Now I can cross myself off the most-humiliated-girl spot. What happened when she stopped the car?"

"I tried to speak first, but she wouldn't let me."

"Of course not." Alice chuckled. "What did she say?"

"She told me she was falling for me, that I was the only guy she'd cared about in a while…" Jack paused. "Her speech ended with the L-word."

"Oh gosh, poor girl. And that's when you told her?"

"Yep."

"And what did she do?"

"Let me just say the one-hour drive back to the city was… *awkward.*" Jack sing-songed "awkward."

"Well, at least she didn't leave you stranded on the hilltop." Alice's mouth trembled with the effort of not smiling. "I would have."

"Nah, Lori might still hope she can change my mind."

Alice's pulse sped up as she asked, "Can she?"

"No way. If I had any doubts, yesterday's trip cleared them up for good." Jack made a gun with his fingers and shot himself in the head. "Worst Friday night of my life."

"Really?" Alice couldn't hide her amusement.

He nodded. "Really. Ice, why don't you turn on your laptop so we can get going. You can give me more grief later. Deal?" Jack added a stomach-flipping wink.

"Deal," Alice whispered, suddenly out of breath.

As she powered on her Mac, her fingers prickled. Both their relationships had ended on the same day; it had to mean something. Today *was* tell-your-best-friend-you-love-him day. She'd wait until they were done with the project to speak to Jack. *Or jump him.* He was single and wouldn't stay so for long; this was her moment. After all, how bad could it go? Not as tragic as with Lori. The worst he could say was no…

***

Alice burst into her three-bedroom apartment, slamming the door shut behind her. Ignoring her roommates' questioning faces, she crossed the entrance hall to her room and flung herself onto the twin bed. Alice hid her head under the pillow and suffocated a scream with the bedcover.

Both of her roommates followed her into the room.

"Are you okay?" Haley asked.

"Hey, what's up?" Madison said.

Alice rolled over on the bed so she lay facing the ceiling. Still holding the pillow over her face, she muttered something incomprehensible.

The mattress dipped as her friends sat next to her one on each side of the bed. "You might have to repeat that without the pillow covering your mouth," Haley suggested, her voice coming from the right.

Alice lifted the pillow to say, "I just humiliated myself in the worst possible way," and then hid her face again.

"How?" Haley asked.

She pressed the pillow harder against her face and shook her head, refusing to speak.

Haley tickled her sides. "Come on, out with it."

Alice thrashed in the bed, trying to make Haley stop. Finally, she tossed the pillow aside. "I surrender!" she yelled. "I'll tell you everything." She recovered the pillow from the floor catching sight of Blue, her pet bunny, hopping away from the commotion. Alice straightened and settled the pillow behind her head, then took a moment to study her friends.

On her left, Madison. An introverted poet in the body of a statuesque blonde who dressed like a boho hippie. Her long, soft curls were always loose, and a book was constantly in her hands, like now. On Alice's right, Haley. An edgy computer science geek with a sleek, dark bob and an urban style. Whenever Haley had something in her hands, it was some techie gadget with software in it. They were both smiling at her encouragingly.

"I hit on Jack!" Alice confessed.

Madison looked down at her with big eyes. "You didn't!" she yelped, her grip tightening on the hardback in her lap.

"I did."

"I take it it didn't go well," Haley said.

Alice groaned. "Worse."

"What happened to our plan of waiting for a gap in girlfriends while you moved out of the friend zone?" Haley asked.

Madison nodded, but kept silent; she was letting Haley run the interrogation.

"The gap presented itself sooner than we thought." Alice told them about the kidnapping debacle. "And you know how Jack is. He would've been dating someone else by Monday, so I... I..."

"Did something stupid and impulsive?" Haley offered.

Alice nodded.

"What did you do? Jump him?"

"I tried." Alice moaned with shame. "I threw myself at him, and he was like 'Thanks, but no thanks.'"

Anxiety broke on Haley's face. "I'm so sorry," she said.

"Me too," Madison added, looking fretful and worried.

Haley took Alice's limp hand, squeezing it. "Did he say why?"

"He said we're friends." Madison and Haley both kept silent, waiting for the rest. So Alice gave it to them. "And that's when I practically begged him for it. And he just kept saying no."

"You begged?" Haley repeated. "Give us specifics."

"He said I was his friend, and I countered by saying he's slept with all his female friends. He told me that's exactly why he doesn't have many left. So I told him Felicity is still his best friend, even though she's female, and he slept with her."

"Who's this Felicity?" Haley asked.

"She's his oldest friend from Indianapolis."

"What happened between them?" Madison asked.

"I don't know the specifics. Only that at some point they had a relationship that didn't end well. And Jack was all like"—Alice started talking in a mock dude voice—"*It took me two years to be friends with her again after we broke up. I won't screw up another friendship.*" She made a finishing gesture with her hands. "End of story."

"Hmm. What happened after that cozy little chat?" Haley asked.

"He told me I was upset about Ethan dumping me."

"Which is sort of true," Madison said. "I still can't believe my cousin broke up with you."

"It doesn't matter, really. I'm not upset about Ethan, I'm upset about Jack."

"How did you leave things?" Haley asked.

"I followed his lead and pleaded temporary 'I-was-dumped' insanity."

"Well, at least you didn't give him the 'I've been desperately in love with you for two years' speech," Haley said. "Harder to take back."

"No doubt," Alice agreed.

"What if Jack was right?" Madison asked. Alice flashed her an incendiary stare, so her friend hurried to explain. "I mean, he's not exactly boyfriend material, and you don't want to be friends with benefits."

"I know he's attracted to me—"

Haley scoffed. "He's attracted to every good-looking female."

"Fair enough, but we have a deeper bond. We're not just friends." Alice pointed a finger at them in turns. "You both said that."

"Yeah, okay," Haley conceded. "But put yourself in his shoes."

"How so?"

Haley sighed. "He's a guy, gorgeous, and he can have all the girls he likes. He enjoys his popularity with the ladies. When he gets tired, or when a relationship gets too serious, he moves on to another girl. But he has you for all his emotional needs. A constant, steady connection that he doesn't risk screwing up by sleeping with someone else. You told me yourself he doesn't have self-control when it comes to sex."

"Well, he does with me." Alice pouted.

Haley gave her an encouraging smile. "Which, in a twisted way, tells you how much he cares about you."

"He can keep Felicity as his emotional backup."

"Felicity is a thousand miles away," Haley pointed out. "You're here."

"And I don't think him confiding in his ex would work so great for you," Madison added. "Do you even know her?"

"I've seen her around campus a couple of times when she came to visit."

"Why don't you talk to her and get an informed opinion?" Madison suggested. "Ask her if it was worth risking their friendship for a shot at love."

Alice shrugged. "I don't have her number."

"Mm, helloooo?" Haley said. "Pity we don't live in a world where finding people on the Internet is just a name search away. I wish there was a website for that. How about we invent it and become gazillionaires?"

"I'm not friending her on Facebook," Alice replied stubbornly. "And I'm not talking to her. I can't risk anything getting back to Jack. I don't even know if I can trust her—what if she's still holding a torch for him? I'd pour my heart out to her, and the next second she'd spill everything to Jack. I'd be digging my own grave."

"You don't know that," Madison said. "Aren't you curious to talk to the only person who can tell you how the friend-girlfriend-friend cycle really is?"

"Even if she said being with him wasn't worth ruining their friendship, it would mean nothing. They may not have been able to make it work, but that doesn't mean it would go wrong with us, too."

"You want to be his girlfriend, and he doesn't want a girlfriend," Haley said flatly. "You could be headed down the same destructive path as Felicity if you're not careful."

"What if he broke up with Felicity because he wasn't in love with her?" Alice insisted.

"And he is with you?"

Alice shrugged. "There's a deep connection between us, something more than a friendship. If, as you said, he relies on me emotions-wise, what do you call that?"

Haley blew out, making her bangs balloon for a second. "Complicated."

"It is. But I'm tired of playing the 'friend' role, pretending I don't have feelings for him. I'd rather try and fail than not try because he's afraid it *could* fail."

"So what do we do now?" Madison asked.

Alice lifted up to a sitting position, lying back against the headboard. "We make him jealous."

"You were with my cousin for months, and Jack never showed signs of jealousy."

"Jack never saw me with Ethan," Alice said. "There's a big difference between knowing someone you like is dating someone else and seeing it with your own eyes."

Madison arched her brows. "So you're looking for a casual hook up?"

"Ew. No!" Alice grimaced. "I just want to show Jack what he's missing."

"How?" Haley asked.

"For once, I'll shed the geek uniform." Alice stuck to a conservative dress code in class, and Jack had never seen her dressed to impress. "It's time he realizes I'm a woman. I could read indecision in his eyes before he said 'no.' He just needs a push."

Madison scratched her cheek before asking, "No chance you saw only what you wanted to see?"

"No, I'm positive, and I'm tired of pretending. I don't want to be his friend. Watching him sleep his way through campus is like dying a slow death. It makes me live in fear that one of his girls will eventually stick around, and she won't be me. I get anxious whenever he dates someone for more than a month, and I'm not interested in being his emotional fix forever." Alice waved one hand in the air dismissively. "If he really feels nothing for me, I'd rather find out now and move on with my life."

A muffled squeal came from under the bed. Alice bent over to reach and pick up Blue. "This is all your fault," she told the dark gray bunny as she stroked his soft fur. "If you hadn't scurried off to his room in our freshman year, I would've never met Jack."

A flashback of that day forced its way into Alice's mind.

***

Alice ran down the hall of her newly assigned freshmen dorm to find Blue. Her stupid roommate had let him out of his cage and then forgotten to close their door. Alice popped her head inside every room on both sides of the hall, asking, "Hi, have you seen a small bunny, dark gray fur?" But no luck.

Her anxiety grew with each passing door—until she reached the end of the corridor and stopped on the threshold of the last room. Inside, a guy sat on a twin bed holding Blue in his lap. He was wearing a simple white t-shirt, black basketball shorts, and man's slides.

And he was SO hot.

Alice barged into the room. "You found Blue," she shrieked, startling both human and bunny.

A pair of dark eyes focused on her and the boy's expression changed from slightly alarmed to interested. Something fluttered inside Alice's belly. Blue had stumbled upon the best-looking boy of the dorm: dark brown hair, square jaw, and a general tousled, bad-boy aura.

Alice lowered her gaze, suddenly self-conscious. His scrutiny felt like having a spotlight pointed at her face. She did a quick mental checklist of the state of her hair, makeup, and clothes. Um, probably not good; she'd run out of her room midway through her unpacking, in cozy clothes, no makeup, and her hair was a recently bleached mess.

"Hello stranger," the boy said, flashing her a mischievous grin.

109

"Hi." Alice pushed an unruly lock of hair behind her ear. "You have my bunny."

The hottie scratched Blue behind the ears, making him purr. I'd purr, too, if it were me, she thought.

"Blue, is it?" he asked.

"Yep."

The boy cocked his head toward her. "And you are?"

"Alice."

"I'm Jack."

"Nice to meet you." Alice took a tentative step forward. "Can I have him back?"

"Wait, don't I get a reward for finding him?" Jack teased.

He should get a reward for finding you, Alice thought. Instead, she said, "Your reward would be that I take Blue back before he poops on you." Did I really just say "poop" in front of a super-hot guy? Alice blushed as she watched Jack's smile switch back from dashing to mildly worried. She closed the distance between them and took the struggling bunny from his hands. At the light brush of skin on skin, a shiver ran through her.

"You start tomorrow?" Jack asked. "Or are you one of the luckies with no lectures on Monday?"

"Definitely not lucky." Alice shook her head. "My first class is at a stupid early hour."

"Same bad luck here. You pick a concentration already?"

Alice frowned. "Concentration?"

"It's the fancy word they use around here for major," Jack explained.

"Oh, that." Why can't they just call it a major? "Chemistry."

"No way, same as me." His face lit up. "You're in Professor Chase's class?"

"Yes." Same major—concentration, whatever—same classes. I'll see you almost every day. Alice did a victory dance inside her head.

"Me too." The "I'm interested" smirk was back on his face. "Want to go together?"

"Sure." Alice clutched Blue more tightly as the bunny tried to leap out of her grasp and back into Jack's lap. "I'm just a few doors down, room 254."

"I'll stop by tomorrow morning. Deal?"

"Deal."

"See you later, Ice."

Alice's face fell a little. "It's Alice."

"Mind if I go with Ice?"

Usually, her name got shortened to Ali or Ally. Lice once, thanks to a mean girl in fourth grade. But never Ice.

"Why Ice?" she asked.

"It has the most beautiful crystalline structure."

Oh! He was flirting with her using molecular structures. If this wasn't perfect chemistry...

Alice left the room and walked down the hall, but then, on impulse, decided to look back. Jack was leaning against his doorframe, smiling. He'd been watching her go.

***

"You would've met Jack in class the next day anyway," Haley said, bringing Alice back to present.

"Yeah, but if it wasn't for this little guy"—she kissed Blue and set him back on the floor—"we wouldn't have gone together. I wouldn't have sat next to him that day, or the next, and now I wouldn't be stuck in the stupid friend zone."

"It could be worse," Haley insisted. "You could've slept with Jack freshman year and now he wouldn't even remember your name."

On Alice's other side, Madison blushed a furious red. She was very self-conscious of one-night stands and guys ditching her afterward.

Alice crossed her arms and pouted. "Say what you like, I'm tired of waiting."

"What's your evil plan to make him jealous?" Madison asked.

"He's going out with the team tonight," Alice said. Jack played varsity basketball for the Harvard Crimson. "He doesn't know I know his plans."

Haley narrowed her eyes at her. "And how do you know?"

"A girl in my photography class is dating a guy on the team. She told me."

"And what are these plans?" Madison pressed.

"Halloween house party; I'm going, and you're coming with me."

"To a party populated by tall basketball players?" Madison smirked.

111

"Who am I to complain? Where's the party? Is it walk-in, or do we need an invitation?"

"It's someone's house off campus, and all Kappa Kappa Gamma are invited."

Their sorority was where Alice, Haley, and Madison had met. After becoming close friends, they'd moved in together at the beginning of sophomore year. Greek life at Harvard wasn't residential, so no sorority house. Both Haley and Alice had been recruited as freshmen, while for Madison Smithson, being a Kappa Kappa Gamma was a family legacy. Just like going to Harvard, and then Harvard Law School. The sorority was also where Alice had met Madison's cousin who, at the time, was a senior and chose to mentor Alice. Now Georgiana was in law school. Weird how many people in Alice's life shared the same surname. Ethan, too, was a Smithson. The only one ever to quit the family's law firm to start his own real estate business. He was the black sheep of the family. *Alice, Ethan could be a golden sheep, you don't care. He dumped you! Stop thinking about that particular Smithson.*

"What about Emily's party?" Haley asked. "I told her we were going."

"Yeah, but her parties suck. We can stop on our way to say hello, stay half an hour, and then join the real paaarrrtyy." Alice bobbed her shoulders up and down to an imaginary tune.

"We're sold on the party switch." Haley nodded. "But just showing up won't be enough to mess with Jack. So…?"

"I've no idea. I figure I'll make it up as I go." Alice looked at her friends with a conspiratorial air. "Your task is to make me as hot as I can be in my costume." She struck a pin-up pose, pushing her chest forward and locking her hands behind her head. "I want to show him what he's saying 'no' to."

"All right, Miss Femme Fatale," Haley joked. "Let's make you irresistible."

Jack

Jack was late. In less than an hour he had to be Halloween-ready, and he was still in the bathroom shaving. This was the last Saturday before the basketball season kicked off, a.k.a. the last game-free weekend for the next five months. To celebrate, the entire team was going to a house party. The address he had was just a few blocks off campus, meaning Jack could get as wasted as he liked with no car to drive.

And he *needed* to get wasted tonight.

What an awful weekend he'd had so far. First, a kidnapping followed by a traumatic breakup, and then his best friend tried to kiss him in the library. Women were crazy; he was past due for a guy's night.

No, not women plural, Jack corrected himself. One woman in particular.

He didn't care about Lori; she'd get over it. Ice, on the other hand… Dodging her once had been hard, but what if she tried again? He wasn't a saint, and her new look sorely tested his self-control. The dark hair was unsettling—*sexier,* even. Not what he was used to. And she'd tried to kiss him! *Don't think about it, Jack.* He'd mistaken his connection with a friend for something more once, hurting Felicity hard. The whole thing had been a disaster, one he wasn't going to repeat with Ice.

Even if it was impossible to forget the thrill he'd felt when she'd come close to him. How their lips had almost touched before he'd come to his senses and pushed her back—

Jack involuntarily jerked his head and cut himself with his razor. He threw the blade in the sink and washed the cut with fresh water. To stop the bleeding, he reached for a paper roll and pressed a sheet of paper on the small wound. This Ice business was affecting him way more than it should. She was just acting out because her boyfriend had ditched her. That was it. When girls dyed their hair and made a move on their best friends, they were acting out. It was nothing more. Ice would be back to normal as soon as she found someone else to date.

Jack frowned at himself in the mirror. All of a sudden, the thought of Ice dating someone else wasn't that pacifying. *What's wrong with me?* Jack had never had a problem with her dating other men. Then again, she'd never tried anything with him before. Since they'd met, he'd kept Ice locked in the friend zone. Okay, maybe not since day one. Jack remembered fondly the girl barging into his room looking for her bunny. She'd been impossibly cute with her messy blonde bun and worried frown. At once, Jack had vowed to make the human bunny his first college catch. But when they'd started seeing each other every day in class, they'd become friends. And now Ice wanted more. *Not going to happen.*

Ice wasn't the "friends with benefits" type—well, no girl was, really. No matter what they said, girls always ended up asking for more. Commitment, a serious relationship, *I love yous,* and all that. Jack wasn't interested in any of it. He was determined to enjoy his college years with no strings attached.

He removed the paper from his jaw. The bleeding had stopped, so he quickly finished shaving and rinsed the remaining gel from his face. The cold water was soothing on his skin, tempting him to dunk his entire head under the icy stream to cool off. One freezing shower apparently hadn't been enough to forget Alice had made a pass at him.

The doorbell rang, announcing Peter had arrived. *Good!* Peter Wells, his best wingman and team captain, was the fire Jack needed to melt his thoughts about Ice. If possible, Peter was even worse than Jack with girls. The Crimson captain was a senior and always dated a bunch of girls at the same time—freshmen to seniors, or even older. Exactly the bad influence Jack wanted tonight.

He dried his face with a towel, then wrapped it around his neck and went to open the door.

"Sullivan, my man," Peter greeted him.

They clasped hands and bumped chests, which resulted in Jack's hand getting smeared with bluish paint. The team had decided to go to the Halloween party dressed as Smurfs. The costume was very basic: white sports shorts, no clothes from the waist up, a white jersey beanie, and a *lot* of blue body paint.

Peter was wearing a team hoodie, for now, one the blue paint would make unusable. But the captain always wore team-branded clothes. His favorite pickup line was to tell the ladies he was joining the NBA after graduation. It wasn't necessarily a lie. Peter was bound to receive an offer from one of the big teams sooner or later. What the girls didn't realize was they'd be long forgotten by then. But just saying the three little magic letters—N B A—kept the WAG dream alive, and the girls fell right and left for Peter. His blue eyes, dark hair, and impressive height certainly didn't hurt, too.

Peter gave him the once-over. "Yo, my man, you're late," he complained. "I need you to get blue and do my back. The lady doctor keeping you busy?"

"The lady doctor was fired," Jack said, closing the door behind his friend. It was another lady giving him pause.

"Already? What happened?"

"She drove me an hour out of the city to show me the beautiful sunset, tell me she loved me, and announce she was ready to move our relationship to the next level." Jack raised his hand sarcastically.

"Ouch!"

"Yeah, tell me about it. I had the worst night yesterday." *And the worst day, today. What the hell, Ice!* Jack shook his head.

Peter took his headshake for disappointment about the doctor. "Come on, my man," he said. "Tonight we're going to find you a hot nurse to replace the doctor and cure your soul. Now put on your white shorts and let's get blue."

***

The Smurf costumes were a rousing success. It was impossible for them to move around the party without being the center of attention. Twenty tall guys were hard to miss in a crowd already—paint them blue, and it became impossible. The ladies seemed to love the idea; the guys scored extra points for daring and originality.

Jack dodged a girl who was pushing through the crowd, sloshing her drink over anyone not fast enough to get out of her way. As she scurried by, Jack noticed the girl's face was smeared with blue paint. At least one of his teammates had already scored. Jack poured himself a beer from a huge keg and took position next to Peter in a corner that offered a strategic view of the house.

From his vantage point, he spotted a group of three girls with potential: a blonde and two brunettes. The ladies had their backs turned, but the rear view did not call for complaints. The blonde was dressed in a short, airy dress, which looked more like a babydoll shirt. She had little white wings strapped to her back. *An angel.* One brunette was clad in a tight, glittery black jumpsuit with only one shoulder strap. From her bottom sprouted a tail she'd laced around one wrist for support, and she had kitten ears. *Meow.* The last girl was wearing a short, sequined red dress and had tiny red horns on the top of her head. *Hell-o.* Jack had a good feeling about the trio.

He nudged Peter. "Angel, devil, or hellcat?"

The captain whistled. "I'll take the kitty catty."

A pang of disappointment stabbed Jack's chest; he would've chosen the kitten, too. Never mind. Angel or devil? As they scoped out their targets, a dude in an unoriginal vampire costume approached the girls and left a minute later with the she-devil. "I'll take the angel, then," Jack said.

"Let's see the faces first," Peter cautioned.

Jack stared as the angel spun around; she was pretty and looked familiar. Where had he seen her? Realization hit him a second before the black kitty turned around and they locked eyes. It was Ice.

Alice

Alice turned her head and met a pair of dark eyes. She pursed her lips, trying not to smile. Jack was a Smurf—genius. His blue face was a mask of surprise—he obviously hadn't expected her to be here.

She whispered in Madison's ear, then dragged her roommate toward Jack and his fellow blue friend—from his impressive height, another basketball player—to say hello. Alice stopped in front of Jack and smiled. He blinked, stunned. He was gaping at her tight costume and not speaking.

"Hi," Alice said.

"Hi." Jack's jaw tensed and his eyes became wary. "Why are you here?"

It was time to let him know she could play *oh so cool.*

"Most Kappa Kappa Gammas came here tonight." Alice casually wrapped her hair to the side, leaving her bare shoulder and neck exposed. "At least, the cool gang did."

"My man," the blue friend butted into the conversation. "Aren't you going to introduce me?"

With all the blue paint covering him, Alice couldn't tell much about the second Smurf's looks. Just that he was super-tall, ripped, and had popping blue eyes.

"Peter, Alice," Jack said without enthusiasm. "Alice, Peter."

"Nice to meet you," Alice said. "I'd shake your hand, but I'm afraid of turning blue." She turned around to introduce Madison, but her roommate was already chatting with another Smurf. "How many Smurfs are there?"

"The entire team," Peter said.

"You play basketball with Jack?"

"Yeah, headed for the NBA next year, hopefully." He made a cute, no-biggies face.

Alice noticed Jack fidgeting uneasily at Peter mentioning the NBA. *Ah, the notorious NBA line.* Alice had heard of this guy: Peter Wells was Jack's preferred wingman, and the NBA reference was his favorite pickup line. Peter was hitting on her and Jack didn't like it. *Perfect!*

"The NBA, wow, how cool!" she said, playing along.

"Hi, Alice." Becky, a fellow Kappa Kappa Gamma dressed as a sexy nurse, stopped next to her. "Fraternizing with the Smurfs?"

"Becky, meet Jack, fellow Chemistry student and the only non-nerd guy in my class, and Peter, future NBA star," Alice introduced, trying to keep her eyes from wandering from their faces to their painted-but-still-very-visible six-packs.

"Hi," Becky said. "The house is full of Smurfs."

"Yep, the Crimson all came as Smurfs," Alice said. "So, whose idea was it?" she asked Peter.

"It was a team decision."

"It's brilliant," Becky said, openly staring at the generous amount of muscle on display.

"So, Becky, is it? My friend here"—Peter patted Jack on one shoulder—"needs some *nursing* back to life. He's recovering from an injured heart."

"Is he now?" Becky peered at Jack, then at Alice, as if she was silently asking, "Is he cool?"

The sultriness in Becky's voice made Alice's skin prickle with ugly emotions: irritation, jealousy, pain, and anger. But she disciplined her features, trying to appear neutral. If Becky ended up sleeping with Jack tonight, she'd be forgotten by morning. It was more important for Alice to act unconcerned.

"Jack's a darling," Alice said aloud, then leaned toward Becky to whisper in her ear, "If you're looking for a night's fun." She tilted her head and winked at Jack, then continued speaking to Becky in hushed tones. "Don't expect anything serious from him." The sisterly code of Kappa Kappa Gamma, and the more general girl code, demanded she warn Becky of what to expect.

The information didn't seem to bother Becky. She turned toward Jack once again, saying, "I'm out of juice." She shook the empty red cup she was holding. "Why don't we go get another drink?"

He chugged whatever was left of his beer and shrugged. "Sure."

As they walked away, Jack peered over his shoulder, catching Alice's eye. Confusion at her attitude was written all over his face. Then they were gone, and Alice was alone with Peter. Madison had disappeared with the other Smurf.

"You're a junior?" Peter asked.

"Yes. You?"

"Senior. And your concentration is Chemistry?"

"Yep."

"Whoa, tough. You're a smart girl, then."

"Were you hoping for dumb?"

"No." He shot her a grin, his teeth too white next to the blue lips. "I like a challenge."

"What's your major?"

"Econ. But hopefully, I won't need it—"

"Yeah, I know…" She waved him off. "Not with the NBA knocking on your door soon." Now that Jack was gone, she didn't have to pretend she cared about an alleged future career as a pro athlete.

"You're not into basketball?"

"Not a sports fan in general."

"Ouch."

"What? Did I ruin your best pickup line?" Alice smiled to soften the blow.

"Touché. Are you from around here?"

"No, I'm originally from Philly. You?"

"Florida. Small town near Orlando."

Alice studied him for a few seconds. "I'm trying to imagine your face without the blue paint."

"Careful with that, I'm told I'm devastatingly handsome."

"And modest, too."

"You really have no idea how I look? Haven't you been to a game? Not even once to see Jack play?"

"No. Jack knows I don't care about sports." He also didn't want her anywhere near his teammates, she suspected. "I don't even know the rules. I get you guys have to throw the ball inside the basket, but that's about it."

Peter chuckled. "I guess in the end that's all that really matters. You should give basketball a shot. It's a beautiful game." He winked. "If you want, I can explain the basics to you."

"It's too loud in here to concentrate on a game's rules."

"Rain check for tomorrow?"

Now he was playing a whole different ball game, but why not play along? If she really wanted to make Jack jealous, Peter would do the trick, and he might be a little treat for her self-esteem, too. She needed someone to look at her in a way that made her feel beautiful. Desirable. And Peter had definitely mastered that particular skill.

"How about you grab me a drink for now?" she asked.

"What are you having?"

"Beer."

"Wait here, I'll be right back."

Peter disappeared behind a corner and was back in a couple of minutes with two blue cups in his hands. He offered her one, saying, "Want to move upstairs? It's too noisy to talk down here."

Dangerous question.

"Sure," Alice said.

Dangerous answer.

She followed him up the stairs, half-curious, half-worried to see if he would try to take her into a room. But Peter stopped at the top of the stairs and sat on a carpeted step. Alice sat next to him, keeping a safe distance.

"I don't bite," he said.

"But you stain." She bumped her cup into his. "Cheers."

"To what?"

"To an evening with a blue guy." She raised her cup, and they both drank.

"Would you get terribly mad if I got some paint on you?"

Alice held his burning gaze. "It depends where."

He took the cup from her hands and set it alongside his on the landing. "How about on your lips?"

"You can try." She smiled. "I promise I'll keep my claws in."

Careful not to touch her in any other way, he leaned in and pressed his lips to hers.

The kiss was gentler than Alice expected. And when it was over, it left her wanting more.

"Is my face blue?" she asked.

"Looks like you have dark lipstick on. Listen, I'm over this party. Did you drive here?"

"No, walked. You?"

"Yeah, me too. Can I walk you home?"

"Let me check with my roommates."

Alice fished her phone out of the small clutch strapped across her torso to text Madison and Haley. Neither texted back.

"I'm afraid my roommates have gone to visit the Smurfs' village," Alice said. "We can go if you want; I just have to grab my jacket, I left it downstairs. You came bare-chested in this cold?"

"Hah, no. I left my hoodie in a room." Peter sprang up and offered her a hand. "I'll go grab it and meet you by the door."

Alice ignored the blue hand and stood up on her own. "Cool. See you downstairs."

Peter let his hand drop and gave her a peck on the lips before hurrying down the corridor.

Alice hopped down the stairs and mercifully found her jacket on its hanger, undamaged. It was always a gamble to leave outerwear unsupervised at house parties; there was a good chance you'd never see it again. As she was pulling on her jacket, Alice caught a flash of white and blue out of the corner of her eye.

She turned around, saying, "You were quick."

But she didn't find the Smurf she was expecting staring back at her. She found Jack.

Jack

"Your face is half blue," Jack said, swiping a thumb from the corner of Alice's mouth down toward her jaw. The blue paint on her lips made him positively murderous.

"And now I imagine you've made it worse," Ice replied defiantly.

"Where are you going?"

"Peter is walking me home."

"Ice, don't." Jack stepped forward but stopped as she backtracked. "I get you're mad at me for what happened today—"

She cut him off. "This has nothing to do with you."

"Don't bullshit me."

"I'm not." Ice stared him down. "Earlier… I was upset about Ethan dumping me. Now I want to blow off steam, and Peter's a charmer. What's your problem?"

Yeah. What was his problem? He'd seen her date before, no problema. He was cool, happy even, with her dating other guys. *But not Peter. Mister NBA was the problem.* Why? Jack wasn't sure, but he knew he didn't want Alice to have anything to do with his captain.

"He's not… What I mean is, I've told you how Peter is with girls. Why would you go home with him?"

"To have fun?" Ice challenged. "Relax! I'm not shopping for a husband."

"Ice, don't be like that."

Alice narrowed her eyes. "Be like what, exactly?"

"This is not you. Come on, I'm taking you home." Jack made to grab her elbow, but she recoiled. He wasn't sure if it was to avoid his touch, the body paint, or both.

"I'm not going anywhere with you. You've made it clear you're only interested in being my friend, and guess what? I don't need a *friend* tonight, I need a *man.*"

As if on cue, a hand slapped his shoulder. "My man!" Peter said. "Keeping my lady company? Where did you put your nurse?"

"She had to go to the bathroom," Jack replied, stiffening. All of a sudden, Peter had become the most irritating person he knew, with his swagger and his constant *my man-ing.*

"Might take the lady some time. I just passed the door and there's a line," Peter informed him. "I'm taking off." Peter leaned in and added in a low voice, "And I hope this kitten doesn't have claws. Then again, that could be fun too."

Jack felt an impulse to throttle his friend. Instead, he made an effort to stay calm. "The party's just started and you're going home already?"

"It's not that great of a party," Alice interrupted. "We're going. If you see Madison or Haley, can you tell them I went home? I've texted them, but just in case..."

"Sure." Jack shrugged. Alice pushed past him to get out. Unable to stop her, Jack tugged Peter's arm and whispered in his ear, "Be nice to her. She's a friend."

Peter gave him a foxy smile. "Hey, I'm always nice to the ladies."

Peter made to follow Alice, but Jack held him back. "I'm serious."

"Chill, my man. I'll treat her with white gloves."

Reluctantly, Jack let him go. He cringed as he watched Peter wrap one arm around Alice's shoulders as they headed for the door. She never looked back.

Suddenly, the party seemed incredibly dull. All Jack wanted was to go home and wash off the body paint that had dried hard on his skin and now stretched and pulled with every movement he made. But going home alone wasn't an option. He'd be stuck thinking about Alice and Peter together. Jack shook the image away. He was overreacting. Ice never slept with anyone on a first date, let alone after a trashy party. She might be mad at him, but she wasn't going to sleep with Peter tonight. And Peter didn't like it when girls didn't sleep with him on the first night. He didn't have the patience to wait. The whole thing would blow up before it even started. Jack had nothing to worry about.

Jack marched to the bar, popped a Jell-O shot in his mouth, and then another. He searched the countertop for a clean cup, filled it with ice from the fridge, poured himself an unhealthy amount of vodka, and topped up the cup with a splash of lemon soda.

"There you are," the nurse said. Jack couldn't remember her name. "I thought I'd lost you."

"I was just mixing myself a drink. You want something?"

"What are you having?" She stole the cup from him and grimaced after taking a sip. "Blech, too strong for me." She gave the cup back. "But I'll do a Jell-O shot. You want one?"

"Sure." Jack dropped his too-strong drink on the counter and took the shot, his third in as many minutes.

Ready for the alcohol to kick in, Jack waited for the nurse to put down her glass before he cupped her face to kiss her. As he moved one hand to her back to pull her closer, she grabbed both his hands and kept them away from her body.

"You'll make me blue," she said, pulling away from him.

"You're already blue," he said, looking at her lips and thinking at once of another set of blue-stained lips.

The nurse giggled and wiped her mouth with a napkin. Jack swallowed another shot and gave one to her as well.

"The Smurfs idea is cool, but it can't be comfortable," she said.

"It was a much cooler costume in theory. But this blue paint is getting really itchy."

"We should wash it off," the nurse said suggestively.

"We?"

"Unless you prefer to shower alone."

"I don't." Jack downed another shot and gestured toward the door. "Let's get out of here."

He grabbed his old sweatshirt from under a couple of dudes sitting on the couch and guided the nurse to the front of the house.

Outside, when the cold night air hit his face, Jack paused. He threw a side-glance at the girl walking next to him. What was he doing? He could go home and shower alone, instead of sleeping with the umpteenth girl who meant nothing to him and whose name he couldn't even remember. Maybe it was time to straighten his head, be serious with someone he really cared about. *Ice.*

Jack was about to open his mouth to say he'd changed his mind, when a slow burning started in his stomach and his vision fogged. It was as if all the alcohol in the Jell-O shots suddenly released into his system. Jack staggered sideways and dropped a heavy arm around the nurse's shoulders, all thoughts of redemption forgotten.

Alice

Now that she was walking home alone with Peter, with Jack out of the picture, Alice didn't feel so bold anymore. What was she doing with a guy she knew nothing about? Was making Jack jealous really worth it? She doubted Peter could give her much more than that. If half the stories Jack had told her about him were true, Jack was practically a monk compared to Peter.

Alice wished she knew what his face looked like without all that blue paint. Not knowing was bothering her more than it should.

"You've gone all quiet on me," Peter said.

"I can't help but think I've no idea what your face looks like."

"We can solve that tomorrow. For now, you can stare at my pretty eyes." He batted his lashes at her.

Alice chuckled. "Is there going to be a tomorrow?"

"I hope so. I've promised to explain how to play basketball, remember?"

"You mean a practical lesson?"

"If you'd like. The coach has left me the keys to the Lavietes Pavilion; it's really cool when it's empty. We could take a couple shots."

"You want me to actually play?"

He stopped and grabbed Alice by the waist, pulling her in front of him. She stiffened, worrying about the paint getting all over her jacket. Then she dismissed the concern; the waterproof fabric wouldn't be hard to wash.

"I'd love to play with you," he said, looking her straight in the eyes. The intensity of his stare dazzled her. "Can we call it a date?"

"Your eyes really are pretty," Alice teased. "So I'm going to say yes."

He leaned in to kiss her. Alice didn't care if this was a mistake; having Peter kiss her was great, and Jack could go to hell for all she cared right now. *This is not you,* he'd told her. But this was exactly her! She was a woman who liked to be kissed by handsome—allegedly—men. She wasn't a nun.

A cold blast of air blew in from behind her, making the hair on her nape stand up and sending a shiver down her spine.

"You're trembling," Peter said, pulling back and massaging her arms with his hands.

"It's cold, and I'm not exactly covered up."

House parties required bringing only the minimum wardrobe. So Alice was standing in the cold of November wearing a flimsy jumpsuit, an older, not-warm-enough jacket, and no gloves, hat, or scarf.

"Yeah, me neither." Peter, with his bare legs, was even more poorly equipped for the chilly air. "Let's get you home."

They walked in silence for another ten minutes until Alice stopped in front of her building. Next to her, Peter kept hopping from one leg to the other. The exposed skin under his shorts sent a shiver down her back.

"This is me," Alice said. "You want to come in? We have a coffeemaker in the hall," she added, to make it clear this wasn't an invitation to her room. "I could make you something hot before you have to walk home."

"Yeah, that'd be great. I'm freezing."

Inside, she made a pot of decaf, which they drank seated at one of the tables. Alice would have preferred the cozy armchairs by the fire, even if it wasn't lit, but she was afraid Peter would stain them. Plastic chairs were easier to wipe clean.

They chatted, enjoying their hot drinks, and Alice soon lost track of the hour. It wasn't until Madison staggered in the front door, barely standing, that Alice realized how much time had passed.

She threw Peter an apologetic look. "I think I'd better go take care of my roommate before she wrecks our apartment."

"Yeah," Peter agreed. "She looks pretty wasted."

Madison was having a silent argument with the elevator. She kept pushing a button that wasn't really a button and started to rage when the little lights signaling the elevator was on call wouldn't light up. Madison increased her efforts, stabbing the plaque with her finger.

"Yep, she does." Alice nodded.

"This dried-up paint is making it painful to talk, anyway," Peter added.

"Is kissing painful too?"

Peter cupped her face with his hands. "I'll take the pain like a man." He kissed her goodnight. "I'll pick you up here tomorrow at two-ish?"

"Sure. I'll leave you my number just in case."

They exchanged contact information, and Peter gave her a quick peck on the lips before jogging out into the night. Alice didn't envy him the walk—or run—home one bit.

Alice joined Madison in front of the elevator. "Here." She pushed the up arrow.

"Was that a Smurf?" Madison asked.

"Yeah."

There was a ding, a swipe of metallic doors, and they stepped inside the elevator.

"I hate Smurfs," Madison said.

"I thought you were with one."

"No, I left for a second to get a drink and, poof, he disappeared with another girl." Madison scoffed. "Story of my life."

Madison had a lot of confidence issues and a huge inferiority complex.

"So, where were you all this time?"

"Haley and I party hopped, and I drank too much."

"You don't say. Where's Haley?"

"She met a guy and left with him."

Alice scoffed. "Another masked dude?"

Haley had been obsessing for months over a guy she'd met at a Venetian Masquerade Ball. After dancing with him most of the night, she'd lost him without ever learning his name, or even what his face looked like.

Madison shrugged. "If that does it for her."

As they reached their floor, Alice helped Madison walk to her room and helped her out of her angel costume. Her friend's beautiful blonde hair was all ruffled and impossibly tangled. It'd be a bitch to comb through the next morning.

"Did our plan work?" Madison asked as Alice tucked her into bed. "Was Jack jealous?"

"I think so." Alice smirked. "The Smurf downstairs was his best friend and favorite wingman. Jack didn't seem happy when I left with him."

"Good for you." Madison patted her on the arm. "Now I have to sleep. I'm really tired…" She closed her eyes and her head lolled to the side of the pillow.

Alice kissed Madison's forehead and retreated to her room. Blue tried to sneak out, but she snatched him up and closed the door.

"Here." She kissed him goodnight and dropped the bunny in his cage, leaving its door open so that if Blue wanted to take a night stroll, he could.

Alice quickly readied for bed, but it took her a while to drift off to sleep. She didn't know what to expect from her date tomorrow. Regardless of what Jack said, Peter hadn't tried anything with her tonight. He couldn't be the bastard Jack had made him out to be. And what about Jack? Had he gone home with Becky? Was he with her right now?

As she tossed in bed, Alice tried to convince herself she didn't care where Jack was or what he was doing. *Or with whom.*

Jack

Jack woke up staring at a ceiling that wasn't his own. He peeked under the bed sheets—he was naked, and his skin had returned to its normal color. The nurse had done a thorough job of cleaning him last night. She stirred beside him, and Jack sighed.

This was the hard part. The wake-up call could go one of three ways.

One: The girl he'd slept with didn't care that this had been a one night stand with no possible future. (This was the best-case scenario.)

Two: The girl *did* care, but pretended she didn't to either save face or to try to convince him she was cool to date. Still good.

Three: The girl did care and was a crier and/or a screamer. Criers and screamers ranked equally bad on the scale of unpleasant, morning-after talks, beaten only by a combination of the two.

Jack really wasn't in the mood for a shouting match. His head was throbbing, and he needed another hot shower—alone this time. Maybe he could sneak out before she woke up. Pity he was trapped against the wall and not on the easy-escape side of the bed. He could try to climb over the nurse without waking her, but it didn't seem likely.

The nurse stretched. "Morning," she said.

Jack sighed again. Time for *the talk.*

The girl got up immediately without trying to cuddle—a promising sign. She got dressed, and Jack did the same, taking in the whole room as he searched for the exit door.

"Stop acting like a trapped animal," said the nurse, who was no longer dressed as a nurse—she was wearing a pair of black leggings and a Harvard sweatshirt. "I'm not going to make a scene if that's what you're worried about. I'll make you a cup of coffee—if you want it—and send you on your way. No drama."

Jack was surprised. He thought he'd seen it all, but this was a new level of unconcernedness. "I'll take the coffee," he said.

"Milk, sugar, black?"

"Black is cool."

The studio apartment was tiny. The bed doubled as a couch, and the kitchenette was stuffed in a small corner with barely a bar and two stools. Jack sat on one.

The nurse placed a steamy mug on the countertop. "Here's your coffee."

"Thanks, mmm…"

"Becky. The name's Becky."

"I knew," Jack lied.

She raised an eyebrow. "No need to pretend here."

Jack couldn't help asking, "So, we're cool?" He usually avoided these questions like the plague.

"Yeah."

"How come?" And here he was asking one after the other.

"I'm too busy with school to have or want a boyfriend. Alice told me you'd be perfect for a night of fun, so this"—she flipped a finger between them—"is it. Plain and simple. No strings attached."

Jack grimaced. "Great!"

This should've been Jack's dream morning-after speech, but somehow it depressed him. He felt *used.* Jack slapped his face with his hands to get a grip on himself; he was turning into a girl. What bothered him the most was that Alice had told this girl—Becky—he was one-night-stand material. It hurt, even if it was true. And why had Alice pushed Becky into his arms? After her stunt at the library, it made little sense.

Yesterday afternoon she'd tried to kiss him, and he suspected there were feelings involved. He was sure it wasn't by chance she'd somehow showed up at the same Halloween party just a few hours later. Had she wanted to make him jealous? He would have assumed that was the case, except the whole night she'd acted as if nothing had happened between them. She'd barely spoken to him, pushed him to hook up with another girl, and then she'd left with Peter.

Jack's blood boiled. If this was all a perverse plan to make him jealous, it was working. The thought of Alice and Peter together made his seat too hot. He'd never been jealous of Alice's boyfriends, but for some inexplicable reason, Peter was different. Jack had to know what had happened, or, hopefully, what hadn't happened between them last night.

He finished the coffee and stood. "Well, Becky, thanks so much for the coffee"—Jack stroked the back of his head with one hand, embarrassed—"and everything else. I'll get out of here." Jack peeked out the window; he had no idea where Becky lived, or how they'd gotten here last night. "Err… Where's 'here?'"

"We're on Litchfield street. It's a quick walk to campus."

"I'm making it a morning run." He was still wearing his sporty shorts and an old sweatshirt. Mornings in Cambridge in November were viciously cold.

Becky stared, unimpressed. "Even quicker."

She walked him to the door and opened it for him; she was kicking him out. It was a weird novelty for Jack.

"Do we hug goodbye?" he asked.

"Sure." She gave him an unconcerned hug and waved him goodbye.

Jack jogged home. He beat his roommate to the bathroom and took a long, hot shower followed by a huge, alcohol-draining breakfast. By the time he was done, it was already mid-morning. It was time to make a call. He scrolled through his contacts with his thumb and tapped on Peter's name.

Peter picked up on the second ring. "Sullivan, my man, what's up?"

"Hey, Captain, you up for a one-on-one game later?"

"Can't do," Peter answered, and alarm bells went off inside Jack's head. "I have a date," he added, confirming his fears.

Jack oh-so-casually asked, "Someone I know?"

"Yep, that girl from your concentration, Alice Brown. I'm giving her a behind-the-scenes of the Lavietes."

Jack ground his teeth and tried to speak in a normal voice. "You guys hit it off, then?"

"Nah." Relief washed over Jack as Peter continued, "Turns out the blue paint was great to attract the attention, but a big turn off for the ladies. How did it go with your nurse?"

"I had her bathe me first," Jack replied smugly.

"Ooooh, my man!" Peter hollered. "I should take that page out of your book. You're a genius."

"So you went to bed early? It wasn't even midnight when you left."

"No, the kitten kept me up talking until her roommate came home wasted."

Jack stared at the phone, not sure he'd heard right. "You were up all night *talking?*"

"Yeah. Your friend was cool, and the paint was too weird anyway.

We'll see how it goes today."

Jack was tense again. "What, do you plan to have sex on the court?" he snapped. "If the coach catches you, you're dead."

"Not on the court." Peter chuckled. "Maybe later. Anyway, your Alice seems more of a slow burner."

Exactly, *his* Alice. "And you're okay with waiting?"

"I kind of like this girl."

Why, of all girls, did Peter have to walk the line for Ice? "That's a first."

"Who knows, my man; maybe she'll take one look at my face and decide I'm gross." Jack doubted it. "She kept saying she was bothered she couldn't picture how I looked under all the paint."

"I'd run for the hills if I saw your ugly face," Jack joked.

Peter laughed. "All right, buddy, I've gotta run too. See you tomorrow at practice, yeah?"

"Yeah, I'll talk to you later."

"Later."

Peter hung up.

Jack stood up and hurled his phone at the bed. It bounced off and landed on the carpet unscathed. Jack kicked it under the bed. What the hell was happening to him? Peter was behaving, and it made him angry instead of relieved. Why was he so mad? *Who* was he mad at? Alice? Peter? Himself?

On impulse, Jack picked up his gym duffel bag and decided to go to the MAC and work off some steam. Staying home and brooding definitely wasn't an option. Instead, he'd do some cardio to sweat out the hangover, and maybe also some weight training. Homework would keep him busy for the rest of the afternoon. Jack couldn't afford to fall behind, not with the basketball season kicking off next weekend.

An evil grin spread on his lips as Jack studied the practice schedule hanging over his bed. He wouldn't have much idle time in the coming months, but neither would Peter have much time to woo Alice. *Aha!*

Alice

Madison staggered into Alice's room, dragging her feet behind her, and sat on the empty bed. "I'm never going to drink again."

Alice stopped leafing through her closet to look at her friend. "That's what every college kid says after a great Halloween party."

"Meh, the party kind of sucked."

"Agreed." Alice nodded. "At least it got me a date."

"About that. What's your plan here?"

"Actually, I don't have one." Alice resumed her shuffling of clothes. "Thinking I could make Jack jealous was stupid."

"I thought it worked."

"Yeah, me too, until I read this." Alice abandoned her closet again, took her phone out of her jeans' pocket, and handed it to Madison. "It's the first message on WhatsApp."

Becky had sent her a too-graphic text about her showering activities with Jack.

"Ew," was Madison's sole comment.

"I know," Alice sighed. "Jack definitely wasn't heartbroken about me going home with Peter."

"So you're dating his friend now? Doesn't he have the worst reputation?"

"He does, but so far he's been nice."

"You like him?"

"Too early to say." Alice shrugged. "Let me see his face first, without all that blue paint."

Madison tapped the phone. "Want me to find the Crimson roster pics on their website?"

"Actually, I prefer it to be a surprise."

"And if he's ugly?"

"I don't think he is." Alice smiled a secret smile. "Anyway, a face alone doesn't do it for me. I need to feel a connection, a spark."

"But isn't he your typical athlete jerk?" Madison insisted.

"Can't say yet." Alice closed the room door before Blue could make a run for it. "I agree with you. On paper, his CV is bad, but last night felt so easy talking to him. It felt right."

"You're giving up on Jack then?"

Alice wasn't sure; the text from Becky had churned her stomach. Her feelings toward Jack right now were more violent than loving.

"I don't know," she admitted. "Jack isn't stupid. He knows yesterday wasn't just about a rebound, no matter what I said afterward. If he wants to make something out of it, he knows where to find me. In the meantime, I'll live my life."

Madison captured a sulky-looking Blue as he hopped near the bed. "With his best friend?" she asked, stroking the bunny.

"Well, I'm not going to stay single and wait for Jack to make up his mind."

"But if you go out with Peter, doesn't that make you off-limits for Jack, even if he's into you?"

"Why?"

"I don't know." Madison shrugged. "Don't they have a bro code—'Bros before Hoes,' or something like that?"

"Huh. I hadn't thought about that." Was she making a mistake? No, Alice couldn't second-guess herself like this. "If they have a secret code, I know nothing about it," she told Madison. "Anyway, it's nothing serious with Peter. He's just a much-needed distraction."

"If you say so." Madison sounded unconvinced. "Have you decided what to wear?"

Alice turned back toward her closet. "No. I've never been on a sporty date before."

"You can borrow my new PINK set if you want."

"You're a lifesaver!" Alice jumped on her bed to hug Madison. Blue squealed in protest.

***

At two p.m., Peter texted Alice he was on his way. She took the elevator to the lobby and waited for him behind the hall's glass doors, avoiding the outside cold.

When a tall guy jogged up the steps, she didn't recognize Peter, not until he waved and smiled from behind the glass. Alice's breath caught in her throat. Peter was a Jake Gyllenhaal lookalike, much better looking than she expected. She reminded herself that looks meant nothing and put her woolen gloves on before opening the door.

"Hey, you," she said, feeling shy.

He gave her a quick hug and flashed her a grin. "So, did I pass the face test?"

Alice beamed back. "You know you did."

He winked. "Shall we go?"

132

They entered Lavietes Pavilion from a secondary access, and Peter led the way to the basketball court. He took off his jacket and beanie. Alice watched him, thinking she'd never seen a guy look that sexy in sportswear. She followed his lead and peeled off her coat, hat, scarf, and gloves, setting them on another plastic chair.

Alice sized up the stadium; it was much bigger than she had expected. Weird that they allowed players to come in when it was closed.

"Are you sure we're allowed in here?" Alice asked.

"Not really."

Alice glared at Peter. "What do you mean?"

"The coach didn't exactly give me the keys; I might've lifted them from him."

"Are you crazy?" Her mouth gaped open before she started to panic. "We could get expelled! You could get kicked off the team…"

"Nah," Peter said, unfazed. "I'm too good a player to kick me off. Relax; no one's coming today. Coach Morrison gave us a free day. Last one of the season, probably."

Alice still wasn't convinced about staying. "How come?"

"We have our first game next Saturday, so no free weekends until March. The coach told us to have fun on Halloween night, rest today, and get ready to sweat on Monday."

Alice let his enthusiasm infect her, and she relaxed. "Did he also tell you to get blue?"

"No, that was the team's personal initiative."

Alice stared around the court. "So this is where the magic happens?"

"Yep. Wait here."

Peter unlocked another door—probably a storeroom—disappeared inside, and came back bouncing an orange ball. He stopped close to her and made the ball spin on his index finger.

"Are you trying to impress me?"

"Are you impressed?"

"Not yet."

"How about now?" Peter turned toward the right basket, bent his knees, and made the shot from half a court away.

Holding her breath, Alice watched the ball fly across the room. It went right through the metal hoop, barely making the net move. Peter was already running after it.

"You're such a showoff," she said after he came back to stand beside her. "So, how does this game work?"

Peter bounced the ball again while he explained. "Varsity rules are different from the real thing." Every two or three bounces, he made the ball loop between his legs in a move Alice was sure was not as easy as it looked. "Each team has five players on the court, and there's one captain."

Alice smiled. "Let me guess—that's you?"

"You guessed right."

He continued with his Basketball 101, and Alice listened patiently. Peter was so passionate he could convert even an anti-sports girl like her.

When Alice's head started to spin with all the rules, Peter finally said, "That's the basics—oh, also, you have to dribble the ball at all times. You can't run across the court holding it. More than three steps"—he stopped the ball and made three demonstrative steps—"and you lose the play. You want to try a shot?"

Alice suddenly felt self-conscious. "You'll have to show me how; my last attempt was in fifth grade or something."

"Come here."

Alice joined Peter at the free-throw line, and he positioned himself close behind her. A shiver spider-walked down her spine. *What have I gotten myself into?*

"Your right foot should be slightly in front," Peter said, his warm breath trickling down her neck. As he helped her get into the right position, all Alice could focus on was how the front of his leg pressed on the back of hers as he pushed it forward.

"Keep your weight on the balls of your feet," Peter instructed. "And hold the ball like this." He was a good foot taller than Alice, and he showed her how to palm the ball by holding it above her head from behind. The demonstration required him to push his chest against her back, making her skin tingle at the touch. "Here, take it."

Alice took the ball from him and he adjusted her hands on it.

"Now bend your knees and push your hips backward." He pulled gently at her waist, bringing their bodies even closer together, and Alice got body-wide goose bumps.

He let go and circled her. "Elbow up." Peter pushed her ball-supporting arm up about two inches.

"You're bossy," Alice said, straightening.

He chuckled. "Knees bent."

Alice crouched again.

"Now do a little jump and shoot."

Alice gathered momentum in her knees and then straightened her body in a fluid motion, releasing the ball as her feet left the ground. The orange sphere soared up in the air and started its descent toward the rim. For one glorious moment, Alice thought it would go in. Then it bounced off the hoop and fell out of the net.

"Almost," she said.

"Not bad for a first try." Peter ran after the ball. "Here, try again." He threw the ball at her.

She caught it and got back into position.

After fifteen minutes of free shooting, Alice's arms began to hurt. She'd never realized how heavy the ball could become. "I'm tired. Can we take a break?"

"Wait here." Peter disappeared again and came back with a blue throw mat. He sat on it and patted the empty space next to him.

Alice joined him. "Have you always wanted to play basketball?"

"Not exactly, but when I turned fourteen I shot up a foot, and I think my height decided for me."

"How tall are you?" Alice studied him, trying to gauge his height in her head. "Six five?"

"Six seven."

"Whoa."

Peter hooked an arm around her waist and pulled her closer. "You don't play any sports, then?"

"I used to do gymnastics," Alice said. "But it was never professional or anything."

"You mean you used to do all those scary jumps and weird contortions?"

"They're not so scary once you get the hang of them."

"Still badass. Want to show me?"

She smiled. "I'm way out of practice. But I can show you a video of when I was eleven."

"I'd love to see it. Did you have one of those sparkly costumes on?"

Alice blushed and changed the subject; she didn't want Peter picturing her in a stupid costume. "How come you're spending your last free afternoon for the next five months with me?"

"There are worse people, no?"

"Thank you very much." She made to swat his shoulder playfully, but he caught her wrist and held it, pulling her toward him.

Alice became suddenly shy under his blue gaze. Even more so when he lifted her chin with his free hand, brushed one thumb across her cheek, and kissed her. They lay back on the mat, still kissing, him on top of her.

The loud sound of a door shutting in the distance interrupted their heated kiss.

"Shit, someone's here." Peter leapt to his feet, and so did Alice.

Peter moved faster than a leopard. He picked up the mat and ran to turn off the light. Alice collected their coats and followed Peter inside a storeroom filled with various training equipment. Peter put the mat back in place, then closed the little room's door. They were left standing in complete darkness.

Peter pressed a finger on her closed lips. "We have to keep quiet," he whispered. "Whatever happens."

"What do you mean?" she hissed, starting to panic.

He brushed his lips against her ear. "Only that if I tickle you, you can't scream." He moved his fingers to her sides and Alice suppressed a giggle, pressing her mouth to his chest. "Quiet," he ordered.

They heard muffled voices coming from the main court, and Peter stopped tickling her. It was scary and exciting, especially when Peter pushed Alice against the vertical pile of mats and left a trail of kisses down her neck. Alice pulled herself up to kiss him on the mouth, completely forgetting the people outside.

She wasn't sure how long they stayed locked in the cramped storeroom, wrapped around each other. But she suspected their kisses lasted well beyond the moment the voices outside went gone quiet.

"I think it's safe to go out," Peter whispered in her ear. "But let me check first."

He moved away from her and used his phone as a torch to find the handle. He pulled the door open, letting in a sliver of faint light.

"I think we're good," Peter said, opening the door completely. "But we'd better go."

They hastily threw on their coats and snuck out of the pavilion by the same door they'd used to get in. Outside, it was already dark. Alice checked her watch; time with Peter had flown by again. They grabbed a quick bite to eat, and then Peter walked her back to her building.

Alice stepped up onto the first step leading to the entrance door. "This way I'm only half a foot shorter than you," she said, placing her hands on his shoulders. Peter wrapped his arms around her waist.

"Have I earned a next date?" he asked.

"You get points for the basketball lesson, but lose some for almost getting us caught." She paused. "However, you do get bonuses for your kissing-in-the-dark skills."

No more encouragement was needed for him to demonstrate those skills again.

"Was that a yes?" he asked after the kiss.

"Yeah." Alice nodded. "What should we do next? Break into the library at night?"

"How about something homier?"

"Like what?"

"Dinner, prepared by yours truly?"

Alice was surprised. "You can cook?"

Peter winked. "One of my other secret skills."

"I'd love to." Alice smiled. "When?"

"Ah." Peter scratched his head. "Between classes and practice, I'm conscripted until next Sunday. Early dinner?"

"It's a date." Alice smashed an imaginary gavel on an imaginary bench. "Sunday sounds great, and I have a busy week too."

Peter's eyes sparkled with another idea. "Hey," he said. "We play McGill Saturday night—why don't you come to watch the game?"

Alice really hated sports, but how could she say no? "Okay. Do I have to get tickets?"

"This one's free admission," Peter said. "Just arrive early to get decent seats."

"Will do," Alice said. He was cooking her dinner; she could endure *one* game. And she would force Haley and Madison to go with her so she wouldn't be alone and bored the whole time.

"I'm counting on it," he said.

Alice gave him another kiss. Then she hopped up the steps and hurried inside her building, feeling giddier than she deemed wise.

Jack

Jack was ten minutes late for his nine a.m. Organic Chemistry class, despite the fact that he'd changed at top speed after practice and ran here straight from the gym. Luckily, the professor had his back turned to the class as he wrote today's lesson plan on the board, allowing Jack to sneak in undetected.

As he jogged down the stairs of the classroom, Jack's muscles ached and his mood was at an all-time low. Coach Morrison wanted to kick off the season with a victory against McGill, resulting in a particularly nasty workout. But it was the short chat with Peter beforehand that left Jack the sorest. As they changed in the locker room, the captain had given him the highlights of his date with Ice the day before. Jack had barely heard anything the coach said all practice, too busy imagining Alice and Peter locked together in that dark storeroom.

He paused halfway down the stairs and searched for the back of Alice's head in the crowded lecture hall. It took him a minute to recognize her as the brunette sitting in their usual spot two rows from the front. The color change was doing weird things to him. He'd never thought he preferred brunettes over blondes or redheads. Yet for Ice, Jack was sure he preferred her as a brunette. He hopped down the steps and took his spot next to her.

"What did I miss?" he asked.

"Not much." Ice didn't turn to look at him, nor did she stop taking notes. "We're just getting started on multi-step organic synthesis. Did you have breakfast?"

"No," Jack whispered. "The coach kept us until the last minute."

Ice abandoned her notepad to reach into her bag and take out an energy bar. This was why she was his best friend. She always carried around a supply of energy bars for him, exactly for days like this. Okay, so Ice was acting normal, showing no hard feelings over Saturday. But Jack couldn't relax—even if he'd dodged an uncomfortable conversation about the library, Ice's date with Peter was still bugging him.

"Here." She also handed him a silver thermos. "There's some coffee left. It shouldn't be cold yet."

"You're a life saver."

Technically speaking, food and drinks weren't allowed in class, but the rule was widely overlooked around campus. Especially where coffee was concerned.

Jack finished his breakfast and tried to follow the lecture. Ice was pretending nothing had happened, and Jack wanted to pretend, too. He wanted to keep his mouth shut but found he couldn't. "Did you have fun yesterday?" he asked.

Alice finally turned toward him with a sharp look. Yeah, dark hair definitely suited her best; it brought out her eyes. She studied his face for a few seconds before speaking. "If you're asking, I guess you already know."

True. They hadn't spoken after the party, and she hadn't told him she was going on a date with Peter. She must've guessed Peter had told him.

"Yeah, Peter mentioned your date this morning."

Professor Procter raised his voice pointedly.

Alice scribbled something on her notepad and edged it toward Jack. Talk later. Deal?

As he read, she underlined the writing twice. A final statement.

Jack mouthed, "Deal," and took out his Organic Chemistry book, determined to finally concentrate on the lesson. He could talk to her between classes.

He had to wait until their lunch break to broach the Peter subject again. They had a morning full of lectures, and after each one ended, Alice was out of her seat, down the stairs, and by the door in seconds. She'd done her best to avoid talking to him. But as they walked toward the cafeteria, she had no escape.

"So," he started, "you moved on pretty quickly from Ethan."

"Not as quick as you, apparently."

"Meaning?"

Alice gave him that seething look again. "Did you have fun taking off all that blue paint?"

Touché. She knew about the nurse. Becky had to have a flaw, right? She wasn't a morning-after drama queen, but she had a big mouth.

"I never said I was in love with Lori," Jack said, trying to justify his actions.

"Neither was I with Ethan," Ice countered.

"Okay, but you were serious about him."

"My bad."

Jack let out an exasperated, "Come on, Ice."

"What?" She played dumb.

"You're always serious when you date."

"So?"

"So you shouldn't date guys like Peter—or myself, for that matter."

Ice stopped walking. "Why do you have a problem with him?"

"He's not good when it comes to girls, trust me on this."

"He's been perfectly nice to me."

"It's only been two days."

"Well, you'd better get used to it." Alice positively glowered at him. "I'm coming to the game Saturday, and we have another date Sunday."

"What?" Jack asked, shocked. "You've never come to a game before."

"You never asked."

"Because I know you hate sports."

"I don't hate sports," Alice said. "I don't particularly enjoy them, but it doesn't mean I can't watch a game. It was fun playing yesterday."

"You had fun playing basketball, or you had fun in the storeroom?" Jack inwardly cringed at how petty he sounded.

"Both, if you really have to know," she hissed.

"You're making a mistake."

"Listen, Jack." Alice rolled her eyes. "Your objections have been duly noted. But right now I like Peter, he makes me feel good, and I want to feel good. I need to. So I'll keep dating him. If or when he does something I don't like, I'll stop. End of story."

"Are you going to sleep with him?"

"What if I am?"

"He'll just use you."

"Why?" She pursed her lips. "You think it's impossible for a guy to want to date me for more than a few months?"

"A few months?" Jack laughed. "With Peter, you'll be lucky if it turns into a few weeks before he moves on to someone else. If he's not already seeing some other girl on the side. It wouldn't be the first time."

"And why can't he be different for me?"

"Guys like him just aren't."

"You mean guys like *you!*" Alice splayed her arms to her sides.

"You're such a hypocrite."

"Why?"

"You sleep your way around campus and now you're bashing Peter for his low moral standards?"

"I'm just warning you." Jack wanted to grab her by the shoulders and shake some sense into her. "If you want to make a fool of yourself, be my guest."

"You know what? Go to hell." Alice's eyes became watery and her lower lip trembled as she repeated, "You just go to hell."

She stormed away, not looking back, and Jack was too mad to run after her. He walked in the opposite direction, heading to a different café.

What was happening to him? Alice was right. He was in no position to judge Peter; their attitude toward girls was the same. Ice should steer clear of them both. Imagining her in bed with Peter made Jack see red. If Alice wasn't going to listen to him, he'd have to distract Peter from her. Yeah, find a hot girl for his friend and have him forget Ice for good. It was all in her best interest. He'd be doing her a favor.

Alice

After their argument on Monday, Alice tried to give Jack the haughty silent treatment. It didn't work; Jack didn't let her go a day not talking to him. At their next shared lesson, he switched on the charm and soon he had her bent in two laughing her head off. After softening her up, he apologized and said he shouldn't be meddling in her love life. Jack explained he had seen many girls hurt by Peter, and that he was simply worried about her. But he understood she was a big girl and that she could make her own decisions. He was just a concerned friend.

Just. A. Friend. Words Alice officially hated.

How could three simple words send her emotions spiraling?

Alice had to get him out of her head. She'd been obsessing about Jack since freshman year; it was about time she accepted they weren't going to happen as a couple. He'd made it perfectly clear he wasn't interested. All that crap about not wanting to ruin their friendship was just that: crap. If a guy, especially one with Jack's sex drive, was interested, it was impossible to be that rational. To have the amount of self-control he'd shown her when she offered herself up on a silver platter. He simply didn't like her, not in the way she wanted him to. She should've known from that first humiliating time he'd made it stark clear he'd never look at her any other way.

****

Alice had spent the entire Saturday afternoon choosing an outfit that would send the message: you want to spend the rest of your life with me, but I'm not trying too hard. It was a difficult one to pull off, especially if she added the keep-me-warm-in-winter requirement. It the end, she'd opted for a homey-sexy look as opposed to outright-sexy: uber-tight jeans, ankle boots, and a cream sweater that hugged her curves in all the right places.

She still couldn't believe Jack had finally asked her to go on a real date with him. "Dinner tomorrow night, deal?" he'd asked her the day before at the end of class. It hadn't been a declaration of undying love, but it was an improvement from meeting up for coffee or going to the library to study. Dinner on a Saturday night meant serious business.

Alice entered the restaurant with a pounding heart and flushed cheeks—reddened not just by the sudden warmth of the place, but by who was waiting for her inside. She spotted Jack sitting in a high-backed booth, half hidden by the booth in front of him. From the entrance, Alice could only see his right side. He was reading a menu.

As if he felt her looking at him, he lifted his gaze and they locked eyes. Alice's world tilted. Hers wasn't a simple crush; she had fallen head-over-heels for Jack. He got up, flashing a wild grin, and walked toward her. As he hugged her hello, Alice inhaled his scent—a mix of his shaving gel and his natural odor—and her stomach exploded with butterflies.

"You came alone?" Jack asked.

He seemed surprised.

"Yeah?"

She followed Jack back to the booth only to see a pretty girl already occupying the seat closest to the wall.

"Ice, this is Olivia." Jack made the introductions. "Olivia, meet Alice."

Olivia? HAS HE ASKED ME OUT TO INTRODUCE ME TO HIS GIRLFRIEND? Alice screamed inside her head. No! This wasn't happening. This couldn't happen.

It could, and it was.

Alice watched the girl get up as if in slow motion. Her bubble of happiness had transformed in a water bubble that slowed everything down and made voices sound deep and distorted.

In her slow motion voice, Olivia said, "Noooice tooo meeeet yoooouuu." She extended a manicured hand.

Muscle-memory made Alice stretch out her arm and take Olivia's hand. Her lips froze in a polite expression—one she hoped didn't look too strained—as she willed herself to sit opposite the happy couple. She prayed she wouldn't start crying in front of them, although angry tears were already welling in her eyes.

Alice dabbed at the corner of her eyes with the sleeve of her sweater. "Gosh, it was windy outside," she said to explain the gesture.

"We were thinking of catching a movie later," Jack said.

At least this torture session would be short-lived. Alice calculated how long her agony would last. It was a few minutes past seven. Surely, they'd want to catch the eight-thirty show, nine at the latest. The walk to the movie theater took fifteen minutes, plus ten to get the tickets... They had to leave in an hour, an hour and a half tops. She could survive sixty minutes of this. She didn't have another choice.

"Do you have any plans for later?" Jack asked.

Alice's plan had been to spend the night in Jack's arms making love to him for the first time.

"Plans?" You mean besides crying myself to death? "I have a... um... sorority meeting."

"They make you meet on a Saturday?" Olivia—the nosy bitch— asked.

"It isn't an official meeting, just first year pledges getting together and hanging out."

"It must be nice to be part of a group." Olivia's over polite smile seemed to imply, "See? This is my little group here: Jack and me."

Olivia had possessively linked her arm with Jack's; she was so irritating, Alice felt a swell of anger, envy, and, possibly even, a tiny surge of hatred. She had a mental vision of grabbing the ketchup and mustard bottles—one with each hand—and squeezing them in Olivia's face until they were both empty. As unrealizable as the fantasy was, it gave Alice the strength to endure the next hour.

***

Olivia, like many others after her, had been but a short footnote in Jack's life. Instead, Jack's newfound attitude of acting as if Peter didn't exist stuck around a lot longer. Alice didn't know what to make of this new approach, but she preferred it to the insistent nagging that had preceded it. Jack constantly telling her how a guy like Peter could never fall for her, to Alice translated as Jack telling her how *he* would never fall for her.

Dating someone else had always been the best way to avoid thinking about Jack not liking her, or Jack's new girl-of-the-moment. Maybe Peter wasn't the wisest distraction of choice, but he was good-looking, charming, and so far he'd treated her with nothing but respect. True, he had a reputation. So what? Alice was just looking for a fun pastime to avoid brooding over Jack. She wasn't going to get hurt; she could handle Peter. And if he dumped her, she'd deal with it. Just as she'd dealt with Ethan breaking up with her. Or, more to the point, telling her she'd never been his girlfriend in the first place and that he didn't want to have casual, meaningless sex with her anymore. *Good times...*

Besides, Peter's flirty texts were the only highlight in her otherwise bleak routine. She'd started to look forward to the little red circle with a white number appearing over her WhatsApp icon. They hadn't managed to meet again after their date on Sunday, as both their schedules were packed: classes, his practices, her sorority commitments. Their few free moments did not overlap, but they chatted a lot through texts, and by the time Saturday rolled around, Alice couldn't wait for their dinner the next day. Peter had promised to cook for her, and she was fascinated. Not many college kids had kitchen skills beyond microwaving premade meals.

"Well," Madison said as they entered Lavietes Pavilion with half an hour to spare before the game. "Harvard certainly doesn't push the bling side of varsity sports"

"Why?" Alice asked.

Alice, Madison, and Haley took three seats close to the front. Peter had told her to come early, but they needn't have worried. The stands were still half-empty.

"I watched a game at Notre Dame once, and it was like going to an NBA game," Madison explained. "They had mega screens hanging from the ceiling, videos, music, cheerleaders… Their pavilion is like a real indoor stadium; this looks like a sorry high school gym."

"I thought people only ever went to Notre Dame to watch football," Haley said.

"Football season was over when I visited."

"Why were you in Indiana, anyway?" Alice asked.

"My cousin from my mother's side goes to school there. She's not a Smithson, so she wasn't destined to Harvard-then-Harvard-Law from birth."

Madison's family ran one of the top law firms in Boston. All Smithson kids were expected to graduate from Harvard Law School. Ethan was an alumnus, Georgiana was attending it now, and Madison would apply next year. Alice remembered how Ethan always complained about the suffocating expectations of his family.

"Is the Harvard team any good at basketball?" Alice asked.

Madison shook her head. "I have no idea."

"Neither do I," Haley said. "Anyway, we're here for the tall, pretty boys, so who cares."

"Speaking of, which tall, pretty boy are we concentrating our attention on today?" Madison asked.

"Peter, I think," Alice said.

"So no Jack?" Madison insisted. "Are you suddenly over him?"

"No, I'm not." Alice puffed her cheeks in exasperation. "But he made it clear I'm not his cup of tea. I thought that if—when—I told him how I felt about him, we'd have one of those Hollywood moments a la *When Harry Met Sally*. Unfortunately, I got more of a *He's Just Not That Into You*."

"But you didn't really tell him how you feel," Haley pointed out.

"Thank goodness for that!" Alice cringed at the thought. "At least it wasn't a complete humiliation."

Madison pouted. "Are you sure an 'I'm madly in love with you' speech wouldn't have made a difference?"

"No difference, I'm sure."

"What about Peter?" Haley asked. "You like him?"

"Yeah. He's fun, charming, and he has pretty eyes."

"Isn't he a bit of a… mmm…" Haley let her words hang.

"Man-slut?" Alice supplied. No point in denying it. "Yeah, I think so.

But I'm not looking for a serious relationship right now."

"As long as you don't get hurt," Madison said.

"I don't care about him enough to get hurt."

A speaker announcing the two teams silenced Madison's upcoming retort. They stopped talking about the boys and concentrated on ogling them.

"I know number 23." Madison pointed at one of the players. "He's in most of my English classes."

Something in her friend's tone of voice made Alice think Madison had a little crush on the guy.

Haley didn't pick up the vibe. "He's super cute," she said. "What's his name?"

"Scott," Madison said sulkily.

Haley checked the Crimson website on her phone. "Number 23, Scott Williams. He's a junior."

"I told you he's in my class."

"Is he single?" Haley asked.

"Why do you want to know?"

"Relax!" Haley said. "What are you so touchy about?"

It was clear to Alice that Madison was getting territorial, but sometimes Haley could be completely blind to other people's feelings.

"Look." Haley pointed at the court. "He's going for a shot." They all followed the ball as Scott let it go and it flew over the court. "Goal!" Haley shouted, lifting her arms over her head.

"This isn't soccer," Madison snapped.

Haley poked her tongue at Madison and turned to Alice. "You should ask Peter to introduce us."

"Sure," Alice said, taking a mental note to never ever do so.

Madison scoffed, but Haley wasn't looking at her and didn't seem to hear. Then the referee blew the start whistle, and the three of them stopped talking and concentrated on the game.

Alice was no expert, but once the game was over, two facts were clear.

One: Peter was the team's star.

And two: Jack had played like crap.

She looked at him now. Even if Harvard had won to McGill 66 to 63, it was clear Jack had a black temper. As if he felt her staring, he turned toward her. They locked eyes, and his frown deepened. Jack quickly looked away and disappeared into the locker room. Ah, hell, if he wanted to be a sour puss for having played one bad game… This was why she didn't like sports much. Alice hated how a won or lost game—or badly played, in this case—could sway the mood of a person, or an entire city, or even a country. It was so stupid.

She caught Peter's eye next. He shot her a grin; his mood couldn't have been more different from Jack's. Peter blew her a kiss and twirled his index finger in a "later" gesture that she knew meant tomorrow. He had been clear that game nights were reserved for the team. She gave him the thumbs-up and blew a kiss back. Peter waved and then focused his attention on an approaching reporter.

Jack

Jack entered the locker room and flung his neck towel down onto a bench. He hurried in and out of the shower before any of his teammates were finished. When Peter eventually jogged into the locker room, Jack was already getting dressed.

The captain did his usual round of high fives and cheered with the rest of the team, then stopped next to Jack. "Sullivan, my man," he said, giving Jack a pat on the shoulder. "It'll go better next time, and we won anyway."

Jack gave him a stiff nod, avoiding catching his eye. He was scared he might punch his friend otherwise. Peter's words of condescension continued to ring in his ears, their implied meaning obvious. Did Peter expect Jack to thank him for saving the game? Fat chance of that. He'd never been jealous of Peter being the better player. Jack cared more about his academic achievements as far as his time at Harvard was concerned. Yet tonight, he was bitterly jealous of Peter's raw talent. He was getting increasingly mad, and it was all Alice's fault.

Jack finished getting dressed, packed his bag, and sat on a bench near his locker to wait for the others to catch up with him. When they were all showered and mostly dressed, Coach Morrison came in for his usual after-game speech. Jack's shoulders slumped, and he prepared himself for another humiliating fifteen minutes.

As expected, praises for Peter were equaled only by admonishments toward Jack. Harsh, but—thanks to the final victory—brief. Peter had cut his rebuff short by winning the game almost single-handedly; it should have made Jack appreciate his captain. It only made him angrier.

After dinner, a few players decided to go for a nightcap somewhere nearby. Jack was tempted to say goodnight and go sulk in the privacy of his room, but then he noticed Peter join the group. A mean idea struck him. If Peter was going, so would Jack. All it took to end Peter's so-called relationship with Ice was for the captain to go home with a pretty girl. Piece of cake! Peter always ended up sleeping with someone after a victory on the court.

They headed for a cheap beer in The Cambridge Queen's Head, a low-key pub on campus. There were six of them in total, the best regular players. Scott and David Williams, two brothers on the team, went to order for everyone while the others secured a table. Jack was puzzled. It was rare for the two brothers to hang out together; they usually avoided each other. Besides blood ties, the two seemed to have little in common. Scott was warm and easygoing, David cold and detached. Jack was pretty sure they hated each other. He shook the thought away; the Williams brothers weren't his focus right now.

Jack concentrated on the crowd in the pub. Being Saturday night, it was busy and packed with pretty girls. In fact, just as Scott and David returned with their beers, two blonde girls strolled by. One had her hair tied up in a high ponytail; she had a cute smile and big eyes. Pretty. Yet her friend was more attractive with her long, straight hair and doll face.

"Did you guys all swallow a bottle of Skele-Gro as kids?" Ponytail asked, while her friend smiled with a flirtatious twinkle in her eyes.

Jack would've usually focused all his attention on the prettiest girl, but tonight he had a different agenda. He chatted up the ponytailed friend, completely ignoring Doll Face. Out of the corner of his eye, he saw Doll Face's temporary confusion at being overlooked. Then the girl shrugged and turned to talk to the other tall guy standing next to her: Peter.

Jack was only half-following his conversation with Ponytail. He was too busy trying to overhear snippets of what Peter was saying to Doll Face. She was exactly his type, much more than Alice was, especially with her new look.

"Are you even listening to me?" Ponytail asked.

"Yeah, sure," Jack lied.

"So what do you think?"

"About what?"

"Forget it. I'm getting another drink." She left.

Doll Face was still talking to Peter when she noticed her friend was gone.

"I'd better check on my friend," she told Peter. Her tone suggested she didn't actually want to. Jack read her imaginary subtitles: "I want you to tell me to ignore my friend and ask me to stay here."

Jack waited for Peter to use one of his usual get-lucky lines. If he left with this girl, his relationship with Ice would end before it even started.

Instead, Peter just shrugged. "Sure," he said, lifting his glass to drain the last inch of his beer. "I'm heading home anyway."

Hit by her second rejection of the night, Doll Face left tight-lipped.

Jack was shocked and unnerved. True, the team never stayed out late or for more than a light beer during the season, but that didn't mean they didn't pick up girls on the way. It wasn't like Peter to pass on an opportunity like this.

The team left together, and they paused outside the pub in the cool night air to say goodbye and part ways. Scott and David headed down Cambridge St. with Matt and Blake, while Peter and Jack left in the opposite direction up Oxford St.

"Dude," Jack said as they walked. "That girl you blew off was hot."

"My man," Peter sighed. "She was."

"How come she's not headed home with you?"

"I have a date with Alice tomorrow."

"Oh, so now you're going exclusive?"

Peter stopped. "Sullivan, if you have a problem with me dating one of your friends, just come out with it and say so."

"I don't have a problem with you dating anyone," Jack lied. "But I care about her and I don't want to see her get hurt."

"So why did you try to fix me up with a blonde doll tonight?"

"I didn't. I was talking to her friend."

Peter ignored his lie. "Listen, my man, I get it. Alice is your friend; I told you, I have my white gloves on." He lifted his hands and wiggled his fingers. "So, did I pass the test?"

Jack nodded stiffly. Peter was too smart for his own good, only he had no idea how badly Jack wanted him to fail, not pass.

Alice

For her date with Peter, Alice decided to wear a long, knitted dress buttoned up at the front and ankle boots. Peter had given her his address, so at five in the evening she left her building and headed for his house. She was both excited and anxious. College guy's houses could be scary. They could range from generally unclean to sanitary service emergency. And the bathrooms… ew. The only boy's room she'd ever seen cleaner than hers was Jack's; he was too fastidious not to clean after himself. Not that it mattered. Other than for group projects, they weren't going to use his room for any extracurricular activities.

She had to stop thinking about Jack. He wasn't a variable in her sentimental equation anymore. She was going on a date with Peter, not Jack. The tall, blue-eyed team captain needed to be her sole focus. What would Peter's house be like? Alice was about to find out. She stopped in front of a mahogany wood-framed house, a duplex actually, and double checked the address before ringing the bell.

Peter came to the door wearing gray sweatpants and a white t-shirt. *Why are guys in sweatpants instantaneously ten times hotter?*

They hugged on the threshold and he showed her inside. The house smelled of eggs but in a good way. Despite this being a college-boys-inhabited apartment, the place didn't look too dirty. Not stark clean, but not gross either.

Alice followed Peter behind the kitchen bar where he had two pans on the stove.

"Mmm." She inhaled deeply. "Smells good. How come you can cook?"

"I'm part Italian on my mother's side. She taught me."

"Wow. Can you speak Italian?"

"Un po'."

"That sounds like Spanish, un poco. How about something more elaborate?"

"All right. Sei bella come il sole."

Alice recognized the word "bella." He must have paid her a compliment of some kind. Hearing him speak Italian was too thrilling to be wise. So she moved on to safer topics. "That was cool. What are you making for dinner?"

"Grazie. And I'm making spaghetti carbonara. Please tell me you're not a trouble-eater."

"Trouble-eater?"

"Yeah, you know, vegetarian, pescatarian, gluten-hater, or something like that."

"I'm not, I swear. I love pasta, and I couldn't live without bacon."

"Great, because this recipe has both. I've opened the wine if you want to pour us a glass."

Alice turned toward the bar where the opened wine bottle and glasses were. This was all very grown up. Much more of a mature date than what she would have expected from a college boy. It was the kind of date Ethan would have taken her on.

She winced at the thought of her ex. Her heart was still a bit sore from the breakup—er, *dismissal.* In the span of two weeks, her boyfriend had dumped her and her best friend had returned her romantic advances with the warmth of an ice block. If it weren't for Peter, she'd be at an all-time low. He was the perfect distraction, one that could cook delicious pasta with loads of bacon in it, judging from the smell.

Alice poured the wine—red, of course—and handed Peter a glass. "So, you live here alone?"

"No, I have a roommate. He's visiting his family this weekend, and he doesn't have classes on Monday, the lucky bastard," Peter said. "He'll be back tomorrow night."

Leaving them alone in the house for the entire evening. *Well-played.* Alice wasn't sure if she wanted to sleep with Peter tonight. As dates went, it was so far so good, but her mind wasn't made up yet. She decided to go with the flow and see where the evening would lead.

Alice didn't comment on the *Home Alone* situation, so she just lifted her glass and said, "Cheers." She clinked her glass against his and they both took a sip.

Peter started working on the sauce while Alice hovered behind him. He bent over a bowl beating raw eggs with a fork and mixing them with some kind of grated cheese. Watching him cook made him sexier than usual. He still hadn't kissed her, although she wished he would.

He lifted the lid off the stockpot, probably to check if the water was boiling, which it was. Then he threw some salt in, followed by the spaghetti, set a timer on his phone, and turned to her.

"Did you enjoy the game last night?" he asked.

"Actually, I did."

"You seem surprised."

"I am a bit. I thought sports were boring, but when you have a team to cheer for, it's exhilarating." She beamed at him. "Congratulations on the win."

Peter shrugged. "Thanks. We didn't play at our best, though, and the season is long."

"Madison said Harvard was a bit on the cheap side, as basketball pavilions go."

"She's right," Peter agreed, surprising Alice. "But a degree from Harvard is a degree from Harvard. There's no topping that."

"So you chose a better school with a less-than-stellar team?"

"Yeah, basically."

"Even if you're shooting for the NBA?" Alice asked.

"Scouts will spot talent no matter the team you play on, and I could get a serious injury at any point in my career. A good degree never goes away."

Peter was proving to be more levelheaded than she'd expected.

"Cheers to that," Alice said, taking another sip of wine.

Peter checked the timer. "The pasta will be ready in a minute," he said, and came closer to her. She was leaning with her back against the kitchen bar, and he trapped her between it and his body. He set his glass on the bar, took hers away, and put it down next to his. "Which means I have exactly sixty seconds left to kiss you."

He wrapped his arms around her back and pressed his lips to hers. Alice's entire body warmed, an electric current spreading through her from head to toe. When the beeping timer put an end to the kiss, Alice wished pasta took longer to cook.

"You can sit down," Peter said, pointing her toward the table. "I'll bring the pasta over in a second."

Alice noticed the laid table for the first time. The living area was an open space that included the kitchen, the main living room, and a small dining area on the side. The table setting wasn't too fancy, but, again, impressive for an alleged college jock.

"Mmm, this is delicious," Alice said after tasting the first forkful of spaghetti. "You have to give me the recipe."

Peter shook his head, smiling. "Not possible. If you want real Italian pasta, you'll have to come to me."

Was he planning another date already? "You mean you want me to knock on your door whenever I'm craving great pasta?" she teased. "That could become a problem."

"With you, it wouldn't be."

Bit cheesy, but Alice let it slide, accepting the compliment. A girl could get used to wonderful homemade dinners and a stream of compliments coming from a smoking hot, tall guy in sweatpants.

"I haven't made any dessert," Peter said once they'd finished eating the pasta.

"Oh, that's all right." Alice patted her belly. "I'm already so full."

"Want to finish the wine on the couch?"

Heat rose in her cheeks. She was certain the couch was heavy-making-out territory. "Sure."

Peter emptied the bottle into their glasses and picked them both up, guiding the way to the living room. They sat almost on top of each other, her legs across his lap, her back leaning against the puffy couch arm. They chatted a little longer, Peter casually stroking her shins as they talked. Her head was spinning a little—because of the wine, or because of Peter, she couldn't tell.

I like him, she realized. *A lot.* The night they'd met, their first date, and now tonight—everything with him was perfect, exciting, new. Peter wasn't the superficial jerk Jack insisted he was.

Jack. She didn't want to think about him or her unrequited love for him ever again. Alice wanted to close that book and move onto a much more interesting read.

When her glass was empty, Peter took it from her and set it on the coffee table. He pulled her fully onto his lap and they started kissing. After a while, he flipped them over and laid her on the cushions, pressing his body on top of hers. That's when Alice knew they weren't simply going to make out and then say goodnight—she was aching for more, and she could tell he was too. Peter was an amazing kisser, and her toes curled as she imagined what he would do to her in a bed.

Alice tried to stay in the moment and not think what it'd feel like if it was Jack on top of her. She needed to move on with her life. She was too old to believe in fairytales; time to grow up. Ethan, Jack… they were her past. Peter was her present.

Jack

Jack wanted to kill someone. A very specific someone. Sulking, he watched Alice walk into their first Monday class with her cheeks flushed from the cold and a dreamy smile on her lips—she was practically *glowing*. Peter hadn't given Jack any specifics at practice, which was the first red flag. But his smug, stupid face and confident smirk had hinted at more than enough for Jack to figure out that his captain had gotten lucky with Ice.

They'd slept together. Jack had no doubts. The thought was like a sucker punch to his guts. He was rotten jealous; there was no denying it at this point. He'd always thought he was fine with Alice being his friend and nothing more, a platonic relationship. *Wrong.* When she'd tried to kiss him, something had stirred in him, and seeing her with Peter was torture. Thinking of them together turned his stomach in a washing machine spinning at full speed.

For the first time, Jack had arrived at a lecture before Alice. He was usually late as he had to run all the way across campus from the gym after practice. Today, he'd managed to get in at the top of the hour and Alice was fifteen minutes late. *Ice was never late.* Had Peter given her such mind-blowing sex that she'd had trouble getting up this morning? Jack's stomach churned again.

What now? Should he tell her? Tell her what, exactly? Accuse her of having had sex with Peter? Demand an explanation? Or go for something more along the lines of, "Hey, Ice, remember the other day when you tried to kiss me and I told you it wasn't going to happen between us because we're just friends? I was kidding. Let's get together."

She would laugh in his face. Coming clean with her now would be a disaster, and Jack still wasn't sure starting a relationship with Ice was right. What if he screwed up again? He'd already lost one best friend because he'd thought he was in love with Felicity when he wasn't. He'd mistaken familiarity and attraction for something they weren't. Was he misinterpreting plain territorial jealousy for deeper feelings here? Jack didn't know what he felt for Alice or if he should be with her; the only clear certainty in his mind was that she shouldn't be with Peter.

If he'd never cared who Alice dated before, why the change now? What if Alice wasn't the problem? Maybe it was Peter. Jack didn't like his captain invading his turf. Yeah, that must've been it. Male competition was his problem, not his non-existing-before-two-weeks-ago feelings for Ice. Jack had better play it cool with both of them. Their relationship would evaporate just like all the other relationships Peter had. He shouldn't worry. This problem would solve itself.

Still, when Alice sat next to him and uttered a cheerful, "Hey!" Jack felt like punching something—no, some*one*.

"Hi," he replied stiffly. "Had a good weekend?"

"Yeah. You?"

"Just the usual: practice, game, homework."

"Yeah, I saw the game. It was, uh, cool."

"I played like crap."

"The team won; it's all that matters."

"Yeah, scoring is all that usually matters with basketball players."

He noticed Alice stiffen in her chair.

"Are you having a bad morning?" she asked.

"You could say that." Jack sneered. "For one, it started with me having to listen to Peter bragging about scoring with you."

"He did *what?*" Alice hissed. "Did he tell the entire team we had sex?"

Jack felt as if he'd just been punched in the stomach. *So I was right—it did happen.* He wanted to lie to her and claim Peter had gone bragging to everyone—what better way to drive a wedge in their relationship?—but he couldn't bring himself to do it. "No, he just told me," Jack admitted. "Actually, he didn't say it—but I can read between the lines. Thank you for the confirmation."

Alice blushed. She hid her face by bending forward to take her notepad out of her messenger bag.

"So how was it?" Jack asked. He couldn't help his morbid curiosity.

"You've never asked me about sex with other guys before," Alice whispered.

"You've never dated any of my friends before."

"Oh, so that gives you kiss-and-tell privileges?" She scowled at him. "I don't think so."

"If it sucked, you can just say it."

"No, it didn't suck. It was the best sex of my life," Alice whispered furiously. "Happy now?"

Yeah, Jack had gotten what he wanted. He basked in the bitter satisfaction of having tricked her into saying what gave pain to no one but himself.

"Mr. Sullivan, why don't you answer the question?" Professor Procter targeted Jack. "You seem pretty busy discussing hypotheses with Miss Brown."

Luckily, Jack's subconscious had been half-following the lecture, and he was able to cook up a half-decent answer. After the rebuke, he and Alice didn't exchange another word for the rest of the class, and Jack made himself promise he would never discuss Peter with Alice ever again—especially not how good his captain was in bed.

Live and let live was truly the best solution. Jack would let Peter ruin everything on his own. No need to interfere or say anything. Peter would dig his own grave, eventually.

***

Jack's do-nothing-and-life-will-take-care-of-it plan failed miserably. Two months later, Alice and Peter were still dating. Peter had either become monogamous or was smart enough not to let Jack catch him with some other girl. To be honest, Jack really believed Peter was being faithful to Alice. What with their super-packed schedule, Jack didn't see how Peter could fit in another woman; it was nearly impossible. The thought gave him little consolation.

Besides his mood, Jack's performance on the basketball field had suffered too. Alice had become a regular presence at their home games, keeping Jack angry and distracted. Not a good combination when you were playing a team game and all you wanted to do was strangle your captain. Coach Morrison noticed something was up, but Jack refused to provide any explanation, so the coach made him play the bench more often than the court.

On top of everything else, his dating life was nonexistent. All of a sudden, women who were not Ice seemed dull to him. Jack didn't see the point in sleeping with any of them anymore. The notion that he didn't want to sleep with anyone else because of Alice surprised and scared him. The only person who knew of this turmoil was his friend Felicity. Over the phone, she'd told him—not without a hint of regret in her voice—that he'd finally fallen in love with someone. And that not wanting to sleep with anyone else because they weren't Alice was exactly what being in love felt like.

Jack didn't know what to do with this unwelcome intel on his feelings. Telling Ice now, when she already had a boyfriend, would be a stupid move. Also, the possibility that she could turn him down left him in a state of panic. Was this how Ice had felt after the library incident? Why had he been so stupid? In the last few months, Jack had relived that afternoon over and over in his head. In every single one of his fantasies, he had scooped Alice into his arms and kissed her back. How could he have been so stupid, and how could Ice have moved on so quickly?

She hadn't told him she loved him—but had she? Was her love for him over, finished, caput? Just like that? Was she in love with Peter now?

Nausea assaulted him whenever he let his mind drift in that direction. Jack needed a break. A break from seeing Alice almost every day and feeling her less close to him with every passing hour. Ice spent more and more of her free time with her boyfriend and ignored her supposed best friend. In response, Jack's ego crouched in a dark corner of his mind like a sulky child neglected by his parents.

Mercifully, winter break was approaching fast. There'd be no time for Alice and Peter to be together. The team was flying to Hawaii over Christmas to play three games in Honolulu. No way would Peter behave himself on a trip where they'd be surrounded by hulu beauties 24-7. *No. Way.*

Alice

Alice and Peter were in the library, heads bent over their respective coursework. It was the weekend before finals week and, for once, Peter didn't have any games to play or prep for. Not that it helped their dating schedule much. Whatever time could be spared from basketball, Peter had to dedicate to revisions. Hence, their "romantic" library date.

Alice stared at her textbook, trying to take in the complex formulas of molecular orbital theory but not really succeeding. She felt guilty for being here with Peter. She'd always done her last minute revisions with Jack, but lately, they didn't hang out much outside classes.

Jack had stopped antagonizing her about her relationship with Peter, and she'd stopped asking him about his dates. She didn't want to know anymore, and he was being uncharacteristically discreet. He hadn't bragged about a new girl in a while. Not that Alice kidded herself into thinking he had not boasted because he had nothing to boast about. Alice didn't know if she felt better or worse not knowing exactly what was going on in Jack's love life. Yet, a new stubbornness compelled her to never ask.

Alice had asked Jack if he wanted to join them for this study session, but he had replied with a curt, "No, thanks!" that had sounded more like "I'd rather walk on broken glass barefooted."

Peter looked up from his econometrics book and asked, "Are you going home for Christmas?"

"No. Every year my parents go on a cruise for Christmas." Alice grimaced. "Be away on the 25th and you can get the cheapest fares ever. My family is more about Thanksgiving. I'll stay here and get a head start on spring term."

"Alone on Christmas Day?" Peter arched his brows. "That's sad."

Alice shrugged. "I'm used to it."

"Why don't you come to Hawaii?"

That had been her latest discovery about the Harvard basketball team. The Crimson weren't free, not even for Christmas. They had to fly to Hawaii to play three games, one of which was on the 25th. Okay, there were worse fates than "having" to go to Hawaii at Christmas time. But still…

"Hawaii?" Alice repeated.

"Yeah, why not?" Peter stared at her expectantly. "We leave on the 21st and we get back on the 26th. I know we have three games, but they usually leave us some chill time in between. My parents can't make the trip, so it'll be just the two of us."

"And the team." *And Jack.*

"Yeah, but I can cut some free time, and it's a week in Maui." Peter's enthusiasm was evident. "It's better than staying here buried under the snow, alone on Christmas Day."

"Yeah, but you'd be busy most of the time with the team, no?"

"True," he admitted. "Why don't you ask your roommates along? You girls could go sunbathing on the beach when I have team duty, and we could hang out the rest of the time."

Alice considered the possibilities. "Madison has to go home at Christmas for sure. Her family's a bit overbearing. But I could ask Haley." Christmas in Hawaii was starting to sound like a real option. "Are you seriously asking me to go to Hawaii with you?"

"Never been more serious."

Alice chewed her pen. "Can I think about it?"

"What is there to think about?" Peter mimicked hula dancing. "What could be better than flying to a tropical beach with your awesome boyfriend?"

Boyfriend. So far, Alice had thought of their relationship as hanging out or casual dating, but Peter had just made it official.

"I can't say yes for sure," Alice conceded. "I have to check flight fares and ask Haley if she can come."

Alice was stalling to gain some time to decide. The truth was, every year since she'd moved to Boston, her parents had given her a very generous Christmas gift, basically a bribe, to appease the guilt of not spending the day with her. She had saved up the money for the past two years—but maybe, for once, she could stop being super responsible and give herself a break. A Hawaiian break.

Alice was both thrilled and wary of Peter's proposal. True, sports could be fun to watch. Yet, whenever the team lost—a fifty-fifty chance so far—Peter became sulky and short-tempered. It could be hard to be near him after a lost game. Jack was a tad less moody about it, but basketball wasn't as important for him.

To be honest, it felt like basketball was the third wheel in her relationship with Peter. It was an all-consuming element in Peter's life with practice almost every day and several games a week, both at home and in other cities. Before, being Jack's friend but not taking a real interest in the game, Alice hadn't noticed how demanding it was.

She had a love-hate relationship with basketball now. Watching Peter play—okay, she kept an eye on Jack too, she couldn't help it—was exhilarating. It was like dating someone in a band. Whenever you put a man on a stage of sorts, it was guaranteed women would find him instantly more attractive. For Peter, it was exactly like that. On the field, he had a huge spotlight on him that made him irresistible. And he wanted to spend Christmas with her.

Christmas in Hawaii with Peter sounded awesome in theory. But what if the team lost? She'd be in a tropical paradise with her boyfriend and a dark cloud of bad temper over their heads. *Not ideal.* Also, it wasn't going to be a cheap or short trip. But if Haley could go, it'd be a fun trip, better than staying in an empty campus during the Christmas holidays. As gorgeous as Harvard was, it wasn't Hogwarts.

When she thought about it that way, the choice was clear. It was between Hawaii with Peter and possibly one of her best friends—two, counting Jack—or Cambridge alone. Mmm. Last year, Madison had invited her to celebrate with her family. Every year, the Smithsons had this huge Christmas celebration at their country house. It had been such a cheery, fuzzy-warm day. And also the day she'd met Ethan. Madison would invite her again, but Alice couldn't accept this time; it'd be too awkward. Ethan probably had no desire to have his ex sprinkled on him on Christmas Day. And what if he brought his new girlfriend? *Ugh.* It'd be a holidays nightmare.

There was no contest. She was going to Hawaii.

***

Alice barged into her apartment barely able to contain her excitement. "Roommates meeting!" she announced.

Haley and Madison were seated at the dining table revising for finals. Madison was studying poetry verses, and Haley code lines. They both lifted their heads, looking grateful for the interruption.

"What's up?" Haley asked, sagging on the couch.

Madison sat next to Haley, and Alice chose the armchair on the side. "Peter's invited me to go to Hawaii with him over Christmas," she said. "The team has to play three games there, and he wants me to go."

"Hawaii? Wow." Haley seemed excited.

Alice beamed. "Would you girls like to come with me?"

Madison's face fell. "I can't go," she said at once. "You know how my family is about Christmas and traditions. I can't skip it."

Alice had expected that. "Haley?"

"How many days would we be there?"

"Less than a week."

"I would have to tell my parents I'm not going home for Christmas and ask them for an expense contribution," Haley said. Then, turning toward Madison, she added, "They're more flexible about holidays than your parents."

"Lucky you," Madison muttered, paling. She gave the impression of swallowing a lump in her throat.

"I'll check with my parents." Haley got to her feet and disappeared into her room.

Madison got up as well. "I have some reading to do," she said, somewhat deflated. She picked up a book and disappeared into her bedroom.

Alice followed her and knocked on her door. "Can I come in?"

"Yes," came Madison's muffled voice from within.

Alice opened the door and leaned against the threshold. "I need to ask you a favor." Alice thought of the first excuse for following Madison. "Can you take care of Blue while I'm gone?"

"Sure, I'll only be gone for Christmas Day."

"Thanks." Alice walked into the room. "Are you okay?"

"Yeah," Madison said a small voice. "Why?"

"You seem upset about Hawaii." Alice sat on the bed next to Madison. "What is it?"

"Nothing. I just thought you were coming to my house again for Christmas." Madison crossed her arms over her chest. "I know I haven't officially asked you yet, but I thought it was implicit."

"Yeah, I know, and thank you." Alice smiled, tight-lipped. "But I can't come to your house this year."

"Why?"

"You know why. Ethan will be there. It'd be too awkward for the both of us."

Madison grimaced and theatrically swatted her forehead with her hand. "You're right. I'm so stupid. I hadn't even thought about it."

"Are you sure there's nothing else?" Alice insisted. Madison was very private about her feelings—she had to have information like this dragged out of her.

"Like what?"

"Is it about that guy, mmm, what was his name?"

"What guy?"

"Number 23, the one you recognized at the game."

"Scott? What does he have to do with anything?"

"He's in your concentration, and I got the impression you had a little crush on him."

"I don't," Madison said, too defensive.

"Haley seemed to like him too," Alice pressed. "You wouldn't be worried about something happening between them while we're in Hawaii, then?"

Madison blushed. "No!"

"Madison, if you like him, just tell Haley he's off-limits."

"As if it would matter." Madison sulked. "If Haley Thomas wants him, she's going to get him. She doesn't even try, and all the guys love her. Nothing I say would make a difference. It's not like he's my boyfriend or anything. I've never said more than 'hello' to him."

"But if you told Haley—"

"No! And promise me you won't say anything to her about it, *ever*."

"Why?"

"Just promise me," Madison said with an anguished face. "Can you?"

"Okay, I promise."

Alice had a hunch she'd just made a mistake. Secrets ruined friendships; nothing good could come out of this one.

Haley barged into the room a second later. "Guess what?"

"What?" Madison asked.

"My parents okayed the Hawaiian trip and, as a Christmas present, they're helping me pay for it."

"That's wonderful," Alice said.

She turned to Madison to study her reaction. Her friend was smiling, but her eyes were sad.

"Come on." Haley, oblivious as always to most of the things happening around her, grabbed Alice's hand to pull her up from the bed. "We have to plan our trip."

Alice stood up and followed Haley out of the room, throwing a dismayed Madison a wistful glance as she closed the door.

***

"Hey, Ice," Jack called, running after her at the end of their last final before winter break.

"Hey." Alice stopped walking and waited for him. "How did you do?" she asked, referring to their Organic Chemistry test.

"Good, I think." He frowned. "Except for question two, maybe. Which of the functional groups did you mark as susceptible to nucleophilic attack? A and B, or A, B, and C?"

"Just A and B."

"Great, me too." He smiled. "How about you? Any doubts?"

"Question four: the most acidic compound was CH_3SH, right?" It had taken her ten minutes to mark that answer. "I always confuse them."

"Yep, that's the one."

Alice let out a relieved breath. "I should be good then."

"What do you say to a hot chocolate to celebrate? Deal?"

"Deal."

Jack was in a bright mood for a change. Since she'd started dating Peter, it had been a rare thing, and Alice missed their easygoing interactions. Given the freezing December temperatures, they headed for the nearest place: a cozy coffee shop called Crema Café. Even the short walk outside was enough to turn Alice's nose and sans-gloves hands red, so she welcomed the puff of warm air that blasted her as she pushed into the coffee shop.

The atmosphere inside, besides being deliciously warm, was also incredibly festive. Red and white Christmas decorations rested on every available surface, and the crowd was loud and cheerful. At four in the afternoon on the last day of finals, pretty much the whole campus was on vacation.

"Grab a table," Jack said. "I'll go order. Chocolate with cream?"

"Yeah." Alice uncoiled her scarf from around her neck. "Medium, please."

"I'll be right back."

Jack scurried off to join the line and Alice couldn't avoid noting how well his pants fitted him. *Bad Alice,* she chided herself, *no more checking out Jack's butt.* She had a boyfriend, one with a derriere just as good as Jack's. Alice had to keep drilling it into her head that she and Jack were just friends. And friends didn't ogle each other's butts. Definitely not.

The only free table was a tiny one in the back that barely seated two. Alice removed her coat, sat down, and waited for Jack while blowing into her cupped hands to warm them. The hot paper cup Jack handed her five minutes later did a much better job of heating her frozen fingers.

"I'm so glad this semester is over," Jack announced, plonking down on the chair next to her.

Close. *Too* close. Despite the place being crowded and the cocoa aroma drifting up from her cup, Alice could still smell Jack's aftershave. It made her stomach contract a bit, so she flooded it with hot chocolate to force her belly to relax.

"Yeah, me too," she said. "This one was hard; not that I've encountered an easy one yet." Alice was babbling. They had spent a million afternoons just like this one. There was no reason to be this nervous. "We should put vodka in this." Alice shook the cup. "It's so vanilla of us to celebrate with chocolate."

"I have a game soon," Jack said matter-of-factly. "Nothing stronger than beer for me."

Alice felt a stab of annoyance. "I should change best friends. You're not daring enough."

Jack's eyes sparkled. He gave her a look that said, "Try me." A hot, red flush crept its way up from Alice's neck to her cheeks. They held each other's gaze for a second longer before the moment was lost. Jack's head disappeared under the table as he retrieved something from his bag.

"To overcome my shortcomings in the fun department," Jack said once his torso was straight again, "I got you something for Christmas."

Alice stared wide-eyed at the tube-shaped bundle he was holding. "Are we doing presents now?"

They'd never given each other gifts before.

"Nah. It's really nothing." Jack shrugged. "I saw it in a shop window the other day and it made me think of you…"

"Can I open it now, or do I have to wait for Christmas Day?"

Jack flashed her a grin. "Go ahead."

Alice attacked the wrapping paper. It came off to reveal a cute pink bunny shape.

"What is this?"

"If you remove the case it becomes an umbrella," Jack said, his voice hesitant.

Alice's heart stopped. She stared at the pink umbrella covered in tiny white dots, unable to lift her gaze to meet Jack's eye.

"I know it's silly," Jack continued. He sounded just as nervous. "But do you remember that night—"

Alice lifted her gaze and locked eyes with Jack. "Of course I remember…"

***

It was a stormy spring night, with rain pouring from the sky by the bucket. Jack and Alice were waiting for Jack's girlfriend to come out of the pub where they'd all had dinner. The atmosphere inside the pub had been humid and suffocating. So much so that when the girlfriend— whatever her name was—had needed to use the restroom, Alice and Jack had preferred to wait outside in spite of the rain. Since that first awful dinner with Olivia, it had become routine for Jack to bring his dates along from time to time when he and Alice went out together.

They took shelter under the pub's ledge, Jack standing in front of her near the door. After a couple of minutes, the door was pushed open, forcing Jack to squeeze her between his chest and the pub wall to keep out of the downpour. Too close. With her back to the wall and Jack looming over her, Alice's skin prickled. Embarrassed, she shifted to the side, keeping under the ledge, making it look as if they weren't together. A bulky guy with a black umbrella came out of the pub. He did a quick scan of the road and focused his attention on Alice.

"Hey, you," bulky guy said. "Bad night to go home without an umbrella. Want a spot under mine?"

Before Alice could do or say anything, he grabbed Alice by the waist, pulling her close to him. His breath reeked of onion rings and beer. It made Alice gag.

"I'm good, thanks," Alice said, trying and failing to push him away. He had her in a viselike grip and wouldn't let go.

"Come on," Mr. Bad-breath said, sending another wave of foul stench her way. "I'm taking you home." He started dragging her down the road.

Jack's deadly-cold voice came from behind them. "She said she's fine."

Mr. Bad-breath stopped. "What's your problem, dude?" He turned toward Jack. "Is she your girlfriend?"

"No, she's not," Jack replied, his voice low.

At the look of controlled fury on Jack's face, the guy tried to justify himself. "I was only offering her space under my umbrella."

"She already has an umbrella," Jack said.

"I don't see any umbrella," the guy protested.

Jack wrenched Alice free. "I'm her fucking umbrella," he growled, shoving Mr. Bad-breath away. A look of furious determination darkened his eyes.

"Whatever, dude." Mr. Bad-breath walked away from a fight he was certain to lose given the resolve in Jack's eyes, leaving them both standing in the rain.

Alice's hair and clothes were getting soaked, but she didn't care. She lifted her gaze to Jack. "That was very Rihanna of you," she said to smooth the tension.

Jack's jaw relaxed, and he flashed her half a smile. Neither of them moved; they just stood there in the pouring rain, staring into each other's eyes. The way he was looking at her made Alice's pulse speed up. He moved a step closer. Oh, gosh, was he going to kiss her?

"Jack!" his girlfriend called. "What are you doing in the rain?" Whatever-her-name-was came and stood next to him, placing him under the shelter of her own umbrella.

Alice was the only one left standing in the rain, her hair and clothing drenched. And her role in the scene shifted from movie-romantic to incredibly pathetic in an instant.

"I guess I'll get going," Alice said. "I'm only a block away." More like four or five.

She spun around, not waiting for a reply, although she did manage to catch the death stare whatever-her-name-was flashed her. Then she hurried off into the rain, not daring to look back and catch Jack's eye.

***

Alice thanked Jack for the bunny-themed gift and managed to nod her way through the rest of the conversation in the time it took them to finish their hot chocolates.

When a solid, minute-long silence lingered between them, she said, "We should get going."

"Well," Jack said, getting up to leave. "Seeya after Christmas." He grabbed his bag from the floor.

Alice got up as well. "Mmm, about that." She wasn't sure why telling Jack she was going to Hawaii was making her so nervous. But she couldn't put it off any longer. "We might see each other sooner than that."

"I'm flying to Hawaii tomorrow, Ice. No chance."

"I know. But when I told Peter I was alone for Christmas, he invited me to Hawaii." She smiled half-heartedly. "So Haley and I are going."

Jack's face fell, sending a chill up both of her arms.

"Don't be too excited," Alice said.

"It's not… I mean," he stuttered, eyes wide with surprise. "You're coming to Hawaii?"

"I am."

"That's great."

His creased forehead and tight-lipped smirk sent a completely different message from "great."

"I'll see you at the airport tomorrow," Alice added, annoyed, but trying not to show it. "We're on the same flight."

"Of course."

Now Jack looked as if he was standing on hot coals. He shifted his weight from foot to foot and seemed eager to get away from her as quickly as possible.

"Well, I'll catch you tomorrow then." Jack took two steps backward. "Gotta go. Bye." He turned on his heel and was gone before Alice had a chance to add anything.

Outside, it had started snowing. Fat, feathery flakes were spiraling down, coating the streets in white frost. Alice shook her head and opened her new umbrella to walk home.

Haley

The Uber driver dropped Haley and Alice off at Logan International Airport super early the next morning. Haley fidgeted all the way through the airline check in and airport security checks. Since they were leaving so early, they had skipped breakfast at home. And Haley was starving. When they finally stopped at a Starbucks near their gate to grab a quick bite, her stomach was already grumbling in protest.

As Haley sipped her grande caffè mocha, a tall guy shuffling through the Hudson News shop across the hall caught her attention. He had his back turned so she couldn't see his face, only his clothes. He was wearing sweatpants and a puffy sports jacket with a hoody pulled over his head.

"Hello?" Alice asked next to her. "Are you listening?"

"No, sorry, I was distracted by the hottie over there."

"Which one?"

"The one in the puffy blue jacket?"

"How can you say he's hot? I can only see his back."

"It's a hot back. I wish he'd turn around." She stared at his shoulders, whispering, "Turn, turn…"

Both Haley and Alice followed the mysterious guy's progress around the shop, but he walked away without once turning his face toward them.

"Aw, pity," Haley said. "Now we'll never know."

Alice rolled her eyes. "I think I'll live."

"That's because you already have a hot boyfriend. We single gals, on the other hand…"

"Need to ogle strangers in airports?" Alice offered.

"Pretty much." Haley laughed.

"So you're definitely over your masked stranger?"

Haley's heart gave a wistful pulse. Last summer she'd gone to a Venetian Masquerade Ball and danced with a masked stranger only to lose him halfway through the night and never see him again. She'd been a bit obsessed ever since. She'd never even seen his face, making the search that much harder. But her mask had been a simple rhinestones application around her eyes that left her face practically bare, so she'd hoped that if she couldn't find him, he would somehow find her. But that had been months ago, and she'd lost faith.

"Not much of a choice," Haley said, "I have to use the restroom. Wait for me here?"

Haley left without waiting for a reply. She searched the ceiling for the restrooms signs and followed them to the Ladies' Room. As she pushed open the door, it banged into someone.

"Oh, sorry," she apologized.

An older woman scowled at her. Haley poked her head inside and saw the room was packed with people waiting in line. There were only four stalls, and one of them was out of order. It'd take her forever to wait for her turn. *Why are women's restrooms always so busy?* The thought gave her an idea. She backtracked from the Ladies' Room and decided to scout out the situation in the Men's Room.

Haley stopped in front of the Men's Room door. She checked behind her shoulders. *All clear.* It was empty inside, and all the stall doors were open. *Go figure.* Haley snuck into the room and went about her business as quickly as possible, rushing outside as soon as she was finished.

Just when she thought she'd made it undetected, Haley bumped into someone on her way out. She found her gaze level with a puffy blue jacket. *The guy from the news shop.* Haley had to bend her neck backward to see his face: green eyes, chiseled features, and a cute smile. He was so tall and *so* hot. Recognition gnawed at her. Where had she seen him before?

The hot guy stepped back. "Pardon me," he said, double-checking that he had the right restroom. "Isn't this the Men's Room?"

"Yeah, sorry," Haley apologized, embarrassed. "There was a super long line for the Ladies' Room, and here was empty, so…" Haley kept looking at his gorgeous face, trying to place it. "I'm sorry, have we met before?" And now she'd just used the oldest pickup line in the book. Great.

"I think I'd remember meeting you." His lips curled upwards in an amused smile. He kept his eyes trained on hers, making her blush. "We could've crossed paths on campus." He jerked his chin toward her Harvard sweatshirt. "I go to Harvard too."

"Going home for Christmas?"

"No, actually. I'm on the basketball team and we're going to Hawaii to play."

That was it! She'd seen him at a game.

"Really?" Haley couldn't believe her luck. "Me too."

He arched his eyebrows. "You play basketball for the Crimson?"

"No." Haley laughed awkwardly. "What I meant was that my best friend is dating your captain, and he's invited her along, so we're going to Hawaii with the team, sort of."

His smile widened. "Small world."

Haley tilted her head to the side. "So it seems."

"It was nice meeting you…?"

"Haley Thomas."

"Scott Williams."

He looked at her expectantly, and Haley realized she was still blocking his path to the Men's Room. They both moved at the same time, bumping into each other again. They did a little dance of moving in the same direction twice before Scott stopped and allowed Haley to move past him. She started toward the café, but couldn't help turning back. Scott was holding the door open, watching her go.

Haley smiled and ran off, eager to tell Alice the news.

Alice

Alice's heart jolted in fear as Haley pounced on her from behind.

"Guess what?" Haley asked, with a smile so big it shined like a lighthouse beacon.

"What?"

"I bumped into Mr. Hot-Back in the restrooms. Alice, he's so gorgeous I could barely stand to look at him without melting. And it gets better." Haley paused for effect. "He's a player for the Crimson; we'll be in Hawaii together for the next week." Haley gave a high-pitched giggle, making Alice flinch. "How unbelievable is that? I mean, it must've been destiny or something, right?"

An ominous feeling of dread wrapped itself around Alice's stomach. "What was his name?" she asked in a flat voice.

"Scott."

Alice's face fell. Why of the twenty guys—okay, eighteen minus Jack and Peter—on the team did Haley have to like the same one Madison liked?

Haley's bright smile faltered. "Please stop. You're overwhelming me with your enthusiasm," she complained. "Something bad I should know about this guy?"

Alice considered breaking her promise to Madison. Instead, she resigned herself to being a passive spectator to this Haley-Scott disaster in the making. "No, not at all," she said. "I know nothing about him, and neither do you."

"I don't need to know anything besides the fact that he's the most epically gorgeous guy I've ever seen."

Alice shrugged. "What if he's a d-bag?"

"Why do you have to be so negative?" Haley glared at her. "What's the matter with you?"

Alice was saved answering by Peter grabbing her from behind and kissing her neck.

"Yo. Here's my beautiful lady," he said.

Alice turned to say hello and instinctively tried to peek over his shoulder to see if he was with Jack. There was a group of basketball players standing nearby, but Jack wasn't with them.

"Yo, everyone," Peter continued loudly. "Meet my better half."

Better half? That was cheesy, coming from Peter. Alice wondered what had gotten into him.

Alice shook hands with the team members she didn't know and introduced Haley. Almost everyone looked at her friend as if she were a bowl of ice cream and they were a spoon. After all, Haley was the only single Crimson groupie. Alice hoped someone could still distract her from Scott.

"Scott, my man!" Peter shouted. "Over here."

Scott and Peter did that thing of clasping hands and bumping chests before Peter introduced Alice.

"Scott Williams, meet Alice Brown. Alice, meet Scott."

Alice finally understood what the Scott fuss was about. Up close, he was definitely a looker, with his dark blond hair and green eyes. Harvard might not have the fanciest basketball pavilion, but they definitely had the best-looking NCAA team.

"And this is her roommate, Haley Thomas," Peter said to Scott.

Scott flashed Haley an amused grin. "I believe we've met."

Haley blushed, astonishing Alice. Her friend never blushed. Haley and Scott immediately started talking, unaware of anything else around them. Alice was worried; both her friends liked the same guy, and it looked like one of them was going to get him. How would Madison react when they came back and told her? She would say nothing and suffer in silence, Alice suspected. *Please let Madison's crush on Scott not be serious,* she thought.

An announcement played in the background.

"Yo, guys," Peter said. "This is our flight. Let's go before the coach comes looking for us."

Peter put an arm around Alice's shoulders and steered her toward the gate.

"So, what is the policy with your coach?" she asked. "Am I allowed to be here? I mean, is it normal to invite people along?"

"Sure. I'd say about half the guys will have their families there."

"Oh, okay."

As they reached their gate and joined the boarding queue, Alice started scanning the crowds again for any sign of Jack. She couldn't spot him anywhere, which freaked her out. He *had* to be coming, so where the hell was he?

Her question found an answer as they boarded. Jack was settled in a window seat all the way to the back. He had his arms crossed over his chest, his head tilted to the side, and he was wearing a sleeping mask. *A sleeping mask?*

How could he already be on the plane, let alone asleep? Even if he'd been the first in line, he must've boarded the plane… what? Five, ten minutes ago, tops? And he knew she'd be there. So why wear the mask before they'd even said hello?

With a sinking feeling, Alice realized that Jack wearing the mask and pretending to be asleep had to be a twisted way of avoiding her. The "why" of it remained a mystery.

Was he mad at her for coming? That must be it. When she told him she was coming to Hawaii, he'd basically fled. But why? Why was it so annoying to have her here? Was it a turf invasion? A mixing of groups he didn't want to be mixed? Was he still worried about her dating Peter? He hadn't said a word about it in two months.

Well, fine then. If he wanted to ignore her the entire trip, he could suit himself. She ignored the gut-twisting spasm of annoyance in her stomach and took her seat next to Peter.

Jack

Under the sleeping mask, Jack squeezed his eyes shut until they hurt. He knew his little act wouldn't accomplish much, but he couldn't face Alice and Peter on their romantic trip. The idea made his stomach cramp. To avoid them completely was impossible, but Jack was determined to keep the interactions to a strict minimum. The break he'd so coveted had transformed into his worst nightmare. And a night tossing in bed dreading the next day had not helped him come to terms with the situation.

From his corner at the back of the plane, Jack listened as Peter let out his usual repertoire of "yo, oooh, my man" as he greeted everybody else. He listened as his captain introduced Alice to the players who didn't know her yet. A bitter tang spread under his tongue. Even the right of introducing Alice to the team had been stolen from him. He should be the one at her side making introductions, not Peter. Still brooding, Jack eavesdropped as Peter maneuvered people around so that he could sit next to Alice. *How sweet.* He wanted to throw up.

Jack kept his eyes shut under the mask and tried not to tense his jaw and mouth. Torture; it was a slow torture to lie still in his seat pretending to be asleep. He was so on edge real sleep was out of the question, even after take-off when the plane quieted down. To be wide-awake, unable to move, and with nothing to do was mentally exhausting. He couldn't check the time on his phone, so he tried to judge by what was happening around him.

The take-off happened on time, which he learned from the captain's announcement. *Six-thirty.* After a while, there was the usual ping of the seatbelt sign being switched off. *Seven?* Only half an hour had passed, and to Jack, it seemed like an eternity. More time passed, and Jack found himself counting the seconds. When would it be safe to stop pretending he was asleep? After they served breakfast and cleared out? Yeah, that was probably his best bet.

Breakfast finally arrived. Jack heard Matt, who was sitting next to him, open a plastic bag. As Matt chewed on his snack, Jack marveled at how loud he sounded. So it was true that when deprived of one sense the others intensified. Eons later, when the flight attendants came back to take the trays away, Jack was itching to take his mask off. Yet, breakfast seemed to have stirred a lot of movement in the cabin. Many people were coming and going in the small aisle between the rows of seats. It was a mass pilgrimage to the restrooms.

At one point, Jack could've sworn he heard Alice's voice somewhere to his right hiss, "*Sleeping Beauty.*" Or maybe he'd just spent too much time inside his own head. Wasn't hearing voices the first sign of going mad?

When he couldn't take it any longer, Jack removed his mask and opened his eyes. *Phew,* he was safe, no one was looking his way or moving around. All passengers seemed engaged with a movie, a book, or they were genuinely asleep. He peeked at the clock. Nine-thirty. Three hours gone, a gazillion more to go. But so far, his avoid-them-at-all-costs plan had been a success.

A short-lived one. Once the plane landed at LAX, where they had to catch a connecting flight, there was no way Jack could avoid talking to Alice. He waited for the plane to empty, postponing the inevitable as long as possible, before he walked out.

For an instant, Jack thought everybody was gone, and he'd be Alice-and-Peter free for a little longer.

Until a hand smacked his right shoulder. "Yo, my man. What's up?" Peter asked. "Where have you been, Sullivan?"

"On the plane?" Jack shrugged.

"You're funny." Peter clearly hadn't caught the sarcasm in Jack's voice. "We're going to grab a burger for lunch. You coming?"

Jack could say he wasn't hungry, but everyone would notice he was acting weird. He'd better keep up at least a tiny bit of appearances. Ice already seemed suspicious. She was standing next to Peter, and from the way she was eyeing Jack, it was clear she wasn't happy with him. "A burger sounds great," he lied. He'd rather eat paper. "I skipped breakfast; I could eat an elephant."

"Didn't you eat on the plane?" Peter asked.

"Nah, I was sleeping when they served breakfast."

Alice scoffed.

Jack ignored her.

"A lady keep you up until the small hours?" Peter asked.

Jack shrugged, neither denying nor admitting to anything. But he accompanied the shrug with a wicked smile that let everyone assume Peter had nailed him.

"Oooh," Peter hollered. "Good for you, man."

Alice didn't comment, scoffing or otherwise.

***

Their motel in Honolulu had a two-story horseshoe layout with a rectangular pool in the middle. Jack's room was on the second floor on the right side of the U; he was sharing with Matt. After an early dinner,

174

Coach Morrison had sent them to bed to rest before their first game the next day. Jack was ready to follow the instructions and hoped Peter would too.

Matt came into the room and collapsed onto his queen bed. "I'm toasted, man," Matt said. "Do you mind if I turn off the lights?"

"No, go ahead. I'm taking a breath of fresh air."

Jack opened the French doors and walked out onto the small patio outside. It was night, but the temperature was still well above seventy degrees. Compared to frigid Boston, this was heaven. Jack stared across the pool. Half the rooms on the other side were dark. Of the illuminated ones, many had their curtains closed. *Not Alice's room.*

It felt a bit stalkerish to spy on her as she sat chatting on the bed with Haley. But Jack couldn't stop staring. He was so relieved she wasn't with Peter, he could hula dance.

His joy didn't last long. Haley and Alice both turned their heads toward the door at the same time. They giggled, hugged, and Haley jumped off the bed. Two seconds later, Peter appeared inside the room. He pulled Alice up from the bed and started kissing her.

Acid rose in Jack's throat. He continued to watch, unable to avert his eyes as Alice pulled Peter back on the bed, where he landed on top of her, never breaking the kiss. Jack felt numb; his body refused to work. The only parts still functioning were his eyes, which were inexorably trained on the gruesome scene before him.

When Peter got to his feet to close the curtains and turn off the lights, Jack gripped the metal rail so hard his knuckles turned white. Jack had no air in his lungs. His skin was on fire. His entire body seemed to burn. This tropical paradise was his personal hell. Jack wanted to scream. He wanted to drag Peter off the bed and beat him into a pulp. But most of all, Jack wanted to be the one on top of Alice. Instead, all he could do was swallow bile.

A loud crash brought him back from his haze. Two windows down from Alice's room, the curtains of another room were shaking, and loud shouts mixed with banging noises were audible even from outside. Someone was fighting.

Jack wasn't the only one who'd heard the noise. In a matter of seconds, Alice's lights switched on and Peter opened the French doors and hopped out on the patio, struggling to get back into his jeans. His head shook left and right as he tried to determine what was going on. A surge of pure joy ran through Jack's veins at the perfectly timed interruption.

"What's going on?" Matt appeared on the patio next to him, his hair tousled and his face still sleepy. "I heard a crash."

Jack pointed at the room with the shaking curtains. "I think it came from there."

"Damn right," Matt said.

At that moment, the curtains collapsed and Matt and Jack had a clear view of what was happening inside. Two guys were wrestling on the floor while a terrified Haley was begging them to stop.

"Who's that?" Jack asked.

Matt squinted his eyes. "Looks like the Williams brothers are at it again."

A wolf whistle came from the other side of the motel. It was Peter. Matt and Jack turned to look at him.

"Guys," Peter shout-whispered. "Can you see what's happening?"

"David and Scott Williams, Captain," Matt shout-whispered back. "Two doors down from yours."

More lights were popping on in other rooms. If they wanted to avoid trouble, they had to pacify the two Williamses before the rumor of a fight reached Coach Morrison.

"I'll go check." Peter gestured toward the room. "Can you guys back me up?"

"We're on it," Matt said.

From their respective patios, Matt, Jack, and Peter all rushed in and out their rooms to go stop the Williamses. Jack knew he shouldn't be happy two of his teammates were fighting. But as he ran down the motel hall, he couldn't help but feel grateful the Williams brothers hated each other.

Haley

Today had been the best day of Haley's life, and it was about to get better. Since bumping into Scott that morning, Haley couldn't stop smiling. They'd sat next to each other on both flights and had spent the whole journey talking. And Haley had discovered Scott wasn't just a pretty face. He was the most amazing guy she'd ever met, and she could see herself falling in love with him in the blink of an eye.

"Are you sure you're okay with swapping rooms?" Alice asked.

They were chatting on the bed in their room.

"Yeah." Haley beamed at her over-concerned friend. "More than okay."

"Isn't it a bit… mmm… quick?"

"Alice, we're going to sleep in the same room." Haley rolled her eyes. "It doesn't mean we have to have sex."

Alice put her hands forward in a defensive gesture. "I'm just saying that if you're not sure, or if you change your mind at any point, you don't have to switch with Peter." She dropped her arms. "I can see him any other night."

Peter and Scott were sharing a room and Peter, playing matchmaker, had asked for a roommate swap. Both Haley and Scott had said yes. Haley was waiting with Alice for the guys to come back from their mandatory team dinner.

"Alice, I'm sure," Haley insisted. "I haven't been this excited about a guy in forever."

"I'm just saying you can take it slow if you want to."

"And I already told you I don't plan to *sleep* sleep with Scott," Haley said. "Just sleep in the same room."

Alice looked at her skeptically.

Haley smiled wickedly. "I'm not saying it's a total hands-off situation. I sure hope there will be some kissing involved."

"Okay," Alice conceded. "Because Peter will be here soon."

Haley giggled. "Hey," she said. "You know what room they're in?"

"No. Peter's coming here, so I didn't ask," Alice said. "Didn't Scott tell you?"

"Yeah. But you know me, I forgot." Haley leaned to one side of the bed to grab the room's phone and dialed nine.

The line connected after two rings.

"Reception, how may I assist you?"

"Hello," Haley said. "Could you please tell me what room Scott Williams is in? I'm here with the Harvard Crimson."

"Mr. Williams is in room 226," the efficient voice replied. "Anything else I can do for you tonight?"

"No thanks, that'll be all." Haley hung up.

As if on cue, they heard someone knock on their door.

"This must be your prince charming," Haley said, getting up to open the door.

She let Peter in, grabbed her overnight duffel bag from the floor, and left Alice and Peter alone.

Haley walked down the hall, staring at the doors. She was in room 230, so room 226 wasn't far. Haley reached it and stared, undecided. She'd been cocky with Alice, but truthfully she was super nervous. She liked Scott so much, and she was afraid he didn't like her back with the same enthusiasm. He'd been wonderful all day, but what if he'd said yes to the room swap only to do Peter a solid? Well, it was too late to change her mind now.

Haley knocked.

A tall guy—presumably another basketball player—came to open the door. He was shirtless with only a pair of fleece pants on. His dark hair was wet as if he'd just come out of the shower. Piercing blue eyes dilated in surprise at finding Haley on his doorstep. Yet, quickly, his gaze shifted in a way that could be described only as… *predatory*.

Haley was struck silent.

"Hello, again," the guy said.

Again? Had he noticed her on the plane?

"What can I do for you?" His tone and lopsided smirk were suggestive.

"Oh, I'm s-sorry," Haley stammered. "I asked the reception for Scott Williams's room and they sent me here."

"Ah, I see." Blue eyes flashed. "They had the sense to direct you to the better Williams brother."

"You-you're Scott's b-brother?"

Why was she stuttering? This guy made her nervous.

He nodded. "David."

Haley was tempted to turn and run. "D-do you know which room Scott's staying in?"

"Were you on the plane with us today?" David asked, ignoring her question.

"Yeah."

"I didn't catch your name."

"Haley."

David casually leaned against the threshold, arms crossed on his bare chest. "So who are you? His girlfriend?"

"No, we met today."

David raised both eyebrows.

"I mean." Haley tried to think how she could make him understand the situation. "I'm here with my best friend. She's dating Peter, your captain. They wanted to share a room, so we swapped. I'm supposed to be bunking with Scott."

The smirk was back on David's face. "Interesting."

"Nothing is going on." Haley didn't know why she felt the need to explain herself to this guy. "I'm just going to sleep in Scott's room, not *sleep* with Scott."

"Well," David said, gently grabbing her hand and locking eyes with her. "If you're ever interested in doing something more exciting than sleeping…" He suddenly pulled her in closer. "You know where to find me."

"David," Scott's voice came from behind her. "Let her go."

Haley tried to free herself, but David held her firmly against his chest.

"And why would I do that?" David asked.

"Can't you see you're scaring her? I won't just stand here and let you intimidate her."

David's jaw tensed. "I don't recall needing your permission to do anything."

Haley was still struggling to push him away from her, but he was not giving an inch.

"David, back off," Scott ordered between gritted teeth.

"Or what?" David asked. He made some sort of weird move and spun Haley around so that now she had her back pressed against him as he hugged her from behind. David bent his head ever so slightly. As he kept taunting Scott, his lips almost brushed against Haley's neck. "What are you going to do, little brother?"

Scott was breathing hard. "Leave. Her. Alone," he repeated, closing his hands into tight fists.

"She's all yours," David said.

He pushed Haley toward Scott, who grabbed her shoulders to steady her.

"Are you okay?" he asked.

"Yeah," Haley lied. She wasn't digging the family drama one bit.

Scott let her go and, before she had a chance to realize what he was doing, he threw himself at his brother. Fury twisted his handsome face in an unrecognizable mask.

"What the hell is wrong with you?" Scott screamed, grabbing David by the throat and nailing him against the wall.

David threw his brother back with equal force, and the two started beating the hell out of each other. They barreled around the room, knocking over furniture as they careened toward the back of the room. They ended up crashing against the French windows with a loud bang.

Haley was crying. She was yelling at them to stop, but she was too scared to go anywhere near them. So she looked on as they kept fighting. At one point, the curtains collapsed, covering their struggling bodies so only a shaking blob of fabric was visible.

Peter came into the room, pausing briefly next to Haley. "Are you okay?" he asked.

Relief washed over her. "I'm fine. Please, just make them stop."

"I'm on it." Peter darted forward and started pulling at the curtains entangled around both brothers' limbs.

"Haley, I'm here," Alice said.

Haley turned around and launched herself at her best friend, hugging her tight.

"What happened?" Alice asked.

Haley tried to reply, but instead of words, she started sobbing so hard against Alice's shoulder she no longer could talk.

Alice

Alice was trying to soothe a sobbing Haley when Jack and another guy— Matt, Alice thought was his name—flooded into the room to help Peter. Working together, the trio were finally able to pull the two struggling bodies apart. As Matt and Jack forced the wrestlers to their feet, Alice recognized one of them as Scott. He didn't look as if he was ready to stop the brawl, and neither did the other contender. Jack and Matt had to restrain them while Peter planted himself in the middle, arms spread wide to keep them apart.

"Shut the door," Peter told her. "We don't need anyone else involved."

Alice let go of Haley, who finally seemed less agitated, and went to close the door.

Scott and the other dude were still struggling to break free of their teammates, but Jack and Matt were fighting back just as hard. Scott's opponent was bare-chested, and his otherwise pale skin was blotched with red patches. He didn't seem to care or notice, being too busy glowering at Scott, whose nose was trickling blood on the carpet.

"You two calm down," Peter ordered. "We can't have Coach Morrison come in here and see you like this."

The mention of the coach seemed to calm down the two hot heads. They stopped struggling. Peter lowered his arms, still standing between them.

"Are you cool?" Peter asked.

They both nodded grudgingly, and Matt and Jack let them go.

As soon as Matt loosened his grip on Scott, he jerked his elbow up to get free. He touched his hand to his nose to keep the bleeding in check, still glowering at the other guy. He looked ready to start fighting again. Instead, Scott turned around and left the room without saying a word.

Haley watched him go with a dismayed look on her face.

"What happened here, man?" Peter asked.

The remaining amateur boxer flattened his wet, disheveled hair back, unconcerned. He was another looker for the team, but something about his face read "mean."

"My little brother must have some anger issues," mean-good-looking guy said.

Brother? This was Scott's *brother?*

"And you wouldn't know anything about provoking him?" Matt said.

Scott's brother wiped sweat from his forehead with the back of his hand. "It's not my fault if he can't control himself."

The door opened again, and another player walked in, presumably the missing roommate.

"Whoa," he said, taking in the devastation inside his room. "What happened here?"

"Scott and David decided to play real-life *Mortal Combat*," Jack explained.

He had not looked at Alice once since he'd walked in.

"We'd better clean this up," Peter said, looking around the room. "Luckily, it looks like nothing's broken."

"Peter," Alice said.

He paused mid-motion to look at her. "Yeah, baby?"

"It's best if I stay with Haley tonight."

Was that a satisfied smirk on Jack's face? Jack bent to straighten a capsized coffee table before Alice could be sure.

Peter walked toward her. "Sure, baby, I'll see you tomorrow." He planted a tender kiss on her forehead.

"Good night everyone," Alice said, purposely avoiding Jack's gaze.

Alice and Haley left the guys to clear up the mess and walked back to their room.

Inside, Haley slumped on her bed and covered her face with her hands.

"Care to tell me what the hell happened?" Alice asked.

"I honestly have no clue," Haley moaned.

"Were they already fighting when you got there?"

"No. Reception gave me the wrong room number." Haley hugged her knees to her chest, resting her chin on them. "They gave me *David* Williams instead of *Scott* Williams."

Alice was shocked. "That really was Scott's brother?"

"Apparently. So I knock on the wrong room and David opens the door. Then he starts acting all cocky and smug." Haley imitated a dude's voice. "*Oh, they've sent you to the better brother.*"

"Was he hitting on you?"

"Oh yeah."

"Did he get physical?"

"He sort of force-hugged me. But then Scott arrived, and they started arguing and… Well, you saw."

"Yeah, heard, too. Scary."

"It was. It looked as if they wanted to kill each other." Haley scrunched her face. "How can you hate your brother that much?"

"So Scott has some family issues, huh?" Alice tried to lighten the mood.

"Mm-hmm. I wonder what the real story is."

"Rivalry?"

"Some competition is normal between siblings," Haley said. "But those two acted as if they completely, utterly loathed each other."

"They were pretty intense," Alice admitted.

"I'm sorry I ruined your romantic night."

"Haley, you didn't do anything," Alice reassured her friend. "Seems to me it was all David's fault."

"He was being a douche," Haley agreed. "But Scott attacked him first."

"Has this changed your mind about him?"

"I don't know. It definitely wasn't a first date to remember." Haley chuckled sadly. "And him running away like that without a word. Weird, huh?"

"They say women are complicated, but guys are even stranger," Alice said. "Should we try to get some sleep?"

"Oh, no!" Haley covered her face with her hands again.

"What?"

"I dropped my overnight bag in David's room."

"I'll have Peter get it tomorrow."

"Thank you." Haley peeked at her from between her fingers. "I don't want to have to see him again."

"You need to borrow some PJs?"

"No, I have a long t-shirt in my luggage I can use."

Haley hopped off the bed to get changed, and Alice dropped her head on the pillow, feeling uneasy. She stared at the ceiling, wondering what else would go wrong on this trip.

Haley

A brief but decisive knock on their door woke Haley early the next morning. She dragged herself out of bed and shuffled toward the door. She peered through the peephole and saw David waiting on the other side. Haley instinctively took a step back.

"What do you want?" she called through the door.

"Good morning, Sunshine." David's ever-mocking voice was muffled on the other side. "I come in peace to return your possessions."

Haley flattened herself against the door to check again through the peephole. David wasn't lying; he had her duffel bag with him. She opened the door.

"How did you know it was mine?" she asked.

"I doubt any of my teammates wear lacy underwear, at least that I know of." David's smug smirk was infuriating. "By the way, impeccable taste."

"Give it back." Haley stretched her arm forward to grab her bag, but David snatched it backward.

"Ah, ah, ah. Not yet," he said, still smiling. "You're going to have to hear me out first."

Haley crossed her arms and took a step back. "Hear out what?"

"I wanted to apologize for what happened last night; it wasn't my intention to cause trouble."

"Yeah, it was." Haley was not about to let his charm fool her. "Why else would you be like that?"

"Well. When an amazingly beautiful girl, who is *not* my brother's girlfriend, happens to knock on my door in the middle of the night, I find it hard not to present her with…" David paused. "Options."

The compliment, no matter how cheesy, made Haley blush. Flattery rarely worked on her, but pair it with piercing blue eyes and uncanny good looks, and it did have an effect.

"Listen," Haley sighed, "I'm not sure what's going on between you and your brother, but I'm not getting in the middle of that."

"Might be too late for that."

"How so?"

"I've my heart set on you now." His blue gaze was intense and unsettling.

"Not going to happen," Haley snapped.

David winked. "Never say never."

"Can I have my bag now?"

David handed it over. "Until next time."

Without waiting for her reply, he turned on his heel and walked back to his room. For reasons inexplicable to her, Haley watched him go and waited until he disappeared into his room before she closed the door.

"Who was that?" Alice asked from her bed.

"David Williams."

Alice straightened with a worried expression. "What did he want?"

"To give my bag back and apologize for last night." Haley sat on her bed.

"Was it okay?"

Haley considered the question. "I don't know; with him, it's hard to say," she admitted. "I don't know if he was serious or if he was mocking me. Maybe he just wants to piss off his brother more."

"Well, it was nice of him to apologize."

"It felt more conniving than nice."

"I could ask Peter what the deal is with the Williams brothers," Alice offered. "No one seemed surprised they were fighting last night."

Another knock came at the door.

"Who is it now?" Haley asked the ceiling.

"I'll place my money on the other Williams brother."

Haley instinctively checked herself out in the wardrobe mirror, fluffed her hair, and opened the door.

"Hi, is this a bad time?" Scott said.

"No, I was already up."

"Hey." He lowered his gaze to the floor, embarrassed. "I wanted to apologize for the disappearing act last night."

"It's okay," Haley lied. "You don't have to explain anything."

"Actually, I do." Scott looked back up. "Team duties start in little over an hour. I was wondering if you wanted to take a walk down the beach with me first?"

Scott was so genuine and sweet. Exactly the opposite of his brother.

"I would love to," Haley said. "Can you give me fifteen minutes to get ready?"

Scott's face brightened. "I'll wait for you in the hall."

***

The sand was cool this early in the morning. Haley had taken her flip-flops off and was walking barefoot on the beach. The sun was still low above the horizon, but its warm rays indicated the temperature would rise soon enough. Scott hadn't said much yet; he had a serious frown and the face of someone thinking too much.

Haley decided to break the ice first. "So that was your brother, huh?"

Scott was still lost in his thoughts. "Yep."

"What's the deal with you two?"

"We were never close." Scott looked straight ahead, his voice

185

emotionless. "But I'm not sure when David started hating me. Maybe he thinks I've stolen his thunder or something by, you know, being born."

"Mmm, so nothing else got stolen between you two?" Haley asked.

"Ah." Scott scratched the back of his head. "Is it that obvious?"

"Well, you saw us talk last night and lost your mind. All that rage wasn't about me."

"No, you're right," Scott admitted. "It was déjà vu."

They walked a little further in silence.

"So are you going to tell me about the girl?" Haley asked when she couldn't hold it in any longer.

Scott didn't try to deny it. "It was a long time ago, in high school. Her name was Brigitte. She was a student from France doing her junior year in the US. Long story short, we both liked her, and she did something David will never forgive me for."

"What?"

"She chose me." Scott stared at the sky.

"That's it?" Haley thought there was a lot more Scott was holding back.

"No, it's a lot more complicated." He finally looked at her. "But enough about the past." He stopped to face her. "What happened yesterday won't happen again. I won't lose control like that... What I'm saying is, I'm sorry you had to see that, and I hope I haven't scared you off for good." He raised both his eyebrows in a cute and interrogative way.

Haley smiled. "You haven't... scared me off."

"Good," Scott said. "Because I've been dying to do this since the moment I first saw you." He cupped her face with his hands and lowered his mouth to hers.

Alice

Christmas Day was the weirdest. It wasn't just the warm weather and floral décor that clashed with Alice's snowy image of the holiday, or that she had to eat a light, quick lunch because the team played later that night. It was being with Jack without really being with him. It felt strange, wrong. She'd always imagined their first Christmas together under different circumstances.

Alice's mood wasn't exactly cheery to begin with. Peter had seriously downplayed how much the team-related activities would keep him busy. If Alice had come alone, she'd have been pissed. Add the fight between David and Scott, the room swap complications, the fact that Jack had been a total bitch the entire time, and there was a distinct lack of *merry* in her Christmas vacation. And it was about to get worse.

The referee blew his whistle three times, signaling the end of the game. Alice stared at the scoreboard, downcast. Harvard had lost. They'd won their first two games, and Alice had hoped the winning streak would continue. But no. Now Peter would be in a bad mood, and their last night in Hawaii didn't sound very promising with a sullen boyfriend.

"We lost," Alice said.

"I don't care." Haley pushed her hair behind her ears. "I couldn't wait for the game to be over."

"Aren't you worried Scott will be mad about losing?"

"He doesn't look too ruffled." Haley waved and smiled at him.

Scott flashed her friend a grin that indeed said he didn't care much about the final score. Haley and Scott had officially become an item. Yesterday, the only game-free day in their trip, the four of them had spent the entire day at the beach. And the new couple had been inseparable; they hadn't stopped kissing for more than two minutes. Last night, finally, they'd managed to swap rooms without incident. After a night with Scott, Haley had come to breakfast with a smile so bright it had told Alice all she needed to know.

Alice watched as the team gathered their gear and disappeared into the locker room. There were only two people with expressions darker than Peter's: Jack's and, well, David's. The older Williams brother didn't seem to have taken Haley and Scott getting together lightly. But he hadn't pulled another stunt since their first night on the island. Instead, he opted to keep a haughty, detached attitude. And Jack… well, he'd been a jerk for the whole trip. Alice couldn't pinpoint exactly what bothered her so much about his behavior. It wasn't just that he'd done his best to avoid her; he acted as if he couldn't stand to look at her. It was clear he was annoyed she'd come on this trip. Why? Had she stolen his preferred wingman? The thought made her bristle.

"Let's go," Haley said. "I can't believe we're flying home tomorrow. I don't want to lose one minute we have left."

Alice followed her friend out of their seats toward the stadium exit. "Yeah, sure."

Her mind was on a completely different page. She couldn't wait to be home and craved the comforting view of the snow-covered campus and the chill, time-of-the-year-appropriate temperatures. But most of all, she wanted to be alone. No Peter and no Jack. This whole trip seemed like a huge mistake and a total waste of money at this point. She would have counted Haley's new romance a success, except that it was with the guy her other best friend had a crush on. All in all, a complete fiasco.

Madison would be devastated. Haley's happiness was so obvious and in-your-face it left no room for interpretation. Alice could only hope Madison's infatuation for Scott wasn't as deep as she suspected. Because from the way he and Haley kept looking at each other, Haley's strong feelings were reciprocated.

What a mess. What a complete, utter mess.

***

Alice's worries proved true the following night. When they arrived back home at the apartment, Alice noticed Madison staring at Haley's ecstatic smile with a look of pure dread.

"Merry Christmas," Madison said. "Only a day late."

Haley twirled around the living room, blind to Madison's discomfort. "It's been a very, very merry Christmas!"

"Yeah?" Madison wringed her fingers, steadying herself for the bad news. "So the trip went well?"

"Better!" Haley spread her arms wide and kept spinning. "I left single and came back in love," she announced in a singsong voice.

Madison paled. "With who?"

"The best guy in the world: Scott Williams!"

Haley was too excited to notice how Madison drained completely of color and had to lean against the couch for support.

"I can't wait for you to meet him," Haley continued. "He's so great."

"Actually, I-I do k-know him," Madison spluttered.

"You do?" Haley was genuinely surprised. "How come?"

"English concentration, remember?" Madison's voice carried a ring of accusation. "I told you when we went to see that basketball game."

"How am I supposed to remember from so long ago?" Haley

dismissed her. "Anyway, he's Superman when it comes to courses."

"What do you mean?" Alice purposely injected herself into the conversation to give Madison a minute to recover.

"He's taking all these pre-med courses on top of his main English concentration, on top of basketball. He's superhuman."

Alice checked she'd heard right. "So he wants to go to Med School, but he's majoring in English?"

"Yeah, says it's his passion." Haley shrugged. "You should ask the other poet in the room." She jerked her chin toward Madison. "I'll never understand why people spend so much time reading all that stuff dead people wrote."

"Just because the only thing you enjoy reading is lines of code," Madison snapped, "doesn't mean all other people shouldn't care about literature."

Haley lifted her hands in surrender. "No one's touching your precious Shakespeare, don't worry. Wow, I can't say a thing about books without you getting all touchy. Hands-off lit, I promise."

Oh, Haley. She had no clue Madison's attitude had nothing to do with literature. It was more of a hands-off-*Scott* issue.

Madison blanked out Haley and turned to Alice. "Did you have a good time too?"

"Yeah, but I got so mad at—"

"I'm hopping in the shower and then straight to bed," Haley interrupted. "I'm beat."

"Good night," Alice said.

"Night." Haley disappeared inside the bathroom.

"You were saying?" Madison asked.

Now that Haley was out of hearing range, Alice asked, "Are you okay?"

"I'd rather not talk about it," Madison said, close to tears. She was visibly struggling to choke back a lump in her throat. "Can you distract me with your own boy problems?"

"Are you sure?"

"Yeah." Madison nodded. "We'll talk about it, but not now. Can I keep Blue tonight?"

"Sure." Alice walked into her room to pick up the bunny. She brought him into Madison's room and sat on the bed next to her. "Here, bunny joy for you."

"Thanks." Madison took Blue and placed him on her lap. He squealed at being handled, then relaxed when Madison started stroking him. "So was it Jack or Peter who pissed you off?"

"Jack, for the most part."

Alice started telling her friend about Hawaii, focusing on how Jack had ignored her, and leaving out Haley and Scott's romance. If Madison wasn't ready to discuss her feelings for Scott, giving her a break was the least Alice could do. And she had enough Jack-complaints to keep talking all night long.

***

The weekend before the start of Spring Term, Alice received a text from Georgiana. Her mentor was back from Paris and she wanted to meet up.

Alice popped her head inside Madison's room. "Hey. You busy?"

Her roommate was lying on her made-up bed, enthralled by some nineteenth-century literary tome.

Madison raised her bespectacled face. "Huh?" Her expression was one of not-so-veiled annoyance that she usually gave when someone interrupted her reading.

"Georgiana is back from Paris," Alice said. "I'm meeting her for coffee."

Madison lowered the book to her knees. "So she didn't stay in Paris? *Pity.*"

"Eh…" Alice could not understand how two people—cousins—she liked so much could despise each other. At least, she knew Madison didn't like Georgiana—she wasn't sure if it went the other way around, too. "I take it you wouldn't want to join us?"

"I'd rather stick a fork in each of my eyes."

"How would you read, then?"

"Audiobooks."

Alice walked into the room and sat on the only chair available next to Madison's desk. "I honestly can't understand why you don't get along with her."

Madison snorted. "And I *honestly* don't understand how you can be so blind to the fact that my dear cousin is a stone-cold bitch!"

"She's always been kind to me."

"You must be part of an elite group of chosen ones." Madison drummed her fingers on the hard cover of her book. "As for the rest of us, we only get to see her Queen Bee side. Everything has to be about her and never anyone else."

"But did she ever do something bad to you?" Alice asked.

"You mean like stealing my boyfriend?"

Now, that explained a lot of things. "She did that? I didn't know."

"Well, it's not like she's going to tell you or even admit it. If you asked her, she'd tell you he wasn't really my boyfriend. That the relationship was all in my head since I had a childish infatuation. And, anyway, she couldn't help it if he loved her and not me."

Alice did not recall Madison ever being with someone in a long-term relationship. "When was this?"

"High school. I was a freshman, and she couldn't stand me dating a senior. She didn't even like him; she did it just to spite me." Madison's features contracted in anger. "She made freshman year a nightmare for me; the day she graduated was the best day of my life."

"Sounds like a long time ago," Alice said. "Couldn't you give your cousin a second chance?"

Madison huffed. "Listen, Alice. I know she's your friend and I'm glad she's nice to you. But we're like oil and water; we don't mix. I already have to spend spring break trapped on a tiny island with her; I want to avoid any unnecessary suffering."

"Okay, okay. I get the message." Alice lifted her hands in surrender. "Where are you going for spring break?"

"Martha's Vineyard. It's my other cousin's—Vicky, the nice one—wedding, and she made it a one-week event in the middle of March on an island you shouldn't touch until late May or June. But never mind, she's the one cousin I love."

Alice chuckled. "Your family is complicated."

"You tell me."

"I gotta go now."

"Have a good time with Maleficent." Madison waved, then stuck her nose back in her book.

Alice stopped at the door. "Are you sure you'll be all right? Is Haley out, too?"

Madison lifted her gaze again. "She's at Scott's, I think. And Alice,

I'm not suicidal. You can leave me alone for an afternoon, I promise."

Madison was trying to appear strong, but Alice could tell she was in a lot of pain.

"Okay. I'll see you later," Alice said. She still felt responsible for what had happened between Haley and Scott. She'd made one of her best friends the happiest person in the world, and the other miserable.

Madison smiled, then made a point of staring intently at her book. The this-conversation-is-over message all too clear.

Alice walked out of the room, guilt comfortably nestled on her shoulders.

***

Georgiana was waiting for Alice at the Starbucks on Broadway. She'd already ordered two venti cappuccinos and was seated at a round table in the corner near the wall-wide window.

"Hey," Alice greeted.

Georgiana's eyes widened. "Whoa, it's you." She stood up to hug her. "Alice Brown! For a moment, I didn't recognize you. This new hairstyle is amazing. When did you dye it?"

"A while ago. I needed a change." Alice shrugged. She had forgotten the last time she'd seen Georgiana, she'd been a blonde. "You look amazing, too."

They both sat down. The weather was freezing, and Alice gladly wrapped her hands around the warm coffee cup.

"I can't be that amazing." Georgiana pinched herself on a cheek. "I'm still super jet-lagged. We landed only last night."

Georgiana loved false modesty. Right now, she had the look of a porcelain doll: perfect skin, perfect hair, no bags under her eyes, and no signs of tiredness on her face.

Alice ignored the bait for compliments. "How was Paris?"

"The usual." Georgiana waved a hand casually. "Cultured, so European and romantic."

"Is everything good with Tyler then?"

Georgiana's boyfriend hadn't exactly been eager to move across the globe for a semester. Georgiana had pulled some serious strings in the exchange program so that she and Tyler could go to Paris. All to keep him away from his best friend Rose—now Ethan's girlfriend.

Georgiana tilted her head to one side, then the other. "Yes and no."

"What do you mean?"

"I think there's still something going on between him and Rose." Georgiana paused and stared at her with big eyes. "By the way, I was so sorry to hear my idiot of a brother dumped you for her. You're so many leagues above her, it doesn't make sense."

Alice waved her off. "Ah, it was a long time ago. I'm over it."

"Dating anyone new?"

Alice took a sip of coffee before saying, "Yeah." She gave Georgiana the highlights of her relationship with Peter. They did the conventional round of Facebook stalking on their phones before Alice brought the conversation back to Georgiana's love life. "So, Tyler and Rose; why are you still suspicious?"

"Have you ever had a male best friend?" Georgiana asked.

Jack. "Yeah, why?"

"If you didn't have an interest in him that went beyond friendship, would you stop talking to him if he moved to Paris for a semester with his girlfriend?"

The thought of Jack in Paris for a semester with an imaginary girlfriend chilled Alice to the bone. She hadn't told Georgiana about her feelings for Jack. The only two people Alice had trusted with the knowledge were Madison and Haley.

So Alice decided to give Georgiana a neutral answer. "If I didn't have feelings for the guy, no. I'd be happy for him to have this opportunity. Why? Rose and Tyler stopped talking because he moved to Paris with you?"

"More or less. In the weeks before we left, Rose went AWOL." Georgiana's eyes sparked maliciously. "I know they didn't talk much, if at all, while we were there, and she moved out of his house a month after we left."

"Wasn't she there only temporarily, to begin with?"

"In theory, yes." Georgiana leaned forward, lowering her voice. "But before Paris, she wasn't even looking for a place. I kept arguing with Tyler about it. Then she gets the house all to herself and moves out in a blink. Why the rush?"

"Is she still dating your brother?"

"Unfortunately, yes," Georgiana admitted. "She couldn't get her claws in my boyfriend, so she stuck them in my brother instead."

"But if she's dating Ethan, she won't be after Tyler anymore," Alice pointed out.

"I don't know." Georgiana leaned back in her chair, unconvinced. "With a girl like that, she might want to have her cake and eat it, too."

"So, what are you going to do?"

"Nothing for now. I'll see how things evolve." Georgiana pursed her lips, determined, before adding, "But I'm not leaving Tyler to her if it's the last thing I do."

Alice secretly thanked the sky above that Jack had never had a girlfriend this resolute. Why was she thinking about Jack, anyway? Her boyfriend was Peter. *P. E. T. E. R.*

"I'll ask Tyler to come to my sister's wedding with me," Georgiana continued. "If he says yes, it'll show how committed he is."

"Ah, yes. On Martha's Vineyard, right? Madison told me about it."

Georgiana winced. "Sometimes I forget my cousin is your roommate. That must be a pain; she's so boring." Georgiana made a gesture as if she was swatting away an annoying fly.

Maybe Madison's prejudices weren't all inside her head.

"We get along well," Alice said noncommittally. "Will Ethan bring Rose to the wedding?"

"He's stupid enough to ask her, I'm afraid." Her friend sighed. "Call it a happy reunion."

"Well, at least you'll be able to study how she and Tyler interact."

"Yeah, that's the only silver lining. What about you? Any fun plans for spring break?"

"Not yet." Alice shrugged. "Something fun with Peter, hopefully. The basketball season will end in early March, so he'll have more free time."

Another trip with Peter. Alice wasn't that eager but tried to be optimistic. A basketball-free, Jack-free trip, had real potential.

Haley

Haley was about to press Scott's doorbell when the door opened and she found herself staring into David's blue eyes.

His face switched from surprised to coy in a heartbeat. "Hello, Sunshine," he greeted her.

"I'm here to see your brother," Haley said.

"State the obvious, won't you?"

"Is he home?"

David shook his head. "Nope."

"We were supposed to meet here at 3," Haley explained. "Can I wait for him inside?"

David smiled that infuriating smirk of his and opened the door wide, presenting the inside of the house to her. "Come on in."

"So you guys live together?" she asked as she took off her scarf and coat and draped them on the back of an armchair in the living room.

"Unfortunately. My parents refuse to pay for separate accommodations." David closed the door and walked back inside the apartment. "So yeah, I'm stuck with my virtuous younger brother as a roommate."

"Why do you always have to do that?"

"Do what?" David raised his eyebrows.

"Speak as if you mean the exact opposite of what you say."

"Oh, that." David chuckled. "It's called sarcasm."

"I get it; you have it in for Scott. But can't you get over it?"

David's eyes blazed. "Get over what, exactly?"

Haley lowered her gaze, unable to meet his eyes, as she whispered, "He told me about Brigitte."

"Oh, yeah?" David gritted his teeth. "And what exactly did he tell you?"

"He told me you both liked her in high school, and that she chose him."

"That's rich!" David's nostrils flared wide as he stared at the ceiling.

"What's rich?"

"That little tale my brother fed you."

"You're doing it again: hinting at some mysterious, hidden truth and never saying what's on your mind!"

"I hate to break it to you, Princess, but with me what you see is what you get." He pointed down at himself. "I don't pretend to be good when I'm not. And I don't pretend to be a righteous son-of-a-bitch when I'm not."

"Again, you don't say it, but you're implying Scott does pretend to be something he's not."

David shrugged, apparently calm again. "Your words, not mine."

"And what would he be lying about?"

"Ah, see." David's smirk was bitter this time. "To lie outright wouldn't be Scott's style. He prefers to omit. That Brigitte story, he conveniently left half of it out so he wouldn't look bad."

"What did he leave out?" Haley asked.

"I'm sorry, I can only give sarcastic, half-true answers... So why don't you ask your *boyfriend*."

David put so much hatred into the word "boyfriend" that Haley recoiled. She wondered how it was possible for the two of them to live together without either of them having killed the other yet.

She refused to let David provoke her. "You're just trying to screw with my head."

"Tell yourself whatever you need to sleep at night."

"I don't need to tell myself anything," Haley snapped.

"Good for you." David walked back to the door and opened it. "I trust I can leave you here without you scavenging the place, yeah?"

Haley sat on the couch and crossed her arms over her chest, glaring at him. "I'll wait right here."

"Perfect. Don't wait up for me." He slammed the front door as he left.

Haley wanted to scream. She shouldn't let him get to her. How did he manage to get under her skin so easily and so quickly?

To distract herself, Haley studied the room, taking in details of the house. Definitely a guy's apartment. The couch was brown leather with plastic compartments to hold glasses or beer cans. She swiped a finger over the rim of one. Everything else screamed model-house as if this were the apartment they used to show for visits; it was all plain furniture. The only personalizing touches were basketball-themed items casually propped here and there around the house, and a huge flat-screen TV.

She wondered what the bedrooms looked like. Could she get away with taking a quick peek? But what if Scott came home and found her snooping in David's room? She'd be so busted. Haley checked her watch; he was supposed to have been here fifteen minutes ago. It couldn't be much longer until he arrived.

As if on cue, Haley heard a key turn in the keyhole and the door opening. She got to her feet.

"Haley, you're here," Scott said. He seemed surprised to find her inside. "I'm so sorry I was late, I was reading and lost track of time."

"It doesn't matter. David let me in."

Scott's face immediately darkened. "I'm surprised he was here. He's usually never at home."

"He was headed out," Haley said. "Said not to wait up for him."

Scott looked wary. "Is that all he said?"

Haley considered how to answer. She didn't want David to stir up problems between her and Scott, which had clearly been his intention, but she was too curious about Brigitte to let it go.

"We had a bit of an argument actually," Haley said, hugging herself.

Scott took three quick strides across the room and braced his hands on her shoulders "Did he do something to you?" he asked, looking at her with a worried expression.

"No." Haley shrugged free and sat down. "He didn't do anything. He said things."

"What things?" Scott sat next to her.

"He said you haven't told me the whole truth about Brigitte."

Scott massaged his temples with his fingers. "What else?"

"Nothing. That's all he said."

"All right." Scott sighed and faced Haley. "David has this idea in his head of how things happened that's not true."

"Okay…"

"Listen, you shouldn't let him get to you like this."

"I know. But I can sense you're not telling me something, and it feels like David's trying to use that against us." Haley was tired of Scott's instant semi-muteness whenever David or Brigitte were mentioned. "So what's the truth?"

"I don't like to talk about that period of my life."

"I get that," Haley said. "But if you don't tell me, I'll never know which one of you I should believe."

Scott scoffed. "See? You're already starting to doubt me. That's exactly what he wants."

"And also why we're talking about it," Haley insisted. "Listen, you can't tell me David's got the wrong idea without telling me why or about what."

Scott sighed. "All right. I'll tell you everything." He leaned his back against the couch and spoke, looking at the ceiling. "Brigitte was my first. The first girl I loved, my first everything. She was beautiful, playful, and she had this impossible-to-resist French accent that would make any guy lose his mind."

"Okay, you don't need to be that specific," Haley joked.

"Sorry." Scott smirked. "Anyway, from the first day she set foot in our school, David had his eyes on her, and so did I. But I was shy and inexperienced and he was not. They started dating almost immediately."

"Then what happened?"

"She was my age, a year younger than David, so we had a lot of classes together and we started talking. She had a compelling personality. It was impossible not to fall for her, especially for a shy guy like me. At one point she started complaining about my brother, said their relationship wasn't working. Finally, one day she told me they'd broken up."

"Was it true?"

"I believed her. I wanted to believe her so badly."

"So, she was lying?" This Brigitte character wasn't growing on Haley. The opposite, in fact.

"Yeah."

"And you couldn't tell?"

"No." Scott shifted position and finally met her gaze. "I never saw her with David anymore, and I had no reason to assume she was lying."

"So you two… what?"

"Exactly what you think. We were together while she was still seeing David."

"I don't understand. What did David do?"

"He didn't know." Scott shook his head. "Brigitte told me we had to keep our relationship a secret. She explained it by saying she didn't want to hurt David's feelings, that it was too soon for us to date openly… blah, blah, blah. I was young and in love, gullible enough to go along with it if it meant I could be with her."

"It didn't last, I take it."

"No. David found us together." The shadow of a bad memory crossed Scott's face. "We got into this huge fight, and then we told Brigitte she had to choose."

"And she chose you," Haley finished for him.

"And that, David will never forgive."

"So you stayed with her, even after she lied to you like that?"

"As I said, I was young, stupid, and in love."

Haley put the last pieces together. "David doesn't believe you didn't know."

"No, I don't think he does. And the fact that I kept going out with Brigitte afterward was proof enough for him."

Haley honestly could not blame him. "How long were you with her?"

"At the end of the year she moved back to France, and David moved on to college. This wound between us has been festering ever since."

"Well, at least now it makes sense why he behaves like that." Haley's head was spinning with all this new information. "Haven't you tried to explain to him how it really happened? It seems to me this Brigitte person was pretty awful."

"In hindsight, she was," Scott agreed. "And I've tried to talk with my brother a million times, but he won't listen."

"I'm sorry for dredging all of this up." Haley squeezed Scott's upper arm. "But I needed to know."

"And I'm glad I told you the whole story."

"Come here," Haley said.

She opened her arms to hold Scott to her chest as she leaned back on the couch. Haley stared at the ceiling, enjoying Scott's weight on her. But as she stroked his hair, she couldn't help but feel sorry for David.

Alice

"You guys," Madison called, strolling across the living room with a huge suitcase in tow. "I'm off. Wish me luck for the worst spring break ever!"

Alice interrupted her own packing and emerged from her room to say goodbye. "Oh, come on," she said. "It won't be that bad!"

"A week stuck on a tiny island with my entire family?" Madison rolled her eyes. "Yeah, it will."

Haley joined them. "If it's any consolation," she said, "I've been conscripted by my parents as well after skipping Christmas." Haley hugged Madison and then eyed Alice sideways. "She's the only one who's going to have a good time."

"I'm sure you guys will have just as much fun," Alice said defensively.

"Yeah." Madison snorted. She lifted one hand and lowered the other as if weighing options on an imaginary scale. "Boring family wedding on freezing Martha's Vineyard." She reversed the height of her hands. "Or amazing trip with hot boyfriend in sunny Miami. Mmm… you're right. It's hard to call!"

"Oh, shut up." Alice shoved her away playfully.

"At least you're going somewhere, and weddings are fun," Haley protested. "I'm just going to be confined at home for a week."

"Trust me," Madison exhaled. "If you'd met even half my family, a week in *your* house would look like paradise."

"You could always meet cute wedding guests," Alice offered.

"I don't know." Madison frowned. "All Vicky's friends are lawyers."

"What's wrong with lawyers?" Haley asked.

"Seriously?" Madison said, incredulous.

"I mean," Haley continued, "aren't you supposed to become one as well?"

A shadow crossed Madison's face. "We'll see." She sighed. "I'd better go or I'll be late. See you guys."

They did a three-way hug, and then Madison left.

"Are you leaving today as well?" Haley asked, once Madison was gone.

"No, Peter is picking me up tomorrow," Alice replied. "You?"

Haley checked her watch. "I have an Uber booked in half an hour. I'd better go finish packing!"

A short while later, Haley called out again to announce she was leaving. Alice hugged her friend goodbye, walked her to the door, and turned around to an empty apartment. She wrapped her arms around her chest, hugging herself. It felt weird to be here alone. Should she call Peter and ask him to spend the night? It would make sense as they had to leave for the airport early the next morning. As sensible as it was, the idea did not appeal to Alice. She'd rather be alone.

You'd rather be with Jack, a treacherous voice echoed in her head.

"No, I wouldn't," Alice said aloud.

Liar.

Alice sank on the couch. Okay, she was lying. The thought of being away from Jack for a week was depressing. Even if they didn't spend as much time together as they'd used to. She still saw him in class every day, and most weekends at games. Even at Christmas, seeing him in small, annoying doses had been better than not seeing him at all.

Alice threw a pillow across the living room and let out a frustrated scream. "Why can't I just forget him?" she asked the ceiling.

No reply came.

****

After an uneventful trip, Alice and Peter landed at Miami Airport mid-morning and took a cab to Peter's house. His parents owned a condo apartment in South Beach, and they'd agreed to let him use it during spring break. Alice couldn't have afforded to pay for a hotel on top of the flight, not after Christmas's detour to Hawaii.

Peter's house was a glassy, two-story apartment. Wall-wide windows and white, minimalist furniture were the main theme. They stopped there only long enough to drop their luggage and change for the beach, and then they were off. When they reached the sandy shore, Peter rented two lounge chairs from a booth and collapsed on his as soon as it was delivered. He was asleep in a matter of minutes.

Alice coated herself in sunscreen and tried to relax by reading a book. Too soon, her skin heated up. The wind wasn't cool enough to counter the smothering midday heat. Half-bored by the book and definitely too hot, Alice decided to take a walk along the beach to distract herself. She dipped her toes in the ocean, then returned to the loungers and picked her book back up. When she got bored again, it was back to the water. She repeated this cycle several times, and Peter slept through all of it.

By the time he finally stirred, Alice was itching to make plans for all the things they should go see and the nice restaurants they could visit. It was her first visit to Florida, and Alice couldn't wait to explore a new city and, possibly, the Everglades and Key West. She'd also heard the Cuban food was great here. Maybe Peter knew a good place to have an authentic taste. He said he didn't.

"Do you think we can drive to Key West?" Alice asked next.

Peter groaned. "Yo, it's a four-hour drive."

"So?" Alice stiffened on her chair. "We have a week."

"There's not that much to see, plus I'd like to relax. Spend the week with my friends here in Miami. It's really not worth it to waste a day to drive down there."

Alice bit her lower lip in frustration, trying to suppress the angry retort that wanted so badly to come out. She really wanted to see the Keys, but this was Peter's vacation too. If he wanted to stay in Miami...

"How about the Everglades? I've always wanted to ride one of those crazy boats with the giant fan in the back." *They look so exciting in the movies.*

Peter shaded his eyes with one hand to look at her. "A hovercraft?"

"Yeah, that's it. Can we go on one?"

"Sure." He tilted his head back toward the sun, eyes closed. "A friend of mine has one he uses to fish. We can get a ride with him."

At least Peter had finally agreed to do *something* fun.

"You want to take a walk down Ocean Drive with me?" she asked.

"Babe, relax." He threw her a reproachful, one-eyed stare. "Can't you just enjoy the sun? I'm chilling here."

Alice fought hard to keep her temper in check. "Is 'chilling' all you plan to do while we're here?"

"Don't worry babe, I have it all planned out. We're having a party at the house tonight."

"A party?"

Shouldn't he at least have asked her if she wanted to have a party on their first night in Miami? Alice was anticipating a quiet, romantic dinner, not a house party.

"Yeah, I've invited a few friends over," Peter said casually.

"Should we buy something? The house is a bit understocked."

"Nah, there's a liquor store a block from the house."

"What about food?"

"They have Doritos and stuff at the store."

This didn't sound like the kind of party Alice would enjoy. She had a sinking feeling this trip would not end well, possibly even worse than Hawaii. "I'm going for a walk," she snapped. "See you back at the house."

She stood up from the lounging chair to go have a look around Ocean Drive by herself. Dread filled her as she thought about the party they were supposed to host in a few hours.

***

At three in the morning, Alice had had enough. What were supposed to be a "few" friends had turned out to be half of Miami. *The worse half.* Peter's friends were either too drunk to talk, or too obnoxious if they could still manage to string two words together. She felt like a fish out of water. There wasn't a single person in the house she wanted to meet or try to chat up. Her head was throbbing, thanks to the loud music drilling a steady boom-boom-boom in her brain. She'd even considered calling the cops on her boyfriend just so she could finally go to bed. Enough was enough.

Alice walked toward Peter and poked him in the shoulder. "I'm going to bed," she said.

"Oh, baby. Already?" He slurred his words. "But the fun is just starting."

"I've had enough *fun* for tonight," Alice hissed, sure that Peter would miss the sarcasm in her voice.

"All right." Peter ruffled her hair, and it took all her self-control not to swat his hand away. "Go to the upstairs bedroom, the guys know it's off-limits."

The fact that the downstairs bedrooms were clearly *not* off-limits made Alice's stomach heave.

"Good night," she said, her tone glacial.

Peter grabbed her by the waist. "Night," he said, then tried to kiss her on the lips. As he drew closer, a whiff of his breath—a disgusting mix of beer and cheap vodka—smacked Alice. Repulsed, she turned her face and Peter's lips landed on her left cheek.

Alice wiggled away and almost ran across the room and up the stairs to the safety of the upper floor. She changed into her PJs and locked herself in the master bedroom. She didn't care that Peter might not be able to come in later in the night. There was no chance in hell she would sleep with him tonight—literally or otherwise. She hoped this horrific first day had been a one-off and that Peter would get all this frat-boy partying out of his system for good. Because if this was how he planned to spend the whole week, Alice could see herself renting a car and driving to the Keys alone.

Jack

Jack walked out of the arrival gate of Indianapolis airport, searching the crowd with his eyes. He spotted Felicity at once; she was holding an iPad with "Mr. Sullivan" handwritten on the screen. He looked at her with fondness. His ex-girlfriend and oldest friend wasn't classically beautiful—short, with squashed features, and a little on the chubby side—but her impeccable grooming and bubbly personality made her attractive. Jack was home because he hadn't seen his parents at Christmas. As for Felicity, Jack suspected she'd come home to spend spring break with him.

Felicity insisted on denying it, but Jack was sure she still loved him. No matter that their relationship had ended more than three years ago. Her feelings for him had always been fiercer and, apparently, longer lived.

She saw him and her entire face brightened. Jack's heart sank a little. Every time he saw her, he couldn't help remembering the day he'd broken her heart. The way she'd cried and screamed how much she hated him. The way his chest had exploded with guilt at causing her so much pain. And the solitude that had followed that summer after he'd lost his best friend.

"Jack!" Felicity waved a hand above her head and ran toward him.

She barreled into him and he scooped her up in his arms, lifting her feet off the ground.

"It's so good to see you," she said.

"You too, Felix." Jack ruffled her blonde hair fondly.

"I can't believe you're here. It's been forever!"

"When did you land?" Jack asked.

"Early this morning. I caught a late flight last night."

Felicity was studying at Berkley. After their breakup senior year, before they'd somehow patched their relationship, Felix had gone to school as far away from Jack as she could.

"But I still look fresher than you," Felix added, eyeing him sideways as they walked toward her car. "What's up with you, Sullivan?"

Jack grimaced. What was up with him was that Ice had decided to spend spring break in Miami with Peter. But Jack wasn't comfortable discussing his feelings for another woman with Felicity. Especially not in person when he could witness all the tiny giveaways of her discomfort in the creases on her face.

Jack shrugged. "Nothing. I'm just tired."

Felicity didn't look convinced, but she didn't press him. They reached her car and spent the rest of the journey in silence, with Felicity driving and Jack staring out the window. She dropped him at his parents' house, and they agreed to meet up later for a beer.

*****

Jack was in his parents' garden in front of the rock fire pit. The sun had set a while ago and Jack had lit the gas fire to keep warm. He was staring at the flames, sipping beer from the bottle, when Felicity walked out from the house and sat on the chair next to him.

"You're worrying your mother, you know," she said by way of greeting.

"My mom?" Jack raised his brows, still looking at the fire. "Why?"

Felicity wrapped herself in one of the outside blankets and dragged her chair closer to the fire. "Maybe because you're sitting outside when it's fifty degrees?"

"I have the fire to keep warm."

"Or maybe it's that you're drinking beer alone, looking sadder than when your Teenage Mutant Ninja Turtles went missing."

Despite his bad mood, Jack's lips twitched. Losing his favorite action figures had been the biggest tragedy of his childhood. He turned to face Felix. "I'm not alone. You're here."

"Open this." She handed him a beer bottle. "Your dad said you kidnapped the bottle opener."

Jack took the bottle, cracked the cap open, and gave it back.

Felicity took a sip and sighed. "Is this brooding still about that girl at Harvard?"

No point in lying. Jack turned toward the fire again and nodded.

Felicity scoffed. "Have you talked to her?"

Jack shook his head.

"Jack Sullivan, look at me."

He did.

"Tell her how you feel."

"What's the point? Ice has a boyfriend."

"That's because she doesn't have all the information."

"You haven't seen them together." A flash of Alice and Peter making out on the bed in Hawaii appeared in his mind's eye. "She's in love with

Peter."

"Or maybe," Felicity said in her I'm-spelling-it-out-for-you voice, "she's in love with you and is using this Peter guy as a distraction because she thinks she can't have you."

Jack glared at his friend. "You don't even know her."

"Believe me." Felicity turned red. "It's very difficult to get over you."

Guilt gnawed at Jack again. It was clear Felicity was projecting herself onto Alice. But Ice wasn't Felicity, and she wasn't in love with him. "Listen, Felix. She's been with Peter for months. They're in Miami now on a romantic getaway. Trust me, she's not in love with me."

"How do you know? Have you ever asked her?"

"Ice wouldn't be dating Peter if she loved me."

"Again, she doesn't have all the info."

"What difference would it make?"

"Jack, can't you see?" Felix sounded exasperated. "She tried to kiss you, and you said you wanted to be her friend. She has no idea how you feel."

"But why date Peter?"

"To make you jealous?"

"Even if she did at the beginning, now they've been together too long."

"Okay, maybe Alice likes this Peter dude, but do you know for sure if she's in love with him?"

"No."

"So stop being such a crybaby and talk to her. What are you waiting for?"

"Peter graduates in a few months."

"So your plan is to wait for him to be out of the picture?"

Jack shrugged. "Maybe." Actually, that was exactly his plan. Peter would get a contract with some big team and move away from Boston. And, yes, Jack imagined himself as the shoulder for Alice to cry on.

"That's a losing strategy."

"Why?"

"If you want the girl, go get her. Don't wait for her to fall into your lap. *Fight.*"

"And what if I lose?"

"You wouldn't be worse off than now. You've got nothing to lose and everything to gain from talking to her."

Jack's eyes reflected the fire's dancing flames. Could Felicity be right? Had he wasted all these months brooding instead of fighting for what he wanted? He had to at least try. Jack pursed his lips in a determined pout. Peter had had it easy so far, but that was about to change.

Alice

Alice didn't drive alone to the Keys. She should have, but instead, she endured a full week of Peter's crazy partying, his sleeping in late, and his constant "chilling." She saw what she could of Miami in the mornings when Peter was so wasted he wouldn't even get out of bed to go to the beach. He had made her hate Miami and everyone from Florida. And the worst part was that he hadn't even noticed something was terribly wrong. By the time they returned to Boston and parted ways, Alice was amazed that she'd managed to keep her cool the entire trip.

Back at her apartment, she finally let out all her frustration as she and her roommates discussed their respective trips from hell whilst doing their nails in the living room.

"You guys," Alice said, scowling at Madison and Haley, "I'm telling you, he was too wasted to help me clean up."

"So you had to clean his parents' place by yourself?" Haley demanded incredulously. She paused in applying her black polish to stare up at Alice, her brush hanging in mid-air. "Why? I mean, what do *you* care if he left the place trashed?"

"I was a guest in his parents' house, too." Alice winced at the memory of the dirty apartment after a week of non-stop partying. "I couldn't leave their house trashed."

"You should've let him handle it," Haley insisted.

"I agree," Madison said.

"Believe me, girls," Alice insisted, "if you'd seen the place, you would've been just as compelled to clean it up." She lifted her shoulders in a gesture of impotence.

"So you were in Florida for a week and all you did was babysit a drunk Peter?" Haley asked.

Alice nodded in misery. "That's depressingly accurate. It's like he had to make up for the entire basketball season and compress five months of lost parties into a single week."

"No romantic drive to the Keys?" Madison asked.

"Nope."

"But you did do something romantic in Miami?" Madison insisted.

"No, not even one dinner." Alice wished she didn't sound so bitter. "I survived on Doritos and hot dogs for a week."

"No Everglades?" Haley offered.

"Too 'touristy' according to Peter, but I managed to have him arrange a ride on a hovercraft."

"That sounds exciting," Haley said. "See, you and Peter did something fun."

"Oh, yeah. His friend drove me around the swamp while Peter drank beer with some other friends back at this guy's fishing shack. Great fun."

"At least your tan looks awesome," Madison said. "Better than family duty for a week."

"Yeah," Haley agreed. "You had the best spring break among the three of us, by far, so please stop complaining about partying too much."

"I would've rather spent the week being cuddled by my mom," Alice said. "I swear."

Haley glowered at her, so Alice turned to Madison, changing the subject. "How was the wedding?"

Madison stopped blowing air on her shiny coral nails and said, "Vicky was a beautiful bride."

"Any cute boys?" Haley asked.

"Not one!" Madison sighed.

Alice stared down at her blue nails, not liking the result. "How was Georgiana?" she asked, as she began to remove the polish with a cotton disk.

Madison winced; a common reaction when anyone mentioned Georgiana in her presence. "Her usual nasty self."

Alice was curious about the whole Georgiana-Rose-Tyler love triangle. "Was Tyler there?"

"Yep. Rose and Ethan were there, too."

Correction: quadrangle including Ethan in the picture.

Alice finished removing the last specks of blue and started applying a nude miracle gel to her pinkie. "So, did you pick up any weird vibes?"

she asked.

"Why?" Haley asked, puzzled. "What's going on?"

Madison launched into an explanation. "My cousin, Georgiana, suspects her boyfriend, Tyler, has a thing for his best friend, Rose. Or, equally bad, that Rose is trying to steal him from her. Only Rose was at the wedding as Ethan's date. He's my other cousin, Georgiana's older brother, and Alice's ex."

Haley raised both her eyebrows. "Come again?"

"I said my cousin Georgiana—"

"Yeah, I got all that the first time," Haley interrupted. "It just sounded too soap-opera to be real."

"So, is it?" Alice asked. "Did any of it seem real to you?"

"Well." Madison thought for a second. "Rose and Tyler definitely seemed awkward around each other. And Georgiana stared daggers at her for the entire week. Moved the target from its usual spot behind my back, actually. But from the way Rose and Ethan were staring at each other the entire time… Sorry, Alice…"

"Don't worry." Alice shook her head. "He's ancient history."

"They seemed smitten," Madison concluded. "So, no, I don't think Rose is trying to steal Tyler."

"What about your cousin and this… Tyler?" Haley asked.

"That, I'm not sure about. I caught him looking at Rose with a brooding expression one too many times."

"So Georgiana wasn't entirely wrong," Alice mused. "There could've been something between Rose and Tyler at one point."

"If there ever was, Rose is over it," Madison said, confident. "And I hope for his sake, Tyler will be over my *sweet* cousin soon, too."

"Oh, come on," Alice chided.

Madison shrugged. "He didn't seem much into her, anyway." She turned to Haley. "What about you? How was your break?"

"In one word, *boring*," Haley replied. "But I didn't have to cook, and my mom did my laundry! She ironed my pajamas. Ironed PJs, can you guys believe it?"

Alice and Madison chuckled.

"I'm being serious," Haley insisted. "It was way too cold to do anything remotely fun—"

"Not as cold as Martha's Vineyard," Madison interrupted. "I

promise."

"Still cold enough to spoil every outdoor activity. Plus, none of my friends was there. They all came back for Thanksgiving or Christmas, but definitely not spring break. It was a desert town."

"What did you do all day?" Alice asked.

"Honestly? I coded, I slept, and I ate my mom's food. I win the price for lamest spring break ever."

"Yeah." Alice smiled playfully. "I'm afraid you do."

"Anyway," Haley continued, "next weekend I'll come up with something amazing to cure our back-to-school blues." She paused to look them in the eyes. "And that, you guys, is a promise."

***

"Roomies!" Haley sang as she burst into the living room the next Saturday. "What do you say we all go out together tonight?"

"Define 'we,'" Madison said.

"Define 'out,'" Alice echoed.

"We, as in *us*." Haley pointed at them in a circle. "Plus the guys. And we're going out as in to some grownup bars." Haley wasn't letting their scarce enthusiasm damper hers. "We're finally all twenty-one. You know what that means."

Madison scoffed. "I'd rather not be the fifth wheel. Thanks, but no thanks."

"Madison!" Haley turned to face her. "You wouldn't be the fifth wheel. A lot of guys from the team are coming. The season is over, and they can finally enjoy their Saturdays like normal people. You could meet someone."

"Yeah, sure," Madison said. "Because that always happens to me."

Madison's neck and cheeks heated; she'd hidden the real reason for not wanting to go behind sarcasm. So far, Alice reflected, her friend had never seen Haley and Scott together. Madison had probably gone out of her way to make sure that didn't happen.

As for Peter and Alice, this was the first weekend after the season's end—excluding spring break—that they could go out together. Even with Haley dating Scott for three months, there hadn't been any previous group dates. A beer with Peter and a random guy or guys on the team on weekdays at the most. But the basketball season *was* over, and change

210

was in the air…

"Is Jack included in the group?" Alice asked, to draw attention away from sulking Madison.

"I'm not sure, but most of the team is going," Haley replied.

"David, too?" Alice asked.

Haley shrugged. "Probably."

Madison threw her a mean stare. "It must be nice having two guys fighting over you."

Haley frowned. "As it happens, it's pretty horrible. What's up with you? Did you eat lemons for breakfast?"

Madison caught herself and blushed a deeper shade of red. "I'm sorry, Haley, it's not you." It was clear to Alice how Madison was trying her best not to be jealous or bitter, but sometimes her repressed feelings got the best of her. "I just got a low grade and can't wrap my head around why."

Haley rolled her eyes. "What did you get, a B+?"

"A-, actually. But I really can't understand why the minus."

Haley turned to Alice. "Are you going to smack her, or should I?"

"Hey," Madison protested. "I'm right here. I can hear you."

Haley blew out air. "So, tonight. Are we on?"

"Sure," Alice said.

"I guess," Madison agreed.

"Great!" Haley clapped her hands twice. "I'll call Scott and organize everything."

While Haley was busy on the phone with her boyfriend, Alice whispered, "Are you okay? You don't have to come if you don't want to."

Madison's lips parted in a sad smile. "I have to face them sooner or later. I won't be able to avoid them forever."

"Okay," Alice continued in hushed tones. "But if it gets too much, let me know. Promise?"

Madison nodded.

***

The downtown bar Haley had chosen was already half full when the three of them strolled inside. It was fancy in an urban way: brick walls with wide, metal-framed windows and high ceilings. Tall, circular tables

211

surrounded a dais in the center of the room.

None of the guys had arrived yet, so the girls got started on cocktails. With her birthday in mid-December, Haley still wasn't over the thrill of legally ordering a drink in a public space. She immediately offered to go order for everyone. They happily let her.

"How are you holding up?" Alice asked Madison.

She grimaced. "You don't have to check on me every five seconds. I can handle myself."

From the way Madison kept gnawing her bottom lip, eyes glued to the entrance door, Alice doubted her friend was going to handle anything well. But she didn't press her further. Haley came back with their drinks and started babbling about something. Alice didn't listen. She was too distracted worrying about Madison.

Haley snapped her fingers in both their faces. "Hey, I'm talking. What's up with you two?"

"Nothing," Alice and Madison said in unison.

After being caught, they both made an effort to act normal and give Haley their undivided attention. At least, until Madison went suddenly pale. Her gaze fixed over Alice's shoulder with that deer-in-headlights expression. Alice turned toward the front of the pub where the heads of several tall guys bobbed above the crowd, heading toward them. Her eyes trained on Jack first, then Peter, Scott, and the many other familiar faces with them. It looked like Haley had been right; most of the team was here. At least everyone old enough for public drinking.

Peter greeted her with a kiss, and Scott did the same with Haley. Madison stared, petrified.

"Hi, babe," Haley said to Scott. "Remember Alice?"

Scott looked at her and said, "Hi."

"And this is Madison," Haley continued. "My other roommate."

A flicker of recognition creased Scott's forehead. "Hi." He smiled as if he'd placed where he'd seen her. "You're in my poetry class."

"Yeah." To her credit, Madison managed to function as a normal human being, smiling only a little awkwardly. "Madison, nice to meet you."

"Scott."

They shook hands, and when Scott turned to kiss Haley again, Madison downed her entire drink. Alice was about to say something when she became distracted by Jack appearing with a flock of girls in tow. They looked like freshmen at best, but they couldn't be. In a bar, it always was twenty-one-and-above only. Fake IDs, perhaps? Jack was shamelessly flirting with three of them at the same time, and he was clearly well on his way to charming the pants off the entire group.

Alice sighed and then followed Madison's lead, downing her drink in one sorry gulp.

Madison

"Oh, look," Madison muttered into her glass, talking to herself. "Haley is going home with Scott. *Super fun!*" She stared at the half-consumed drink in her hand, waiting for a reply, and decided it was better to finish her cocktail rather than trying to talk with it. Madison tilted her head backward and chugged. What in the hell had made her agree to come out with *them* tonight?

Two hours into the evening and Madison was ready to call it quits. She'd masochistically stalked Haley and Scott most of the night and had had enough. If Haley—who had insisted so much on this "night out drinking," only to sip a single cocktail and ignore her friends to be with her boyfriend—was going home, so could Madison. She had drunk enough to be tipsy, and the constant thumping in her temples promised a mean hangover the next day.

Madison was about to follow the happy couple out when another member of the team leaned his elbows on the table next to her now-empty glass. "They make my stomach turn, too," he said.

Madison detached her gaze from Scott and Haley to stare up at the newcomer. To call him "hot" would have been an understatement. "And you are?" she asked.

"David. Pleased to meet you." He smiled a confident, lopsided grin that screamed *danger.*

Madison's lips parted in a surprised O. "You're the infamous brother." It figured that Scott's brother would be even better looking and into Haley just as much as his younger sibling.

"I hope you didn't believe everything you heard about me."

"Why?" Madison cocked her head to the side. "I've only heard good things. Are they not true?"

Whoops, she was flirting. *So?* David looked just as pissed off at the leaving duo as she was; so what if they mourned together?

Trouble shared is a trouble halved.

David jerked his chin toward her empty glass. "Want another one of those?"

"Sure, why not?"

Or possibly double-trouble.

"You go to Harvard too?" David asked, once he was back with their drinks.

"Yep," Madison said between sips. "What's your concentration?"

"Statistics. Yours?"

"Ew. No offense, but I can't stand numbers."

David smiled genially. "None taken."

"I'm studying English Literature and Poetry."

David raised his eyebrows. "I hope you're not as much of a tormented soul as my little brother."

Madison blushed at the mention of Scott. "I hope 'tormented' isn't the first word that comes to mind when one looks at me."

"Definitely not." Davis brushed his right thumb across her cheek. "'Beautiful' would be more appropriate."

The rosy tint on her cheeks grew a deeper red. "Want to dance?" Madison asked, for lack of other responses.

David pinned her with his blue gaze. "I'd love to."

"Great!"

Madison gulped down the remains of her drink and grabbed David's hand to lead him to the dais in the center of the room. It was already crowded with throngs of partygoers having a good time. She made to turn to face David, but he spun her round and wrapped his arms around her from behind. As they started swaying in time to the music, David's chin brushed the top her head. He was so tall. Having him so close, Madison moved rigidly as a stick at first. Until David lowered his head and whispered, "Relax," close enough to her ear to send shivers down her spine.

Maybe it was the one-too-many drinks, or the hot guy standing behind her, or the one that had gone home with her best friend. Madison didn't care; she let her inhibitions melt away. She was happy to just dance to the fast rhythm of the music, pressing herself against the solid wall of David's chest. She lost count of how many songs played before the dancing changed to full-scale making out. David was a great kisser.

Her phone started vibrating in her small leather clutch. Madison ignored it, too engrossed in the kiss to stop. But when it kept on vibrating, she pulled back with an embarrassed, "Sorry" to check out who it was.

She had two missed calls and a text from Alice asking where she was and saying she was heading home.

"It's Alice," Madison said. "She's going home. You want to go, too?"

David smiled. "I'm having fun right here."

"Yeah, me too. Do you mind waiting here while I go say bye?"

"Not at all." David grabbed her by the waist and pulled her close to kiss her lightly on the lips. "Don't make me wait too long."

Madison blushed. "I won't." She took two steps backward, never breaking eye contact, and turned to push her way through the crowd to go tell Alice she was staying.

Haley

Haley left Scott's apartment early the next morning. She had a ton of homework to do before Monday and an entire program to code that she'd left to the last minute. Scott walked her halfway to a Starbucks, where they had breakfast together, and then kissed her goodbye. Haley sleepwalked the rest of the way home; the coffee had not been strong enough to wake her up properly. Mercifully, it took her only five minutes to get to her building and take the elevator up to her floor.

Pushing open the door to her apartment, Haley was startled to find a tall, dark-haired, bare-backed guy in her kitchen. Haley couldn't see his bottom half from behind the bar, but she hoped at least that part was covered up. The mysterious dude was standing in front of their opened fridge, acting as if he owned the place. The mere stance of his shoulders exuded arrogance. He took his time to examine the contents of the fridge and settled on Haley's 2% milk. With the milk carton in his hands, the dude grabbed a glass out of the cabinet above the sink and poured himself a drink.

The theft of her milk shook Haley out of her shock. She kicked the entrance door shut with force, to make sure it made enough noise to startle the thief. *It did.* As the door slammed shut, the dude's shoulders jerked. But the milk thief didn't turn around. He finished drinking his milk, taking his time, and then placed the used glass in the sink without washing it.

Haley's nostrils flared. "That's my milk you're drinking," she accused.

Slowly, deliberately he turned around, and Haley found herself staring into a pair of piercing blue eyes. *David.*

"Morning, Sunshine," he purred. His lips parted in a lopsided grin. "I apologize for abusing your hospitality." He made a mock bow. "I'll buy you a new carton."

Haley narrowed her eyes to slits. "What are you doing in my house?" she hissed.

"I'm a guest."

"I never invited you here."

"*You* are not the only person living here."

His eyes never left hers, causing a soft blush to creep up her cheeks.

"What do you mean?" she asked, even if a sneaking suspicion was already making her heart beat faster.

"Your roommate is a lovely girl," David said. He walked out from behind the bar.

Please let him not be naked, please let him not be naked, *Haley chanted in her head.*

He rounded the corner, revealing that he was wearing the same pants he'd had on last night. Haley was both relieved and somehow disappointed at his being half-dressed. Before she could stop herself, her eyes traveled down his chest and over his sculpted stomach, coming to rest just above the open button of his pants.

"See something you like?" he asked, cocking one eyebrow.

"*No.*"

David closed the distance between them until he was so near Haley could feel the heat coming from his body. "I'll see you later, then." He gave her that mocking grin again. "Or not."

Haley poked him just below the collarbone, pressing hard on his chest. "Hurt her and—"

"What?" he challenged, inching even closer, his face a breath away from hers. "What are you going to do, Princess?"

Haley held his gaze. "You don't want to find out," she hissed.

David stepped backward. "Relax," he said. "Contrary to popular belief, I can be a gentleman when the need calls for it." Without waiting for a reply, David walked into Madison's room and closed the door behind him.

Haley was left standing alone in the hall, her face so hot she was sure she must've had steam coming out her ears. She glared at Madison's door, then stormed inside her own room.

Throwing her coat on the bed, she searched her bedroom for something that would help distract her. Haley sat at her desk, stabbed the "on" button of her laptop, and opened a blank C++ page. Programming always calmed her, but today it was life or death. It'd keep her from bursting into Madison's room to drag the bastard out by his hair.

With one hand clenched on the mouse and the other drumming on the wooden desk, Haley tried to focus on the program. The blinking cursor teased her, waiting to be moved, making her brain feel as empty as the blank page. David's smug smirk kept appearing in her mind's eye, erasing everything else. She couldn't remember the simplest input command. When squealing giggles echoed in the adjoining room, Haley's concentration failed, and her mood blackened even more. This David situation was not working for her; she had to do something to stop him.

***

Haley remained in her room until she was sure that both David and Madison had left the apartment. Not that it did her any good. She hadn't accomplished anything the entire morning and was still fuming from her short encounter with David. When it seemed safe to come out, Haley tiptoed into the living room, still wary of her own house. Alice was sitting at the dining table doing homework.

Haley strolled toward her. "We need to talk."

"Hey." Alice lifted her head from her chemistry book. "I didn't know you were home."

Haley sat in the chair opposite to her. "Did you know who else was here?"

"Yeah."

From her tone, Alice didn't seem too happy either.

"How did it happen?" Haley asked.

Alice dropped her pen and closed her book, resting her elbows on it. "After you left with Scott, I went home with Peter. Madison told me she was having fun, and that she was staying. I didn't know that it was David providing the entertainment and charming his way to her bedroom."

"What do you think about it?" Haley asked.

Alice leaned back in her chair, crossing her arms. "What do *you* think? You seem to have a definite opinion on the subject."

Haley lowered her gaze and bit her bottom lip. She was ashamed of her train of thought.

"Come on," Alice encouraged. "Spit it out."

Haley scrunched her face. "Promise you won't judge me?"

"Why would I?"

"What I am about to say is horrible, and you might think I'm a presumptuous bitch."

Alice smiled reassuringly. "I'm sure I won't."

"Okay." Haley inhaled, and prepared to say the unsayable all in one breath without pausing. "I think David is sleeping with Madison only because he wants to mess with me to make me jealous. I'm not saying Madison is not likable or anything; she's absolutely likable. I just don't think *he* likes her. Am I the most arrogant person in the world and the worst friend ever for thinking that?"

Alice shook her head. "No. Unfortunately, I agree with you. I don't like David. Something about him is off, and he's taking advantage of Madison. But I'm not sure why."

"Do we tell her?"

"NO!" Alice shouted. "Never. You can never say anything about it to Madison."

Haley had not expected a reaction so strong. "Whoa, relax. Why can't we talk to her?"

"I'm sorry for yelling at you," Alice apologized. "It's just that Madison is already so insecure around guys. We can't put more doubts in her head. She looked so happy this morning."

Haley felt like gagging. "I'm glad I didn't see that." David's behavior was literally making her stomach ache. "So what do we do? We tell the guys to do an intervention on his side?"

"Why?" Alice asked skeptically. "You think he would listen?"

"No, probably not."

"And I wouldn't put it past him to tell Madison."

"You're right…" Haley suppressed a frustrated scream. "We can't sit here and watch him play with Madison's heart. So?"

"I'm sorry, but that's exactly what we do: *nothing*."

"Nothing? How can—"

"Haley," Alice interrupted. "I know you're worried. I am, too. But if we try to do something, anything at all, we'd be playing his game. He'd use it to hurt Madison or you, try to get between you two. Ignore David long enough and you'll be calling his bluff."

"I hate sitting here doing nothing!"

"I know." Alice reached across the table to grab her hand. "But it's the right thing to do."

"I hate him." Haley squeezed her friend's hand. "I was giving him the benefit of the doubt, but now…" She shook her head. "I hate him."

"It's hard to think he's Scott's brother."

"Yeah, right? Now Hawaii makes a lot more sense. Imagine having to put up with him your entire life."

"Poor Scott," Alice agreed.

"Let's talk about something else." Haley let go of Alice's hand to pull one foot up on the chair and hug a knee to her chest. "Is everything all right with you and Peter? You've seemed off lately."

A dark shadow crossed Alice's face. "Wrong topic."

"Okay. So what was up with Jack last night? He was flirting with all breathing things."

Alice's cheeks heated up. "Even more wrong topic."

"Why? You're not still into him, are you?"

Alice stared her down. "Haley, I love you, but this is your third strike."

"But you've been with Peter for how many months now—?"

"I'm not talking about it, so drop it," Alice hissed. Then, regaining her cool, she added, "Can we talk about something not boy-related?"

The two of them stared at each other blankly.

Alice cracked first, bursting out laughing. "Look at us," she chuckled. "We're two promising, bright Harvard students and all we can talk about is guys."

"If you want, we can discuss the latest Kardashian drama," Haley said genially.

Alice scowled at her, still smirking. "I'd rather not. How about we just do our homework?"

"Fine!"

Haley pushed her chair back and went to retrieve her laptop, ready to spend the rest of the day brooding.

Alice

Haley's mood did not improve over the next few weeks. Alice kept catching her walk around the house with pursed lips and a morose frown. Madison was at the opposite end of the emotional spectrum. She waltzed through the apartment with a happy, distracted air.

Alice was torn. She was happy Madison was taking a break from her heartache over Scott and Haley. But her dating David was an awful idea. To discuss the issue with Haley was out of the question. Her other roommate wasn't aware of the full extent of the problem. Haley kept insisting on an intervention whenever the subject came up, which was a no-no. Only two other people knew everyone involved: Peter and Jack. Alice had to open up with one of them or she would go mad. But which one?

Alice stared at the ceiling of her room, trying to ignore her inner voice which screamed for her to confide in Jack. It was getting harder every day. Her relationship with Peter had been deteriorating ever since spring break. On the outside, everything seemed fine. Deep down, the excitement had worn off and their differences were becoming too evident to be set aside much longer.

A sudden bang made Alice jolt in her bed, and Blue went running under the bed, squealing in terror. Alice hopped off and tiptoed to her door to check out what was going on outside. Madison and David were standing in the entrance hall kissing.

Alice cleared her throat. "What's going on?"

Madison broke the kiss and David answered, "Darling Haley seems to be in a mood." He looked smug and self-satisfied.

Alice narrowed her eyes at him. "I wonder why."

David shrugged innocently.

Madison threw her a questioning look. "Is something wrong with

Haley?”

"No," Alice lied. "Have fun, guys. I'll see you later." She disappeared back into her room before Madison could ask more questions.

***

"Can we go somewhere private to talk?" Alice asked Jack as they exited their last lecture the next day.

His mouth gaped open before he asked, "Am I in trouble?"

"No." Alice smiled. "Not you."

"Where do you want to go?"

"Somewhere no one can overhear us."

"Secret stuff, huh?" Jack grinned. "How about the Chem Lab?"

"We're not allowed in there."

"Neither is anyone else; it's the perfect place for secret meetings."

"All right, but if we get caught and kicked out of school, you get to explain it to my dad. Deal?"

"Deal."

They walked down the hall furtively and waited for the hall to be empty before sneaking inside the lab. Alice sat on the teacher's desk and Jack stood before her with an expectant frown. Glass beakers, vials, and jars of powdered ingredients surrounded them.

"It's Madison," Alice said, and for just a second, she could've sworn Jack paled. "She's sleeping with David."

Jack raked his hand through his hair. *Was that relief on his face?*

"I assume that's bad news?" he asked.

Alice drummed her heels on the desk's wooden panel. "What do you think?"

"David's on the team, but we don't hang much. He's a loner."

"Exactly my point."

"Yeah, but you haven't dragged me to a secret meeting just to tell me this, right?"

"No, there's more," Alice admitted. "But you have to promise you won't tell anyone. Deal?"

Jack made the Boy Scout salute. "Deal."

"Madison is secretly in love with Scott."

"David's brother?"

"Yeah, Haley's boyfriend, too," Alice clarified. "Haley doesn't

221

know, and she can't find out."

"Okay."

"But we think—Haley and I, that is—that David is only using Madison to screw with Scott and Haley."

Jack scratched his head. "And you concluded this how?"

"David tried to make a pass at Haley several times; it seems too much of a coincidence for him to date our roommate next."

Jack was not convinced. "Why would he do it?"

"To make Haley jealous."

"That would work only if Haley... I mean, is she? Jealous?"

"She won't admit it, but I think she is a little." Alice nodded. "David has a unique way of getting under Haley's skin."

"So his diabolical plan is working." Jack let out a mocking evil laugh.

Despite the seriousness of the discussion, Alice chuckled. "Yeah, Haley is brooding half the time. But Madison is the real problem." Alice's cheeks heated with worry. "She's so insecure around guys, and she's only ever dated d-bags. You know, the type who only use her for cheap one-night stands. Madison can't know David is using her, too. And if he breaks her heart..."

Jack looked away as if he was embarrassed. Was he self-conscious about treating women poorly? *He should be.*

"Is this too much girl talk for you?" Alice asked.

"No." He met her eyes again, still wary. "But I don't see what your point is."

"I need advice." Alice groaned. "What would you do in my place? If Haley and Madison were your friends."

Jack thought a while. "Honestly? Nothing," he said.

Alice breathed in relief at Jack coming to the same conclusion she had.

"If David only wants to make Haley jealous," Jack continued, "and she does nothing, this little act will become boring for him in no time. The best advice I can give you is to tell Haley to act as happy as she can around David, instead of letting him know she's pissed off."

"Yeah, you're right. I'll do exactly that." Alice hopped off the desk. "Thanks for listening."

Jack pulled her into a hug. She wished she never had to let him go.

***

Back home, Alice tapped on Haley's door and slipped inside without waiting for permission.

"Can I talk to you?" she whispered.

"Why are we whispering?" Haley used the same hushed tones.

"Because I don't want Madison to overhear us."

Haley beckoned her to the bed where she was already under the covers with her laptop on her knees. "What's up?" she asked.

"David."

"What did he do?" Haley hissed, making room for Alice on the bed.

"Nothing." Alice paused. "Nothing new, I mean."

"So?"

"It's you."

Haley mouthed, "Me?"

"Yeah, you," Alice confirmed. "You can't glower at him every time you see him around the house."

"But—"

"And you can't disappear into your room and slam the door when you catch them kissing, either."

Haley pouted.

"I know you're mad." Alice squeezed her friend's knee. "But right now you're right where he wants you, and David knows it."

Haley chewed her lower lip. "So what do I do?"

"When you see them, smile, be pleasant… act as if you don't care…"

"But I do care."

"Which is why you have to do this."

"You're right. I've been an ass." Haley pursed her lips in a determined expression. "I'll fake-please the shit out of him."

"That's my girl talking." Alice stared at her watch. "Gosh, it's late." She yawned. "I said my piece, I'll go."

Haley pulled her into a hug. "Thank you for the tough love."

"You're welcome." Alice got up. "Night."

"Night."

Alice sneaked out of Haley's room as silently as she had walked in and tiptoed across the hall. She headed to her room, but changed her mind mid-course and paused in front of Madison's door. *Hell, in for a penny, in for a pound.* It was time for a second pep talk.

Again, Alice gave a soft knock and slunk in, uninvited.

"Hey, do you have a minute?" she whispered.

Madison closed a book and looked up at her. "Why are you whispering?"

Alice made her way to the bed. "I don't want Haley to overhear us." *Deja vù, anyone?*

Madison frowned. "I have a feeling I won't like the next thing that's going to come out of your mouth. What is it?"

Alice decided to cut straight to the chase. "Scott. Why are you dating his brother?"

"Why not?"

"Isn't it weird that one minute you like Scott, and the next you're dating within the same gene pool?"

"Scott is with Haley," Madison replied, annoyed.

"Yeah, for now."

"Are you suggesting I should save myself for Scott in case one day they break up?" Madison sounded bitter.

"That's not what I meant."

"What, then?"

"I'm just saying that, considering your feelings for Scott, it could be a bad idea to date his brother." *His bastard of a brother, more accurately.*

"I don't have feelings for Scott."

Okay, Madison was in full-blown denial.

Alice crossed her arms and arched an eyebrow at her friend.

Madison dropped the book she'd been reading on the nightstand and leaned forward on the bed, reaching for Alice's hands. "Listen, I had a silly crush on Scott, but that's over." Alice wasn't convinced but let Madison finish, anyway. "Before Haley introduced us, we hadn't spoken once. He was the cute guy in my class I liked to look at and fantasize about."

"So it was never something serious?" Alice asked, still skeptical.

"Just a fantasy."

"And David? Are you guys serious?"

"It's early days." Madison smiled, and Alice had to master all her self-control not to flinch. "I don't know what's going to happen."

"Please be careful, okay?"

"Why?"

Alice shrugged. "Scott seems like a good guy, and he hates his brother."

"Does that make David a villain?"

"No, it just puts him on my watch-list."

"You're so scary," Madison joked.

Alice lifted her hands, scrunched her face, and let out a terrifying zombie growl.

Madison chuckled.

Alice patted the bed. "I'll let you get back to your book." She made to get up, but Madison pulled her back onto the bed.

"Wait a second," Madison said. "Now it's time for pep talk number two."

Three, actually. Alice was surprised, so she asked, "What did I do?"

"What's going on with you and Peter?"

Alice groaned. "It's too late to have this conversation."

It was Madison's turn to arch an eyebrow.

"Okay," Alice said. "What do you want to know?"

"Are you in love with your boyfriend?"

Alice didn't have to think for a second. "No."

"Then what are you doing with him?"

"It helps with other things…"

Madison did not relent. "Like pretending you have no feelings for Jack?"

Alice ignored the question. "I should've never come into your room."

"Too late for that."

"What do you want me to say?"

Madison leaned back against the headboard. "I don't want you to say anything. Just listen for once."

"Go ahead." Alice rolled her eyes. "Say your piece."

"I'm not touching the Jack topic for now," Madison started.

"Thank you for your clemency," Alice said in a worshipping voice. "Oh, sage roommate."

Madison ignored the jibe. "So, Peter. When you started going out with him, he made you happy. Everyone could tell. But lately…"

"Is it so obvious?"

"For people that know you? Yes." Madison confirmed the fears that had been gnawing at Alice's side since spring break. "What happened?"

"In the beginning, it was new and exciting." Alice stared blankly into the past before concentrating on Madison's worried eyes. "Lately, I'm realizing how different we are. I mean, spring break was a nightmare. We're so different. We only work..." Alice blushed. "Physically. Everything else feels off."

"Why are you still with him, then?" Madison pinned her with a stare. "Were you hoping the school year would end and you wouldn't have to break up with Peter because he would just move away?"

Nailed it. "Is that bad?"

"Duh!" Madison made a silly face. "It's always better to have a clean cut."

Alice shook her head. "I came here to dispense my wisdom, and you kicked me in the butt instead." She pouted. "Now I'm going to go mope alone in my room." Alice stood up and Madison didn't stop her this time.

She laughed. "You do that."

Alice waved goodbye. "Night."

"Night."

Alice returned to her room and collapsed on her bed with a heavy sigh. Talk about food for thought—between her roommates' love lives and her own, she had enough thinking material for ages.

***

Alice stared in the mirror. A plain white t-shirt, a pair of light-wash jeans, and white sneakers seemed like an appropriate breakup outfit. Lectures were over and, with Peter's graduation looming over them, Alice wanted to end their story before finals week. Peter had been a whirlwind of excitement in her life, but their relationship wasn't forever and ever. It had never been.

In the past month and a half, Alice had kept appearances up. It had been easier to pretend everything was fine than to face up to her real feelings. Now it was time to grab the Chicago Bull by the horns. It was only a matter of time before he moved to Illinois, anyway; his agent had been super positive about the Bulls making an offer. There was no point in staying together. It was only a matter of who said it first.

Now that she thought about it, this would be the first time Alice was doing the dumping. In all her previous relationships, even when she'd known things weren't going well, she'd always allowed the other person to call the shots. Not this time. Strangely, the prospect of being single didn't make her feel insecure. Alice wasn't scared of being alone anymore. Was this what growing up meant?

She knew calling it off with Peter was the right thing to do. That fact didn't help her lack of experience in breaking the news, however. She'd done an extensive Google search on the dos and don'ts of the process. After being on the receiving end so many times, Alice should've been much more of an expert, but right now her mind felt blank. Honestly, there had never been a breakup modus operandi that had made her feel better about what was happening. She did a mental recap of the Internet's advice all the same. The main dos were to tell him before anyone else (Madison didn't count), to be one-hundred percent sure and honest—but not brutal—and to do it in person. She had that covered. The don'ts included not using empty clichés, not asking for a "break," and, apparently, public spaces were a huge no-no. That's why Alice had asked Peter if she could drop by his house later, *yes,* and if his roommate was going to be there, *no.*

Peter opened the door to his house with a smile so dashing, a little something fluttered in Alice's belly. A million doubts immediately attacked her brain, and she tried to chase them away. A strong physical attraction wasn't enough to stay with a guy.

"Hey." He pulled her into a crushing hug.

"Hey, yourself."

Peter let her inside the house, whistling a happy tune.

"You're in a good mood?" Alice asked guiltily; she was about to ruin that for him.

"Oh, baby, you've no idea. I just got *the* call." He stared at the ceiling. "I'm in."

Alice could tell his mind was a million miles away.

"In…?"

"The NBA." He cupped her face and stamped a kiss on her lips. "A two-year contract."

"That's great." *And also the perfect excuse.* "Where, Chicago?"

Peter did a stupid, hip-hop victory dance. "Yep."

"Amazing." Alice's smile tensed. This was the perfect moment to tell him.

"What's up, baby? You look so serious."

Alice sat on the couch. "Can we talk for a minute?"

Peter looked at her warily. "All right." He sat next to her.

"This year with you has been… the most exciting of my life, and I'm glad I've gotten to know you…"

Peter's face darkened. "But?"

"But you're moving to Chicago. You'll have this electrifying new life and I'm super happy for you, I am, but I'm staying here. You'll be traveling a lot, meeting so many people. I'm not going to fit in that life, and I guess we've always known this—us—wasn't forever."

Peter remained silent for a second, then said, "Be honest, Alice. We'd be having this conversation even if Chicago wasn't in the picture, right?"

"True," Alice admitted. Peter was so sharp sometimes. "Listen." The next part was the hard one. "I love spending time with you, and we have a great chemistry, but…" She paused. "I'm not in love with you. And you aren't with me, either, are you?"

The L-word had not made an appearance in the six months they'd dated.

"I'm not sure." Peter looked crestfallen. "You're the first girl I really liked."

"That's because I'm super awesome," Alice tried to joke, but she felt choked. Saying goodbye wasn't easy, no matter how sure she was. "If you were in love with me, you'd be sure. It isn't something you can half-feel."

"I've never been in love, so I wouldn't know. Have you?"

Yes, with Jack. I still am. Alice blushed. "Only once, and it sucked." *It still sucks.*

"*This* sucks," Peter complained. "I didn't think we would say goodbye today."

"But you knew we would, eventually?"

"Yes, I guess I did." Peter opened his arms. "Come here." He pulled her onto his lap, and she nestled her chin on his shoulder. "I know you're right, baby," he said, stroking her hair. "It's just that I'll miss you."

"Me too." Alice sniffed. "But it's not like we're breaking up because we hate each other. We can always keep in touch." She pulled back to look at him.

He seemed to consider but shook his head. "Nah, we both know it wouldn't work."

"No, probably not. I have no past experiences to relate to. You're the first ex I'd like to keep in touch with." Alice fought back tears. "But you'll be too busy fending off cheerleaders and fans, anyway."

Peter's eyes were so blue, and his face so gorgeous. He wasn't making this easy on her.

"Can't we keep seeing each other until we're both in Boston?" he asked.

For a moment, Alice was tempted to say yes. What difference would a month make? But it'd only be a slower death—what was the point?

"I couldn't stand it." She shook her head. "It'd be like going around with a stick of dynamite and a ticking clock attached to our backs. It'd be horrible."

"You're right. A clean cut is best." Peter stood up, scooping her into his arms and carrying her with him. "But don't think for a minute I won't see to you one last time."

Alice giggled and let him take her to his room. Ah well, give it to Peter to know how to say goodbye in style. *Best. Breakup. Ever.*

***

The school year was over. Finals were over. After exiting their last exam, Alice and Jack strolled around campus enjoying the warm mid-May sun on their faces. As they headed across Cambridge Common Park, Alice recognized Rose and Tyler talking on a bench nearby. They were immersed in conversation, both their faces dead serious. Should she text Georgiana?

Alice decided to mind her own business. She grabbed Jack's arm to pull him back. "Do you mind if we go the other way?"

Jack cut her a surprised look. "No, why?"

"No reason."

Jack looked unconvinced but didn't press her, so they headed in the opposite direction toward Harvard Yard. They wandered around aimlessly for a while, mostly in silence, until they stopped for a Frappuccino. Jack walked in to get their drinks and Alice waited at a table outside. It took him only five minutes to order and join her.

Alice studied him. He'd been fidgeting in a nervous way all day, and it wasn't like him to stare into space as he was doing now. Maybe before an exam, when he was mentally studying, but definitely not after. He was acting as if he was rehearsing a speech in his head.

229

"Something on your mind?" Alice asked.

Jack's eyes flickered to her face, troubled, before he looked ahead and spoke, "Ice, I know you're with Peter and I shouldn't say anything—"

"We broke up."

His face whipped toward hers so fast she was afraid his neck would snap. "Really? When?"

"Two weeks ago."

"That long." Jack seemed hurt she hadn't told him.

"He didn't tell you?"

"With the season over we don't hang out that much." Jack shrugged. "How did it…? I thought you…"

"Loved him?" Alice finished the phrase for him. "No. Peter is fun, but I don't love him. There's only so far you can go in a relationship if you don't love someone. We lacked the spark."

"So it wasn't because of the NBA? Matt told me about the Bulls."

Alice smiled mischievously. "Actually, that gave me the perfect excuse to break up. The long distance scenario, and how it would've never worked."

Jack blinked. "You mean *you* broke up with him?"

"Yeah. Don't look that surprised. And don't worry, he wasn't too heartbroken or anything." Alice paused, gathering the courage to ask, "What about you? Any new girl on the horizon?"

"No, no one. I haven't found my spark either."

Jack looked at Alice as if there was more he wanted to say.

"Well, it must be hard." She chuckled awkwardly. "My roommates and I are probably the only three girls on campus you haven't slept with."

Why did she always have to blab stupid things when she was nervous?

Jack's neck flushed scarlet and his jaw tensed. "Right."

Alice frowned. "Why did you blush just now?"

"I didn't." He flashed her a dismissive grimace.

"Yes, you did. I told you my roommates and I are the only three people on campus you haven't had sex with, and your neck turned fifty shades of red."

Jack lowered his gaze to the floor. He looked guilty, like someone who'd been caught. But caught at what?

"Oh gosh," Alice gasped, bringing a hand to her mouth, realization washing over her. No, it couldn't be true! She felt tears welling in her eyes and she, too, stared at the floor. "Haley or Madison?" she whispered.

"It was nothing."

"Haley. Or. Madison?" Alice repeated through gritted teeth, keeping her gaze trained on her sneakers.

"Madison."

A blade cut through Alice's heart. "When?"

"It was a one night stand at the beginning of freshman year; she wasn't your roommate then, and I didn't know you knew each other."

Alice did a mental timeline of her friendship with Madison. They'd met as pledges at Kappa Kappa Gamma. But they hadn't become close friends until toward the end of freshman year when they'd moved in together. Alice hadn't told Madison about her crush on Jack until several months later. *Still.* At one point Madison must have realized.

Fighting back the tears, Alice said, "And the two of you just happened to both forget to tell me you'd slept together?" Alice waited for a sob to die in her throat before she continued. "What did you have, a secret meeting agreeing not to say anything?"

"No, you know I would never—"

Alice glared at him, not caring that her eyes were probably bloodshot by now. "No, Jack, at this point I don't know."

He paled and whispered, "I think we both decided it wasn't worth discussing."

"Mmm, usually people keep secrets about things that matter." Anger was mounting inside Alice. "Not the other way around."

"Well, it didn't… matter. It wasn't that big of a deal."

"Sure. Nothing is ever a big deal with you."

"What's that supposed to mean?"

Jack's embarrassed face in the Chem Lab flashed before her eyes. "When we spoke in the Chem Lab, that's why you were so weird. I told you guys only ever used Madison for sex, and you were one of those guys." Alice wanted to gag. "And you said nothing!"

"What was I supposed to say? Yeah, I had sex with Madison once. So? Why are we arguing about Madison?" He slapped one hand on the table. "It was ages ago, and it meant nothing. Why are you so mad?"

"You still don't know, do you?" Alice turned her face away. "She's my best friend and you… you…"

"What?"

Alice couldn't keep her feelings bottled up inside any longer. She stared into his dark eyes and spilled it all out. "I'm in love with you, Jack. I have been since freshman year. I had to watch you go through girl after girl, and I hated every single one of them because I was jealous. I spent years hoping one day you'd notice me, or realize I wasn't just a good friend to talk to whenever you didn't have a date or someone to screw."

"Alice, I didn't know," Jack said pleadingly.

"Oh, I know *you* didn't know. But guess who did know?" People around them were staring, but Alice didn't care. "Try and guess one of the two people I confided in. Yeah, *Madison*. And all this time she never told me she had sex with you, and just by chance you never told me either." Alice stared at the sky, blinking. Gravity wasn't helping in keeping the tears in. Still looking up, she added, "I'm an idiot, but I'm not that stupid. I've probably been a running joke between the two of you this entire time."

Alice pushed her chair backward, making an angry scraping sound, and walked away as the first tears rolled down her cheeks.

Jack ran after her. "Alice." He grabbed her by the shoulders and forced her to turn. "I've been the idiot this entire time. You're the most wonderful person I know, and I should've realized a long time ago we weren't just friends." For an instant, the snake of Alice's hope lifted its head, ready to destroy all her rational thoughts as she waited for Jack to tell her that he felt the same, that he loved her. Instead, he added, "Madison was nothing."

Just like that, a mental image of her best friend naked in bed with Jack appeared before her eyes, and Alice couldn't take it. It made her so jealous her blood sizzled. Her stomach churned, and suddenly, she was scared she might throw up.

"Nothing, huh?" she hissed, shoving Jack away.

He kept hold of her arm. "Ice, please."

"Let me go," Alice screamed, yanking her arm free. She turned on her heel and ran away, tears flying behind her in the wind and heavy sobs shaking her entire body.

Madison

Madison was home alone. She was lounging on her twin bed reading a paper for class when a loud pounding on the apartment door startled her. The insistent sound of fists meeting with wood told her the noise wouldn't stop until whoever was out there was let in. And to have all that intensity, it had to be a male someone. She left her unfinished paper on the bed and went to open the door.

"Jack!" Madison was taken aback.

She barely had time to take in his crazed expression before Jack burst past her into the house, yelling, "Is she here?"

"Who? Alice?" Madison closed the door behind him. "I thought she was with you."

"She was."

Jack searched the apartment with his eyes as if he expected Alice to jump up from behind the couch and yell, "Surprise!"

Madison touched him gently on the back. "Jack, she isn't here."

Jack clenched his fists. "I need to find her!"

"What happened?"

Jack turned to face her. "She knows."

"Knows?" Madison frowned. "Knows what?"

"About us."

Madison suppressed a groan; she was scared and relieved all at once. The squashing weight of the secret was finally gone, but now the consequences of the truth were about to come back and bite her. Since the day Alice had pointed out her tall, brown-haired classmate as her crush, Madison had felt a gut-wrenching guilt. Every time Alice spoke about Jack, a stone settled in the pit of her stomach. Madison knew she should've told Alice she'd had sex with Jack the moment she'd recognized him, but she hadn't. She'd panicked instead. And after that first encounter, the more Madison kept quiet, the harder it became to talk. The fear of Alice shunning her, and of Haley choosing Alice over her, had been too much. For the first time in her life, Madison had met two girls she adored who wanted to be her friends. She didn't want Alice to hate her for something that had meant nothing, so she'd kept the secret. And so far, so had Jack.

Madison narrowed her eyes at him. "Why did you tell her?"

Jack raked a hand through his hair, his face tormented. "I didn't. It sort of… came out."

"How?" Madison hissed. How could something this big "sort of" come out?

Jack flinched. "She told me you three were the only girls on campus I hadn't slept with. When I didn't laugh along with her joke, she guessed the truth. It was one thing to not tell her, but when she asked me, I couldn't lie to her face."

"Oh." Madison covered her forehead with her hands. "Now she's going to hate me."

"Not as much as she hates me," Jack countered.

Madison didn't want to play the who-will-Alice-hate-more game. Jack had no idea why Alice was so upset. "You don't understand," Madison said.

"I do. She told me everything."

Madison doubted it. "Oh, really?"

"Yeah, really," Jack sneered. "She told me she's had feelings for me from the moment we met, and that she only ever told you and Haley. She said now it all felt like a bad joke. That we were having a laugh behind her back, or something."

It was worse than Madison thought. "Oh, no."

"I tried to tell her what happened with us meant nothing." Jack raised his hands defensively. "No offense."

Madison was well past the point of being stung by this comment. Their night together had meant nothing to her, either. Alice needed to understand that. As her mind raced to find ways to make Alice see the truth, Jack's last words penetrated her worried haze. Madison studied him. "Alice told you she was in love with you, and all you said was our night together was meaningless?"

"I didn't have time to tell her much else before she ran away. Any idea where she could be?"

"Maybe." Madison started pacing the room, thinking aloud. "There are a couple of places she could've gone to cool her head."

"Come on, give me directions so I can get going."

"No." Madison stepped back. "I need to explain everything to her first. Alice needs to be ready to listen to whatever you have to say."

"Madison." Jack's tone was low and his jaw tense. "I should speak to her first."

"Why? Because you did such a great job in the last conversation?"

"I don't need your permission," he snapped.

"No, but you need hers."

"Damn it!" Jack turned and punched the closest wall.

Madison jumped back, staring wide-eyed at the small dent Jack's fist had left in the drywall.

He wasn't moving now. He had his arms braced on the wall next to the dent, his shoulders heaving with forced breaths, and his head dropping low.

"Jack," Madison said. "Alice will need time before she's ready to talk to you."

He turned bloodshot eyes on her. "And what's different about you?"

"It's not the same."

"Why?"

"Because she isn't in love with me!"

Jack's jaw sagged. He closed and opened his mouth twice to retort, but nothing came out.

"You'd better go." Madison opened the apartment door and pushed a shocked-into-silence Jack out. "I'll ask Alice to call you, but you need to give her some space."

Jack didn't speak. With a dejected air, he turned on his heel and jogged down the hall. He would probably keep searching for Alice, but that wasn't Madison's concern right now. She shut the door and started pacing again. *What next?* She needed to find Alice and explain.

A minute later the door opened again and Haley shuffled into the house.

"Was that Jack I met in the hall?" Haley removed her jacket and hung it in the closet. "What was he doing here?"

Madison didn't answer. What would Haley think of her?

Haley gasped. "Is that a hole in my wall?"

A sob escaped Madison's lips.

"Mad, are you okay?" Haley dashed toward her. "Are you crying?"

Madison couldn't keep it together any longer; she hugged Haley and started crying. "It's bad, Haley, so bad," Madison wailed. "She will never forgive me."

"Who? Who has to forgive you, and why?" Haley pushed back to look at her. "Please sit down and tell me everything." Madison let Haley drag her to the couch. "What's going on?" Haley demanded.

Madison looked up at her friend and made her confession. "I slept with Jack."

"What?" Haley let go of her hands as if she was infected. "Now? *How could you?*"

"No, not now." Madison dropped her head into her hands. "Years ago, when we were freshmen. I didn't know you or Alice back then. I had no idea she liked him. But I never told her."

"Okay." Haley seemed to calm down. "Not as bad. So what was Jack doing here?"

"He told Alice." Madison straightened up and sobbed out the rest. "Apparently, Alice snapped and told him she was in love with him, that it was all a bad joke because I was one of the two people who knew and I never said anything."

"Mmm, I see why that could be a problem." Haley slumped back on the couch, pressing her palms to her eyes as if that could help her think.

The silence was unnerving. "Do you hate me?" Madison asked.

Haley lowered her hands and straightened up. "Of course not. You made a mistake is all."

"Thank you." Haley's understanding meant the world. "What do I do now?"

"Find Alice and talk to her." Haley made a huffing sound. "Where do we start?"

"I think she's on the roof. She always goes there when she's upset."

"How do you know?"

"I just do."

"See, you're a much better friend than I am."

"I'm sure Alice doesn't feel that way right now." Madison shook her head. "You want to come up with me?"

"Why?" Haley didn't sound keen. "Isn't it better if you talk alone?"

"I need you there to give an impartial, non-emotionally-involved perspective. And just in case she tries to throw me over the railing."

Haley sighed and stood up. "Let's go."

Alice

Alice leaned on the railing of her building's rooftop, staring at the Charles River and the Boston skyline in the distance. She wasn't really taking in the view; her mind was blank. All she could feel was the wind brushing against her face and pushing her tears backward. Mid-Spring and the late afternoon air was still cold in Cambridge.

Alice heard the rooftop's heavy metal door open and close. She didn't turn to look, but she was sure Madison had just walked outside. Her dear friend must have had another behind-her-back chat with Jack.

Still not turning, Alice said, "Go away. I don't want to see you."

"Alice, please, just hear me out," Madison pleaded.

Alice turned to face her ex-best friend and was surprised to find Haley standing beside Madison. She directed her fury at Haley first. "Did you know?"

Haley paled at the harshness of her tone. "No, I didn't. I swear."

Alice relaxed a little; at least she had *one* loyal friend who hadn't lied to her every day for the past two years. Haley approached her, and they hugged.

"I think you should hear Mad out," Haley whispered in her ear.

Alice pushed Haley back. "I don't care what she has to say."

"Alice, it meant nothing," Madison said.

"If I hear anybody else saying it meant nothing, I'm going to scream. People don't hide meaningless things; they hide the important stuff."

"But it wasn't important."

Alice narrowed her eyes. "So why keep it a secret?"

"I was scared you wouldn't want to be my friend any longer." Madison looked haggard: her face was red, blotchy, and covered in tears. The wind blowing against her made her appearance all the more tragic by giving her a halo of golden locks. But Alice wasn't about to be mollified by the act. "You'd just told me how deeply in love you were with Jack, and I didn't know what to do. I panicked. And after I didn't say anything that first time, it became harder and harder to tell you."

Excuses. These were all empty excuses. "Well, guess what? Now we're no longer friends. So there you go. Good job."

"Please don't say that." Madison sounded desperate.

"Alice," Haley said soothingly. "Maybe you should try to calm down."

"Why? She's a liar. She lied to you too, you know."

"To me?" Haley took a surprised step backward. "About what?"

"Alice, don't," Madison whimpered.

"She'll be after your boyfriend next." Alice knew she was being mean, but right now all she wanted was to hurt Madison as much as she'd hurt her.

"Scott?" Haley asked, moving her gaze back and forth from Alice to Madison. "What about Scott?"

"She likes him," Alice said.

Haley set her gaze on Madison. "Do you?"

"Yeah, I do. I did." Madison was becoming frantic. She was crying so hard she had trouble speaking. "But I would never try anything with your boyfriend, you have to know that. She's just being mean right now."

"How long have you liked him?" Haley asked. She didn't sound as mad as Alice had hoped.

"Forever," Madison confessed. "I told you he was in my English classes."

"So why didn't you say anything?"

"Because it doesn't matter!" Madison screamed. "It never matters. Scott doesn't want me. He never even noticed me before you started dating him. Guys never like me; they always like *you* or *you*." Madison pointed at them each in turn. "Never me. So what was the point?"

"The point is being honest with your friends!" Alice yelled back.

Madison ignored Alice. "Haley, I never tried anything with Scott, and I never would. I'm with David."

Alice scoffed. "Yeah, about David—"

"Alice, shut up!" Haley froze her with a stare.

Alice's heart skipped a beat; she'd almost delivered a blow she would've never been able to take back. But Madison wasn't stupid, and the withering look on Haley's face was too much of a giveaway.

"David what?" Madison asked.

Alice shrugged. "Nothing." She looked away, ashamed for what she'd almost said.

Haley kept silent.

"Who's keeping secrets now?" Madison asked.

No one replied.

"Fine!" Madison shouted. "You want to hate me for something that happened before I even knew you? Go ahead. Take the moral high ground because both of you are always so perfect. I'm out of here." Madison ran back to the door and disappeared down the stairs.

"That went well," Haley said, slapping her hands on the sides of her thighs. "Does she really like Scott? She told you?"

"She didn't have to, Haley." Alice rolled her eyes. "To anyone looking, it was pretty obvious from the first basketball game we watched."

Haley shook her head. "I never knew."

"I know. Subtle intuition isn't really your thing."

Alice walked back to the railing, and Haley followed her. "Is that a nice way to say I have my head stuck too high up my rear end?"

Alice chuckled coldly. "Let's say you're not the most observant person."

"Is that why she's sleeping with David?" Haley groaned. "That makes it even worse."

"I've no idea how her mind works. Believe me, I don't."

Haley kept quiet for a minute before saying, "Alice, what you were about to say—"

Alice didn't let her finish. "You don't have to tell me. Thank you for stopping me. I'm so mad, and I just wanted to hurt her…"

Haley sighed. "I get that she wasn't one-hundred percent honest, but—"

"It's Jack, Haley. Madison had sex with him." Alice kept imagining them together.

"Is the problem that she slept with him, or that she didn't tell you?"

"Both." Alice focused on the glistening water of the distant river, trying to let her eyes see only what was in front of her and not what her mind kept picturing. "I can't stand to look at her."

"Can you really blame her for not coming clean before?"

Alice turned to face Haley. "Why are you on her side?"

"I'm not," Haley hurried to say. "But can't you see she had a reason to be scared to tell you? Alice, your gut reaction is to hate her, and it would've been the same two years ago. Only now, you have a solid friendship that can take the hit. You didn't back then." Haley paused, most likely to give Alice time to process what she'd just said. "Can you honestly tell me it wouldn't have changed anything? She made a mistake because she was scared to lose you. Can't you forgive her?"

Alice shook her head. Madison was only half the coin of her emotional turmoil.

"What is it, Alice?" Haley insisted.

"I told him I loved him." Alice couldn't even say his name. "There's no taking it back this time."

"And how did he react? Did he say anything?"

"I can't remember." Alice wiped a tear from her cheek. "Something about Madison not being important. I'll have to change schools. I can't go here and see him every day for the next school year."

"That's a bit melodramatic." Haley waved a hand dismissively. "And finals are over, so you don't have to see Jack for the entire summer if you don't want to. But you can't ignore Madison."

"Aren't you mad at her?" Alice asked.

"About Scott? Why would I be?"

"Why wouldn't you?" Alice insisted.

"Can't you see that not telling me she liked Scott was the most selfless thing to do?"

"How?"

"She could've called dibs on Scott," Haley explained. "But instead of having the 'I will have him or no one will' attitude, she let me date him. And I think she didn't want me to know about her feelings for him so that I wouldn't feel guilty about being with him."

"You make her sound like a saint," Alice said, resentful.

"What do you think was her motive? And why didn't *you* tell me?"

Alice had no other explanation for Haley's first question, so she ignored it and answered the second one. "It wasn't my secret to tell."

Haley crossed her arms and stared her down. "So there are secrets it's okay to keep, and others that are not?"

Alice hated when Haley was right. "I hate your cold logic."

"Do you hate Madison too?"

"No, not really," Alice admitted.

"Then you should let her off the hook." Haley walked away and beckoned Alice to follow. "Let's go downstairs so we can all talk without freezing our asses off."

***

When they entered Madison's room, it looked as if her wardrobe had vomited all her clothes on her bed. She had two suitcases open on the floor and she was scurrying between them and the bed, throwing in things at random.

Alice kept closer to the threshold, but Haley barged in, asking, "What are you doing?"

"I'm moving out," Madison said while she walked up and down, hauling clothes. "I'll stay at my parents' house, be out of your hair for good."

"Madison, stop!" Haley placed herself between the bed and the suitcases. "We don't want you to go."

Madison stopped and looked at Haley. "Aren't you mad at me?"

"No, of course not."

Madison popped her hip and propped a hand on her waist. "How come you don't care that I used to drool over your boyfriend?"

"For one," Haley said, "I know you never tried anything with him and never would. And I'm glad you allowed me to date him guilt-free."

Madison's lips parted in an astonished O-shape.

Alice followed the exchange, knowing it was her turn to absolve Madison next. As if on cue, Madison peeked at her over Haley's shoulder, her eyes still wide with fear.

"I don't want you to move out either," Alice said.

Madison went limp and collapsed to the floor. She landed in a sort of butterfly yoga pose and started ugly-crying again. "I'm sorry," she kept repeating between sobs. "I'm so sorry…"

She wasn't faking her pain. Something in Alice shifted; she sat on the floor next to her friend and hugged her. "I know," she said, stroking Madison's hair.

They did a Ping-Pong of respective apologies and half-choked sobs until Haley interrupted them. "Enough!" Haley was never one to dwell on sorrow. "This mess is not going to clean itself." She pointed at the cemetery of discarded clothes surrounding them. "Come on, you two." Haley offered them one hand each and pulled them up. "Madison, you take your things out of the suitcases. I'll put them back on hangers, and Alice, you hang them in the closet."

Alice found it helpful to concentrate on a practical task, and even if Madison still avoided catching her eye—they would probably walk on eggshells around each other for a while—Alice knew they'd be okay.

Their friendship was strong and it could recover from this blow.

Yet a suffocating pain still lingered in Alice's chest; the hole there wasn't healing. Making peace with Madison had not been enough. Her heart was still shattered. Her friendship with Jack was over. For the first time in her life, Alice found herself preferring no-Jack to my-friend-Jack, and that, she feared, would not change.

***

As they worked on restoring the wardrobe as a team, Madison's phone started ringing. She dropped the dress she was carrying to take the phone out of her pocket. "It's Vicky, my likable cousin," she said. "I'd better pick up; she never calls unless it's important." Madison swiped a finger on her phone and paced around the room as she talked.

With the chain of work interrupted, they all paused to listen to the phone call.

"Hi, Vicky, what's up?" Madison asked.

Pause.

"Yeah, I'm okay. I had a bit of a rough day." Madison threw an apologetic glance at Alice, and Alice made an effort to smile. She couldn't believe that less than an hour ago she'd been ready to toss her friendship with Madison into the garbage.

"She's *what?* For real? How?" Madison fired questions at the phone. "You're not joking?" She sounded incredulous. "When? So soon? All right, you too. Love you." Madison hung up and turned to Alice. "You're never going to believe this!"

"What?" Alice asked, wary. She'd had enough surprises today.

"Georgiana is pregnant, and she's getting married to Tyler."

Alice was too shocked to speak.

Haley frowned. "Isn't she in grad school?"

"Yeah."

"Were they trying for a baby?" Haley asked, the hint of an accusation in her voice.

Madison smiled. "Vicky wouldn't give me specifics, but I have a suspicion there's more to the story than she let on…"

The possibility of a trick pregnancy was enough to leave Alice, Madison, and Haley gossiping and laughing together, the tension of the morning finally gone.

***

Alice and Madison received the invitations to Georgiana's wedding on the same day. Haley wasn't invited to the wedding as she didn't know Georgiana well; she'd only ever seen her in freshman year at sorority meetings. The letters arrived as all three roommates were chilling in their living room. Madison and Alice opened the heavy cream envelopes while sitting side-by-side on the couch. The wedding would be in two weeks' time.

Madison broke the silence first. "It seems my pregnant cousin is having a shotgun wedding before her bump starts showing."

Since their argument, Madison had been quiet and subdued. But in the last few days, it had gotten worse. Her face had become paler, the bags under her eyes more pronounced. Alice couldn't remember the last time she'd seen Madison smile. Still, she had not asked. They were being perfectly normal with each other, but some sore feelings lingered.

"I still can't believe she's having a baby," Alice said, turning the card in her hands.

Georgiana had called Alice to deliver the happy news right after Madison had spoken with Vicky. Later, Madison had integrated the information with what she'd heard through her family's grape vine. The gossip was that Georgiana had deliberately stopped taking the pill to get herself accidentally-on-purpose pregnant.

"It's a pretty obvious consequence when you go off the pill," Madison said flatly.

"Are you sure that's true?" Alice didn't want to believe her mentor would sink so low to keep a man. Georgiana was smart, beautiful, and, to the outside world, the incarnation of confidence. "You think there's no chance it was one of those rare cases where the pill actually didn't work?"

"What?" Madison snorted. "That famous zero point one percent?"

"It could be," Alice insisted.

"No, it couldn't." Madison shook her head. "Georgiana did it on purpose."

"I agree with Mad here," Haley butted into the conversation, still tapping on her iPad. "The pill not working is the most overused excuse for getting pregnant by *accident*."

"Why would she do that?" Alice asked.

"To force the poor guy to marry her," Madison said.

"Yes, but why?"

Madison shrugged. "Because she wanted to marry him? I don't know."

Alice changed the subject. "So you're going to be a bridesmaid?"

"Unfortunately."

"Isn't it a good thing? Maybe she wants to reconnect with you."

"It's not a good thing, it's family politics," Madison said, sounding sure. "I'm her cousin, so I get a spot on the bridesmaids' roster. Tomorrow I have to go to a bridal shop and stomach Georgiana parading around in white gowns. I'm dreading her choice of bridesmaid outfits."

Alice was surprised. Weddings were Madison's thing; she was a hopeless romantic and loved them. But today, she sounded bitter. Even if this was Georgiana's wedding, why was her friend being so cynical and negative about everything?

"Oh, come on. If there's one thing you can't say about Georgiana, it's that she doesn't have a sense of style," Alice said. "She'd never pick ugly dresses, it'd ruin her ceremony."

"I hope you're right."

"You want to go together that day, or do you have special bridesmaid duties?" Alice asked.

"No. We should go together from here." Madison blushed.

Why the blush? Maybe she wanted to bring a date. Alice checked her invitation; it said plus one. "I mean, if you want to go with David—"

"No!" Madison said, too quickly. "Why would I want to go with him? We're not even dating anymore."

Haley perked up on the couch and, while Madison wasn't looking, they exchanged a completely silent conversation made of shrugs, wide eyes, and mouthed words: *"Did you know?"* … *"No, you?"* … *"No. What do you make of it?"* … *"No idea."* … *"If he hurt her, I'm going to kill him."* … *"I'll help."*

"Mad, are you okay?" Haley asked.

Madison shrugged. "Sure." She turned around with a fake smile plastered on her face. "So, the wedding." Madison's tone was upbeat and her change of subject so abrupt, Haley and Alice exchanged another we'll-get-to-the-bottom-of-this-later look. "I have to be there early to get my hair and makeup done by a professional. My dear cousin doesn't trust my grooming skills. I bet you can get special grooming privileges, too."

"You think?" Alice was skeptical although not about getting free hair and makeup.

"Yes. Unless…" Madison paused.

"What?" Alice asked.

"Are you sure *you* don't want to bring a date to the wedding?"

"One-hundred percent."

"Are you still avoiding Jack?"

"Yes."

"Why?"

"I'm too ashamed." Alice forgot Madison's troubles and concentrated on her own. "I told him I loved him. Worse, I told him that I've been carrying a torch for him since freshman year. I also yelled about being jealous of all his girlfriends. I can't stomach the idea of facing him after all that."

"Is he still calling you every day?" Haley asked. "He's called me only twice this week."

Jack had been harassing Haley—the neutral party in all this—almost as much as he had Alice.

"Yes," Alice confirmed. "Less often, though. We're down to two missed calls per day."

"Don't you want to know what he has to say?" Haley asked.

"Yes and no," Alice confessed.

"Why not?" Madison.

"I can't take what I said to him back this time, Madison. I can't pretend I was acting out because I was on the rebound from Ethan. Saying I love you, I've been in love with you for three years, is pretty final. We can't go back to being friends, it'd kill me. It's goodbye for good this time. I'm not ready."

"What if he has something different to say?" Haley asked.

"Like what? That he's finally realized he loves me, too? This is not a fairytale, and Jack is no Prince Charming."

Alice stood up from the couch and braced her hands on the window frame. Whenever she rehearsed her angry declaration to Jack in her head, her face burned with shame. I'm in love with you… I have been since freshman year… I had to watch you go through girl after girl… I hated every single one… I was jealous… I spent years hoping one day you'd notice me…

The humiliation was too much.

"When he came here searching for you," Madison said cautiously, "he didn't look like a worried friend."

Alice stiffened. She didn't want to discuss Jack with Madison; the wound was still too fresh. "What did he look like, then?" she asked.

"To be honest, like a crazed lover. He punched the wall."

Instinctively, Alice turned to stare at the wall and found her roommates staring, too. "Yeah, right."

"I'm being serious," Madison insisted.

"I saw him, too," Haley said. "He looked desperate."

"Did he say anything specific?"

"No, but—" Madison started.

"No, exactly," Alice snapped. "Can we drop the topic now?"

"What would you like to talk about?" Madison asked. "I've got no love life to complain about."

"So you ended it for good with David?" Haley asked.

"Yes." Madison winced. "Better no love life than a crappy one."

"What—" Haley started.

"I don't want to talk about it," Madison hissed.

"Are we doing a bachelorette?" Alice changed the subject completely. It was clear whatever had happened between Madison and David was still too raw.

"No," Madison said. "Since Georgiana's pregnant, we'll do a bridal/baby shower two-in-one."

"When?" Alice asked.

"Next weekend."

"Okay, so we have the shower next week, and the wedding the week after?"

"Correct," Madison confirmed. "And tomorrow is shopping with Bridezilla, but that's just for *lucky* me."

"What am I going to do alone for two weekends?" Haley asked.

"Want to swap lives?" Madison asked. "What do we need? A shooting star, or something? Find me the star, and I'll make the wish in a heartbeat."

Haley rolled her eyes. "Your family can't be that bad." She turned to Alice for confirmation. "Right?"

Alice took Madison's side. "The Smithsons can be overbearing at times."

"The voice of truth." Madison made a thank-you gesture and sighed. "I hope three weekends in a row with my family won't send me to therapy."

***

The next weekend, Alice followed Madison up the front steps of her aunt and uncle's massive townhouse for the bachelorette/baby shower. Madison stopped on the doorstep, visibly reluctant to go in. Alice stepped forward and rang the bell.

Georgiana opened the door. "Alice! I still can't get over the hair, so fabulous." Georgiana hugged her and then switched her attention to Madison. "Madison," she said with a tight-lipped smile. "You might want to try a blowout sometimes; I hear it does wonders for unruly curls. Come on in, everyone's outside."

Madison rolled her eyes, then took Alice's arm under hers and guided her through the house toward the backyard. Okay, Alice thought, so Georgiana really was a bit bitchy with Madison.

The setting outside was stylish in an overwhelming, pastel-colors way. Pastel decorations, pastel gazebo, pastel food, and pastel-wrapped presents. Pastel pink seemed to be the dominant color.

"Is she having a girl?" Alice asked.

"I think it's too soon to say," Madison said.

"There's a lot of pink here."

"Eh, you know Georgiana." Madison shrugged. "She probably thinks she can influence the sex of the baby by sheer willpower."

Alice looked down at the bright, rainbow-patterned present in her hands. "Let's go drop this off."

They walked toward a table piled with presents, and she deposited hers on top. It clashed so badly with the harmonious pastel theme that Alice immediately removed it from the top and hid it at the back.

"Where's yours?" Alice asked.

"No idea. My mom was in charge of the presents from our side of the family. Probably something expensive," Madison added, her voice tainted by jealousy. "It's not like I'm going to spend my own money on my bitch cousin."

247

"How about your unborn niece?"

"Or nephew," Madison pointed out. "Let's see how he/she turns out first. Hey, why don't we go say hello to my mom?" Madison pointed at a stylish woman in the distance and steered Alice that way.

Alice loved Madison's mom. Of all her friend's relatives, she was the most easygoing and probably the one who'd passed on to Madison her boho style. Alice suspected it had a lot to do with the fact that Madison's mom had not been a Smithson from birth.

"Did you pick the bridesmaid dress?" Alice asked as they walked.

"No, *she* did."

"What color?"

"*Pastel* lavender," Madison said mockingly.

Alice suppressed a laugh. "Is it bad?"

"No, you were right," Madison conceded. "She's too stylish to pick a hideous dress. Hi, Mom…"

They chatted with Madison's mom until Mrs. Smithson was called away to solve a catering problem, and then they headed back to the buffet.

Alice was trying to decide what to eat when Georgiana waltzed over and grabbed a light-blue pastry. "Alice," she said. "Try these azure ones, they're delicious. Madison," Georgiana continued. "You might want to stick to the white pastries, they're sugar-free. You know, in case you're watching your weight."

Alice half-choked on a bite of her "azure" tart. Georgiana definitely was snarky with Madison in a way she'd never seen her be with anyone else.

A loud crash resounded in the background, and they all turned in the direction of the noise. A server had tripped and dropped an entire tray of glasses.

"Those idiots," Georgiana snapped. "Ladies, excuse me; I have to go make sure this party doesn't get ruined by substandard house help."

Alice smiled awkwardly and, out of the corner of her eye, caught Madison throwing away the cake pop she'd only half eaten.

Alice could pretend not to have seen, but she felt the need to say something. "You know you can eat the whole tray if you want. You don't have any weight issues."

"No." Madison sighed, that air of lingering, unexplained sorrow crossing her eyes. "She made me get my dress half a size smaller than my usual. So she's right, I need to watch what I eat."

"No, you really don't." Alice picked up another azure tart and pushed it into Madison's hand. "Eat this, it's really delicious."

Madison grabbed it and bit half off, smiling. "Mmm, you're right… these are divine."

Alice wished everything in life could be solved with a blue—sorry, *azure*—tart.

***

The day of the wedding, Madison and Alice left their apartment to drive together to the Smithson's country house in Madison's car. Madison was wearing her lilac, one-shoulder strap bridesmaid gown, and Alice was in a simple blush cocktail dress. Alice had not dared wear anything that wasn't pastel. They'd left their hair loose and wore no makeup, as per wedding planner-issued instructions. A professional would take care of them before the ceremony started.

At the house, the whole pampering process was extremely efficient. A stern-looking wedding planner ushered them to a small room to change into black silk kimonos and then moved them into different rooms, one for each beauty task: hair, makeup, nails, and a final station where they got back their (steamed) dresses. The wedding planner and her assistants kept muttering, "Divide and conquer."

Throughout the entire process, Alice was alone. She never caught a glimpse of the bride or Madison until she was ushered back into a changing room and found her roommate already there. Madison, who usually never wore makeup, looked stunning in her gown with her golden locks arranged in a complicated chignon. When Alice was dressed, too, a scary assistant ordered them to go wait inside the church, which was even-in-heels-walking distance.

The first guests had already started to arrive and Ethan was helping his father welcome everyone. Many voices were overlapping, the typical Boston accent mixing with a southern lilt. The groom was originally from Texas. Alice shuffled through the entrance door with Madison at her heels, trying to avoid catching Ethan's gaze; she hadn't seen her ex since their breakup.

For now, Madison sat with Alice on the bride's side of the church, halfway to the back. Yet, soon, she would have to go backstage to make her official entrance as the ceremony began.

"Is the best man a woman?" Alice asked, squinting her eyes.

"Yep, Rose," Madison confirmed. "Ethan's girlfriend."

"You're right!" Alice exclaimed. "I didn't recognize her primped like that; if it wasn't for the chignon, you could take her for a guy."

"Yeah, Georgiana forbid her from wearing a dress or doing her hair in any style other than a low chignon."

"Seriously? Why?"

Madison shrugged. "I guess she wanted to make sure no one stole her thunder. As if." She snorted.

Rose was talking to the minister. Alice felt weird watching her; it was like spying, in a way. Maybe it was normal to be fascinated by the woman your ex-boyfriend had chosen over you. The visual stalking of her old rival didn't last long. Rose soon finished her conversation and vanished through a door on the right of the altar, presumably where the groom was waiting.

At that moment, Ethan walked past them and disappeared behind the same door as Rose. He didn't recognize Alice, or he pretended not to. After five minutes, he came back out and nodded to the priest. The groom and best woman followed and took their spots at the altar.

"I have to go," Madison said. "I'll catch up with you later." And she was gone.

The wedding march started playing a few minutes later as the bridesmaids and bride made their way down the aisle. The minister started talking and before Alice knew it, the ceremony was over. *It doesn't take long to change your life forever.* She tried to wait for Madison to walk back to the house, but her friend was in the thick of the crowd with the rest of the family so Alice decided to fly solo.

At the house, the reception was taking place in the gardens. Waiters were already passing out champagne flutes and some aperitifs, so Alice grabbed a flute of the bubbly. She removed her shoes to walk on the grass, feeling strangely isolated amidst the crowd of guests. Weddings did weird things to a girl's emotions.

Alice's mood didn't improve during lunch. She didn't know anyone at her table, which was obviously the singles table—seven women and a grand total of three guys sat around her. A perfect reproduction of the dating men-women split. For Alice, it was an effort to sustain polite conversations for the three hours the five-course meal required. So, when the dessert buffet was announced, Alice seized the opportunity immediately and shot out of her chair to stretch her legs.

Rose

Rose left Ethan at their table and strolled around the dessert buffet. She took a plate and piled it with all sorts of treats. As she reached the chocolate bonbons, Rose noticed a pretty girl throw her a furtive glance and then lower her gaze just as quickly.

The girl's face looked familiar, but… *different* was the word. As if something was not quite as it should be.

"Hi," Rose said, unable to keep her curiosity in check. "Have we met before?"

The girl gaped at Rose, eyes wide with… surprise? Fear? It couldn't be fear. Who would be afraid of Rose, and why?

"Just the once," the girl said, her tone not exactly warm. "I was a blonde when we last met, though."

Rose tried to mentally Photoshop the girl's long dark strands into golden ones, seeing if she could guess where they had met.

The girl cut her memory exercise short by saying, "I'm Alice." She paused. "Ethan's ex."

Rose couldn't help blushing. The image of a pretty blonde girl staring daggers at her the night she'd met Ethan popped into her mind's eye. He was dating Alice at the time and had broken up with her to start dating Rose.

Alice was more striking as a brunette; the new hairstyle made her appear more mature.

"Alice, sure. I'm Rose. I don't believe we were properly introduced before." She offered her hand, hoping Ethan's ex didn't hold too much of a grudge. After all, it had happened almost a year ago.

Alice seemed to consider for a second before taking her hand. "Nice to meet you," she said, and quickly let go. The ex piled more chocolates on her plate and took a step backward. "I have to go back to my table. It was nice seeing you again."

"Yeah, sure."

Rose watched Alice run away, then made her way back to her own table. Ethan was gone, so she sat down to enjoy her mini desserts. While she was eating, the band started playing and people all around her stood up to dance.

"Miss Atwood," Ethan said, appearing next to her. "May I have the honor of a dance?" He bent forward in a hint of a bow and offered his hand.

Rose let go of the chocolate pastry she was holding. Ethan was so much better than chocolate. She marveled once again at how much she loved him. Especially when he played the gallant, gentleman hero.

She took his hand, smiling. "Most certainly, Mr. Smithson."

Ethan led her onto the dance floor. They'd never danced together, not this formally, at least. But they were doing a great job of it all the same.

"Where did you learn to dance?" he asked.

"I had to partake in the renowned Dallas Symphony Orchestra League Presentation Ball for debutantes," Rose said jokingly. "What about you? I didn't know you could dance so well." She was honestly surprised—he was leading her like a professional.

Ethan's jaw tensed slightly. "Sabrina made me take lessons when we were engaged."

"Oh, I'm sorry." Rose was horrified.

"Don't be." Ethan smiled his most dashing smile, making the corners of his eyes go all crinkly and igniting a sparkle in them. "At least something good came out of that engagement." He squeezed her hand.

Rose squeezed it back. It was the first time he'd spoken about Sabrina in a lighthearted way. Rose liked to take credit for this newfound easiness about his past.

"Speaking of exes… did you know Alice is here?"

"I haven't seen her, but it figures." Ethan spun Rose away and made her pirouette back. "Alice is Georgiana's young sister or little sister; I never understood sorority tiers very well."

"She's dyed her hair. She looks good," Rose said provocatively, prodding Ethan's feelings for his ex.

"You look good." Ethan pulled her closer. "I'm not sure if the fact that I find you hot while you're dressed like a boy should scare me or not," Ethan teased as he and Rose waltzed across the dance floor—a platform that had been set up in the middle of the Smithson's family home garden.

"I'm about to cut into your dilemma," Rose said. "Do you think the style-gestapo will flay me if I let my hair loose? This chignon is killing me. And the bow tie is strangling! How do you guys wear these around your neck every day?" She started pulling some pins out of her hair.

"Here, let me help…" Ethan pulled her to the edge of the garden and started working his fingers through her hair.

When the last pin came loose, Rose shook her head and let her hair cascade down onto her shoulders. Ethan was already undoing the bow tie.

"I have to stop now, or I'll end up undressing you completely. It wouldn't be very proper."

"No, it wouldn't, especially not with your mother staring at us. She's been watching us like a hawk all day. What's up with her?"

"Ah, my dear." Ethan grinned. "I'm afraid that with my sister's nuptials, I remain the sole Smithson sibling yet to be matched. I'm pretty sure my mother has designs on you."

"Aren't two weddings in six months enough for her?"

"Is the thought of joining yourself to me in holy matrimony so unappealing to you, Miss Atwood?"

"What? No, I-I mean…" Rose was stuttering, her face searing red. "Are you serious?"

"Why not?"

His stare was like burning ice.

"I thought you w-were against getting married."

"I'm against girls shopping for rings after one date. I'm not against getting married to the woman I love."

"Are you proposing?" Rose's heart was beating way too fast.

"Now, don't go getting a big head, Miss Atwood…"

She swatted him playfully. "Jerk."

He grabbed her hand and pulled her into a kiss.

"I love you," Ethan whispered. "One day, I want you to be my wife. What do you say?"

"One day." Rose couldn't help but smile like an idiot. "I love you, too."

"Now that my noble intentions are in the open, can I bring you to my room?"

Ethan and Rose discreetly disappeared behind a bush and ran across the lawn toward the house, holding hands and laughing like a pair of kids.

***

The inside of Ethan's house was so stylish it was scary. It was an impeccable mix of rustic and modern design, a balance hard to get right. From tiny objects to each major furnishing element, everything was placed perfectly. Nothing left to chance. It was impressive but somehow made the place feel more like a museum than a lived-in home. All this flawlessness could get suffocating. Rose felt for Ethan. Being a Smithson really came with a lot of pressure attached. *Imagine being an unruly kid in this house.*

Rose followed Ethan up the stairs and through a corridor with too many white doors to count. He stopped in front of one toward the end, pausing with his hand on the handle. "You're about to have a glimpse into my teenage lifestyle." He flung the door open and a loud snore came from within.

Sprawled on Ethan's bed was a bulging, middle-aged man, fast asleep.

"Rose, meet Uncle Frank." Ethan sighed. "He must've decided my room was as good a place as any to fall asleep."

Rose giggled, taking in what she could of Ethan's room before he closed the door. She took inventory of his life when he was younger. Items of an over-achiever: awards, certificates, sports trophies. But also a cool, popular kid: a rock band poster, shots of him posing with his friends and lacrosse teammates. His smile was already irresistible, even back then. Then there were the obligatory family photos, stored in elegant frames his mother must have bought. They showed his well-adjusted side: his parents, Ethan with his sisters, and a photo of the entire Smithson clan.

The door clicked shut, and they tiptoed away, careful not to wake the sleeping man.

"We'll have to take one of the guest rooms." Ethan turned on his heel and headed back toward the beginning of the hall.

He opened a random door. Before Rose could peek inside, Ethan roared and rushed into the room. Rose made to follow him but stopped dead on the threshold. She raised a hand to cover her mouth as she stared at the scene before her eyes in shocked silence.

Ethan was holding Tyler against the wall by the neck of his unbuttoned shirt. On the rumpled bed lay a cowering girl, her eyes big with fear. Rose took in her wrinkled bridesmaid dress, messed up hair, and kissed-away lipstick, and the reality of what had happened here hit her in the stomach.

"I'm going to kill you, you bastard," Ethan hissed in cold rage. He drew his elbow back, closing his hand into a tight fist, and cranking his arm back to punch Tyler in the face.

Rose jumped forward and took a hold of her boyfriend's arm before he could land the blow. "Ethan, stop!" she yelled.

"What?" He turned toward her, glowering, his eyes crazed. "Are you going to defend him, even now?"

"No, no," Rose hurried to say. "But think: you can't reduce his face to a pulp without having to explain what's going on to everyone downstairs. That would be even worse for Georgiana."

For a split second, Ethan seemed not to care what anyone would say. But he took a deep, steadying breath and lowered his arm without hitting Tyler. Instead, he yanked Tyler off his feet and hurled him across the room, sending him crashing against a wooden dressing table. The dresser capsized and Tyler careened to the floor.

"What are you guys doing?" Vicky, Ethan's other sister, stepped into the room. "I could hear the noise from downstairs." She took in the scene and closed the door behind her before demanding again, "What's going on here?"

Where Ethan's rage was intense and outspoken, Vicky's was calm and controlled, but no less brutal. Her blue eyes, the same color as Ethan's, were cold and smoldering at the same time.

Ethan was leaning against the wall, looking exhausted. He made an I-can't-talk gesture and shook his head.

Vicky turned to the girl on the bed next, who said, "I'm sorry" and began to sob.

Rose was the only one cool enough to speak. "We came into the room and found them on the bed. Tyler must be drunk."

She threw a reproachful look at her best friend. Tyler was sitting on the floor with his elbows resting on his bent knees and his face hidden in his hands.

Vicky's cold fury turned toward the bridesmaid first. "Madison, I know you've always had it in for Georgiana, but this?" She waved a hand between the girl and Tyler. "On her wedding day?"

"I'm s-sorry," the girl whimpered.

"She's your cousin!" Vicky barked. "We're family, for goodness' sake."

"P-please don't tell my parents." The girl's eyes seemed to become wider still.

Vicky seemed about to spit a gruff retort, but instead, she took a deep breath and started pacing in circles, staring at the floor and holding her chin in one hand. She stopped and said, "We're not going to tell anyone." The middle Smithson sibling took turns staring down everyone present. "What happened here today doesn't leave this room."

"Are you kidding me?" Ethan raged. "Our sister married this scum bag, who couldn't be faithful to her for half a day. Gigi has a right to know; she could get an annulment or something."

"Our sister isn't going to want an annulment," Vicky said.

"Not even after this?"

"I don't think so." Vicky shook her head. "Georgiana is too stubborn to admit she was wrong, and she's still pregnant with his baby."

Rose heart broke a little as she watched pain and anger mix on Ethan's face. "It doesn't mean they have to stay married," he said, "not if this is how it's going to be."

"Ethan." Vicky was not backing down. "I'm sorry to break it you, but as much as I love her, our sister lied to him about being on the pill. She maneuvered to get herself pregnant. Georgiana forced this on him, knowing what she was doing all along."

Rose agreed with everything Vicky was saying, and she was glad that for once she wasn't the one who had to tell Ethan. Whenever Rose tried to point out that this was a two-person mess, and that Georgiana wasn't exactly an innocent victim, Ethan left on the jealousy wagon, making it all about her history with Tyler. He'd never forgiven Rose for not allowing him to tell Georgiana that Tyler had cheated on her with Rose. Ethan was convinced Georgiana would not be pregnant now if she had known. Rose wasn't so sure, and to have someone else reason with him was a welcome novelty. They'd already had too many arguments about

Tyler and, frankly, defending her best friend was getting harder and harder. Rose was ashamed of him, and also of the tiny part of herself that was relieved it wasn't her that had married Tyler.

Rose stared up at Ethan, the man she loved with all her heart, the man who'd saved her, and she wished she had a way to comfort him. He looked so anguished.

"Well," Ethan said, then took his rage out on the ottoman at the base of the bed with a violent kick. "No one forced him to propose or to cheat on our sister on their wedding day!"

The statement seemed to give Vicky pause. She crouched on the floor next to Tyler. "You. Hey, you!" She snapped her fingers in his face. "Look at me."

Tyler slowly lifted his head.

"What happened here?"

Tyler

"I freaked out," Tyler said, barely able to focus on Georgiana's sister crouched next to him. "People kept telling me all these marriage and new-daddy jokes, and I just started downing one drink after the other, and I lost it…" What a pathetic excuse. He was pathetic. If he couldn't keep it together for a few hours, how was he going to manage a lifetime? "I don't know what I'm doing."

"Fair enough. Listen." Vicky paused until Tyler's eyes focused on hers. "I know you didn't ask to be a father, but you're going to become one, anyway. As our nephew or niece's dad, you're part of the family now no matter what." Vicky was talking in a calm, polite voice that surprised Tyler. "Now, you can be a good father even if you're not married to our sister," Vicky continued. "Was this a last minute case of cold feet, or is it how you plan to behave from now on?"

Tyler's pulse raced. What did he want? He wanted to be a good dad, and for his child to grow up with two parents. So what was he doing here?

"Th-this is not…" he stuttered. "It wasn't… I want to try."

"Okay. You get this one pass." Vicky raised one finger eye-level between them. "And that's it."

Ethan emitted a disbelieving grunt from his corner. Tyler didn't dare look at him. Of all the people in the world, why did it have to be he and Rose who had walked in on him? *Still better than my pregnant wife,* Tyler thought. The weight of what he had almost done to his wife made him sick. What if Ethan and Rose hadn't been here? Would he have had sex with Georgiana's cousin? *Probably, yes.* What the hell was wrong with him?

Vicky stood up. "Go wash your face and pull yourself together." She offered him a hand and helped him up off the floor.

Tyler did as he was told and disappeared into the en-suite bathroom. He didn't dare meet anyone's eye, particularly not Rose's. In one look, he'd be able to read all her thoughts, and he couldn't cope with the reproach and disappointment he was bound to find written in her dark eyes. Tyler gently closed the door behind himself and braced his arms on either side of the sink. He stared in the mirror.

Someone he didn't like stared back. Georgiana wasn't perfect, but she didn't deserve this. More than everything, his unborn child did not deserve to come into the world in a broken family. He'd been stupid and weak. Tyler shook his head. How had this whole mess even started?

During the banquet, Tyler remembered shuffling around the tables alongside Georgiana. She'd made him take turns greeting all the guests. His relatives, her relatives, friends from Boston, friends from Texas, there had been so many. Every group ready to offer advice or words of wisdom. Tyler had smiled and endured it. They had drunk a toast at each table—well, Georgiana hadn't, she was sticking to virgin mimosas—but Tyler had downed one glass of champagne after the other. He'd needed the alcohol to endure jab after jab about married life, newborns, and shrinking bank accounts. His anxiety had grown with every new joke. He had another year left in school, and yet he was already expected to provide for a wife and a child. Tyler came from a wealthy family, as did Georgiana, so money wasn't a problem—in theory. Provided he kept asking his parents for support. With Georgiana's expensive tastes, he couldn't buy a bigger home, repay student loans, and sustain a family without economic help from his parents. So that was his independence flying out the window, and it *sucked.*

When the meal finally ended, Tyler had left his table with the excuse of needing some air. He had gone to hide behind a tall hedge that shielded him from view. The girl, Madison, Georgiana's cousin—he hadn't known she was her cousin at the time—was there hiding, too. They'd started talking, then he'd asked her if there was a place he could wash his face. She'd shown him to the downstairs bathroom, but there was a line so they'd gone upstairs. Madison said he could use one of the guest rooms, and before he knew what was happening, they were kissing on the bed instead. He was cheating on his wife three hours after they got married.

Never again.

He'd be a father soon. It didn't matter if Georgiana had tricked him, that he hadn't asked for this, and that he was scared as hell. He already loved this child with all his heart; nothing else mattered.

Tyler stared hard at himself, vowing not to be the kind of d-bag who cheated on his wife. Turning on the tap, he splashed cold water on his face. This had been his wake-up call. Vicky was right—the situation sucked. But since he had decided to marry Georgiana, he had to give the marriage a fair shot.

Tyler finished washing his face then straightened his spine, his jaw set with determination. He buttoned his shirt, adjusted his cuffs, and re-did the knot of his bowtie until it looked impeccable. There, the image of the perfect groom. One pass, Vicky had said. That's all he needed; he would not screw up again.

Rose

After sending Tyler to get it together in the en suite, Vicky turned toward her cousin, who was still sobbing on the bed. "Did you come here in your car?" she asked. "Can you go home right away?"

"I drove here, but I came with my roommate."

"Your roommate?" Vicky seemed surprised. "What's her name? How come she was invited?"

"Alice. You met her," the girl said.

Is it possible the roommate is Ethan's Alice? Small world, Rose thought. A furtive glance at Ethan confirmed that, yes, it was the same Alice.

"Alice is Georgiana's friend, too," the disgraced bridesmaid continued. "She came to our house for Christmas the year before last, and she was at the baby shower. We were talking about her on Martha's

Vineyard, remember?"

"I was getting married I don't remember anything anyone said to me that week, but I remember her from Christmas…" Vicky stared at the ceiling pensively. "A cute blonde, right? I didn't see her in the crowd today or at the shower."

"She's a brunette now."

"That explains it, then," Vicky said matter-of-factly. "It doesn't matter, anyway. You can't tell her about what happened here."

"Alice is my best friend," the girl protested. "She won't tell Georgiana."

"Madison, listen to me." Vicky closed the distance to the bed. "I'm not kidding. You can't tell anyone about this. Promise me."

The girl looked scared again. "Okay, I promise. I won't tell anyone."

"Can you ask your roommate if she can get a ride with someone else?"

On impulse, Rose said, "We can give her a lift."

Ethan arched his brows. "Are you sure?"

Rose nodded.

Noticing the underlying tension in Ethan's question, Vicky asked, "Why the face? You know her, too?"

"Alice and I dated a while ago," he explained.

"Seriously?"

Ethan shrugged.

"Ah well, that's taken care of. Madison, are you sure you're okay to drive? Did you drink?"

"No, not much."

That's a lie, Rose thought. From the state of her, Madison wasn't wasted, but she wasn't anywhere close to sober either.

"Are you sure?" Vicky echoed Rose's worries. "We can call a car if you're not okay."

"I'm good," the girl insisted. "I can drive."

"Okay."

Rose wasn't convinced, but Vicky was calling the shots and Rose didn't want to contradict her.

"Here." Ethan's sister handed their cousin a wet wipe. "Clean your face," she instructed.

Madison's mascara was running in rivulets down her flushed cheeks.

She scrubbed her face with the tissue, making her skin even blotchier. Under all that melted makeup, the girl was stunning. Blue eyes, high cheekbones covered in cute freckles, and otherwise regular features that made her a classic beauty. Madison freed her hair from the half-undone, elaborate chignon all the bridesmaids had, letting loose a cascade of golden looks. Even more beautiful. Yet her face, for all its beauty, was twisted ugly with remorse, shame, and a mix of other complicated emotions Rose couldn't discern.

Vicky waited for her to be finished cleaning herself before she spoke again. "Do you know how to get out of the house from the back?"

"Yes." Madison nodded.

"Okay. I'll call you tonight and we'll talk this through. But not a word to anyone else."

Madison grabbed her clutch from the bedside table and fled the room. Watching her run, Rose couldn't help the gush of pity in her chest.

"Ethan." Vicky turned her attention on him next. Solving one problem at a time, snap-snap-snap. "Can you please go grab an aspirin and some water?"

"Yeah." Ethan threw a murderous stare at the bathroom where Tyler was still holed up. "It's better if I get out of here." He exited the bedroom.

"Will Madison be all right?" Rose asked.

"What makes you ask that?"

"She seemed really…" Rose paused to find the right word. "Broken."

Vicky hugged herself. "Madison has always harbored a major inferiority complex toward me, and toward Georgiana especially. And everyone else, really: her friends, the girls in her sorority, you name it. My sister didn't help cure any of her insecurities either. You know how she can be."

Rose was surprised to hear Vicky hint again that Georgiana was far from perfect. She knew the two sisters were close, and she'd assumed it meant they were alike. In reality, they couldn't have been more different.

Vicky kept going. "And my whole family is so damn competitive that growing up a shy, reserved kid… Madison hasn't had an easy time of it. Don't worry, I'll call her later and talk with her. Really talk. I'm not going to point the finger. Ethan has never understood the female pecking order of this family, but I do, and I'm sorry to say Madison has been at the bottom her entire life."

The more Vicky talked, the more Rose liked her. "At least she can count on you," she said.

"Madison is like another younger sister." Vicky braced her hands on the bed's footboard. "I can at least try to understand the perverse train of thought that brought her to behave like she has today. After years of being bullied by Georgiana, she probably saw this as retribution."

"Bullied?"

"Bullied is too strong a word." Ethan's sister waved a hand. "Outshined, teased. Let's say Georgiana usually wins the competition to get the most attention at the dinner table. Madison is fragile. She doesn't know how to stand up for herself. So she probably decided to backstab Georgiana, get the other end of the stick for once. It makes me sick to my stomach that my family is so messed up."

"It's not," Rose said.

Vicky raised a skeptical eyebrow.

"Well, maybe a little," Rose conceded. "But the important thing is that you stick together no matter what."

"I hope you're right. What about your friend in there?" Vicky pointed to the still-closed bathroom door. "Do you think Tyler will be capable of keeping his word, or do I have to send home all the bridesmaids?"

Rose considered the question for a few seconds. "Usually, he's on his best behavior for a while after he's messed up. Especially with something as big as this. I know he wants to try, but he probably feels trapped by so many responsibilities he didn't ask for." Rose shrugged. "I'm sure he will be a great father and he will *try* to be a good husband."

"It's more than I would've done in his place."

"Really?"

"Yeah. I love my sister," Vicky said fiercely, "in the same way you love your cat after he's peed on your favorite rug. The way she tricked Tyler into becoming a father is inexcusable. No matter how you look at it."

"Still, Georgiana doesn't deserve this." Rose stared at the crumpled bed sheets.

Vicky gave her a long stare. "That's kind of you. I know you two have your own history and don't like each other much."

"Yeah... we... uh..." Rose didn't know what to say.

"But I do like you," Vicky added. "I want you to know that. I've never seen my brother this happy."

Rose was taken aback. Vicky was proving to be one of the coolest people she'd ever met. Rose smiled and nodded. "I like you too."

Ethan came back into the room with a bottle of spring water and a plastic vial of aspirin tablets. "What are you two smiling about?" he asked gloomily.

"Nothing," they both answered.

Ethan passed the water and tablets to his sister.

"Thanks," she said. "You two go. I'll stay with the groom until he's good enough to come back out."

Ethan gave his sister a stiff nod and moved outside the room. Rose smiled at Vicky one last time and then followed him. He was already headed for the stairs.

"Hey, come here." Rose grabbed his hand to stop him and hugged him.

"Please." Ethan tried to push her back, but she wouldn't let him. "Don't even try to defend him."

"I wasn't going to." She took Ethan's face in her hands. "I want to know how *you* feel."

Ethan's jaw relaxed, and he stopped struggling to get away. "I can handle it."

"Are you sure?"

"Yeah, I have you." He finally placed his arms around her waist. "I'm good."

Rose kissed him. "I love you."

"I love you, too. Now, let's go before people start wondering where everyone went."

"Right." Rose smirked. "And we have to tell Alice she just earned herself an awkward ride home."

Alice

Alice spotted Rose and Ethan coming out of the house. She had to admit they were a beautiful couple. After everything that had happened with Jack and Peter in the past year, Ethan was ancient history. But still, seeing your ex and his new perfect girlfriend so in love wasn't exactly ideal.

They seemed to be walking in her direction, so Alice turned her back to them and grabbed a flute of champagne from a passing waiter. Surely they would try to avoid her just as much as she was trying to avoid them. The last thing Alice expected when she turned back was to find them standing right behind her as if they wanted to speak to her. She almost choked on her drink and recovered just in time to avoid making a complete fool of herself.

"Hi, Alice," Ethan said. Rose smiled apologetically.

"Hi," Alice replied warily.

"Madison wasn't feeling well," Ethan said. "She had to go home and asked me to tell you."

Alice had seen Madison drink more than one glass of wine. Should she even be driving? "Is she sick?" Alice asked, the embarrassment of facing her ex replaced by worry for her friend. "What did she have?"

"Nothing serious. She was just a bit lightheaded."

Ethan's jaw kept twitching as he spoke. That, added to the way Rose was shifting uncomfortably from one foot to the other, and Alice was positive they weren't telling her the whole story.

Alice dropped her glass on a nearby table and reached into her clutch for her phone. She had one new text from Madison.

Not feeling well, heading home

Alice scrolled through the chat, but there were no other messages. Things didn't add up. She lifted her head and asked, "Is Madison gone already?"

"Should be." Ethan shrugged.

His hostile attitude was pushing Alice's buttons. Was he mad at Madison? Because she wasn't feeling well? "So you let her drive home alone when she was feeling lightheaded?" Alice pressed him. That didn't sound much like Ethan; it didn't sound like any of the Smithson clan.

"It wasn't that serious."

"But serious enough she had to go home."

Alice wasn't sure why she was trying to pick a fight, especially with her ex. But she wanted to find out what it was that they weren't telling her.

"Anyway, Madison should have texted you to tell you," Ethan said, ignoring her question point blank. "Since she was your ride, we can give you a lift home."

A lift home with her ex and the girl he'd dumped her for? *Hell no!*

"Err." Alice put the phone back in her purse to gain a couple of seconds. She had to wiggle her way out of this situation. "Yeah, she did text me. Don't you worry, guys. I can call an Uber to get home."

"I live just off campus," Rose said. "It's not a problem for us to drop you off. It'd cost you a fortune to get a car to come all the way here and back to Cambridge."

Ethan's girlfriend was being so genuinely kind and warm, it was impossible to say no. And Alice wasn't good at thinking on her feet. *Madison had better be seriously ill.*

"Okay, then," Alice sighed. "When do you guys want to go?"

"After they cut the cake?" Ethan looked at Rose who nodded.

"All right, that's settled," Alice said. "I'll see you later, guys." She walked away as quickly as she could without appearing to be running.

Not long afterward, the band stopped playing and the wedding planner took the stage to ask all the guests to group on the lawn for the cutting of the cake. They formed a big semicircle around a small round table covered with a white cloth. On top of it stood the wedding cake— a five-layer tower decorated with a waterfall of pale pink-and-white sugar flowers.

Alice waited to see where Ethan and Rose would go, and positioned herself on the opposite side, at the back of the crowd. When all the guests were settled, soft music started in the background and Georgiana and Tyler made their appearance from inside the house. The bride and groom crossed the garden holding hands, Georgiana looking positively radiant in her amazing high-low hem gown and Tyler appearing too pale for his own good. He was smiling, but something was off. His smile looked forced. Was he nervous?

As the bride and groom took their place behind the small table, Georgiana's older sister discretely emerged from the house. Victoria scanned the crowd, then joined Ethan and Rose. They all started whispering furiously to one another, heads bent in a close circle. The argument seemed to become heated, so much so that Vicky made a "be quiet" gesture, peering over her shoulder. Alice's suspicions flared up again. It looked like the three of them were discussing some big secret the guests shouldn't overhear.

Ethan went quiet and fixed his gaze ahead. Rose was studying his face apprehensively. Why? Alice followed Ethan's stare: he was glaring at the groom with murder written all over his features. Alice had never seen him so livid. Vicky's mouth, too, was set in a thin line, and she sported a deep frown. Georgiana appeared to be the only unabashedly happy Smithson sibling. What was all the drama about?

A cheer erupted from the crowd as Georgiana and Tyler joined hands and sunk a knife into the cake's top layer. Alice drained her glass and walked back to her table to wait for a slice of the wedding cake as did most of the guests. She wasn't hungry; she'd had enough of the wedding banquet, and her stomach was knotting tighter and tighter at the prospect of her awkward ride home. But, apparently, it was bad luck to leave a wedding without having a bite of the cake. And she could use some good fortune.

The cake was too sweet, so after the first perfunctory bite, Alice left the rest. She was about to go search for Ethan and Rose when Georgiana appeared by her side.

"I'm throwing the bouquet," the bride announced, taking Alice's hand. "You have to come."

Alice followed her and joined the crowd of eager-looking—to say the least, belligerent to be more accurate—single girls ready to catch the prize. Around her, crazed women started pushing and shoving, so Alice decided to move to the edge of the swaying crowd.

"All right, ladies," Georgiana yelled, and winked at Alice. "Here it goes. One… two… three…"

The bouquet soared high in the air and almost hit Alice in the face before she caught it. A disappointed groan resounded around her. The bouquet felt heavier than she'd imagined. *Fat chance I'm getting married within the year,* she thought.

Georgiana barreled into her, yelling, "I knew you'd catch it!" The bride pulled her into a hug, the beading on her dress scraping Alice's skin at multiple points. "Thanks so much for coming. I'm sorry we didn't get to talk much today, but everyone wanted a piece of me."

"Of course." Alice smiled. "You're the most beautiful bride in the world."

"I have to go now." Georgiana was more hyper than a hamster on a wheel. "Tyler and I have to say our goodbyes before going."

"Are you leaving for the honeymoon tonight?" Alice asked.

"Yeah." Georgiana nodded. "We'd better hurry. I'll call you when I get back, all right?"

"Sure, have a great time."

They hugged again, and Georgiana waltzed away in a whirl of white organza. With no excuses left to delay the inevitable, Alice sighed and started searching for Ethan and Rose. It was Rose who found her instead.

"Alice, here," she called, pushing her way through the crowd to reach her. "We're ready to go if you are."

"Are you sure you wouldn't rather I took a cab?"

"This far out of the city? It'd be expensive," Rose said. "Listen, I understand this might be awkward for you…"

"Well, a bit," Alice admitted. "Isn't it for you, too?"

"Honestly, I'm cool if you're cool. Ethan, too." Rose smiled. "But if you don't want to go with us, I understand; that's why I came looking for you alone. I thought maybe you didn't want to say anything in front of him."

The more Rose talked, the harder it was not to like her. Plus, Ethan's annoyingly kind girlfriend was right: paying for a cab would be a pain. And Alice wasn't exactly swimming in money at the moment. As for Uber, one tiny, money-forgetting-ATM-detouring incident last year had made her passenger score drop and now drivers ducked her requests.

Alice made up her mind. "I'm cool."

Ethan was waiting for them at the front of the house, now transformed into an unofficial parking lot. Luckily, they'd come in the pickup, so Alice wouldn't have to squeeze in the back of his sports car.

"You're still at the Botanic Gardens?" Ethan asked, catching her eye in the rearview mirror.

Alice blushed, thinking she'd had sex with him there, in her room. "Yeah, still there."

The awkward trio spent the ride in silence; each of them busy with their own thoughts. Alice didn't pay attention to the road, so when Ethan pulled up in front of her building, she was startled they'd already arrived. She was about to get out of the car when she froze, her hand on the door handle, her pulse out of control.

Jack was sitting on the steps of her building.

***

Spotting her, Jack sprang to his feet. "Hey," he said, jogging toward her. "Whose truck was that?" He frowned at the leaving car.

"Ethan's," Alice replied, not offering any further explanation.

Jack's face darkened. "Are you dating him again?"

Alice's shoulders slumped forward. "No." She was tired of playing games. "He and *his girlfriend* gave me a lift back from Georgiana's wedding. Madison and I went together in her car this morning, but she had some kind of crisis and left mid-party." Alice searched her clutch for her keys and headed toward the door. "I should probably check on her."

Jack trailed her. "Yeah, I saw her go inside."

Alice narrowed her eyes at him. "How long have you been waiting here?"

"Pretty much all day."

The admission jolted Alice's heart, but she decided to ignore it. "Did Madison look all right?"

"She wouldn't speak to me. But she had puffy eyes."

Alice made to insert the keys in the lock. "Then I should definitely go see if she's okay."

"Wait." Jack grabbed her elbow gently. "Can we talk, please?"

"It's been a long day," Alice protested. "And I can't stand on these heels any longer."

"Let's sit down then."

Jack pulled her away from the door and toward a nearby bench.

Alice let him at first but then chickened out. Jack ambushing her like this was too much. One ex in a day had been enough, and even if Jack wasn't officially an ex, it still felt that way. "I think I really should go check on Madison." She resisted his pull.

"Look," Jack said, peeking over her shoulder. "There goes another bridesmaid to take care of Madison."

Alice turned around. Victoria, Georgiana's sister, was ringing the bell to her apartment.

"How did you know she's a bridesmaid?" Alice asked.

"Same long, lavender dress as Madison." Jack shrugged. "It can't be that popular."

Alice's resolve not to talk to him softened. "I don't know if I should be scared you just used the word 'lavender' or not."

Jack shot her a grin—an interiors-melting one.

"Come on, Ice. We need to talk. And Haley's here, too." Jack jerked his chin at the building entrance. "Madison is taken care of."

Alice turned her head. Haley and Victoria were standing in front of the door, having some kind of argument. Alice finally gave in. With Haley there, Madison would be fine. She let Jack drag her the rest of the way to the bench.

Jack looked nervous and wasn't talking, so Alice prompted him. "What are you doing here?"

"You wouldn't take my calls."

Because the next time we talked, I'd have to say goodbye to you, Alice thought. Better get it over with quickly. "Okay, so what is it?"

"I came to apologize," Jack stated simply.

"For what?" Alice snapped. "For sleeping with my friend, for not telling me, or for something else?"

"All of it, and more."

Alice panicked. "I can't do this, Jack. I can't."

"Do what?"

"Have this conversation with you." He frowned. So Alice explained, "The 'we can't be friends anymore' conversation."

"Sorry, but we'll talk about how we're not going to be friends." Jack tapped a finger on his thigh. "Right now."

A crack spread through Alice's heart. "So you agree." She stared at the floor. "We can no longer be friends?"

"Is that what you want?" Jack asked. "To be my friend?"

She looked up at him. "No."

"Good, neither do I."

"And what do you want?"

Jack pinned her with his stare. "You, Ice. I want you."

Air escaped her lungs as she spiraled down a vortex of possibilities. Then fear kicked in. "Yeah, right," she said.

"Is it really that hard to believe?"

"The only time I tried to kiss you, you did everything you could to push me back. So, yeah, it is."

"You caught me off guard. I didn't expect it. I didn't know how to react." Jack gathered his thoughts. "I didn't even know how I felt, and by the time I had a good idea, you were already dating Peter."

"And now you know?" Alice asked, still skeptical.

He locked eyes with her and closed the space between them. "Yes."

"And how is that?"

Jack brushed the hair away from her face. "We're not *just* friends," he whispered, never lowering his gaze. "We never were."

Alice wasn't ready to accept these words. She'd waited too long to hear them. "And you realized this when?"

Jack looked at the sky in a way that said, "You're not going to make this easy for me."

No, she wasn't.

He trained his eyes back on hers. "I think I first realized it—subconsciously, at least—on umbrella night. When that dude grabbed you. When he pulled you away, and you struggled to get free but couldn't, I wanted to beat him into a pulp."

"That was a year ago," Alice noted.

"I know, but again from the first moment I saw you with Peter..." Jack made a strangled noise with his throat. "All I've wanted to do is smash his face. I've been rotting with jealousy ever since."

Could this be true? Was Jack really saying... *What was he saying?*

"Was the umbrella at Christmas..." Alice paused, appalled. Not sure what to ask. "Was it some sort of encrypted message I should've deciphered to... to what?"

"I didn't put that much thought into it. I saw a bunny-shaped umbrella, it reminded me of you, of that night, and I wanted to give it to you."

Alice narrowed her eyes at him. "Were you pretending to sleep on the plane the next day?" she asked, her voice daring him to deny it.

Jack frowned, a red flush creeping up his neck. "I had been waiting for a break ever since you started dating Peter. I couldn't wait to leave for Hawaii because I knew you and him wouldn't be together. That I wouldn't have to guard my shoulder in case I bumped into you two on campus, or change libraries because you were already there, *with him.*"

Alice stared at him, her mouth gaping open. That was exactly how she'd behaved around Jack's girlfriends all along. *Avoid. At. All. Costs.* Hope bloomed inside her chest.

"So, yeah," Jack continued. "When you told me you were coming along, I freaked out. I didn't want to deal with you and him on my trip. So I pretended I was sleeping."

"You said you were tired because you'd spent the night with someone," she accused.

Jack shook his head. "Peter said it, and I let everyone believe it." His shoulders sagged forward. "Because it was better than the alternative, than you learning the truth."

Alice raised her eyebrows in a silent interrogation.

"That I'd spent the night awake, dreading seeing you and Peter together every single day of the trip."

Alice tried to imagine what being on a trip with Jack and one of his girlfriends would do to her. *A slow death.* But, still, she couldn't let herself believe him. If she did, then… no, it would hurt too much.

"The night I met Peter," she said, ice in her voice, "you went home with Becky."

Jack didn't lower his gaze. "Ice, you want a list of all the stupid things I did?"

Alice nodded.

"If you promise to listen to everything else I have to say, I'll give it to you. Deal?"

"Deal."

Jack smiled, relieved, and took her hands in his. "From the moment I saw your lips stained blue, I hated Peter. *Hated* him. I wanted to be the one kissing you. But did I say so? No. I did what I do best and got drunk out of my mind and slept with the first girl I saw."

Jack talking about sex with other girls was like having an invisible hand wrap around her heart and have it suddenly squeeze. Alice bit back the bitter retort already forming on her lips and forced herself to remain silent. To listen.

"Then the next morning I woke up in her apartment," Jack said. The only emotion in his eyes was regret. "And she threw me out, and it felt… pointless. I was tired of being with people I didn't care about—"

Alice interrupted him by wrenching her hands free. They immediately felt too cold, and she wanted to put them back where they'd been. But Jack talking about the girls he'd slept with was making it hard for her to sit still and listen to him. She pinned him with a stare, asking, "So you haven't slept with anyone since—what, October?"

"No," he replied, unflinching.

Alice's eyes widened. "Don't mock me, Jack. You expect me to believe you've gone"—she counted on her fingers—"seven *months* without sleeping with anyone?"

"No one since Becky."

There wasn't a trace of hesitation in his voice or features. A little smile spread on Alice's lips, and she couldn't stop it. "Go on," she said. "With the list of stupid things you did."

Jack reclaimed her hands. "Umbrella night, I wanted to kiss you." A black hole opened where her stomach should've been. "And that day at the library," Jack continued, "the same. But I was scared of history repeating itself, like what happened with Felicity, and I couldn't bear to lose you the same way I lost her. *Not you.* So I pushed you away and spent an hour taking a freezing shower; not that it did me any good. Then at the party you acted as if nothing had happened, you pushed your friend on me, and you kissed Peter."

Alice felt the need to admit some of her own stupid actions. "I was trying to make you jealous."

"It worked." Jack flashed her a mischievous grin. "After your first date with Peter, I lost my mind. I was even more stupid."

"How?"

"I told you not to date him because he was bad for you. And when that didn't work, I tried to have him hook up with some random girl to prove my point and make you ditch him."

Alice couldn't stop the foolish smile tugging at the corners of her mouth from spreading, or the small fire that was now burning in her chest. "You're really bad," she said.

"I am, was." Jack squeezed her hands. "My next tactic was to ignore you, and him. To pretend you didn't exist, or that the two of you weren't together."

Alice knew that particular tactic all too well; she'd used it many times on him.

"Then there was Hawaii, and I couldn't fool myself anymore," Jack said. "So I pretended to sleep to avoid you. That night, when I saw Peter come into your room—"

"You saw that?" Alice asked, shocked. A furious blush invaded her face. "How?"

"My room was directly opposite to yours. David and Scott Williams fighting was the best thing that happened in Hawaii. When I saw you head back to your room with Haley, I was happy. I was glad two of my teammates had almost beaten each other to death if it meant you got to spend one less night with Peter."

Alice's mind was exploding. "Why didn't you say anything?"

Jack scoffed. "Coming from you, that's rich."

Alice pulled her hands away from his grip again and stood up. "Excuse me?"

Jack sprang up from the bench and was in her face in a blink, crowding her. "You say you've known for years, so why didn't *you* say something sooner?"

"I tried." She glared at him. "You rejected me."

"And you claimed to have been on the rebound."

"Are you saying you believed me?"

"No," Jack admitted. "I never said anything after that day because you were with Peter. It didn't seem right."

"And trying to have him sleep with other girls was right?"

"That was a week into your relationship. You hadn't slept with him yet. When you became steady, it seemed wrong to try to break you two apart. I didn't want to hurt you." Jack paused. "And when you broke up, I messed up again."

"Madison," Alice whispered. That invisible hand was back at her heart and squeezing. "Was that another one of the stupid things you did?"

"Not telling you was stupid. And, yes, it was deliberate." For once, Jack was owning it. "Have you ever wondered why I never as much as looked at someone in our concentration, or at one of your close friends—"

"You slept with Becky."

"You pushed her on me," Jack protested. "And she's not a close friend."

"And why were close friends and people in our concentration off-limits?"

"Ice, you know why. It felt like crossing a line," Jack explained. "One I crossed with Madison, but only because I didn't know you'd meet her in the future and become best friends."

"And why didn't you cross that line, knowingly?"

"To leave the door open."

"The door to what?"

"You and me."

"Jack, you're contradicting yourself every five seconds. First, you didn't know. Then, you've always known… None of this makes sense." Alice took a step back. "I'm too tired for this. I'm going inside."

Jack grabbed her by the shoulders gently, keeping her in place. "No, you're not," he said. His tone was final. "I know I'm not making much sense, but I've come to tell you something, and you need to hear me say it."

Alice's heart was beating too fast. She couldn't speak.

Jack's right hand traveled from her shoulder to her neck, ending up buried deep in her hair. "I love you, Ice. And I'm not afraid. I won't be stupid again and not kiss you. Even if it is just this once." His other hand moved down to her lower back, and he pulled her close to him. The hand at the back of her nape tilted her head upward, and Jack's lips brushed against hers.

Alice's knees buckled. She wrapped her arms around his neck for support, her fingers slipping through his dark hair. A million times she'd imagined kissing Jack, but none of her fantasies could have prepared her for the real thing. Everything inside her melted. All her fears, all her insecurities, all the pain and jealousy. It was all gone, obliterated by this kiss.

Jack broke the kiss. "I love you," he whispered.

"I lo—" Before Alice could say it back, he was kissing her again, and this time her knees really did give way.

Jack scooped her up into his arms and began to carry her away from her building.

"Where are you taking me?" Alice asked, losing herself in his eyes.

"Home. With me. And I'm never letting you go ever again. Deal?" Jack flashed her that mischievous grin she loved so much.

Alice beamed back at him. "Deal."

End of Book 2

MY BEST FRIEND'S BOYFRIEND

JUST FRIENDS BOOK 3

CAMILLA ISLEY

Haley

"I don't have an umbrella," Haley called, shouting to be heard over the rumbling summer storm. "Do you?"

"No," David yelled back. "And I don't care."

He hurried past her out of the cover of the library porch and ran down the steps. When he reached the bottom, he tilted his face up and closed his eyes. In a matter of seconds, he was soaked.

"What are you doing?"

David looked at her from across the street, he was walking backward toward the center of Harvard Yard. "Come here. It's only water."

Haley didn't know what possessed her, but she did as he asked. She ran off the porch and joined him in the middle of the park. The sensation of the rain on her skin was electrifying as she spun on her toes, arms opened wide. Haley looked upward and laughed and laughed, unable to stop—until she pirouetted right into David's arms. The smile died on her lips as he caught her wrists and held her hands close to his chest, leaning his head down…

She tried to pull back, a ragged breath catching in her throat. "David, don't."

David's lips brushed her forehead in a soft, wet kiss. "I wasn't going to," he whispered. "The next time we kiss, you'll want to just as much as I do now…"

Two Months Ago

Madison

Madison fled the room and closed the door behind her, pausing a moment in the hall to catch her breath. Her hand was still wrapped around the doorknob, and her rib cage bobbed up and down in panicked gasps. Tears blurred her vision, and her temples were exploding with a mix of fear, shame, and the first signs of a killer hangover. Now that she was alone, the enormity of what she'd almost done hit her in the chest, guilt stabbing at her heart. *No*, she didn't have a second to spare thinking about the betrayal. Her number one priority was to get the hell out of her grandparents' house.

The Smithson country mansion was a two-story building with ten plus bedrooms and a three-acre garden with a pool. Even if the property belonged to her grandparents, Madison and her cousins had basically grown up here. But now the familiar walls of the upper-floor hall seemed to be pressing in on Madison, ready to crush her in their wake.

No one was up here, save for the people in the room she'd just left. Madison let go of the handle as if burnt by an electric shock and stumbled down the hall. She hopped down the stairs, careful not to trip on the hem of her bridesmaid dress, and paused on the last step to check the ground floor. The gardens were swarming with wedding guests, but the house itself was empty except for a few servers scurrying in and out of the kitchen.

All clear.

Running as fast as her high heels would allow, Madison covered the distance from the bottom of the stairs to the main door in a blur of lavender silk. Then she was out. No one had seen her, no one had called after her.

Good.

She could have handled a random relative or a guest, but if she'd run into Alice, or worse, her mom, they would have seen right through her. And what if she'd run into Georgiana?

The thought made her shiver, making her walk across the front-yard-turned-parking-lot all the more difficult. Her spiky heels kept sinking into the fine white gravel, causing her to stumble with every step as she traipsed toward her car. Madison considered taking off her shoes, but she doubted walking barefoot on pebbles would prove any more comfortable.

A few more wobbly steps got her to her SUV. With trembling hands, she fished her car keys out of her clutch to unlock it, then collapsed into the driver's seat. Only after hauling the door shut and putting a darkened window between her and the house did Madison finally feel safe.

She rested her head back against the seat, closing her eyes and taking a few deep breaths. When she'd calmed down enough to drive, she kicked off her shoes, threw them onto the passenger seat, and put the car into drive. But the row of cars parked in front was too close for her to get out. She maneuvered the car back and forward a few times, trying to steer it at an angle that would allow her to exit, but the SUV was too big.

Losing any composure she'd just tried to recover, Madison started screaming and crying, hitting the wheel in violent blows of desperation. Why did nothing in her life ever go according to plan?

"Why? WHY?" She kept shouting it over and over again. "WHY?"

When her throat began to hurt from the screaming, and her hands started to go numb from slamming her palms against leather-covered plastic, Madison instead gripped the wheel and desperately turned her head left and right in search of a solution. But she was one hundred percent trapped. What now? She couldn't go back to the reception and seek out the cars' owners. No, there were too many people on her "avoid-at-all-cost list" she didn't want to risk bumping into: Ethan, Vicky, Rose, Alice, Tyler, Georgiana…

With a sinking heart, Madison realized she'd never be able to show her face at another family gathering ever again. Later; she'd think about all that *later*. Now she had more pressing issues to solve. On a whim, Madison glanced at the rearview mirror—behind the SUV was nothing but spotless green grass and an intricate flower bed.

Well, sorry, Grandma, Madison thought as she switched the gear to reverse.

She hit the accelerator with enough force to jump up the curb separating the lawn from the gravel and reversed into the flower bed. Pushing the gear back to drive, she pressed her foot all the way down and the car screeched forward, leaving deep tire marks in its wake. Her grandparents' otherwise pristine front garden, ruined. She'd never hear the end of it if they found out it had been her, but at the moment she was too frenzied to care. Half of the family already hated her, so why not start working on pushing away the half that still cared about her?

The drive home seemed to take forever. When Madison finally pulled up in front of her building, she was still feeling nauseous. The pounding at her temples had not stopped, and the stomach-churning anxiety gnawing at her guts had not passed. She parked the car in her reserved spot, killed the engine, grabbed her shoes and clutch, and got out of the SUV barefooted holding up the hem of her dress—without heels, the skirt was too long.

Halfway to her building, Madison stopped dead in her tracks. Jack Sullivan was sitting on the front steps with a forlorn expression—the look of someone who'd been waiting for a long time.

Perfect. Just freaking perfect!

If there was one person missing from Madison's "avoid list" at the wedding, it seemed the dude had decided to show up at her place instead. Oh, he wasn't here to see her—she knew that. Jack was here for Alice, her roommate. But the last thing Madison needed right now was to be reminded of another guy who'd used her for easy sex and then forgotten all about her. Of another time she'd been too quick to jump in bed with a dude she'd just met. Of another betrayal that had almost cost Madison one of her best friends.

Jack didn't look like he was about to go away anytime soon, and Madison was too exhausted to wait for him to leave. She needed a shower, her bed, and a Xanax. Keys clutched tightly in her hands, she marched forward.

"Madison, hey," Jack said, jumping up. "I was—"

"Leave me alone," she replied. "I don't want to talk to you."

"Oh, okay." He backed off a step. "Do you know when Alice will be home?"

"I said leave me alone!" Madison yelled, brushing past him and shoving her key into the lock. She let herself in, then slammed the door in Jack's shocked face.

To hell with him, too.

In her room, she wrestled with the zipper to get out of the gown, threw the shoes in a corner, and headed to the bathroom for a hot shower.

Thankfully, the apartment was empty. No one around to ask her what had happened or to demand an explanation for her shitty behavior, which she still didn't begin to understand herself.

Yes, her life was a mess. Guys hated her, or used her and then threw her in the garbage once they'd had their fun. And her cousin Georgiana was the queen bee of bitches. *But nothing can justify the fact that I almost slept with Georgiana's husband on their wedding day.*

Was it because she'd wanted revenge? Or was she just so pathetic that even the most insignificant flattery from a handsome man made her lose control of herself?

"What's wrong with me?" Madison asked the empty bathroom.

She tried to wash away the shame and humiliation with the scorching water, rubbing her skin raw until it was all blotched and red. But no amount of scrubbing could cleanse the emotional stains off Madison's conscience.

Wrapped in a towel, wet hair loose on her shoulders, Madison collapsed on the bed ready to forget she existed. Unfortunately, the world wasn't as ready to forget her. Just as she was starting to doze off—thanks only to anti-anxiety drops—her phone rang. The muffled ringtone came from inside the clutch she'd dropped on the desk, only a few feet away from the bed but out of reach. Madison glared at the small bag, resentful someone had woken her when all she wanted was to be unconscious. She was pondering what would bother her more—to keep listening to the ringtone, or to get up and silence it—when the sound died on its own. *Finally, something goes right for once.*

But Madison had only just started getting cozy again on the pillows when the ringtone filled the room once more. This time, she dragged herself out of bed to find out who was calling.
Vicky.

Despite the way her cousin had reacted back at their grandparents' house—preferring comprehension over judgment after walking in on her sister's husband kissing a bridesmaid—Madison groaned. She stared at the phone still ringing in her hands, but couldn't bring herself to answer. The shame was too much. No matter if Vicky was the most understanding person in the world, Madison wasn't ready to talk to her. Filled with guilt, she let the call go unanswered, hoping her cousin would give up.

It didn't happen. Nothing ever happened the way Madison wished it to. When Vicky called again, Madison let that call, too, go unanswered. Then she turned off her phone and sank back on the bed, finally sure nothing would distract her from the void of her existence.

At some point she dozed off, and she must have slept for a few hours, because when she woke up the sun was starting to set. Madison straightened up against the headboard, her neck sore from falling asleep on wet hair. She blinked, trying to clear her vision. A shiver ran through her entire body; the air conditioning in the apartment was set on a low temperature, and the towel she'd been wearing had almost entirely slipped off.

Madison rubbed her arms with her hands, then climbed out of bed and went to fetch a pair of clean PJs. She was just pulling on the bottom half when the buzzer rang. Had that been what had woken her up?

Gingerly, she shuffled through the living room to the entrance hall. Their building had video intercoms, and their camera showed a distressed Vicky fidgeting with the button. She was still wearing her bridesmaid dress—an exact replica of the lavender gown now adorning the floor of Madison's room.

What now?

Madison didn't want to talk to her, but Vicky must've been worried sick to rush all the way here as soon as the wedding had ended. *I should have texted her to say I'd gotten home fine, but didn't feel like talking, not left her hanging. Can I do anything right?*

Well, there was no escape now. Vicky was here, probably wondering if Madison had died in a horrible car crash. Madison picked up the receiver just as the buzzer rang again.

"That's my buzzer you're abusing," Haley's voice drifted out of the intercom. "Can I help you?"

Madison's eyes snapped to the small screen on the wall. Haley—her other roommate—had just walked into the frame, and was now talking to Vicky. The girls seemed unaware Madison could overhear them.

"Yeah, sorry," Vicky said. "Hi. I'm Victoria Smithson, Madison's cousin. I was looking for her."

Haley gave Victoria a once-over. "Didn't you see her at the wedding?"

"Yeah. But I wanted to make sure she got home okay."

"Couldn't you call?"

"Her phone is off," Vicky said, looking annoyed. "Is there something wrong with me wanting to see my cousin?"

"No, of course not. It's just that in the two years we've lived together, this is the first house visit any of her relatives have paid her. Odd, right? Especially since you've spent the entire day together." Haley's cold logic wasn't missing a beat. "Did something happen?"

"No!" Vicky was too quick to say, and Madison could pick up Haley's skeptical expression even on the tiny black-and-white screen. "I only wanted to check if she got home safe."

"Well, her car is in our reserved spot." Haley pointed to the side and then crossed her arms. "Doesn't seem damaged in any way, so we can assume everything's fine."

"I'm sorry, but do you have something against me?" Vicky snapped. "Why can't you just let me in?"

"It's nothing personal, but don't you think that if Madison wanted to talk to you she'd have her phone on? Or she would've let you in herself." Haley turned toward the camera with a pointed look.

Instinctively, Madison took a step back. It was as if Haley was staring right at her through the screen.

"Listen, something did happen," Vicky said. "It's a family matter, and I can't discuss it with you, but Madison and I need to talk."

"Yeah, the problem is I can't shake the feeling Madison is doing her best to avoid you. If something is bothering her, she can talk to me."

"No!" Vicky yelled, frustrated. "She can't talk about what happened with you."

"Uh-oh, why not? Is she forbidden? She's not a kid you can boss around, you know."

Vicky stuttered something intelligible, her embarrassment bound to confirm Haley's theory.

Madison's roommate instantly went on the aggressive. "Aren't you supposed to be the good cousin?"

"I *am* the good cousin…"

Madison couldn't watch any longer. "It's okay, Haley," she said into the speaker. Both heads snapped toward the intercom. "Vicky is only trying to help."

"Oh, Madison." Vicky stepped so close to the camera that her face took over the entire screen. "Are you okay?"

"Yeah, I'm fine. Sorry I didn't pick up the phone, I was too…" She couldn't say, *"Ashamed."* "Well, you know, I didn't feel like talking."

"Madison, you need to talk to someone," Vicky insisted.

"Does it have to be you?"

Vicky turned sideways and looked at Haley. "You really stuck your neck out for my cousin."

"She's my best friend," Haley said simply.

"Please take care of her tonight, and whatever she tells you, please keep it to yourself."

"You can trust Haley," Madison jumped in. "She won't say anything."

"Seems I've been outvoted," Vicky sighed. "I'm going home, Madison. When you're ready to talk, please call me, okay?"

"I promise. And, Vicky… thank you."

Madison watched her cousin wave toward the camera as if to say she had nothing to be thanked for, and then Vicky turned on her heel and disappeared off the edge of the screen.

Haley frowned at the camera in an "explanation time" way, and said, "Since you're there, why don't you buzz me in?"

Madison took a deep breath, then pushed the button. This was not a conversation she was looking forward to.

She positioned herself on a stool at the kitchen bar with a direct view of the entrance to wait for her roommate's arrival. The few minutes Haley took to ride up in the elevator and reach the apartment seemed to last forever. When she finally got in, Madison's heart was in her throat. Talking about the wedding fiasco would force her to admit what had happened, even to herself.

"So," Haley said instead of *"Hello."* "Who do I have to beat?"

"Me, unfortunately," Madison replied, getting up from the stool. "I'm the villain in this one."

"You?" Haley hung her jacket on the rack behind the door and dropped her backpack on the carpet. "What did you do?"

Before confessing, Madison sought the comfort of a hug, clinging to Haley and collapsing on her shoulder in a fit of sobs. Haley caressed her hair and murmured soft, soothing words.

After Madison had calmed down enough, Haley said, "Get in bed,

I'm making tea."

Madison followed the order and waited under the covers for Haley. She came in a few minutes later with two steaming mugs and settled next to her, sipping the tea and waiting for when Madison would be ready to talk.

Between muffled sobs, Madison managed to spill out everything. "At the wedding, I kissed the groom," she confessed. "Georgiana's husband. Ethan and Rose walked in on us making out in one of the guest rooms. Ethan and Tyler began to fight and Rose was trying to stop Ethan from smashing Tyler's face when Vicky came into the room and took charge of everything. She gave Tyler a pep talk and tried to calm Ethan down, then she sent me home," Madison concluded, keeping her sad tale as short as she could. At the end, she turned toward Haley, prepared to find judgment and disappointment written all over her best friend's face and finding neither.

"Okay," Haley said. "Now I can see why Vicky was so worried about someone outside the family knowing."

"Because I'm a horrible person, the worst."

"You only made a mistake. Okay, a big one, but that doesn't make you a horrible person for life. What I don't understand is…" Haley frowned. "Were you aware the dude was the groom? I mean, were you out-of-your-mind-drunk or something?"

Madison wished she had at least plausible deniability. Wouldn't it be great to be able to say she was so drunk she hadn't realized who Tyler was? But she couldn't. "I knew," she confessed. "And I was tipsy, but definitely not drunk."

"So what made you do it? I know your other cousin is a total bitch, but you're not mean or vindictive. Did Georgiana do something bad today? Was kissing the groom a crazy revenge play?"

"Yes and no." Madison covered her face with her hands and shook her head. "Georgiana was her usual nasty self, but nothing out of the ordinary. She didn't say or do anything I haven't heard before… It's just that lately, with everything that's been going on, I haven't been myself."

"Why? What's been going on? What are you talking about?"

"The fight with Alice about Jack… Haley, she *says* she's forgiven me for sleeping with Jack, but she hasn't, not completely, at least, and I miss our friendship so much…"

"Alice!" Haley seemed to have just remembered they had another roommate. "Where is she?"

"Still at the wedding, or getting here. Ethan is giving her a ride; his girlfriend lives near campus."

Haley low-whistled. "Awkward."

"Another thing she can hate me for."

"Come on, Maddie, Alice doesn't hate you."

"I'll agree with you if she doesn't come home tonight." Madison mustered a small smile. "Jack was waiting for her downstairs when I got here, seemed like he'd been there all day…"

"Ah, I didn't see him, think he got her?"

"One can hope."

"Anyway, about today… I know you, Maddie. The fight with Alice wasn't enough to drive you to a make out session with your cousin's groom on their wedding day."

Madison looked away, blushing. "No, but it got me to mull over that period of my life… Freshman year?"

"What about it?"

"Nothing special. I just met a lot of assholes that year who weren't exactly nice to me, and neither was Jack." Madison threw her mug-free hand up before Haley could say anything. "I'm sure he's going to make Alice happy, it's clear he's in love with her, but back then…"

"No prince charming, I get it."

Madison scoffed. "Nowhere near."

"Maddie, you're circling around what's really upset you."

"I'm only saying I was already in a fragile state of mind when David rocked the boat for good."

Madison felt Haley stiffen at the mention of David—her boyfriend Scott's brother.

"How?"

"Our breakup wasn't pretty."

Haley sighed. "Tell me everything."

Madison stared at the wall, gaze unfocused, as a memory of that day danced before her eyes.

***

"I've told you a thousand times I don't want to meet here," David said

as he opened his apartment door to find Madison standing on the other side. "Hello" and "come in" apparently forgotten.

"Yeah, but Scott is at my place with Haley, so I thought it'd be okay to hang here for a change," Madison said. "Plus, I didn't want to be there right now."

David finally moved aside to let her in. "Why not?"

"Alice and I had this huge fight. It's all solved in theory, but I'd still rather not be at home."

"You and Alice? Not Haley?"

"No, why would I fight with Haley?"

"No reason, apparently." David sounded annoyed—no, more like disappointed. Madison came closer to hug him, but he shuffled away. "I don't have time for this."

"Why? School's over. You only have to wait for Commencement Day. Are you nervous?"

"No."

Madison fished in her bag for a gift-wrapped book. "This is for you: my graduation present."

David arched an eyebrow as he took the gift. "What is it?"

"A collection of my favorite poems."

David chuckled at first. "Priceless, that's priceless." Then he laughed bitterly. "Can you really be that stupid?"

Madison flushed in mortification. "You don't have to read it if you don't want to."

David threw the book across the room, the wrapping paper tearing as it hit the wall. "I'm not my brother!" he shouted. "I don't care about the words of other tormented souls who've been dead for centuries."

"It's only a present, no need to be such a dick about it."

David pinched his nose. "This isn't working out."

"What isn't?"

"You, us, this."

Tears Madison had fought hard not to shed started to roll down her cheeks. "Why?"

"I can't stand you. All you do is talk, talk, talk"—David mimicked the action with his hand—"all the time. I can stand you only when you're asleep."

"What are you talking about? We've been dating for two months and

you never said a thing."

"A mistake, clearly."

"If you hate me so much, why go out with me at all?"

"You had your purpose. Seems it's run out."

"What purpose?"

"Madison, I need you to leave." David pushed past her and reopened the door.

"But—"

"GET OUT!"

***

"I had no idea what to say, Haley, I basically fled the place… It was so humiliating," Madison said, concluding her tale. "It made me feel… I don't know, worthless."

"You're not worthless," Haley hissed, pulling her into a tighter hug.

There was a fury in her friend's words that made Madison lift her head to look Haley in the eye. "What's up with you? You seem angrier than I am."

"It's David. I *hate* him."

"Yeah, well… You tried to warn me about him. My bad I didn't listen."

"No, you did nothing wrong. He's a jerk."

"Yeah, but I'm not such an angel, remember? Anyway, between him, the Alice/Jack drama, and my family… I lost it today."

"Tell me how it started, precisely."

"With a ketchup spill." Madison chuckled bitterly. "So ridiculous! During the buffet, I had ketchup on my fingers after eating a slider burger… I was looking for a napkin when I almost bumped into the bride. Georgiana was a mean bitch as always. She said something about me being a pig and how I was fatter than her even if she was three months pregnant." Madison closed her eyes. "At that moment I hated her, Haley. I'd never felt a loathing so strong. She made me sick. I wanted to grab her by the hair and smash her face into the mayonnaise dip."

Haley scoffed. "She sounds precious enough."

"But of course I didn't do anything; I just stood there and let her walk all over me. I smiled, cleaned my hands on a napkin, and got back to my table, which, being a bridesmaid, was the same as the bride and groom.

For the entire lunch, I had to stomach Georgiana ranting on about how perfect her life was… Tyler was seated right in front of me and seemed equally rattled by Georgiana's ramblings. I caught him looking at me more than once and I was happy about it. It was like my little secret revenge against Georgiana. I was thinking, 'You might've forced him to marry you by getting pregnant accidentally-on-purpose, but he doesn't love you.'"

"So you *wanted* to sleep with the groom?"

"Not really, I was happy with him eye-flirting with me, but then things got out of control. By the end of the meal I just needed to get out. I couldn't stand Georgiana a second longer, so I walked away to get some air. I was hiding in the garden behind a hedge when Tyler found me. He was being all nice and cute and charming, and I thought, 'Screw Georgiana.' I wanted to hurt her. I wanted to hurt myself and all my family… It's hard to explain. I knew I was doing something wrong and self-destructive, but I wanted to do it anyway."

"And all of this because of David?"

"David, Georgiana, Alice, Jack, my life in general…" *The fact that I'm in love with your boyfriend,* Madison added inside her head. "Your pick."

"But in the end, nothing unrepairable happened," Haley said. "I mean, it could've been horrible, but it wasn't. Vicky seemed more worried than mad."

"You didn't see the glare in Ethan's eyes. He's never talking to me again."

"I'm sure that's not true. He'll come around if you leave him time to process." Haley squeezed her hand supportively. "He probably has no idea what a bitch his sister can be. Vicky will give him a reality check."

"Mmm, I wouldn't be so sure. Ethan has such a blind spot when it comes to Georgiana."

"But not Vicky?"

"No, she loves her sister, but can still see Georgiana's many flaws. Vicky is the only person in my family I feel close to."

Haley grimaced. "I'm sorry I gave her such a hard time."

"Thanks for being my champion, by the way." Madison smiled at her friend. "I'm sure your protective attitude let Vicky know her nut-job of a cousin was in good hands."

"You're not a nut job."

"Wish I could believe you."

"But you had a hell of a day. Why don't you try to sleep it off?"

"Will you stay with me?"

"Sure, let me just get changed."

Haley went to her room and came back wearing a pastel rainbow unicorn onesie covered in little multicolor stars. She snuggled under the covers next to Madison and comforted her until she fell into a dreamless sleep.

Alice

Alice woke up smiling. Even if her brain was still half-unconscious, the joy was too strong not to seep through all the layers of her mind. She was so used to waking up being the hard part, the moment when she'd have to remember it had all been a dream. That she wasn't Jack's girlfriend, that they hadn't made love all night, and that he'd never see her that way. Not today.

Today reality surpassed all fantasies. Her toes curled under the sheets as memories of how they'd spent the night IRL flashed before her eyes. *Yeah, definitely better than every dream could ever hope to be.* For a brief moment she doubted herself; could that really all have happened? Slowly, Alice lifted her lids, eyes focusing at once on the very naked proof that, *yes*, it had been real.

Jack was lying on the bed next to her. Head tilted to the side on the pillow, dark hair ruffled in all directions, and not a sock on his body. She ran her fingertips down the length of his collarbone and arm, all the way to his wrist and back up. She needed to touch as well as see before she could let herself believe Jack was in love with her after they'd been just friends for three years.

A pang of fear made her chest contract. How would their relationship change now? How would they transition into being boyfriend and girlfriend? Would everything be different? Better? Worse? Would sex ruin everything?

Her mental rant was interrupted when Jack opened one eyelid to peek at her sideways. "Ice, I can hear you thinking too much."

"I'm not."

Jack turned sideways to stare at her properly, elbow bent on the pillow, head propped on his hand. "So you weren't getting all inside your head worrying about how our friendship is ruined forever, and how we're doomed, and wondering how long before we break up?"

"No?"

"Good." He pushed a lock of hair away from her face. "Because we're never breaking up."

"How can you be so sure?"

"I love you."

Alice's insides melted. It wasn't the first time he'd told her, but the words were still so new on his lips. She reached up to touch his face, again wanting to make sure he was real and not just a dream. "I love you, too," she whispered back.

Jack pulled her into his arms. "Now that you're mine, I'm never letting you go, Ice. Deal?"

"Deal." Alice giggled. "But at some point, you'll have to let me go home."

"Why?"

Alice pointed to the floor, where her cocktail dress from the wedding lay in a pool of blush chiffon. "As lovely as that dress is, I can't go around all day wearing it."

Jack's mouth curled at the corners. "Fine by me. I prefer you naked anyway."

"You have a roommate," Alice chided. "And I need to check on Blue. Remember the little guy who introduced us?"

"Remind me to buy him some expensive bunny treats." Jack smiled. "Can you have breakfast in a cocktail dress?"

Alice's stomach grumbled in reply. "Starbucks' patrons don't judge, and I'm starving."

She'd eaten plenty at the wedding, but they'd skipped dinner altogether last night. They'd been too busy doing… what Jack was starting to do now…

Alice's body tingled under his touch, and with a playful smile, she said, "Now, now. Just because you got lucky once…"

"Oh, yeah?"

Alice squirmed under his gaze.

Jack's grin was wicked. "So it was just a one-off?"

Whatever sassy reply Alice was trying to come up with was silenced by Jack's lips. Oh, gosh, he was *so* going to get lucky any time he wanted.

***

Alice was fighting hard not to sing her joy to the world as she unlocked the door of her apartment. With a full belly, the phantom of Jack's lips all over her body, the more visible trail of beard burns all over her face and neck, and the echo of those simple, life-changing words—*I love you*—ringing in her ears, Alice was walking on a cloud and sporting a smile so wide her cheeks ached.

The smile, however, was short-lived. It died on her lips as she spotted Haley's anxious expression. Her roommate was standing in the living room holding her chin with one hand in a pensive pose. When she heard Alice come in, instead of saying *"Hello"* Haley pressed a finger to her lips and pointed at Madison's door with her other hand.

"What's going on?" Alice whispered. Haley closed the distance between them and made to push her back out the door, but Alice resisted. "Wait, I have to get changed and take a shower."

"The shower can wait," Haley whispered back. "We need to talk. Put something on and meet me on the roof. Please be quiet, I don't want Madison to wake up."

Begrudgingly, Alice shuffled into her room and changed into a pair of sweatpants and a T-shirt. She checked Blue's cage. It had already been cleaned and the bunny fed. Well, even if they didn't let her shower, at least her roommates were good for something.

That's when Alice remembered Madison had come home from the wedding in tears yesterday and she'd left Haley to deal with the mess, not sparing the matter a second thought until now. She hadn't even texted Madison to ask her how she was. And from Haley's urgency, the issue was far from solved.

I'm a horrible friend.

Now filled with worry, Alice hurried to the rooftop.

"What's going on?" she asked as soon as she set foot outside.

Haley turned to face her, eyes positively murderous. "I'm going to kill David Williams. I hate him, Alice, I hate him so much."

"Why? What happened? What did he do?"

Haley sighed. "I've been authorized to tell you everything, since Madison wants you to know, but she's not in the right state of mind to repeat the whole story…"

The more Haley talked, the more Alice started to connect all the dots from the previous day and weeks. The blue shadows under Madison's eyes. Her pale face, newly cynical view on weddings, and general subdued attitude. Madison pretending the breakup with David had been unimportant, and her refusal to discuss it. Alice had blamed Madison's sudden reticence on their argument over Jack, but deep down she'd known something else had to have happened. It seemed David Williams had happened! And one of her best friends—*yours truly*—abandoning Madison at a time of need had happened. Even after she'd learned about their breakup, Alice hadn't asked, because her pride and heart were still sore after discovering Jack and Madison had had a one-night stand in freshman year. And Haley had probably been too clueless as usual to notice—they usually had to spell things out for her where people's feelings were concerned. Haley could talk to robots, but she found people much harder to read.

As Haley wrapped up the full story, more pieces fell into place. Madison's sudden disappearance from the wedding the day before. Ethan, Vicky, and Rose confabulating in a close circle. Ethan's homicidal expression when he looked at Tyler. And the groom's pale and frazzled appearance.

What. A. Mess. No wonder Ethan was giving me attitude yesterday, *Alice thought. At least now it made sense.*

"…And then there's Scott," Haley concluded. "Madison likes him more than she's letting on, doesn't she?"

Well, ding-dong, Haley. That took you long enough to grasp.

"Mmm," was all Alice mumbled, not wanting to confirm Haley's fears, regardless of how well-founded they might be.

"Mmm?" Haley turned toward her, crossing her arms over her chest. "Is that all you have to say?"

No, *Alice thought.* I want to tell you how happy I am. How crazily, stupidly in love I feel. I want to savor the joy at least for twenty-four hours without being pulled into more drama.

Alice chided her inner self for being so selfish. One of her friends was in pain and all messed up. No matter what Madison had failed to confess, she'd always been there to support Alice through every Jack crisis. They had spent endless movie nights in whenever Jack had a new date and Alice was too depressed to go out. And Madison hated watching TV, she only loved books.

"We have to do something," Haley insisted.

"Yeah, but..." Alice pulled her hair up into a ponytail. "What *can* we do? I mean, other than being around and being supportive?"

"I don't know, Alice. I feel so guilty. She's in love with Scott, isn't she?"

"I can't honestly say," Alice said vaguely.

Haley threw her a no-bullshit look.

"Okay," Alice conceded. "I suspect she's more into Scott than she's letting on."

"Wonderful!" Haley pressed her hands to her temples.

"Hey, it's not your fault. You don't have to feel guilty about dating him."

"But how could I not? I'm his girlfriend. Remember how much you used to hate Jack's girlfriends? How can Madison stand to live with me?"

"First, those are a lot of questions, and second, I'm sure Madison doesn't hate you."

"Would you not hate me? Just a few weeks ago you wanted to claw her eyes out for sleeping with Jack, *once*, three years ago. And I've been with Scott for the past six months, right in her face! And I'm not even considering giving him up because I'm just so in love with him... but then, it's impossible not to feel guilty about how happy I am."

Alice nudged Haley shoulder-to-shoulder. "So is Scott *the* one?"

Her friend smiled. "I suspect he might be. I've never felt this way for anyone."

"Not even for the infamous masked dude from last summer?"

"Please don't remind me about that." Haley hid her face behind her hands. "I dance with a masked stranger at a party, kiss him, never learn his name, and spend the next six months obsessing over him. How lame is that?"

"Sounded pretty romantic when you were telling us the story." Alice started talking using what she called a "movie trailer" voice. "A lonely dame at a ball rescued by a mysterious masked gentleman who sweeps her off her feet, leading her in a passionate dance—"

"He was a horrible dancer."

"It's the thought that counts." Alice continued talking in her movie voice. "A romantic stroll in the gardens under a thousand fairy lights, and then, at the stroke of midnight, an epic kiss…"

Haley laughed at her theatrics, but said, "It wasn't midnight, I'm no Cinderella, and it's the dude who fled the ball without telling me his name. Sometimes I even wonder if that night was real. You know when something seems so 'too good to be true' that you ask yourself if it wasn't all a dream?"

Haley had just described how Alice had woken up that morning, and she couldn't suppress the little smirk that escaped her lips. "I know."

Haley caught the smile and flashed a grin back. "Tell me, Miss Brown, are those beard burns all over your face?"

Alice couldn't keep it inside any longer, she told Haley everything. How Jack had waited for her in front of their building, how he'd told her he was in love with her, and how they'd spent the night and the best part of the morning.

"Great!" Haley scoffed sarcastically. "So we're both the happiest we've ever been and our best friend is at an all-time low. Alice, I love Scott so much… and he loves me back… a-and I don't know how to shield Madison from all that."

"For one, we don't rub our happiness in her face."

"And for two?"

"We have to avoid becoming two of those cheesy couples that do things only in pairs. We have to keep going out with a wider group of people—singles and couples—and include Madison as much as possible. And when she has a low day and needs a girls' night in, we tell the beloved boyfriends to beat it."

"And you think that will be enough?"

Alice shrugged. "It's the best we can do; we can't fix her love life for her. When Madison's ready, she'll find the right guy. In the meantime, our job is to be around as much as possible and to force Madison to be social."

"She likes parties more than I do."

"True, but what guys do you usually pick up at parties?"

"The wrong kind. Gotcha."

"Anyway, there won't be many parties, at least for a while." Alice sighed. "Not with almost everyone gone for the summer."

"Right. Only the best are left." Haley smiled, staring at the Boston skyline in the distance. "I could never spend a whole summer home."

"Me neither, I'd be bored out of my mind."

"And also lovesick over Jack."

"Especially lovesick over Jack." Alice flashed her friend a megawatt smile. "So how's your schedule for summer break? Are you going to be super busy?"

"Nah." Haley toyed with a lock of hair, curling it around her fingers. "I'm taking three summer courses, but I should be able to stick around a lot. You?"

"Same for me. I'm doing an internship at a pharmaceutical company downtown, but it's mornings only." Alice grinned. "Jack applied for the same program without telling me, you know, when we weren't speaking…"

"I like his style."

"Yeah, me too. You know what Madison is doing?"

"A literary research project for her department."

"And Scott?"

"He applied for a few internships, something to do with pre-med school. But no answers so far, I think. We haven't really discussed it yet."

"Okay, so everyone will be here for the summer," Alice said. "Now that we have a plan, can I go shower?"

"Yeah, thanks for the pep talk." Haley pulled her into a hug and added jokingly, "Now you can go wash Jack off."

They both laughed and stumbled toward the elevator, still hugging each other. They were a team; they could solve any problem if they stuck together.

Haley

Haley spent Sunday at home with her roommates. They baked cookies together, and Haley and Alice made an effort to avoid any boy talk. The strain was clear on Alice's part; she was bursting with happiness and it was obvious she had to check herself not to smile and hum love tunes under her breath 24/7. For her part, Madison put on a brave face and let them organize the day for her.

But being a good friend had meant ditching her boyfriend for most of the weekend. So as she knocked on Scott's door early on Monday afternoon, Haley was super eager to jump into his arms.

When he came to open the door, Haley's breath caught in her chest. That face. Those eyes. That mouth.

Despite the fact that they'd been dating for six months, he still had that effect on her. Today he was wearing a bright blue tank top that made his muscled arms stand out, a pair of white basketball shorts, and his feet were bare on the wooden floor. His dirty blonde hair was already streaked golden from the first real sun of summer, and he'd never looked better.

Scott smiled. "Hey."

The smile brightened his entire face, from his sexy lips to his emerald green eyes.

"Hey, you," Haley breathed when Scott hugged her.

He smelled like he always did: soapy, manly, delicious. But when Haley pressed her face into Scott's chest, guilt suddenly flared through her. Haley was here in his arms, and Madison was at home, *alone.* They were in love with the same guy, and that was a problem without a solution. One of them would always end up being hurt. Unless, of course, one of them stopped loving him.

But how could you not love Scott? It was inconceivable. He was gorgeous, smart, kind, and sexy as hell. He was also a bookworm like Madison. They'd been sharing the same Lit classes for years. Haley could just picture her best friend adoring Scott from a distance, too shy to talk to him. She was equally glad and sad Madison had never mustered the courage to speak to Scott. If she had, Scott could've been Madison's boyfriend now; they had so much in common. They both were words people, whereas Haley preferred numbers.

But, hey, opposites attract.

And as guilty as Haley felt, there was no way she would ever give up Scott.

He pulled her into the apartment and shut the door, his lips slowly making their way from her neck to her mouth.

"It's only been a day, but I've missed you," Scott whispered in her ear.

Haley mumbled something back, too distracted by the cute, tiny freckles scattered all over his shoulders. All she wanted to do now was take off his top and feel that hard chest pressed against hers as she dug her nails into his muscled back. She started kissing the freckles, one by one. And Scott must've been a mind reader, because in a swift move he took off the tank top, draping it over his other shoulder.

"Easy, tiger," Haley joked, pushing him toward his room all the same.

He flashed her a grin. "From the way you're looking at me, I thought you were the tiger."

Yeah, that was exactly how she felt. Like a hungry cat ready to pounce.

Haley kicked the door shut and pushed Scott onto the bed. Then she almost jumped into his arms, losing herself in the kisses of the boy she loved so much. And at that moment there wasn't space for anyone else in her mind. There were only Scott and his kisses.

***

The guilt waited until a couple of hours later to sneak back into Haley's mind and start whispering in her ear about how selfish she was for being so utterly happy.

"Are you sure you're okay?" Scott asked.

They were cozied up on his bed. Haley had stolen his tank top—she loved wearing his clothes—which reached almost to her knees.

Basketball players are tall. Haley winked to herself for dating one who, at present, was left shirtless next to her.

Haley shuffled across the bed and dropped her head onto that beautiful, smooth-skinned chest. "Yes, sorry." She kissed one of his flat-muscled pectorals. "I'm just a little distracted."

A little distracted. That's one way of putting it.

Haley was positively torn between two loyalties. On one side stood Scott. She wanted to tell him everything, not to keep secrets from him. But then there was Madison. Haley couldn't expose her friend's feelings to him. If the roles were reversed, Haley would be humiliated by his knowledge. Neither could she discuss how disgusting his brother's behavior toward Madison had been when David had dumped her. She had to put Madison's need for privacy before anything else; her best friend was fragile and needed to be protected. But it still sucked not being able to tell her boyfriend why she was in such a bad mood.

The front door slammed shut and Haley jolted in Scott's arms.

"Sounds like my charming roommate is home," Scott said.

The risk of bumping into David had been a calculated one when Haley had asked Scott to meet at his place. Better than Madison running into Scott at their apartment. Plus, Haley couldn't make love to Scott with Madison in the adjoining room. It would break whatever was left of her friend's heart.

"When is he moving out?" Haley asked. "I mean, isn't school over? Shouldn't he get on with his life, get a job somewhere, or something?"

Scott sighed. "I'm afraid that's not David's plan."

"What do you mean?"

"He's doing a summer internship at an investment bank in downtown Boston, and he's starting his MBA at Harvard Business School in the fall."

"So he'll be here for another two years."

"Yep."

"And he's not moving out…"

"Nope. But at least he won't be on the basketball team any longer. I'll see him less than ever and so will you especially…"

It'd better be that way.

Haley wasn't sure she could control her rage around David. There was something in him that made her go to extremes. She'd never thought she'd be able to loathe someone, *really hate*, but David had proved her wrong.

"…Would you want to go?"

Where?

Scott had kept on talking and was now looking at her expectantly. He wore a little frown, but was trying hard to smile as if he wanted to be casual about what he was asking, when in fact it was something he cared deeply about. But *what* was he asking?

"Go where? I'm sorry, I got lost in thought again." Haley forced herself to stop twirling her hair and pay attention. "Where are you going?"

"Damn, you really are distracted." Scott's face fell with disappointment. "Are you sure you don't want to tell me what it's about?"

"I'm sure," Haley said, and made a move-on-with-what-you-were-saying gesture while squeezing his hand to show him her worries did not concern their relationship.

Scott rolled his eyes, but he let it go. "I said that you'll have to see even less of my brother if you come to California with me this summer."

Haley's chest contracted with sudden fear. "Since when are you spending the summer in California?" Haley disentangled herself from Scott's arms to stare at him.

"I wasn't until this morning."

"What happened this morning?"

"I got this." Scott handed her his phone, an email opened on the screen.

Haley quickly skimmed the text. It was an official acceptance notice for Scott to shadow a certain Dr. Kendrick Allen, a neurological surgeon.

"I know it's last minute," Scott said as Haley kept reading the details of the email. The internship started on June 20—*only two weeks from today*—and ended on August 26, the week before the fall term started. *Two months without Scott.* "But I never expected Dr. Allen to accept my application. This guy is like the best in his field, he's leading this revolutionary research program on neuro—"

"I can't come," Haley interrupted him. "You know I'm taking summer courses."

"I thought you were just considering it. You never told me you actually enrolled." Scott's eyes widened. "Summer School, huh?"

Haley stared at the bedspread, her finger picking at a loose thread. She knew Summer School sounded uncool. "I like the different crowd." She shrugged. "And there's always interesting people from all over the world with all these unique backgrounds and coding experience."
Oh, hell. Did that come out as lame and geeky as it sounded in my head?

Scott lifted her chin with a finger. "Well, that settles it, then. I'm not going."

"But it's an incredible opportunity."

"I have a backup internship in Boston. I never thought Dr. Allen would pick me."

"Because he's the best."

"He is, but the doctor here in Boston is amazing too."

"But not *as* great." Haley sighed. She didn't want Scott to go. But for him to lose such a once-in-a-lifetime opportunity because of her... "Two months isn't a long time," she lied.

Two months without him would stretch on for an eternity.

"Haley Thomas, I'm not going anywhere without you," Scott declared. "I love you, and I don't want to spend a single day apart. End of story."

A warm fuzz threatened to turn Haley's inside to jelly. Scott's gaze was so intense, and he sounded so sure. She stared at the phone still clutched in her hand. Scott had until Friday to accept—or refuse. The offer would stand for four more days.

"Don't reply today," she said. He was about to protest, but she stopped him. "Please, take all the time you have to think about it. I want you to be sure. An opportunity like this is too important for you, for your future career. Take at least a couple of days to think it over."

"I will, but I'm not moving to California without you."

***

Dating varsity basketball players had its cons. Haley would've loved to spend the entire evening with Scott, but tonight he had to go meet a few of his teammates for an outdoor basketball game. Last winter, basketball had been the silent third wheel in their relationship and even now that the official Harvard Crimson team training had stopped for summer break, the game was still a huge part of Scott's life. He spent almost as much time training now as during the regular season, and never missed an opportunity to play.

So, after spending every last possible second with Scott, Haley was running late. She'd just left his apartment and was hurrying home, wondering why phones had the special ability to lose themselves inside a woman's bag.

Haley rummaged again in her maxi bag, but her hands kept coming in contact with all sorts of different things; everything but a phone. And she needed to call her mom ASAP. She could picture her mother already staring at her smartphone, fretting as she waited for Haley's call.

Miranda Thomas was the techiest of her parents and the one who could always be relied upon to pick up whenever Haley called. She would then put the call on speaker for Haley's dad to take part. Weekly calls were Haley's special ritual with her mom and dad. She rang them every Monday and Friday night—and tried to never miss an appointment.

Haley rattled her bag and attempted another blind search, but with all the stuff cluttered inside, she couldn't find the phone. Especially not while she was speed-walking across campus.

Frustrated, she stopped near a bench and, with a sigh, knelt next to it and up-ended the overfilled bag onto the seat. When something disappeared into the folds of her maxi bag, there was no other way of luring it out. But even after a forensic examination of all the objects scattered on the bench seat, her phone was still MIA.

A flashback of taking the phone out of her bag to check her texts and dropping it on Scott's nightstand shot through Haley's head. Unfortunately, there was no follow-up memory of taking the phone from the night table and putting it back into the bag.

Haley groaned, swatting the bench.

The phone was at Scott's apartment, and Scott was at a game that would last at least two hours, maybe more. But Haley had to call her mom—she checked her watch—*right now.*

This left only one solution. After all, the other Williams brother *was* at home. Haley groaned again. She really didn't want to confront David. Not today. Not ever. But what other choice did she have? She could hurry home and Skype her parents instead, but the thought of her phone being alone in the same house as David Williams gave her the creeps. And since her mom would probably call her way before she could get home and in front of a computer, David would know the phone was there because he'd hear it ringing.

Shoving everything back into her bag with a sweep of her arm, Haley got up and hurried back toward Scott's house.

***

"I forgot my phone," Haley said, skipping the pleasantries and barging into the apartment past David.

"Hello, Sunshine," he said, using his usual mocking tone. "Would you like to come in?"

"I'm just picking up my phone and then I'm gone."

"You mean this?"

Haley stopped halfway toward Scott's room and turned around.

302

David stood there looking at her with an arrogant, self-satisfied face that demanded to be slapped. An infuriating lopsided grin was stamped on his cruel lips. He must've picked up her phone from somewhere because he was wiggling it tantalizingly between his thumb and index finger.

She marched back to where he was standing. "Give it back." Haley made to grab the phone, but he raised his arms over his head, way out of her reach.

Damn basketball players and their being super tall—*or ex-basketball players, in this case.*

"Say please," David taunted.

Haley gave up the fight to reach the phone and stared him down. "David, stop it. I need to call my mom; I don't want her to worry."

"Miranda? Looovely lady."

"How do you know my mother's name?"

"Before you got here, she'd already called three times and, as you said, we wouldn't want the lovely Miranda to get worried, so I picked up and acted voicemail. You're welcome."

"You looked into my phone?"

David scoffed. "Don't worry; your lovey-dovey, emoji-filled texts with my brother would be too boring for me to spy on."

"I want my phone back."

He took a step forward so that now he was towering over her, crowding her space, his gaze intense. "Say. Please."

A familiar scent Haley couldn't quite place—one associated with a positive memory—filled her nostrils. Confused, Haley backed away instinctively. "Stop doing that."

"Doing what?" David asked, acting all innocent.

"The flirty eyes thing, and the charming act… I want nothing to do with you."

His eyes flared bluer, if that was even possible. "Now," he said, tossing her the phone. Haley caught it and quickly texted her mom to say she'd call her later. All the while David kept talking. "There's really no need to be rude. If you're mad you can't withstand my charms, that's your problem, darling."

"Your charms?" Haley hissed, pressing Send and fixing her narrowed gaze on him. "What charms? Yeah, you've pretty eyes and a pretty face, but that's it. You're mean and cruel for no reason. The way you hurt

Madison makes me sick, you—"

"Your friend is just another stupid girl in love with my soppy brother. Madison didn't care about me enough for me to really hurt her. She used me as a rebound, same as I did her. But speaking of hurting Blondie..." David snapped his fingers, then pointed one at her. "I bet your relationship with dear old Scotty is doing more damage to her right now than I ever could."

A blow too close to home. Haley was at a loss for words.

"Ooh." David smiled, satisfied. "Seems I've touched a sore point. I apologize, Sunshine."

Rage flared in Haley's chest. "You don't even try to deny you used her. How can you be so arrogant after everything you've done? You should be ashamed of yourself."

"You confuse me for someone who cares about your opinion, little miss 'I like to judge.'" His next words came out in a low hiss. "None of this matters to me. None of it."

"Then why do you even bother to tease me all the time?"

"Oh, that?" David asked, his voice mocking again. "That's just for fun. I enjoy watching how hard you try to deny the obvious chemistry between us."

"There's no chemistry between us," Haley spat. "I wouldn't touch you with a ten-foot pole if you were the last guy on earth."

"Might be too late for that, my dear."

"What do you mean?"

David started walking toward her, slowly, deliberately. Haley backed away until her shoulders came in contact with the living room wall. David stopped a few steps short of where she was standing and covered the top half of his face with his hands. He lifted the index finger of each hand to show only his eyes through the narrow gap, giving the impression he was looking at her through a mask.

And then he bowed.

***

"Would you do me the honor of this dance?"

The guy bowing in front of Haley was staring up at her through an elaborate black mask. His eyes were a dazzling electric blue and the corner of his mouth was turned up in a lopsided grin that promised

304

danger.

"But of course." Haley did a coy little curtsy and took the stranger's hand. "Mister…?"

"Giving you my name would defy the purpose of us wearing masks," the man said, taking her hand and straightening his back. He was remarkably tall, a good full head taller than Haley.

"My gentle sir, you find me at a disadvantage," she said, keeping up the pretense of speaking like gents and dames while he led her toward the dance floor. "How is it fair when my face is practically bare and yours almost entirely covered?"

Haley's mask for the Venetian Masquerade Ball consisted of a few strategically placed stick-on Swarovski crystals scattered around her eyes. But the stranger's mask covered the majority of his face, leaving only his lips visible. And those sparkly blue eyes.

He leaned forward and whispered in her ear, "Then I'm all the luckier for it."

If the costume party had been dull up until the mysterious man's appearance—and definitely not worth the investment in her rented princess gown or the ticket's cost—it seemed the night could still turn around.

Keeping at the edges of the dancing crowd, they started swirling in time with the music. Neither of them had a clear idea of what they were doing, but Haley hoped her long skirt made enough of a show to cover for their poor dancing skills. Not that she cared much, anyway; she was too entranced by the blue eyes of the man leading her so inexpertly in what had officially become the most romantic dance of her life.

Not being able to see the guy's face was both enticing and infuriating. He could be anyone and no one. And the only detail the mask didn't leave to the imagination—his full lips—didn't help steady Haley's breath. A hot flush warmed her skin; she had become too sensitive to the touch of one of his hands on the small of her back. And to his other hand holding hers, to the way sharp electric tingles shot down her arm from where their skin touched.

"I've never seen eyes as green as yours," he said.

Haley wanted to reply that the blue of his was no joke either, but it seemed corny to repeat the same compliment he'd just paid her. "You have pretty eyes, too," she said, almost out of breath.

His gaze was so intense it was squeezing the air out of Haley's lungs. They didn't say much afterward; in fact, they didn't speak at all. Haley and her masked stranger stared wordlessly into each other's eyes, green into blue, while they kept doing a poor impression of a waltz.

Haley wasn't able to explain the force of the insta-connection, the way it made her pulse race and her breath short. The music, the costumes, the elegant hall; it all seemed to disappear, reducing Haley's world to those blue eyes and full lips and the thousand faces that could be hiding under the black mask.

Maybe love at first sight was a thing. Even if it turned out she had no idea who this man was, she still felt an ease, a sense of belonging, that she'd hardly ever experienced with any of her exes.

Distracted by her own thoughts, Haley stepped on the stranger's toes.

He winced under the mask and said, "What do you say we take a stroll outside? It's getting scorching hot in here." He rolled a finger on the inside of his shirt's collar. "And we've demonstrated our awful dancing skills enough for one night."

Haley swatted him playfully. "Who are you calling an awful dancer?"

He smiled wickedly and offered her his elbow. Haley linked their arms together and followed him outside, where the temperature was a bit cooler thanks to a crisp evening breeze abating the late summer heat.

The villa where the party was being hosted resembled more a European palace out of a fairy tale than a countryside mansion in Massachusetts. With its imposing size, light brick architecture, turrets, and large windows, it was more castle than house. And its gardens were just as stylish, a mix of flower beds and shrubs organized in symmetric geometrical patterns and lit with a thousand fairy lights.

There was a small gazebo in the center of the garden, a wrought iron structure covered in white roses silhouetted against the dark night sky. Without speaking, they both headed toward the flowery cage. It seemed like a good place to talk—or not talk.

When they stopped underneath the arch, the tension in Haley's body spiked. She felt edgier than the first time she'd kissed someone.

"You make me nervous," she told the stranger.

He held both her hands close to his chest as he faced her. "Good nervous or bad nervous?"

"Good, I think."

He tilted his head at her questioningly, and Haley started to over-talk. "I don't know your name or what your face looks like, but I feel like I've known you forever. Can you at least tell me if you're from around here? Will I see you again after tonight?"

"I go to school in Cambridge. I'm about to start senior year."

"Me too. You go to Harvard? What's your major?"

"Shh…" He pressed a finger to her lips. "So many questions…"

Haley kissed the finger in what she hoped was a sensual gesture, then guided his hand down to rest on her waist. "So little answers…"

The charming stranger joined both his hands behind her back and pulled her against his body. Less than an inch separated their faces now. For the first time, Haley's nostrils filled with his scent—a mix of sun-kissed skin and a citrus aroma, bergamot or orange. A fragrance that was woody, citrusy, and salty at the same time. It made her think of a sunny day on a boat in the middle of the Mediterranean. It's what Haley imagined all those male models from D&G perfume commercials must smell like.

The mysterious man spared her the time to take another ragged breath before he closed the distance between them. Their lips finally connected, and despite them not dancing anymore, the world still seemed to spin around them. She clung to him—to his chest, to his shoulders, to his neck—the only firm point in a dizzy, swaying universe. The kiss didn't start softly or tentatively; like everything else between them so far, it was forceful right from the beginning. Not just intense, but deep, powerful, passionate… and somewhat more meaningful than every kiss Haley had ever given or received. In the arms of this mysterious man, Haley felt helpless and secure at the same time.

When he let go of her mouth, he left a trail of gentle kisses down her neck, then brushed a thumb down her cheek and over her lower lip. Haley wasn't sure she was made of flesh and bones any longer; she was worried her body might melt under the stranger's touch.

She was about to pull his face down to hers once more when angry shouts and a crashing sound reached them from inside the house. Haley turned to check what the commotion was and caught sight of several security guards running after another impressively tall guy. The "fugitive" was heading in their direction.

"Oh-ho," the masked stranger said, "looks like we've been found out."

"Why? You know that guy?"

"Yep, we came together."

"What did you do?"

"We aren't exactly invited guests to this party."

"How did you even get in??" Haley asked.

"Climbed over the fence. And now I have to go."

"But—" Haley began. Her mystery man cut her off by pulling her into a passionate but hurried kiss. She was still collecting herself when he winked, stepped away, and walked backward toward the gate.

The runaway friend had now almost reached them; as he raced toward the gazebo, he yelled, "We gotta beat it, my man!"

The masked stranger bowed one more time to Haley, wearing that impossibly sexy, wicked grin, and then he was running away.

"Wait!" she shouted as she watched him go. "You haven't even told me your name…"

Still running, the unknown man who had stolen Haley's heart turned his head and smiled again, his lips forming an answer, the sound of which got lost among the shouts of the security guards chasing after him…

***

A year later, as Haley relived the memory as if in slow motion, the lost answer became suddenly clear. Finally, she was able to read the word on the stranger's lips… David.

"It was you?" she asked the real-life David standing in front of her.

"In the flesh." He bowed lower, before removing his hands from his face and straightening up.

Time seemed to stop for Haley as they stood immobile facing each other, blue eyes locked on green ones. Haley didn't know what to do, say, or even what to think. She was too busy trying to breathe normally and ignore the electricity filling the air. Thank goodness her back was already pressed against the wall; she leaned on it for support.

David couldn't be the masked stranger, he couldn't. Oh, but he was… there was no denying it. The startling blue of his eyes was the same. Haley lowered her gaze slightly… and his full lips were the same. How had she never noticed before?

"Don't look at me like that." He took a step forward. "You know I can't resist you when you do."

Haley moved her lips to voice a reply, but her mouth had gone dry. The hard drive of her mind had just received too much conflicting information; it was in override, and her brain couldn't compute anymore.

"S-stay r-right where you are," she stammered.

David took another step forward.

"David, no."

Haley tried to dodge him by shifting to the side, but he was quicker. "No?" He grabbed Haley's shoulders and pressed her harder against the wall—his sun-kissed and salty fragrance invaded her nostrils. "Tell me you don't want to kiss me again. Tell me that night didn't stay with you for a long time, because it sure did stay with me."

Yeah, it had. But it didn't matter now. This was David. *David.* The same guy who had hurt Madison so badly, the same brother Scott hated so much. He was the same D-bag who enjoyed playing games with other people's feelings. He had said it himself: this was all a joke to him.

"Back off," she shouted, pushing him away with all her force. "What happened that night changes nothing."

Stumbling backward, he laughed, full of scorn. "Tell yourself whatever you like."

Haley straightened the strap of her bag over her shoulder and walked past him, heading for the door. "I'm leaving."

"All right, Sunshine, but please try not to dream too wildly about me tonight."

With one last glare, Haley flung the door open and fled the apartment.

***

"So the dude in the black mask was David?" Alice asked from her spot on the couch next to Haley. "Like, for real?" Her roommate was still reeling in shock from the revelation—just like Haley, no matter that she'd had a couple of extra hours to digest the news.

Haley fluffed a pillow and leaned back, hugging it to her chest while she tucked her knees neatly under her chin. The position prevented her from nodding, so she mumbled a "yep" back.

Madison was perched on the armchair in front of them, equally shocked. She was staring at Haley wide-eyed, apparently too weirded out to speak.

"Wow, I mean, just whoa," Alice said, fluttering her hands. "Why did you think he waited so long to tell you?"

Ah, that was a very good question. Haley had no clue what the answer might be.

"What if he was waiting for the moment it'd hurt the most?" Madison spoke for the first time since Haley had got home and told her best friends of the dreadful discovery. "Did something happen between you and Scott?"

"No," Haley said. "Nothing out of the ordinary. I have no idea why David chose today of all days to remove the pin from the grenade."

"So," Alice asked tentatively, "is it a grenade?"

"Well," Haley scoffed. "David and I kissed. How do you think Scott is going to take the news?"

"It happened before you even met him. Scott can't get mad about it." *Haley threw Alice an icy stare she hoped sent the message:* Yeah, because when you found out Madison had slept with Jack before she even met you, that made you so not care…

Madison caught the stare and blushed.

Alice, too, got the unspoken memo all right and grimaced. "But you didn't know, and it's not like you hid the kiss from Scott on purpose."

"Scott will look at me in a different way. This entire beef between him and David started over another girl they both dated back in high school. So I think Scott is definitely going to mind if his girlfriend happens to have a past with his brother."

"Did David try to steal Scott's girlfriend or something?" Madison asked.

"It was shadier than that," Haley said. "This French girl, Brigitte, came to their school for an exchange program in her junior year. She was in the same grade as Scott, and a year younger than David."

"Same as you…" Madison interrupted.

"Yeah." Haley didn't like the parallels one bit. "Anyway, apparently she was unbelievably beautiful and had this impossible-to-resist accent…"

Alice raised a skeptical eyebrow.

"…and she was a total bitch," Haley continued. "She started dating

David right away, but Scott told me they had like almost every class together, and they talked, and he was in love with her, and things with David weren't going well, blah, blah, blah. Long story short, Miss Brigitte told Scott she'd broken up with David when she hadn't, then started dating him too."

"How's that even possible?" Madison asked.

Haley shrugged. "I only heard Scott's side of the story. She told him it was too soon after her breakup with David for them to date openly."

"Okay," Alice said slowly. "So she kept her relationship with Scott a secret. But if she was still officially dating David, how could Scott not notice?"

"I don't know," Haley said, exasperated. "She must've been an evil mastermind, making sure she went out with David only when Scott wasn't around."

"For how long?" Alice again.

"I. Don't. Knoooow." Haley was tired of answering all these questions, especially since none of them were bringing her any closer to deciding what to do next. Specifically, how to tell Scott. "Whatever little Scott told me, I had to drag out of him, and already it was harder than a dental extraction."

"Ew." Madison made a gagging impression.

Haley rolled her eyes. "Anyway, I'm not sure *how* it happened. The only certain fact is that at some point David found them together, confronted his brother, and asked Brigitte to choose. She chose Scott, and because Scott kept dating her, David doesn't believe Scott didn't know she'd been cheating on David with him."

Alice low-whistled. "Talk about family intrigue."

"See why I'm not ecstatic history is repeating itself?"

"This is completely different," Alice insisted.

"Totally," Madison agreed. "Hey, do you think David recognized you right away?"

Haley closed her eyes, trying to remember the first time she'd met David—without him wearing a mask, at least. Haley and Alice had been in Hawaii for Christmas, playing groupies for the Harvard basketball team as Alice had been dating the team's captain, Peter, at the time. That trip had also been when Haley had met Scott. And since Peter and Scott had been sharing a room, Haley had agreed to swap roommates so that

Alice and Peter could bunk together. Except reception had confused Scott Williams with David Williams, and they'd sent her to the wrong room. She'd knocked on a door expecting to see Scott, and had found herself staring into David's blue eyes instead. Had he recognized her at once? Haley squeezed her eyes tighter, pressing her hands to her temples. When David had opened the door and found her on his doorstep, all he'd said was: "Hello, again."

Had that *again* meant everything… or nothing at all? Had he simply recognized her from the plane ride? Haley couldn't tell, because immediately after saying hello David had acted like a total jerk, and then Scott had arrived, and then they'd started beating the hell out of each other and trashing the hotel room as they fought.

How didn't I recognize him? Haley asked herself. *His lips, his eyes, his scent…* There'd been a moment when David had pulled her close and held her against his bare chest, just as Scott had turned the corner of the hall and found them talking. David had kept Haley tucked into him for a few long instants to make his brother mad, but he hadn't smelled of citrus and the sea then. He must've used a different soap since they were staying in a hotel and he'd just gotten out of the shower. Or he must've not had the time to put on cologne…

"Hel-lo?" Madison called her back to present.

"Yeah, sorry." Haley rubbed her eyes and opened them. "I'm not sure if he recognized me right away, Maddie. With David, it's always hard to tell what's going on inside his head."

"You know nothing," Alice joked. "You're worse than Jon Snow!"

Haley grabbed a pillow and playfully smothered Alice with it. "You guys aren't helping. I need to decide what to do."

"Hey, I'm innocent here." Alice stole the pillow and positioned it behind her back. "So, is this revelation making you feel any different about David? Does it make you question your relationship with Scott?"

Haley couldn't help but notice the way Madison perked up in her armchair. Almost as if she hoped Haley would say yes. *Sorry, Maddie.* "No, I love Scott," Haley said, looking away.

"Are you sure?" Alice insisted. "When you came back from the Venetian Ball last summer you seemed pretty taken up with masked Dav—"

Madison's super loud ringtone filled the room, interrupting Alice.

"Hello?" she picked up. "No, sure… You do that… No… Yes… I'm on my way." All frenzied by the call, Madison stood up. "Guys, I forgot it's my book club night. I should go or I'll be late." Then she sat back down. "I mean," she added, chewing her lower lip between words. "I can stay if you need me to." And then she started babbling. "It's not like I can't skip one night, even if I'm president of the club. I'm here for you. The chapters we're discussing tonight aren't all that interesting anyway; we're still nowhere near chapter twenty-two or chapter twenty-nine…"

Haley goggled at Alice to check if she had any idea what Madison was rambling about, but her other roommate shrugged and shook her head.

"…but, still, I'm president of the club, and I proposed this month's book—the classic *not* the retelling—so perhaps I should go?"

Madison finally went quiet, even if she kept torturing her lower lip with her teeth.

"Go," Haley said. "I'm fine. I mean, I'm not fine, but you can't do anything about it. And I have Alice to help psychoanalyze me."

"Are you sure?"

"Yep!"

"I'll make it up to you, I promise."

Madison stood up again and, bending at the waist, she pulled Haley into a bone-crushing hug before disappearing into her room to get dressed. She dashed back out all of three minutes later looking adorably crumpled in a frilly short dress with ruffles. Her style was completed by messy hair pinned on top of her head with a pencil, a frayed leather messenger bag strapped across her chest, and giant black glasses covering half her face. She was beautiful in a sexy-but-innocent librarian way, if only she'd realize it. If Madison gained just a dash of self-confidence, she'd be able to get any guy she wanted.

Well, not *any* guy. Not *my* guy.

But there was no reason for Madison not to find a gorgeous, loving, and caring boyfriend.

Haley still couldn't understand why her friend seemed only to fall for the bad boys. Scott being the one decent-guy exception, but also the only guy Madison had never approached.

"I'm going," Madison said. "Call me if you need anything."

Haley smirked. "Aren't cell phones banned from book club

meetings?"

Madison's eyes widened, her expression crestfallen.

"I'm joking," Haley said.

"Ah, of course. Well, bye, girls."

Madison blew them each a kiss and then was gone.

After the door clicked shut, Alice waited for all of two seconds before attacking Haley again with questions. "Now tell me, how do you really feel?"

Haley winced. "I don't knooow." She collapsed theatrically on the couch.

"Mmm… I sense a lie by omission here," Alice insisted.

"Please stay out of my head."

"Please let me in so we can sort out this Williams brothers situation."

"And how do you propose we do that?"

"When I say 'David,' what's your gut feeling?"

The little air pocket Haley felt in her belly was not the reaction she wanted to have after hearing his name. "Sometimes, I'm sort of drawn to him," she confessed. "It's this inexplicable, almost animal thing. He makes me tick, not sure why, because I genuinely dislike him. But whenever I'm near him I'm on edge… and knowing how good a kisser he is doesn't help."

"So you're attracted to him in all his bad-boy glory," Alice said, smirking. "Your body wants him and your mind can't cope."

"Is that even possible?"

"Apparently so." Alice paused for a second before asking the next question. "Have you ever been tempted to… act on this attraction?"

"Hell, no." Haley straightened up. "I'm with Scott, I love Scott. He's the sweetest, most adorable…"

"Hot," Alice suggested.

"…*incredibly hot* boyfriend in the entire world."

"So why are you so worried? If you're not having any existential which-brother-should-I-date doubts, what's the matter?"

"Alice, I know I'm okay. But what about Scott? I don't want to lie to him, but…"

"Lie? Why should you lie?"

"He's going to ask me if I liked the kiss. What should I say?"

"Ah."

"Yeah, ah! What if he starts asking all the wrong questions? Like, did I think about the kiss after it happened…? Should I tell him the truth and say I spent the next six months obsessing over his brother?"

"Err… probably not. You should downplay it a bit."

"In short, lie."

"In short, sugarcoat the truth a little for the greater good?"

"See why I'm not eager to have that conversation?"

Alice pulled Haley's feet onto her lap and started massaging her ankles. "Eager or not, you'd better rip off the Band-Aid. No good can come from waiting."

Haley groaned. "You're so completely right. I hate you."

"Aw, come on, you know you love me. Even when I'm painfully right."

"I do." Haley smacked her lips in a loud air kiss. "Any suggestion on the best way to tell Scott?"

Madison

"Madison, hey," a familiar male voice called from behind her. "Wait up."

She turned to find Scott waving at her. All the air left her lungs, leaving Madison breathless. Usually, when she saw him, she'd had time to prepare. But to meet him in the street by chance just like that, Madison was caught off guard. He was looking glorious in basketball shorts and a loose tank top, a cool sackpack strapped to his back. Her eyes roamed the length of his bare, muscled arms up to his shoulders, collarbone, chin, mouth… And those eyes… they were the darkest green in the soft light of the street lamps.

"Hey," Madison managed to mumble. "What are you doing here?"

"I just came from the park," he said, catching up with her. "There's a basketball court there, so we go play sometimes. Didn't expect it to last this long, but we ended up with a tie and had to do a re-match."

"Did you win?" Madison asked with a smirk.

"Of course." Scott winked. "Want to walk home together? Your house is on the way to mine."

Did she want to walk home with Scott? *Yes, please.*

"What are *you* doing out so late?" he asked, and gave her a subtle once-over that made shivers spider-walk from her heels up the back of her legs and all the way up her spine to her nape. "Not playing basketball, I guess," he joked.

"Book club night." Madison smiled shyly as she started walking. "The discussion got a bit more heated than anticipated and we finished late…"

"Oh, which book?"

"*Northanger Abbey.* We're reading the classic version alongside a modern retelling that stirred a literary fire."

"The retelling, is it any good?"

"Why? You enjoy reading Jane Austen?"

"Hey, I might be a dude, but we're not all like Mark Twain. I love Jane; I don't want to 'dig her up and beat her over the skull with her own shin bone' every time I read *Pride and Prejudice.*"

"So have you read it many times?"

"Ah, it's a truth universally acknowledged that a book lover has to read it more than once."

Scott was walking her home, and now, on top of looking gorgeous in his sporty clothes, he was quoting Jane Austen at her. Could a guy get any more perfect? Madison bit her lower lip so forcefully she almost drew blood. How was she supposed to get over him? *But I need to… I have no choice. Scott doesn't want me, he'll never want me. He has Haley… why would he ever spare me a second glance?*

"So," Scott continued, "is *Pride and Prejudice* your favorite Austen novel?"

"Nah, I'm more of a *Persuasion* kind of girl. I identify better with Anne Elliot than Elizabeth Bennet."

Scott gave a slight double take. "Not searching for your Mr. Darcy, then?"

You are my Mr. Darcy.

STOP IT, her conscience raged inside her.

Madison cleared her throat to hide her internal battle. "It's not about the hero, but the leading lady. Lizzy is too fierce, and I'm not. And my family… they can be pushy, just like the Elliots."

"You mean they persuaded you to break off an engagement with the love of your life?"

Madison giggled. "No, it's more of a modern-day issue."

Scott raised his eyebrows interrogatively.

"My dad wants me to become a lawyer to join the family business," Madison explained.

"Ah, and you don't want to?"

"No, never have."

"What would you want to do?"

Madison stared up at the night sky, wondering why she was pouring her heart out to Scott. She never discussed her plans and dreams for the future with anybody, so why open up to him? *You know why...* Yeah, she did. But what good could come of it?

"I'm sorry," Scott said. "You probably don't want to discuss your entire life plan on your way home on a random Monday night."

"No, it's not that." Madison turned to look at him and found his bright green eyes trained on her. It made her knees go soft. "It's just that when you ask someone what they want... I mean, I doubt there's a harder question to answer, right?"

"Touché."

"If I had to tell you my biggest dream, it'd be to be a writer. To live in a small, remote cottage on the beach on the coast of Maine. Somewhere cold, with a view of a lighthouse, and only the sound of waves as a companion."

"Sounds tempting..."

"You like to write, too?"

"Yeah, I love it."

"Fiction, poetry...?"

"A bit of both. You?"

"Mostly fiction... I like stories."

"So what's stopping you from following that dream?" Scott challenged.

"My father would never accept it. The only other Smithson who refused to be a lawyer is my cousin Ethan..."

"I'm sure they didn't burn him at the stake."

"No, but his father told him Harvard was no longer free for kids who didn't play the good little lawyer. So you see why I'm worried about becoming a penniless writer with so much debt on my shoulders. I would have to find a more reliable source of income. A job I could actually stomach that still had to do with books..."

"Like?"

"Like becoming a teacher, or working at a publishing house, or even a publishing startup."

"Seems like a good plan."

"More brave than good. I'm not sure I'll ever find the guts."

"Would you rather do a job you hate to make your dad happy?"

"No, I'm just saying that whatever I do, someone is going to be disappointed, and it won't be easy either way."

"No," Scott agreed. "Nothing worthwhile ever is."

Did that apply also to love? Madison wondered, and then she shifted the focus of the conversation away from herself. "Have you always wanted to be a doctor?"

Scott smiled. "So Haley has been talking about me?"

"She has."

I also might've had this little stalking habit of knowing everything about you even before you met her. But let's ignore the details, shall we?

"Anyway, being a doctor has always been the dream for me. A real stethoscope was my favorite toy as a kid; I never considered anything else..."

"What kind of doctor do you want to be?"

"Neurosurgeon."

Madison tried hard not be impressed. "Why?"

"The brain is the most fascinating organ in the entire human body; it can do the most extraordinary things..."

Or turn perfectly normal human beings into silly, lovesick girls who'd give up everything for a kiss from the boy they loved. *No, bad Madison. Scott is Haley's boyfriend... and even if he weren't, he'd never be interested in you.*

"I bet your parents are happy about you becoming a neurosurgeon," Madison said.

Scott's lips parted in a foxy grin. "They're not too cross about it, but the academic is going to be challenging enough for me."

"I'll take your word for it, science books are the only kind I avoid. Oh..." Madison stopped abruptly; she'd almost walked right past her building. She was so comfortable talking with Scott she hadn't been paying attention to the road. "We're here. Thanks for walking me home."

"No problem." Scott smiled again. "You think Haley is still up?"

Oh. *Oh.* So that was why he'd walked her home. Scott wanted to catch Haley before she went to bed, probably only to give her the most romantic goodnight kiss and then go home.

"She was when I left earlier, can't say for now. You want to come up and check?"

Yeah, Madison, invite him up to see a girl who's not you. Smart move.

Why was she torturing herself like this? Was she really so desperate to spend five more minutes with Scott that she'd even put up with seeing him with Haley?

Yep!

For Madison, loving Scott from afar, spending time with him was like poking a wound or scratching away a dried scab. Nothing good could ever come out of it, but she couldn't control the impulse.

"I should probably text her." Scott unlocked his phone's screen. "It's pretty late."

He typed a quick text and they both waited to see if Haley would reply.

"She must be already in bed," Scott said after a while. "I'll catch up with her tomorrow."

Madison was about to insist for him to come up when she remembered the whole "Haley kissing David at the masquerade" drama. Maybe her best friend wasn't ready to see her boyfriend and have "the awkward talk" with him.

"Yeah, right. Now that I think about it, she mentioned she was having an early night," Madison said. "This is goodnight, then."

"Night."

Scott pulled her into a quick goodbye hug, turned on his heel, and jogged away into the night. Madison stood there at the bottom of the steps of her building, dumbfounded. Her skin burned in all the spots where it had just connected with Scott's. Her nostrils filled with his scent of clean soap mixed with a sheen of light sweat, probably from the game. And her eyes trained on the tall figure quickly disappearing into the darkness.

Haley

Haley stared at Scott's text, aghast. Fear paralyzed her even if the message only said:

She gaped at the simple line of text while keeping her phone on the lock screen. If she didn't open the text, he wouldn't know she'd read it, meaning he'd think she was asleep, meaning she wouldn't have to reply or, *worse,* talk to him. Via text or in person, it didn't matter. Haley was so utterly terrified of the next time she'd have to talk to her boyfriend that her first irrational instinct was to postpone the moment. Even if she knew she was only making things worse.

The entrance door opened and then clicked shut, signaling that Madison had gotten home. Haley and Alice had said goodnight a while ago, but Haley was still wide awake. She was in bed, staring at the ceiling and trying to draft an I've-kissed-your-brother-but-it's-not-a-big-deal speech in her head.

Long, gut-wrenching conversations weren't her thing; she was more about short, direct communication. But how else could she explain to Scott all the layers of her feelings? Make him understand how much she loved him... and how little she cared about his brother.

Maybe it didn't have to be so complicated. How about starting with a simple goodnight text? Haley unlocked the screen and typed:

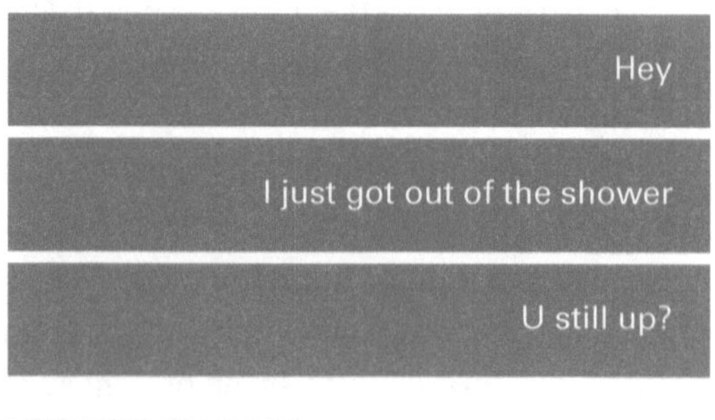

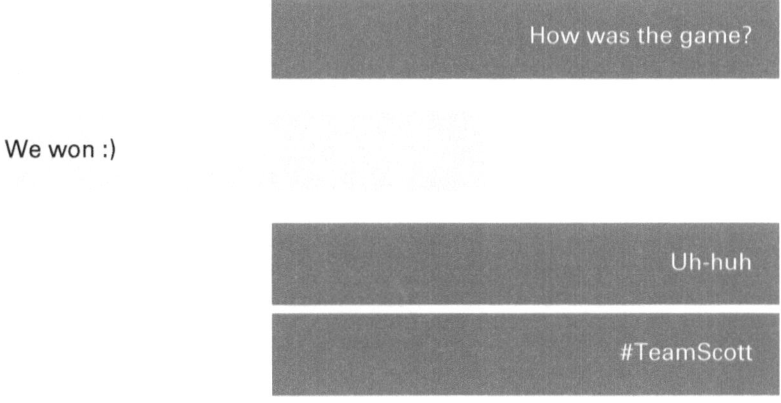

We won :)

Haley paused, undecided on what to type next. She *was* #TeamScott. Every cell in her body wanted him. David didn't matter, he'd been a summer fantasy almost a year ago and a real-life jerk for the past six months. He was mean and cruel, and this was only his latest stunt to try to ruin his brother's life. Haley wouldn't let him. She needed to make Scott understand. Her phone beeped again.

I was just outside your building

Wanted to kiss you good night in person

Now you'll have settle for an emoji

:*

Haley's heart contracted with a little pang.

I ♥ you too

Goodnight

:*

She had nothing to worry about. Scott loved her, and he would believe her.

***

Haley wasn't feeling nearly so confident the next morning when she had to decide how and when to face her boyfriend. She used every possible excuse not to talk to him, in person or over the phone. Texts were okay for now. Haley had convinced herself that since she couldn't break the news with a text, it was perfectly normal not to mention the kiss in them. It wasn't like lying by omission.

She avoided him all of Tuesday, and on Wednesday morning, as she read Scott's early morning texts, she was ashamed to feel so completely relieved he'd be too busy to see her until later tonight. He had sent her a good morning kiss followed by a string of cute complaints:

Morning

:*

I'm so over the emojis

The real thing is so much better

Seems like forever I haven't seen you

And today I'm busy all day

I won't be home until later tonight

Going downtown to interview at
Massachusetts General Hospital

For a different pre-med program

They're going to give me the tour of the
hospital afterward

So it'll take a while

Enough to give Haley a few more hours to prepare for her confession. But she couldn't postpone it any longer. Tonight, she must tell him.

Haley picked up her phone and hit reply.

I miss you too

Good luck for the interview

But you don't need it

They'd be crazy not to pick you

Call me when you get back

I need to talk to you tonight

There's something I have to tell you

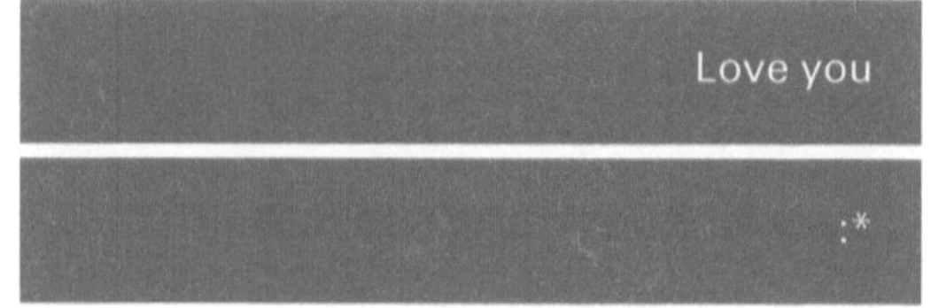

Haley had roughly eight hours to prepare herself. She should draft a speech and perhaps rehearse it on Alice. In normal circumstances, she would've asked Madison for help, since she was the best of the three of them with words, but she couldn't ask her friend to play Cyrano de Bergerac for her and Scott. Haley complimented herself on the literary quotation—totally learned from the Steve Martin and Daryl Hannah movie *Roxanne*.

Help or not, she had a job to do. Haley jumped off the bed and sat at her desk. Feeling particularly romantic, she decided to leave her laptop off for once and write the speech the old fashioned way using pen and paper.

Her decision proved a bad one for the environment. By the time she had a speech that satisfied her, the floor of her bedroom was littered with crumpled sheets of discarded drafts. But Haley was happy with the final result. After hearing her words, Scott wouldn't be able to turn her down. Now all she needed to do was to shower, make herself look pretty, and wait for her boyfriend to call.

Scott

On Wednesday night, Scott walked into his apartment lost in thought. The visit at Massachusetts General Hospital had gone well, and he was optimistic they'd accept him. So why did the thought make him so gloomy? Unconvinced, he peeked at the brochure still clutched in his hands. What was he complaining about? Massachusetts General was a top-tier hospital, and Dr. Salinger—Scott's would-be assigned doctor— was an excellent neurosurgeon.

But not the best.

Okay, not the best, but close. And this internship would be here in Boston, where he could stay with Haley all summer instead of them spending it three thousand miles apart.

Right.

He would get another chance to work with Dr. Allen. Sure, because opportunities like that just happened to rain on pre-med students, especially after they'd turned down medicine luminaries once already. Dr. Allen would simply sit there and wait for the wonderful Scott Williams to be his shadow whenever he chose.

Who am I kidding?

Students all over the U.S. would kill to get picked for that job, to be part—even if only as an observer—of Dr. Allen's research project. And the doctor had picked him, Scott. And he was about to turn down the offer, for a girl. But he'd do anything for her.

"Hello, brother." David's voice made him jump. Scott hadn't seen him half-hidden behind the kitchen bar. "Sorry, I didn't save you any dinner."

"Get lost, David."

A rundown with David was the last thing Scott needed right now.

"That's the best you can do? Ladies and gentlemen, please welcome on stage Scott Williams..." David banged a fork against a glass a couple of times and then dropped both into the dishwasher.

Scott refused to take the bait.

"No speech?" David continued. "I'll admit I was expecting more of a powerful opening."

"I said get lost."

"Oh, come on," David said, coming into the living room. "What's it gonna be?" He crouched slightly, hopping from one foot to the other and bringing his fists in front of his face in a defensive stance. The movements of a boxer in the ring. "Hook to the face?" David swung his elbow up and punched the air. "Sucker punch to the stomach?" He threw a low punch with his other hand. Then he straightened up—the boxing demonstration apparently over. "Personally, I'd prefer a raging shouting match. I would hate for us to get physical again. No one around to save your skinny ass this time."

Scott frowned. What the hell was David talking about?

"Wait, wait. Oooooh..." David's sneer widened. "You don't know..."

"Know what?"

Scott hated being at a disadvantage with David, and it looked like he was right now. David knew something that Scott didn't. Something that made David happy and that would, presumably, make Scott feel just the opposite. So much so that his brother had expected Scott to attack him as soon as he'd laid eyes on him. What was it?

"She hasn't told you…"

She. David meant Haley, Scott had no doubts now. His blood ran cold through his veins, and he rolled his fingers into tight fists, crushing the hospital brochure he was still holding.

"Told me *what?*"

"Oh." David shrugged and waved him off. "I wouldn't want to meddle."

Scott moved in a blur—in two quick strides he was on his brother. He grabbed David by the collar of his T-shirt and pinned him against the wall. They were almost nose to nose. "What did you do?" he hissed.

"I kissed her, brother." David spat the words in his face. "It was long and passionate. And she enjoyed every second of it."

Scott let go of his brother and staggered backward. He felt like he'd been hit multiple times in short sequence. Only David had used words instead of fists. "You didn't."

"Ask her if you don't believe me." David straightened the collar of his T-shirt. "We were reminiscing about it just the other night. Now, if you'll excuse me." David grabbed his phone and put it in his jeans pocket. "I had plans for tonight." He put on his black leather jacket and, with one last sly smile, he left.

Scott reeled backward until he hit the couch. David was a bastard and an asshole, but he wasn't a liar. He'd never said he'd kissed Haley if it wasn't true.

When had it happened? Was that why Haley had been kind of off lately? Scott had had the impression she'd been dodging him in the last couple of days… and now he'd found out why: she didn't want to confess.

No! The Haley he knew, the Haley he loved, would never cheat on him, especially not with David. She hated his brother. At least, that was what she'd always told him.

But David is no liar.

Scott's world tilted. He grabbed the couch backrest for support as angry tears streamed down his cheeks. In a blind rage, he punched the

cushions in hard, fast strokes until his hand began to hurt. Taking deep breaths to try to calm himself, Scott took out his phone. He opened the messenger chat with Haley and scrolled through the past few days' conversations. Nothing in her texts pointed to a betrayal; they were full of sweet words, cute emoji, and I love yous.
But David is no liar.

He shuffled the chat to the end, his eyes resting on the last string of texts from her.

Call me when you get back

I need to talk to you tonight

There's something I have to tell you

Love you

:*

Was "there's something I have to tell you" code for "tonight I'll admit I've cheated on you and dump your ass to be with your brother"? Could Haley really like David? Kiss him? It seemed so impossible…
But David is no liar.

Why else would she have kissed him?

Scott was still looking at the chat, searching for clues, when an email flashed into his inbox and invaded the top half of the screen. It was from Dr. Allen's office in California, reminding him they were still waiting for an answer from him about the shadowing program.

He loved Haley so much, and the last thing he wanted was to spend the summer away from her. But was he being stupid and naïve to give up an opportunity like this for a girl? Until an hour ago, Scott would've been sure the answer was no. He could already picture himself marrying Haley, one day after they were done with college and both had a job. He was devoted to her, and her to him. She wouldn't cheat on him, she just wouldn't…

But David is no liar.

The notion was like a drill into Scott's brain, and after hearing it so many times in his head, he started to believe it.

Jaw clenched, Scott wiped the tears from his cheeks with the back of his hand. He opened the email and, after reading the complete message, he tapped an impulsive reply...

Haley

Seven, and still no call. Haley was losing her mind. For the past hour, she'd been sitting at the dining table in her apartment staring at the black screen of her phone. She'd done all she could to postpone seeing Scott, but she'd spent the afternoon wishing time would fly faster... now that she had her speech ready, all this waiting was getting to her. And Scott should've been home by now.

"That phone will disintegrate in your hands if you grip it any harder," Alice said, staring at her dubiously. "I'm trying to make dinner here, but your anxiety is ruining my cooking chakra."

"Sorry," Haley said, releasing the hold a little. "I'm waiting for Scott to call. We're having the big talk tonight."

The book Madison was reading tumbled to the floor as she straightened abruptly. "You still haven't told him? Why?"

Haley shrugged and grimaced guiltily. "I've been busy, and so has Scott. I'm telling him tonight."

"Haley!" Madison pressed her palms to her cheeks, shocked. "But he lives with *David*. What if the jerk tells him first?"

A sense of unease sneaked around Haley, tightening around her chest like an invisible rope. "David's never home, and he wouldn't."

"Um, hello?" Madison was getting all worked up. "Are we talking about the same person? Because the David I know wouldn't miss an opportunity like that to make people miserable. Especially his brother."

The unease worsened. Haley looked up at Alice chopping vegetables behind the kitchen bar for reassurance, but judging from her friend's worried expression, Alice seemed more aligned with Madison's line of thinking.

"Why don't you call him?" Alice said. "Instead of torturing yourself waiting."

"Okay."

With a pounding heart, Haley unlocked the screen and dialed Scott's number…

"It went to voicemail," Haley said, staring aghast at her friends.

Madison frowned and Alice stopped chopping her veggies.

"What do you think it means?" Haley asked.

"He could have forgotten to charge his phone?" Alice said tentatively.

Madison kept quiet; she just chewed her bottom lip like she did whenever she was nervous.

"Oh, no. No, no, nooo. If David got to him before I could explain… no!" Haley panicked. "I have to call him. Madison, do you have his number?"

"Scott's? No, why?"

"Not Scott's, David's…"

"Ah." Madison blushed. "Yeah, sure. I'm sending you the contact."

Maddie sent you a contact

David

Haley saved the number and pressed call.

He picked up on the third ring. "David's phone." There was music in the background and David sounded surprised, probably because he didn't recognize her number.

"Did you tell Scott?" Haley asked without preamble.

"I think I recognize that lovely tone of voice." The background music dimmed. Wherever he was, David must've moved to a quieter spot. "Nighty-night, Sunshine. What can I do for you?"

"Did you tell him?" Haley repeated.

"Tell him what?"

"David," she warned him. "I'm not in the mood for your games."

"Okay, fine. My brother and I had a heart to heart earlier."

"What did you say to him?"

"You sound worried… I only told the truth."

"What truth?"

"That we kissed, and that you enjoyed it… if memory serves me well."

Haley lowered the phone and closed her eyes, holding back the tears that were already threatening to spill.

After a few steadying breaths, she lifted the phone back to her ear, saying, "You know that's not the truth."

"No? Where's the lie?"

"Did you make it sound as if I cheated on him?"

"I stuck to the facts. No more. No less."

"So did you tell him the kiss happened before I even met him?"

"Um, that detail could've slipped my mind."

"You bastard."

"Ah, but I seem to remember that half-truths like I'm-not-lying-but-I'm-not-telling-you-everything made you tick."

"What are you talking about?"

"It worked pretty well for Scott when he told you how I was mad at him because a girl in high school chose him over me, forgetting to say I was *with* that girl when he started screwing her behind my back."

"I don't have time for this." Haley hung up. "You were right," she told Madison. "David is an asshole and I'm an idiot for leaving him the space to work his stupid tricks." It was adrenaline alone that kept Haley from collapsing in tears. "What do I do now?"

"Go find Scott," Alice said.

"You need to explain everything to him," Madison added. "It will be fine, he loves you."

"Go," Alice repeated. "Don't waste another second."

Haley jumped up, grabbed her bag, and dashed out of the house at a run.

Madison

"You think she'll make it?" Alice asked.

"Scott lives only a few blocks away, she'll get there in time," Madison said. "From the sound of that call, David must have just told Scott. There's nothing Scott could have done in the last few hours that Haley can't fix."

"Yeah, you're right. Scott doesn't seem like an impulsive guy. He wouldn't just head out and hook up with a random girl for revenge."

"No, never." Madison shook her head. "That's not him."

"Did you have dinner?"

"Not yet."

"Want some salad?" Alice offered. "I made extra."

"Sure."

Madison watched Alice set the table for two and plate the salad. They sat and started eating together.

"Mmm," Madison mumbled after the first forkful. "This is delicious, what's your secret?"

"Balsamic vinegar glaze."

"Awesome."

"So…" Alice paused. "Besides having an amazing cook for a roommate… how's everything else going? We didn't really get to talk after the… ah… wedding."

"Yeah, sorry for bailing on you and making you go home with Ethan and Rose, that must've been awkward."

"Your cousin was a bit grumpy, but now I understand why. And his girlfriend… Well, Rose is too damn nice to dislike, even for me. Plus, I found a nice surprise when I got home." Alice couldn't help smiling a little. "So I can't complain."

"Yeah, your surprise tried to talk to me, but I blew him off." Madison paused to swallow. "I'm so happy you guys are finally together, you deserve to be happy after waiting for so long."

"Maddie, it's only been a few days." Alice dropped her fork and stared into space. "But it's like everything I imagined, only ten times better."

Alice's smile was so radiant, and Madison tried to match its warmth, but how could she when her chest had transformed into a huge empty box with nothing in it?

Alice must've noticed, because she said, "Haley told me David has not been very *gracious* about your breakup."

Madison scoffed. "What else could I expect? You warned me about him, everyone did, but I didn't want to listen. I don't know, David seemed like a perfect distraction. And the breakup didn't hurt so much because I didn't care about him. I honestly wasn't that into him. He was a pretty face and great sex—don't tell Haley…"

"No way." Alice's eyes widened. "Our roommate is already confused enough."

"Anyway, it wasn't *because* we broke up that it got to me, it was *how* it happened. When David gets mad, he's scary and mean… I've never had a guy yell at me like that… And now I'm just glad it's over."

"And what about Scott?" Madison was about to deny everything as usual, but Alice anticipated her. "And please don't say you haven't got feelings for him," Alice added, "because we both know that's not true. I get why you don't want to talk with Haley about it, but I'm here. You can trust me, and you need to open up to someone about it. So, out with it."

Madison pushed her empty plate away and after flattening her palms on the table, she rested her forehead on the back of her hands. "Am I that obvious?"

"Only to me." Alice squeezed her arm. "Is it getting any better? It's been a few months now…"

Madison stood back up, shaking her head. "In a way, it's getting worse."

"How?"

"Before, Scott was this cute guy in my class I admired from afar. But since he's been going out with Haley, I got, you know, to meet him. He started talking to me. When we have a class together, he stops to say hello or sits near me. The other night I bumped into him when he was coming back from a basketball game—"

"Yeah," Alice said. "Jack was out playing too."

"Anyway, Scott walked me home." Alice raised an eyebrow. "Only because he wanted to see if Haley was still up," Madison justified herself. "And we talked about books and what we like to write. Oh, Alice, knowing Scott makes it so much worse. I want nothing more than for all these stupid feelings to melt away. I don't want to like him. I don't want to feel this way about him. But I can't control it, it won't just go away. No matter how wrong it is."

"It'd be wrong only if you tried to steal him from Haley. This way it only sucks. And I know exactly how you feel; I spent the last three years of my life with that same exact feeling…"

"Yeah, but you got the guy in the end. I can't even hope for that because it'd mean Haley is heartbroken. I just don't know what to do."

"Listen, Maddie." Alice took her hands in hers. "Who knows if Scott and Haley will stay together, or if you'll ever get to be with him, or even want him anymore? You could meet someone who sweeps you off your feet tomorrow… And our lives are going to be so completely different in a year when we graduate, anyway. You just have to be strong and pull through. And whenever you feel like banging your head against the wall, or when you feel the impulse to do something crazy and stupid like, I don't know, kiss the groom at someone else's wedding…" Alice gave her a little squeeze that let her know it was okay, that she understood what had brought Madison to that extremely bad choice. "You come to me instead. Madison, you've always been there for me when I was down for Jack. I know I've been distant lately, but that's only because I'm an idiot. I got mad and petty, and I'm sorry…"

Madison's eyes prickled with tears. This was the first real conversation she'd had with Alice after the Jack fight. Their friendship hadn't felt the same since then—at least, not until today. And now Alice's warm smile told her things were finally back to how they were before—minus the weight of untold secrets looming over their heads.

"No, it's all my fault," Madison said, tears rolling down her cheeks. "I closed up in a ball of misery and left everyone who cares about me out. But I love you, and I missed our friendship so much."

Alice, too, was sniffling a little. "I know, I love you too. Together we can get past anything."

"Thank you," Madison whispered. "I don't know where I'd be without you."

They hugged and shared a good old cry, just like best friends do.

Haley

"Scott, open the door." Haley pounded her fist on it again. She'd been trying to convince Scott to let her in for five good minutes now. She was hammering the door with one hand and compulsively pushing the doorbell with the other. "Scott, I know you're in there. Open up. Please, I need to explain to you. It's not what you think."

"How is it, then?" his strangled voice came from inside.

Haley stopped the attack on the door. "Please let me in." She rested both her hands and her forehead on the cold surface, imagining Scott on the other side doing the same.

A few long seconds stretched out before the lock clicked. Gingerly, Haley pushed the door open and stepped into the apartment. Scott was facing away from the entrance, presenting her with the sight of his broad shoulders. Haley closed the door behind her and stepped forward. "Scott…?"

He turned, face red and blotched from crying, eyes bloodshot.

"Oh, Scott." She made to throw her arms around his neck, but he stepped away.

"Is it true?" he asked in an angry whisper.

"It's not what you think."

"Actually, it's very simple," Scott said in a glacial tone. Then he shouted, "Did you kiss him or not?"

"I did." Fresh pain registered on Scott's face, making Haley's heart crack. "But I didn't know who he was, or that he was your brother. I hadn't even met you yet."

Confusion now marked Scott's features. "What are you talking about?"

Haley dared to take another step forward; she grabbed Scott's wrists and dragged him toward the couch, where they both sat down. He seemed too shocked to protest. "Last summer," she explained. "I went to this masquerade ball upstate. It was one of those stupid parties where everyone has to wear a period costume and a mask—"

Scott yanked his wrists free. "Why are you telling me—?"

"Please let me finish," Haley interrupted. "Let me tell you the whole story, and then I can answer all your questions. Okay?"

He nodded.

"That night at the party, I met a guy. He was wearing a huge mask that covered most of his face. I danced with him, we took a walk in the park, and he kissed me."

"I don't need to hear about all the guys in your past."

"You need to hear about this one."

"Why?"

Haley sighed. "Because it was David."

The look of confusion on Scott's face intensified. "I don't understand."

"David and I met that night, we kissed, and that was it. Immediately after the kiss, the security staff came running after his friend because they were crashing the party. The guards chased the friend all the way through the garden to where we were standing. They ran away together, and I never saw his face or learned his name. I didn't recognize David in Hawaii, but I think he recognized me, and that's why he acted so aggressive from the start."

"You kissed him a year ago?"

"Yes."

"And you didn't know who he was?"

Haley shook her head.

Scott stood up and started pacing around scratching his head. "So this is all a twisted comedy of errors?"

Haley wasn't sure what a "comedy of errors" entailed, and the situation couldn't be any less comic, but she nodded all the same.

Scott's features relaxed for a moment. Then his jaw tightened again. "How long have you known?"

"Only since Monday night. When I left here after seeing you, I forgot my phone. I came back to get it and David started acting all nasty as usual. We got into a fight, and that's when he told me."

"Is that why you've been avoiding me the past few days?"

"Yes," Haley admitted.

"Because you like him."

"No, Scott. I love *you*."

"Then why didn't you tell me?" He was near yelling again.

"Because I was afraid!" Haley shouted back, standing up from the couch.

Scott seemed taken aback by her sudden scream. "Of what?"

"That you would look at me differently, that you wouldn't want to be with me anymore…"

Scott shook his head. "He made it sound as if you'd cheated on me."

"I didn't." Haley took a step forward. "I would never do that to you. I've just been stupid, I should've told you right away… but I was so worried. I thought waiting a couple of days wouldn't be such a big deal. I should've known David was going to be a dick about it. I'm sorry."

Scott sank back on the couch, dropping his head into his hands.

"Scott?" Haley sat next to him.

He looked up at her. "I wish you'd told me right away."

There was a haunted look in his green eyes that made Haley shiver.

"Why?" she asked in a trembling voice.

"David never lies," Scott said. "When he said you two had kissed, I... I..."

"You what?"

"I believed him..."

There was something he wasn't telling her. "And?"

"I took the internship in California."

Haley breathed a sigh of relief. For a moment she'd imagined Scott going to town to make out with the first girl he saw. But the next second she wondered if Scott moving to the other side of the country was really any better.

"To punish me?" she asked.

"No. Yes. I don't know. I was blinded by rage and it sort of happened."

"How could it *sort of* happen?"

"I was looking at your texts from the past few days, trying to figure out what was happening, and they sent me a follow-up email. Without thinking, I replied that I was going."

"Because you wanted to get away from me."

"From you both." Scott lowered his head. "I thought you were going to leave me for him."

Haley took his face into her hands and lifted his chin. "Scott, look at me." He did. "I will never leave you for him. I love *you*. It will always be you."

Scott pressed his lips to hers. An urgent, passionate kiss that mirrored all of Haley's feelings. The way he pulled her close, the intensity of his need, was fueled like hers by the dread of losing each other, by the relief at it not being so, and by the longing already present for the time they would have to spend apart.

Scott lifted her bodily from the couch, and without ever breaking the kiss or saying another word, he brought her to his bedroom. They made love as if it was the first and last time, their bodies speaking to one another the way words never could...

***

Haley stared at the moonlight filtering through the blinds, at the faint silver sheen it cast over Scott's room, making the silhouettes of his dresser, desk, and wardrobe barely distinguishable in the darkness. Scott was lying next to her on the bed, head resting on her chest as she stroked his hair.

"Can't you sleep?" he asked.

"No, sorry. Too many emotions today." Haley gave a soft chuckle. "I'm still pumped full of adrenaline."

Scott shifted positions and propped his head on an elbow as if to stare at her, even if in the darkness it was impossible. Haley could only distinguish the black contour of his straight nose. "Is adrenaline all that's keeping you awake?"

"Also guilt for not telling you about the kiss right away," Haley said. "And anger for leaving David room to come between us. I should've never done that." She sighed. "But Scott, after everything you told me about Brigitte, I would've hated for you to see me differently. For you to think I was the same as *that girl* from your past."

Scott cupped Haley's face with one hand. "Hey, you're nothing like Brigitte. She was a liar and a schemer, a mean girl who enjoyed toying with people's lives. You only made an honest mistake. We both did. I, too, left David room to play his tricks. I should've trusted you. No matter what he claimed, I should've called you instead of taking his word for it and making life-changing decisions in the heat of the moment."

"Yeah." Haley wasn't able to keep a bittersweet note out of her voice. "I hadn't pinned you down as impulsive. You always seem so calm and reflective."

"I am impulsive when it comes to you." He tapped her nose with a finger in an affectionate gesture. "You make me literally lose my mind, usually in a good way. But today… when I thought I'd lost you… to him. I went off the wrong deep end."

Haley didn't say anything, so Scott asked, "Are you worried because we're going to spend the summer apart?"

Haley traced his profile with a finger. "I'm not thrilled you're going away for two months, but I'm happy you took the internship, honestly. It was too good an opportunity to pass up on, just for me. And I'm not worried about us, I trust you completely."

"And I trust you." Scott pulled her closer. "But the idea of spending so much time apart… I don't want to."

"Two months will fly by," Haley lied.

"Come with me," Scott breathed down her neck and started kissing her collarbone.

The sensation was so good, Haley was almost ready to throw all her other obligations out the window and say yes. But she couldn't.

Pulling back, she said, "I can't. Even if I wanted to, it's too late to get a refund on tuition, and I can't just throw all that money away."

"And I can't stay." Scott sounded heartbroken. "I already confirmed with Dr. Allen's staff, and I wrote to Massachusetts General to notify them I've accepted another offer."

"Gah, you've been thorough." Haley sniffled, trying not to burst into tears. "You must've really hated me."

"I could never hate you." Scott stamped a soft kiss on her lips.

"But you're going to California."

"Unless I want to spend the summer doing nothing, I have to."

Suddenly cold, Haley lifted the bedspread over her shoulders. "Where does that leave us?"

"In a long-distance relationship for two months?"

"You don't want to take a break?"

"No, never. Why would I want a break? I'm in love with you."

"So the fact that I kissed David doesn't change the way you feel about me?"

Scott stiffened next to her. "The thought of his lips"—he traced hers with a finger—"on this mouth makes me want to punch a wall. I'm jealous of my brother and he is jealous of me in a way it's hard to explain if you don't have a sibling… But the past doesn't change how much I love you, not for a second."

"Are you sure?"

Scott pushed a lock of hair away from her forehead. "After David told me about the kiss, I wanted to die, to disappear, to go as far away as possible… and now I'd give anything to take it all back, but I can't. I've always wanted to be a doctor and I need this internship. I've been so stupid to believe—"

"No, you haven't." Haley laced her fingers with his, bringing their joined hands to rest over her heart. "David never lies," she said. "It's something he knows you've always trusted, and he used it against you, but it's not your fault for believing him."

"I just keep wishing that I'd waited a few hours. Or I think about what would have happened if I hadn't seen the email. I'm torturing myself imagining everything else that could've stopped me from sending that damned response."

"And my brain is stuck in a loop of 'if only I'd told him sooner.' But I didn't and you didn't and there's nothing we can do about it now. David twisted the truth and used it against us, but we can't let him win."

"He's already won, he got exactly what he wanted… to keep us apart."

"It doesn't matter where we are, physically. We're still going to be together. David hasn't won anything."

"It still sucks."

Haley scoffed. "Agreed."

She noticed that Scott wasn't asking any questions about the kiss. How it'd been. If Haley had enjoyed it. If she'd thought about David after that night. He had asked if she liked David while they were still in the middle of a shouting match, but nothing afterward. Maybe Scott didn't want to know. Or he could be afraid of what answers she might give him. And he'd be right, because the truth wouldn't make the kiss any easier to digest for him.

If he ever asks, I'm not going to lie, Haley promised herself, before shifting the topic to more practical aspects. "When does the internship start?"

"June 20th… It's a Monday, but I'll have to get to California a couple of days early to find a place to live and get settled."

"So you're basically leaving in a week."

"I haven't planned anything yet."

"And you won't have much time to plan," Haley said, straddling him. "Because I'm going to want to spend every minute you have left here together." She kissed him.

"Hey." Scott ran his hands down her lower back. "It's just a summer… nothing will change."

"You promise?"

"I promise."

Scott

Scott didn't bump into his brother again for the next two days. On Friday morning he found David seated at the kitchen bar wearing a suit and eating cereal out of a bowl as if he didn't have a concern in the world.

Scott stopped dead in the middle of the living room, undecided on what to do. A part of him wanted to scream at his brother, to beat him into a pulp. But at the same time, he wanted to pretend David didn't exist.

"Oh, come on, brother," David said. "No need for that disapproving scowl. I've heard the princess come and go these past few nights... Guess all is well again in paradise?"

"No thanks to you."

Scott had to muster all his self-control not to get dragged into another argument with David. Better to skip breakfast and leave before he did something he'd regret.

But his brother wasn't as ready to ignore him.

"May I ask why you stole the coffee maker?" David said, in a perfectly conversational tone. "Is caffeine deprivation your ultimate revenge strategy?"

"The coffee maker is mine and I can do whatever the hell I want with it."

"Are you finally moving out?" David asked. "Couldn't help but notice you're getting all boxed up. How are you going to afford a new place?"

"If you really have to know, I'm moving to California for the summer for an internship."

"Woooh." David smiled viciously. "I hope my little slip of the tongue had nothing to do with your sudden decision to move cross-country."

"What do you want me to say, David? That your mastermind plan to ruin my life worked? Well, bravo." Scott clapped his hands mockingly. "You're officially a dick."

David licked his spoon and dropped it into the bowl before saying, "At least now you've tried first-hand how fun half-truths can be."

"What are you talking about?"

David's blue eyes flared. "You know what."

"Not Brigitte again. How many times do I have to tell you that I didn't know?"

"How convenient..."

"I can't do this again, you refuse to listen—"

"Oh, I hear you just fine. Pity I don't believe you." David got up from the stool and rounded the kitchen bar, his eyes searching Scott's face. "Were you really dumb enough not to notice? Not to ever wonder?"

Scott didn't reply.

"Come on, Scotty, say it," David pushed. "Let it out, you'll feel better afterward, I promise."

"I DIDN'T KNOW!" Scott shouted, exasperated.

"Didn't know?" David spoke in a quiet hiss, his cold fury topping Scott's blunt anger. He took a step forward and shoved Scott backward. "Or didn't *want* to know?"

David gave him another push until Scott's back was pressed against the wall. In a quick move, his brother jagged his forearm against Scott's throat, leaving him just enough room to breathe. "Tell me, brother," David said, still speaking in a soft, angry whisper. "Whenever Brigitte told you not to make your relationship public, to keep it a secret from me, you never suspected it might be because she was still *with* me? Never?" David pinned him with a glacial blue stare. "Not even once?"

Scott lowered his gaze, unable to sustain his brother's glare. The truth was that, deep down, he had suspected something was wrong with the way Brigitte had behaved. Scott hadn't known for sure, but he had preferred to look the other way. To pretend he believed her version one hundred percent.

"There." David gave him another light shove and then let him go, bouncing backward. "Feels good to finally admit the truth, doesn't it?"

Scott wiped his mouth with the back of his hand. "What do you want me to say?"

"Apologize for once. Admit you didn't care if what you were doing was wrong, because you wanted Brigitte more than anything you'd ever wanted in your life. And even after you found out the truth, you still didn't care…"

"I am sorry, David. I've been sorry for a long time. But can't you see she strung both of us along? We both loved her, and she probably didn't care about either of us. Can't we just let that go? Start over?"

"Nice speech. One I could've respected if you hadn't decided to fish in my pond again."

"*Your* pond?" Scott scoffed. "Because you kissed a girl one night, a girl who couldn't even tell who you were?"

"It was a rather special kiss."

"I've been with Haley for the past six months, in case you haven't noticed. I never knew you'd met her first, and now it's too late to call dibs."

"Seriously? You didn't know? Is that your good-for-all excuse?"

"Haley is with me now. Forget the fantasy and open your eyes to reality."

"I want what I want, brother."

"Keep your hands off her," Scott threatened.

"That, brother, is only for Haley to decide."

"She hates you."

"Mmm... maybe..." David's mouth curled up at the corners, his eyes sparkling with malice. "Well, then, you have nothing to fear." He straightened his tie and jacket and opened the door. "I only hope she doesn't get too lonely while you're gone..." David waved mockingly. "Bon voyage."

Haley

Scott's last week in Cambridge seemed to fly by for Haley in no time at all. Being both still free from any other commitment, they spent every minute available together—mostly in bed. But all too soon, the last day before the departure arrived.

Haley barged into her apartment, eager to grab a change of clothes and be back on her way toward Scott's house.

"Hey, you're alive," Alice joked from the kitchen. "I'm making coffee, want some?"

"Hi... no, thanks. I'm just going to pick up a few things and go back to Scott's place. It's our last night together."

"How're you holding up?

"Super-duper," Haley said sarcastically. "I'm kinda in a hurry... Mind if we talk another time? Tomorrow I can tell you all about how sad and depressed I really am."

"Yeah, about that." Alice stepped into the hall to face her. "I wanted to give you a heads-up..."

"About what?"

"Did you have anything special planned for tonight?"

"No, Scott and I are just going to hang out at his place. Why?"

"Good, because the guys are planning a send-off party, Jack told me about it."

Haley didn't think it possible, but her mood worsened dramatically. The last thing she wanted tonight was to *party*. Parties were for celebrations, and there was absolutely nothing to celebrate here. "A party?"

"More of a dinner, really. I told Jack to tone it down as much as he could."

"Can't you tell him to call it off entirely?" Haley hated the way she sounded super petty, and the fact that in the span of a week she'd become the neediest, clingiest girlfriend. But she couldn't help being selfish. Scott was leaving and every minute they weren't alone together felt like wasted time.

"Too late for that." Alice shrugged apologetically. "Jack left only a few minutes ago, but he was going to give Scott a call." Disappointment must've shown on Haley's face, because her roommate hastened to add, "But I'll ask him to book a table early and I'll make sure they keep it short. I'll also tell Jack and the others not to insist on going for drinks afterward. Sound good?"

Haley relaxed. Alice was only trying to help, and Scott's friends had a right to say bye to him before he left. As much as she hated it, Haley would have to share. "Yeah," she said, pulling Alice into a hug. "Sorry for being so snappish, I'm in an awful mood."

Alice patted her back supportively. "I know, babe."

Just as they pulled apart, the apartment door opened again.

"Hi, roomies," Madison said, coming in. "What's up?"

"I was telling Haley the boys are organizing a dinner for tonight to say goodbye to Scott."

"Aw." Madison unconsciously lowered her gaze to the floor for a second before staring back up at them. "Sounds fun."

"Can you make it?" Haley asked, to let Madison know she was invited.

"Mmm… yeah, I'm free tonight."

"Great. Can I also ask you a favor?"

"Sure. What do you need?"

Haley felt super shitty for what she was about to ask, but Madison was still one of her best friends. And they had an unspoken agreement not to let the fact that they both were in love with the same guy change their friendship. And if Scott were any other guy, Haley wouldn't have had a problem asking her best friend for a favor… so…

"Can I borrow your car tonight?" Haley asked. Madison was the only one out of the three of them with a car. Her entire family was from Boston and she'd literally just driven a few blocks from home to come to Harvard. "I want to give Scott a ride to the airport; I would hate it if he had to take an Uber."

"Yeah, of course." Madison smiled, her cheeks reddening. "Do we need to drive tonight?" she asked Alice.

"No, Jack wanted to keep it walking distance."

"Perfect." Madison grabbed the keys from the small cabinet in the entrance and handed them to Haley. "The tank's full, you should make it to Logan Airport and back without troubles."

"Thank you." Haley took the keys and hugged Madison. "You're the best."

"No problem."

"Well, I'd better get going." Haley put the keys in her bag so as not to forget them, then dashed for her room, saying, "I'll see you both later."

***

Less than an hour later, Haley was lounging on Scott's bed, back against the wall, MacBook open in her lap. She was keeping him company while he packed. And to distract herself from the reality of Scott's largest suitcase lying open on the floor, Haley was playing around with some data. The self-assigned task was to organize a large set of scattered figures into a statistical report that would make sense. Yeah, a geek at heart.

Haley was focused on a particularly dense section when Scott's voice penetrated her concentration. "I know you wanted to spend tonight alone, but Jack called—"

"Alice told me about the party," Haley interrupted. "No worries. You know who's going to be there?"

"Just you girls and a few of the guys on the team, the ones still around."

"Is David still MIA?" she asked.

"Yep," Scott said, folding a sweatshirt. "Haven't seen him or heard from him since our latest brotherly chat."

Haley abandoned her numbers for a second to watch Scott. "It's good that you finally discussed the Brigitte issue, though, isn't it? It's the first step to fix your relationship…"

"Brigitte isn't the issue between us anymore… you are."

"Then you have no issues at all because I'm with you and that's never going to change."

Scott squatted low, turning his back to her as he rearranged a few items inside his almost-full suitcase. "So that kiss really meant nothing to you?" he asked, almost casually. "Because David keeps hinting it was a big deal."

Ah, the dreaded question had finally arrived.

Haley squirmed on the bed. Alice's advice to play down the truth rang in her ears. But she'd promised to herself she wouldn't lie to Scott. "I was caught up in it at the time." She watched his shoulders tense. "But more in a fairy tale fantasy sort of way. It wasn't real… And, honestly, I hadn't thought about it in forever, because now I have you."

Scott got up, a slight grimace on his face. His expression said he didn't like what he was hearing, but he thanked her for the honesty.

"TMI?" Haley asked.

"No." Scott walked toward her. "You kissed David. I don't like it, but I'll have to deal with it." He leaned in to retrieve a stack of underwear from the chest of drawers near the bed, throwing a peek at her Mac's screen as he bent. "What are all those numbers?" Scott asked, as if nothing of importance had been said, the let's-change-the-subject subtitle all too clear.

"A baseline of data. I'm trying to build a sorting algorithm."

"My eyes cross just looking at it. I've always hated calculus and math."

"Maybe the theory, but once you see what you can do with all the formulas, it's amazing. Like, here, take this data—when it's raw and unprocessed, it's pure chaos… but when the algorithm sorts and organizes the numbers, they begin to tell a story."

Scott threw a skeptical glance at the sheet. "Sorry." He shrugged. "Still looks like gibberish. I prefer stories told in words. Numbers were never my thing."

Haley rolled her eyes, disappointed. Scott never shared her

enthusiasm for computers and programming. And whenever he tried to enlighten her on the beauty of poetry, she often found herself half bored to death. The only novels Haley enjoyed reading were sci-fi sagas and the occasional vampire novel—books all too commercial for Scott's literary fiction tastes—and she preferred to watch the movie versions of most books anyway. Both Scott and Madison would gag if they heard her say this aloud.

She pressed save and shut her laptop; it was getting too warm on her legs, anyway. Haley threw a wistful glance at the brimming case on the floor. "Almost done here?" she asked, tearing her eyes away from the suitcase and its implied meaning. Scott was leaving her… Tomorrow, he'd be gone. *It's only two months,* she kept repeating to herself.

"Yeah, I need socks…" He took them out of another drawer and shot six balled pairs into the suitcase, basketball style—feet in a slightly staggered stance, body elongated, arms up, and six flicks of the wrist— sending all the tiny balls to land precisely in the center of the suitcase. He looked sexy as hell, like whenever he was on the basketball court. "…And I'm done."

He smiled, and Haley couldn't resist—she swung her legs off the bed and pulled him to her before he could go close the suitcase. She rested her hands on his hips, looking up at him. "So what's the latest housing plan?"

"I've booked a Holiday Inn for tomorrow and Friday night. And I have six housing appointments scheduled; I hope to find a place before the weekend."

"I liked the one near the beach."

Haley had helped him sort through the Craigslist listings to choose which appointments to book.

"Of course you liked that one." Scott dropped his hands on her shoulders, his thumbs caressing her trapezius muscles. "But it's also the farthest away from the hospital, and everyone says traffic sucks in California."

"It's not like you'll be driving."

"No, exactly. I hope the condo two blocks from work will be cool."

"The apartment-share with the residency student?"

"That one."

"Aren't residents supposed to be super busy and never at home?"

Haley's hands sneaked under Scott's tank top and up his lower back. "Don't you want to meet someone who'll introduce you to loads of people? You don't know anyone over there."

"I don't expect Dr. Allen to be a nine-to-five kind of guy; shadowing him will be worse than any residency. There won't be much time for me to get social."

"I wish I could believe you." Haley pouted jokingly. "You'll meet tons of blonde Californian beauties and forget all about me."

Scott gently pulled at the ends of her just-above-the-shoulders bob. "Pity I have a thing for brunettes…"

"You do, huh?"

"I do." Scott's smile disappeared, and he became suddenly serious. "I'm going to miss you," he said, dropping his forehead to hers.

"Me, too." Haley lifted her chin to kiss him.

In a blur of passion and longing, they tore each other's clothes off and rolled onto the bed, their limbs so entangled it was impossible to tell where one body started and the other ended…

***

"We're going to be late," Haley said, her mind still hazy from all the goodbye sex.

If nothing else, Scott's imminent departure had given her the best week of sex of her life. There was something to be said about making love knowing you were about to be separated from your partner for a long time. It heightened everything. Every kiss, every touch, every sensation was more urgent, intense, powerful…

Scott groaned, stretching beside her. "I don't care…"

"The sooner we leave," Haley grazed the skin of his neck with her teeth, "the sooner we can come back and do this again."

"I'm convinced." He flashed her a roguish smile and hopped off the bed.

They took a quick shower—*together*—and managed to get to the restaurant only ten minutes late. To their relief, they weren't even the last to arrive. Alice and Jack beat them to it and, judging from the healthy glow on both their faces, for the same reason.

Once they were all seated, Haley fought hard to keep a smile plastered on her face. But inside, she couldn't help the relentless countdown her brain had initiated. Her stupid mathematical mind enjoyed providing her with a set of depressing numerical stats Haley could've gladly done without. 12 hours until Scott's plane left. 720 minutes. 43,200 seconds. 72 days before he came back. 1,728 hours. 103,680 minutes. And a ridiculous number of seconds. Okay, now she could get Scott's hatred for numbers.

How was she supposed to endure all that time without him? It wasn't that Haley had never been single, or that she didn't know how to be on her own. But in the last six months, she'd relinquished most of that independence to her relationship. She'd gotten used to Scott's presence by her side. To always have his support, to see him almost every day, to make love to him whenever she wanted, and to always be able to count on him... And now she'd have to learn how to be alone all over again.

Besides disturbing numerical statistics and even gloomier thoughts, Haley was having a hard time deciding what she found more annoying about this farewell party. The way Madison kept trying—*and failing*—not to stare at Scott adoringly. How Alice seemed to pick up on everything and kept alternating worried side glances between Haley, Madison, and Scott. The frankly tasteless jokes the "boys" kept bouncing off Scott about Californian beauties. *Hello? His girlfriend is sitting right next to you, assholes.* Or the fact that every minute they spent at this restaurant was a minute less Haley could have Scott all for herself.

Usually the most social and outgoing in her group of friends, tonight Haley felt like a bratty child who hadn't gotten what she'd wanted for Christmas. While her family was all happy and busy celebrating, she was left alone sulking in a corner—ignored.

Get a grip, *she told herself.* You're ruining this for Scott, stop being a total bitch.

Haley took a deep breath and got up to go to the restroom. A splash of fresh water on her face and she'd be as good as new and back to being a decent human being and not a sorry girlfriendzilla.

She'd barely made it to the hall leading to the restrooms when someone grabbed her from behind.

"I know you'd rather be back home," Scott breathed down her neck. "Me, too."

Goosebumps traveled all the way down from Haley's nape to the tip of her toes.

"Busted?" she asked, turning around.

Scott nodded, opening his arms invitingly.

Haley burrowed her face in his chest. "I'm sorry, it's your goodbye party and I'm ruining it for you. But I can't help being in an awful mood."

"Hey." Scott made her look up. "You're not ruining anything. I know every minute we spend here seems like a minute less we can be together, but I promise I'll make it up to you."

Scott had a wicked twinkle in his eyes and Haley couldn't help but smile and ask, "Make up for it, huh? How?"

Scott whispered the mischievous answer in her ear and made to lead her back to the others before she could reply.

"Hey," Haley protested, "what if I really needed the restroom?"

Scott flashed her a grin. "Did you?"

"No," Haley admitted, and let him pull her away.

Back at the table, they spent the rest of the evening eye-flirting with each other. The entire dinner didn't seem wasted time anymore, just a long session of hands-off foreplay. Haley couldn't stop smiling—for real this time. Never in her life had she had this much complicity with anyone. Not a guy. Not her friends. Only Scott. It would always be Scott.

***

Hours later, in Scott's room, Haley was staring at the dark ceiling, a whirlwind of sad thoughts swirling ceaselessly inside her head. After a night together that needed to last them two months, they were both spent and could not have made love another time even if they'd wanted to.

"You're not sleeping," Scott said, turning on the bed to face her.

"Neither are you."

"I can't sleep with you so awake next to me."

Haley huffed the hair away from her face. "Sorry, but I don't want to sleep."

"Why not?"

"Because you're here now and sleep is a waste of time." Haley sighed. "I can sleep tomorrow all day if I want to. Hell, I can sleep every day for the next two months… but not tonight, not while you're still with me."

"Night… it's almost dawn already."

"Wilt thou be gone?" Haley whispered. "It is not yet near day."

Scott propped himself on an elbow, surveying her. "Are you quoting Shakespeare at me?" he asked with a grin barely visible in the faint light that preceded dawn. "I thought you hated verses and plays and poetry…"

"I do." Haley smirked.

Scott frowned in the semi-darkness.

"End of the nineties," she announced in a dramatic voice, "Leonardo DiCaprio and Claire Danes co-star in the most epic movie of the decade…"

Scott groaned. "*That* movie, seriously?"

"Hm-mmm," Haley hummed. "*Romeo + Juliet* was one of my favorite movies growing up. I learned it almost by heart."

"You liked the movie, or Leonardo DiCaprio?"

"Bit of both."

Haley smiled, and Scott tickled her sides. The game soon ended in a kiss, and when Scott pulled away, he didn't move back to his side of the bed. He knelt half on top of her, caressing her hair.

"I appreciate the literary quote," he said. "But we're nothing like Romeo and Juliet."

"No? Feels a lot like it."

"What? Like we're star-crossed lovers who just got married in secret because our families are mortal enemies and now I've killed your cousin and I'm being exiled?" Scott taunted.

"No," Haley said, her tone serious. "Like you have to leave and I don't want you to."

"I have more care to stay than will to go," Scott recited theatrically. "I'll stay and lose my flight… Haley wills it so."

"No, she doesn't. Haley wills you to go do your wonderful internship and learn everything you can from your superstar doctor. But she wants you to stay at the same time… if it makes any sense?"

"Completely, because I want to go and to stay just as much."

As if on cue, Scott's phone lit up, and the alarm started beeping.

"But you have to go," Haley said.

Scott gave her a peck on the lips and sat on the bed to silence the phone. Haley knelt behind him, hugging his back.

She leaned in and bit his earlobe. "Think we have time for one last bit of fun before your exile?"

Scott didn't have to be told twice. "My snooze time is pretty long." He dropped the phone and turned, pinning Haley on the bed underneath him. Turned out they still had some steam in them.

***

The drive to the airport was a sad business spent mostly in silence. Haley was busy driving Madison's car and getting too much inside her own head, and Scott was evidently exhausted after a sleepless night. Haley knew him well enough to see he was already focused on all the things he needed to sort out before Monday.

After a quick breakfast outside of the security check barrier, the time to really say goodbye came. Tears already welling in her eyes, Haley followed Scott toward the gate as far as non-passengers were allowed. She kept her gaze trained on the floor the entire time to hide her puffy red eyes, and when they stopped, Scott had to lift her chin to make her look at him.

"Please don't cry," he whispered, pulling her into a hug.

Haley inhaled his familiar scent, and that did it—the last shred of self-control she'd hung to slipped away, and she started sobbing uncontrollably.

"It's okay," Scott said, caressing her hair. "I'll be back in no time."

"I know, I'm just being silly."

"No, you're not." Scott pulled back slightly and cupped her face in his hands. "I love you."

"I love you."

He kissed her one last time—okay, more three or four kisses all rolled into one heart-wrenching goodbye—and then he walked away.

Haley watched him go through security until Scott was on the other side. He turned to flash her a sad-ish grin while he raised the hand holding the plane ticket in a final farewell gesture. And then he was gone.

The moment Scott disappeared behind the corner, a cold, heavy stone replaced Haley's heart.

Be fickle, Fortune, *Haley thought, feeling just as ill-divining as Claire Danes in the movie,* for then I hope thou wilt not keep him long. But send him back.

Back to me, and fast... Haley took the poetic license of adding.

***

Scott was gone, and the only thing that made Haley get out of bed on Monday morning was the start of summer classes. After a weekend spent holed up in her room watching *Romeo + Juliet* on repeat, Haley was glad something was forcing her to react. With two grad computer science courses and an advanced statistics class on her plate, she hoped she'd be too busy to mope over Scott.

He'd called every day since he'd gotten to California, but talking over the phone was a poor replica of a real-life conversation, and every single time he'd been in a hurry. Too many things to set up, too many places he needed to be. And he hadn't even started working yet. If things kept going this way, she'd be lucky if they managed to talk for more than ten minutes at a time.

Unfortunately, the first week of school proved all her fears right. The classes were demanding, but not nearly challenging enough to absorb Haley completely. She still had plenty of time to feel lonely. After almost seven months dating Scott, she was used to being held, kissed, and cuddled. The lack of physical contact was taking its toll, and the difficulties in talking to each other were rattling her emotionally. Conversations with Scott were officially counted in minutes—single digits—and not hours.

Saturday morning, still in this state of mind, Haley was positively scared of spending another full weekend in her room. She worried she'd end up with another forty-eight-hour marathon of tragic love movies and endless tears… so she decided to go to the library to do her homework. Usually, she didn't care to use a shared space to study. Library goers had a tendency of rolling their eyes at her constant keyboard click-clacking that made Haley uncomfortable. But staying home wasn't an option today. In a public location, Haley would have to get her act together, concentrate on her assignments, and she definitely wouldn't be able to watch any movie or cry.

Of all the facilities available on campus, Haley settled on the Widener Library. If she really had to go study somewhere, she might as well pick Harvard's flagship library. The building was an impressive brick rectangle, its front lined with huge white pillars that stood at the head of a flight of steps. Inside, the larger study room, Widener Loker Reading Room, had an old-style feel and was even more impressive with its high-vaulted light-green ceiling that let in plenty of natural light.

The place must've been a lot emptier than during a regular term, but still, all the long rectangular tables had two to three students already seated at them. Haley shuffled to the back of the room, toward a table with only two busy seats at the opposite ends. On the left, facing Haley, was an Asian girl in a red cotton sweater with long dark locks, her neck bent over a set of open tomes. On the right, there was an empty chair with a messenger bag strapped across its back and a laptop opened on an Excel sheet.

Haley's first instinct would've been to grab a seat in the middle, but the Excel sheet had caught her attention. Whoever was working on that model was doing a really poor job. To be fair, Haley could understand the base logic they'd applied. But they were going at it all wrong... a few lines of well-thought code inside an Excel macro could solve the problem in a matter of minutes. Otherwise, it'd take them hours...

Careful not to make it scrape, Haley drew back the second to nearest chair to the abandoned laptop and sat down, setting up her MacBook on the table. Where to start? The STAT S-106 homework assignment seemed to be calling to her. And while she worked at it, the fella next door could get a better idea of how data should be handled. Secretly, Haley hoped that whoever was going to sit next to her would realize how good of a job she was doing and plead for her help. She couldn't help it. When it came to numbers, she was such a show-off.

Shuffling the syllabus out of the way, Haley found the paper with the first homework assignment. Question one looked easy, a straight statistical analysis of a given pool of data, complete with Mean Absorbance Ratio, and prevalence calculations. Question number two, instead, was the open-ended kind Haley hated:

```
The Boston Mayor is determined to
assess the population satisfaction
with the performance of the Police
Department (PD) and the District
Attorney (DA) office in all the
city's counties.

You are in charge of the team
contracted to do the study and must
```

```
report to the Mayor.

- Who should you poll? Do you
attempt a census or opt for a well-
designed controlled poll/survey?

- What sample size(s) would you
use? What criteria do you need to
satisfy to argue about the
validity of your final
conclusions?
```

The assignment continued with more stupid open questions. Ugh, what a waste of brainpower… going over the methodologies to acquire the data was so boring. Essential for any analysis to ever make sense, but still boring. Haley wanted to play with the numbers, not the methodologies they were collected with.

Let's get the dull questions out of the way first.

Haley was working on the first point—Who should she poll?—when the mysterious next-door neighbor showed up. Haley recognized him a second before their eyes met, from the light scent of citrus and sun-kissed skin that filled her nostrils.

Open-mouthed and wide-eyed, she lifted her eyes and met David Williams' gaze, the same shocked expression mirrored on his face. With his dark hair tucked behind his ears and wearing a simple white T-shirt, faded jeans, and sneakers David looked… well, there was only one way of putting it: *hot.*

Haley cursed under her breath. All of a sudden, a day spent in her room crying seemed like the better alternative.

"Hi," he whispered.

No mocking grin, no challenging attitude. He sat in his chair and, with a few clicks of the mouse, he revived the laptop screen that had gone dark in the meantime.

Haley was still staring at him, ready to pack her things and go, when—eyes still glued to the screen—he added, "We're in a public library, Haley." *Haley.* Not Sunshine or another stupid nickname. "I'm here to work, no need to fidget."

Haley shut her still open mouth and imitated him, turning her eyes to her Mac and trying to concentrate on her homework. She could do this, ignore David and complete her assignments. Haley reread the first question.

Who should she pool?

Well, who was interested in the service levels of the Boston PD and DA? All adult residents of the Boston area counted, for sure. But should she also include non-resident students? Did minors count? Did tourists count? Did David Williams count?

She jotted down the questions—all minus the last one—to justify the inclusion or exclusion of the different groups in her final answer.

What sample size should she set on?

That depended on the margin of error she was ready to accept, and on the desired responses confidence level—to account for the statistical probability of people lying when interviewed.

And what was the statistical probability of her picking the one chair next to David Williams on a campus with more than twenty-two thousand students and over seventy separate library units?

On a regular day, fooling around with percentages and deviations—even for stupid open-ended questions—would've intrigued Haley, but on this particular morning, she was having serious troubles concentrating. What with having to fight the urge to spy on David and what he was doing every five seconds. And what with his distracting aftershave that she could barely—but definitively—detect.

Maybe she should rethink her strategy—start with the heavy-handed numerical problems first, and research the philosophy of statistical analysis later. Yeah, okay. But why was David so blatantly ignoring her? And why was it bothering her if he did? Wasn't it what she always asked of him, to leave her alone? Yeah, which he never did. So why start today?

Careful not to be too obvious, Haley threw a side-peek at David. Contrary to her, he appeared very concentrated on his analysis and was still sorting through his data—*manually*. Could it be that David Williams wasn't the issue? Maybe the nagging at Haley's sides came from the poor way such a beautiful set of raw data was being handled. That must be it. She should show him how models were built, and move on with her homework.

"You're doing it all wrong," Haley whispered.

David turned toward her. "Excuse me?" he asked in an equally low voice.

"Your model." She pointed at his screen. "If you keep doing it like that, it'll take you forever."

"I bet that was the point."

"Uh?"

"My boss dumped this"—David tilted his head toward the laptop—"and five other models to build on me last night saying he needed them ready for Monday morning, but granting me the special privilege of working from home. So I suspect he wanted to make sure I spent every second of the weekend slaving over this."

"You have five more?"

"Yep."

"If you keep going at that snail's pace you'll never finish."

"Thanks for the cheer up." His signature mocking grin finally made an appearance. "Now I'd like to keep working if you don't mind."

"I could show you how to make it a quick job," Haley said. "You'd be done in no time."

David arched both his eyebrows in surprise. "And why would you do that?"

"I can't help myself when it comes to numbers," Haley blabbed without thinking, opening her defenses up for an easy gibe. She'd served it to him on a silver platter.

Haley watched a twinkle appear in his blue eyes, the phantom of the easy retort she was sure they were both thinking: *You mean you can't help yourself when it comes to me.*

She waited for him to rip away, but he didn't. David only smiled, he turned his laptop toward her, and said, "Knock yourself out."

Haley shifted her butt into the chair next to him and avidly set her hands on the almost-virgin dataset. "To do a good job, you need to clean the data first. Then you can start elaborating them…"

"And how do I do that?"

Haley started lecturing him on everything that he was doing wrong, and David stoically took a notebook out of his bag and began to take notes on all his unforgivable model-building mistakes. He watched Haley sort through his first model in less than an hour, asking her to explain what she was doing step by step. And she did, enjoying both the work and the chance to show off her mathematical skills.

Admiring her new model all shiny and pretty on David's screen, Haley felt better than she had all week. With a big smile, she said, "And that's how it's done."

David low-whistled, careful not to make the sound too audible. "Thank you," he said, his gaze more intense than ever.

Despite herself, Haley blushed. "You're welcome. Now I'd better get back to my own work."

She considered returning to her chair, but the gesture would look ridiculous at this point. So she simply pulled her laptop closer and resumed working on her homework questions. And in a weird way, David's nearness stopped bothering her. Haley was still hyperaware of his presence next to her, of his unmistakable scent, but most of the uneasiness she usually felt in his presence had gone. Perhaps because for the first time since Christmas, he'd behaved like a normal person and not a psychopath. The library was a good influence on him.

So Haley spent the rest of her Saturday working side by side with David, answering his questions whenever he hit a snafu in his model building, and even forgetting to eat lunch altogether. When an attendant came to tell them they were ten minutes past closing time already, she was utterly surprised. Even if it was already late afternoon, the sun, being late June, was still high in the sky and the room as luminous as in the morning. So nothing had alerted Haley of the passing of time.

Outside, they stopped on the steps for an awkward goodbye. As long as they'd been cocooned in the protected environment of the library, it had seemed all fine and uncomplicated to sit next to David for an entire day working together. But now that they'd moved outside, Haley was second-guessing the choice she'd made to stay.

"Hey, I'm starving," David said, breaking the silence. "Want to grab a bite?"

Now, going out to dinner with David was a definite no-no.

"No, thanks." Haley pulled at the strings of her backpack. "I have to go and call Scott," she said, blurting out the first excuse that came to mind. Probably not even an excuse. She hadn't checked her phone all day, library's policies and all, and she really had to call Scott. Also, it was good to remind them both that even if he was thousands of miles away, Scott remained the huge pink elephant standing right next to them.

A dark shadow clouded David's features. "Sure," he said, descending a step. "Well, I'd better get going. Bye."

"Bye."

Faster than she could say *"Williams brothers,"* he was hopping down the remaining steps and sprinting away.

Haley sat on the edge of the porch with a sigh. Unhooking her backpack from one shoulder and rolling it from back to front, she fished her phone out of the small pocket at the base. She unlocked the black screen and saw five missed calls—all from Scott.

Crap.

After plugging in her headphones, she tapped his name.

He picked up on the second ring. "Babe, where have you been? I've tried to call you so many times." He sounded hurried.

"Yeah, sorry. I've been at the library all day, doing homework. I even forgot to eat lunch, and I had my phone on silent."

Why was she leaving out the part where David had been there too?

You know why.

I've done nothing wrong, Haley argued with herself.

Such a pretty little liar...

"Haley, I'm sorry..." Scott said. "I had time to talk before, but I can't now."

"Oh." So the one time she could've had a real, longer-than-a-few-minutes conversation with her boyfriend, she'd spent the day—doing what, anyway?—with his brother and hadn't checked her phone once. Haley wanted to kick herself. "Going somewhere?"

"Yep. Dr. Allen's assistant just called, he's removing a brain tumor today, and I'm invited to watch the procedure."

"Will it last long?"

"Hours, eight to ten." So she wasn't going to hear from him again today. "And the patient will be alert the entire time, isn't it exciting?"

How Scott could get so enthusiastic about spending ten hours watching one person crack another person's skull open and fiddle with their brains—*while the poor dude was awake*—was out of Haley's comprehension, but she tried to sound supportive all the same. "Wow, brain surgery... sounds thrilling."

"Um, listen, I really gotta bounce. Call you tomorrow?"

"Sure."

"Love you."

"Me too."

The words had barely left Haley's lips when the line clicked off. She was tempted to hurl her phone down the steps; it seemed so satisfactory when people did it in the movies. But in real life, it'd only leave her with no phone, or with a seriously damaged one, and she doubted broken technology would lift her mood. A stomach cramp reminded Haley of the skipped lunch. Better get home and order a pizza.

Haley stood up, resenting the warm June sun caressing her face. Never had she hated a summer so much.

***

The subconscious is a tricky mechanism, a gray area of the mind that allows individuals to lie to themselves. Haley's most private thoughts must've been safely stored in that gray matter when she walked into the library the following Saturday. How else could she tell herself that she wasn't hoping to catch David there again? That there was no particular reason she'd chosen today—exactly a week after she'd bumped into David—to return to the Loker Reading Room. That, on the contrary, she actively wished for him not to be there. And that when she spotted him seated in the same exact spot as the previous Saturday, it wasn't relief she felt.

Now, part of her suspected there was something fundamentally wrong—or if not outright wrong, at least dangerous in a playing-with-fire way—in her actions. But her subconscious still allowed her enough wiggle room for her to sincerely tell herself that it was okay. That there was nothing wrong with spending time with David. That she hadn't been looking forward to the weekend since Monday. And that it was for personal hygiene reasons she'd showered that morning—and blow-dried her hair and put lip gloss on.

"Hey," she greeted him.

Yeah, nothing wrong with spotting that same relief reflected in his eyes as soon as they set on hers.

"Hey, Miss Robot."

Miss Robot. No more Sunshine, but not even Haley.

Haley raised both her eyebrows. "I'm not Sunshine anymore?"

"Miss Robot sounded more appropriate."

Haley half-smiled, half-grimaced, loving the nickname but hating that she did.

"I hoped you'd show up," David said, his smile so genuine that it almost shattered Haley's fickle mind barriers. But David's next comment made it okay to ignore the alarm bells. "I have a new modeling challenge for you."

They only shared a common interest in numbers and Excel spreadsheets. It was okay to hang out, nothing wrong with that.

She sat on the chair next to him and asked, "Are you always supposed to work on weekends?"

"It's investment banking, they're not famous for leisure working hours. And it's your fault if I monumentally pissed off my boss."

"My fault, how?"

Someone nearby coughed in a reproachful way, so David lowered his tone considerably when he said, "You had me deliver him a set of six perfectly built models."

"Wasn't that the point?"

"No, as it turns out." David drew his brows close together in a mock-serious expression. "The point was for me to spend every waking hour of the weekend sweating cold, knowing I wouldn't be able to complete the assignment. I should've pulled a couple of all-nighters, and then walked into the office on Monday looking like a properly humbled intern. My boss didn't appreciate the swag…" David smirked.

Yeah, Haley could just imagine the scene. David had swagger enough for ten interns.

She ignored his smug expression and asked, "And you work at this lovely place… because?"

"It's where the best of the best work… it's like joining the military and applying to be a Navy SEAL. The training is going to be a bitch, but if you survive, you're part of an elite force."

"That saves lives and protects the country; you only want to swim in cash."

"It's not about the money…" David pierced her with a stare. "…It's about the challenge."

Haley couldn't sustain that gaze and busied her hands with a stack of notes. "Anyway, is the new model punishment?"

"Boss wanted to make sure I spent the whole weekend working this time. He doesn't know I have a secret weapon."

"And what if I hadn't shown up?"

He held her gaze a moment longer than Haley was comfortable with. "But you did."

Right. Better to bring the conversation back on safer ground. "What's the new model about?"

"What do you know about the stock market, volatility, and risk management?" David challenged.

Haley smiled and cracked her knuckles. "Show me the math."

***

Haley didn't forget about lunch this time—at around midday, hunger bit at her. Still, she was undecided if she should say anything, as she was sure that if she mentioned taking a break for lunch, David would try to join her.

So?

Would sharing a sandwich be all that different from building a model together? Somehow it sounded more compromising—*date-ish.* But when her empty stomach let her know with an angry grumble that it couldn't care less about her moral reserves, Haley asked, "I'm going out for a sandwich, care to join me?"

David lifted a finger toward her, eyes still trained on the screen. "Give me fifteen minutes. I need to finish one thing first."

"O-kay."

Haley looked back at her own screen, off-putted. Not that she had expected David to fall at her feet with gratitude for a simple invite to lunch—well, actually, she had kind of expected it. He should consider himself lucky that after everything he'd done, she was still talking to him—helping him, even. Ungrateful little brat.

Haley was about to put him in his place when his concentrated frown stopped her. He seemed oblivious to her mood shifts. In fact, he appeared so focused on his work that Haley relaxed. Making her wait wasn't personal; Haley was the same when she was so caught up in programming—she didn't see or feel anything else. Not hunger, and definitely not hurt feelings.

Suppressing a sigh, she kept working on her program, throwing him side-glares from time to time—even if she understood the work-frenzy, she was still famished.

361

A good twenty minutes later, David shut his laptop and they headed out. They grabbed two sandwiches from a kiosk and went to eat them seated at an outside table bathed in the warm July sun. It would've been almost too hot, if not for the cool breeze constantly blowing that made the temperature just perfect.

"You're staring," David said, eyeing her over his half-eaten sandwich.

True, Haley *was* staring. "Who are you?" she asked, narrowing her eyes at him. "And what did you do with the real David?"

"You're looking at him."

"So if you know how to be a normal person, why do you usually act like a jerk?"

"Pardon me?"

Now that she'd started, Haley wasn't about to back down. "Excluding today and last Saturday, you've always acted nasty around me."

"Sorry if I wasn't a jolly good fellow while I had to watch you drool all over my brother."

Haley stopped her hands halfway to her mouth and lowered the sandwich. "Excuse me? You were a poster child for douche central right from the moment you opened the door of your room in Hawaii. I wasn't even with Scott back then."

"I was flirting"—David batted his lashes jokingly while he smiled—"and you were giving me the cold shoulder."

"I wasn't."

"Oh, pluhease." He rolled his eyes theatrically. "You were already so much into my brother there was nothing I could've said to make you change your mind."

Ah, but there was something you could've said, Haley thought, and hoped her emotions wouldn't show on her face.

No such luck. David saw right through her, and when he spoke next, it was as if he'd read her mind. "Not *that*," he said. "I wanted you to like *me,* not a fantasy we both had ages before at a summer dance."

"You still could've been nice," Haley chided, praying she wasn't blushing. Her cheeks flared up whenever she thought about the night of the masquerade. "And why tell me about the ball so much later, then?"

David licked a smidgen of sauce off his fingers. "What can I say? I'm not perfect."

Haley scoffed. "Duh-uh."

"What's that supposed to mean?"

"You really hurt Madison, you know?"

"Oh come ooon, I already told you Blondie was never that into me."

"Regardless of her feelings, you can't expect to yell horrible things at a girl and not have her take them to heart—especially someone as sensitive as Madison."

"I'm sorry, okay?" David scrunched the paper that had been holding his sandwich in a tight ball and hurled it at a nearby bin, his aim impeccable. "I was having a bad day, and I snapped."

Haley swallowed the last bit of her sandwich, then said, "It's not me you should apologize to."

"In a way, I should, though."

Haley didn't reply; she just kept watching him reproachfully. Her expression said: *I'm listening.*

David dragged his chair closer to hers. "I'm sorry I acted like a jerk around you this whole time. It was only because I was angry at Scott for something that happened years ago—and because I was jealous. And I'm sorry I told you about us, about the kiss, the way I did…"

Haley arched one eyebrow.

"And, yes, I'm sorry I made it sound to Scott as if it had just happened. I thought he was going to get mad for a few hours and then get over it. I didn't know he would move halfway across the country five minutes after I told him."

"But you're not so sorry he's gone." Haley scowled.

David's eyes twinkled with mischief and he grinned. "No, I'm not a saint."

Haley wanted to keep glowering at him but found it hard. Her lips seemed to stubbornly want to curl up in a smile.

Features contracted in a mask of innocence, David asked, "Am I forgiven?"

"You're on probation," Haley conceded. Without giving him room to gloat, she got up, walking all the way to the garbage bin to throw away her trash, and added, "Let's go back inside and finish our work."

"At your command, Miss Robot."

Haley made a point to press her lips tightly together and not smile. *Damn,* it was really hard to keep a grudge against the dude. Haley silently cursed herself for being so soft.

Alice

A week later, on Saturday afternoon, Alice knocked on Madison's door.

"Come in," her roommate yelled from inside the room.

Alice opened the door and stopped dead on the threshold. "Whoa, what's going on in here?"

Madison was sitting on the floor surrounded by sheets of printed paper that were scattered all over the carpet in apparent chaos.

"I'm deconstructing *Don Quixote*."

No kidding, Alice thought. "Literally?"

"No, not literally." Madison rolled her eyes as if everyone should know what deconstructing a book meant. "But I need to check different chapters at once to—"

"I'm already late," Alice interrupted, before Madison could launch into a didactic explanation.

Madison stared up at her with a face that said: Well, you're the one who came into my room asking what I was doing… so?

"I wanted to give you a heads-up," Alice explained.

The confusion on Madison's face deepened.

"I'm meeting Georgiana for coffee." Madison's confusion turned to shock, then to shame. "We're going to Crema Café in case you're going out and want to… uh… avoid the place."

"So the newlyweds are back from the honeymoon," Madison said, more to herself than Alice. "They've been gone almost a month… Thanks for letting me know. I'll definitely avoid Harvard Square. Are you going right now?"

"Yep."

"I'll head out with you." Madison stood up, revealing the only tiny circle of carpet not covered in paper. "I could use a break from all this mess." She grabbed her battered leather bag, a paperback from her nightstand, and slipped into a pair of flats. "I'm ready."

"You're taking a break from reading a book by reading another book?" Alice asked, tilting her chin toward the paperback in Madison's hands as they headed out of the apartment.

"This?" Madison scoffed. "This is genre fiction; it's the definition of a break. And I wasn't reading *Don Quixote,* I was deconstructing it. This"—she tapped the book and then pushed the "down" button of the elevator—"is just a story, something I don't have to study, or analyze, or—"

"Deconstruct," Alice offered, entering the elevator.

"Exactly. I can get lost in the narrative without thinking, take a break from everything else, and travel to a different place."

In the lobby, Alice pulled Madison into a hug, saying, "All right, have fun on your break."

"You too."

Madison held the entrance door open for her and they both stepped outside, heading in opposite directions.

***

"Sorry I'm late," Alice said as she arrived at Crema Café.

Georgiana was already there, sitting at a table for two, but as soon as she spotted Alice she got up to welcome her. Her bump wasn't showing yet, but Georgiana still seemed rounder, softer. Not in a weight-gain way. Alice couldn't explain it; it was as if Georgiana's edges had been smoothed, making her sorority big sister a gentler version of her former self.

"Don't worry," Georgiana said, air kissing her. "I got here only a minute ago."

"Wow." Alice smiled, taking in Georgiana's tan and pregnancy glow. "You look fantastic."

"Oh, please. I'm a fat cow." Georgiana sagged back in her chair. "None of my clothes fit anymore."

Inside her head, Alice rolled her eyes. Georgiana was such a drama queen—at over four months pregnant she was barely showing and must've only gained a few pounds, tops.

"A good excuse to buy new ones?" Alice joked. Then she put on her poker face as she asked, "So, how was the honeymoon?"

Georgiana was a close friend and Alice wanted to make sure she was okay without revealing the huge secret Madison had entrusted her with. Plus, there were some truths better left untold. Alice doubted telling a pregnant woman that her husband had almost had sex with a bridesmaid—*and a close relative*—on their wedding day would help anyone.

"Curaçao was amazing," Georgiana said breezily. "The beaches, the weather, the food, the tiny colored houses… everything!"

How about the groom? "And with Tyler? Everything good?"

"Super," Georgiana added, too quickly. She plastered a smile on her face that screamed forced.

"Are you sure?"

"Yeah." Georgiana waved her off. "My husband—how cool is it to say that?—he just worries too much."

"About what?"

"Oh, pfff… the baby, the house, law school. I told him everything is going to be fine, no need to change our plans."

Eyes goggling a little, Alice quickly caught herself and reined in her surprise, schooling her face into a neutral expression. Georgiana sounded as if she believed having a baby wouldn't change a single thing in her life.

Alice cleared her throat and asked, "So you plan to go back to school in the fall?"

"Yeah, why wouldn't I?"

Because of the little human growing inside you who's going to want out in the middle of the school year? *"Won't it be too difficult with a newborn baby?"*

"You sound just like Tyler now. When the baby comes, we'll hire a nanny to help. We can go to the library to study and I can skip a couple of lessons if the baby needs me…"

Georgiana seemed way too optimistic about the impact a baby would have on his parents' lives. But once Georgiana made up her mind about something, there was no changing her opinion, so it'd be pointless to argue with her. "Glad to hear you're not worried."

"I'm not, no need to stress. By the way…" Georgiana leaned forward conspiratorially. "Want to know the sex of the baby?"

"You found out?"

"Had my ultrasound on Monday." Georgiana unconsciously rubbed her tiny bump. "It's a girl," she announced.

"Awww, that's amazing."

"I know." This time Georgiana's smile was positively radiant. "We couldn't be happier."

Without getting up, Alice bump-scraped her chair closer to Georgiana and pulled her into a side hug. "I'm so happy for you."

"A life is growing inside of me." Again, Georgiana's hand went to her belly. "I can't describe how weird and fantastic and unbelievable it feels."

"Sounds overwhelming…"

Georgian's face became really serious. "Sometimes it is, especially how much I already love this little person I've never met. But it's also so scary to know she'll depend on me for everything…"

"Well, you *and* Tyler," Alice said. "Are you worried he's not going to be a hands-on dad?"

"Oh, no. I'm sure he'll be a wonderful dad."

"So how are things between you two, I mean, baby aside?"

"Great, really." The fake smile was back. "He only worries too much."

Alice wasn't sure if Georgiana was purposely refusing to admit there were problems in her relationship—well, marriage—or if she wasn't ready to face the reality as of yet, and was lying to herself. But it was clear the "trouble in paradise" topic was off-limits, so Alice switched subjects completely. "Have you started looking at names yet?"

"Not really. But I bought this on the way here." Georgiana pulled a pink book—titled *Baby Girl Names*—from her bag and opened it. "Want to help me scroll through?"

"Sure."

They both bent their heads over the book and rolled names off their tongues for the rest of the afternoon.

Madison

For her break, Madison chose a coffee shop a good thirty-minute walk away from Crema Café. She ordered a Chai Tea Latte—her favorite—and settled at the most secluded table in the café. With a wall on one side and a huge column on the other, she was screened from the other patrons and could read her escape book in peace.

But after only a few chapters, she got distracted by a female voice on the other side of the column that sounded oddly familiar. A girl had just asked someone why they had to come all the way over here and couldn't meet nearer to campus.

"Georgiana is meeting a friend at Crema Café," a guy replied. "I didn't want to risk running into them."

Madison shrank in her chair—her pulse quickened, and her entire face was suddenly burning with embarrassment. That was Tyler sitting on the other side of the column—as in, Georgiana's Tyler. And now that she'd placed him, it was easy to recognize the other voice as Rose's. Brilliant!

Apparently, the world wasn't done playing sick jokes with her. And now I'm trapped.

Madison couldn't get up without them spotting her. And no matter how hard she tried to stare at the words printed in her book, she couldn't avoid overhearing their conversation.

"So, where do you want to start?" Rose asked, an edge audible in her voice. "Hard topics first?" Tyler must've nodded, because Rose kept talking. "What got into you at the wedding?"

Madison wanted to evaporate. She'd never felt more uncomfortable in her own skin—and she'd felt pretty damn uncomfortable in it most of her life.

"I honestly don't know why I did what I did," Tyler said.

"I mean, I get the girl was a blonde goddess…"

A blonde goddess? Were they really talking about her? Madison never thought of herself as beautiful. She usually placed herself in the "not entirely ugly" category, at best.

"It wasn't because of the girl, Rose, she could've been anyone."

Now, that's flattering. Madison scoffed inside her head. It was always nice to be reminded how un-special she was.

"What was it, then?"

"Nothing and everything. Until my wedding day, doing the right thing by Georgiana sounded fine—noble, even. But then I was in front of a minister promising to be with her for the rest of my life, and it all became real. I was married—I *am* married—to a woman I'm not sure I love enough, only because she's carrying my baby."

"Still, trying to sleep with a bridesmaid doesn't seem like an optimal solution."

"Rose, I promise you I'm done with all that shit. I'm never going to cheat on anyone ever again. If my marriage doesn't work out, I'll end it in a clean way. I never want to feel as low as that day ever again."

Makes two of us, Madison thought.

"Whoa, already talking divorce? You've only been married a month. Did the honeymoon go that bad?"

"Not the honeymoon… it's just that I don't recognize my life anymore. We found out on Monday that we're having a girl…"

"Yeah, I heard through the family grapevine," Rose said, probably meaning Ethan had already told her. "Congratulations."

"Thanks."

"Have you talked names yet?"

"No, but I told Georgiana all the names Mark Wahlberg runs off the bear in *Ted* are off-limits."

Rose laughed. "Fun scene."

"Anyway," Tyler continued. "We found out the sex on Monday, and I came home two days later to find Georgiana had transformed your room into a *My Little Pony* nightmare. There's pink everywhere."
Sounds like my cousin, all right.

"Not my room anymore," Rose said. "And you had to decorate it anyway, no?"

"Okay, but she didn't even ask me, she just did it, exactly the same way she got pregnant. Do first, ask later."
Definitely Georgiana's style.

"Have you tried to talk to her about it?" Rose asked.

"No. Honestly, it's hard to talk about anything with her these days. She's completely delusional about the whole 'becoming a parent' thing."

"Delusional how?"

"For one, she has this picture in her mind where we go back to school in the fall like nothing has changed."

"When is the due date again?"

"January 4."

"Okay, so provided she doesn't experience complications, she could complete the fall term with little trouble. But what about winter?"

"Exactly my point. She plans on hiring a nanny and expects everything else to stay the same. We already had endless arguments with me trying to make her understand how it won't be a breeze with a baby crying all night. Or that if she breastfeeds, well, a baby needs to eat every couple of hours. She won't be able to go to class in the morning, forget about our daughter for an entire day, and come back at night."

Madison heard a muffled chuckle.

"Not funny," Tyler protested.

"I know, I'm sorry," Rose said, amusement still audible in her voice. "But I never thought you'd be lecturing me on breastfeeding timing."

"I'm not lecturing you, I'm trying to lecture *her,* but she won't listen."

"Georgiana is the younger sibling, the baby of the house." *More the spoiled princess of the house,* Madison commented inside her head. "She's never been around real babies, so she's being a bit naïve, or over-positive."

"Yeah, but what will happen when stuff gets real?"

"Come on, Tyler, you're not giving Georgiana enough credit. She's a force of nature, and she's not the type to give up. You're in a privileged position already because you don't have money issues. And what Georgiana says is true: you can hire help, and it's going to make a huge difference." Tyler made a scoffing noise, and Rose quickly added, "Let me finish. I know the situation is not ideal, but you can make it work, school-wise. I'm sure HLS has a million facilitations for students who are parents."

"Maybe, but Georgiana refuses to ask the Dean of Students Office."

"So *you* ask. You're going to be a parent, too. Go to the office and ask them yourself, so that when—*if*—Georgiana has a meltdown, you'll already have most of the answers."

"Yeah, I could do that..." Tyler said.

"Duh-uh." Madison could almost hear Rose rolling her eyes. "But how you'll manage school is not the real issue here, Ty," Rose continued. "You and Georgiana are married... I thought you could fall back in love with her, but after the wedding and after talking with you today, I'm not so sure. What do you feel for her?"

There was a long moment of silence until Tyler said, "I care about her... deeply. But more in a she's-going-to-be-the-mother-of-my-child way. I want to take care of her and protect her, but romantically..." Another long pause. "I don't love her that way, not anymore. I'm not in love with my wife and I don't think I'll ever be again..."

And at that moment, something Madison had never imagined being possible happened. For the first time in her life, instead of being jealous of Georgiana, Madison pitied her. Not pity felt in a superior or spiteful way, but genuine, sorrowful commiseration.

***

Tyler and Rose spent another good hour chatting and, by the time they were done, Madison's bladder was about to explode. She was sweating cold from the effort of not getting up and running to the restrooms—damn Chai Tea Latte. But if it would've been super awkward to be seen when they'd arrived, making her presence known after eavesdropping on them for two hours was not an option. Madison preferred to pee in her pants—or skirt, in this case. She even forced herself to wait ten good minutes after she heard them leave before hitting the ladies room.

After her break gone wrong, Madison needed a serious pick-me-up, and what better place to lift her spirits than the Widener Library? With its retro vibes and extensive book collection, it was the one place that put Madison in a great mood simply by stepping through its doors.

Madison took the long road to get to the library, cutting across Harvard Yard to avoid having to cross Harvard Square. Georgiana and Alice were probably gone too by now, but with her awful luck, Madison preferred not to take chances.

Jogging up the steps of the tall, rectangular building, Madison already felt more positive. She stepped inside, pausing a second to admire the twin monumental stairs leading to the upper floor, the huge vaulted windows, the dome, and the majestic chandeliers. Neck bent backward, eyes closed, Madison inhaled the scent of knowledge, of culture, of possibility…

She headed directly for the Loker Reading Room, reflecting as she walked if she should try again to finish her escape book or reread *Don Quixote* in a traditional way. It could help to have the whole narrative fresh in her mind before she went back to deconstructing the book. She pulled her—*intact*—copy of the classic novel out of her bag and, nose stuck into the first pages, she strolled on autopilot toward the Loker Room without paying much attention to where she was going. She was so familiar with the building that her feet led her there without much help from her brain.

Still concentrated on the book, Madison lifted her gaze briefly to find an empty chair and sat down, already completely absorbed by the story. No matter if she'd read it a thousand times, *Don Quixote* would forever

371

be one of her favorite books. Madison could identify so well with the protagonist—even if he had a few loose screws. Alonso was a bookworm and a hopeless romantic who'd read so many romances he was convinced he could bring chivalry back and undo all wrongs. And he'd decided to do so under the pseudonym of Don Quixote de la Mancha. Like Alonso, Madison preferred to believe she lived in a more romanticized version of the world and often hoped her life would turn into a fantastic story. The reality of it was so dull…

If I ever write a novel, *Madison thought,* I'm definitely going to write under a pseudonym, something epic. *She sighed.* A girl can dream…

Forty-five minutes later, Madison was close to tears—she was reading the scene where all of Alonso's books were burned and the poor knight, while desperately looking for his library, was told a magician had stolen all the books and made the room disappear—when an outburst of laughter distracted her from the most tragic passage.

With a pretty convincing stare of death in her eyes, Madison's neck snapped up to search for the source of the noise. One thing she couldn't stand was people being noisy at the library. The only two patrons who didn't have their necks bent over a book were a boy and a girl sitting at the farthest table in the back of the room. They were facing the wall, so Madison couldn't see their faces, but something about them sent alarm bells to her brain.

The boy said something, making the girl laugh again. Their tone was low enough for the voices not to carry over to where Madison was sitting, but the girl's laugh was loud, and it was disrupting Madison's concentration. Eyes squinted in reproach, Madison was about to get up to go ask them to keep it down or leave when the girl turned to the right, pushing a lock of hair behind her ear.

Madison gasped as she recognized her best friend. Her jaw dropped open and her gaze snapped to the guy. His face was still hidden, but his dark hair, broad shoulders, and Harvard basketball team T-shirt were dead giveaways.

As she forced her mouth shut, a million questions and ugly emotions crossed Madison's mind. What the hell is Haley doing with David Williams? Why do they look so cozy with each other? How can Haley be nice to him after what he did to me? How dare she do this to Scott? *And then Madison's thoughts turned even uglier.* Is she cheating on

Scott? With his brother? Are they friends? How can she be friends with David? Does Scott know?

And finally the one thought Madison had never dared voice, not even to herself: *She doesn't deserve him.*

I'm cursed, *was Madison's next realization.* Why do I have to run into all kinds of awkward people and situations today?

Two opposite impulses took hold of her. One side of her wanted to get up and run outside as fast as she could. The other wanted to stay and watch—absorb the evidence of Haley's betrayal toward her, and toward Scott. When Madison's thoughts spiraled from observing from a distance to taking a picture and sending it to Scott anonymously, she realized how poisoned she was by the sheer, bilious envy she felt for Haley and Scott's relationship. She had to leave before she did something stupid and reckless that she wouldn't be able to take back.

Wondering what in the hell had possessed her when she'd thought to get out of the house to *relax*, Madison slammed her copy of *Don Quixote* shut and stormed out of the library.

***

"You're not going to believe the day I had," Madison said to Alice, sagging on the couch next to her in their apartment.

"That bad, huh? What happened? I thought I'd spared you the worst…"

"Maybe you did, but the second and third worst definitely happened."

"What do you mean?"

"Guess who I ran into?"

"Who?"

"Who else would want to steer clear of the place where you were meeting Georgiana?"

Alice stared at her blankly.

"Tyler and Rose, catching up," Madison announced.

Alice's eyes widened in horror. "No!"

"Uh-huh. They had the same idea and chose a café on the opposite side of campus. Pity I was there already."

"Did they see you?"

"No, I managed to stay hidden the entire time and almost peed my pants for the effort."

Alice chuckled. "Oh, gosh. Please tell me about it…"

Madison was just finishing relating the first horrible half of the afternoon when Haley glided inside the apartment as if walking on a cloud.

"Hi, girls," she greeted them. "I'll be out in a sec, save some of the juicy gossip for me." And then Haley disappeared into her room.

Madison narrowed her eyes at the door.

"She's definitely more cheerful these days," Alice said. "I mean, a month ago, when Scott left, she didn't want to get out of bed, and now she's dancing on air."

Now that Madison thought about it, Haley hadn't been heartbroken over Scott leaving for a while. Not that Haley had ever complained openly, but her sadness had been evident to those who loved her. Until Madison had stopped noticing Haley being inconsolable. Because her friend had not been that sad anymore.

"Hey." Alice snapped her fingers to attract Madison's attention. "What's with the pouty face?"

Madison stopped staring daggers at Haley's door and turned toward Alice. "I might know why she's so cheerful."

"And?"

"I saw her at the library getting all cozy with David."

"Williams?"

"Uh-huh."

"Cozy how?"

"They were making a mess of the place with their laughing fits."

"Madison, what are you implying?"

"Nothing, just telling you what I saw. Haley doesn't seem heartbroken over Scott leaving anymore and she's shacking up with his brother while he's gone."

Alice scowled at her. "Haley would never cheat on Scott."

"So what was she doing with David?"

"Maybe they're friends." Alice shrugged.

"Since when? Since she's found out he was the kiss of her life?"

"You're jumping to conclusions and it's not fair."

"I'm not jumping to anything; I'm only saying that something is off here. Has she told you she was seeing David in any capacity: friend or lover?"

"No, but—"

"Me neither," Madison interrupted. "So why hide it if she's doing nothing wrong?"

"I don't know, maybe the topic simply didn't come up?"

"Seriously, Alice?"

"What do you want me to s—"

"Shh," Madison whispered. "She's coming out. Humor me; let's see if she lies about it."

Alice threw her a reproachful stare that said: *We shouldn't pull this bullshit on each other.* But she kept silent all the same.

"So," Haley said, settling herself on the armchair opposite to them. "What are you girls up to?"

"I was just telling Alice what an awful day I had." Madison tried to keep her tone calm, even if all she wanted to do was scream, *"You have the best boyfriend in the world; how can you be so disloyal to him? You don't deserve Scott's love!"*

"Really?" Haley asked. "Why? What happened?"

Madison gave her the short version of her unfortunate encounter with Tyler and Rose, and then asked, "What about you? What did you do today?"

"Oh, nothing special, I was at the library all day, studying."
No mention of David.

Madison flashed an I-told-you-so stare at Alice, who said, "I thought you didn't like the library. Were you working on a group project?"

"No, I was alone," Haley lied through her teeth, and Madison bristled on the couch. "I just needed to get out of the house, and I'm digging the library lately."
The library, or David Williams?

Alice stared at Madison, at a loss for words, Haley had straight out lied, and now even Alice couldn't deny something was up.

***

Madison was coming back home from the gym the next day when she spotted David Williams walking toward her from the opposite direction. She froze for an instant and, before he could see her, she turned on her heel and hurried away.

"Hey, Blondie," someone called.

It had to be him; he was the only person in the world who called her Blondie. Madison quickened her pace. She'd be damned before she stopped to say hi to David Williams.

"Oh, come on. I know you've seen me." He was getting nearer. "Would you stop and wait for me?"

Madison turned her head to half-yell, "No, I won't!" then continued striding away.

"Come on, Blondie." David caught up with her and, stepping in front of her to block her path, added, "I only ask for five minutes of your time."

"Five minutes too long," Madison said, crossing her arms over her chest. "What do you want?"

"To talk to you. Can I get you a coffee or something?"

"No. Way."

"Please." He made a cute, pleading face that made him look more handsome than ever. *Bastard.* "I'll get you a Chai Tea Latte. Let me say my piece, and I'll be on my way."

And he'd somehow remembered her favorite drink. *Double bastard.*

Madison frowned. Why was David being so nice? What did he really want? She was ashamed to admit curiosity was getting the best of her. Was it a coincidence that David wanted to talk to her precisely the next day she'd caught him and Haley together? But he didn't know they'd been busted. So what could he possibly want?

Against her better judgment, Madison lifted her index finger in front of her in what she hoped would look like an intimidating gesture. "One drink," she conceded.

"One drink is all I need," David said, heading toward the Starbucks across the street.

Madison sat at a small table outside while he went inside to order. In the ten minutes it took David to get their drinks, Madison second-guessed her decision a million times. More than once, she was tempted to leave, and at one point, she'd almost gotten up.

"You're still here, Blondie," David said when he finally got out, offering her a paper cup and sitting across from her.

Could he read minds now?

Madison took a sip of her drink—delicious, with a pinch of vanilla just as she liked it—and waited for David to talk. Her body language sent a clear message: *not gonna make it easy for you.*

David sighed, once again reading her attitude all too well. "So…"

"So," Madison half-repeated, half-scoffed.

He rolled his cup in his hands a few times before he lifted those impossibly blue eyes and stared right at her. "I wanted to apologize. I've been an asshole to you, and I'm man enough to own up to my mistakes and say I'm sorry."

Madison stared at him, flabbergasted. Of all the things she'd imagined he'd say, somehow *"Sorry"* hadn't made the list. Why was he apologizing to her? Why now? It sounded too good, too decent, to be true coming from certified bad-boy David Williams. A heartfelt, sincere apology was so much out of his character that maybe it *was* too good to be true. A flash of him laughing in the library with Haley passed before Madison's eyes, and she narrowed them at him.

"What's your angle here, David?"

"No angle, Blondie, just a plain and simple apology."

"Yeah?" Madison rested her elbows on the table, leaning forward. "So you're not hoping the second I leave here I'll run to tell Haley what a reformed man you are?"

"As a matter of fact"—David mirrored her posture, leaning forward on his elbows—"I wanted to ask you to keep this conversation private, just between the two of us."

Madison reclined back in her chair and crossed her arms over her chest, studying him for any obvious sign that would give away the lie. She found none. Still, she didn't trust him. "You're telling me not to do something and hoping I'll do it anyway."

"No, I'm not playing mind games here." His nostrils flared. "I'm trying very hard to apologize to you for the crappy way I treated you."

"So why don't you want me to tell Haley?"

His blue eyes pinned her to the chair. "This apology is about *you* and no one else."

"Stop lying, I saw you two getting all cozy at the library yesterday. You're trying to steal her from right under Scott's nose while he's away."

"Blondie, let me tell you something. In love, there's no stealing. People who get 'stolen' *want* to be stolen. If Haley loves Scott and wants to stay with him, there's nothing I could ever do or say to change that. Nothing." David shrugged. "Do I want Haley? Yes. Do I hate that she's dating my brother? Yes. But this conversation between us has nothing to do with Haley. I'm trying to do the right thing by you."

"Why now?" Madison insisted. "You expect me to believe you suddenly had an epiphany and decided you weren't going to be an asshole anymore?"

"As much as everybody likes to paint me as the bad guy, I'm not all bad." David shrugged. "The way I treated you was crap. You're right, I was an asshole—big time. A total dick… Guilty." He lifted his hands as if in surrender. "I went out with you for the wrong reasons and ended things like a complete douche…"

"What reasons?"

David lowered his gaze before speaking up again. "I wanted to make Haley jealous by dating her roommate… there, you have it. The ugly truth, bare and exposed."

"You admitted you want Haley, and that you started dating me only to get at her. How the hell am I supposed to believe this is not all a contorted ruse to look good for her after you screwed up by showing your true colors with me?"

"Because those aren't my true colors," David snapped. "It's what I've been trying to tell you all along. I have a bad temper and sometimes I act like a total jerk. When I get angry, I lash out. I'm aware I'm not always the nicest guy, but this is not all a diabolical plan to look good for Haley. I'm here to say sorry to *you*, and only *you*." He let the words hang in the air a few seconds before going on. "What I said the day we broke up… I snapped, but I don't really think any of the things I said."

"Really?"

David put a hand over his heart. "I swear."

An evil little smile surfaced on Madison's lips. "So you don't think that I talk too much?" She arched an eyebrow at him.

Why could she be this bad ass only with people she didn't care about?

David's mouth curled at one corner, and he smartly avoided the question. "You're beautiful, smart, and any guy would be lucky to have you."

Despite herself, Madison was mollified. "Then why be so mean?"

"Part of my shitty personality, I guess." David rolled his eyes. "Come on, Blondie… Of all people, I thought you'd understand what got me so worked up. Cut me some slack, no?"

"Me? Why me?"

"We both know I wasn't your first pick of the Williams brothers," David said with disconcerting blatancy.

Cheeks aflame, Madison tried to deny it. "I don't know what you're talking about."

"No need to lie, Blondie. I never judge." David's blue eyes seemed to be piercing right through Madison's soul. "The night we met, I saw the way you stared at my brother and I saw the way you looked at them together. Tell me it wouldn't be much easier if Scott was dating a nameless stranger. Or that it wouldn't hurt less if he loved someone you didn't know at all, someone you could hate freely. Someone you could hope he'd break up with as soon as possible. Instead of someone you care so much about." David scoffed bitterly. "The more you care, the more it hurts."

Speechless, Madison stared into his eyes for a long while. In their expressive blue, she could now discern the pain of older and newer scars. Brigitte and Haley, two girls who'd chosen his brother over him. Was that pain so visible in her own eyes, too? Was that why Haley behaved awkwardly around her sometimes?

Madison swallowed and nodded at David. In a weird way, she'd never felt more understood than right now by this guy she'd thought she hated. Not by Alice, and certainly not by Haley. In a thin voice, she said, "Please don't tell him, Scott has no idea."

David nodded back. "Your secret is safe with me, Blondie."

"And stop calling me that."

"All right, Barbie." He flashed her a crooked grin. Guess there wasn't too much reforming David Williams; he'd always play the handsome bastard part. "Are we good?" he asked, standing up and offering her his hand.

"You've earned the benefit of the doubt." Madison took his proffered hand and let him lift her up. Eyes level, she added, "Nothing more."

"That's all I ask." David Williams smiled and pulled her into a comradely hug.

The world was weird.

***

If David Williams deserved the benefit of the doubt, so perhaps did

379

Haley Thomas. Maybe Madison had been too quick in judging her best friend. From the way David had talked about Haley, there was nothing strictly romantic going on between them. Madison still thought Haley was playing a dangerous game, but the jury hadn't rolled a verdict yet.

Oh crap, and now she was thinking like a lawyer. Being part of the Smithson family did leave its legal mark, no matter how hard one tried to escape it.

Demoralized, Madison shuffled a few sheets of paper around on the floor. She was getting nowhere with this research project on *Don Quixote*. She felt like she, too, was fighting against windmills. Not because her enemies were imaginary, but because she was fighting a losing battle.

Madison collected all the scattered pages that had been resting on the floor for the past week and decided to call it a day. Her mind was too crammed with thoughts, doubts, and conspiracy theories for research work. She hadn't told Haley about her little chat with David. Mostly because she still wasn't one hundred percent sure Haley hearing about his redemption had not been his motive all along, and the apology all an act. But she also hadn't confronted Haley about seeing them together at the library. And the number of secrets they were keeping from each other was growing sickeningly fast.

Could a friendship already put to the test by a shared love interest survive so many deceptions? Madison loved Haley, but a small part of her couldn't help hating her too. She wanted to see Haley happy with her boyfriend and at the same time desperately wanted them to break up. Madison wanted everything and the opposite of everything, and it was driving her crazy.

A knock on the door made her lift her gaze from the pages. "Come in," she called.

"Hey." Alice poked her head inside the room. "Haley and I are going to watch an impromptu basketball game, Jack's playing, and then everyone's going for dinner… You coming?"

"Yeah." Madison nodded. "I need a break, just give me five minutes to get ready."

"Sure, we'll be outside."

Madison didn't feel like being in a skirt, so she pulled her dress over her head and hopped into a pair of skinny jeans and a white T-shirt that said: *the book was better*. Flat sandals on, hair up in a messy bun, and she was ready. At the last second, Madison grabbed a paperback from her desk just in case the game got boring.

Alice

"Did you know David was playing?" Madison hissed in her ear.

"No, I swear," Alice replied. They'd just arrived at the gym and already there were troubles. "Jack said the game was among guys on the team, but I assumed he meant *this* year's team."

"Hey, babe." Jack hugged her from behind, making Alice forget about the tension between her roommates. "You made it."

She turned in his arms and fastened her hands behind his neck. "You know I'm a sucker for tall guys in basketball shorts."

Jack put on a cute frown. "And by tall guys in basketball shorts, I hope you mean just *this* guy."

"And who else?" Alice smiled and pulled his face down to kiss him. It still amazed her she could do it whenever she wanted.

"Dude." Someone nudged Jack from behind. "You ready to go?"

Alice broke the kiss and briefly made eye contact with David Williams, who jogged backward calling, "Come on, Jack, we need to get started on some warm-up drills."

It was a two-against-two match and it appeared Jack and David were on the same team. Matt Lucas and Blake Donovan were on the other. Both Matt and Blake were from the Boston area, so they'd stayed for the summer.

Jack turned toward the indoor basketball court, saying, "I'll be right there." Then he whispered apologetically to Alice, "Duty calls."

"You didn't tell me David would be here," Alice whispered back.

Jack's eyes widened. "Why? Is there still drama going on? I thought everything was good." He stole another glance at his teammate. "Did he do something bad?"

Alice was about to answer *"yes"* automatically when she realized that this time, no, David had actually done nothing wrong for a change— unless going to the library had become a crime. "No, not really," she reassured Jack. "But I need to update you on the latest crisis. Now, go bag the game."

Jack stole a peck on her lips, saying, "A kiss for luck," and then joined David.

Still high from the kiss, Alice backtracked to go sit with her friends on the gym floor at the margin of the court. But the moment her butt hit the PVC, she felt like she could cut the tension between her two other roommates with a knife. Madison was scowling at David—and at Haley, too, sometimes—and Haley seemed very busy looking everywhere but in David's direction.

Alice sighed and decided to hit pause and ignore them. She was here to enjoy watching her boyfriend play, not to become an unwilling witness to a silent cat fight. She turned all her attention on him and the game.

Jack looked ridiculously gorgeous running and leaping around, his face set in a concentrated frown every time he tried to outsmart an opponent with his drills or when he prepared for a throw. Alice was grateful to whoever had decided to make basketballs so heavy. The weight had shaped every muscle in Jack's arms, and whenever he wrapped those toned biceps around her… *Get a grip, girl.*

Mid-match, Alice realized she was still positively ogling Jack. Not that there was anything wrong with that, but… After ignoring her roommates for the whole game so far, she turned to check on them. A quick side-glance was enough to leave Alice horror-struck. Haley wore a rapt expression as she watched David run—pretty much the same one Alice must've sported a few seconds ago looking at Jack—and Madison had on an affronted pout as she stared daggers at Haley staring at David.

Alice returned her eyes to the match for a second, appraising the disruptive element. She imagined David Williams as an extraneous molecule ruining a perfect chemical reaction… because, no matter if she had eyes only for Jack, the senior Williams brother was really something to look at tonight—or every other night.

He was dressed in a matching dark blue tank top and shorts and his black hair—pulled back from his forehead by a thin white hairband— seemed so dark it appeared to have midnight-blue streaks in it, which only made his eyes pop more. Like all the other players, he was tall and fit, but David also had that bad-boy aura and lopsided grin that added a charm unique to him. Rugged. Handsome. *Dangerous.*

Alice watched as Jack threw the ball halfway across the court in a quick pass. David caught it firmly in his hands and crouched, only to then spring up in a jump, aiming for the basket without a moment's hesitation—his feet an inch shy of the three-point line. The orange sphere flew over Matt's head, who tried and failed to block it, and landed squarely in the center of the metal ring, almost without touching its borders. The only sign of its passage was a soft swish of the net.

Haley cheered and clapped her hands.

Madison scoffed, visibly annoyed.

"What?" Haley turned toward her, smiling. "We're here to cheer Jack's team, no?"

"Sure," Madison snapped again. "*Jack's* team."

Alice stared up at the gym's roof, wondering if there'd ever be harmony again among her friends. But the night's tension only escalated when the match ended—three games to two for Jack and David—and the guys disappeared into the locker room to take a shower, leaving the girls alone with their unspoken beef.

Haley's anger bubble popped first, and she turned toward Madison with thunder in her eyes. "Care to share why you've had the face of someone swallowing lemons all night?"

"Something *soured* my evening," Madison said.

When Madison turned the bitch on, she could get nasty really fast.

"What's your problem?" Haley asked.

"My problem is what's happening between you and David."

"Nothing is going on between us," Haley said, her tone too angry not to be defensive.

Madison scoffed. "Yeah, keep lying… It's what you do best."

Haley jumped up from the floor. "Excuse me?"

Madison got up, too, and Alice had no choice but to imitate them. She placed herself squarely in the middle to keep her best friends from clawing each other's eyes out.

"I saw you at the library the other day," Madison spat. "You were with *him*, don't deny it. And when I asked you about it you lied."

Haley's mouth fell open, a furious blush spreading on her face, but instead of backing off, she narrowed her eyes and hissed, "If you already knew, why ask?"

Madison crossed her arms over her chest. "I wanted to see if you'd lie about it." She stared Haley down. "You did."

"Girls." Alice tried to inject herself into the conversation. "Why don't we all try to calm down?"

"You tell her," Haley said, pointing at Madison. "She's the one looking down on everyone else from her high tower."

"At least I'm not being shady."

"Neither am I!"

"So does Scott know you hang out with his brother?"

"It's none of your business." Haley glowered at Madison one last time. "I'm out of here," she said to Alice. "I'm sorry, we'll hang next time."

Without another word, Haley stormed out of the gym.

Alice waited for her to be gone before she scowled at Madison. "You really had to do that, didn't you?"

"Why are you glaring at me?"

"Because, Madison, Haley is your friend. *Haley.* You should always be on her side. Even if she was having a full-blown affair with David, you should still be on her side."

"But—"

"No buts. Haley hasn't judged you once, no matter what you did." Alice paused to let her point get home. When Madison's face shifted from haughty to embarrassed, she continued. "I know you're holding her to higher standards because of Scott, but you can't act out this way. It's not fair."

Madison looked close to tears. "Yeah, you're right. None of this is fair. I'm out of here too. See you at home."

In a few quick steps, Madison left the gym, slamming the heavy metal door behind her. Alice sighed and pulled her hair up into a ponytail. She was wrapping the hairband when Jack took advantage of her exposed neck and pressed his lips to the sensitive skin just under her ear, saying, "Hey, where did everybody go?"

Alice turned around; the boys were all showered and ready to go. "The girls left. They had stuff to do at home." She tried to ignore the disappointment on David's face at seeing Haley gone.

Jack arched his brows questioningly, and Alice made a face that said: *Don't ask.*

"Oh, okay."

"Can I still hang with the boys?" Alice smiled.

It was Matt who replied, sporting a wide grin. "You're basically one of us."

Jack wrapped an arm around her shoulders. "Well, let's go. I'm starving." Whispering in her ear, he added, "No more drama for tonight. Deal?"

"Deal."

They all walked out of the gym, and Alice was positively ashamed to be relieved that her friends—and their toxic vibes—had left so that she could enjoy a drama-free dinner with her boyfriend.

Haley

"Haley, wait," came Madison's voice from behind her.

Instead of slowing down, Haley picked up her pace—*Yeah, petty as hell.* But Madison had rubbed her the wrong way tonight. She wasn't sure why she'd lied—*omitted*—to her roommates about being friends with David. But Madison's judging reaction had let her know she couldn't confide in them anymore, or at least not in Madison.

"Haley," Madison called again. "You can't avoid me; we live in the same house."

"Fine!" Haley stopped and spun around. "What do you want?"

Madison caught up with her. "To apologize."

Haley was thrown off by the unexpected declaration but still wasn't ready to give in and just forgive Madison for being the biggest bitch. "I'm listening."

"I'm sorry for going nuclear bitch on you, but why didn't you tell us about him?"

"Are you here to apologize, or to ask more stupid questions?"

"Both. I'm sorry I turned all high-and-mighty on you, but I'm not sorry for calling you out on the lie."

Haley tapped her foot on the curb. "Given your wonderful reaction, can you really blame me for not telling you?"

"Is that the only reason you didn't say anything?"

"I know David is still a sore point for you." Madison kept looking at her, unconvinced. So Haley continued, "And I don't need anyone's judgment for being his friend."

"His friend?" Madison asked. "Haley, you're in denial."

"Denial? How dare you—"

"I saw you together, okay?" Madison shouted, interrupting her.

"So? We were building a model. I help him out with coding sometimes. Big deal. It's not like we were making out or banging each other on the table."

"No, it was so much worse."

"How could it be worse?"

"Because it isn't a sexual thing, Haley, you like him. The fact that he's mystery-kiss-masked guy, that you met him first, changed the way you see him."

"Madison, David and I are only friends. I'm with Scott."

"So why are you doing this to him?"

"And since when have you become the Scott police?"

Madison's cheeks flared red.

"That's what I thought," Haley said ruthlessly. "Guess what? *My* life, *my* boyfriend, *my* choices. Keep your nose out of it."

Pain flared behind Madison's eyes. "Fine. It's just hard to watch you throw away the perfect guy for his douche bag of a brother. When it all comes crashing down on you, don't come crying to me."

Madison pushed past her and kept walking toward their house.

"I won't!" Haley yelled after her.

***

The fight with Madison nagged Haley's conscience for the rest of the week. So much so that she almost didn't go to the library on Saturday. But the atmosphere inside the house was positively poisonous, and she needed to study, and the library really did help her be more productive. You could go to a different library, *a voice echoed inside her head.* Well, I don't want to. And I'm not going to let Madison dictate my life.

David was already at their table when she arrived.

"Bad mood?" he asked after taking one good look at her.

"Please don't ask." Needing a distraction, she said, "Do you have any vicious models for me to crack today?"

David dipped his head in a mock bow. "I hear you, vicious model on its way."

After pulling up the file, he offered his laptop to her. Haley sat next to him and happily forgot about Madison's accusations for the rest of the day.

***

As usual, it took an attendant to kick them out for Haley and David to leave the library. They were outside saying goodbye when an insistent vibration in her backpack distracted Haley. She rummaged blindly for her phone until her hand clasped around the slim rectangle. Haley stared at the caller ID on the screen: *Mom.* Weird, they just had their weekly chat last night and her mom never called on a weekend unless something was wrong.

"Mom," she said. "What's going on?"

"It's your father," her mother said, a tremor in her voice.

"Dad? What about Dad?"

"Oh, Haley, he's had a heart attack."

The ground disappeared from beneath Haley's feet. She felt like she was about to faint. "When? How? Is he okay?"
Please let him be okay, please let him be okay.

"He's in surgery right now… Before… we were outside taking care of the garden and I don't know what happened… he just collapsed."

"But what are the doctors saying?"

"The surgeon is optimistic, but they won't tell me anything for sure until he's out of the OR."

Haley made a split-second decision. "I'm coming home."

"Yeah, I figured you'd want to. We're at Mercy Hospital."

"I'll be there as soon as I can."

"How are you getting here?"

"I'll catch a flight or the bus, I don't know."

"Please be safe. I have to call Uncle Tim now."

"I will, Mom, bye." Haley pressed End and immediately googled flights. There were none going out of Boston Logan to Buffalo after five in the evening. "Damn," she cursed. The bus took forever. "I need a car."

She was about to call Madison, when David said, "I'll drive you."

Haley had forgotten he was standing right next to her. "You have a car?"

"Yeah."

"Would you really drive me home?"

"Not would, *am.*"

387

"But Buffalo is a seven-hour drive."

David checked his watch. "If we leave now, we can be there by midnight."

Haley swallowed. "Thank you."

David gave a curt nod. "Do you need to go home to get something?"

"No, I just want to leave."

"Let's go, then."

***

David's car was a midnight-blue pickup. He drove it in silence, following the navigator's instructions on his phone without trying to make small talk. Haley was glad. She wasn't in the mood to talk. She wasn't in the mood to do anything. All she wanted was to get home as fast as possible and be with her family, and David seemed to understand that.

They only stopped once to fill the tank and go to the restroom. David ate a cold sandwich while he drove, but Haley's stomach was too cramped up with worry. David didn't insist on her eating, and once again, Haley was grateful that he let her be. No awkward, *"I'm sorry."* No stupid, *"How are you feeling?"* questions. And no *"You should try to eat something,"* crap. David drove her in silence, the hard resolution of getting her to Buffalo as soon as possible etched on his rugged features.

Haley's mom called again halfway through the trip with the good news that her dad was out of surgery. The doctors had said everything had gone well, and that now they only needed to wait for her father to wake up. The biggest lump eased in Haley's throat; her dad was going to be okay. She would get there in time. She would see him again.

After the call, Haley's phone died, making her curse under her breath. She'd spent too much time on Google, learning everything she could about heart attacks, recovery, and prevention, consuming all the battery. She hadn't thought to buy a charger at the gas station, and she certainly didn't want to stop again now.

"What happened?" David asked, probably worried the call had been bad news.

"My phone died," she said.

"I don't have a charger, but mine still has half the battery if you want to call Scott," David offered.

And, once again, Haley appreciated how much effort it must've taken him to say that.

"You don't need it for directions?"

"It says to go straight for the next two hundred miles. I can manage." David freed the phone from its case on the air vent and handed it to her.

"Thanks." Haley dialed Scott's number and waited on the line. It rang, and rang, and rang… "He's not picking up."

"Probably because it's my number. Try a text."

"No, it can wait until tomorrow." The truth was Haley feared Scott would go into full panic mode and ask her all the questions she didn't want to answer right now. "Mind if I give your number to my mom, in case she needs to get a hold of me?"

David shook his head and didn't add anything else for the rest of the trip.

At exactly ten minutes past midnight, he pulled over near the main entrance of Mercy Hospital.

"Go," he said. "I'll find a parking spot."

Haley didn't need to be told twice; her hand was already on the car door handle. She thanked David again and rushed out of the car and inside the towering building. Her mom had texted her the floor and room they were keeping her dad in, so Haley headed straight for the elevator. She had to meander through a few halls and pass many doors before she spotted her mom standing in the threshold of a room.

"Mom," Haley shouted, probably too loud for a hospital, especially after midnight.

Her mother turned and smiled; she looked tired but relieved. "Monkey," she said, using Haley's pet name.

Haley flew into her mother's outstretched arms and, resting her forehead on her shoulder, she finally cracked down. She started sobbing convulsively while her mother gently stroked her hair, whispering soothing words. "It's okay, Baby Monkey. We got scared, but it's all good now."

"How's Dad?" Haley lifted her head, wiping the tears from her face with the sleeve of her blouse. "Can I see him?"

"The doctors will be out in a minute, and they'll let us in afterward."

While they waited, Haley bombarded her mom with questions, since the doctors weren't around to interrogate. Miranda responded as well as she could. They'd told her that the heart attack had been minor as only a small portion of tissue had been involved, and that they'd been able to remove the clog during the surgery. The prognosis for her dad was a speedy recovery, provided he took better care of his health and stuck to a wholesome diet.

She learned this last part from a young doctor who she'd roped into questioning. "I'll make sure he never touches a slice of bacon in his life ever again," she swore.

The doctor smiled and said, "Seems like Mr. Thomas already has the best care. Would you like to see him?"

"Yeah, can we go in?" Haley asked eagerly.

"Yes, but only for a few minutes. Your father needs to rest right now."

"We won't be long, I promise."

Shyly, Haley entered her father's room. His face brightened as soon as he spotted her on the threshold. He was pale as a ghost, hooked to too many machines to count, with tubes jutting out of his body all over, but her dad was smiling at her.

"Dad." Haley rushed forward, ready to hug him, but stopped just before the bed, afraid of hurting him. She took hold of his left hand instead. "I got so scared."

"I know, Baby Monkey." His voice sounded coarser than usual, but his eyes were alert and full of life. "I promise I won't do it again."

Haley fought back tears again. "We won't let you," she said, wrapping her free arm around her mom and pulling her close. "At the cost of making you a vegan," Haley threatened.

Her father chuckled at the mock threat and pressed his right hand to his chest as if it hurt, which it probably did.

Haley paled.

"Too soon for jokes, Baby Monkey," her dad said. "Now you both go home and have a good night's rest."

"But, Dad, I just got here."

"I'll see you tomorrow, Monkey."

"Come on, Haley." Her mom pulled her closer. "We need to go, your father needs to rest."

Haley planted a kiss on her dad's forehead and left some space for her mother to do the same, before they both walked out wishing him goodnight.

David was waiting for them seated on a chair in the hall outside her dad's room. When he spotted them coming out he got up, his face pale, worried, and tired.

Haley steered her mom toward him and made the introductions. "Mom, this is David, the friend who drove me here."

"We talked on the phone a few weeks ago, right?" her mom said. "Nice to meet you in person, and thank you for bringing our daughter home safe."

David shook her hand. "It's a pleasure, Mrs. Thomas. I'm glad I could help. How's Mr. Thomas?"

"Already well enough to boss us around and order us to go home."

"I'm glad to hear it." David's mouth stretched in a close-lipped smile. "If you're going home"—he scratched the back of his head—"is there a motel nearby you could suggest?"

"Oh, don't be silly." Her mother scoffed. "You're staying with us."

"I wouldn't want to intrude, Mrs. Thomas," David—suddenly the most educated, parents-presentable boy on Earth—said.

"No intrusions." Her mom smiled warmly. "Plus, I came here in the ambulance and we could use the ride home." She spared Haley a wink. "And please, call me Miranda."

"Thank you, Mrs.—Miranda. I'll get the car out front; you can wait for me downstairs." David nodded at Haley, then sprinted toward the elevator.

Haley had followed the conversation between him and her mother with mixed feelings: it was so weird to have David here in Buffalo, meeting her family—*staying at her house.*

"So that's David, huh?" Her mom asked with a shrewd smile. "*Not your boyfriend, I take it?*"

"David's just a friend, Mom."

"A very good one to drop everything and drive you across the country at a moment's notice."

Haley shrugged. "I guess. Can we go now? I'm really tired."

***

Staring at the roof of her childhood bedroom, it took Haley a long time to fall asleep. The worry-induced adrenaline of the day was still pumping in her blood, but mostly it was the thought of David sleeping in the adjoining room that kept her awake. Haley wasn't sure why the idea made her so restless, but the whole David-in-her-childhood-home scenario seemed so improbable, so out of context. If she'd ever imagined introducing someone to her parents, it had been Scott she'd pictured coming to Buffalo, not David. And definitely not under the present circumstances.

To be honest, the fact that he'd been her hero today wasn't helping either. It was so much easier to disregard David when he was acting like a jerk and hurting everybody. This new knight-in-shining-armor attitude was confusing. It forced Haley to see the good in him, and she couldn't help but like what she saw.

A stab of guilt made her chest contract. These were dangerous thoughts to have, and Haley was too exhausted to even begin to investigate what they might mean. She tried to empty her brain and, after several minutes of tossing and turning, fatigue got the best of her and she finally fell asleep.

***

When Haley came down to breakfast the next morning, David's truck was no longer in the driveway.

"Has David left already?" she asked her mom, accepting a warm cup of coffee.

"Yeah, he got up at the crack of dawn, said he needed to head back to Boston." Her mom placed a bowl of cereal in front of Haley. "Something about having work stuff to finish before Monday."

Haley nodded, realizing just how much giving her a ride had cost David. His boss had given him a ridiculous amount of data to analyze, and even if Haley had helped him a little with the coding on Saturday, he still had plenty to do. And with a seven-hour drive back home, he'd have to work all afternoon and part of the night to finish. Haley felt awful for him.

"Can I say something?" her mother asked.

"I won't like what you're about to say, will I?"

"That depends."

"But you're going to say it anyway."

Her mom nodded.

Sighing, Haley sat on a stool and started eating the cereal. "Go ahead."

"David… isn't your friend."

Haley dropped the spoon into the bowl, milk splashing all over. "I thought you liked him."

"I do." Her mom paused to grab a towel and clean the mess. "The problem isn't that I don't like him, it's how much he likes you."

"Mom, I already told you there's nothing between us."

"Maybe not on your side." Miranda sighed. "But that boy is in love with you, Monkey."

Haley's pulse raced. "No, he's not."

"You're blind if you can't see it, or you're in denial."

Great. Second time in a week someone told her she was in denial. Well, she wasn't!

Deaf to Haley's protests, her mom continued dispensing unrequested motherly advice. "I know you're very much in love with Scott, but, Haley, if you don't like David that way, don't lead him on. You'll only end up hurting him."

Haley kept her lips stubbornly shut.

"And, Monkey, if you *do* have feelings for him, the sooner you admit it and decide which brother you want, the better for everyone."

Haley refused to acknowledge a word of what her mom was saying. She was with Scott, and they were in love. End of story. "Visitor hours are about to start," she said. "We should get going."

***

Despite her father's many attempts to send them away, Haley and her mom ended up spending most of Sunday at the hospital. Haley had not bought a new charger yet, and she didn't check her messages until later that evening after they'd stopped at a convenience store to buy one and returned home. There were two texts from Scott, and a few missed call alerts.

Without a moment's hesitation, Haley tapped his name, yearning to hear his voice, to be comforted by her boyfriend. In the past twenty-four hours she'd run on adrenaline alone, but now that the worst of the fear had passed, the stress, exhaustion, and weariness were catching up with her.

After three empty rings, Haley knew Scott wasn't going to pick up. She let the call run anyway until the line disconnected on its own. Close to tears, she typed a quick text.

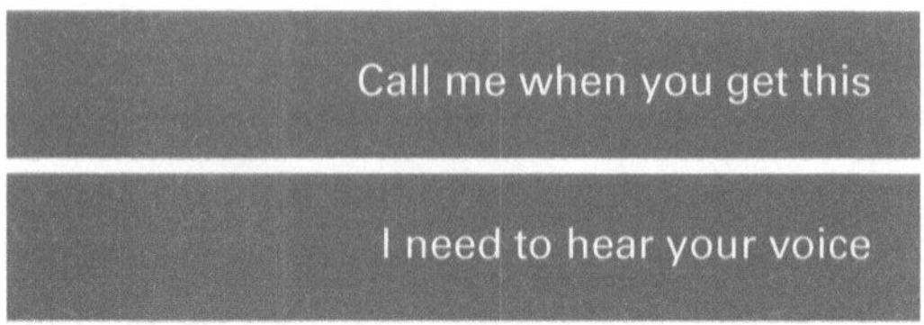

Haley collapsed on the bed, curling into a ball and hugging the phone to her heart. Being in a long distance relationship sucked. She needed Scott, not just his voice. Haley needed to feel his love on her skin. His arms wrapped around her, his lips on hers, their bodies pressed together as they made love. She felt so freaking lonely without him.

While in the midst of contemplating how alone she was, Haley must've fallen asleep, because suddenly she was jolting awake to the sound of *Lovefool* by The Cardigans—Scott's personalized ringtone from *Romeo + Juliet*.

Still groggy with sleep, she unstuck the phone from her left cheek and swept her finger on the screen to answer. "Hi."

"Hey," Scott's voice came warm from the other side. "Did I wake you? I know it's late in Boston, but I saw your text and I thought I'd call anyway."

Haley rolled on the bed to face the ceiling. "I'm not in Boston."

"No?"

"I'm at my parents' house…"

Haley poured out all her anxiety and fear from the past twenty-four hours.

"I wish I could've been there for you," Scott said when she was done talking. "I'm so sorry you had to go home alone…"

I didn't… As her heart skipped a beat, Haley heard nothing else of what Scott said. David had driven her here, and Scott didn't know.

"I didn't come home alone," Haley blurted out before she could change her mind. She lifted up on the bed and tucked her knees under her chin. "David drove me here."

There was a long silence before Scott said, "David?" His tone was suddenly cold and detached.

"Yeah, we were at the library when my mom called. There were no more planes out of Boston to Buffalo and I didn't know what else to do. The train or bus would've taken forever…"

"You were *with* David?"

"No, Scott. We just happened to be in the same place at the same time. I was studying, he was working… Sometimes I bump into him when I go to the library."

"So it was a coincidence he was there when your mom called…?"

"Yes. My phone died last night. I called you from his number to tell you."

"That was you?"

"Yeah."

Scott was silent for a few long seconds. "Why him? Why couldn't you go with one of your roommates?"

"I had zero time to think. David was there, and he offered to give me a ride, and I didn't want to waste any time going home—"

"Did he meet your parents?"

"Just my mom."

"Just your mom, huh?" Scott sounded petty as hell.

"Scott, don't be like that—"

"Wait, is he still there?"

"No." Haley gripped the comforter and closed her fist into a tight ball, crushing the fabric. "He slept here last night, but was gone before I woke up this morning."

"At your parents' house?"

"Yeah, in the guest room."

"Ah, hell, if he was in the guest room."

Blood pounded in Haley's temples. She'd wanted to call Scott to be comforted, not to get sucked into a major fight over David. "Scott, it was nothing shady."

"Yeah, Haley, nothing shady at all. Only, when I left a few weeks ago you swore you hated my brother, and now out of the blue you're bringing David home to meet your parents."

Haley let go of the comforter and massaged her forehead to ease the throbbing. "He didn't meet my parents because my dad is too sick to meet anyone, okay? David was only doing me a favor as a *friend*."

"Since when are you two friends?"

"He apologized a while ago for being a dick, and I guess we've been okay since then."

"And why didn't you tell me?"

"It wasn't a big deal."

Scott scoffed. "Not a big deal, huh? Damn, Haley, first the kiss and now this."

"I called you last night to tell you. It's not my fault you didn't pick up!"

"But it's your fault you were in a car with my brother. There were a million other people you could've asked for help."

"Yeah, maybe. But all I wanted to do was to get home. I thought my dad was going to *die*… I didn't care about anything else at that moment."

"I get it that you were worried—"

"No, Scott, I don't think you're getting any of it."

"What did you expect me to say? To be okay with David playing the hero and you letting him… Why him? Of all people, why did it have to be my brother?"

"BECAUSE HE WAS THERE AND YOU WEREN'T!" Haley shouted, exasperated. She caught her breath, regretting the outburst. "I didn't mean it like that…"

"No, sure." Scott sounded hurt.

Haley felt even more spent and emotionally drained than before falling asleep. "Scott, really, it came out all wrong. I'm just exhausted."

"I should let you get some sleep, then."

Without waiting for a reply, Scott ended the call. Haley didn't have the energy to call him back; besides, she was done arguing and having to justify herself to everybody. She'd done nothing wrong, and if this was the maximum level of empathy Scott could show her after what had happened to her dad, he could go to hell. As tears rolled down her cheeks, Haley grabbed a pillow and used it to choke her sobs until she fell asleep again.

Scott

Scott hung up with Haley and, with a few quick, angry sweeps of his thumb, he pulled up David's number and pressed call.

His brother picked up on the fourth ring. "Ooh, hello, to what do I owe the pl—"

"Stay the hell away from my girlfriend, David," Scott yelled into the phone.

He was still trembling with suppressed fury after speaking with Haley, and he needed to vent his anger on the one person responsible.

"Calm down, Scotty, you seem to be in a bit of a rage."

"How dare you—"

"What? Help your girl at the moment she needed it the most? What are you mad about, exactly?"

"Must've been nice to play the hero. Pretending to be a friend when you're not…"

"I never kept my intentions secret, brother."

"Have some decency. Haley is *my* girlfriend."

"Oh, I see. So your morals have shifted, now? Isn't a brother's girlfriend fair game for you? What changed?"

"Cut the crap, David. I don't want to get sucked into the Brigitte fight again. We were freaking teenagers, get over it."

"Oh, using the I-was-too-young excuse? Have you finally outgrown the I-didn't-know one? Come on, Scotty, you can do better than that."

"What were you doing with Haley, anyway?" Scott felt guilty for not trusting Haley's version, but when his brother was involved, he lost all rationality.

"I bumped into her at the library. I'm sure you're not so insecure that you don't even want your girlfriend *talking* to other people."

So Haley had told the truth. Still, Scott wasn't satisfied. "You didn't just talk to Haley, you drove her home for seven hours, met her parents, and slept at her childhood house."

"And what should I have done, genius? Let her drive home alone in the state she was? Let her wait the night for a flight? Put her on an eleven-hour bus ride? What? She tried to call you to tell you; pick up your phone next time."

Scott cursed himself for the umpteenth time for not answering the call. He'd seen David's number flash on his screen and had ignored it.

By his silence, David must've known he'd struck a chord, because he twisted the knife deeper. "By the way, it's always nice to know I can count on you in case I'm in an emergency."

"Spare me the lecture. You're a dick."

"I'm a dick? You're mad because you weren't there when Haley needed you the most."

Scott's grip on the phone tightened. "And whose fault is that?"

"Not mine. I'm not the one applying to cross-country internships before checking if my girlfriend is okay with it."

"The only reason I took the internship is that you lied to me."

"Technically, I didn't lie."

"Technically, you're an asshole."

"Scott, let me give you some brotherly advice: your girlfriend just went through the most horrible night of her life and, instead of comforting her, I assume you've been a petty bitch…" Scott hated when his brother was right. "Do yourself a favor and get over your wounded ego. As much as I hate to say this, Haley needs you right now—a better version of you, at least."

"Why are you telling me this?"

"Because I care about her." David didn't just care about Haley; it was in the tone of his voice. He was in love with her. This wasn't a petty revenge or him being a jerk for the heck of it. They were in love with the same girl, *again.* The realization hit Scott in the stomach like a sucker punch. "And I don't want you to make my job too easy," David added, switching back to being an ass. "Wouldn't be fun otherwise."

Scott ignored the jibe and said what was really on his mind. "I'm sorry this happened again. I didn't know you had a past with Haley when I met her."

"Don't go soft on me, brother." There David was, doing it again—hiding his real feelings behind sarcasm. "If you don't mind, I have a ton of work to finish for tomorrow, and it's the middle of the night here."

"David?"

"Yeah?"

"Thanks for making sure she got home safe."

"You're welcome."

Haley

You have one new audio message from Scott.

Staring at the writing on the screen, Haley hesitated. The message was several minutes long. What would Scott say? Would he break up with her? Haley couldn't stomach the idea. She stared at the message for a while. Then, with trembling fingers, she opened the recording and put the phone on speaker.

"Hey, it's me… I know you probably hate me right now, but I need to say this… I'm so sorry for last night. You were down, and I acted like a jerk. I should've been there for you, and instead, I made an awful situation worse. I feel like shit thinking about how I behaved…

"Sorry I didn't get how hard it's been for you and your family… It's just that after basically living in a hospital for a month, a heart attack begins to sound almost like a bad cold. And I'm not saying it was, I'm trying to explain why I might've lost perspective. Haley, I… I…

"What I'm trying to say is that I've been a total dick. I thought about what was best for me and not you. After hanging up with you, I called David to yell at him, too… and I have to say, he put me in my place. Totally in a David-ish way…" Scott chuckled in the recording. *"Serves me right, I guess. In the end, I'm glad my brother was there to drive you and make sure you got home safe, and I'm so glad your dad is okay…*

"Haley, please forgive me. I'm so, so sorry…" Scott's voice sounded choked. *"I hope you're willing to give me another chance. I love you…"*

Without checking the time—in either city—Haley called him back.

Scott picked up on the second ring, sounding half-asleep. "Hey."

"Did I wake you?"

"I'm glad you did, I was having a nightmare anyway."

"What nightmare?"

"One where my perfect girlfriend broke up with me for being the greatest idiot."

A smile crept on Haley's lips. "Funny you said that, I was having the same bad dream."

"Any guy would be crazy to break up with you."

"So you're no longer angry with me?"

"I consider myself lucky you're still talking to me. Can we pretend last night never happened?"

"Yes… yes!" Now Haley's smile stretched so wide her cheeks hurt.

They were still on the phone an hour later when her mom called from downstairs, "Haley, we have to leave in twenty minutes… Are you up?"

"I'll be right down, Mom," Haley shouted back, and then added into the speaker in a normal tone, "I have to go, talk later?"

"Okay. How long are you staying in Buffalo?"

"Until tomorrow, or Wednesday at the latest. I wrote to my professors to explain the situation, and they all said it'd be okay to skip a couple of classes. But it's finals week next week, so it's back to Boston even if I don't want to."

"Your dad will be fine."

"Yeah, everyone keeps telling me so. But I'd still prefer to spend more time here."

"HALEY!" An impatient shout drifted up from the bottom of the stairs.

"My mom is going crazy," Haley said. "I really have to go."

"Okay. Say hi to your parents and call me when you get back from the hospital."

"Will you be home?"

"Dr. Allen's schedule is all right today."

"Okay, gotta go. Love you."

"I love you too."

When Haley and her mom arrived at the hospital, there were two huge flower bouquets in her dad's room. Both were from Scott. The one for her dad was white, yellow, and blue—the Buffalo Sabres' colors, he was a huge hockey fan—and the other was red roses for Haley.

"Seems like our Baby Monkey is dating a very proper young man," her dad said with a huge smile on his face.

"Yeah." Haley opened the card—it simply said: *Sorry, I love you*—and joined her dad in smiling. "The best."

***

After a thousand reassurances from the doctors that her father wasn't going to suddenly get worse, but only better, and a million promises from her mom that she'd put him on a healthy diet and make sure he rested, Haley was ready to leave.

She caught the last flight from Buffalo to Boston on Wednesday night, and both Madison and Alice came to pick her up at Logan Airport in Madison's car. From the moment Haley spotted her two best friends' worried faces as they waited for her at the arrival gate, she knew that even if there had been tension between them lately, they were going to be fine. No matter the petty squabbles over boys, they'd always be there for one another.

As soon as she passed the barrier, Madison and Alice ran toward her pulling her into a crushing three-way hug. They brought her home and cuddled her to death until all three were too tired to keep their eyes open. It became even clearer how worried her roommates had been when Alice tiptoed into her room to leave a half-asleep Blue with Haley. The tiny bundle of fur was the ultimate pick-me-up of the house. He was the sweetest bunny, he loved to be picked up, to cuddle, and if scratched behind the ears he'd start to purr like a cat.

Haley thanked her friend and gladly snuggled Blue close to her chest, falling asleep to the comforting sound of his gentle bunny-purring.

The final days of class were busy enough not to let Haley's mind wander too far over what could've happened to her family. Over what would eventually happen when her parents became old. If she had had nothing to do, she might've slipped down a rabbit hole of catastrophic scenarios filled with hospitals and tubes and sick people.

But before she had time to notice, it was the weekend again. As she jogged up the steps of the Widener Library early on Saturday morning, Haley kept moving her hair around—side to side, up in a bun, down again—and readjusting the straps of her backpack. This would be the first time she'd seen David after he'd driven her home. Would he even be there? Would the easy, we-play-around-with-coding-sometimes relationship they'd established over the past month be changed? Scott had said he and David were okay now, but was he telling the truth? Or only saying what Haley wanted to hear?

When she reached their usual table, David wasn't there, and the pit of hard disappointment that hit Haley low in her belly scared her to death for a moment. But she didn't have time to analyze her gut reaction to David being missing because she soon heard his voice come from behind her, "Hey, Miss Robot, you're back."

She turned, at a loss for words. There were a million things she wanted to tell him—to thank him for making a horrible day slightly less horrible, for being her hero without asking for anything back, for making Scott understand instead of trying to work him up more.

The emotions must've shown on her face, because David's features turned serious—his signature lopsided grin evaporated, and the twinkle in his eyes switched from playful to intense.

"Come here." David pulled her into a hug.

Haley didn't want to ask herself why it felt so good to be in his arms, if it was right or wrong, or what it meant. For a few instants, she let herself live in the moment. She was starved for affection and she needed a comforting hug.

David let her go, saying, "Your dad will be fine, he gave you a scare, but it's over now."

"Right." Haley very un-sexily sniffled. "My mom has already gotten rid of all the salt in the house."

"No." David made a mock-scared face. "And what if the Sanderson sisters were to attack?"

Haley smiled. "I didn't take you for a *Hocus Pocus* fan." Weird how David always managed to make her smile. "We'll think about it when Halloween comes."

"You've got work to do?" David asked, pulling back a chair to sit down.

Haley imitated him. "Yeah, finals begin on Monday." She sat down and sighed. "Sadly, no laptop for me today."

"Me neither. What did you do?"

"Why? You did something and they took your laptop away?"

"My boss was so pissed off I completed the last assignment that he moved me to analog crap."

Haley lowered her gaze, taking more time than necessary to fish her notebook out of her bag. "I'm glad you managed despite the seven-hour detour."

"I had a good teacher." David winked. "What's your excuse for being technology free?"

"A crazy professor." Haley shrugged. "He says we completed enough coding assignments with our homework and midterms. For the final, he wants us to become the computer."

"Meaning?"

"We have to show we not only know how to code, but also that we understand what each command triggers inside a machine. So we have to do all the corresponding calculations by hand."

"Because?"

"Apparently so that if humanity was ever caught in an apocalypse that destroyed all existing machines, then we'd be able to program new ones from scratch."

"Awesome." David grinned.

"Lame." Haley rolled her eyes. "What's your poison for today?"

"One of our clients was stuck in the Middle Ages and kept physical-only books. And guess who has to check they were dematerialized correctly?" David dropped two gigantic piles of paper on the table. "Copy of the original against a printout of the digitalization."

"Isn't that a waste of a Harvard-graduated brain?"

"It's not about the sophistication of the work, it's about letting me know I'm at the bottom of the food chain and testing if I'm a quitter."

"Are you?"

David flashed her one of his intense, electrifyingly blue stares. "When I want something, I never give up."

On that note, Haley blushed and decided it was probably better to study for her exams. Pen in hand, she bent her head low over her exercise sheet and started working. David did the same next to her.

***

Half an hour before closing time, a dark shadow crossed over the library.

Haley lifted her gaze to the ceiling. Where there had been bright squares of light a few moments ago, now there were only dark-gray patches.

"Maybe we should go before it starts raining," she said.

"Too late for that, Miss Robot," David said as the first raindrops spattered the roof. "Are you finished?"

"One exercise left. You?"

"It'll take me all weekend to finish. No cheating this time." David shrugged and went back to work.

"I'm done," Haley announced ten minutes later. "We should get going; it seems like it's getting worse."

Now there was a steady hammering of water hitting glass.

"Yeah." David dropped his pen and stretched his right hand. "Library's closing in fifteen minutes anyway."

They both packed their things and headed downstairs.

The moment Haley pushed open the lobby door, a strong gush of warm wind pushed back against her, carrying a spray of water in its wake.

Head bent low against the wind, Haley stepped out. Despite it being five in the afternoon, there was so little light that the day had turned to night hours early. Dark clouds the color of lead crowded the sky, rain unloading off them in large, fat drops—a perfect summer storm.

"I don't have an umbrella," Haley called, having to shout to be heard over the rolling thunder. "Do you?"

"No," David yelled back. "And I don't care."

He hurried past her out of the cover of the library porch and ran down the steps. When he reached the bottom, he tilted his face up and closed his eyes. In a matter of seconds, he was soaked.

"What are you doing?"

David looked at her from across the street, he was walking backward toward the center of Harvard Yard. "Come here. It's only water."

Haley didn't know what possessed her, but she did as he asked. She ran off the porch and joined him in the middle of the park. The sensation of the rain on her skin was electrifying as she spun on her toes, arms opened wide. Haley looked upward and laughed and laughed, unable to stop—until she pirouetted right into David's arms. The smile died on her lips as he caught her wrists and held her hands close to his chest, leaning his head down…

She tried to pull back, a ragged breath catching in her throat. "David, don't."

David's lips brushed her forehead in a soft, wet kiss. "I wasn't going to," he whispered. "The next time we kiss, you'll want to just as much as I do now…"

There. Haley couldn't pretend anymore that David didn't have feelings for her. She lifted her eyes to meet his. "David, I care about you, but I'm in love with Scott. That's never going to change."

"Never is a long time. You can't deny that what we've been doing here means something…"

"David, we're friends." Haley tried to pull back again, but he wouldn't let her go.

"You're a liar, Haley." David's eyes flared up with dark emotions. "You're lying to me, and you're lying to Scott, and most of all you're lying to yourself."

"Don't do this to me, David, please don't."

"I'm not doing anything, only telling you how things are. I won't lash out again or try to do stupid things to make you jealous, and I won't try to get between you and Scott. But I want you to know how I feel. I want you to know that when you're ready to admit that you feel the same, I'll be there." He tightened his grip on her hands, but not in a way that hurt. "I won't go away, Haley. I'll always be here for you." David pulled her wrists up and kissed her knuckles. Then he locked his impossibly blue gaze on her. "I love you."

***

Walking home under the pouring sky, Haley didn't feel the tickle of the droplets landing on her face, or the rain soaking her clothes and sneaking down her spine. All she could feel was the echo of David's words: *I love you.* The intensity of his stare as he said them, and the ghost of his lips on her forehead.

Okay, let's calm down, Haley thought. It was perfectly normal not to remain indifferent when someone declared his undying love in the most romantic rain shower ever. But David wasn't just anyone, he was David. He was the boy in the mask, the one who'd saved her at her darkest moment.

Haley vowed to avoid him for a while. She didn't have the mental ease to deal with his—*or her*—feelings right now. Luckily, their casual little ritual of spontaneous Saturday meetings at the library had no more reason to exist. Summer School was over, and there were no more excuses—*need,* it had very much been a practical need—for Haley to go to the library.

True to expectations, finals week kept Haley busy. Between last-minute revision sessions, the amount of work she had to recoup from the four days she'd spent in Buffalo, and the exams themselves, her mind didn't have much time left to dwell on boys telling her they loved her in the rain.

On the first Friday in August, Haley came home from her last exam feeling positively drained. And she wasn't done yet; she still had to pack her bag, as she was leaving for Buffalo the following day. But all she wanted to do was curl up under the blankets—maybe stealing Blue from Alice again—and sleep.

Her roommates had different plans. They'd both been waiting for her to get home, and ambushed her as she entered the apartment, shouting, "Happy birthday!" and blowing into a pair of ridiculous party blowers that made a hideous noise.

Oh, no. No. No. No. The last thing Haley wanted was a birthday party. She hoped the surprise ended at the blowers and chocolate-glaze cupcake with a single candle on top that Madison was now bringing forward.

Forcing a smile on her face, Haley said, "Thank you, guys. You didn't have to." She was about to blow the candle when Madison stopped her.

"Wait, you have to make a wish first."

I wish my bag will magically pack itself, and to have an early night tonight.

Haley was a practical girl.

"Done," she announced. "Can I blow now?"

"Knock yourself out." Alice smiled.

They all cheered as the tiny flame blew out. Alice promptly took the chocolate cupcake away and cut it into three slices, doling one out to each of them.

Haley took a bite and closed her eyes, savoring how creamy and delicious the cake was. "Umm, this is heaven."

"Yep," Alice agreed, scarfing down her slice.

Madison was still licking her fingers when she peeked at her watch and announced, "Come on, Haley, you have two hours to shower and get ready. Then we're taking you out to celebrate."

Haley suppressed a groan and tried to put a conciliatory expression on her face. "Guys, I'm super thankful for the surprise, but can't we just stay in and binge watch romcoms?"

Madison threw Alice an I-told-you-so stare before saying, "Absolutely not. We have plans."

"But I still have to pack my bag to go home, and I leave super early tomorrow."

Madison looped her arm under Haley's elbow and steered her toward her room, saying, "Which is why we took the liberty of packing for you." Madison pushed the door open to reveal Haley's bag standing open on the floor, packed to perfection. Clothes, shoes, and makeup cases were arranged in tidy rows, and all the space was occupied with the maximum possible efficiency. Haley had never seen a suitcase better organized.

"Now, chop, chop." Madison playfully spanked her to prompt her to enter the room. "We're on a schedule."

"Okay, okay." Haley rolled her eyes and pushed Maddie out the door.

She started donning her clothes and, still in her underwear, she grabbed a clean towel to go shower. With a sigh, she threw a wistful glance at her packed-to-the-brim bag. Well, at least one half of her birthday wish had come true.

***

When she came out of the steaming shower, she found the girls eating pizza at the kitchen bar.

"Wait, are we staying in or going out?"

"In for food," Madison said. "Out for fun."

"We're meeting the others at a bar in downtown Boston," Alice explained. "But we wanted to eat first and avoid getting drunk on an empty stomach."

Haley hoped to avoid getting drunk on any kind of stomach, and she also wondered who "the others" meeting them downtown were. But the pizza smelled delicious, so, with one pink towel wrapped around her body and another one around her head, she sat next to Madison and grabbed a slice.

For three girls, the giant pizza sitting in front of them disappeared alarmingly quickly.

Brushing her hands together to get rid of the crumbs, Haley asked, "What's the dress code?"

"Dressed up," Alice said, shrugging apologetically as if to say: *not my fault.*

"High heels?" Haley asked, disgruntled.

Both her roommates nodded.

"Are we going to walk?"

"Hell no," Madison said. "We'll call an Uber as soon as we're ready and"—she looked at her watch—"we should get a move on."

They all hopped off their respective stools and paused in the hall.

"Meet again here in half an hour?" Madison asked.

They all nodded and disappeared into their rooms. But of course, in less than five minutes they all ended up in Madison's room, exchanging makeup, curling each other's hair, and trying on outfits.

Haley opted for a white dress with spaghetti straps and an empire waist, Madison for a colorful, flowy dress, and Alice for a classic little black dress. And, voilà, they were only slightly late when their driver dropped them off at the designated bar downtown.

Inside, their usual crowd of friends was waiting for them. Mostly girls from their sorority and guys from the team: Matt Lucas, Blake Donovan, Jack… and, of course, David Williams. He was drinking a beer with his elbow propped against the bar, talking to Becky, another soon-to-be-senior Kappa Kappa Gamma.

Becky had a bit of an easy-girl reputation. She'd slept with Jack the previous year—way before he was with Alice—and from the way she was flirting with David now, she looked like she wouldn't mind going home with him tonight.

Haley grimaced involuntarily. The idea somehow didn't sit well with her. Not so much what—*who*—Becky did or didn't do. Everyone male or female was free to have sex or not have sex with however many people they wanted. But the certainty that she didn't want Becky and David to sleep together tonight struck Haley like a bolt of lightning, sending a weird current down her spine.

He lifted his gaze and their eyes met, causing another stream of electricity to course through Haley's body. This was the first time they'd seen each other after David had told her he loved her. Even at a distance, and even in the faint lights of the bar, the blue of his eyes sparkled. David's mouth curved up at one corner and he waved.

"What are you looking at with that long face?" Madison asked, and then followed Haley's gaze to the bar. "Who the hell invited *him*?"

"Come on, Maddie." Alice rolled her eyes. "He's friends with everyone we know, and he's Haley's friend, too. Right?" She turned to her for confirmation.

Haley blushed profusely and nodded, hoping the dim lights would cover her flush.

"Whatever," Madison said, and marched off to the opposite side of the room to go talk to Matt.

"I need a drink." Haley plastered a smile on her lips. "Join me?"

"Can't wait for a Cosmo, they make the bestest here." Alice linked her arm with Haley's and they joined Jack and Blake in the line to order.

There, Alice let go of Haley and wrapped her arms around Jack's waist, a megawatt smile brightening her face at once. "A Cosmo for your girlfriend and another one for the birthday girl."

Jack turned around, his smile matching Alice's, and bent down to steal a kiss. "Two Cosmos for the ladies on their way."

Haley felt a little pang of envy. Their happiness made her miss Scott so much more. It'd be another three weeks before he came back, and it still seemed like an eternity. Haley looked away from the happy couple, and her eyes landed on Madison next, guilt replacing envy at once. At least she had a boyfriend who adored her and who'd be here soon; what about Maddie?

Following Madison with her gaze as she moved across the room, Haley was surprised to see her friend stop next to David. At once, Becky made herself scarce and Madison and David began to talk in hushed tones. He was smiling, and she was scowling—without looking really mad.

For the first time, the reality that Madison had actually had sex with David—*multiple times*—struck Haley like a blow. They had that intimacy peculiar to ex-lovers. Madison looked too comfortable for her own good.

Everything Madison did lately confused Haley. First she was dating David, then she was in love with Scott. And after David had broken up with her in the worst possible way—if one was to believe her version of the story—there she was talking to him as if they were a pair of old friends. From the way she acted whenever he showed up in their group, Madison seemed to still hate David, so what business did she have talking to him?

Haley wished she could hear what they were saying.

Madison

Madison had not asked Haley a single question about her emergency road trip with David. If Scott knew and had nothing against it, neither did Madison. Even if she suspected David was gaining too many points with Haley. But their friendship had been on the mend since Haley had come back from Buffalo, and Madison didn't want to risk ruining this newfound balance with indelicate questions.

But there was nothing wrong with probing the other party interested.

"Still playing the good boy part?" Madison asked.

"Not playing any part, Blondie." David smirked. "It's not my style."

"And how's your diabolical plan to steal your brother's girlfriend going?"

"Why? Hoping I'd get a move on?"

"That's not—" Madison started defending herself, but then she noticed David's amused face and swatted him instead. "You're still a jerk."

"Oh, come on, Blondie, I'm only teasing you a little."

Madison scoffed. "Why are you here?"

"To wish Haley a happy birthday. Is that against the law?"

"David, I know you… You have the charm on."

"Are you charmed?"

"I'm immune."

"Ouch." David brought a hand to his chest. "Now you're hurting me, Blondie."

Madison scowled at him. "I will if you mess with Haley."

David arched an eyebrow. "Am I still on your watch list?"

Madison wasn't sure. "I'm glad you were there for Haley during the crisis with her dad, but I'm not sure your gesture was one hundred percent selfless."

David made a cute, I'm-innocent face. "No?"

"Stop playing dumb. I bet you enjoyed being the hero."

"Is that how Haley describes me now?"

Madison smiled despite herself. "You're impossible."

"And you're charmed."

"Am not."

David smirked but didn't say anything.

Madison chewed on her lower lip.

"Come on, Blondie, spit out whatever you're dying to say."

"David, I know you care about Haley. But sometimes the best way to show someone you care about them is to back off and let them be happy with someone else."

"The way you do, Blondie? And how much good has that done you?"

"Now you're being mean again."

"No, I'm telling the truth, just like I always do. Now, if you'll excuse me…" He pushed past her and disappeared into the crowd.

Madison watched him go, not knowing if she still hated him to death or if he was growing on her.

Haley

Fed up with watching David and Madison flirt—it definitely looked as if they were flirting—Haley excused herself and went to the restroom to calm down.

What the hell?

Madison had even smiled at him at one point. Funny way to show her hatred. And what about David? So much for being in love with her, and for promising he wouldn't try to play mind games or make her jealous… And why was it that simply seeing him talk to one of her friends made her jealous?

They used to be together.

So? What place do you have being jealous?

Haley shook her head. *None.*

Still, she couldn't shake the feeling. And it annoyed her.

Haley entered the restroom and stood in front of the mirror. She didn't really need to use the toilet, so she decided to fluff her hair and reapply her cranberry lip gloss.

On top of everything else, Scott still hadn't called to wish her happy birthday. Sure, he'd sent a cute message with a silly picture that morning, but nothing else all day. He was probably locked in an OR, but Haley wished he'd make the effort to find the time to call.

When she could no longer pretend to be fixing her hair, Haley dropped her lip gloss in her clutch and headed out, checking her phone for new messages. There were none.

"Hello, Birthday Girl." David's voice startled her halfway down the corridor to the main bar.

Haley lifted her gaze from the screen to find him propped against the wall, arms crossed over his chest. He'd clearly been waiting for her.

"What? Are you stalking me now?"

"Oooh." That infuriatingly sexy grin spread on his lips. "Feisty, aren't we? I like it." He lowered his gaze to her legs. "The heels, too."

"What do you want?" Haley didn't know why she was being so rude.

"Only to wish you a happy birthday."

"You could've done it as soon as you saw me."

"True." David pushed himself off the wall and searched the folds of his jacket. "But I wanted a little extra privacy to give you this." He took a small box out of an inside pocket.

"What is that?"

"A birthday gift, obviously."

Haley softened at once. "David, you can't give me gifts."

"What? Now a *friend* can't give you a present for your birthday?"

Haley scowled at him. "A *friend* could. Is that what we are... friends?"

Lips curling up only at one corner of his mouth, David said, "This is a one hundred percent friendly gift." He handed her the small box.

"What is it?"

"Open it."

Haley did, and gasped when she discovered a stunning dark-silver locket inside. It was an engraved oval in a Gothic style, beautiful and perfect. "David, thank you, it's gorgeous. You shouldn't have."
He really shouldn't have.

"May I?" he asked.

Haley gave him the necklace and turned toward the wall, holding her hair up. David came closer, looping the necklace around her neck and fastening it at her nape. His fingers grazed her skin, and shivers spread down her spine. Haley had to make an effort not to shudder under his touch.

"Now," he said, letting the chain fall in place. "You wouldn't think I'd buy you jewelry, right?"

Haley scoffed, facing him again. "No?"

David reached for the pendant. "It's a secret container." He flipped the locket open to reveal a hidden USB key inside. "Thirty-two gigs of data at your disposal anytime you need it, Miss Robot."

Haley smiled. This really was the perfect gift for her. "A girl never knows when she might need extra gigs."

Just then, Haley's phone started ringing. *Lovefool.*

"It's Scott," she said. "He hasn't wished me happy birthday yet."

David's smile faltered slightly. "I'll leave you to it. See you later."

Haley watched him go, filled with mixed emotions. She waited until he'd turned the corner to pick up.

"Hey," she breathed into the mic.

"Hey, are you out celebrating? I can barely hear your voice over the music."

In the hall the music was less loud than in the main bar, but it was still loud, especially to talk over the phone.

"Give me a minute; I'll go outside… Here. Can you hear me now?"

"Loud and clear. Happy birthday!"

"Thanks."

Tires screeched on the concrete, distracting Haley. She lifted her gaze and spotted a familiar truck crossing the road and merging onto the MA-28 toward Cambridge. She only got a side-peek at the driver, but enough to recognize his slight frown. The same one he had on whenever he was concentrating on the road—she should know, she'd spent seven hours watching him drive not long ago.

Haley's chest contracted a little at seeing David go. Was he mad at her? He couldn't be. At least, he didn't have any right to be. Maybe it was better this way for everyone. On impulse, Haley's phone-free hand closed around the locket dangling from her neck.

"Haley, are you still there?" Scott's voice brought her out of her trance.

"Yeah, sorry. What were you saying?"

"I was asking if you're having fun."

"Yeah, the girls organized a surprise party, they made me a birthday cupcake, fed me pizza, and now we're in downtown Boston to celebrate with everybody else."

"Sorry I can't be there." The hurt was audible in Scott's tone.

"It's as if you were."

Only it wasn't. Not really.

There was a pause. Was Scott thinking the same? Instead, after a while, he asked, "Is David there?"

"He was." Haley didn't want to lie. "But he left early."

"Oh."

Was it an I'm-upset-he-was-there *oh,* an I'm-happy-he's-gone *oh,* or something between the two?

"Anyway," Haley continued. "I'm doing it more for the girls than for me. My birthday wish was to have an early night. I leave at five tomorrow morning."

"That's the saddest wish ever."

"Well, nothing great has happened lately."

"Haley?"

"Yeah?"

"Stare up at the sky."

Haley looked up at the dark blue sky. There wasn't a cloud in sight. "Okay?"

"Can you see the stars?"

"Uh-huh?"

"I'm looking at the same stars…"

Finally, a small smile crept on Haley's lips. "Are you going all cheesy romantic on me?"

"You bet I am! I promise you, Haley, this is the last birthday you spend alone."

"I wish I could kiss you right now."

"That sounds like a much better wish. Tilt your head up and send a kiss to the stars… They'll pass it over."

Feeling silly, but also giddily romantic, Haley gazed up, pressed her hand to her mouth, and blew a kiss to the sky. "Done! It should get to you in approximately… mmm… six hours, assuming kisses travel as fast as planes."

"I won't go to bed until it gets here. Now, go enjoy your party. I love you."

"I love you, too."

With one last glance at the sky, and then at the spot where David's truck had disappeared, Haley walked back inside the bar.

***

The day after the birthday party, she left for Buffalo. Her mom had been super excited when Haley had announced she'd fly over to celebrate her birthday with them, and that she'd stay home for as long as she could. It had been ages since she'd stayed in Buffalo for more than a few days. Usually, even for the holidays, Haley never stayed more than a week.

At first, between the celebrations, the catching up with her parents, and the rest of the family's entourage—grandparents, aunts, uncles, cousins, and old friends—it was a family-reunion honeymoon. Haley

414

was so grateful her dad was home that she didn't care about following the lifestyle of a fifty-five-year-old couple.

But after almost two weeks at home, Haley—as much as she loved her parents—couldn't stand living with them any longer. Her dad, usually the life of the party, was mostly sulky about his new healthy-but-unsavory diet. And her mom had started bugging Haley about all kinds of annoying house chores. The day Miranda Thomas told her she should clean up her room, Haley knew she had to get back to Boston. It was only ten days before the official year start, and every single one of her friends was going crazy over the massive end-of-summer party Blake Donovan was throwing.

Blake was on the basketball team, and was also apparently a rich kid with a summer house in the country, complete with an Olympic-size outdoor pool. And since his parents were away in Europe, he'd decided to put the empty house to good use.

In their roomies WhatsApp group, Madison wouldn't stop going on and on about the party—for a generally quiet introvert, she had a weird love for parties—but even Alice showed some excitement. Haley was torn; the date of the party would be only a day after Scott came back from California. She wasn't at all sure she'd be ready to share him with the world after only one night together.

But, party or not, Haley craved to be home in her own apartment. Free to eat or not eat at whatever weird hour of the day or night she pleased. Free to leave her dirty socks on the floor for as long as she liked without the socks police—aka her mom—yelling after her. And as much as she loved her dad, she was too young to follow his no-salt-no-bacon-no-nothing-remotely-yummy diet. Definitely time to hug her parents goodbye and go.

***

Despite her flight being over an hour late, Haley was in a positive mood when she landed in Boston late on Friday night. Only a week until the party. And only a week before Scott came back from California. She took an Uber home and after a quick hello to her roommates, she went to bed.

But sleep didn't come easy; Haley was too excited. Scott was coming home in only seven days. How would it be to finally have him back?

Excitement quickly turned to worry. What if California had changed Scott?

And what if being alone here has changed me?

If nothing else, one thing had already changed for sure.

When Scott had left, Haley had positively hated his brother. But now they were friends of sorts, and David… he loved her, and she hadn't told Scott about his confession. Should she? Did Scott know anyway? No matter how much the two brothers claimed not to stand each other, they always seemed to get the other like no one else could.

Would it be weird to go to Scott's apartment and see David there? Yeah-ah.

David had promised not to be a jerk anymore, and that he wouldn't try to come between her and Scott. And Scott had seemed to accept Haley's friendship with his brother after her dad's heart attack. But would the three of them all living in the same city again tip the balance?

The next morning, Haley was still nervous. As always when she needed to calm down, she turned to coding. Only she didn't have an assignment or any inspiration for a new program. She just sat there staring at the black screen while fidgeting with the necklace David had given her for her birthday. Since that day, she'd never taken it off or used the USB key hidden inside. Haley weighed the ball of metal in her hand and then, on impulse, she opened the locket and plugged the tiny key into her laptop.

The memory was empty except for a folder called *Miss Robot*. Haley opened it. Inside there was a single JPEG file also named *Miss_Robot*. With trembling fingers, Haley clicked on the picture.

A black and white portrait popped up on the screen, its lines crude and sharp, but the final result no less powerful for it. Haley stared transfixed at the raw sketch of her face.

Was this how David saw her? Beautiful, but strong and also… mysterious. It wasn't so much that she looked pretty in the drawing. It was the expression he'd immortalized—one of deep concentration Haley had never seen on herself—that struck Haley. Yeah, maybe she'd never seen that expression because when it came on she was too busy with whatever she was doing to look in a mirror.

And who would've guessed bad-boy David Williams had an artistic side? And was he really that much of a bad boy anyway? Or was it a mask he wore? A different kind from the one he'd had on the night they'd met. Was it a cover he put on every day to pretend nothing touched him when the exact opposite was true?

Haley still had David's number saved on her phone from the night Madison had forwarded her the contact for her to call him and ask if he'd told Scott about the kiss. She couldn't help but scoff and shake her head at the memory. That David had been a royal D-bag. But not the David who had driven seven hours to get her home to her sick dad. And not the David who had told her in the most romantic summer storm that he loved her. And not the David who had drawn this sketch.

Rolling her phone in her hands—left, right, left—Haley was itching to call him. Maybe a call was too much; a simple text would be better. She typed an easy-going:

Unoriginal, but safe. He probably wouldn't even see it or hit her back, and then it'd be fine. Unfortunately, three pulsing dots appeared on the screen almost immediately; David was composing a reply.

Hey?

Haley could almost picture the surprised-but-pleased frown on his face.

Easy with your perfect posing skills

No, I know

You're a natural

Some time passed with neither of them texting until a bubble appeared again on Haley's screen.

The library is not the same without you

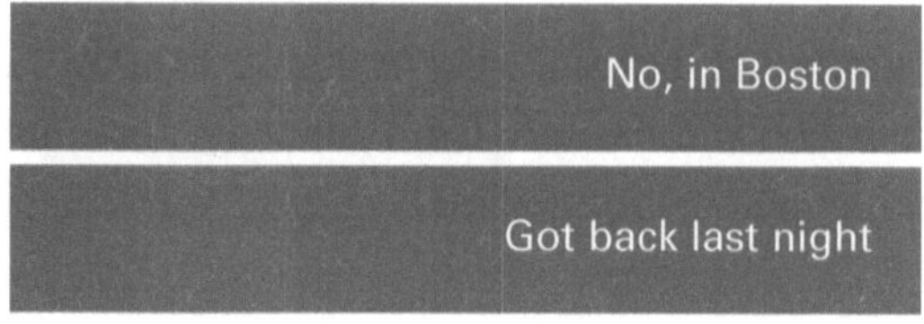

Yep, you still in Buffalo?

For no reason, Haley's heart beat super-fast as she typed:

Want to grab a beer later?

That sounded dangerously like a date. And as if reading her mind, David's next text came in pronto:

It's not a date

Still, Haley did not reply.

Okay, Miss Robot

Let's do it this way

I'll be at The Plough and Stars

The Irish Pub down Mass Ave.

At around 7

If you feel like joining

You know where to find me

I'm not coming

Haley finally typed.

I'll still be there

In case you change your mind

I won't

Never say never

Gotta get back to work now

See you later?

Haley did not reply this time. She locked the screen and shut the phone in a drawer as if it had suddenly become radioactive. Texting David had been a bad idea. An awful, stupid, wicked idea.

***

The tiny clock window on Haley's laptop kept teasing her. She tried to concentrate harder on the job she was doing—she'd settled for updating her coding cheat-sheet with everything she'd learned over the summer—but the task was dull enough to leave her mind free to roam. Plus the little, ever-changing numbers on the digital clock and their implied meaning kept distracting her.

The house was silent. For once, both Alice and Madison were out, and Haley was left alone to listen to the sound of silence. Or, more like the sound of a thousand imaginary clocks ticking away the seconds inside her head.

At 6:28, she wondered what David was doing, if he was getting ready to go out. She imagined him at his house smiling his crooked smile in front of the bathroom mirror.

And at 6:39, Haley pictured him putting on his black leather jacket and walking outside the apartment.

For the next fifteen minutes, Haley mapped in her head David's walking progress from his house, up on Cambridge Street, left onto Prospect, and finally right onto Massachusetts Avenue.

At 7:05, Haley figured David must be at The Plough and Stars waiting for her. How long would he wait before he accepted she wasn't going?

By 7:09, Haley realized she was already monumentally late, and she had to go now if she wanted to reach the pub before David left. Surely he wouldn't wait more than half an hour. He wasn't that desperate.

On impulse, she got up from her chair, making it scrape on the floor. No time to get changed. Haley checked herself out in the mirror; her eyes were red from staring at a screen all afternoon, and her hair not as bouncy as if she'd just washed it. Her clothes were no better; her dark gray jeans and black flimsy tank top over a white T-shirt weren't exactly sexy-wear, but David never seemed to have a problem with how she looked or dressed.

David.

Haley sat on the bed, fidgeting with the locket hanging from her neck. Was she really going to meet him? Why not? Why make such a big deal out of it? It was only a beer with a friend. No, it wasn't. David didn't want to be her friend, and Haley... she didn't know what she wanted. What?! No, no. She knew. She wanted to be with Scott one hundred percent. Nothing else. *No one* else.

Pity her boyfriend had almost disappeared in the last few days. Scott had been even more sparse than usual with his texts and they hadn't talked in what seemed like forever. After two months without seeing him or talking to him for more than ten minutes at a time over the phone, Haley had started wondering—secretly, in a dark space at the back of her mind—if the epic romance she'd thought they'd shared had not entirely been inside her head. Scott would be home soon, true, but would their relationship be the same? Could they just pick up where they'd left as if nothing had changed?

And was seeing David an unasked-for complication?

Oh, forget it. She could go have a beer with David without it having any apocalyptic, life-changing meaning. It was only a drink.

Right.

Haley stood up, grabbed her leather bag from the chair next to the desk, and walked down the hall of her apartment. Before opening the door, she fished out a tube of lip gloss and coated her lips in front of the hallway mirror, smacking them together in an imaginary kiss. There, she was ready.

Grabbing her keys from the plate on the small cabinet propped against the entrance wall, Haley threw the apartment door open and gasped, blinking several times while the rest of her body froze in utter shock.

Scott was standing on her doorstep. In the early sunset light filtering through the hallway windows, his perfectly tousled curls shone dark honey-gold, streaked with sandy highlights from his summer in California. His skin was tanned and dotted with even more adorable freckles than usual. His ripped chest and arms made Haley want to be crushed into a never-ending embrace. And his lips, curled up at the corners in a timid, nervous smile, were begging to be kissed.

Haley's pulse raced and butterflies exploded in her belly. How could she have thought even for a second not to be in love with Scott? Now that he was standing in front of her, it was clear her feelings hadn't changed. She'd never stopped loving him. Scott was her guy. It would always be Scott.

"Hey," Scott said.

Haley's lips broke into a wide, incredulous grin. "You're back a week early."

"Surprise."

"Is that why you disappeared in the last few days?"

A mischievous smile appeared on his face. "Are you mad?"

"No." Haley shook her head.

"Going somewhere?" Scott asked, tilting his chin toward the bag looped over her shoulder.

Haley blinked, confused. She honestly couldn't remember where she was headed. "No, I wasn't going anywhere," she said. She stared into Scott's sparkling green eyes a moment longer before he pulled her close and their lips collided.

End of Book 3

I don't WANT TO BE FRIENDS

JUST FRIENDS BOOK 4

CAMILLA ISLEY

David

She wasn't coming.

David cast another furtive look at his watch. At a quarter past eight, Haley was an hour and fifteen minutes late. No, not late, because she'd never meant to come. Earlier, the whole "meet me, I'll be there waiting for you regardless" bit had seemed a wonderful idea when he'd proposed it to her. Teasing. Romantic. At least, when he'd been so sure she'd show up. Now, he'd turned into a sorry dude: David—*Pathetic*—Williams, stood up by the girl of his dreams, drinking alone in a bar.

What a waste of a Saturday night.

David had come to The Plough and Stars early. He'd ordered his first beer at six forty-five and drank it in small sips, pacing himself, not wanting to be tipsy when Haley arrived. His second beer had gone down a lot faster. By now, he'd lost count of the rounds.

"Can you close my tab?" he asked the bartender.

The bartender nodded efficiently. He walked to the cash register and came back with David's credit card and a bill to sign. David wrote his name on the receipt, his handwriting more flourished than when he was sober. Then he stumbled off his stool, drained the last two inches of lukewarm beer in his glass, and dropped it on the counter with more force than he'd intended.

"Sorry," David apologized.

The barman curled his upper lip and gave David an unimpressed look as he swiped the glass off the counter without comment, probably accustomed to sloppy drunks.

Taken aback by the barman's evident contempt, David's hands curled into fists as icy rage flooded his system. He was itching for a fight, but the last lucid part of his brain nagged at him that causing a brawl in a bar near campus was not the smartest idea. And he wasn't really angry at the bartender, anyway. A pair of green eyes flashed in his mind. No, he was definitely mad at someone else.

Outside the pub, hot air dripping with humidity blew in David's face, doing nothing to help him sober up. Why did Boston have to turn into a swamp every August? With a disgusted wince, David stared up at the brick buildings of Cambridge, trying to orient himself. After taking a few tentative steps up Massachusetts Avenue, he realized he was heading the wrong way and turned around, dragging his feet all the way home.

David was no less drunk when he unlocked his apartment door twenty minutes later. He careened inside the house and realized at once that something was off. *Different.* David frowned, unable to identify what was wrong, but definitely sure something had changed since he'd left earlier that night. He scanned the living room and kitchen area for a clue, but everything seemed just as David had left it.

Then he saw it: Scott's door, an inch ajar. That door had remained firmly shut for the past two months. David narrowed his eyes and walked toward his brother's room. Pushing the door open, he saw a huge suitcase parked next to the bed. His worst fears confirmed: Scott was home.

His brother was back in Cambridge from his summer internship in California a week early. Why? And where was he now, if not here?

David's body reacted to the answer an instant before his brain connected the dots. His heart contracted in a spasm, and he missed a breath. There was only one place Scott could have gone: to see his girlfriend. Haley.

"Ooooh, perfect." A bitter sneer spread on David's lips. "Welcome home, brother," he said to the empty room, and then punched the door with so much force that the skin on his knuckles split. His opponent— *the wooden door*—took the hit and bounced back with no lasting damage sustained. The same couldn't be said for David's fist.

With a throbbing hand, and a dark mood none improved after the punch, David stumbled over to the freezer. As he took out a bag of frozen peas and applied it to the back of his hand, his gaze landed on a bottle of vodka sitting at the bottom of the compartment.

Like most drunk people, the idea of getting even more trashed was incredibly appealing to David.

He dragged the bottle out, smiling. "Hello, baby," he told it. "Why don't we keep this party going?"

With the bag of peas precariously balanced on the back of his injured hand, David dropped the bottle of vodka on the kitchen counter and went hunting in the cabinets for shot glasses. He found six and arranged them in an orderly row on the countertop.

One-handed, he opened the bottle and poured the first shot, saying, "For my brother." Then he poured another. "And his lovely girlfriend,

Haley. I wish them a happy life together." Each statement was followed by a shot glass being filled. "To myself, for playing the part of the fool again. And to Brigitte, who tried to teach me a lesson many years ago I don't seem to want to learn."

David stared at the one remaining empty shot glass, trying to decide who he should dedicate it to. Unable to come up with another toast, he shrugged. "To me again, because I'm worth it."

David filled the last glass and threw the empty vodka bottle into the sink, where it landed with a loud clunk. Unmoved by the noise, David lifted the first glass and toppled the contents into his mouth. One by one he brought the small glasses to his lips, banging them on the counter once he'd downed them. The vodka burned his throat as he swallowed, and it spread like acid when it reached his empty stomach. But David didn't stop until all the glasses were dry, by which point he was irredeemably intoxicated.

Head spinning, he staggered to his room and, fully-clothed, fell face-down on his bed and passed out.

Madison

Madison woke with a groan, the morning light burning through her closed eyelids. Why could she never remember to close the blinds? Not that hard, right? All she had to do was turn the stick and the slim metal panes would seal themselves off, keeping the light out and allowing her to enjoy a Sunday morning lie-in. But, no, she always forgot, and those rotten, pupil-stabbing sunrays woke her up at the crack of dawn, *pronto*.

Pity, she'd been having the best Scott dream ever. Right before she'd woken up, he'd walked into her bedroom, ripped off his shirt, and told her he wanted her.

"Ah, hell," she huffed, throwing off the sheets and getting up.

Now that she was half-awake, the building pressure in her bladder became too strong to ignore. Barefooted, garbed in only a matching pair of pale pink panties and a flimsy tank top, Madison dragged her feet off the bed and headed for the apartment's shared bathroom.

Madison was too busy rubbing the sleep out of her eyes to pay much attention to where she was going. So, she was utterly stunned when she almost crashed nose-first into someone walking out of the bathroom.

Someone really tall, and mostly *naked.*

Madison's jaw dropped as she stared up into Scott's emerald green eyes. He was standing in front of her, bare-chested and wearing only a pair of unbuttoned jeans, with an apologetic smile stamped on his sexy lips. Exactly as he had in her dream.

She blinked.

Am I still dreaming? Isn't six in the morning a little too early to start hallucinating?

"Hi," the hallucination said, in a fantastic impersonation of Scott's low, masculine voice. "I thought no one would be up this early." Imaginary Scott proceeded to fasten the button on his jeans, visibly embarrassed.

The pull was inexorable, and Madison's gaze was drawn to the gesture. Her eyes traveled down his flat-muscled chest, skimmed over a sculpted, rock-hard six-pack, and came to rest on the deliciously inviting V of muscles disappearing below the jeans waistband.

Mmm, Madison thought, chewing on her lower lip. *Well, if I really have to hallucinate something, high-five, imagination.*

"Madison?" the hallucination asked. "Are you all right?"

"Never been better," Madison said, smiling like a fool.

"Oh, okay." Imaginary Scott shifted on his feet.

Madison didn't care if he seemed uncomfortable; this was her dream, so she might as well take the lead. She raised her hand and splayed it across Imaginary Scott's chiseled chest. But when her fingertips came in contact with warm, living flesh, Madison gasped and retracted her hand as if burned. "You're real!"

He chuckled. "Last time I checked."

"But you're in California," Madison protested.

"I came home a week early to surprise Haley," Scott—the real, not one-bit Imaginary Scott—said. "Sorry if I startled—"

"Oh, gosh," she interrupted. "Oh… oh." Shocked, Madison pressed one hand over her mouth while the other moved down to cover her panties. Oh dear goodness, she was standing in front of Scott wearing close to nothing and acting like a complete fool.

She flushed red head to toe, and, following her hand with his gaze— *his turn to gawk*—Scott's cheeks pinked as well.

With another awkward smile, he repeated, "I thought nobody would be up this early… Sorry."

Madison couldn't take a second longer of this exchange. She pushed past him, muttering a hurried, "Excuse me," and barged into the bathroom, locking the door behind her.

Breathing heavily as if she'd just run ten miles, Madison rested her shoulder blades against the wooden door. *Crap. Crap. Crap.* She hit her head back against the wood in time with the imprecations. Then she realized Scott might be able to hear her and stopped before she made an even bigger fool of herself.

She took long, steadying breaths, trying to slow her heart down. But the stubborn idiot seemed to be settled on run mode, making her gasp like there wasn't enough oxygen in the room. Embarrassment and shame burned a steady fire in her lower belly.

Madison collapsed down, her butt hitting the cold tiled floor, while a million thoughts crossed her mind.

Scott was back. He'd just seen her half-naked, hair disheveled, and probably sporting a horrible case of morning breath. Madison exhaled into her cupped hand and smelled it.

Shit.

What the hell was Scott doing in her bathroom at six in the morning?

He must've spent the night here, making love to Haley in the adjoining room while Madison had been sleeping next door, clueless. And they'd probably make love again soon.

Double shit.

This last image lit a different kind of fire in Madison's guts. Flames of anger and disappointment. Flames of envy flaring into hate. Hate for the best friend Madison couldn't legitimately hate, and hate for herself for all these contrasting feelings that kept eating at her.

And now there really wasn't enough oxygen in the room, maybe not even in the entire apartment. Madison needed out. She used the toilet only because her body forced her to. Then she turned the lock and opened the bathroom door a crack, poking her head out to make sure the hall was clear. Scott was gone, so she sprinted back to her room, pulled on a pair of sweatpants and a T-shirt, grabbed her gym bag, and fled.

The campus gym ran various group classes, and Madison was hoping to burn off her bad mood with something up-tempo and high-intensity. But the only thing on this morning's schedule was Hatha Yoga. Madison scoffed; she wasn't in the mood for anything relaxing, calming, or even remotely of the feel-as-one-with-the-universe philosophy. She needed to drive her body to its limits, so she wouldn't have any energy left to think about what had happened—or to imagine what might be happening at this very moment in Haley's bedroom.

Head bent low so as not to make eye contact with anyone, Madison jammed in a pair of earbuds and stepped on the first available treadmill. She set the machine on the longest and hardest program and selected a random cardio workout playlist on Spotify. But even with her feet flying on the mill and music pounding in her ears, Madison's brain was still functioning at full capacity, damn it. And her heart, despite being busy pumping blood at 160 beats per minute, still had time to break over and over again like it had been doing for the past eight months. Eight long months since the day Haley had come home from Hawaii and announced she and Scott were an item.

How much pain could a broken heart cause? There had to be a limit...

Because I can't take this anymore, Madison thought.

Scott's two-month internship in California had put a false sense of security in her. With him gone, away from Haley, it hadn't been so bad. There had been no sudden stabs in her chest when she ran into him on campus, or when she caught an intimate stare between him and Haley— or, worst of all, when she saw them kissing.

With Scott and Haley's relationship on hold, Madison had coddled herself in the false idea that she was getting over him. That these stupid feelings would go away. That she wouldn't feel so damn miserable all the time anymore.

Nope. Not for you, Madison. Not a chance in hell.

This morning's encounter with Scott had been the proverbial cold shower, her false sense of security promptly washed away. The illusion she wasn't in love with Scott gone.

So, what now?

Alice's words from their last "Scott" discussion echoed in her mind. *"Listen, Maddie,"* Alice had said. *"Who knows if Scott and Haley will stay together, or if you'll ever get to be with him, or even want him anymore? You could meet someone who'll sweep you off your feet tomorrow... And our lives are going to be so completely different in a year when we graduate, anyway. You just have to be strong and pull through."*

Alice was right. All Madison had to do was to be strong and pull through. She'd already suffered eight months of this. She could survive twelve more.

I can do it!

I have to be strong and pull through, Madison repeated inside her head. Eyes focused forward with a newfound determination, Madison pumped up the speed of the treadmill and ran and ran and ran toward the new finish line she now saw standing before her. Graduation was only a year away. Her life would change. Everything would change. And she'd be finally free…

Haley

"I may have traumatized one of your roommates," Scott said playfully, snuggling back under the covers next to Haley.

"What do you mean?" Haley asked, still groggy with sleep.

They had done little *sleeping* the night before, and Haley wouldn't mind staying in bed for another month. All she wanted to do was to drop her lids, burrow closer to Scott, and rest.

"I bumped into Madison on the way back from the bathroom. It was… awkward."

That woke Haley up, all right. She was so tired of the guilt tainting her relationship with Scott. But whenever Madison appeared in the picture, she couldn't help herself. After discovering Madison was secretly in love with her boyfriend, Haley had sworn never to spend the night with him here, in the adjoining room to Madison's. She'd vowed to do everything humanly possible to spare her best friend's feelings. But last night had been so unexpected… spontaneous, unplanned. Her happiness at seeing Scott again had obliterated all other thoughts. Scott had come back to her; nothing or no one else had mattered.

"Why? What did she say?" Haley asked.

"Not much. She made some weird comments; she was probably still sleeping. When she realized she was standing there in her underwear, she locked herself in the bathroom."

Great. Haley groaned inwardly. *I spend one night here with Scott and, of course, Madison had to bump into him the next morning.*

The front door slammed shut.

"Think it's her leaving?" Scott asked. "I hope I didn't offend her. I assumed no one would be up this early."

"Don't worry." Haley turned and wrapped her arms around his neck, dropping her head on his chest and deciding to postpone the drama. Right now, all she wanted to do was enjoy her boyfriend being back after so many weeks apart and not brood over anything else, period. "I'm sure she's not offended."

***

Several hours later, when the need for food overcame all other base needs—namely, sex and sleep—Haley and Scott finally emerged from her room, both completely dressed this time.

Alice, her other roommate, was in the kitchen making a sandwich, and when she spotted Scott her eyes widened. "Oh, hello! When did you get back?"

Scott waved. "Just last night."

They hugged. "Tired of all that sun and palms?" Alice joked.

Scott let Alice go and wrapped an arm around Haley's shoulders. "More missing what was at home."

"I bet." Alice nodded understandingly. "You guys want a sandwich?"

"Actually…" Scott scratched the back of his head. "I'd better go home, I barely set foot in last night. I don't even think David knows I'm back."

David.

The name sent a chilly current coursing down Haley's spine. Their text exchange from last night scrolled through her mind.

Want to grab a beer later?

It's not a date

Okay, Miss Robot

Let's do it this way

I'll be at The Plough and Stars

The Irish Pub down Mass Ave.

At around 7

If you feel like joining

You know where to find me

I'm not coming

I'll still be there

In case you change your mind

I won't

Never say never

Gotta get back to work now

See you later?

Dammit. Had he been waiting for her all night? Well, she'd told David she wasn't going, but he hadn't believed her. And the truth was she would've gone if Scott hadn't shown up unannounced on her doorstep. Haley imagined David waiting for her at the pub alone. She pictured his expression changing from cocky self-assurance when he first arrived, to bitter disappointment—*anger?*—as time passed and she didn't show…

"Hey, are you okay?" Scott asked her, frowning slightly.

"Yeah," Haley said. "Just a bit lightheaded. We skipped dinner *and* breakfast."

"Right. I got so used to skipping meals at the hospital, I don't even notice anymore."

Alice arched a brow. "Aren't doctors supposed to promote a healthy lifestyle?"

"Besides being the worst patients, they're also the worst role models for a decent life-work balance," Scott said. "All right, I'm going." He leaned in to kiss Haley on the forehead. "And you girls, don't forget to eat your vegetables," he joked.

They all laughed, and Haley walked him to the front door.

Scott paused on the threshold. "I'll call you later, okay?"

"Mmm-hmm."

He gave her a soft kiss on the lips and left. Haley shuffled back to the kitchen, climbed on a stool, and dropped her head on the bar.

"Sandwich?" Alice asked, somewhat sarcastically.

"Yes, please."

Haley heard a plate being placed next to her face and Alice climb on the stool beside her, but still, she didn't rise up.

"Okay, what's with the desperation act?" her roommate asked. "Aren't you happy Scott is back?"

"Yeah," Haley groaned, finally straightening. "Of course I am."

Alice made a "So what?" face.

"It's just that everything around us is so complicated."

Alice took a bite out of her sandwich and waited for her to elaborate.

"This morning Scott walked out of the room for like... five seconds, and he bumped into Madison."

"Oh."

"From what I gathered, he was half-naked, and she was half-naked, and she didn't take it very well. I always try not to sleep here with him. But last night..."

"It's okay, Haley." Alice nudged the plate toward her. "Eat up. Madison knows you're with Scott. Okay, bumping into him out of the blue might've been a shock, especially if she was wearing only underwear—you know how shy she is—but you have to stop the guilt tripping. You're doing nothing wrong."

Haley chewed a bite of her tuna sandwich and found it difficult to swallow.

"What else aren't you telling me?"

"David."

"Mmm… Not overjoyed his brother is back, huh? He had you all to himself for two months."

Alice's words stung a little. "What's that supposed to mean?"

"Listen, Haley, I'm not Madison, and I have no beef with David, but even a blind person could see you two got close over the summer…"

"So?"

"I don't know." Alice shrugged. "You tell me, you brought him up."

"He asked me to go out for a drink yesterday, as friends…"

"And?"

"I said I wouldn't go, but he's impossible. He told me he'd be waiting for me anyway."

"And were you going to meet him?"

Haley nodded.

"And that's when Scott showed up on your doorstep."

Haley nodded again.

"And David spent all night waiting for you in a bar… And, let me guess, you feel guilty about that, too?"

"I do. It's like wherever I turn, my relationship with Scott is hurting someone. I'm uncomfortable here because of Madison, and now it'll be horrible at his place, too, because of David."

"So David makes you uncomfortable… how?"

"Not you, too."

"Sorry?"

"First Madison, then my mother, and now you. I'm tired of people asking if I have feelings for David."

"Well, do you?"

"I just said I don't want to talk about it."

"But I think you do, and I'm the right person for the job."

"Why?"

"I'm on your side. I don't care which Williams brother you date, and I don't care if you have feelings for both. Correction, I *do* care, because you're my friend, but I don't judge. You wouldn't be the first girl who has feelings for two guys, and I'm not trying to be your moral compass, only a friend."

"Okay."

"Would it be easier if I asked questions?"

"Yep."

"Okay, let's start with the easy ones. You don't hate David anymore, right?"

Haley tried to fly back in time three months and summon up all the anger and contempt she'd felt whenever she'd thought about David... The jerk who'd treated Madison like a doormat. The lying bastard who'd made Scott accept the internship in California. But all those hard feelings had been gone for a long time.

"No."

"And you consider him a friend, at the very least."

"Uh-huh."

"But he likes you."

"It's a little more complicated than that."

"How?"

"He... might've said he's in love with me."

Alice's eyes bulged out. "What? When?"

"Over the summer. Remember the mega storm right before the term ended?"

Alice nodded.

"He told me standing under the rain in the middle of Harvard Yard."

"Romantic much?"

"*Notebook* worthy."

"And what did you say?"

"That I love his brother."

"Oh, harsh! And he...?"

"Promised he'd wait for me. For when I was ready to admit I have feelings for him, too."

"Well, I guess that brings us to the only question that matters. Do you have feelings for him?"

Haley stared at her lap, shaking her head. "I wish I could tell you 'no' and mean it. But the truth is I don't know anymore. The only thing I know for sure is I want to be with Scott."

Alice took her hands. "Well, then there's only one thing you need to do."

"What?"

"Make David understand that's where you stand, with no more room for interpretation. It'd be cruel to give him false hope. Have you been one hundred percent clear with him?"

"I—I…" Haley scrunched up her face into a dubious expression. "Ninety-five percent?"

Alice squeezed her hands, giving her a *"make sure you close that five percent gap"* stare, and Haley nodded. She'd have to talk to David as soon as possible. What a great conversation to look forward to.

Scott

Scott entered his apartment and immediately caught a whiff of an out-of-place smell that, if he had to define it, he'd name: House After a Rave Party Eau De Toilette. But it made little sense; David wasn't the type to throw house parties, and the place was too clean for a party to have happened recently, anyway.

After dropping his wallet and keys on a low cabinet, Scott moved into the kitchen to get a glass of water. Here the stench worsened, the after-party smell mixing with the distinctive funk of something rotting. A quick glance around the kitchenette, and the source of the mystery stink was easily explained.

Six empty shot glasses stood arranged in a neat row on the counter. Scott lifted one and sniffed it: *vodka*. So, apparently, his brain associated vodka with house parties. That made sense. But the weirdest discovery was a bag of frozen peas left unopened to melt under the direct sunlight filtering in through the window.

Scott picked the bag up, which went all limp and mushy in his hand, and he had to suppress a gagging reflex as he sealed it inside several trash bags. He closed each up with three or four tight knots to prevent the stink from coming out and dropped the bundle into the bin. He'd take it downstairs later.

What the hell had happened here? Why would David get drunk on vodka and leave a bag of frozen peas to rot on the counter? Sometimes his brother was really mysterious.

After opening the window to let fresh air in, he stacked up the tiny glasses and dropped them in the sink, where he found an empty bottle of vodka. Yeah, David must've had quite a night. Shrugging, he threw the bottle into the glass bin, rinsed the glasses, and put them in the dishwasher. Then he decided he'd better check on his brother.

David's door was ajar, and Scott approached cautiously. If David didn't know he was back, he could have a girl in there. Why use *six* shot glasses unless he was playing some sort of game? David wouldn't be drinking that much on his own, would he? Six vodka shots seemed a bit over the top even for him. But a quick peek inside David's room confirmed that they were alone in the house.

His brother was lying on the bed, face down and fully clothed—white T-shirt, jeans, white sneakers—very much with the air of someone who had drunk half a bottle of vodka on his own the previous night.

He lay so still that Scott wondered if he was breathing. A soft poke to David's side produced a loud snore, confirming he was alive. Scott shook his head. *What the hell, bro?* He seriously considered leaving David "as is," but then he'd just be bothered by the image of his brother's poor bedding situation.

So, with a sigh, Scott decided to undress him using a bottom-up approach, starting with the shoes. Mid-disrobing, he noticed the swollen, caked-in-dried-blood knuckles of David's left hand. Had he been in a fight? With whom? Scott shook his head and continued rolling David left and right to remove his clothes. When he had him in his boxer briefs and T-shirt, his brother finally stirred awake.

"Scotty," David said with a slur. "Welcome home, brother."

Scott struggled with David's limbs to tuck him under the sheets. "Missed me?" he asked sarcastically.

"Threw a party in your honor last night."

"Really?"

"Yep, I had so much fun."

"I see," Scott said, playing along. David was too delirious right now to be making any sense. "How about I get you an aspirin?"

"Stop being so fucking nice," David said, angry all of a sudden.

His brother struggled to straighten up, but as soon as he managed to right himself into a sitting position, he must've become dizzy because he collapsed back on the pillow.

"I don't feel so good," David concluded.

No shit, Scott thought.

"Wait here," he said. "I'm gonna get you that aspirin and something to clean the hand."

Without waiting for a reply, Scott moved into the bathroom, took the pills and disinfectant out of the cabinet above the sink, and returned to the kitchen to get a glass of water. Before heading back to David's room, he grabbed his phone out of his pocket and dialed Haley's number.

Haley

"Miss me already?" Haley said, picking up the phone.

"Yeah, of course," Scott said.

"But that's not why you called."

"No, it's that… I don't think it's a good idea for you to come here tonight. I know I just got back, but—"

"Why?" Haley asked, her stomach contracting with a sneaking suspicion.

"It's David." Scott sounded worried. "I've never seen him like this."

The knot in Haley's guts tightened. "Like what?"

"He's stinking drunk, and he's babbling about throwing me a 'welcome home' party last night. Totally insane. All I can tell you is that I found an empty bottle of vodka in the sink and David passed out on his bed. I think he got into a fight with someone."

Haley swallowed. Oh gosh, it sounded worse than she'd thought. If David had known Scott was back, he'd also have known why she'd stood him up last night.

"In a fight?" Haley asked. "Why would you say that?"

"Because his right hand looks like he's put it through a meat-grinder."

"Oh."

Haley couldn't explain the injury. She only hoped David hadn't done anything stupid.

"Listen," Scott continued. "I'd better go check on him, but you stay home. He's already moody enough. One second he's all peace and love, and the next he gets angry for no reason. David's not a very good drunk."

No kidding.

"Okay," Haley agreed. "I'll see you tomorrow, then?"

"Yeah, I'll call you when I wake up. Love you. Bye."

"Bye."

As Haley hung up, the front door opened and Madison walked in.

Oh, hell… let's jump from one broken heart right onto the next…

"Hi," her roommate said, smiling.

Not the reaction Haley had expected.

"Hey?"

"So big surprise last night, huh?"

Madison was acting as if she didn't care at all. She was all sparkly eyes and bright smiles, making Haley's chest surge with gratitude. Madison really was the best friend in the world. If their parts were reversed, Haley wasn't sure she'd be able to be so gracious.

"Yeah." Haley finally allowed herself a tentative smile. "Heard you had a little surprise yourself this morning. I'm sorry, I—"

"Oh, that… Pffff…" Madison waved her off and turned to hang her bag on the rack behind the door. "I'll admit I wasn't expecting to run into Scott…" Madison kept fidgeting with the bag a while longer than necessary. *To hide her face while she talked?* "It was… weird. Didn't expect a boy in here. I was half asleep and probably made no sense."

Madison turned at last, pink cheeks bright with embarrassment, but softened by a no-big-deal smile.

"So you're not upset?" Haley asked.

"No. Nooo. I mean, it *was* awkward…" She shrugged. "But that's it."

Madison's eyes sent Haley a clear message that her friend probably wasn't able to express in words—a silent plea of *"Can we pretend this never happened and that I'm not in love with your boyfriend?"*

Haley nodded, agreeing to Madison's unspoken request. Deciding to change the subject, she said, "Hey, what are you doing tonight?"

"No plans yet. There's a book presentation at a bookstore downtown I'd like to see, but I don't feel like going all the way to Boston alone."

"Why don't we go together? We can hit the event and then stop for a bite somewhere."

"Are you sure?" Madison looked hesitant. "Don't you want to be with Scott?"

"Scott's having David problems."

"David problems?" Madison frowned. "Already?"

"Uh-huh. Let's get ready first, and then I'll tell you everything?"

"All right. Meet here in twenty?"

"Yeah." Haley pulled Madison into a hug and added, "Thank you."

"For what?"

"For being the best friend in the world." Haley held her tighter.

Madison squeezed hard, too, and in that simple gesture, they shared another million unspoken words.

***

By the next morning, Haley was dying to see Scott and itching to learn if David had pulled any more drunken stunts. She woke up way earlier than usual for a non-school day and managed not to call Scott right away. For the better part of the morning, she kept herself busy with mundane tasks she usually postponed until they became super urgent. She sorted the alarming pile of both dirty laundry—*to wash*—and clean laundry—*to put back in the closet*—she had accumulated before visiting her parents, then cleaned her room and emptied the suitcase she hadn't had a chance to unpack yet. She figured she might as well get all those things sorted before school started and she got too busy.

But when by eleven-thirty Scott still hadn't called, Haley's patience had officially run out. Her bedroom was cleaner than when she'd first moved in, and she'd even done the kitchen and bathroom. With no more housekeeping distractions available, she grabbed her phone and called her boyfriend.

Scott picked up after several rings, his voice sounding all groggy with sleep. "Morning."

"Morning?" Haley said jokingly. "It's almost noon."

"Hey, I'm jet-lagged."

"You were in California, not Japan."

"Still, it's only barely past breakfast time for me."

"Luckily for you, I love brunch. Want to grab a bite together?"

"Sure."

"Should we go out or stay in? I mean… is everything okay over there? Is David okay?"

"Mmm… I have no idea, I'm still in bed. Hold on. Let me check."

Rustling, scuffing noises cracked out of the speaker as he got out of bed. Then the sound of a door opening, footsteps, another door, footsteps again… and, finally, silence.

"He's gone," Scott announced.

"Gone? Where?"

"To work? His internship shouldn't be over yet."

Haley had no trouble believing that. From the way his boss had made David slave over work assignments every single weekend for the past two months, it made sense they wouldn't let him off until the very last day of summer break.

"Is he going to be okay?"

"I suppose. He slept all of yesterday and I made him drink two bottles of Gatorade, so he should be fine. Except for that hand, maybe."

Haley hoped so. For now, physically "well enough to go to work" was all she wanted to hear about David; she still wasn't ready to investigate his bruised ego, or worse, broken heart.

"So what do you want to do for lunch?" she asked. "Should I come over?"

Haley was already warming up to the idea of an empty house and Scott all to herself, when he said, "Why don't we do something outside? I've spent the last two months locked in a hospital with artificial air and artificial lights. I could use a day outdoors."

"You want to go hiking or something?" Haley asked, unconvinced.

The great outdoors weren't exactly her thing.

"How about the beach?"

"The beach? You've turned surfer boy on me. Err… you do realize we're in Boston, right? Not exactly famous for its beaches."

"Come on, who cares? Yesterday I looked up a few spots we can check out. I just want to spend a few hours with you, relaxing in the sun and doing nothing all day. No brothers, no roommates… only me and you."

"Well, when you put it like that." A wide smile spread on Haley's lips. "Give me half an hour."

"Okay, come here when you're ready. My place is closer, and we have to take the Red Line at Central."

"I'll buzz you when I get there."

***

The trip to the beach turned out to be longer and sweatier than Haley would've liked. It took them about forty-five minutes and one T line change to get to Revere Beach. But nothing could dampen her good

442

mood. Scott was here, they were together, so who cared where they went or what they did?

As expected, the beach was nothing special—a thin strip of sand just off the road, with nondescript concrete buildings in the background. But at least the ocean was blue, and the place brimmed full of people. The waterfront closer to the road had been fenced off to make space for a sand sculpting competition. Different teams of four to six people buzzed around with various tools, busy building impressive sand structures of sea monsters, buildings, ships, people, and many others. Food trucks lined the back of the fenced area, the smoke drifting up from their grills and permeating the air with the delicious aroma of smoked meat. And off in a corner, at the end of the sculpture display, a band was playing live on a stage.

Haley and Scott walked by the various sculptures, admiring the works of art and marveling at the level of detail the artists were able to impress on the sand. When they reached the final sculpture, a mermaid sitting in an open shell, they bought a pair of Chicago-style hot dogs and found a spot at the edge of the crowd to settle down on the beach and eat with more privacy.

"Mmm, so good," Haley said after her first bite. She eyed the overflowing toppings and sauces incredulously. "I mean, it should be disgusting, but it's delicious."

Scott laughed. "It really should be disgusting."

Haley licked her fingertips after finishing the last bite. She watched Scott shove the rest of the hot dog into his mouth and then wipe his hands with a napkin. The early afternoon sun made his hair shine blonder than ever; he'd let it grow over the summer, and now an unruly lock kept falling on his forehead. He pushed it behind his ear, only for it to fall back after a second. His sunglasses were too dark to see his eyes, but his sexy smile more than compensated. It made Haley wish they were alone.

"What?" he asked, probably sensing her scrutiny.

"It's nice, you know? Being here and doing nothing with you. I missed that."

"I missed it, too. I'm sorry for the disappearing act. I know I haven't been the most present boyfriend this summer, not even over the phone…"

"Stop." Haley leaned forward. "We already talked about it. Working with the best neurosurgeon in the country was too good an opportunity to pass. You don't have to feel guilty for going. Plus, it's all in the past now. Yeah, it's been a tough two months, but we're here now. Together. And we don't need to worry about being apart. We only have to enjoy each other."

"I plan to do a lot of enjoying," Scott joked.

Haley smirked. "You can start by helping me with the sunscreen." She fished a bottle of lotion out of her beach bag and handed it to him. "Or I might turn into a lobster." The skin on her shoulders was already starting to burn.

She hopped on Scott's towel and sat in front of him, facing away toward the ocean. Haley pulled her hair up to give him better access, shivering when the lotion landed cold on her back. The shuddering passed as soon as Scott's warm hands started kneading it into her skin, leaving Haley free to enjoy the gentle massage.

When Scott stopped, she asked, "Are you sure you got all the spots? UV protection is really important."

"UV protection, or getting a free massage?"

Haley tilted her head over her shoulder to look at him. "Both."

"Great, since it's my turn now."

Haley turned completely, kneeling in front of him. "I love you," she whispered and leaned in to give him a soft peck on the lips. "I'm so happy you came back early."

"Me, too."

He hooked his hands on her hips and pulled her closer for a more thorough kiss. Mmm… if only summer could last a little longer…

***

Later that night, they stopped outside Scott's building to say goodbye.

"Don't go," he pleaded, holding her hands.

"I'm full of sand and I need a shower."

"You can shower here."

"But I don't have any clean clothes."

"So borrow something from me. You steal my clothes all the time, anyway."

Haley was about to give in when an ominous thought popped into her head. "Is David home?"

The other Williams brother had remained safely out of her mind all day, making her forget all about the hard conversation she needed to have with him, and the subsequent unavoidable hurt feelings. But now the sudden, real prospect of bumping into him was just too upsetting. Today had been perfect, and Haley wanted to remember it like that. No drama. No fights.

Scott gazed at the parking lot across the street. "His truck isn't here. He must be gone."

Well… if David wasn't at home…

"Okay," Haley agreed with a bright smile.

Inside Scott's house, they showered together and Haley borrowed one of his T-shirts to put on afterward. On her, it basically looked like a mini-dress. As underwear, she used a spare bikini and left her feet bare; no risk of catching a cold. They ordered a pepperoni pizza for dinner, watched a movie, and went to bed early, both tired after a long day at the beach. If she had to relive only one day for all of eternity, this would be the one she chose. As Haley fell asleep cuddled in Scott's arms, the notion that David had not yet come home briefly crossed her mind, only to be dismissed at once. Nothing had spoiled the best day of summer so far, and she wouldn't let anything ruin it now.

When she batted her eyes open next, daylight already filtered through the blinds. Her throat felt like dry earth left cracking under the sun. The pepperoni pizza had been super salty.

Without paying much attention to where she was or what she was wearing, Haley, still half asleep, lifted the arm Scott had wrapped over her chest and wriggled off the bed to go grab a glass of water.

She was heading for the fridge when a voice startled her.

"Good morning, Sunshine."

David's voice.

Clad in a dark suit, he sat at the kitchen bar eating cereal out of a bowl. His spoon-wielding hand was wrapped in white gauze and caught Haley's attention for a second before she lifted her gaze to meet his icy blue stare. He'd stopped eating and was eyeing her with an unreadable expression. Anger? Hurt? Scorn? All three?

Whatever emotion his face showed, the use of the wrong nickname hit Haley like a slap, jerking her fully awake at once. He hadn't called her Sunshine in months, and, okay, she'd already guessed he wouldn't be calling her Miss Robot anymore, not with Scott back, but she'd hoped they could've settled on a neutral 'Haley.'

Apparently not.

"David. Hi."

He gave her one last appraising look, then sneered. "I have to say… your taste in jewelry is much better than your taste in clothes."

Embarrassed by the comment, Haley lowered her gaze to the hem of the long T-shirt—*Scott's T-shirt*—she was wearing, which reached just above her knees. On reflex, she closed one hand around the pendant dangling from her neck. David's birthday present to her. Since he'd given it to her two weeks ago, she hadn't taken it off once.

"Don't be like that," she pleaded.

His eyes flashed. "Be like what? I merely criticized your fashion sense, or lack of thereof—"

"It's not that, David, and you know it. You're back to acting like a dick for no reason. We've gotten along all summer. Why can't you—"

"Things change," he interrupted.

"Nothing has changed. Scott is back, like you knew he would always be, and we're together. No news there."

"Sorry I'm ruining your reunion honeymoon with my bad mood."

"Stop the jerk act… This is not the real you."

"No? Why?" He dropped the bowl and spoon down on the counter and walked toward her. "Because I was nice to you a couple of times? Who said that wasn't the act? I'm only making it easier for you, *Sunshine.* Am I not?"

Such venom spilled from his words that tears welled in Haley's eyes. "Don't do this, David, don't be like this. I thought we could be friends?"

"Friends?" David let out a bitter, mocking laugh. "No, Haley, sorry… I can't be your friend."

"So what was this summer for you? A joke?"

"I'd call it more a mistake."

"Why?"

"I can't be in your life, not as a *friend.*" David pointed at Scott's half-open door. "With him gone, I could pretend… hope… fool myself. But now… now, it's too damn hard."

"But David—"

"Why? Why would you even want to be my friend?"

"Because I care about you."

"Well, Haley, my feelings run a bit deeper, so you see how that might be a problem…"

"So you'd rather cut me off completely."

"Don't you understand?" Eyes flaring, he took another step toward her. "I can't see you with him. It kills me to know you're here, just one step away, but a whole universe apart. I don't want to hear your voice coming from under his door at night, or talk to you the next morning." He gave the T-shirt another seething glare. "Right now I can't even stand to look at you wearing his clothes… and I sure as hell don't want to be your friend."

Haley swallowed, lips trembling. "If that's how you feel. Do what's best for you."

"I will. I'm not the one with a problem admitting my real feelings."

Still glowering, David turned on his heel and marched out of the apartment, slamming the door shut behind him. Haley stood still, alone in the middle of the living room. She was breathing heavily, more shaken than she'd like to admit, and with a tightening in her chest that was hard to ignore.

It's better this way, her rational self tried to console her. *You can't have your cake and eat it, too.*

It wasn't fair to ask David to be her friend when he was in love with her. To stand by while she continued on her merry relationship with his brother. No, it wasn't fair. But the prospect of David being a stranger did nothing to lift Haley's mood.

And this mess was all his fault, anyway. He was the one having a sudden change of heart, after going above and beyond to become her friend over the summer. He had made her see his good, kind side, his devil-may-care personality… a taste of freedom. And now he couldn't just take it back. Nothing had changed; Scott had always been in the picture. David had always known… *even when we pretended it was just the two of us…*

With shaking hands, Haley grabbed a glass from the cabinet and filled it under the tap. The long, full gulps she swallowed did nothing to help her heartbeat slow down to normal. Seeing David so hurt had crushed her. Or maybe she was hurting, too, at the unwelcome awareness of having lost him for good.

Whatever the reason for the smoldering pain in her chest, one thing was clear: yesterday's carefree mood was already a distant memory. It seemed like whenever she and Scott saw each other—no matter where, her house, his house, wherever—someone got hurt. And the constant guilt kept on wearing Haley down.

Before going back into Scott's room, she made a quick dash into the bathroom to splash a handful of cold water on her face, hoping to clear the clouds around her mind. But as she climbed back into bed next to her boyfriend, she was still unsettled. Thank goodness he still slept like a baby. If he'd heard even a snippet of her conversation with David...

How could I ever explain it to you?

As she lay in bed, staring at the ceiling and seeing only a pair of wounded blue eyes staring right back, Haley's phone vibrated on the nightstand. She picked it up, finding a series of texts from Alice.

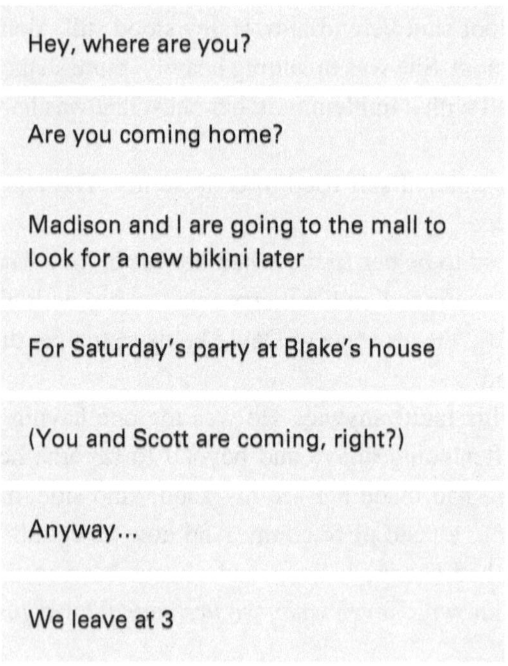

Haley stared at the screen for a few seconds. What better distraction than a trip to the mall and an afternoon of mind-numbing shopping with her best friends?

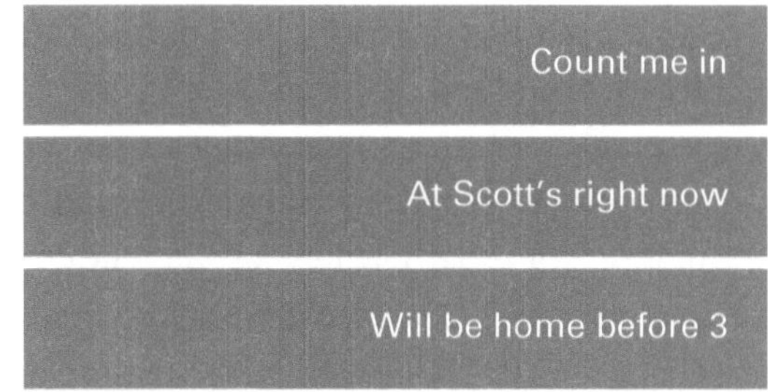

She put the phone back on the bedside table and snuggled in closer to Scott. She kissed his cheek while he still slept, dropping her head on his chest afterward and closing her eyes.

Will it always be so hard?

***

"Black or white?" Madison asked, holding up two identical bikinis, save for the color.

"Isn't the white one transparent?" Haley asked.

Madison stretched her hand inside the fabric to check if it was see-through. "Doesn't seem so."

"What about when it's wet?"

"Oh." Madison's face fell. "You're right."

She put both hangers back in place.

"How about a print?" Alice suggested, pulling out a gorgeous top. Asymmetrical, ruffled, with a trim made of mini pompoms. The fabric was in a pale pink shade with a budding flowers print.

"Wow." Madison's eyes widened; the boho-chic in her clearly couldn't resist. "This one's amazing. I'll try it on. Does it have a bottom, too?"

"Here." Alice handed her both pieces.

"You two pick one and join me in the fitting rooms. I want your opinion before I decide."

"Yes, boss," Alice joked. "You go ahead, we'll be right there."

Alice waited a while after Madison was gone before she spoke again. "See something you like?"

"I'm going with black," Haley stated.

"Like your mood?"

Haley's head snapped toward her friend.

"Yeah, it's that obvious," Alice confirmed. She took the top Haley had in her hands and switched it for another one. "If you have to go with black, at least try for an interesting shape."

The new top Alice had given her was a faux-wrap, cold-shoulder bikini top. Not exactly Haley's style, but what the hell. She already had a ton of plain, monochromatic black swimsuits, so if she had to spend the money she might as well mix things up a little.

"You make me live dangerously," Haley joked, selecting a pair of slips to match the top.

"And are you really making me ask?"

"Ask what?"

"The reason for the black mood."

Haley winced. "I saw David this morning. I walked into him coming out of Scott's room while wearing only one of his brother's T-shirts. He…"

"Was a douche?"

"He tried, but he really couldn't keep it up. In the end, I think he was just hurt."

Alice sighed. "At least now he can move on."

"Yeah, but it's never nice to cause someone pain."

"I know." Hands full of bikinis, Alice gave her a quick hug. Then, pulling back, she asked, "Nude or navy?"

Haley was glad Alice wasn't pressing the David topic; the less she thought about him, the better. She pointed to the nude halter bikini top with a high crochet neck. "When Jack sees you wearing that, he's going to pass out."

Alice put back the navy one and winked. "Perfect."

"What took you so long?" Madison complained, when they joined her in the fitting rooms.

She'd already changed into her swimsuit, and Haley honestly didn't get how her friend could be so insecure around guys. At five-foot-ten, not only was she statuesque, she simply was drop-dead gorgeous with her long, curly hair and big blue eyes.

"What do you think?" she asked, biting her lower lip.

"Buy," Alice said.

"Definitely buy," Haley confirmed.

Madison's entire face brightened up with a smile, the self-doubt gone.

"Yeah, I love it, too. Let me see yours…"

* * *

They all ended up buying the pieces they'd tried on, and by Saturday morning Haley had to confess that some of her roommates' enthusiasm for this end-of-summer party had finally infected her. Everyone had been blabbing nonstop about how epic the party was going to be for weeks. The host, Blake Donovan, was on the basketball team with Jack and Scott, and had a huge house in the country—currently parents-free—with a massive pool and, apparently, could afford to throw an unforgettable party. Madison had proclaimed it'd be Gatsby-worthy, and even Alice had been talking about little else for the past few days. Haley didn't see what the big deal was; it sounded like any other house party, only fancier. But she was game to spend a day with her boyfriend and all their friends lounging by the pool, sipping cocktails—it was rumored Blake had hired a professional barman—and eating burgers right off the grill.

"Does Scott need a ride, too?" Madison asked. She was driving Haley, Alice, and Jack in her SUV.

"No, he's carpooling with David."

"So they're finally cool with each other?"

Haley shrugged. "Seems that way."

Haley actually had no idea if the brothers were cool. She hadn't asked Scott, and she sure as hell hadn't asked David. But from the way Scott had talked about his interactions with his brother since he'd gotten home, it sounded as if David hadn't been a bitch to him.

Oh, no. He's saving all his complaints for me.

Haley hoped Blake's house was big enough for her and David to be able to politely ignore each other. Just like old times… before he'd told her about their in-incognito kiss, before he'd forced her to like him, before he'd confessed he was in love with her.

Aaaaaaand… let's not think about that.

Clad in their brand-new bikinis and matching cover-ups, all three roommates walked out of their apartment to go meet Jack downstairs. It was only ten in the morning, but the party was supposed to last all day and maybe part of the night as well. So they'd timed it to get there early, but hopefully not first.

451

Twenty minutes later, Madison, following the car GPS, turned into a private alley and pulled up in front of an impressive building. A first look at Blake's country place confirmed that at least some of the buzz surrounding the party had been justified.

"I thought your country house was big," Alice said to Madison, mirroring Haley's awe at the size of Blake's house—*mansion, palace really.* "But compared to this, it looks like a studio flat."

"That's not *my* house," Madison said pointedly.

"Shall we go in?" Haley interrupted them.

"Yeah, let's go," Jack said.

The main door stood wide open—Blake wasn't that concerned with security, apparently—and they followed the instructions of a sign stuck to the door that read:

THIS WAY

$$\rightarrow$$

Underneath, a giant arrow pointed to the French doors across the room. The entrance hall was mostly empty space, except for a corridor made of two rows of red-rope stanchions that forced them to follow a straight path ahead. To either side of the stanchions were an open kitchen with a huge island and a dining space on one side, and a modern, elegant living room on the other. It was easy to see why Blake would be worried about a bunch of drunk college kids wreaking havoc in here.

When they reached the French doors, there was another sign stuck on the glass.

IMPORTANT: CLOSE ME ONCE YOU'RE OUT!

They exited and did as instructed, closing the doors behind them, only to find another sign on the other side.

PARTY'S OUTSIDE. YOU DON'T NEED TO GET IN HERE.

THERE'S A BATHROOM BY THE POOL HOUSE

Oh, so there was a pool house, too?

To reach the actual pool, they had to walk down a flight of steps, pass an outside kitchen/dining area with a barbeque and two massive wrought iron tables complete with white sunshades, and cross a wide stretch of perfectly even green lawn. Behind the barbeque, a guy in a cook uniform was already busy setting up the grilling station.

They all walked down the stairs open-mouthed, admiring how the lower level of the garden opened on the Olympic-size swimming pool, attached Jacuzzi, cabana-style pool bar, and the pool house in the background. The whole pool area was surrounded by wooden chaise lounges with thick, plush padding, two roundish daybeds, and a row of white umbrellas.

Damn!

"I call dibs on the daybed," Haley yelled, running there.

She jumped in the center of the spacious mattress and, turning around, she let herself fall on the mound of pillows that formed the backrest. Alice and Jack settled their things on a double chaise lounge on her left and Madison took a single one on her right. Now all that was missing was a cocktail in her hand and Scott by her side.

Still no sign of him. Haley checked her phone and promptly found a text.

We're running late

David had to drop by the office to turn in
his last work assignment

We'll be there in an hour or so

Whoa, investment banking really gave no one a break. Had David been up all night working? Haley wondered if she could've helped him speed up the process with her programming like she used to, or if they'd stuck him with one of those stupid analog projects. A pang of sadness tugged at her chest; she had no clue, and whatever David did was off-limits to her now. She'd only ever be able to get second-hand info from Scott on what was going on with his brother. But she had to get used to the idea they weren't friends anymore. They weren't anything at all.

Time for that drink.

As if on cue, Jack announced, "I'm going to the bar. What do you girls want?"

Madison straightened up in her chair and shaded her eyes to check out the bar. "Do you think the guy in the cabana is a real barman? He looks professional enough."

Everyone followed her gaze.

Jack shrugged. "I guess so."

"So he can mix up anything we want?"

"I can ask, but give me a back-up just in case."

"I'll take a Mai Tai, but only if they grind the ice. Otherwise, make it a vodka tonic," Madison said. Then, probably noticing that she'd just sounded a tiny bit "spoiled princess," she blushed and added, "Please?"

"No problem." Jack nodded and turned to Haley. "You?"

"A vodka martini, stirred not shaken, but only if they have olives. Otherwise..." She paused, pretending to think, but watching the dismayed expression on Jack's face, she quickly added, "Relax, I'm joking! Vodka whatever is good."

Jack smiled. "One blended Mai Tai, or vodka tonic; one vodka whatever; and you, babe?"

"Just a soda," Alice said. "I don't feel like drinking yet."

"Are you sure?" Jack asked, worried. "Are you okay?"

"Yeah, just pacing myself."

"All right, I'll be right back."

Haley waited for him to be out of earshot before asking. "Why aren't you drinking? Are you pregnant?"

"Oh my gosh, noooooooooo!" Alice shouted. "What the hell, Haley?"

"Sorry, but you've been blabbing about this party for too long to come here and not be drinking... What's up?"

"I got my period this morning, and the cramps were killing me, so I took a couple of painkillers. The instructions said not to drink alcohol while taking the pills, so I have to wait for a few hours."

"Oh, I'm sorry. Are you okay now?"

Alice flashed her a sly smile. "The drugs worked like a charm."

"Why didn't you tell Jack?" Madison asked.

"Because then he'd worry about me all day and ask me how I'm doing every five seconds, and I want him to have fun today."

"You're so sweet. Can I borrow you as my girlfriend?"

Alice blew Madison a kiss. "Sorry, I'm taken."

"Speaking of bad drinking habits," Haley said. "We shouldn't drink on an empty stomach, and it smells like the grill is operational. I'm getting a burger. You guys want one?"

They both said yes.

"Bacon, cheese, BBQ sauce?"

Alice nodded, while Madison said, "No bacon for me, thanks."

Haley couldn't resist making a little fun of her friend. "Is any cheese okay, or should I ask for a specific one?"

Nonplussed, Madison answered, "I prefer Swiss, but any kind is fine, really."

Haley tried to keep a straight face but cracked when Alice started chuckling.

Madison stared at them. "Why? What did I say?"

"Nothing, Miss 'I'll Take a Mai Tai But Only If They Grind the Ice.'"

"But the Mai Tai sucks if the ice isn't blended."

"Sure it does." Haley rolled her eyes. "I'll be right back."

Haley could still hear Madison complain as she walked away.

"I'm not posh, am I?" her friend asked Alice.

"No, honey. But sometimes you do sound a bit high society."

Whatever Madison said back, Haley was too far away to hear.

Two burgers, one vodka whatever, and a Mai Tai—because it turned out they *did* grind the ice and the blended Mai Tai was really delicious—later, Scott finally arrived.

Even from a distance, he and David were hard to miss. True, there were plenty of tall dudes around since half the invitees were on the basketball team, but the Williams brother had that special magnetism about them. Standing there on top of the steps, searching the crowd with their eyes, they looked like the yin and yang of Haley's heart. Scott, with his summer-blond hair, dressed in a dark blue tank top and trunks, and David, in white head-to-toe with his mop of I've-just-rolled-out-of-bed midnight-black hair.

Haley stretched up on the mattress, waving her arms in the air for a few seconds before Scott spotted them and both the Williamses walked toward them. Haley watched David approach, trying to fathom how he'd behave today. He had dark shades on, and the part of his face that was visible—nose and mouth—gave nothing away. When he reached the daybed, he greeted them with a curt, "Ladies." Then he gave Jack a quick nod and turned on his heel, saying, "I need a drink."

So it was a "pretend Haley doesn't exist" kind of day. Whatever.

She decided to concentrate on the brother who didn't come with a side of grouchy pie.

Haley shuffled onto the bed to make room for Scott and patted the mattress. "Come here."

He hopped on and pressed her against the pillows to give her the best "Hi, there" kiss, making all thoughts of David fly out of her head.

Pushing back, Scott smiled down at her. "What did I miss?"

"Not much. Just the best free cocktails and food of your life."

"Mmm, sounds like I have a lot of catching up to do. What are you all drinking?"

"Mai Tais," Haley explained. She was already tipsy. "Blended, not with the chunky ice."

Madison groaned from her chaise. "You'll never let me live that down, will you?"

"Sorry, no."

Scott frowned at Haley. "You prefer the ice cubes?"

"Oh, no. If it weren't for Madison here, I'd still be drinking sorry vodka whatevers."

"And how many did you have?" Scott asked, amused.

Haley took his hand and hopped off the bed, pulling him with her. "Come with me to the bar. It'll all make sense after you've had a few."

They didn't run into David at the cabana or back at their little corner of the garden. For a while, it seemed like the older Williams brother had disappeared into thin air. But as quickly as he'd vanished, David reappeared an hour later, only to keep his "ignore Haley at all costs" attitude live.

He sat on Madison's chaise. "Blondie," David said matter-of-factly. "We need to talk."

"Okay. Talk," Madison said.

"You're sadly out of a drink, and this conversation needs to be alcohol-supported. Can I offer you anything?"

"It's an open bar party."

"Well, in that case"—he stood up and offered her a hand—"let's go take advantage."

Only half-reluctantly, Madison took his hand and followed him toward the bar/cabana on the other side of the pool.

Haley made a conscious effort not to watch them, not to notice the way Madison seemed unable to keep a straight face at whatever David was saying. Weren't those two supposed to not be on talking terms? Whenever Haley saw them together, something stirred in the pit of her stomach. A snake of many coils: truths too hard to face, emotions too twisted to follow, and thoughts too dark to acknowledge.

Pretending not to look wasn't really helping; she needed to block David out of her life completely. She fished a bottle of sun lotion out of her bag and physically turned her back on Madison and David, asking Scott to help her reapply the sunscreen. As Scott's hands massaged the tension out of her shoulders, Haley finally relaxed.

Madison

Madison waited until they reached the other side of the pool to ask, "What do you want?"

"Hey, hold back on the hostility. I come in peace."

"Really?"

"I'd ask what's with the terrible mood…" David took a sip from his transparent plastic cup. "But I feel your pain, Blondie, quite literally."

A little smile forced itself on Madison's lips. "At least the brooding look suits you."

"Whoa, a compliment, Blondie? Careful there, I might think you're warming up to me again."

"Don't go getting a big head. I've only removed you from the undesirable number one spot."

"And who have I been replaced with?"

Involuntarily, Madison's eyes shifted toward Haley and Scott. They were talking as he massaged sunscreen on her back. Just as Madison looked over, Scott pressed a kiss to her friend's neck. Haley laughed and turned to kiss him full on the lips.

David followed her gaze. "Ah! The happy couple. Revolting, I know. So I've asked you here because I have a proposition for you."

"Last time you propositioned me, it didn't end so well."

"Oh, come on, it wasn't all bad, was it?"

Madison scowled.

"Anyway, this one is a much more straightforward endeavor."

Madison cocked her head and relaxed her frown, shooting David a skeptical look she hoped would read as: *I have reservations, but I'm listening.*

David caught the message. "I was thinking," he said. "Since we're partners in suffering, and we're at a party with plenty of free booze, what do you say we get absolutely trashed together?"

"I drove here."

"So did I, but Blake said I can crash in one of the guest rooms."

"Well, that solves *your* DUI problem."

"You can crash with me."

Madison crossed her arms over her chest and turned to study him. "David, what kind of game are you playing?"

"No game. I'm looking for a partner in crime. I'm not hitting on you, or proposing we do something unbecoming." He smiled wickedly. "I'm only asking if you'd like to drown your sorrows in alcohol with me. It's always sad to be a lonely drunk."

"And it's better to be a couple of drunks?"

David made a silly face. "Much, much better."

"And what about the others? We both had passengers."

"Blondie, let me tell you a secret…" He leaned in closer and whispered in her ear, "It's about time you did what's best for yourself."

Madison smiled. "You'd be a wonderful life coach, if only you weren't proposing I get shit-faced."

"Well, if you prefer to just stand here and enjoy the show…" David tilted his head in the general direction of Scott and Haley suggestively. Madison's eyes followed, and a quick glance was enough to make her stomach churn. "Be my guest."

David made to move away, but Madison grabbed him by the arm. "Wait!" If she had to endure the stomach sickness, she should at least have fun in the process. The others could find another ride home, or call an Uber. Or better yet, she'd lend them her car and return home with David the next day. Alice wasn't drinking, anyway. And Madison didn't have to babysit them. "I've changed my mind. I want to get drunk."

"Now we're talking." David smiled his signature lopsided smile and offered her his hand, asking, "What's your poison?"

Madison took his proffered hand. "Blended Mai Tai. They make the best ones here."

"Fine taste, Blondie…" David linked their arms together and steered her toward the pool bar. "You never cease to surprise me."

David ordered their drinks, and after passing Madison her Mai Tai, he raised his glass. "What should we toast to?"

"Why do you ask me?"

"You're the poet."

"Oh, so you've finally warmed up to the 'accursed and tormented soul' lifestyle?"

"Sometimes the heart leaves you no choice."

"All right," Madison said. Then she took a deep breath and put on a mock-serious expression. "It is the hour to be drunken!" she proclaimed in a solemn tone. "To escape being the martyred slaves of time, be ceaselessly drunk. On rum, on poetry, or on unrequited love, as you wish. But be drunk."

David looked at her, speechless for a second. "And you came up with that handy piece of depressing poetry on the spot?"

"No." Madison beamed at him. "It's Baudelaire—reinterpreted, of course."

"Well…" David bumped his cup into hers. "To whatever you just said."

He took a long sip and so did Madison, relishing the cool taste. The danger with Mai Tais was that they went down so smoothly; the orange juice made them fresh, and the sugar disguised the rum all too well. Madison soon lost count of how many they'd ordered—but the barman sure seemed to be awfully familiar with them by now.

Halfway through their umpteenth Mai Tai and borrowed-from-dead-poets toasts, angry shouts distracted them from their drunken mission. Two dudes who looked even more wasted than they did appeared about to start a fight near the pool, just a few feet away from Haley and Scott's daybed. A tall, bulky guy with blond hair was arguing with another shorter, but equally bulky, brown-haired guy. Chests puffed out, brows set in menacing frowns, they yelled insults at each other. The blond guy was bare-chested, while the shorter guy wore a ridiculous Hawaiian shirt.

Each guy had two or three dudes standing behind them, ready to intervene if the fight got serious. Madison didn't recognize any of them; there were far too many people at the party to know everyone.

Turning back to David, she asked, "Did you know Blake had so many D-bag friends?"

David shook his head. "I doubt half the people here are even his friends, but I don't care if a couple of losers want to beat the hell out of each other. We can just sit back and enjoy the show."

A loud crashing sound made Madison look back to the scene. It appeared that Tall Guy had pushed Short Guy into a chair that had capsized, and now Short Guy was returning the favor. Tall Guy stumbled backward, losing his footing. As he flung his arms out in a desperate attempt to stay upright, he sent the entire contents of his glass spilling upward in a wide arc.

Unfortunately, the arc trajectory ended right on top of Haley. She let out a loud screech and jumped up from the lounger, wiping the sticky liquid from her body as well as she could with her hands.

In a matter of seconds, Scott was on his feet and marching purposefully toward the now full-fledged brawl—the friends of Short and Tall Guy had joined in the scuffle, pushing each other around and making everyone around them flee. Everyone except Scott, who was almost on them.

"Unless," David sighed, "my brother decides to play the hero and enters the melee, in which case..." He dropped his glass on the bar. "I have to help him defend the family's honor."

Haley was now trying to convince Scott to give up his quest, shouting at him to come back, that she only needed a quick shower. But Scott seemed deaf to her pleas. Of course, he would be the knight in shiny armor for the girl he loved.

Pity that's not me.

David seemed to have a less chivalrous assessment of the situation. "What a fool," he said, pushing off the bar.

In the time it took David to walk from the cabana to the pool, Scott reached Tall Guy—who, tall as he might be, was still three or four inches shorter than either Williams brother.

The brawl was still roaring, but Not So Tall Guy had been pushed to the edges, and now he seemed more preoccupied with the newcomer towering over him.

"You spilled your drink on my girlfriend," Scott said, with such palpable fury that Not So Tall Guy was quick to go on the defensive.

"Yeah." David materialized by their side, taking a menacing stance next to Scott. "Kind of a dick move."

Outmatched two-to-one, Not So Tall Guy let go of his boldness rather quickly.

"Sorry, dude," he said to Scott. "I didn't mean to."

"You should apologize to her," Scott said, still visibly furious.

Not So Tall Guy wasted no time. He waved to Haley, yelling, "Sorry!"

"It's okay, I'm fine," Haley shouted back. "Scott, please come back here."

"See, it's all cool," Not So Tall Guy said.

David nodded to his brother and withdrew from the scene. Scott gave Not So Tall Guy one last withering stare, then started retracing his steps as well.

What happened next went down so fast that Madison took a couple of extra seconds to process it. One moment, Scott was peacefully walking back toward Haley. The next, he was falling into the pool, pushed inside like a human domino piece; two guys had careened into Not So Tall Guy, who, in turn, had fallen backward into Scott—back to back—propelling him into the water. But Scott was already at the edge of the pool and, before he plunged into the water, he hit the back of his head on the stone edge.

Haley's scream of terror shook Madison out of her momentary inertia. She dropped her glass and ran forward. David was much quicker to react. With an angered roar, he pushed everyone aside and, without removing his clothes, plunged head-first into the water, which was now tinged with blood, an ominous red nebula spreading from one corner to the rest of the pool. Scott's body lay unmoving at the bottom.

Haley

Haley didn't realize she was still screaming until Alice wrapped her arms around her and made her stop. They watched together as David disappeared underwater. He resurfaced in a few seconds, dragging

Scott's inert body with him. Jack jumped over a lounger and joined them at the edge of the pool in an eye-blink.

"Call an ambulance," Jack screamed back at the girls.

Haley couldn't move. She couldn't do anything; she just stood there, trembling like a leaf, watching as Jack helped David drag Scott's body out of the water. Alice still had her wits about her and was quick to reach for her phone and call 911.

David and Jack laid Scott gently on the grass. He wasn't moving, and gave no sign he was alive. David bent his head sideways, putting his ear close to Scott's mouth, probably to check if his brother was breathing. The look of utter desperation on David's face as he straightened sent a chill down to Haley's core.

"Damn it!" David screamed, water from the pool mingling with tears streaming down his cheeks. "Don't you do this to me."

He pinched Scott's nose closed with one hand and began mouth-to-mouth resuscitation. He blew air into Scott's mouth four times and then, letting go of his nose, checked again for any sign of breathing.

"Come on, Scott, come on," David yelled.

Desperation mixed with sheer determination on David's face as he pinched Scott's nose closed again and started puffing air into him again. Halfway through the third breath, Scott's chest convulsed. David hastily helped his brother roll to the side as he vomited water. Once the spasm was over, Scott lay unconscious and deadly white. David bent his ear to Scott's mouth a third time and, this time, he straightened up with a crazed smile on his face.

"He's breathing. Someone call an ambulance!"

Jack threw Alice an interrogative stare, and she said, "We already did."

Everything happened in a blur next. The paramedics arrived quickly, and put an oxygen mask over Scott's mouth before moving him onto a stretcher and into the ambulance. David jumped in with them, and Haley watched them go, still too stunned to say or feel anything.

Her hands wouldn't stop trembling as she got changed into something clean, and she kept on shivering even though it was eighty degrees outside.

Alice, the only one of them who had had nothing to drink, drove them all to the hospital in Madison's car. They left the car in the parking garage and hurried toward the emergency room. Walking inside, Haley was assaulted by an unwelcome déjà vu. Unnatural neon light flashing past, careworn faces, and that typical hospital smell of disinfectant and despair. The same that had clung to her for days after visiting her father at Mercy Hospital in Buffalo. She'd almost lost him less than a month ago, and now she risked losing Scott as well.

No. Haley clenched her teeth with determination. *Scott will be fine.*

They found David pacing barefooted in the general waiting area. His clothes, a light white T-shirt and white board-shorts, left a trail of water droplets behind him and clung to his body like a second skin. He was a portrait of controlled fear: head bent low, gaze trained on the floor, and one hand rubbing his chin in a worried gesture.

"Man," Jack said, putting one hand on David's shoulder. "I've brought you a change of clothes." He produced a small bag Haley noticed for the first time.

David took the bag and stared at each of them in turn. When his blue eyes settled on Haley's, it was like staring into a mirror. Pale and weary, David looked as if he'd lost ten years of his life.

"Where's Scott?" Haley asked in a trembling voice.

"They're running a few tests on him."

"Did they tell you anything?" Alice asked.

David shook his head. "They wouldn't say much. Just asked me what happened, how he was revived, and then told me they needed to check his wound before they could tell me anything. He's getting an MRI…" David's jaw kept twitching as he spoke, and he wasn't able to stand still. "…or something." David smiled a bitter smile. "I'm afraid I've got no clue what that means. Scott's the neurosurgeon in the family. But they assured me giving him mouth-to-mouth was the right thing to do. Now we can only wait for the test results."

"Man, go put on some dry clothes," Jack insisted. "We'll be right here if anyone shows up."

David thanked him and disappeared into the closest restroom to get changed.

The girls sat on a couch nearby. Jack gave Alice a quick hug and then said, "I'm going to the hospital store to see if I can find a pair of shoes for David."

Alice kissed his cheek, and they all watched her boyfriend ask a nurse for directions and vanish down a side hall.

"Thank goodness for him," Alice said. "He's the only one who's thinking straight."

Haley nodded, making an effort to stop her lower lip from trembling. Seated in the middle between her friends, she lifted her hands, palms up, silently asking them to hold them. On her left, Alice's hand was warm and dry; on the right, Madison's was cold and clammy. Madison hadn't uttered a single word so far and, from the way she held on to Haley's hand, she must be just as shaken.

David came back from the bathroom wearing Jack's clothes and a deep frown. He stopped in front of them, looking like he was lost in thought.

"What's the matter?" Alice asked.

"I don't know if I should call my parents."

"They would want to know," Alice offered tentatively.

"Yeah, but my dad is in Hong Kong for work right now, and I don't want to scare my mom while she's home alone… But if it's something bad and I didn't call them…" David paused, visibly choked by emotions.

"How long before the doctors have the MRI results?"

"A couple of hours."

"You can wait to hear what they have to say and then alert your parents," Alice suggested. "That way you'll be able to give them better information."

"Yeah," David agreed. "It's not worth it to scare them." Then, looking straight at Haley, he added, "Scott will be all right."

Haley swallowed and nodded. She wanted to believe David, to share his positive attitude, but not until she spoke to Scott. Not until she saw his green eyes sparkle with life.

***

"David Williams?" a young doctor called after a while.

Haley had no idea how much time had passed. It could have been minutes or hours.

"Yes, Doctor, I'm here." David stepped forward.

"If you could follow me, I'd like to give you an update on your brother."

David turned toward the group of people standing behind him.

Besides Haley, Madison, Alice, and Jack, now all the guys from the team had joined them in the waiting room. With the school year about to begin, everyone had returned to Boston after summer break, and they'd all come to the hospital. Except for Blake, who had to deal with the police back at the country house since they'd opened an investigation into the accident.

"Please, Doctor," David said, "whatever you have to say, I will have to repeat it to them, and I'm afraid I'll do a very poor job."

"All right." The doctor sighed, clearly not pleased at having such a wide audience. "Your brother suffered a head injury. He needed stitches, but there's no skull fracture. However, the scans showed a small hematoma we hope will reabsorb on its own. We want to keep him here under observation for forty-eight hours at least."

"So, he's fine?"

"We'll only be able to give you a definitive answer once he wakes up. We've kept him sedated for now." Finally, the doctor smiled. "But, yes. Your brother should be out of the woods."

Haley let out a long exhale. She felt like she'd been holding her breath for the past few hours, and now she could breathe again.

"Can I see him?" David asked.

Haley got up to join him, but the doctor threw her an apologetic glance. "Sorry, it's only family at this point." Then, turning to David, he added, "Please come this way."

David returned half an hour later with a much more relaxed look on his face. "Scott's sleeping like a baby," he said, attempting a joke.

"When can other people visit him?" Haley asked.

"Sorry, they're not letting anyone who's not family in until tomorrow, or the day after. But you can have a peek through the glass. I'll show you to his room in a moment. Guys," David addressed all the people in the visitors' area. "Thank you all for coming, but you should go home now. There's no point in waiting here. I'll text you as soon as there's news."

The announcement was followed by a manly display of affection made of several back slaps, bro hugs, and hand-wrestler handshakes. Soon enough, all the guys had said goodbye and filed out of the hospital.

When everyone except Haley, Madison, Alice, and Jack had gone, David asked, "Did you guys bring Scott's phone?" He smiled regretfully.

"Mine got toasted in the pool, and I still have to call my parents."

"Yeah." Jack, ever the cool-headed one, fished the phone out of another sack and handed it over.

David stepped away to have some privacy.

"You guys should go home," Haley told her friends.

"You're not coming?" Alice asked.

"No, I'm staying. Even if they won't let me into his room, I'd go crazy at home. I prefer to be here."

David came back a few minutes later, hands shoved in his pockets.

"How did it go?" Alice asked.

David puffed his cheeks, blowing out air. "As well as one could expect. My mom will come as soon as she can. She's calling my father now."

"I'm sorry, man." Jack put a hand on David's shoulder. "Can we help in any way?"

"No. Thank you, guys… for everything."

"We're going to go," Jack said, letting go of David's shoulder. "Call if you need anything."

David nodded and stared at Haley questioningly.

"I'm staying," she said.

After saying bye to everyone else, Haley followed David to Scott's room. Through the glass, Scott looked pale but serene, lying on the hospital bed with his back kept in a slightly raised position. He wasn't intubated but had an IV jutting out of his left arm and a gauze bandage around his head that resembled a white tennis player's headband.

Haley rested the tips of her fingers on the cold glass. "So the doctors said he'll be all right."

"He will," David whispered, standing right behind her. "He has to be."

"I got so afraid." Tears she'd been holding back all day finally rushed out. "There was blood everywhere," Haley sobbed. "If it wasn't for you, I… I don't know… I feel like I'm living my life in and out of a hospital. Everyone I care about is getting sick…" She was spinning down a dark rabbit hole of doom and gloom.

"No one is getting sick." David pulled her into a hug, and Haley's nostrils filled with the acrid smell of chlorine, David's usual scent of summer and the sea washed away by the pool water. "Scott had a dumb accident, but he's fine. And your dad is fine, too. We got scared today, that's all."

"Scott wouldn't be alive if it wasn't for you! The doctor said it, too. You saved his life."

"Hey." David let her go and grinned. "Don't sound so surprised."

"You care about him."

"He's my little brother."

"Yeah, but from the way you two act around each other… You always behave as if you hate him."

"We have a complicated relationship." David tilted his head, frowning slightly. "Usually there's a girl standing in the middle…"

Haley's heart skipped a beat.

"…But Scott is my family. I would never let something bad happen to him. On that note…" David took a step back. "I've been told it's good to talk to unconscious people, helps their brains"—David twirled a finger in the air near his temple—"mend, or stay active, or something. I'll go check if they have a book I can read to him at the hospital store. Can I leave you at the wheel?"

"Yeah, I'll call you if something happens."

"Right." David scratched the back of his head. "Remember to use Scott's number," he said, before jogging away.

He came back about twenty minutes later with a dark-covered paperback and an air of mischief about him. After looking around furtively, he said, "All right, here's the plan. The doctors are making their rounds in half an hour and the nurses are changing shifts right now. I can cover you for five minutes."

"What do you mean?" Haley asked, surprised.

"As much as I'm sure my suave voice has extraordinary healing powers, I'm positive five minutes of hearing you talk to him will do much better for Scott's brain than anything else. Come on." He opened Scott's door. "I'll knock when it's time to come out."

Haley gave him a grateful smile and snuck into the room. With David's words fresh in her ears, Haley started talking at once, doing her best to keep her tone even as she spoke to her unconscious boyfriend.

"You gave us all a scare today, you know? But my honor is intact, at least." She laughed softly. "But next time, please try to ignore the drunken hotheads, yeah? I wouldn't be able to survive something like today twice. I… I was so scared. The moment I saw you fall into the pool, my heart stopped. Scott, the blood was everywhere. I was sure you had none left in you. I thought… Well, I guess I didn't think much at that moment. I sort of lost it."

Haley took Scott's hand. It was cold and dry. "You should've seen David. He went berserk… I've never seen him so… so… *emotional.* Your brother loves you, you know, even if he sometimes makes it so hard to see, he really does. He snuck me in to let me talk to you, even if for only five minutes—"

A sharp knock interrupted Haley's speech.

"And now I have to go before the nurses discover me and kick me out." Haley leaned down to stamp a kiss on Scott's forehead, the part still free from bandages. "See you tomorrow. I'll be just outside."

After opening the door only a crack, Haley poked her head out. David beckoned her to come out and shut the door behind her. No one was around; they'd gotten away with it.

"Are you going to be all right out here alone?" David asked.

"Yeah. Maybe I'll go get a book myself." Haley lied, she didn't have the focus to read right now—but David didn't need to worry about her on top of everything else. She tilted her head toward the paperback in David's hands. "What did you buy?"

David turned the book in his hands. "A thriller. It's supposed to be good." He shrugged and shifted back and forward on his toes before saying, "I'd better get going. Knock if you need something."

Haley gave him a curt nod and went to sit in the empty row of chairs in the small atrium in front of Scott's hallway. Wrapped in eerie silence, the Neurology wing of the hospital offered little to do other than stare at the wall and think. Haley shifted her butt to find a comfortable position, then let her emotions run wild.

Her mind flew to Scott at once, to the months they'd spent apart, and to the few days they had had together since he came back… and, especially, to the hole that had appeared in her chest when she'd seen him lying unconscious on the lawn while David tried to revive him.

David.

He was everything and the opposite of everything: good-hearted and cruel, kind and scornful. He had so many layers Haley doubted she'd ever be able to peel them all off and find the real David, or if it was even a wise aspiration to have.

After a long time sitting, Haley lay down and shifted her blank staring from the wall to the ceiling, her brain still buzzing with questions. As her lids started to droop with exhaustion, one final, ominous thought crossed Haley's mind. She fell asleep wondering if it was possible to be in love with two people at the same time.

***

Haley woke up the next morning with her face resting on a small white pillow and her body under the cover of a hospital blanket.

And where did you two come from?

The answer came to her lips almost immediately. "David."

She straightened up, groaning at the pain in her sore back. Pillow and blanket or not, hospital chairs were most definitely not a comfortable bed. Stretching her neck left and right, Haley stood up, wrapping the blanket around her like a poncho. She peeked into Scott's room through the glass; nothing had changed from the night before. Scott slept while his brother read to him. David's voice didn't carry out of the room, but it was funny to watch the little expressions he made as he narrated the story. A small frown here, a surprised face there. He grimaced and then pouted in an "aha" sort of way, completely absorbed in the story. And even if Haley couldn't hear a word of what he said, she had a clear sense of where the book was going, or when the hero faced a trial or scored a point.

"Hey," someone close by said, making her jump.

Haley turned to find Madison standing in the hall next to her.

"Hi." Haley greeted her friend with a hug. "What are you doing here?"

"We couldn't sit still back at the house."

"We?"

"Jack and Alice came with me. They stopped at the cafeteria to get coffees for everyone. Are there any developments?"

"No. The doctors will take him off medications later in the day. We can only wait."

"How are you?"

Haley wrapped herself tighter in the blanket. "I'm holding in there." She turned her gaze once more to the inside of the room.

Madison imitated her. "Is David reading to Scott?"

Haley nodded. "Yeah, he said something about keeping Scott's brain stimulated while he's unconscious."

"What's the book?"

"A thriller. Something with a famous actor on the cover. I can't remember the name."

Madison narrowed her eyes at the paperback and scoffed. "Leave it to David to torture Scott with mass-market fiction even on his sick bed," she said jokingly, speaking like a true book snob.

Haley studied her friend. "I know you're not a fan of David's, but—"

"David's all right," Madison interrupted.

Haley coughed in shock. "Even after what he did to you?"

Madison hesitated, staring at the floor and chewing on her lower lip.

"What is it?" Haley asked.

"He apologized to me a while ago."

"When? Why didn't you tell me?"

"He asked me not to…"

Haley frowned questioningly.

"When he apologized, I had just spotted you two together at the library, so I accused him of having an agenda; of apologizing only because he hoped I'd report to you so that he'd score points. That's when he made me promise not to tell you, to convince me the apology was about me and not you."

"You still could've told me."

"I wasn't sure the gesture wasn't a reverse psychology trick, and I wasn't convinced he had no angle."

"And you are now?"

"Yes, I believe he was sincere. David can be horrible, but he's also good sometimes."

Nailed it, Haley thought, then added aloud, "That's why you've been talking to him again."

"Uh-huh."

Haley would have asked more, but they were interrupted by Alice and Jack bringing the coffees. Soon after that, a procession of nurses and doctors began when the time to wake Scott up arrived.

The young doctor from the day before closed the blinds. As before,

David was the only one admitted into the room. He came out what seemed like an eternity later with a big smile on his face.

"Someone would like to see you," he told Haley.

The last lump of worry Haley didn't realize she still had in her throat vaporized, and she hurried inside. Scott was sitting on the bed, his back resting on a mound of pillows. He was pale and had bluish circles under his eyes, but he was smiling... even more when he spotted her.

"How are you?" she asked, approaching.

"I'm... still recovering from the realization that I've become a sorry, college frat boy cliché."

"Oh, so you're playing the 'let's-joke-about-it' angle?"

Scott smirked. "Too soon?"

His green eyes sparkled and his smile was sexier than ever. He winked, and Haley knew everything was going to be fine.

Madison

Will I see him today?

First-day-of-school jitters mixed with unrequited-love anxiety as Madison walked into the Baker Center building, the facility where a lot of Humanities classes took place. The first course of the fall term was a creative writing workshop Scott should be attending, head injury permitting. She hadn't seen him since the previous week at the hospital. After two days in observation, Scott had been discharged with the doctors' recommendation that he be kept under constant supervision for at least a week. So Haley and David had taken turns playing nurse, meaning Madison had seen little of her roommate since release day.

Haley had temporarily moved in with Scott, and her visits home had been quick and targeted. She'd come to grab a change of clothes, drop off her dirty laundry, and not much else. When asked about Scott's recovery, she'd say he was doing fine and everything was okay. Answers not nearly satisfying enough for Madison.

She tried not to resent Haley; at least, not more than usual. That first night after the accident had been hard. When everybody had gone home, Madison had wanted to stay. Even if visitors for Scott were still forbidden, she'd wanted to wait outside his room to be close to him, just like Haley had done. But Madison didn't have that right because she wasn't his girlfriend, and asking to stay would've been too weird for everyone. An implied reminder of an awkward truth everybody knew and nobody wanted to discuss.

Well, except for David, maybe. He was always game for a self-pitying chat about the "happy couple." Madison half-scoffed, half-smiled.

Anyway, Scott didn't know about Madison's feelings for him—at least, she hoped he didn't. But she could trust Haley with her secret; she'd never tell him, even if Scott was her boyfriend. And neither would his brother. So explaining to Scott why she'd felt the need to camp outside his hospital room for a whole night would've been *inconvenient,* to say the least.

Catching a glimpse of herself in the hall's windows, Madison checked out her reflection, hoping the extra care she'd put into her makeup and outfit that morning wouldn't be too evident. Satisfied with what she saw, Madison stepped into the classroom with an inhale of anticipation, her heart beating a little faster than usual. But a quick scan of the intimate space revealed Scott hadn't arrived yet.

The classroom was super small. Teachers liked to keep workshops limited, and this one was no exception, with only twelve students admitted. An oval, wooden table occupied most of the space and, around it, half of the thirteen chairs were already taken.

With a sigh, Madison took a seat with an empty chair on either side. Scott could be late; there was still time for him to walk in and sit next to her. Four students had yet to arrive, which gave Madison a fifty-fifty chance of spending the next three hours sitting beside Scott. Those odds reduced drastically when Clare Montgomery came in a few minutes later and sat on Madison's left.

Still one free spot, Madison thought, throwing a hopeful glance at the empty doorway.

With little to do before the professor arrived, and not wanting to stare at the door like a hawk, Madison busied herself organizing her notepad and pens on the table. At five minutes to one, a towering shadow appeared in her peripheral vision, making more than one head turn—female heads. Madison followed their gazes to the threshold, dismissing the newcomer with a quick glance.

Two seconds later, she did a not-so-subtle double take. It was Scott, wearing a longish military green shirt and faded jeans, looking unbelievably gorgeous with a new half-shaved, half-long undercut hairstyle so different from his usual that Madison hadn't recognized him at first.

"Scott." She jumped up from her chair. "You made it."

"Hey." Scott smiled, and the whole room seemed to brighten.

"How are you?"

"Great…" He gave her a quick hug and took the chair next to her, earning Madison a few eye-daggers from her fellow female students. "…all things considering."

"What's up with the hair?" Madison asked.

Scott turned his head to show her his nape, passing his hand on the lower, buzz-cut half. "I felt ridiculous going around with a huge bald patch in the back of my head, so I shaved half off." A large adhesive bandage was still plastered on the spot where he'd hit the pool rim. Turning back toward her, he added, "I still have to get used to it."

Well, me, too. The top of Scott's hair now fell on his forehead, seeming much longer than it had before, and the style really suited him.

"Why? You look great," Madison blabbed. She instantly regretted the spontaneous comment and tried to rein in the furious blush that threatened to make an unwelcome appearance whenever she was this close to Scott.

"Haley likes it, too. But it's good to have a second opinion." Scott winked.

Madison's stomach flipped, and she scrambled to find a different subject other than how good Scott looked. "So you've recovered from having to listen to a thriller feast for a whole night?" she joked, feeling one hundred percent like the book snob she was.

"David is a pretty good narrator, actually."

"Still, I would've picked a Jack London novel if I had to read to you for twelve hours straight."

Scott turned his gaze on her and studied her for a second. "He's my favorite author. How did you know?"

Madison's face heated up, *again.*

Good job, Madison, she chided herself. *Reveal your little stalking habits, won't you?*

"Oh, really? London is one of my favorites, too," Madison lied.

"Really?" Scott's face brightened up at once. "Which one of his books do you prefer?"

Madison was struggling to find something to say—she had read *The Call of the Wild* for another course and remembered doing an allegory study on *White Fang*, but that was as far as her Jack London knowledge went—when the professor came in, greeting all of them with a severe, "Good morning, class," that snuffed out all conversation.

Ding-dong, saved by the proverbial bell.

Phew.

And it's only the first day, Madison cursed inside her head. *How am I going to last a whole year?*

I have to be strong and pull through, she repeated to herself. *Be strong and pull through.*

The school year couldn't have started in a worse way, and now she had to actually read all of Jack London's novels back to back—and preferably before the next class she'd share with Scott.

Georgiana

Georgiana felt strangely self-conscious walking the familiar halls of Caspersen Student Center with her bump clearly showing for the first time since she'd gotten pregnant. At the end of the spring term her stomach had still been smooth and flat, but over the summer a giant bubble had popped out of her midsection and, at twenty-two weeks pregnant, no amount of color blocking or smart dressing could disguise her giant belly.

Eyes followed her as she strode toward her class, trying to project her usual confidence. The indiscreet stares didn't really bother her; Georgiana was used to making heads turn. Over the years, she'd grown accustomed to the extra attention; basked in it, really. Rich, beautiful, and the daughter of one of the most powerful and recognized lawyers in Boston, usually people wanted one of two things when they looked at her: to date her, or to be her.

But not today. Guys were throwing surprised side-glances at her stretched-out belly, and then, horror-struck in a glad-it's-not-me way, they'd stare at Tyler walking beside her. But what rattled Georgiana the most was how girls showed the same attitude. Instead of envying her, they seemed to pity her.

Um, hello? I'm married to the most gorgeous guy in our year, what's with the pity-party?

For the first time since getting married, Georgiana realized that not everyone dreamed of having a husband and a family, at least not as early in life as Georgiana would have both. Yeah, right. These were career-hungry women. The halls of Harvard Law School probably weren't the best focus group for proud stay-at-home-mom wannabes. Not that Georgiana was ever going to be a stay-at-home anything.

Still, Georgiana was relieved when what had felt very much like a walk of shame ended. Unfortunately, things did not improve once inside the classroom.

For one, Rose was there. The bane of Georgiana's existence, not only was she Tyler's best friend, but also Ethan's girlfriend. They were the two most important men in Georgiana's life, her husband and her brother, and Rose had her claws sunk deep in both. And if that wasn't already enough, today her nemesis looked too attractive for her own good in her prim class uniform—dark jeans, light-blue V-neck sweater with a white shirt underneath, blue blazer, and women's derby shoes. Plus, and what irked Georgiana the most, Rose was thin like a stick.

And for two, the sneers in here were far worse than outside. It didn't take Georgiana long to catch her fellow female students staring at her belly in groups of two or three, and then gossiping among themselves in hushed tones with their heads bent together. Again, not a single envious face among them, only derision and pity.

Georgiana let Tyler slide into the middle seat and took the outer seat of the row—with the baby pushing on her bladder, she had to go to the restroom so often that letting Tyler sit next to Rose was a strategic necessity. Gosh, these seats were uncomfortable. Her bump barely fit under the narrow table that spanned the entire row of chairs. Georgiana soon realized she wouldn't be able to bend forward and take notes. Oh, hell. Never one to give up, Georgiana placed her tablet on the table and opened the new dictation app she'd bought foreseeing this eventuality.

A sudden burst of laughter made her snap her neck up. She swept the room with a burning, ice-cold stare until her eyes came to rest on a group of three girls who used to hang on Georgiana's every word. Now they giggled among themselves while purposely not looking at her.

Let's see how much you're going to laugh when your ovaries are all dried up and you're still spinsters living with their ten cats like lonely, crazy cat ladies, Georgiana thought bitterly.

The school year couldn't have started in a worse way. And now she had to pee, *again!*

Haley

Last first day of school ever, Haley thought, with the same melancholy she remembered from her first day of senior year in high school. Only this time, graduation was the real thing. There wouldn't be a new school the following year; only work, and the beginning of a different phase of life. Job applications and adult responsibilities were concepts scary enough for Haley to almost second guess her decision of not applying to grad school. But the one thing she wasn't going to need for sure in this new, grown-up life was more debt. No need to be scared of the future, anyway. Different didn't necessarily have to mean worse.

Right.

Still, she couldn't avoid looking at the buildings, the halls, and the familiar faces of her fellow Computer Science students with a bit of ruefulness as she walked into her first class of the day.

The professors, however, didn't seem to share any of her nostalgic musings. Her schedule was pretty packed already, and each of her instructors opened their lectures with a right-off-the-bat, we-don't-want-to-waste-any-time teaching approach, which didn't leave Haley much time to romanticize over the past and the future as she was barely able to keep up with the present.

So much so that the end of the last lecture of the day came almost as a surprise. All melancholy lost and glad the day was over, when Haley walked outside the main SEAS building, the sun warmed her skin, and the air still smelled like summer.

Smiling, she fished her phone out of her bag.

Scott picked up on the second ring. "Hi, babe."

"Hey, how's my favorite patient?"

"Tired."

"You didn't overdo it today, did you? The doctors said you should take it slow."

"I did, I promise… Just had a long day."

"Yeah, me, too. Where are you now?"

"Crossing Harvard Yard as we speak. You?"

"I was heading toward your place, but I'm too tired to cook. What do you say we grab a bite together?"

"Perfect, also because I suspect we left an empty fridge at home."

"It was David's turn to go grocery shopping."

"And I'm sure he'll go, but I'm hungry now and who knows when he'll be back."

"Yeah, I'm starving, too. Meet me at the bookstore?"

"Perfect."

"I'll get to you in five."

***

If the day could've been described as one of the last of summer when they entered Pinocchio's to grab a square-cut slice of pizza, the weather had definitely switched to "Hello, fall" when they walked out.

"Oh, it's raining!" Haley shouted, opening the restaurant's door to get out.

She made to run under the downpour, but Scott grabbed her waist and pulled her close to him—her back to his chest—under the shelter of the restaurant ledge. "Come here, silly," he murmured. "You'll get all wet."

Haley struggled to breathe, trapped in his grip. No, not trapped… only *torn*. Splintered in two. One part of her wanted to be exactly where she was: warm and dry, safely wrapped in Scott's arms. Secure, protected. But there was another part of her that wanted to run free in the rain, to be wild, spontaneous, and who cared if she got wet…

"It's only water…" a familiar voice whispered inside her head.

Haley tried to stop the thought before it took shape in her mind, but she was too late. Already an image of David standing under a summer storm and beckoning her to join him had invaded her thoughts, clear as day.

His dark, wet hair plastered to his forehead as he caught her wrists and held her hands close to his chest. The intense look in his eyes as he leaned his head down. The phantom of his lips on her forehead after he'd kissed her. A whispered promise: *"The next time we kiss, you'll want to just as much as I do now…"*

477

And then, his rage. *"You're a liar, Haley. You're lying to me, and you're lying to Scott, and most of all you're lying to yourself."*

And the dark emotions in his eyes as he'd made another promise.

"I won't go away, Haley. I'll always be here for you." David's words echoed inside her head with the same intensity as if he were saying them to her now. *"I love you."*

Haley leaned back against Scott, gripping his arms more firmly. No, she definitely couldn't think about that day… not now… not ever…

Alice

On the first day of school, Alice woke up with a start long before the alarm clock was scheduled to go off. On impulse, before even fully opening her eyes, she grabbed her phone and checked her texts. Jack had disappeared on her the day before, and she'd gone to bed worried. It wasn't like him not to reply to her messages or at least to reach out to wish her a good night.

As soon as she touched the screen, a multiple text notification appeared. Alice sighed in relief and opened the chat. Unfortunately, the unlocked phone revealed two clipped, not so comforting, possibly I-don't-love-you-anymore speech bubbles:

No 'good night,' no kiss, no 'I love you.' Alice scrolled up to her part of the chat.

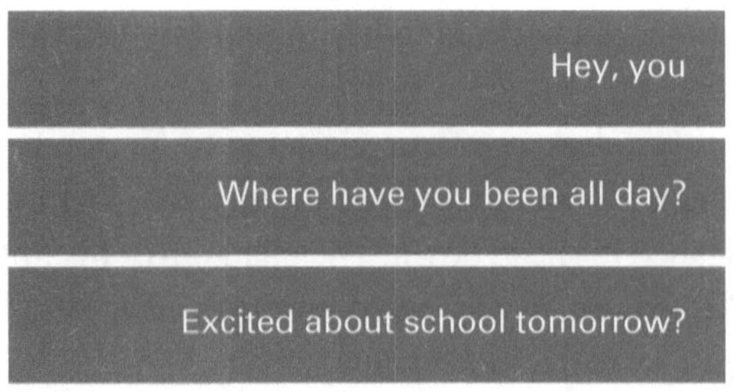

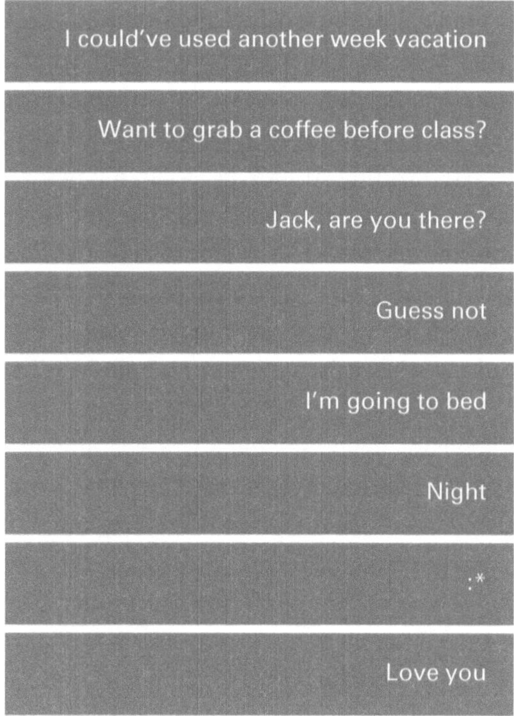

She honestly didn't see where she'd gone wrong with her texts. Okay, she'd asked him where he was twice, but only because he hadn't hit her back. That couldn't be labeled as oppressive or clingy, right? So what was up with him? Was he already getting tired of her? No, *impossible.* This was the old, insecure Alice talking. Jack's Ice was confident her boyfriend loved her. So why was Jack being such a—*Okay, let's stop right there... Keep calm and don't insult the boyfriend. You're going to see him in a few hours and everything will be fine.*

I hope you're right, Alice concluded her mental rant with herself.

After a quick breakfast and a gigantic cup of coffee, she put extra care in choosing her outfit and doing her hair and makeup, feeling half-silly, half-cute. After all, Jack had now seen her in every possible state: dressed up, down, not at all, with spot-on makeup, with morning-after panda eyes. Maybe he hadn't seen seriously hangover Ice yet, but that was it.

Ready and pampered, Alice walked to the Science Center, enjoying the still warm sunrays of late August. Along the department hall, she passed a boy and a girl—clearly freshmen, from the way they stared around themselves, disoriented—and shook her head with fondness. She remembered another couple of freshmen three years ago, who'd stood with their heads bent close over a map, trying to figure out where the hell they were supposed to go on their first day of school.

Not needing to look at a map anymore, and alone, Alice navigated the corridors and stairs of the building with the casualness and confidence reserved for senior students. The first lesson of the day was a large one, and so it took place in one of those movie-theater type classrooms: rectangular—longer than it was wide—with sloped floors and rows of chairs with attached mini-desks on each level.

Alice poked her head inside to check if Jack had already arrived. For Chemistry major students, this was the auditorium where most of the large classes took place, and they had a favorite spot: the first and second chairs in the center, next to the stairs, three rows back from the front. No one was sitting there yet, so Alice quickly hopped down the steps to grab the two seats. She sat in the one farther away from the stairs, placing a notebook on the other one to save it for Jack.

Once settled with her desk up and notepad ready to take notes, Alice turned toward the back of the room to search for her missing boyfriend. Nothing. She pulled her phone out of her bag—five to nine, and still no sign of Jack.

Alice was about to send him another text asking where he was, when a quick succession of flashbacks passed through her mind. They all involved Jack complaining about girls who "kept texting him and didn't get the message" while he tried to ghost them. Most of his breakups had consisted of him simply disappearing until the poor girl eventually *did* get the message.

Am I that girl now?

A lump of dread clogged Alice's throat, and she had to swallow. With clammy hands, she grabbed her water bottle and sipped a few gulps to calm herself. Not that it worked very well. Especially since the professor—Mr. Harrison, a new guy—had just walked down the stairs and Jack was still MIA.

It wasn't like Jack to be late. Had something happened to him? Horrible accident scenarios started playing in her head. But then she remembered that Jack *had* replied to her texts. No matter how short, unsatisfying, and unloving his reply had been. So her boyfriend probably wasn't lying in a hospital somewhere. That was something, at least.

He could still be at the gym. The basketball team had an informal meeting scheduled that morning. That fresh intel came from Haley—whose boyfriend had *not* gone incommunicado—but the meeting was supposed to be only a pep talk, and it should've ended well before their 9 a.m. class started.

Whatever Jack's reason for being missing, texting him now that Harrison had arrived wasn't an option anymore. With the advent of social media and other distracting apps, smartphones had officially become teachers' number one public enemy. All professors seemed to lose their bearings at the mere sight of one in the hands of a student in their classes. So, not wanting to destroy her participation score on the very first lecture, Alice promptly stashed the offending piece of smart tech away.

All throughout the lesson, however, she sneaked glances behind her shoulders whenever Harrison was busy writing on the blackboard. Eventually, on her eighth or ninth try, she spotted Jack sitting in the last row, his face half-hidden in the shadows. He was looking straight ahead and gave no sign of having seen her.

She kept looking at him for as long as she dared, but she had to turn back to the front of the room without having met his eye. This made no sense. Why was Jack sitting back there? Well, he could've arrived so late that he hadn't wanted to attract too much attention toward himself by walking down the stairs.

But usually, whenever Jack was late for class—which happened a lot once regular practice with the team started, and he had to run to lectures straight from the gym—he'd wait for whatever professor to turn around and jump into the chair she'd saved for him at the first good occasion.

Not today, it seemed.

For the next hour and a half, Alice wasn't able to concentrate on the lesson. Not a word of what Harrison said filtered through her mental noise. By the end of class, she had no idea how they were going to be graded, how many midterms they'd have, when—*if*—there was going to be a group project, if the groups would be decided by the students or assigned, and when the first homework was due. Not to mention the actual content of the lecture. The board was filled with molecular structures, and Alice had no clue what they were supposed to do.

For the entire morning, there'd only been one recurring thought drilling a hole through her brain. Jack was mad at her. He was clearly avoiding her… putting distance between them. Why? *Why? Why? Why?* The question kept pushing on her skull from the inside-out and left no space for anything else.

Familiar with Jack's avoidance techniques, Alice shot out of her seat the second Harrison dismissed them and ran up the stairs, barely managing to catch up with him as he walked out of the class.

She grabbed him by the elbow. "Hey."

Jack turned toward her and didn't smile. "Hi."

Alice came close to kiss him, but he pulled free of her grip, saying, "Not here. It's not professional."

Professional? They'd been working together at a pharmaceutical company all summer, and Jack had had no problems kissing her in the hallways. And this was only school. True, it was their first day of class as boyfriend and girlfriend, and they hadn't discussed an on-campus PDA policy… but… Jack had never refused to kiss her. Except… that day at the library, when she'd first tried to kiss him and he'd turned her down without room for interpretation.

Alice forced the déjà vu away and vowed to keep calm and try not to kill her boyfriend. "Why didn't you come sit next to me?" she asked in a neutral tone.

"I was late. I didn't want to come down to the front row with the professor looking."

"That never stopped you before."

"I knew the teachers. Harrison is new."

It all sounded so reasonable, so plausible, and also so much *bogus.* Alice couldn't shake the feeling Jack was lying to her. She was about to call him out on it when he spoke again.

"Let's go, we're going to be late for our next class."

Seething inside, she followed him along the hall to their next lesson— a lab this time. Even though they shared a station, the situation didn't improve one bit. Jack didn't look at her once and didn't speak a word the entire time unless it was related to the experiment they were conducting. And by now, Alice was so mad she was fine with not talking to him. She took it out on the lab equipment instead, handling the various alembics and test tubes with far less care than they deserved.

If Jack wanted to be an asshole, he could be her guest. She would be an asshole right back. But, *just maybe,* he wasn't the wisest to be such a jerk to his girlfriend when, with a few, well-mixed chemicals, she could cook up an explosive and torch him to the ground. Especially not when she had all the ingredients all nicely lined up in front of her.

Steady, Alice. Keep calm and do not torch your boyfriend.

When the lab was over, Alice decided to keep her mouth shut and see what Jack would do. They had no more classes for the day, so she was curious to see what his next excuse would be. She didn't have to wait long.

As soon as they stepped out of the building, Jack said, "I have to go meet Coach Morrison."

"Didn't the team meet already this morning?"

Jack shrugged. "He asked me to meet him again for lunch."

"Okay, see you later?"

"Yeah, sure. I gotta go now." He took a step backward, as if to make it clear she wasn't getting a goodbye kiss. Not that she wanted one. Right now, all Alice wanted to give Jack was a goodbye punch. "I'll see you around."

"You'll see me around?" Her nostrils flared. "Jack, what's up? You've been weird since last night—"

"I don't have time to do this right now." He jogged another couple of steps back, and added, "I've got to go."

Jack turned on his heel and sprinted away.

On the way home, Alice had to fight back tears. When she got home, she stormed inside, so angry she even scared Blue, her pet bunny, when she banged the door to her room shut. What now? Being the first day of school, she didn't have much to do. No papers to write, no studying, no reading… nothing. She was free to stare at the ceiling and keep asking herself what she'd missed. She tried to read a book—something Madison had insisted she read—but of course not a single printed word filtered through the Jack haze.

Eventually, the four walls of her bedroom made her so claustrophobic that she moved into the slightly more spacious living room. And that's where Haley found her when she came home much later: sitting on the couch, staring into space, nibbling at her fingertips.

"Hey," Haley said, frowning at her. "What have you done to your nails?"

"They were collateral."

Haley's frown deepened. "For what? Are you alone? Is Madison home?"

"She put her 'go away, I'm reading' sign on the door, so she must be in there."

"What's up with you?"

"Jack is mad at me." Alice dropped her elbows on her knees, bouncing them up and down in a nervous gesture as she kept staring into space, waiting for an answer to appear out of thin air. "And I've no idea why."

"Could it have to do with the article?"

Alice's head snapped up, and she focused on her roommate, who was now occupying the armchair in front of her. "What article?"

"The one about Peter. He gave an interview to the *Chicago Sun-Times,* and they've re-posted the piece on the team's website. You haven't seen it?"

"No. I don't regularly check the Crimson's website."

"Hey, don't shoot the messenger. Scott told me about the interview; I just got back from dinner with him."

"No, sorry, I'm not mad at you. Is Scott doing okay?"

Haley mmm-hmmed yes, so Alice continued, "I've been going crazy since last night. First Jack disappeared, and then today he's been..." Alice took a breath. "...*not very nice.* You think it has to do with this interview?"

Haley shrugged. "Scott said Jack was as much fun as assembling IKEA furniture at the team meeting this morning."

Oh. *Ooooh!*

"Do you have a link to the article?"

"Wait." Haley took her tablet out of her bag, unlocked it, tapped multiple times, and handed it to Alice. "The good stuff is at the bottom."

Alice paused a second on Peter's picture. Well, there was no denying it: he looked dashing, smiling at the camera in his red Chicago Bulls uniform, muscular shoulders peeking out of the tank top and bright blue eyes piercing the screen. She skim-read the first part of the article and scrolled to the near end as Haley had suggested, stopping when she caught the words *broken hearts.* She backed up a little and started reading.

"So, Peter, did you leave any broken hearts back in Boston?"

"Only mine."

"A bad relationship?"

"Actually, a perfect one."

"And what happened?"

"My girl told me our lives were about to change. I guess she wasn't much into the long-distance scenario."

"I'm so sorry to hear that. Whoever that girl is, she surely let go of a wonderful man. But good news for all our single ladies here in Chicago…"

Alice stopped reading. She returned the tablet to Haley and grabbed her phone to text Jack with a vengeance.

Have you been horrible to me all day
because of that stupid article???

Alice stared intently at the screen, registering the moment Jack received the text and the instant the chat app signaled he had read it. She kept her gaze so laser-focused it might've burned through the glass. Soon after Jack had read the text, the three little dots signaling he was typing a reply appeared and disappeared several times before an actual reply came in. It was a short:

Maybe

Relief washed over her.

You have no reason to worry

You know that, right?

No, I don't

He made it sound like you broke his heart or something

You said you never were that serious
That you never loved him

And I didn't

Peter must've been exaggerating for the press

He's probably going to use his alleged broken heart as a pickup line

You know how he is

Did you tell him we are together?

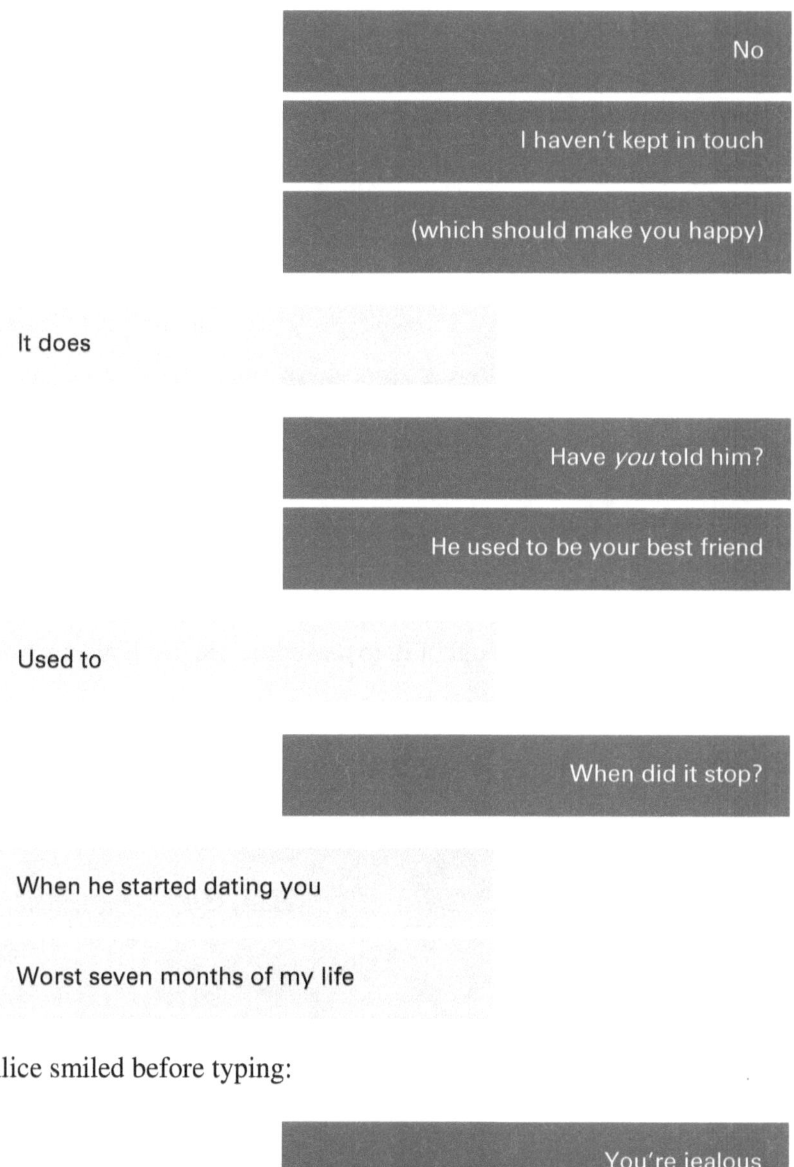

It does

Used to

When he started dating you

Worst seven months of my life

Alice smiled before typing:

I'm not cute

And I'm not joking

Having to watch you with him

Every day...

You can't understand

I can

No, you really can't

Alice scoffed. The nerve of him! She started typing a list of names, careful to leave Madison's out of it, to make him see just how much she got it.

Okay

Sarah

Point made

Elizabeth

Samantha

I get it

Alyssa

Taylor

Jennifer

Jessica

You can stop now

Julia

Emma

Kayla

Megan

Nicole

How do you even remember all of them?

Lori

Becky

Because each and every one of them
was a stab through my heart

Now *you're* cute

I'm not cute

Can I come over?

There's something I really want to tell
you

If it's not:

Sorry for being the crappiest boyfriend
today, I will never ever do that again

No!

I mean I have something to tell you
besides

> Sorry for being the crappiest boyfriend
> today, I will never ever do that again

When he knocked on her door half an hour later, Alice's instincts were torn between kissing him and slapping him. She went for the kiss first, and then she not-so-lightly punched him in the chest.

"Don't you ever scare me like that ever again. Deal?"

He flashed her that boyish-but-roguish smile she loved so much. "Deal."

She hugged him and kept her face buried in his neck for such a long time that, at one point, Haley shouted, "Get a room!"

Alice lifted her head and whispered, "That's not such a bad idea."

She pulled Jack backward into her room, pushed him onto her bed, and kicked the door shut behind her. Straddling him, she said, "So, how much groveling are you prepared to do?"

"All the groveling you require."

"Good. And you have to tutor me as well. I didn't get a word of what Harrison said this morning."

Jack smiled a mischievous smile. "I can work with the student-teacher scenario."

"Uh-oh," Alice scoffed. "I don't think so. It's going to take a while before you get some, Mr. Sullivan."

He pouted and made a cute face he knew she couldn't resist.

"I'm serious." She tried to keep a straight face and failed miserably. "So what was it you wanted to tell me?"

Jack beamed at her. "The coach asked me to be team captain!"

Alice let out a loud squeal and collapsed on Jack, hugging him and kissing him. "That's fantastic. Amazing! Did you expect it?"

Jack's face turned serious. "I think it was between me and Scott, and with the injury so fresh, I suspect the coach didn't want to put too much pressure on him."

"I'm sure you would've gotten it anyway. You're going to be a wonderful captain!"

Jack placed his hands on her hips, his thumbs massaging her sides while he stared up at her, gaze intense. "I'm sorry for today, I really am. I behaved like shit, but when I read the article… Peter is still a sore point for me…"

"I know, but next time just *talk* to me. I don't care if you want to yell at me or tell me to go to hell. If you're mad, let it out. We can't solve anything if I don't know what's going on inside this pretty head of yours." She poked him on the forehead. "Deal?"

"Deal."

"Now you can tell me you love me and start with all that groveling, yes?"

Dead serious, Jack said, "I love you." Then he flipped her on the bed, so that now he was on top, and started kissing her neck. "And I know exactly the kind of groveling you need…"

Haley

After a first week of school made of free evenings, the basketball team came knocking on Scott's door pronto on week two. Scott had not yet been cleared by the doctors to play basketball. They wanted to monitor him for another couple of weeks and do another scan before they permitted any intense physical exertion. But Coach Morrison insisted that he attend all of the team's practice sessions anyway—to familiarize himself with the new team members, the new playing schemes, and, more generally, to keep him in the loop.

Since the basketball team had kidnapped Scott, Haley was spending Thursday night at home, doing nothing. She was sitting on the couch living vicariously through the lives of her 237 Facebook friends. The distraction earned her more than one reproachful look from Madison, who insisted time spent on social media was a total waste, and why didn't she read a good book instead? *Reading is good for mental health, it improves memory, reduces stress, boosts brain function, blah, blah, blah…*

Her roommate was probably onto something, but right now all Haley wanted was a bit of not-so-stimulating Facebook snooping into the lives people wanted her to believe they led, with a side of the occasional my-life-sucks, self-pitying post.

At least, that had been the plan. The danger in navigating the Facebook waters was that all kinds of friend-*ships* could sail by. In this case, a certain other Williams brother she hadn't heard from in a while appeared out-of-the-blue on her feed.

Haley stared at David's post, frowning.

David Williams is feeling naughty at
Monroe C. Gutman Library

That was weird. David never checked in on Facebook. Was it a coincidence he'd shared his location tonight? Did he know Scott would be at practice?

Haley didn't care if it was a plot; they hadn't talked about their friendship since that horrible first morning after Scott had come back from California, and she needed to get a few things out. She checked the time of the post… only ten minutes ago.

She jumped up from the couch and, after feeding Madison a lame I-forgot-I-had-a-project-meeting excuse, she grabbed her coat and bag from the hall and was out of the apartment in a blur.

At the library, she searched the café and study room, but there was no sign of David anywhere. She circled back, trying some of the smaller rooms, but still nada. She went back to the main room and settled at a table, ready to admit defeat. After lying to Madison about having a group project meeting, Haley couldn't walk back home only twenty minutes after leaving. So she took her laptop out of her bag and resigned herself to a dull hour of killing time on the internet. Until…

Haley's phone flashed with a new text message… from David.

Are you stalking me?

Haley jumped in her seat, turning her head left and right, but he was nowhere to be seen.

I wouldn't call it stalking

You basically invited me here

Really, how?

By posting a public "check in" on Facebook

(Which you *never* do)

On the first night Scott is busy with training

You check my profile often?

Haley shook her head. He was being impossible like always. And it was driving her crazy to be blind when he clearly had eyes on her.

Stop looking for me

You won't find me unless I want you to

He was so damn infuriating!

Why are you here?

Because I miss you, was Haley's first instinctive response. But no way would she type that. She bought a few seconds by rolling the phone in her hands. What to write?

Stop trying to come up with a politically correct answer

Just tell the truth

Haley made to pack her things and go when, out of nowhere, David materialized in front of her and took the chair on the opposite side of the table.

Blue eyes flaring, he asked, "Why are you here?"

"Because I missed your company, all right? Happy?"

The corner of his mouth curled up into that infuriating-but-oh-so-sexy lopsided grin. "You really couldn't bring yourself to say you've missed *me*."

Haley glared.

"Fine, all right." David threw up his hands with a little shrug. "I'll take what I can get. So what's been going on with you lately?"

"Madison told me you apologized to her," Haley blurted out.

She'd been dying to tell him she knew forever.

"Glad to know I can trust Blondie with a secret."

"Why did you ask her not to tell me?"

David shrugged with his eyebrows. "The apology wasn't about you."

"Why do you make it so hard for people to see the good in you?"

"Because I'm not a *good* guy. Not all the time, at least. I am good and I am bad and I'm all the shades in between, and I don't want to have to live up to anyone's expectations. You're already dating the right brother if you want a Good Samaritan, or the one who pretends to be."

"Now you're being snarky again."

"Snarky? Me? I'm only telling things how they are. We all have our flaws. But the thing that makes me just go crazy is that because my brother projects being a goody-two-shoes, everyone assumes he's perfect. Scott wants so much to be the good guy he'd never admit he'd done anything awful even if he has."

"We're not talking about Brigitte again, are we?"

"Well, it's the perfect example. Scott goes behind my back, steals my girlfriend, and somehow I'm the bad guy."

"You can't judge him on a single thing that happened ages ago. Besides Brigitte, when has he ever hurt anyone?"

"That's a big besides."

"No, it's not. And stop making this about Scott—"

"Let's make it about us, then," David cut her off. "Why are you here, really? Are you tired of living the righteous life? Are you looking to live dangerously? Why come all the way here just to see me? Don't tell me it's because we're friends. Is that really all I am to you?"

No. You're the stranger who stole my heart with a summer kiss, you're the friend who drove me seven hours in the middle of the night just to get me home in time, the boy who made me run under the rain, the man who apologized to Madison and asked her not to say anything. The answer popped into Haley's mind, unbidden. *You're the person who makes me question everything.*

And you're Scott's brother.

With that last thought, Haley's already ragged breath worsened. "I can't be here."

Before she could get up, David grabbed her hands from across the table, his blue eyes flashing. "You can run away now, but you can't outrun your feelings."

"I'm in love with Scott."

David stared her dead in the eye. "Are you saying that to convince me, or to convince yourself?"

Heart beating so fast in her chest it might break out, Haley fought back the tears. There was a vortex of emotions wreaking havoc in her, shattering everything it found in its path. And Haley feared that if she stayed here a second longer, there'd be nothing left behind.

"David, let me go," she pleaded.

He did so without a word, his eyes burning ice as they tore into hers. Haley couldn't hold that gaze; she was too weak. So she fled the room, feeling the lingering touch of David's stare on her long after she'd walked out of the library.

Away. She had to stay away from him.

***

In no time at all, the relaxed mood of the first weeks of school vaporized, and all Harvard students found themselves swept into the middle of the fall term with homework accumulating, massive studying to be done, and midterms looming over them. And in just over a week, the basketball season would officially kick off.

Scott would be busier than ever. Haley still couldn't fathom why anyone would *voluntarily* submit to the pressure and the schedule-nightmare strain of playing on a college varsity team. But Scott loved the game, and so did Jack—Alice was as puzzled—and so had David, and Peter, and everyone else on the team. So there must be something to it the "girls" weren't grasping.

But before the no-drinking, not-a-weekend-without-a-game-until-March season started, the players—as per Coach Morrison's concession—still had their last free-pass-for-all night: Halloween. This year the thirty-first would be on a Monday, so all the parties around campus had been scheduled for the preceding Saturday—a.k.a. today.

As was tradition, the basketball team would go with a group costume. This year they'd picked Minions costumes—ironic, since the shortest guy on the team was six-foot-two. They'd been Smurfs the previous year. Haley chuckled at the thought. How much had changed that night. Alice had gone out to make Jack jealous and had ended up dating Peter instead. Hence the Christmas Hawaiian trip, and Haley's meet-cute with Scott—*and the not-so-cute introduction to unmasked David.*

Last year, Haley had been single at Halloween. Her heart had still been harboring an irrational hope—a gut-twisting hope that squeezed the breath out of her whenever she caught sight of a black feather—of running into a certain masked stranger…

And let's not go there.

After their unofficial meet-up at the library, David had disappeared. No more subtle Facebook invitations, no texts, no nothing. Haley hadn't seen him on campus, and at his and Scott's house, he was a ghost, always coming in late and dashing out before anyone was awake. If Haley got thirsty in the middle of the night, she'd learned to deal with the urgency and wait until she'd heard the front door open and shut before going out to fetch a drink.

It was hard to believe it was Halloween already. It had only been a year ago she didn't—*exactly,* kisses under the stars didn't count—know either Williams brother. It all seemed like ages before.

"I'm not sure about this," Madison said, bringing Haley back to the present.

All three roommates were in Madison's room, doing their official "dress rehearsal" for the night. After much debate and not many choices available—it had taken them forever to decide on costumes, and all the good ones had already disappeared off the racks—they'd settled on being chipmunks. Haley was Alvin in a red sweatshirt, black leggings, and long, pulled up red socks, Madison was Simon, with blue socks and sweatshirt, and Alice was Theodore in green.

"We're basically dressed for the gym," Madison insisted.

"We can still add the initials," Alice offered, standing in front of the mirror next to Madison and holding a big, cut-out "S" made of white adhesive paper close to her chest.

"Then we'll be dressed for the gym and lame," Madison said. "I still think we should've gone like handmaids."

Madison had wanted to go dressed as characters from *The Handmaid's Tale* by Margaret Atwood.

"And how is the red-nuns look any better?" Haley said. "I like this costume. It's easy, comfortable, and we can wear sneakers."

"But it's so simple," Madison protested. "Do you think people will get it?"

"If we put on the initials," Alice insisted. She grabbed Madison by the shoulders and spun her around. "We can stick them on the back." She held the "S" near the middle of Madison's back.

Madison turned her head over her shoulder to stare in the mirror. "They're not so lame like that."

"And we can all draw whiskers on our faces and get hair-bands with ears," Haley said. Madison was warming up to the chipmunks idea, and they needed to strike whilst the iron was hot.

"I still have my cat ears from last year," Alice said.

Madison turned to face her, affronted. "We're chipmunks, not cats."

"I'm sure they'll have chipmunk ears at the store," Haley mediated, trying not to laugh at Alice's dismayed face. Madison was definitely taking this costume thing a bit too seriously.

After several trips to different costume stores—because, no, they couldn't use mice ears; they were too black, too big, and too round—one YouTube makeup tutorial on how to draw the perfect rodent nose and whiskers on one's face, and much hair curling, they were finally ready.

The party house was the same as last year, a six-room, double-story townhome that had a ground floor large enough to host such a big party. It wasn't a "one party every weekend" situation; the guys living there only threw a few big parties every year, and Halloween was hands-down their best. They put the extra care in decorating the house, garden, and back patio with pumpkins, spiders in their webs, skeletons, and such.

Thanks to their sneakers, Madison, Haley, and Alice had an easy time walking the few blocks to get to the party house. And thanks to their sweatshirts, they didn't need to risk bringing a coat and losing it, or having it ruined by party hazards. They'd walked last year, too, but without heels, it was a much quicker, less painful business.

Halfway to the destination, they bumped into a horde of Minions. In head-to-toe yellow and with an average height well above six feet, they were easy to spot. Less easy was for Haley and Alice to identify their respective boyfriends. When they did, they couldn't help but laugh. Scott and Jack were silly adorable in their yellow onesies with big, round, fake eye goggles on top of their heads.

Scott kissed her and frowned at her sweatshirt. "What are you supposed to be?"

Madison pushed past them, muttering, "Told you no one was going to get it."

"We're *The Chipmunks,*" Haley explained, and she turned around to point at the big "A" on her back. "I'm Alvin, Madison is Simon, and Alice is Theodore."

"Oh, I get it now. Shouldn't you girls be speaking in shrill little voices?"

Haley obliged him, trying to make a good impression of that I-just-inhaled-helium-from-a-balloon little voice. "I can talk like this all night if you want."

"Nope, just kidding. Your usual voice will do just fine." He offered her his elbow. "Shall we?"

Chipmunks and Minions made their way to the house together and, since there were so many of them, they had to queue at the entrance and enter in smaller groups of two or three. Haley was impatient to get in, but just a few minutes after reaching the back of the living room, the main party area, the walls were pressing in on her.

The atmosphere inside the house was suffocating in comparison to the crisp air outside. With the party already in full swing, throngs of boys and girls were drinking, sweating, and dancing body-to-body to the hard beats of the loud music blasting from a set of giant speakers positioned on either side of the fireplace. It wasn't just the volume of the music that felt oppressive; whoever was in charge of the playlist had gone full horror on them, and was spinning one dark, violent tune after the other.

Also, the lights were all off, the only illumination coming from a thousand fake candles scattered all over and a few fairy lights strung over doorways and around the fireplace. Still, the scarce light produced long and gloomy shadows on the walls, made even spookier by the great number of party-goers clad in blood-splattered, grotesque costumes who had taken Halloween too literally. Not to mention the many hooded figures hovering around.

Haley shivered despite the heat. Oh, please, she was being silly. It was Halloween. Costumes were supposed to be gruesome, and as for the stale air, they just needed to open a window or two. She tackled the closest one, relishing the fresh intake of cool air. But she couldn't spend the night breathing out of a window, so she beckoned Scott to follow her out of the living room and into the somewhat less crazy kitchen area. A cool beer was what she needed.

Haley almost chugged the whole cup in one sip, and refilled from the keg, needing more.

What's wrong with me?

Something about tonight didn't sit right with her. Same as in horror movies when the innocent sorority girl doesn't realize the killer is watching her, and she's about to die.

Mmm, hello? No one's going to murder you. I promise, Haley's inner self chided.

Yeah right, no need to stress.

Haley took another sip of beer and followed Scott back into the living room. She searched the walls for another window to open… and froze.

Deep in the shadows, passing behind the dancing crowd, a mask caught her eye. Black and full-faced, with only holes for the eyes and a triangular opening at the bottom for the mouth and chin. The mask looked as expensive as Haley remembered it, with its silver beading, black feathers, and a surface so smooth it appeared to be made of the finest porcelain.

When Haley's eyes met with the blue ones peering out of the black mask, the throbbing beat of blood in her body sped up. Her throat clenched, making absorbing the scarce oxygen in the room all the more difficult. The temperature inside seemed to grow even warmer, making it impossible for Haley to breathe. Or move at all. She was only able to stare into David's eyes as he approached the patio doors, moving behind the mass of sweaty party-goers swaying in rhythm with the music—vampire girls dancing sexily with each other, witches grinding against their zombie partners, and all kinds of monsters throwing their hands in the air.

The black tux costume bestowed on David an eerie glamour, like a modern-day vampire prince, making the boy behind the mask even more handsomely wicked. Stopping by the French windows, he fixed the feathered and jeweled mask on his face and bowed his head in a barely perceptible nod.

Palpitations, followed by sweaty palms and a light head, were Haley's first response to the sight of David wearing *the* mask. The unexpected appearance of a ghost from her past was too much. She was reacting in ways she didn't like, but couldn't ignore. He had power over her; Haley could no longer deny it. But she could choose not to act on it.

Feeling as guilty as if she'd done something wrong, she stared up at Scott. He seemed unaware that his brother had joined the party. He just stood there peacefully sipping his beer and nodding his head in time with the awful music.

Haley stared back at David. He was now leaning against the wall next to the patio doors, regarding her with a satisfied little smirk that seemed to say, *"The ball's in your park."*

"Hey, Scott." Matt's voice made her turn again. "I need a teammate for beer pong. You in?"

Scott looked down at her. "Do you mind?"

"No, not at all. Go ahead."

The timing was perfect. While Scott played, she could go discreetly kill his brother. With all the fake blood around, no one would notice. Tonight, she could get away with murder.

"You're not coming to cheer?" Scott asked her.

"No, actually, I need a breath of fresh air."

Scott kissed her and followed Matt toward the beer pong table in the farthest corner of the room opposite to the patio doors. *How convenient.* Haley waited until they were a few throws into the game and completely absorbed by it, before marching toward David.

"What the hell?" she said without preamble, shoving him against the wall with both hands.

"Whoa-oh, calm down." He smirked under the mask. "I like it feisty, but I have my limits. Should we pick a safe word first?"

"David, cut the crap!" she yelled, part out of frustration and part to be heard over the deafening music. "You disappear for two months and then you show up like this?"

"Like what?" he asked, infuriatingly calm.

"Wearing the same mask you had on the night we met."

"Oh, you mean this little trinket." He readjusted the elastic behind his head. "This was expensive. It's good economy to wear it more than once."

"Why here? Why tonight?"

"It's Halloween, in case you haven't noticed. Masks are all the rage."

He was being impossible, and the music, the heat, the artificial fog…

"I need some air," Haley said. She slid the patio door open and walked out. "Do not follow me," she ordered, slamming the door in his face.

Not two steps out, and she heard the door slid open again. Without turning, Haley walked to the railing and gripped it with both hands. Soon someone was standing right behind her.

"Why shouldn't I follow you?" David whispered, his mouth close to her ear, so that Haley could feel his breath blow softly down her neck.

"I'm in love with your brother," she said, sounding rather desperate.

"So you are," David said—angry, merciless.

Haley wriggled sideways and turned around to face him. *Bad move.* He was the exact replica of the boy she'd fallen in love with that night at the masquerade. Because he was the boy of the masquerade. Only now he was so much more.

Her head spun with memories from the summer ball. The flirting, the dancing, and David kissing her. The touch of his lips on hers, his arms wrapping around her body—

No. No. No. A walk down memory lane wasn't a wise choice. Right now she needed to get out of this conversation and go find Scott.

"You can't keep doing this," she said, in what she hoped was a composed, rational voice. "You keep going hot and cold on me. First we're friends, then we're not, and then you pull a stunt like this. What do you want?"

"*I* keep going hot and cold?" he hissed. "I don't think so. I only came to a Halloween party wearing a mask—"

"Stop lying!" Haley yelled.

"You stop lying!" David shouted back. He took a step forward, grabbing her by the shoulders. Eyes locked on hers, he hissed, "What do *you* want?"

He was too close, and Haley's chest heaved. She was dangerously close to tears, and the few beers she'd had were enough to make her too damn emotional to answer that question.

"Is everything all right here?" Scott's voice interrupted.

Haley's eyes snapped to him, hoping darkness and the whiskers painted on her face would help conceal how upset she was.

"Yeah," she said, trying to master a normal tone and shrugging free of David. "I was just going to come look for you. Did you win the game?"

Scott didn't appear convinced, even less so when David spun around and greeted him. "Hello, brother. Nice gear," he said, eyeing the Minion costume sarcastically.

"David."

Scott seemed confused. After the accident at the pool, and the way David had taken care of him in the following weeks, he wasn't so quick to get angry with his brother. But now Scott was staring between his girlfriend and his brother with a deep, worried frown.

"I didn't know you were coming," he finally said.

David shrugged. "Oh, you know. This is the only half-decent party near campus. I'd better get back inside before all the pretty girls are taken." He sent a pointed look Haley's way.

She watched him move back inside and braced herself for the inevitable questions, but Scott only asked, "Are you sure you're okay?"

"Yeah, it's just so stuffy inside."

"Not anymore. They've opened all the windows. I was coming to open the patio door as well when I saw you out here... The situation seemed *tense*."

"Not really, just—"

"There you are." Madison barged through the now-open doors, interrupting her. "I've been looking for you everywhere. We're playing girls versus boys. You have to come now or we'll lose the table."

Haley shrugged and looked up at Scott, "Do you mind?"

"No." He forced a smile, clearly not happy their conversation had to stop. "Who's on the boys' team?" he asked Madison.

"You, Jack, and Matt. Come on, you two, hurry up." Madison beckoned them inside and, without waiting to check if they were following her, she pushed her way back toward the beer pong table.

Haley plastered a smile on her face. "Come on, she'll kill us if we don't get there in two seconds."

Scott stared at her for a moment longer, his expression seemingly saying, *"This conversation isn't over."*

She nodded in acknowledgment and went back into the house where, with all the windows open, the air was breathable again and not faint-inducing. Eager to have an excuse to drink more and not have to explain the whole David-in-the-black-mask situation to Scott, Haley joined Alice and Madison at their end of the table, yelling, "Ladies throw first!"

***

"You're upset," Scott said—a statement, not a question.

Ah, so he hasn't forgotten, Haley thought ruefully.

They'd been walking in silence toward her house for a good ten minutes now, and after an entire night of drinking and partying with no mention of the David Factor, Haley had hoped Scott had dropped the topic for good.

Apparently not.

"I'm not upset," Haley said, keeping her eyes on the concrete.

"Okay, but you were before when you were talking to David. Why?"

Different brother, same annoying questions.

"It was nothing, Scott, let it go."

Scott stopped, but Haley pretended not to notice and kept walking to see if he'd follow her. He didn't, so she had no other choice than to stop and turn to face him. "You really want to do this now, at two in the morning, while we're freezing our asses off in the middle of the street?"

"I don't know, Haley," he said, his features so serious that not even the Minion costume could infuse humor into the situation. "What is it we're doing?"

"Discussing your brother, *again.*"

"Well, there'd be no need to discuss my brother *again* if I hadn't found you talking to him with the face of someone whose cat just died. And don't tell me it was nothing because I'm not an idiot."

"It was that stupid mask, okay? Are you happy now?"

"What mask? What's wrong with the mask?"

Haley stared at the ground. "It was the same one he was wearing the night we met."

"And by *the night you met,*" Scott said in such a tense, cold, un-Scott voice that Haley had to look up at him. He was speaking through clenched teeth, his jaw tense. "What you really meant *is the night you kissed him.*"

"What do you want me to say? I can't cancel the past."

"I'm not worried about the past."

"What's that supposed to mean?"

"Look at you. My brother shows up wearing a stupid mask, and you get upset, then pretend nothing has happened all night—nice act, by the way—and finally, when I ask you about it, you try to bullshit me."

"I wasn't bullshitting you, I just thought it wasn't important."

"Do you often get so upset about unimportant stuff?"

"Why do you have to make such a big deal about it? David came to the party wearing that mask to provoke me, and it worked. You know how he is; he's the master at pushing a person's buttons."

"No, Haley, he's a master at pushing *your* buttons. Can you stop pretending for a second?"

"Pretending to do what?"

Scott studied her for a long moment. "The only thing I can't tell is if you're just lying to me, or also to yourself…"

Different brother, *definitely* same annoying questions.

"Lying about WHAT?" Haley shouted back.

Scott stared at her dead in the eye, and when he spoke next he did so in a tone so calm it bordered on vicious. "Do you have feelings for my brother?"

Haley wanted to say 'no,' to shout it. But somehow her throat seemed to have clogged up and her mouth didn't open. Eyes wide, she could only stare at Scott, unable to speak. They stood like that for an eternity, looking at each other while an unconfessable truth was being shared between them.

Scott's jaw tightened, and he broke eye contact first. Gaze now fixed on the curb, he said, "Let's go. I'm walking you home."

Haley fell into step next to him, not sure what to say, her heart beating as fast as if she'd been running. In the end, she could only come up with a lame, "I'm sorry."

It came out strangled, and it didn't convey nearly a tenth of what Haley was feeling.

"It's my fault," Scott said. "I went away, and that's all he needed to weasel his way into your life."

"Scott, it's not your fault. Whatever David has over me, it doesn't matter. Scott, stop." She placed herself squarely in his path and grabbed him by the shoulders. "I'm in love with you. I chose you, and I choose you every day."

He gently but firmly shook her off. "See, Haley, the thing is: it shouldn't have to be a choice. Least of all one you have to make every day."

"What are you saying?"

"Honestly? I don't know. Maybe you were right. We shouldn't be having this conversation at two in the morning."

They walked in silence the rest of the way to her house. In front of her building, she climbed up a step so that their eyes were level, and asked him if he wanted to come up.

"Not tonight," he said. "I think I'm just going to walk home and clear my head."

Haley nodded, close to tears for the second time that evening. Same sadness, different brother.

Haley bent her head, touching her forehead to his. They stayed like that for a long time, until she finally said, "I'll see you tomorrow and we'll talk, okay?"

Scott pushed away from her and nodded, before walking away into the cold night.

***

In part because of what had happened with David and Scott, and also thanks to one game too many of beer pong, Haley spent the night tossing and turning in bed. Nightmares of zombies and vampires who alternately assumed the faces of either Scott or David tormented her all night, until she woke up in a pool of sweat.

She showered and ran to Scott's apartment with her hair still wet, not caring if David was there or not. When Scott opened the door, she threw herself into his arms and kissed him with a desperate passion. Without a word, he scooped her up into his arms and brought her to his bedroom, where they made love with that same desperation. And the physical closeness seemed to cure the argument.

Scott didn't bring up David anymore, and Haley carefully avoided the topic as well. And if conversation felt stiff and tentative at first, they returned to normal interactions in a couple of days.

So, on the first Thursday of November, five days after the dreadful Halloween party, Haley headed toward Lavietes Pavilion with her roommates to watch the opening basketball game of the season: Harvard versus MIT. A super competitive game between next door neighbor schools. Jack had provided the tickets, and once inside the gym, Alice led them to their seats in the center bleacher only a few rows back from the basketball court.

"I need the restroom," Alice said as soon as she was out of her coat. "You guys need something from the concession stand?"

"No, I'm good, thanks," Madison said.

"Me, too," echoed Haley.

Alice left, and Haley concentrated on the players doing their warm-up drills… until her vision was blocked by a tall body.

"Hello, ladies." David had materialized in front of them, clad in a Crimson-supporter outfit: Harvard Crimson long-sleeved T-shirt and baseball hat, jeans, and sneakers. Popcorn in one hand, a soda in the other. "So nice of you to reserve me a spot."

Haley gasped. Her nostrils filled with his familiar day-on-a-boat-out-at-sea scent, and she met his eyes for an instant before quickly looking away. Not that it saved her from receiving a Taser-like electric shock. David carried on as if nothing weird had happened between them, sliding in front of her to go sit next to Madison, one seat down from Haley.

"That's Alice's seat," Madison protested.

"Here." David lodged the soda between his legs and used his free hand to remove his baseball hat and throw it on the empty chair to his left. He wiggled on the seat to push aside Alice's coat as well. "She can take my spot. I like to sit in the middle."

"What are you doing here?" Madison insisted.

"Hey, I might not be on the team anymore, doesn't mean I'm not a fan."

Haley made a point of keeping her eyes trained on the court below them and not looking at him. It was too soon. For the past few days, she had purposely forbidden her brain from wandering anywhere near the David topic, but the fact remained that Scott had forced her to admit there was something between them. And now Haley's stupid heart wouldn't let her take it back.

"Oh, hello," Alice said, surprised when she came back to find her seat taken. "You're in my seat."

Haley made an effort to follow the conversation, pretending she was looking—and thinking—elsewhere while she used her peripheral vision to track David's every movement.

He patted the chair next to him. "You've been moved to the left."

"Why don't *you* move to the left?"

"Come on, Alice, be nice. I promise I won't bite." Then he flashed her one of his most dashing smiles. "Popcorn?"

To Haley's dismay, Alice capitulated. She took a handful of popcorn and sat down just as the referee whistled to signal the game had started. They all followed the match in silence until about ten minutes in, when everyone around them, David included, shot up from the bleachers, yelling angrily against the referee.

Haley, Madison, and Alice were pretty much the only three people still seated in the whole stadium.

"What's going on?" Alice asked, once David was back in his seat.

"As the current and former girlfriend of two team captains, you know an awful little about the game."

"I hate watching sports. I'm a hero just for being here."

"Well, you came to see all Peter's games, so now you can't miss one of Jack's, can you?"

Alice glared at him.

"Oops, wasn't I supposed to say that? Are we pretending you and Peter never happened?"

"Why don't you harass someone else?"

"Well, your friend over there is doing all she can to pretend I don't exist." Haley did her best not to respond to the provocation, or even give notice she'd heard him. "And, as for Blondie here," David continued.

"I've harassed her enough for a lifetime—"

"A-men," Madison interjected.

"So that leaves just the two of us," David concluded.

"I'm such a lucky girl." Alice scoffed. "On second thought, since I'm stuck with you…" Alice smacked David on the leg, just above the knee. "I always say the wrong thing to Jack after a game, and I have a feeling that if I say 'congratulations for winning' tonight, he'll bite my head off. Care to explain why, even though we're winning, Jack has his 'game-over' face on and Coach Morrison looks like he's about to have an apoplectic fit? If he shouts any louder, he'll spit out his vocal cords all the way over here."

Haley kept her eyes trained on the game, but that didn't stop her from eavesdropping on David and Alice. The truth was none of the girls understood much about basketball, and she, too, never knew how to talk to Scott after a game. So it'd be nice to have someone finally explain it all. Even if she couldn't openly acknowledge she was interested in what David was saying.

"Jack and the coach are mad because we're playing like crap," he explained.

"But we're ahead by twelve points. How can we be playing like crap and still lead by so much?"

"Well, that's easy: the other team is playing worse than us. If we were up against a half-decent team, they'd be hammering us."

"What are they doing wrong?"

"For starters, the new guy, number 1." David pointed at the court. "He has some big shoes to fill."

"Whose shoes?"

"Peter. He's replaced him as shooting guard—"

"Which is?"

"As the name suggests, the player who takes the most shots. He's usually the scoring leader, the MVP." David pointed to three imaginary spots as he spelled out each letter. "Most. Valuable. Player."

"And the guy isn't good?"

"Oh, no, the guy *is* good. But Peter was *phenomenal*. Let's just say this guy is not getting drafted by the NBA next year."

"I think I'm not gonna use that as a talking point with Jack."

David chuckled. "Wise girl."

"So what role is Jack playing?"

"Point guard. He's the game-maker, the one responsible for bringing the ball down the court and launching offensive plays. He directs the team."

"And he's doing a poor job?"

"No, the captain's the only one keeping up last year's standards."

Haley couldn't pretend not to be listening anymore. She turned toward David and asked, "Are you saying Scott's a bad player?"

"Hey, hello there." He waved at her.

Haley glared at him.

"I'm afraid Scotty isn't at his best tonight."

"What's his role?" Madison asked.

"Center. He's the team's muscle."

"So what's he doing wrong?" Haley asked.

"Almost everything tonight."

"Why?"

David studied the action taking place at the moment, his eyes roaming the court as they followed his brother around. Haley imitated him. MIT had the ball, and their number 12 was trying to find an opening into the Crimson defenses, that much was clear. The MIT guy with the ball passed it to a teammate close to Matt. This other guy caught the ball, feinted to the right, then sprung left instead, dribbled away from Matt, shot the ball toward the rim, and... missed. Scott jumped up in synchrony with another player from MIT, both of them reaching out for the ball... and the other guy got it, turned, and dunked it right into the hoop with both hands.

Admittedly, not Scott's best play. She turned to David to see if he had more of an insight.

David frowned, still studying the game. Finally, he whispered, "He's afraid."

"Afraid? Of what?"

"Of taking a hit to the head." David turned toward her. "He's supposed to be physically dominating the adversaries, getting the rebounds, blocking defenders, and opening other players up for driving to the basket... But look." He pointed to the court. "As soon as he sees as much as an elbow coming his way, he shies away."

"Oh." Haley was worried now. "It's the fall, isn't it?"

"Must be." David shrugged. "He never had this problem before."

"So what now?"

"If he keeps playing like that, the coach will bench him."

"Can you help him?"

David tilted his head to the side and studied her for a second or two with that impossibly sexy smirk of his. "When you ask it like that," he said, winking, "you know I can't say no."

David

"Rise and shine," David announced in a sing-song voice, entering his brother's room on Sunday morning, three days after Scott's dreadful performance at Thursday's home game.

Scott was sleeping like a baby and barely stirred under the covers.

That won't do, David thought. With a vicious sense of satisfaction, he slid the blinds open and let the bright daylight do the dirty work for him.

True to expectations, Scott woke up with a groan, shouting, "Go away!" and trying to shield his eyes by burrowing his head under the sheets.

"Nah, ah, ah." David reached for the other end of the comforter and pulled in the opposite direction.

Scott jumped up into a sitting position and glared at him. The look could've worked, save that it was clear Scott still had morning foggy vision and couldn't properly focus on objects or people.

In fact, his brother rubbed his eyes before saying, "What's wrong with you?"

"C'mon, Scotty, you don't want to spend the day in bed. The sun is shining and I'm dying to shoot a few hoops."

"What? You want to play basketball? No way."

"I've made you breakfast."

"Huh?"

"Breakfast is ready, the court is booked, and now all you have to do is get your ass out of bed." David snapped his fingers twice. "Chop, chop."

"David, I hate to break it to you, but the last thing I want to do today is play basketball. Practice and the games are enough, and Sunday is my day off."

David stared at the ceiling with the air of a martyr. "Well, I tried the sugar coated version…" He sat at the foot of the bed and patted his brother's legs. "If the simple joy of shooting a few hoops with your big brother isn't enough of an incentive, let me tell you how today is going to play out. You'll quit the Sleeping Beauty act, get out of bed, and eat the breakfast I prepared for you with all my brotherly love. Then you're coming with me to the gym, and we're going to play."

"Or else?"

David flared his nostrils. "Or else Coach Morrison is going to realize you're playing like a scared little girl and bench you for the rest of the season. Thursday night you were lucky MIT was full of crap. But the first team with a smidgen of talent is going to crush you, and you'll let them because you're afraid of a little confrontation. So today I'll rough you up until you're all set and good to go. Sound right?"

Scott shot him a glare. "It was *one* bad game."

"You missed nine rebounds out of ten. You got away with it once, but next time… Coach Morrison is going to catch on sooner or later. It took me about five minutes."

Scott finally threw the covers away and swung his feet off the bed. "What's this lovely breakfast you made?"

"Milk and cereal." David smirked, standing up.

"You've got to be kidding me," Scott said under his breath, getting out of bed.

"Hey, there's coffee, too."

***

The more awake Scott became, the more hostile he turned toward David. It was as if he'd remembered he was supposed to be mad at David but had forgotten in the few minutes after waking up. They ate breakfast in silence and walked to the gym in silence, the only sound that of the basketball David was bouncing off the concrete.

Once at their destination, David ran into the indoor court, putting on a little dribbling exhibition. Then he bounced the ball in a wide arc off the floor, leaped high, and slammed the thing. He caught the ball as it swished through the net and dribbled it back to where Scott was looking at him, unimpressed, from the midcourt line.

David and Scott stood in the center circle, facing each other like gladiators in the arena.

"You ready?" David asked.

"Do I have a choice?" Scott said.

"It's your life," David said, dropping the ball at Scott's feet.

"Yeah, it is." His brother picked up the ball while David spread his feet and arms, ready to defend.

David jerked his chin at the ball. "Let's see it."

Scott pulled up and let go of a twenty-footer.

Swish. It was in.

David ran to the basket to grab the ball and slung it back to Scott, then dropped back into his defensive stance. "C'mon, Scotty, that's cheating. We need to go *head* to *head*. Know what I mean?" David snickered.

Scott just blinked at him. Then he pulled up and sank another.

David retrieved the ball again. "That's how you wanna play it?" He resumed his position. "I've got all day."

Scott pulled up again and buried another one.

That was it. David gave him the ball again, but this time he crowded right up next to Scott.

"What happened to all day?" Scott asked. Then he started to dribble, putting the ball on the floor for the first time since their mock game had started.

With a spurt forward, he drove for the basket, only to have David smack the ball away.

"Is that all you got, brother?" David taunted. "Because if that's your best game, you're benched for the rest of the season." With that, he slashed through the lane, shot, and scored.

Scott flared his nostrils, annoyed.

David fired the ball back at him. "Show me what you have."

Scott dribbled, feinted right and darted left, but David saw the move coming and was on him in an instant, taking the ball away again. He pivoted on his heels, bolted for the basket, and scored again. And again. And again. And again.

"Is your butt already getting comfortable on the bench?" David taunted, before he flung the ball back at his brother.

As soon as his fingers had a secure grip on the ball, an enraged Scott charged at him like a bull. He threw a shoulder into his chest and spun hard, catching David's nose with a vicious elbow thrust. David bent at the waist, holding his nose with his hand as a few droplets of blood dripped down. In the background, he heard the ball swish past the net.

"You had enough?"

Scott's angry voice made him turn.

"Why stop now?" David asked, pulling up the bottom of his tank top to wipe his face. "You're just starting to get the gist of it."

Scott pushed the ball on his chest. "Be my guest, but you won't score again."

David snickered. Then he backed off and worked a crossover dribble, trying to set his brother up. He faked left. And when Scott leaned, David darted right. He went past Scott in a flash, gaining a straight shot to the basket. David leaped and let go of a sweet finger roll. But before it reached its height, Scott pinned it against the backboard, blocking David's action. And the next. And the next. And the next.

David came down from another failed jump and stared at his brother. "Look who's back."

Scott glared at him.

"Is that all the gratitude I get for helping you?"

"Helping me?" Scott discarded the ball to the side with an angry throw and marched on him. "Were you also trying to help me on Halloween?" He shoved David back with both hands.

David staggered a few steps backward. "Uh-oh. Someone is pouty…"

"Stay the hell away from me, David, and from her." Scott glowered at him one last time, adding, "I mean it." Then he stormed out of the gym.

"You're welcome," David whispered to the thin air.

Haley

"I'm about to make a proposal that might be very unpopular," Alice announced, coming into the living room.

It was Friday afternoon and, instead of gearing up for an evening out, the girls were all wearing sweatpants, ready to watch the Stanford vs Harvard game on TV that was scheduled to start in less than an hour at 5 p.m. Crazy as it sounded, the game was neither in California or

Massachusetts, but it would take place in Shanghai. Apparently, both the Crimson and the Cardinal wanted to do a little brand-building, despite being already well-known internationally.

"What is it?" Haley asked, just as Madison said, "If you're about to suggest we renounce popcorn because it's not healthy, you're out."

"It's not food related," Alice said.

Both Haley and Madison stared up at her expectantly.

"I thought," Alice said, wringing her hands, "we could invite David over to watch the game with us."

The proposition earned Haley's roommate two sets of raised brows.

"Before you say 'no,' hear me out." Alice raised her palms to forestall any protest. "I know you both have your issues with him, but... He was really useful last week when he explained everything that was going on play-by-play. First time I could talk to Jack about a game. And David's probably going to watch the game anyway... so I figured..."

"I don't think it's a good idea," Haley said unequivocally.

She hadn't told the girls about Halloween. If she had, she was sure Alice would've never proposed anything like that. And she wasn't planning on telling them now, but still, David in her house, while Scott was away, was a big, fat *no!*

Unfortunately, Madison had the opposite reaction. She shrugged and said, "I don't mind. If we have to watch the damn game, we might as well understand what's going on. It's so boring when we can only count the points."

With one roommate convinced, Alice turned to Haley with a pleading expression. "Please? David really helped last time..." Haley was about to say 'no' again when Alice continued with her argument. "What if he's watching the game at home all alone and sad?"

Haley scowled. "Think more at a bar and with a girl on his arm."

Alice switched to a passive-aggressive approach. "Okay, if you don't want to, I'll drop it."

Haley puffed her cheeks up and let the air out in an impatient huff. "How important is this to you?"

Alice joined her hands in prayer. "Very, very important. Crucial to my relationship's health."

"Oh, come on," Madison said, coming to Alice's aid. "The game is more fun when David's explaining it."

True.

But you have unexplored feelings for the guy, a voice retorted inside Haley's head. *Best to avoid him.*

Also true.

But if she said 'no' now, the girls would sense she wasn't telling them something. And Haley really didn't want to have to explain the whole Halloween drama now. Better to say 'yes' and hope David would refuse. It was Friday night, after all, he probably already had plans. Yes, he'd definitely say 'no.'

Wrong!

Less than half an hour later their doorbell rang, and David waltzed into the house carrying a Coors Light six-pack and four pizza boxes.

"Hello, ladies, I come bearing gifts." He dropped everything on the coffee table. "I have beers and I have pizza. Double cheese, pepperoni, and two regulars. You get your pick."

"Amen," Madison said, launching herself at one of the pizza boxes.

Haley stole a glance at him and cursed herself for the tiny electric jolt meeting his blue eyes gave her. In response, David's mouth curled up at one corner as if he'd just read her mind. He winked at her before sitting comfortably on the couch between her and Alice.

Haley tried to make herself small and shrink away as much as she could. But nothing could shield her from his conspicuous presence next to her… Hell, this was going to be a long evening.

***

"Can you believe the team had to go to China to play a game?" Madison asked during the half-time break. "I mean, freaking China! It's a different continent."

"At least they'll be home for Christmas this year," Alice said. "I couldn't have afforded another trip to Hawaii."

"So what are you doing?" Madison asked. "Aren't your parents going on their usual Christmas cruise?"

Alice beamed at them. "Going home with Jack. He's already invited me. I guess I'm meeting the parents."

"Ugh, I'm getting diabetes just looking at you," Madison said jokingly, then turned to Haley. "And what about you?"

"Yeah," David said, inserting himself into the conversation. "Are you coming home to *meet the parents?*"

He stared at her with a half-challenging, half-mocking little smirk. The fact that going home with Scott to meet his parents would mean also spending the holidays with David, in the same house, was not lost on Haley.

She'd already met their mother in a brief encounter back in August while Scott was still hospitalized. But to spend the holidays at the Williams' house would be a whole different ball game.

"I haven't discussed it with Scott yet," Haley said, choosing a neutral reply. "But I can't bail on my parents for two Christmases in a row, especially not after this summer."

"Oh, right," Madison said.

David only mouthed a cocksure "Pity" at her.

"The game's back on," Alice said, grabbing the remote and turning up the volume. "Come on, guys, we're only two points down."

The words had barely left her lips when Stanford scored again.

"Only four points down?" Alice said, dismayed. "Why are we doing such a poor job?"

"We're letting them take the lead," David said. "It's always them going ahead, and us trying to catch up. Our defense sucks."

"Is it Scott's fault?" Haley asked.

"In part," David confirmed.

"Is he still afraid?"

"No, I cured that. But he's angry, and he's making poor judgment calls."

"Angry about what?"

David turned to look at her. "I don't know, you tell me. Trouble in paradise?"

"No!" Haley wasn't about to discuss her relationship issues with the guy who was causing them.

"Then Scott must be wearing his angry *mask* for no reason," David replied, putting extra strain on the word 'mask' to let her know he wasn't buying any of her bullshit.

Haley shot him a not-taking-the-bait look and concentrated on the game, which, from then on, only got worse. So far, Harvard had managed to keep in pursuit of the Cardinal within a margin of four to five points, but the gap started increasing to eight, ten, and even twelve points toward the end.

With only ten seconds left on the clock, Harvard was down by nine. Not ready to give up, Jack was slashing through the lane in a last attempt to bring home two more points, but the referee blew his whistle three times before he could shoot. The game was over.

"And that, ladies," David said in a resigned tone, "is how you lose."

***

Scott didn't come back from China until late next Sunday night. With midterms so close, they could only hang out together to study. So, on Monday, they met at a private study room at the library. Scott barely kissed her hello before opening a biology textbook and burying his nose in it. Since they had to do homework, it made sense not to talk much, but Haley sensed Scott's silence went beyond that. It felt… hostile.

Initially, Haley pinned the bad mood on the lost game against Stanford. After all, who'd be happy to fly fifteen hours to China only to lose in front of thousands of local spectators and even more college basketball aficionados back home? But, according to David, Scott had been playing like crap because he'd been angry… So if he'd started the match already in a bad temper, losing would only have aggravated the issue, but it wasn't the cause…

Haley shifted in her chair. "Are you sure you're okay?" she asked, for what must've been the third time.

"Yes."

"Is it basketball?"

"No."

"So you're not having any trouble playing?"

Scott kept his eyes trained on the pre-med textbook he was highlighting. "What's that supposed to mean?"

"Seems you have a harder time defending since… the accident…"

"And since when have you become a basketball expert?"

"I'm not, but David said—"

Scott's neck snapped up so fast Haley thought it might break. "David? When did you see him?"

"We watched the games together."

"Games, plural?"

"He came to the MIT game. It's a public space," Haley added

defensively, seeing his dark look. "And Alice invited him to our place to watch the Stanford game. She needed someone to explain what was going on with the game so she could discuss it with Jack later, and David is the only person we know who understands basketball."

"Why didn't you tell me?" Scott demanded.

"Wow, Scott, calm down, do I have to fill in a log every time I see David now?"

"You shouldn't be seeing him at all."

"What? Are you going to have to approve all of my friends now?"

"David is not your friend, as you made very clear on Halloween."

There. The resentment that had kept bubbling under the surface since Halloween was finally seeping through the cracks. No matter if they hadn't discussed it, or pretended the issue didn't exist. David's shadow was always with them. And it made Haley feel so angry and so guilty.

"So David is on the list of people I can't see. What's next? Are you going to pick the clothes I can wear?"

Scott stared at her, shocked. "That's not fair, Haley, I'm not some jealous psycho. What would you do in my place? Would it be okay for you if I hung out with a girl who…" Scott trailed off, apparently unable to frame what the equivalent would be. A girl he liked? A girl he had feelings for? What had he wanted to say?

"Listen. For the MIT game, David just showed up at the gym and sat between Alice and Madison. I could either go and miss the game, or stay and not make a big deal out of it. And for the Stanford game, Alice invited him to our place, and—"

"You could've said 'no!'"

"I did, but she insisted so much it would've been weird if I kept saying 'no.' I would've had to explain…" This time Haley left the phrase hanging.

"Explanations are hard, aren't they?" Scott said, his tone bitter.

He looked down at his hands and kept silent for the longest time. When he finally lifted his gaze, his eyes were all red and shiny. "I can't do this, Haley. Not anymore…"

Haley's body reacted as if she were free-falling, even while sitting perfectly still in her chair. She stared at Scott filled with dread and, oddly enough, relief. Since Halloween, something had shifted in their relationship, even if they'd both pretended everything was the same.

David had been on her mind more often than not, and Scott seemed to have picked up on her indecision, even if he hadn't said a word about it. Until now.

"Come on, Haley," Scott continued. "We're past you trying to spare my feelings… You can admit it."

"Over the summer…" Haley paused to gather her thoughts. "Something changed… between David and me."

"When you found out about the kiss?"

"Maybe that was the start, but then it became much more than it ever used to be. I never had real feelings for him, not even after the kiss. And I never lied to you, and I don't want to lie now…"

"So what happened?" Scott's voice shook. "What changed?"

Haley looked at him with teary eyes. "You went away," she admitted. "In the beginning, I missed you so much… But all summer we spent days without having a meaningful conversation… Whenever I called, you were too busy to talk, or it wasn't the right moment. That is, if you even picked up the phone at all. It never seemed like you missed me… and I guess because of it, I sort of stopped missing you… It felt like you weren't there for me, not just physically, but emotionally, too…"

"And David was?"

Haley swallowed and nodded. "With you gone, it was like I couldn't breathe anymore… But David… he bulldozed his way into my life and forced me to let the air in again… and my first gasp of it was a big laugh."

"So it was all my fault… because I left?" Scott said, again not angry, only bitter. "You're saying I practically drove you to him… He told me, you know?"

"Told you what?"

"That he was gonna steal you while I was gone. I just never thought you would've let David into your heart…" Scott paused, then asked, "What is it exactly that you like about him? I mean, I get it, he was there when your dad got sick, but…" Scott stared at her, at a loss for words.

"David makes everything feel new and… unpredictable. I'm a different person with him. He changes me, challenges me, and… surprises me. When we're together, I'm no longer sure of anything. He makes me question everything. When I'm with him… it's like… I'm free."

"And I'm your cage?"

"Not a cage. With you, I feel loved and safe and protected."

"And are those such bad things?"

"No, just different things."

"Things you don't want anymore…"

"Scott… I'm sorry. I never wished for any of this. It just happened. I hadn't even fully realized it until—"

"Yeah, exactly when did you realize you had feelings for my brother?"

A million flashbacks passed through Haley's mind, followed by just as many questions. *The day he told me about the kiss? All those afternoons together at the library? When he drove me home to my father? The night he gave me this necklace?* Haley's hand unconsciously wrapped around it. *When he saved you from the pool? When he stayed up all night to read to you at the hospital? When I found out he wouldn't let Madison tell me about his apology to her? On Halloween night?*

All of those moments had made her fall for him a little, but the truth of it was all in a single instant spent together under the rain. *"I won't go away, Haley."* David's words rang again in her mind. *"I'll always be here for you… I love you."*

"Last summer," Haley confessed. "He told me he loved me—"

Scott scoffed. "I guess that's another little thing you conveniently forgot to tell me."

"No, I chose not to."

"Why?"

"I didn't want to come between two brothers…"

"Yeah, great job with that."

"I'm sorry."

"Why drag it out for so long if you've known for months?" he accused.

"Because I didn't *know*-know. Because it was all so confusing. And because I still love you. Before I could start thinking about the way I felt for David, you came back, and I was so happy to see you… Then there was the accident, and that day at the hospital I was so scared to lose you… I thought whatever I'd imagined having with David had to be… nothing real, nothing important…"

"And now?"

"Now I don't know what I want anymore…"

"What, or… who you want?"

Haley kept silent.

"Did you two ever…?"

"No, Scott, no! How can you ask me that? I would never cheat on you."

"At this point I don't really know, do I?"

"I'm sorry."

"For what? Because you want him?"

"It's more complicated than that. There isn't a switch I can turn that says 'stop loving Scott, love David instead.'"

"Love? You *love* him?"

Haley could only stare back at Scott.

"And you love me, too?"

She nodded.

"But you're in love with only one of us…"

Madison

A quick peek at her watch told Madison that Scott was already twenty minutes late, which was pretty unusual for him. They'd reserved a study room at the library to finish the next revision of their group project and, with the assignment due tomorrow, they really couldn't afford to waste any time.

The project—a co-written short story that had to be cohesive, but with two clear, distinct voices—had been presented in their second class, and Madison and Scott had teamed up at once. Now they were halfway through, with Madison writing in the POV of a young witch, while Scott penned her very sarcastic talking cat.

Fed up with just sitting there and waiting, Madison started revising her side of the story. And by the time Scott arrived, she was so immersed in the narrative that he startled her when he plunged into the chair next to her.

"Sorry I'm late."

Late, Madison scoffed inside her head. *What a pity we're not working on euphemisms.*

She was about to berate Scott for letting her do all the work when she took a second look at him: one-day stubble, dark sunglasses, messed up hair, and a foul reek of…

"Are you *drunk?*" she accused.

Scott sneered. "Mostly hungover."

Madison's eyes bulged. "But it's the middle of the day. Are you okay?"

"Haley and I broke up. By definition, I'm not *okay.*"

A million different thoughts and emotions hit Madison in the guts like sudden punches: elation, guilt, sorrow, hope, elation again, followed by the same guilt. Then, finally, the need to know exactly what had happened. Who had broken up with who, and why?

"How can it be?" she asked

"So you haven't talked to her?"

"No. Last night she came home and shut herself in her room. We assumed she had homework to do or something… What happened?"

"Apparently…" Scott removed the sunglasses and, elbows on the table, he pressed both his palms against his closed eyes. "She has feelings for my brother."

Ah, yeah, there's that…

Scott finished rubbing his eyes and turned his bloodshot gaze to her, studying her reaction. "And you don't seem surprised."

"Scott, I—"

"Please," Scott interrupted her. "If you're about to spin me some bullshit, don't. I've already had enough of that."

"I wasn't going to, but Haley is my best friend…"

"And what about me? Am I not your friend?"

Oh, Scott, you're so much more than that.

"Of course we're friends, but—"

"No buts. Did you know she had feelings for David, or not?"

"I suspected it, but the one time I confronted her about it, she denied it."

"Why did you confront her?"

"Because I'd seen them together."

"Where?"

"At the library."

"Damn, I hate libraries." Scott stared around the room with contempt. "What were they doing?"

Madison cursed herself for not being able to keep a poker face. The interrogation was making her so uncomfortable. She didn't want to spill the beans on Haley, but… Scott deserved to know the truth.

"Nothing, really," she explained. "They weren't doing anything specific except for laughing." Scott's face turned even grimmer, as if instead of "laughing" Madison had just said they were banging each other's brains out on the table. "It was more of a vibe I picked up."

"And when you confronted her about it, what did she say?"

She pivoted the argument on me for having feelings for you… Yeah, definitely not going to say that.

"She swore they were only friends," Madison said as neutrally as she could.

"Yeah. Just fucking friends."

"Scott." Madison put a hand on his arm. "I don't think she was lying. Not consciously, at least."

"When did I lose her? When she learned about the kiss?"

"No, that night she was only worried about how you'd react when she told you. She still hated David back then…"

"So when did it change?"

"I guess when they started meeting at the library. David… he can be charming if he wants to…"

"Okay, now I seriously despise libraries. Can we get outta here?"

Madison threw a glance at their half-finished story… Homework didn't matter right then.

"Yeah," she said, pressing Save before closing her laptop. "Let's go."

Scott stared at the computer, aghast. "Oh, I'm so sorry, the project! I wasn't thinking straight. We can stay and finish it."

"No, it doesn't matter, really." Madison shrugged. "We were almost done, anyway."

"I don't want you to have to finish alone."

"Scott, you're having enough of a bad day to also worry about homework. Trust me. Let's get out of here."

Scott held her gaze for a long moment. "Thank you."

Outside, they walked in silence in the freezing November air with no particular destination. Wrapped in a heavy coat and shielded by a wooly beanie, scarf, and mittens, Madison still couldn't help shivering a little. But Scott seemed immune to the cold. He wore no hat, scarf, or gloves, and kept his jacket with the first two or three buttons undone, but he didn't seem to feel the bite of the wind.

Scott spoke first. "Do you think it would've been different if I hadn't gone to California?" He stared into space straight ahead, as if searching the horizon for an answer.

"Hard to call…"

Scott stopped walking and turned toward her. "You went out with David. What did you like about him?"

Madison reflexively widened her eyes at the blunt question. "You really want me to answer that?"

"Probably not, you're right. But when you two broke up you hated him, too, right? And now you don't anymore… How does he do that? How can he be such a douchebag to everyone, and people just keep on giving him chances…"

Madison stared up at him in surprise, a fierce blush heating up her cheeks. Did Scott know about her breakup with David?

"Nobody told me anything," Scott clarified. "But I can pick up on things… at least when other people are involved. Guess I'm not as good at reading my own girlfriend—sorry, *ex*-girlfriend."

Madison started walking again. "I did hate him for a time…"

Scott fell into step next to her. "And then?"

"He apologized."

"You think he was sincere?"

"I do."

"You never suspected it was just a move?"

"To look good for Haley? Oh, yeah, I did. And I told him, so he asked me not to tell Haley about the apology to let me know it was all about me…"

"And did you?"

"What?"

"Tell Haley."

"Not at first…"

"But eventually?"

"Yeah."

"When?"

Madison was reluctant to answer.

"When?" Scott repeated.

"The day after the accident… David was reading to you at the hospital, and I made a joke about him torturing you with bad fiction, so Haley asked me if I still hated him, and I said 'no' and told her why."

"So I go into a coma and he gets extra hero points for saving my life, and also for apologizing to you… no matter he had to apologize because he was a total shitbag in the first place. Why does everyone prefer him?"

It was Madison's turn to stop. "I don't prefer him. Scott, I can barely tolerate your brother. I'm… I can't even say. Haley must be out of her mind to choose him over you."

Scott stared at her, slightly open-mouthed, and if Madison's cheeks were heated before, they were about to melt right now.

Why don't I come out and tell him I'm in love with him? I mean, I only have to spell it out for him for it to be any clearer.

"You really think that?" he asked.

"Yeah, he's… *David,* and you're you, and there really is an ocean between the two."

"You say that only because we share the same weird literary tastes."

"Absolutely. You're the only guy I know crazy enough to write about a talking cat."

Out of the blue, Scott pulled her into a hug. "Thank you, Madison," he whispered. "I was a drunken mess before talking to you, but you made it better."

Madison let herself get lost in the embrace, feeling a bit stalkerish. Scott was hugging her as a friend, and instead, she was savoring the warmth of his body pressed close to hers while her heart raced out of control in her chest. His strong arms wrapped around her… his lips almost kissing her hair…

That's it! You've been enough of a perv for tonight.

"Hey," Madison said, using all her will to pull back. "It's what friends are for."

***

That evening, after saying goodbye to Scott and going back to the library to finish their project—it took every ounce of Madison's willpower to plow through the revisions, considering all her brain wanted to think about was: Scott is single, Scott is single, Scott is single—Madison finally made it home way later than she'd planned.

"Oh, there you are," Alice greeted her. She was making grilled cheese sandwiches in the kitchenette. "Where were you?"

"Is Haley home?" Madison whispered, ignoring the question.

"Yeah, why?" Alice whispered back.

Madison stalled by removing her coat and various anti-freeze props and hanging them on the entrance hall's rack. Before she told Alice, she wanted to make sure she wasn't going to smile. Madison hated herself for being so happy about the breakup, but she couldn't help herself. Yeah, Scott was miserable, and seeing him so beaten down had been heartbreaking, but he would recover and maybe… just maybe… And Haley… it wasn't like her best friend was going to be alone for long… she was probably already dating David…

Madison schooled her face in a grievous expression and joined Alice in the kitchen.

"So, apparently Haley and Scott broke up."

"WHAT?!"

"Shhhhhh," Madison hissed. "She'll hear you."

"What?" Alice hissed.

"Scott and I were supposed to work on our group project today, but he turned up an hour late looking like a mess… he was half drunk and one hundred percent out of it."

"And why did they break up?" Alice asked, copying Madison's hush-hush tones.

"She has feelings for David."

"Ah," was all Alice said. No surprises there.

"Have you seen her?"

"No."

Madison chewed on her lower lip. "Should we check on her?"

As one, they nodded and moved in front of Haley's door.

Alice knocked, saying, "Can we come in?"

No reply came from the other side, so they shared another let's-do-this glance and then tentatively opened the door. Haley was lying on the bed, fully clothed, legs crossed at the ankles, gaze lost on the ceiling. She had earplugs on and it took her a moment to realize she was no longer alone.

"Hey." Haley removed the earplugs and straightened up, crossing her legs. She took one look at their serious expressions, and said, "So you've heard."

They joined her on the bed, sitting on opposite sides.

"How are you?" Alice asked.

Haley blinked. "Dazzled, to be honest… I didn't cry."

Madison frowned. "And that is bad because…?"

"I'm numb. It's like I can't feel anything… and I'm scared it's only a matter of time before I realize what a horrible mistake I made and my heart is going to get ripped out of my chest."

Madison didn't have a response to that. She could only agree, for obvious reasons. But Alice seemed at a loss for words as well.

"How did you find out?" Haley finally asked.

To which Madison blushed for the millionth time that day.

"You saw him," Haley guessed. "How was he?"

"A mess," Madison said. "But he was… functioning." It was the only word Madison could think of to describe the state Scott had been in.

"Does he hate me?"

Madison shook her head. "No, he's still very much in love with you…"

Haley's mouth twisted into a grief-stricken, possibly guilt-tripping grimace.

"I'm sorry," she said.

"Hey." Alice reached out to grab her hand. "It's a breakup, not the end of the world. But are you sure it's what you want?"

Alice had asked the question Madison dared not voice, too afraid of the answer.

"I mean," Alice continued, "this was rather sudden. You never said a word. What happened?"

Haley told them the behind-the-scenes of "Haley and The Williams Brothers" that had taken place on Halloween night. And how she and Scott had both pretended none of it had happened for two weeks. But how, yesterday, at the mere mention of David's name, he'd flipped and Haley hadn't been able to deny she had feelings for both brothers.

"It wasn't fair to keep going," she concluded. "Scott deserves a person who's one hundred percent into him, and I couldn't be that person anymore."

"So… have you seen David yet?" Madison asked.

"No, and I'm not sure I'm ready yet. I need space… Alice?"

"Yeah?"

"Can you make sure Jack keeps an eye on Scott? With basketball going to shit and us breaking up, I'm worried he'll flip out…"

"Sure, no problem," Alice said. Then, seeing how Haley still seemed completely zoned out, she added, "Hey, it's going to be fine. Scott's going to be fine."

"I know, but the last thing I wanted was to come between two brothers, especially after their history with girls. It's true that relationships come and go, but family should be forever. They're brothers, and no matter how they act, deep down they love each other and would go to the end of the world for each other. I mean, did you see how crazy David went that day at the pool?"

"Yep," Madison and Alice said in unison.

"I don't want to ruin their bond, but I'm afraid I did exactly that."

The three of them stared at each other, neither sure how much truth Haley's words held.

David

After a long day of school, David came home glad he'd toughened up with an investment banking internship over summer break. All his fellow HBS students seemed so stressed about their projects, midterms, and deadlines, but for David, business school felt more like a vacation after the summer he'd had and his nightmare of an ex-boss.

He turned the key in the lock and pushed the entrance door open. Or, at least, he tried. Something heavy was blocking the way on the other side. David did some extra shoving and, finally, he was able to open the door enough to sneak into his own house through the crack. He closed the door behind him and inspected the tower of boxes that had been blocking it. There were five carton boxes in total with various names written in blue marker: tech, kitchen, bath, bed, and mix.

A quick look around the apartment notified David of all the new empty spaces: no coffee machine in the kitchen, no stereo in the living room, the Michael Jordan poster gone… All of Scott's stuff. And, at last, David's gaze settled on the two big suitcases parked behind the couch just as Scott emerged from his room, rolling another bag in place to join the others.

"Going somewhere?" David asked.

Scott shot him an unreadable look. "Yeah."

"Where to this time? Alaska?"

"Nope," Scott said, standoffish. "Just a couple of blocks down the road."

With that, his brother walked back into his room, presumably to finish packing. David leaned against the kitchen bar column, crossed his arms over his chest, and waited. He watched as Scott reemerged from his bedroom with yet another box and filled it with the last few of his possessions still scattered around the house.

"Listen," David said. "I'm all for you claiming your independence and flying away from the nest, but how are you going to afford to live on your own?"

"I'm not going to."

"Okay, then. What about the rent here?"

Scott dropped the box and turned to face him. "I'm switching with Matt. He's moving in with you, and I'll go live with Jack. The rent is about the same, so I'll keep paying my half here and Matt will pay for his place, but we're swapping."

"Well," David said, taken aback. "Thank you for consulting me. I have nothing against the dude, but shouldn't you have at least asked if I was okay living with him?"

"No."

"No?"

"No."

"What's going on? Why the sudden change?" David raised an arm and sniffed underneath his armpit. "I don't stink, I promise."

"Obviously you haven't heard." Scott took a step forward. "Haley and I broke up."

"Oh."

The two brothers stared at each other for a long time, a non-verbal communication of mixed emotions passing between them. Scott visibly angry, bitter, and so freakily calm David worried he was going to go Charlie Manson on him. And David, trying to keep a straight face while his heart was pounding in his chest. He didn't like to see his brother this way, but...

"You want to blow off steam?" David suggested. "Go get drunk, brother-bond over a good old Irish ale?"

Scott eyed him in an I-dare-you sort of way. "Let's not pretend for a second like this isn't the best day of your life," he said, glacially cold. "I'm going out."

"Where?"

Scott pulled on his coat. "Out."

"All right, I won't wait up for you."

"Yeah, don't," Scott said, just before slamming the door shut behind him.

David grabbed a beer from the fridge and, after knocking it open on the countertop, he crashed on the couch, taking a sip. So Haley was single… What did that mean?

He pulled his phone out of his jeans pocket and checked it for texts. Not a peep. Mmm. He toyed with the phone for a while. He didn't want to make a move on Haley while his brother's body was still warm, but he'd already waited for so long… But what to do? Write a text? Ask her out? Nah… too simple… he needed to come up with something special. But then, he'd never been one for grand gestures, and at this point, all that really mattered were Haley's feelings. Either she was into him, or she wasn't. Maybe, in this case, less was more… all he needed was an opportunity.

Haley

David.

Haley's breath caught in her throat as she walked out of her last class of the day and spotted him waiting on the other side of the road. He had the frozen-over air of someone who'd been waiting out in the cold for a long time: red nose, beanie pulled down almost to cover his eyes, and arms tightly wrapped around himself to keep warm.

She crossed over to him. "David."

"Still me."

"How long have you been here?"

"Scott told me about the breakup. I'd say I'm sorry, but I'm not."

Ah, so they weren't circling around it.

"What did he say?"

"Oh, you know my brother. He's a real talker…" David rolled his eyes. "The guy just went on and on about it. Wouldn't shut up."

"So he didn't tell you why?"

"Nope." David moved a step closer. "Why don't you tell me?"

"I'm not in love with him anymore." Haley chose the easier half of the truth. She couldn't tell David she loved him, not yet… It was all still too confusing.

"Mmm…" David's mouth curled up into a little, satisfied smile. "Interesting… Anyone else on your mind?"

Oh, gosh, if he kept looking at her like this Haley was sure she'd melt. She swallowed. "Can we not do this right now?"

"Too soon?"

Haley nodded. "I need space, and we can't do this to him so soon…"

David's smile widened, and he closed the distance between them. "So, Miss Robot." He cupped her cheeks. "There's a 'we,' is there? And what was that you were thinking of *not* doing?"

Haley couldn't help but smile.

He held her gaze for a long time, his thumbs caressing her skin. He pressed closer, making Haley gasp.

"You want to kiss me," he said. It was a realization, not a question.

"Yes," Haley said.

"Good." David leaned in closer but pressed his lips only to her forehead. Then his mouth moved to whisper in her ear. "Pity I have to give you space."

Shivers that had nothing to do with the cold weather spider-walked down Haley's spine, and there was a warm explosion in her lower belly. Heart pounding, she stared up into his teasing blue eyes. Coherent speech abandoned her, and Haley felt very much ready to throw all precautions out the window and grab him by the collar of his coat to kiss him. But David stepped back.

"Don't get too comfortable," he said. "I'll come knocking on your door soon." And with that he walked away, leaving her all hot and bothered in the middle of the street.

***

He didn't call or text the next day, nor the next, nor the next. He didn't wait for her outside another class, either, until days of radio silence turned into weeks. Before Haley realized it, November was gone and finals week was looming over them.

532

Not even an impatient heart could keep a Harvard student from studying. Well, not exactly. Haley's revision was only half-disrupted by nagging thoughts of David, doubling the time it took to get anything done.

Why couldn't she push him out of her mind? He was ignoring her, and it bothered her. But he was only doing as she'd asked, leaving her space. So why was she so mad at him?

You should make the next move, an insistent voice whispered in her head.

True.

David had laid it all bare last summer. Haley knew where he stood. Now she had to tell him where her heart was… with him. Ah… but knowing what one should do and actually doing it were two completely different things. So, instead, Haley buried her head under the sand—or under coding textbooks, in this case—and concentrated on passing her finals with top grades.

With the examinations over, it was time to go home to Buffalo. And now it was too late to talk to David. She didn't want to have the "I love you, too" conversation and then have to leave and not see him for two weeks.

I'll clear my head over the break and call David when I come back, Haley promised herself.

Her last night in Cambridge was spent, as was tradition, with her roommates, swapping presents. They sat on the living room rug next to their plastic Christmas tree, each with two gift-wrapped bundles in front of them. Blue, Alice's bunny, was comfortably snuggled under the tree, sleeping.

"Should we take turns, or open them all at once?" Madison asked.

"All at once," Alice said.

"Yeah," Haley agreed.

"Okay, ready… go!" Madison yelled, and the unwrapping frenzy began.

Haley opened Madison's present first. There was a book: *The Night of Wishes* by Michael Ende. Whenever Madison gave a gift, no matter the occasion, it was always a novel—to spread the book love—plus something else. Haley peeked at the first page to read the dedication:

A Christmas story with a talking cat... to keep your mind off boys.

Haley smiled and opened the second bit of the present. A brand-new phone case in a gorgeous shade of red. Haley's old one was all battered and scratched.

"Thank you, Maddie," Haley said. "I love it."

"And I love yours." Madison held up her "I read past my bedtime" throw pillow in front of her. It had a silver background made of an antique-looking calligraphy and the main writing was pink.

"What did Alice get you?" Haley asked.

"TA starter set," Madison said proudly, showing off her new stationery supply kit. "I still can't believe Professor McKenna offered me a position for next year." Madison paused and chewed on her lower lip. "Now all I have to do is tell my dad I'm not going to law school."

"It'll be fine," Alice reassured her, wielding a rose gold makeup brush in the air, whose handle was in the shape of a mermaid tail.

Once the various books, accessories, makeup tools, and house décor items were unpacked, Alice got up and asked, "Hot chocolate with marshmallows? Raise your hands if you're in."

Two hands promptly shot into the air.

Alice came back five minutes later with three steaming mugs in her hands. She handed them each one and then, teary-eyed, she said, "A toast." She raised her mug. "Living with you guys has been the best… I don't know where we'll be next year… if we'll keep living in the same apartment, or even in the same city. But I wanted to say you're my best friends… and that's never going to change… Cheers!"

All three definitely shiny-eyed, they bumped mugs, yelling, "Cheers!"

Haley sipped her hot cocoa and stared out of the window at the snowflakes lazily making their way to the ground, feeling overwhelmed by how much her life was about change… not just at the end of the year after graduation, but in a little over two weeks when she'd be back and ready to talk to David.

Scott

"MOM!" David shouted from the top of the stairs. "Why is there a gym in my bedroom?"

Scott and his brother had just gotten home early on Christmas Eve after a short—unfortunately, shared—car ride from Boston to Poughkeepsie. The four-hour door-to-door trip had been the most Scott had seen of David since he'd moved out of their apartment, and he'd already had enough. He'd considered taking the bus home, but then he would've had to explain to his parents why he couldn't stand to be in a car with his brother, and that would've been even more unbearable.

But at least it was going to be a short stay. The team had the last game of the year scheduled for the thirtieth, and Scott had claimed he had to be back in Boston on the twenty-seventh, meaning he would leave here the day after Christmas.

When they'd arrived home, David had said a quick hello to their parents and then hurried up to the second floor, taking the stairs two at a time, to drop his bag. But now he was standing on the landing, arms crossed over his chest, looking at their mother with a questioning frown.

"Oh, dear," their mom—a five-foot-two woman nobody believed could've produced two such tall boys—said. "I forgot to tell you we've redecorated. You guys are in the guest room."

"Together?" Scott asked.

"Yeah, you're going to bunk together, just like old times."

Perfect, Scott thought, while trying to keep a straight face. Being under the same roof with David again would already be difficult, but to share a room would be… *hell!*

He crept up the stairs carrying his duffle bag. First he checked his old room, hoping their mother had gotten confused and only David's room had been re-purposed. But, no, as soon as he opened the door, that hope was lost. In place of his twin bed was a huge mahogany desk, and his old desk and wardrobe had been replaced by neatly organized bookshelves. The whole room held a distinct feminine vibe: pale colors, assorted flower pots, and medicinal herbs posters hung on the walls instead of his Metallica ones. So if David's room had become a gym, his was now Mom's home office.

Sighing, Scott closed the door and headed for the guest room, taking in with grim resignation the matching set of twin beds on opposite sides of the room. The headboards seemed to have been laser cut in the middle and split in two, meaning the beds might be pushed together and become one, depending on the guests.

David had already claimed the bed by the window.

"I picked the window seat," David said, turning as Scott dropped his bag on the free bed. "You mind?"

"Whatever," he said, and then got out of there as fast as he could.

The house wasn't big, but large enough that he could limit unnecessary David-interactions to a minimum. Scott only hoped his parents wouldn't pick up on the lingering tension. More like parent, singular; his dad had never been able to read the nuances of his kids' behavior. But Mom… she was a different animal.

Dinner was painful to endure. They didn't see their parents that often, so there was little chance they'd let them go quickly. Small talk and David's presence had to be endured. Scott did his best to be polite and pretend he was doing great: in school, with the team… Luckily, no one asked about his non-existent girlfriend. Admittedly, he took a more passive approach to the conversation, answering questions directed at him and never initiating an exchange. But that was his all-out best.

Hours later, in the dark of their shared bedroom, the oppressive silence made it clear neither of the two brothers was sleeping. When Scott couldn't take it any longer, he asked, "So… you've seen Haley around?"

David's reply came pronto, proving he wasn't sleeping, either. "I've *seen* her, but we're not together if that's what you're asking…"

"And by that, you mean not *yet…*"

"She's asked me for space, and I'm giving it to her."

"Real smooth, brother!"

Scott heard his brother shift position in the darkness.

"Instead of mourning the girl who doesn't love you anymore," David said, "why don't you concentrate on the one who's been in love with you all along?"

"What girl? What are you talking about?"

"Oh, you know. Tall, blonde, big blue eyes."

Scott stared at his brother's dark silhouette, puzzled. "Who?"

"Barbie librarian—does it ring a bell? Yes? No?"

"You mean Madison? She isn't in love with me, we're just friends."

"Gosh, you're even dumber than I thought," David said mockingly. "Trust me, the girl's a goner for you."

"You know what? I'm sleeping on the couch."

Without another word, Scott grabbed his pillow and comforter and headed downstairs. As he stared at the living room ceiling, he found he wasn't able to shake David's words off. Visions of blue eyes and blond hair kept swiping before his eyes. Her kind smile and cute freckles… Madison, in love with him? Was it possible? And, finally, one question above all the others…

Do I want it to be true?

***

The next morning, once everyone had cleared the kitchen after breakfast, Scott stayed behind to help his mother with the preparations for the Christmas meal. It was their special "thing," and Scott had missed the tradition last year. It had seemed worth it at the time, because he'd met Haley in Hawaii, but now the entire past year felt like such a waste.

"And how have you been doing?" his mom asked after a while.

He shrugged while peeling potatoes for the mash—she'd yet to promote him to more noble tasks like the stuffing of the turkey or the glazing of the ham. "I'm great, thanks."

"So is everything okay between you and your brother?"

"Yeah, sure."

"Is that why you slept on the couch last night?"

Busted.

He'd gone back to their room before anyone in the house had woken up, and he thought he'd gotten away with it. But nothing escaped his mother.

Scott kept quiet, so his mom continued. "I couldn't help but notice you seem subdued, while your brother is trying hard to pretend he's not out-of-his-mind-happy."

Damn, the woman had superpowers.

"Am I getting close?" she asked. And when Scott still said nothing, she insisted, "Is it a girl again?"

Scott startled at that. "What do you mean *again?*"

"Oh, Scott, please. You think I'm such an idiot I can't read my own two sons? It's like David's high school senior year all over again… Only the roles are reversed this time. He's on cloud nine, and you're pissed. Did David do something?"

"David…" Scott desperately wanted to say 'yes.' But other than coming onto Haley, David had done nothing entirely shady. He'd made it very clear he wanted her and would do everything he could to get the girl. And as much as Scott sought to blame his brother for sending him to California, the truth was he'd wanted to go. And if all it took for Haley to stop loving him was for David to woo her, then maybe it was better they'd broken up now.

Scott knew all of this *in theory*. But still, he couldn't control the suffocating pain in his throat whenever he thought of her, or the sensation of his heart being ripped out of his chest whenever he imagined her with his brother. "He's always been very upfront about how he felt for Haley."

"Are we talking about the brunette I met at the hospital?"

Scott nodded.

"So you've broken up?"

"Yep."

"And now she's with David?"

"It's only a matter of time."

Scott couldn't anticipate what his reaction would be when it happened for real. As much as he hated himself for it, hearing David say they were not together yet had left him so relieved.

"She seemed like a lovely girl," his mom continued. "But I'm sure there are plenty of other girls out there who'd be more than happy to go out with you."

Madison's face flashed before his eyes, but he shook the idea away. He wasn't going to let David play mind games with him.

"Maybe," Scott conceded. "But right now it all seems pointless."

"Give it time," his mom said, and steered him around to hug him. "It'll get better, I promise."

Scott let himself be cuddled, marveling at how such a tiny woman was able to dispense so much comfort.

After some rocking and gentle shoulder-patting, his mom sniffled and pushed back, saying, "Now, back to your peeling, you slacker. This dinner won't prepare itself."

Madison

On Christmas Day, Madison and her parents arrived at the family's country house in the early afternoon. The official dinner wouldn't start until five, but it was tradition for the Smithson clan to gather ahead of time and chat while nibbling snacks—accompanied by bubbly, thank goodness—and to exchange presents before the main meal.

Everyone was there: Vicky and her husband Robert, Ethan and Rose, a very pregnant Georgiana with Tyler, her aunt and uncle, her grandparents, and Uncle Frank—who wasn't exactly a relative, but who participated in all family gatherings. He always ended up drunk and asleep sooner rather than later.

Madison sat on an armchair strategically positioned so that her grandparents' giant Christmas tree would shield her from her father's view. She sank deep into the plush cushions and observed the rest of her family in silence, trying to avoid meeting anyone's eye.

Ethan, Vicky, and Rose were at the top of her no-eye-contact list. The three people who'd found her making out with Georgiana's husband on her wedding day. Each seemed to regard her with either patronizing or disheartening attitudes. Rose was all kind smiles, and Madison appreciated Ethan's girlfriend for the effort, but couldn't help registering the lingering pity behind her dark eyes. As for Ethan himself, Madison didn't dare look at him at all; he loved his sisters and was super protective of them, meaning that by extension he had to hate her. Vicky was the nicest, as usual, but still, Madison felt like blushing whenever their gazes crossed.

Then she had to avoid Georgiana for the exact opposite reason. "Gigi" didn't know about what had happened on her wedding day, and Madison dreaded her cousin would find out just by glimpsing into her guilty eyes. And even if that fear was absurd, it was wise to leave Georgiana alone under any circumstances. She was invariably nasty to Madison, and now that she was pumped full of estrogen, who knew to what new extremes she could go.

And then there was Tyler, who Madison had to avoid at all cost for obvious reasons.

Ah, and her father, who had just vowed a few hours ago to never speak to her again. Thinking about it, that could actually be a huge improvement. Better he never spoke to her again, rather than yell at her nonstop for being stupid, naïve, a hopeless dreamer, or regale her with the shouted version of the whole "if you want to live the life of a starving artist be my guest, but don't expect to have access to my money while you play around with your stories instead of living in the real world" sermon.

Yep. Her father hadn't taken well the news of her refusal to apply to law school. And, true to expectations, he'd skipped the cajoling and bribing phases altogether to jump right into the classic Smithson-angry-dad-who-blackmails-his-kids-with-money power play.

So Madison sat in silence in her chair, drinking more wine than she ate food, and watching the "Georgiana Show." Her cousin was only ten days away from her due date and was talking about everything ranging from labor horror stories and delivery room breathing techniques, to diaper changing best practices, to a painfully detailed account of the nanny auditions she'd held so far.

When she couldn't stomach any more of it, Madison grabbed another flute of champagne and escaped to the veranda to have a moment alone. It was dark in here, the only illumination coming from the fairy lights strung all around the house and the bluish snow-reflected glow of the garden. At four thirty in the afternoon, it was already night time. But, between natural and artificial lights, her grandparents' garden was well lit, and Madison could admire its snowy outline. Outdoor furniture, shrubs, flowerbeds, the pool… everything was covered in a thick coat of dusty snow, leaving only the silhouettes of what was lying underneath. If it kept on snowing, soon nothing would be recognizable anymore. The garden would transform into a white desert, with dunes and slopes forged by the strong wind that had been blowing on the outskirts of Boston since last week.

A shiver crept down her spine; it was colder here on the veranda. The thick glass enclosing the room was not enough to keep out the freezing cold that was attacking the entirety of Northern America. Madison grabbed a blanket, wrapped it around her shoulders, and kept on staring out of the glass walls while sipping champagne.

She was still contemplating the snow when the sound of footsteps startled her. Turning around, she was surprised to find herself staring into Ethan's cold blue eyes. They held each other's stare for an instant before Madison lowered her gaze to the floor, already blushing in embarrassment.

"Oh," Ethan said. "I didn't think anyone would be here. I needed a moment alone."

"I'll get out of your way," Madison promptly replied, dropping the blanket back on the couch and making a quick dash for the door.

But Ethan grabbed her by the elbow before she'd cleared it. "Hey, you don't have to go."

Now she was forced to hold his gaze, and she could read only disgust in his eyes. "Please, Ethan, no need to pretend. I know Vicky gave you the be-nice-to-your-damaged-cousin speech, but she isn't here… so no need to pretend, really."

Ethan arched his brows. "What's that supposed to mean?"

"I see the way you cringe every time you're around me. So let's just avoid each other and not make this any more awkward than it needs to be."

Instead of letting her go, Ethan gently grabbed her by the shoulders. "Madison, I'm not mad at you. I mean, if I can stand to sit down at dinner with that prick my sister married—"

"See, Ethan, that's the problem. I don't want anyone in my family to have to stand my presence." She shrugged free of his grip. "So I'll just go."

Ethan, however, didn't seem so ready to let her go. He jumped backward and blocked her path to the door, saying, "That came out wrong. I'm not mad at you…"

Madison just narrowed her eyes at him.

"I know I scowl at you sometimes; Rose already chided me on that. But it's because looking at you reminds me of what happened that day, and I get mad whenever I remember my sister is married to such a"—he growled, and flared his nostrils—"Anyway, Madison, we're family. One mistake, or even a thousand mistakes, couldn't change that."

Madison swallowed, all choked up. "Really?"

"Come here." Ethan pulled her into a tight hug. "Is this why you're hiding out here?"

"Yes, and no." Madison sniffled, pulling back. "It's mostly my dad."

"Why? What did Uncle John do?"

Madison studied Ethan for a second before replying. Well, if there was another person in the family who could understand her, it was the other non-lawyer black sheep of the flock. So Madison opened up to him. "I told him I'm not applying to law school, and he didn't take it well."

Ethan let out a low whistle.

"You're the only other Smithson to turn down the Smithson *Legacy*," Madison said sarcastically. "Does it get better in time?"

"Me? I'm a pathetic loser compared to you. I went through the ropes of going to law school, passing the bar, and living the miserable life of a corporate lawyer for a whole year before I found the guts to say enough. You're a rock star."

"Yeah, but you were the first to rebel. Was it worth it?"

"Totally." Ethan became super serious. "Madison, if you're sure you don't want to be a lawyer, believe me, it's a thousand times better that you've said so right away. You can't force yourself to change. Trust me, I tried, and it didn't work. I became more miserable with every passing day until I exploded and had to call it quits. This way you save four or five painful years of life no one could ever give back to you. And Uncle John will come round. You're his only daughter."

"Which only makes it worse." Madison chewed on her bottom lip. "At least your father had spares. Vicky is already in the company, and Georgiana may join when the baby is old enough, but I'm an only child. If I don't join Smithson and Smithson, our side of the family is out, full stop."

"That's not true. Uncle John doesn't have to sell his partnership, and if your kids want to become lawyers, they'll always have a place there."

My kids? Madison scoffed inside her head. *Assuming I don't die a spinster.*

"But Smithson and Smithson is our fathers' dream," Ethan continued, "not ours. And it's not fair of them to expect us to give up our dreams for theirs."

"So I made the right choice?"

"One hundred percent. I'm not saying it'll be easy, but you're saving yourself a lot of grief by ripping the Band-Aid now. Did the threats already start?"

"Yep. I'm cut-off from his money. Whatever that means."

"At the worst, it means paying back your tuition. Do you already have a plan in mind?"

"He hasn't asked for anything yet, but he's promised to cancel all my credit cards. Anyway, I can apply for a student loan to finish the year, and I hope I'll manage next year by cutting back a little."

"You know what you'll do once you graduate? I mean, I'm here if you ever need help, financially or otherwise."

"Let's hope that won't be necessary. They offered me a scholarship for grad school for a research project I'm working on, and one of my professors wants me to be a TA." She smiled and shrugged. "Anyway, if things take a turn for the worse, I can always sell the car."

"Damn, our fathers are real assholes." Ethan wrapped an arm around Madison's shoulders and steered her toward the door. "Let's go pretend to be one big happy family, if only for Grandma's sake."

"Hey." Madison turned her head to look up at him. "You never told me why you came to hide out here?"

Ethan flashed her a wicked smile. "Oh, that. I'm about to do something very stupid, and I just told Grandma, meaning I can't change my mind now." It was clear from his tone that Ethan wasn't going to elaborate further, so Madison followed him to the dining room, wondering what in hell he could possibly mean by "something very stupid."

***

They were just past the appetizers when Georgiana dropped her fork with a loud clattering of silver on porcelain and let out a pitiful whimper.

"Are you okay?" Almost everyone around the table asked a variation of the question at the same time.

Georgiana stood extra still for a few seconds, and finally smiled. "False alarm. It was a small cramp, but nothing serious."

The other thirteen people at the table, Madison included, let out a collective sigh of relief, and the first course was served. From that moment on, however, Madison couldn't help noticing Tyler watching Georgiana as if she were a time bomb, being extra attentive to her cousin's every movement. Especially since Georgiana kept wincing as if in pain from time to time. Until the winces became full grimaces of pain, and Georgiana grabbed her belly and groaned.

Once again, every head at the table turned toward Georgiana, who grimaced again and announced, "I think the baby wants out."

She might as well have shouted, *"Ready, steady, GO!"* because at once everyone dropped glasses, cutlery, bread… whatever it was they had in their hands, and jumped up from the table shouting orders or asking questions.

"We need to drive to the hospital." Georgiana's mom.

"Did you bring your bag?" Tyler.

"I'm getting the car." Both Ethan and his dad.

"Ahhh, it hurts." Georgiana.

"Deep breaths." Vicky.

"Oh, dear." Grandma. "A new baby on Christmas Day."

"Someone get her coat." Madison's father.

"It reeeeah-haaally hurts." Georgiana again.

In a coat-grabbing rush, everyone was up and moving across the hall to get to the front door. Georgiana was supported by her mom and sister, as she suddenly seemed in too much pain to walk on her own. It was amidst all the frenzy that Ethan rushed back to his chair, unceremoniously yanked his jacket from the back of the seat, and made the world stop for a few seconds.

Everyone in the room—Georgiana included—froze to watch a small, velvety red box fly out of his jacket's pocket in a wide arc and land on the living room rug. It popped open to reveal a white gold ring with a single, square-cut diamond set on top.

Rose stared at the tiny box, transfixed. Her hands moved up to cover her mouth. Then she looked at Ethan with tears already welling in her eyes.

"Well…" Ethan smiled oh-so-charmingly with his devil-may-care attitude. "That's not how I intended to do it, but since we're here." He got down on one knee to retrieve the red box and then, turning it toward Rose, he asked, "Rose, will you marry me?"

The entire room waited in silence for Rose's answer. Even Georgiana made an effort not to scream through what must've been a really painful contraction, judging by how she scrunched up her face and bit her lower lip, struggling not to cry out.

"Yes," Rose said, tears running down her cheeks. "Yes, yes, yes."

She knelt in front of Ethan and kissed him for a long moment, before letting go and allowing him to slide the beautiful ring on her finger. Madison realized it was Grandma's ring—that must've been the very stupid thing Ethan had referred to earlier: he'd asked their grandmother for the ring.

Cheers and claps erupted all around and were promptly interrupted by an inhuman scream coming from Georgiana. "Can we get a move on, people?" she yelled. "I'm kinda having a baby here!"

So it was that the Smithson family spent Christmas Day in a waiting room at Massachusetts General Hospital, and that, at 11:49 p.m., the beautiful Jane Smithson Bronfam came into the world as a screaming, healthy baby girl of seven and a half pounds.

Haley

Haley was in the kitchen with her mom, spending Boxing Day afternoon doing a sweet nothing after the eating marathon that had been Christmas Day. They'd even allowed her dad some diet leeway, and with everyone in a joyful, festive mood, the celebration had passed in a vortex of cheers, good food, family anecdotes, and present unwrapping.

Like many of her fellow students, Haley had the impression the entire month of December had slipped through her fingers in a heartbeat. She'd taken a long breath at the end of the term, to then survive in a revising-exam-taking apnea for twenty days and then, boom, boom, boom: pack, go home, and finish all the last minute Christmas shopping until the twenty-fifth finally arrived. And today, with the holiday behind her, was the first essentially calm day of the month. Which, unfortunately, meant she'd had plenty of time to think.

She would've liked to sleep in late, but no, she'd found herself staring wide-eyed at the ceiling at dawn, unable to shake off the fact that no one special had wished her a merry Christmas. Next, she'd wondered who she wanted that someone special to be. Blue sparkly eyes and a crooked grin had appeared in answer. *David.*

Haley hadn't been surprised at how clear a reply her subconscious had provided. In the one and a half months since the breakup, she'd been taken aback by how easily her life had kept going. No tears, no desperation, no sense of hopelessness. The only explanation she could give herself had been that the real mourning phase of her relationship with Scott had passed during the summer. When she'd had to learn day by painful day not to rely on him, not to see him, not to talk to him… and also when she'd started falling out of love with him…

Ironically, she'd sort of hoped to be heartbroken. A part of her still couldn't believe she was letting go of such a great guy. One stubborn piece of her heart couldn't reconcile with not having any more feelings for a boy she'd fallen so hard for. But that was the reality of it.

The only thing that made Haley's heart beat these days were memories of little moments she'd had with David. She'd walk around with a silly, secret smile stamped on her lips after remembering something David had said, or a cute face he'd pulled, or his concentrated frown while he tried to solve a difficult problem… And more than once, she'd cursed herself for not kissing him the day he'd waited for her after class. The echo of his whispered words in her ear when he hadn't kissed her—*"Pity I have to give you space."*—was enough for her to break out in an all-body case of goosebumps.

"Oh!" Her mom gasped, stopping dead in front of the kitchen's window and yanking Haley out of her introspective moment.

Haley wiped another one of her secret smiles from her lips and, dipping a cookie into her tea, she asked, "What's up?"

"Nothing, really." Her mom shrugged the question off. "The neighbors are… mmm… building a weird-looking snowman."

"Something worth seeing?"

"*No!* No. I mean, not really."

Miranda moved away from the window and took the stool next to Haley, looking pensive. She sat quietly for a while. Then, out of the blue, she asked, "I couldn't help but notice the lack of text messaging and late-night calls. Is everything all right, honey?"

Haley guessed she must tell her sooner or later. Even though she spoke to her parents twice a week during the school year, she was very private when it came to her romantic life, and hadn't told them about the breakup yet.

"Scott and I broke up."

"Mmm…" Atypically, her mom didn't say 'sorry' or offer words of comfort. She only asked, "Why?"

"I'd really rather not talk about it."

"Was it because of the brother?"

Ah, mothers! They were a dreadful species.

"Mom, I'm serious, not now."

Even more peculiarly, her mom didn't insist. Instead, she came out with, "You should go for a walk outside."

"Are you delirious? It's thirty degrees out there, and I'm drinking tea."

"I'll make you another one later," she said, grabbing Haley's mug and emptying it into the sink.

"Hey," Haley protested. "I was drinking that."

"Oh, hush, the sun is shining and it's a beautiful day." To Haley's utter dismay, her mom started pushing her out of the kitchen. "Out, out… you're too young to stay shut in here and drink tea all afternoon like an old lady."

Okay, something was definitely up with her mom. This was highly unusual behavior. Haley was not in the mood to deal with mommy-strangeness right then, so she donned her coat, beanie, scarf, and Ugg boots, and headed outside just to shut the woman up.

Haley stepped out onto the porch, scanning the neighborhood to decide if she should head right or left. She froze in surprise when she spotted a familiar face leaning against a familiar midnight blue truck, waiting for her.

Her heart skipped a beat.

At that moment, she felt like Molly Ringwald in the final scene of *Sixteen Candles*—minus the eighties bridesmaid dress and warm weather. Just like Jake Ryan in the movie, David was staring up at her with a small grin on his handsome face. Haley could almost hear the notes of *If You Were Here* by the Thompson Twins as she hopped down the steps of her parents' front porch with the same shy anticipation as an insecure sixteen-year-old Sam Baker.

"Hi," she said.

He watched her approach. "Hi."

"What are you doing here?"

"I figured you've had enough space."

Judging from the tight pull she'd felt in her chest when she'd spotted him standing outside her home, he was right. She stepped closer. "You must be freezing, waiting out here," she said softly.

He gestured to his truck. "I've only been waiting for about a minute.

I got out of my car when I saw your mother waving at me and giving me the thumbs up… I figured you'd come out soon enough."

Haley turned her head over her shoulder to check the kitchen window. There was a rustling of curtains and then nothing else, as if someone had been spying and now was gone.

Mothers! Really, an impossible breed.

"Can we talk?" David asked.

Haley nodded, and walked around and slid into the passenger's side. David climbed into the driver's seat, his long legs and tall frame filling the space next to her.

He started the truck and turned on the heat—even though the inside was still warm—leaving the gear in Park.

"Let's go somewhere, please?" Haley asked.

As much as she was eager to hear what David had to say, she didn't want to do so within reach of her mother's prying eyes.

David smiled and switched the truck into Drive. "You're the expert; tell me where to go."

She guided him to a small park just around the corner from her house. It usually wasn't that scenic a sight, but in winter, coated in snow, with ice crystals as natural decorations, and blue fairy lights wrapped around the various tree trunks, it gained a romantic winter-wonderland vibe.

David parked in the deserted lot and left the car on, warm air blasting all around them from the vents.

Haley angled herself in the seat toward him, unwrapping the scarf from around her neck just to have something to do with her hands. "So? Why are you here?"

Without saying a word, he raised his hand to cup her cheek and leaned forward to kiss her. A long, deep kiss.

"I'm done waiting," he said when he pulled back.

Fair enough. Now that they were together, so close in the confined space of his truck, Haley was done waiting, too. The test was over. She didn't miss Scott. He already felt like a distant memory, and she couldn't believe she'd ever thought of Scott as "the one" because it all paled compared to what she was feeling now as she held David's deep blue gaze.

He ran a finger along her cheek, his voice soft but firm. "So what's it gonna be, Haley?"

She leaned in and kissed him again, sliding her arms around David's neck and pulling him closer until things got so heated that she forcefully had to pull away.

She slid her hands inside her coat and wrapped it more tightly around herself, not because she was cold, but because she was afraid that if she got her hands on David again, she wouldn't be able to pull back this time. "Where do we go from here?"

"I have to be back in Boston by the second—grad school sucks, and all." David rolled his eyes. "But we can go wherever you want for the next couple of days…"

"Any place in mind?"

"Doesn't matter. I'm not planning on letting you out of the room much."

Something melted in Haley's belly, and words failed her.

David winked and put his hands back on the wheel. "Let's get you home now. You need to pack."

***

Haley's parents didn't object to her early departure; especially not her mom, who confessed her secret membership to the #TeamDavid club. And after her dad had given David a thorough grilling on driving on ice, interspersed with not-so-subtle make-my-daughter-suffer-and-you'll-deal-with-me threats, they were good to go. The most obvious destination was to spend a few days at Niagara Falls State Park. The drive was only thirty minutes from Buffalo, and there were plenty of cozy and romantic cabin lodges not too far from the falls.

Reservations made, all they had to do was follow the GPS instructions which, after a long drive along the I-190 N, brought them to a less beaten, winding road.

"If I didn't know better," David commented, observing the forest-y surroundings, "I'd say you're taking me somewhere you'll be able to do as you please with me…"

Ah… well, yes, they'd be… pretty isolated.

"I figured this way we wouldn't have to remember that annoying 'do not disturb' sign."

David flashed her a wolfish smile, giving Haley's insides another good twist.

Will it ever stop? Haley wondered if he'd always have this effect on her. A part of her hoped he would, and the other was scared to death at that same possibility.

They drove around another few bends, until the road ended in a clearing at what appeared to be the main resort lodge. There were no other cars in the driveway, and the guy they'd talked to over the phone had seemed surprised they'd requested a cabin. These accommodations were more popular in the summer when it wasn't this freezing outside.

David parked in the spot with the least snow and, after hopping out of the truck, they headed for the small wooden house that must serve as reception.

"Ah, you're here already," a short man greeted them from behind the counter. Without wasting time, he grabbed a set of heavy-looking keys and a map and rounded the desk to give them the basic instructions. "You're in cabin eight. We weren't expecting anyone so close to Christmas. Usually, our winter guests prefer to come closer to New Year's Eve and stay only a couple of nights, but I have you down for six nights, correct?"

"Correct," David confirmed.

"With such short notice, we only just turned on the heating in your cabin. It might take a while for the room to get to a decent temperature. But you're free to wait here as long as you like, and there's a fully functional fireplace in your bungalow already equipped with three days' worth of firewood."

"*Heat* won't be a problem," David said with such a straight face that Haley wondered if she was so randy she was reading double entendres into every innocent phrase. But then David sent her a wicked smile that gave her no doubt what he really meant. A shiver of anticipation ran down her spine.

"Very well," the clerk said, and proceeded to show them on the map how to get to their cabin. "We don't offer room service," he concluded. "But there's a convenience store two miles up the main road that's open 24/7, and of course all the restaurants in town. Please let me know if you'd like any recommendations."

"Great," David said, taking the map and keys.

"Again, if you need anything at all, call me. You have my number."

Within minutes they were back in the truck, cruising along an even smaller road surrounded by thick forest on both sides. Along the way, they passed a few other bungalow-style guest lodges, until they finally reached number eight: a tiny log cabin in the middle of the woods.

As the receptionist had predicted, the inside wasn't much warmer than the outside, and Haley eyed the fireplace as her last hope. The rest of the cabin was simple and very earthy, but with a modern-chic vibe. Everything was made of wood: roof, walls, floor, furniture…

The layout was pretty basic: an open space with a small kitchenette and dining area on one side, a large space in front of the fireplace covered by a giant white rug of several sheep skins joined together, a door to the side that must lead to the bathroom, and a giant king-sized bed at the back of the room. Haley's eyes lingered on the bed longer than on everything else.

Coming in, David didn't seem concerned by the low temperature. He closed the door behind them, set their bags near the bed, rather business-like, and removed his coat so he could work on building up a fire. Haley watched, impressed, as he crumpled a few newspaper pages into paper balls, threw them into the fire pit, and started building an orderly pyramid of progressively thicker logs.

She sat on the rug in front of the fire, not removing her coat or any of her cold weather accessories. Hat, scarf, gloves… she kept everything on. "I never knew you had such a handy side," she teased.

He peeked at her over his shoulder, a dangerous promise in his eyes. "There's still much you don't know about me."

I'm sure we're going to close the gap tonight, Haley thought, swallowing.

Once the fire was up and burning, David settled on the rug next to her. "Still cold?" he asked.

"Not so much…"

She made to remove her beanie, but David caught her wrist midair. "Let me."

He knelt in front of her and, moving tortuously slowly, pulled off her hat. Then he gently unwrapped the scarf from around her neck, and pulled off her gloves, one first, then the other, his eyes never leaving hers. The buttons of her coat were his next victim and, once he was done, he pushed it off her shoulders. The boots went next, followed by her socks. As he pulled her sweater over her head, he paused to look at her for a few long moments, as if he needed to etch every second into his mind. She used the pause to sneak her hands under his sweater and lift it up. Ever the collaborative, David tugged it off his back in one fluid motion and discarded it next to the mounting pile of her clothes.

Then his lips were on hers, all restraint finally gone. He laid her backward on the rug and climbed on top of her, careful to keep his weight on his elbows. As they kissed, other useless clothes were shed. When they were down to only their underwear, he stopped again. David looked at her with such burning intensity that Haley was overwhelmed by the strength of her feelings; *their* feelings.

"I love you."

Haley reached up to cup his face. "I think I do more than love you…"

David smiled down at her. "What's that supposed to mean?"

"That I've never felt something so…" *Strong, intense, overpowering…* no word seemed big enough. "So…"

"Shhh…" He pressed a finger to her lips. "I know…"

He leaned down and kissed her again, and again, and again. And as they made love for the first time, there was no more need to talk… their eyes spoke for them. And their lips, and their hands, and their bodies…

***

"I like that face," Haley said, rolling over in bed to place her chin on David's naked chest. After a long time spent on the rug the night before, they'd finally moved to the bed.

"What face?" David asked.

"Relaxed, unguarded… serene."

"I'm happy."

"And I'm starving," Haley said, sliding out of bed and regaling David with a full view of her naked rear side. "How about breakfast?"

"You can't ask me about breakfast looking like that," David protested.

"Well, sorry, but I really am starving."

Haley moved next to the fireplace to put on yesterday's clothes, and she was just pulling up the zipper of her jeans when David grabbed her from behind. Shifting the hair away from her neck, he started trailing kisses from right below her ear down to her collarbone. "Are you sure I can't interest you in a rematch?"

Haley laughed and wriggled away. She bent to get her sweater, and picked up David's clothes, too, pushing them into his hands. "Clothes on. You're treating me to breakfast." She watched him obediently put his pants and shirt on, and then, with a coquettish smile, she added, "Also, we might want to stock up a little, just in case we don't feel like going out much in the next few days."

David's eyes darkened. He pulled her close and whispered, "You're right, we need to stock up."

***

On the first day of the new year, Haley and David were all packed and ready to get back to the real world. They'd played house for six amazing days, cooking meals, making love, building a snowman, making love, going on cozy restaurant dates, making love… They'd even ventured out of the cabin to visit the frozen-over falls. But now it was time to return to Boston, and time for a big reality check. As much as Haley loved it, they couldn't live in a bubble forever.

"You got everything?" David asked, scanning the room for any forgotten items.

"Yeah. Listen, David, before we go, we need to…"

"No. No, no, no." David pushed a finger on her lips. "Don't…"

Haley pulled his hand aside, interlocking their fingers. "You don't even know what I want to say."

"No, but I'm assuming it starts with 'What happens when we're back in Boston?' and ends with 'We need to tell Scott.'"

"He should know."

"Not right away."

"He already knows there's something between us. I mean, it's the reason he and I broke up. Didn't you talk at all when you were at home?"

"Yeah, he asked me if we were together."

"And what did you say?"

"I said 'no' because at the time we weren't together."

"All the more reason to come clean."

David took his phone out of his pocket. "So, what? You want me to call him now and tell him?"

"Not over the phone. But as soon as we get back to Boston we're going to tell him, okay?"

David shrugged. "I hope you'll still like me with a black eye or two."

Haley smiled and cupped his cheek. "Even with a broken nose." She rose on tiptoes to kiss him.

"I see you've mastered the carrot and stick thing," David joked after the kiss.

"Is it working?"

"Like a charm." David pressed his lips to her forehead. "Listen, the Crimson have an away game against Vermont tomorrow. We'll tell him when he comes back… And tonight… we can have another selfish night all to ourselves…" He gave her a long kiss.

Haley kept her arms wrapped around him after breaking the kiss. "And I'm supposed to be the expert on the carrot and stick thingy, huh?"

David smirked. "Shall we?"

Holding hands, they exited the cabin and got in the truck, ready for the long drive home.

***

After being gone from her apartment for a good ten days, Haley needed a serious round of grocery shopping. She'd spent two nights at David's place and hadn't had any time to go to the supermarket until now. Plus, she needed to busy herself with something mundane, not to think about how tonight was the night David would tell Scott about their relationship. They'd debated for a long time if they should tell him together, but Haley had suggested David do it alone. They were brothers, and they needed to work out their issues.

Haley was pushing her cart through the cereal aisle when she spotted a familiar figure a few feet ahead of her. She froze, undecided on what to do, just as Scott turned and their eyes met. The initial look of surprise on his face was quickly replaced by a mix of hurt and contempt. He held her gaze for a few impossibly long seconds. Then, without a single word or nod of acknowledgment, he walked away.

Well, then.

"Scott," she called. "Wait."

Haley left her cart behind to run after him. "Are we at the point we can't even say hello to each other?"

Scott stopped and turned to face her. "You're sleeping with my brother. Kind of puts a damper on things."

His words, cold with suppressed fury and lined with harsh resentment, were like a slap in her face. "Scott, I'm… how…?"

"How do I know? Matt told me you spent the night at my old place. I assume it wasn't to play Scrabble. How convenient for you… all you had to do was switch doors."

Matt! They'd crossed paths for ten seconds on New Year's Day as he was leaving the house to go to Vermont, and neither Haley nor David had imagined he'd tell Scott.

"Scott, I'm sorry you found out that way. David wanted to be the one to tell you."

"Oh! Is that what the 'we need to talk' text was about? Well, you can tell him he can save his speech."

"I'm sorry."

"Well, so am I."

After another withering look, Scott dropped his grocery basket on the floor and stormed out of the supermarket without buying anything.

***

"He'll come round," David reassured her later that evening.

They were in his apartment, cuddling on his bed.

"I don't know, David, you should've seen his face. I think we really hurt him."

"He can survive, believe me. I did it for a year."

"It's different. I was never with you before."

"Didn't change the way I felt about you."

"Now you're just trying to sweet-talk me."

"What if I am?" He pushed a lock of hair away from her face. "Would it be so bad? Is it too selfish for me to want to enjoy this moment, just me and you, without worrying about anybody else's hurt feelings?"

"A little."

"Well, sorry to break it to you, but I'm selfish. I take what I want and do what I want… and right now the only thing I want is this…" He pressed his lips to hers, silencing any further protest she might've had.

Scott

If nothing else, the discovery of Haley and David's relationship refocused Scott's anger on the basketball court. Where his fury had been pointless before, now he channeled his aggressiveness into a single aim: winning. He launched himself into one physical confrontation after another, his fear from the first game long gone. Almost as if now Scott *wanted* to get hurt.

The new style soon showed its consequences in an ever-growing number of faults being added to his box score, but also an outstanding tally of successful rebounds and blocked offensive actions. Coach Morrison didn't appear to mind the change much. As long as Scott kept it under the per-game fault limit, Morrison seemed fine giving him more leeway than his teammates. After all, he was supposed to be the muscle of the team.

So Scott poured all his efforts into basketball and training until winter recess was over and classes resumed, providing him with the added distraction of homework and his med school pre-application. Best way to keep his mind off things—off people.

And eventually, day by day, game by game, his heart started to mend. The part of him that had loved Haley, and then hated her, finally leaned toward a non-emotion closer to indifference. If he saw her in a supermarket now, he was sure he'd at least be able to complete his shopping without running away.

It was in this state of mind that Scott walked into his only literary class of the term, three whole weeks after finding out about Haley and David. He was early, so he took a seat at the almost empty table and waited for the other students and professor to show. He was busy staring into space, thinking about nothing, when someone said, "Hi" and took the chair on his right.

Madison.

Scott hadn't thought about her or what David had hinted at since Christmas, but now that she'd magically appeared next to him, he couldn't help but wonder...

"Hey," he said, looking her straight in the eyes.

They *were* big and of the deepest ocean blue.

She was beautiful, there was no denying it, and today she looked cute with her hair pinned in a messy bun by a yellow pencil, and with her librarian-style, extra-large glasses perched on her nose.

Madison held his gaze for barely half a second before looking away to take a notepad out of her school bag. A faint blush spread on her cheeks.

Mmm, interesting, Scott thought.

"So, how were the holidays?" Madison asked, clearly trying to appear nonchalant but still coming off flustered.

"My brother slept with my ex. Not my best Christmas."

"Oh." Madison covered her mouth with her hand, then lowered it to say. "I'm so sorry, I wasn't thinking…"

"Nah, it doesn't matter," Scott reassured her. "I've moved on."

"Really? How? I mean, good for you."

"I realized Haley and I were never a good fit, you know? We had so little in common…"

Madison stared at her blank notepad for a while, then asked, "So you're over her?"

Scott shrugged. "Getting there…"

"Great." Madison blushed again. "For you…"

"Hello, class." The professor walked in. "Welcome to the advanced fiction-writing workshop. I know we all probably had a long day, and a four-to-seven lecture time is never ideal, but we all have to work with what we're given… so I'll keep the introduction brief. I'm Professor Mitchell." The instructor paused to write her name on the board. "And I'll be your teacher for the spring term…"

Everyone started jotting down notes—well, everyone except for Madison, who was frantically searching for something. First, under her notepad, then in her bag, and even on the floor.

"This course will focus on the structure, execution, and revision of short fiction, with a longer project due for your final assignment…"

As Professor Mitchell kept going with her introduction, Scott whispered, "What are you looking for?"

"…throughout the whole term, we will read and discuss literary fiction from a craft perspective, concentrating on revision as well…"

"My pencil," Madison whispered back. "I can't find it."

"…the teaching approach will be primarily the discussion of student work…"

Scott leaned forward on his elbows. "You mean the one in your hair?"

"…with the aim of improving both writer-ly skills and critical analysis…"

Madison grasped at her messy bun, searching for the pencil. In one fluid motion, she freed it from its knot, sending a cascade of golden locks tumbling down her shoulders. Scott stared, mesmerized. At four in the afternoon, the sun was already setting and a warm orange glow was filtering through the window, hitting Madison's face with just the right light. Scott took in the halo of blond curls, her big blue eyes, and he also noted new details… like the cute little freckles that dotted her nose and cheeks. He frowned. How had he never noticed how beautiful she was?

"What's with the Heathcliff scowl?" Madison asked.

And she made literary quips, too.

"…Needless to say, *participation* is a key element of your final grade," the professor concluded, looking pointedly in their direction.

Scott threw Madison a so-busted, let's-be-model-students-from-now-on stare, and they spent the rest of the class in utter silence unless it was to say something course related.

***

After class, Scott and Madison made their way out of Baker Center together. Even if he'd had a super long day, and practice with the team was scheduled for an ungodly hour the next morning, Scott didn't feel like going home yet, so he went out on a limb and said, "Hey, you want to grab a bite?"

He wasn't sure what he was doing, and he didn't have a hit-on-Madison agenda. He was going with the flow, following his instincts, which told him being around Madison felt good. Plus, she was so cute when she blushed, just as she was doing now at his invitation. Scott was sure he had dinner in the bag, when she surprised him.

"Err… I would love to." Madison looked away, even more uncomfortable. "But I really can't."

"Oh, right," Scott said. "No, I mean…"

"It's not what you think…"

Scott tilted his head questioningly.

"This is really embarrassing, but I'm totally broke at the moment."

Definitely not the answer Scott had expected.

"Broke? How?"

"Actually, it's all your fault." Madison smiled. "Remember last summer, when you told me to follow my dreams?"

Scott's memory flashed back to the night they'd met on the street and walked to her house together. "To be a writer?" he asked.

"More not to be a lawyer." Madison sighed. "I told my dad I'm not applying to law school, and, in true Smithson fashion, he cut me off."

"That's awful."

"I know, but I'm his only child, and it's a hit for him to let his legacy within the firm go." Madison shrugged. "Anyway, I've applied for a student loan, but until it kicks in I can't afford dinner out…"

"That's not a problem. Dinner's on me."

There came the cute blush again. "No, I couldn't…"

"Come on, I still owe you big time for our last group project. You covered for me when I was out of it, and I never got to thank you. The least I can do is feed you…"

Madison stared at him, a new spark in her eyes. "When you put it like that… Where to?"

"Shake Shack?"

"Sounds perfect."

Madison

"What's with the dreamy face?" Alice asked the second Madison walked into the living room.

Madison checked the house to make sure Haley wasn't there, then said, "I might've gone on a non-date with Scott."

"Define non-date, please?"

"Oh, you know, a date that isn't really a date…"

Alice closed the textbook she was highlighting and stared at her with a puzzled expression.

"How can I explain it?" Madison took the chair in front of Alice at the long rectangular dining table the three of them often used to study. Books and papers could be spread out on it much more comfortably than on their respective smaller desks. "It's like, it starts out innocently enough: two friends grabbing a bite together after a long afternoon class. And then, BAM, in the middle of dinner you suddenly realize you're on a date… sort of…"

Alice smiled. "So how did this non-date go?"

"It was just perfect, and…" Madison stopped and started chewing on her bottom lip.

"That's not exactly a perfect-date face," Alice noted.

"You think Haley will have a problem with it? Should I ask her first?"

"*Ask* her?"

"Yeah, I mean, am I breaking a girl code here? You know, like never date your friend's ex, or something?"

"Well, she didn't ask your permission to go out with David, did she?"

"No, true. But David and I never were in a serious relationship, while Haley and Scott dated for almost a year."

"And dumped him because she's in love with his brother. You're in the clear… I mean, if something is happening with you and Scott, you should definitely be upfront and tell her, but not in an asking-permission way."

"Right."

"So…" Alice leaned forward on her elbows. "Is something happening between you and Scott?"

Madison couldn't help but smile. "I'm not sure… but he was different today. For the first time, it felt like he was seeing me as a woman and not, you know, a friend, a classmate, or Haley's roommate. I can't explain it in words, but something changed…"

Alice grabbed her hands across the table. "I'm so happy for you."

Seeing her friend's bright smile made Madison dial back a notch. "I don't want to get my hopes up too much. It's really nothing at the moment." Then a horrible thought crossed Madison's mind.

"What?" Alice asked.

"You think he's over Haley? He was pretty beaten up when they broke up."

Alice turned serious, too. "Hard one to call, but if he's being flirty with you…"

"So he wouldn't want to try to make Haley jealous by going out with me?"

"No, never… Why would you think that?"

Madison pulled her hands free and waved Alice off. "His brother did just that."

"Yeah, but that's David. Scott's a good guy… he'd never stoop so low."

"Mmm…" Madison stared at the fake wood-grain of the table, tracing its curls with a finger.

"Madison." Alice knocked on the table to make her look up. "Scott is nothing like that, I promise."

"It doesn't matter, really. I'm probably building castles in the air… I'm sure Scott saw tonight only as dinner with a friend."

"Hey," Alice said with a devilish smirk. "Want me to do some investigative work?"

"What do you mean?"

"We could ask Jack…"

"No, no… Already too many people know how I feel about Scott. I don't want Jack to know, too."

"Err…" Alice cleared her throat.

Madison gasped. "You already told him!"

"I might've said something a while ago. But don't worry, Jack is like a tomb. He won't say anything."

"But they live together!"

"Which is why we can ask him if Scott seems to be in a good mood. I mean, if he walked into the house with a smile matching yours, you have your answer."

The idea was too appealing for Madison to refuse, so she nodded.

Alice grabbed her phone and beckoned Madison to come sit next to her. Madison rounded the table, and they bent their heads together as Alice typed.

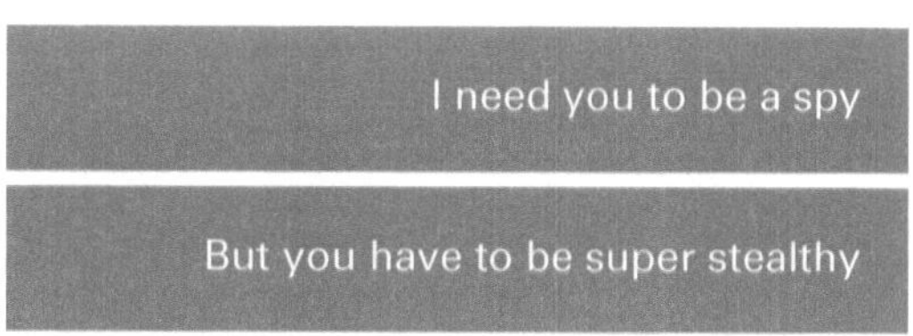

Dots appeared over Jack's name in the chat until his reply came in.

Okay?

Yes?

How does he seem?

What do you mean?

Is he acting strange?

Mmm... Sort of

Meaning?

He's whistling under his breath

Ask him how his day went

Do I have to call him honey?

No, smartass... :)

Just ask him about his day, please?

The chat stood blank for a while until Jack's answer finally came in.

Says it's been his best day in a long while

Alice and Madison looked away from the chat and up at each other, both sporting cheeks-aching smiles.

Scott

After a lot of cajoling, Scott convinced Madison to let him buy her dinner the next Wednesday, and the next. He was already working out a strategy to make her say 'yes' to a repeat tonight when she surprised him.

"So," Madison said as they exited Baker Center. "Where can I take you to dinner tonight?"

"You're taking me out?"

"Yes." She smiled coyly.

Scott studied her. "Your student loan kicked in?"

"Better than that… my mother kicked in."

She made a suspenseful pause, and Scott waited for her to elaborate.

"She told my dad that if he was free to make my last year in college a nightmare and force me to take on student debt, she was free to have him sleep on the couch." Madison smirked. "I don't think he made it past the first night."

Scott low-whistled.

"So now I'm back on a drastically reduced allowance, and I can treat you to a grand dinner a la tacos and fries… You in for Mexican?"

"Mexican sounds perfect."

***

Much later, when the check arrived, both Madison and Scott reached for it.

"Hey," Madison protested. "I said dinner was on me."

"Are you one of those feminists who never let men pay on a date?"

"If this were a date, I might let you pay."

Scott held onto the leather folder tight as he stared into Madison's blue eyes. "So let me pay…"

The blush that ensued had to be the fiercest yet. Madison let go of the folder and settled back in her seat, lowering her gaze. Scott slipped a few bills in, and they walked out of the restaurant without saying another word.

563

They'd been walking for a full block when Madison surprised him with a direct question. "So this was a date?" she asked, steadily looking at the curb.

Scott opted for an equally daring answer. "I'd like it to be."

"Why? I mean, you've never..." Madison stumbled over her words. "What changed?"

"I had a bit of an eye-opener," Scott confessed.

Madison stopped walking and turned to face him, bolder than he'd ever seen her. "What does that mean?"

Scott smirked teasingly. "David might've mentioned something over Christmas break..."

Now, this had to be the best, neck-to-forehead tomato red face ever. Her eyes were open wide and her mouth formed the cutest, shocked little 'O' shape.

"What did he say?"

Scott shrugged. "He hinted a beautiful, smart girl might have feelings for me."

Madison groaned. "Now I want to kill your brother."

Scott chuckled. "Welcome to the club."

A smile lit up Madison's face. Then the rest of what he'd said seemed to register in her eyes, and she turned serious again. "You think I'm beautiful?"

Scott stepped closer, pushing her long curls behind her ears and cupping her cheeks. "Very." Then he leaned in and kissed her. Madison kept still at first, too shy or too shocked to move. But after a few moments, she responded to the kiss with a passion Scott had not expected. Not that he was complaining.

After the kiss, he walked her home, both of them maintaining an embarrassed silence. When they stopped in front of her building, Scott wasted no more time with shyness. "Can I hope for a second date?" he asked.

Madison blushed and nodded.

"I have two home games this weekend against Columbia and Cornell, but I'm free Saturday morning. Want to grab a coffee?"

"Yes," Madison replied in a whisper.

Scott pulled her closer and gave her a soft kiss on the lips. "Until then..."

Madison

For their official second date, as two certified book-worms, Madison and Scott went to a reading from an author they both loved in downtown Boston. Afterward, they stopped to have coffee in a quaint, one-of-a-kind coffee shop near the bookstore. There were a lot more kisses involved, and Madison found herself unable to stop smiling. Not even when, later that evening, she had to get ready to go watch the Crimson play. Her almost non-existent love for the game rekindled at once.

"Maddie, are you ready?" Alice called from the hall.

"Just a second!" Madison shouted back. "I'll be right there."

Haley hadn't come to a basketball match since game one of the season, back at the beginning of November, but Madison had kept going to keep Alice company. And, yes, also to watch Scott play. But tonight was the first night she officially had a reason to go: Scott had asked her.

Madison fluffed her hair in front of the mirror and was about to exit her bedroom when she overheard Alice and Haley talking on the other side of the door.

"Are you sure you'll be okay at home all by yourself?" Alice asked.

"Yeah, I have tons of homework to do," Haley reassured her.

"Is David coming over?"

"No, he's going to the game."

"Oh." Alice sounded surprised. "So why don't you come, too?"

"I don't want Scott to see me there."

Madison's heart sank. Did Haley believe Scott still had feelings for her?

Thankfully, Alice asked the very same question. "But he's moved on from you. So what's the issue?"

"From me, yes, but not from what happened with his brother. They were still bickering over Brigitte after they'd both been over the girl forever. I want to give them space. They're brothers… they have their issues, but deep down they love each other. They just have to stop being so damn stubborn…"

Madison sighed with relief. On Wednesday night, when she'd come back home after Scott had kissed her, she'd waited a reasonable amount of time to allow herself to become stable and coherent enough, and then she'd knocked on Haley's door to tell her. The conversation had been pretty smooth. Madison had told Haley about the kiss, and her friend, after a moment of shock, had wished her and Scott to be happy, saying neither of them could hope to find a better person. Madison was relieved to know now that Haley had been sincere.

Yes, the situation would still be strange for a while, but Madison hoped that, in time, the we-both-dated-the-other-brother-first awkwardness would go away.

"Madison," Alice called again. "We're going to be late."

With a deep breath, Madison opened the door. "You can stop yelling. I'm here."

***

Just as they were about to get seated at Lavietes Pavilion, someone grabbed Madison from behind and gently pushed her one seat over.

"This is my seat, Blondie," David said, sitting on the chair between her and Alice.

Madison glared at him.

"Whoa, what's with the smoldering look?"

"I'm not talking to you," Madison said, crossing her arms over her chest and stubbornly looking away.

"May I ask why?"

Madison turned, pointing a finger at him. "You told Scott I had feelings for him when you promised you'd never do that. I'm *so* mad at you."

"Mmm, interesting, because last I heard, my little slip of the tongue sent my brother flying right into your open arms."

Madison opened her mouth to argue but found herself at a loss for sarcastic retorts.

"So." David smiled, as cocksure as ever. "What you really mean by 'mad' is how grateful you are I've knocked some sense into my brother's head, right?"

With Haley's words fresh in her mind, Madison asked, "So, how are things with you and Scott?"

"Oh." David shrugged. "He knows he owes me."

"Owes you?"

"Yeah. If it weren't for me, he would've said 'no' to California, and now he wouldn't be dating the only girl right for him."

Alice scoffed on David's other side. "Oh, gosh, you *are* smooth."

"You have a problem with me, too?"

"As long as you keep my best friend happy, no, I don't."

David stretched in his chair like a cat. "Glad we can all be one happy family." Then he nudged Madison's shoulder. "Come on, Blondie, away with the scowl. You know you can't stay mad at me…"

Madison's lips twitched, and she rolled her eyes. The dude really was impossible.

"Friends?" David asked, and she nodded.

"Friends."

Just then the referee whistled, and all eyes turned to the game. Madison shouted in encouragement. Finally, she could cheer for the boy she loved with no need to hold back…

***

Madison had to wait another three days to see Scott again. Between conflicting class schedules, his basketball practice sessions plus biweekly games, and her book club, it was difficult for them to find a quiet moment to meet. So, Wednesday nights had become their fixed date amidst the chaos of the rest of the week. They'd spend three good hours eye flirting in class, then go out to dinner together. Or at least they had so far.

"How about something different tonight?" Scott asked, as they walked hand-in-hand out of class.

"What did you have in mind?"

"Dinner at my place. I'm cooking."

An electric current ran through Madison's body. In the month they'd been going out, more or less officially, they'd only made out so far, but going to Scott's house could mean a lot more would happen tonight. Madison quickly did a mental checklist of her legs and bikini waxing status… *Phew, all good.*

"You can cook?" she asked.

"A very limited set of dishes."

"So what's on the menu tonight?"

"I can make a mean steak."

Madison lifted up on her tiptoes and gave him a quick peck on the

567

lips. "How mean?"

Inside Scott's apartment, Madison rubbed her hands together to warm them up. February was almost over, but the weather didn't appear to be improving. The temperature was still in the low thirties, and it had snowed again only two days ago.

Scott hugged her from behind and, pushing her hair out of the way, he pressed his lips to her neck in a soft kiss. "Cold?" he asked.

The kiss spread a warm fuzz through her from the tips of her ears down to her frozen toes. Madison leaned back into him. "Not really… Not anymore."

At that, he spun her around and kissed her properly. Things heated up pretty fast, and soon Madison found herself pressed against the wall, burning hot inside her coat. All she wanted was to get rid of the several layers of clothing separating her and Scott and really touch him, skin on skin.

"Err-hem," someone coughed to their left.

Scott pulled back at once, and Madison stared up at him in confusion for a while, as if emerging from a daze. Then she turned her head to the left, where Jack was standing. He was looking at them with half a smirk—part embarrassed, and part male comradeship.

"Sorry guys," Jack said. "I would've let you carry on, but you're basically blocking the door."

Both Madison and Scott quickly moved out of the hallway, leaving the path free for Jack.

"You going out?" Scott asked.

"Yeah, I'm seeing Alice," Jack said. Then, with a knowing little grin, he added, "Probably going to spend the night. You guys have a good time." And he was gone.

Butterflies exploded in Madison's belly. They'd be here alone all night.

Scott hung his coat and cleared his throat. "So, dinner…"

Madison followed his example by hanging her coat next to his and joined him in the open kitchen. "Yeah, you have to show me this special recipe of yours."

Scott opened a bottle of red wine, and Madison sat on the counter, far away enough from the stove so that oil wouldn't spritz on her. She admired Scott's kitchen skills as she sipped her wine. The steaks didn't take long to cook and, after helping him set the table, they sat down to eat.

"Mmm," Madison moaned at her first bite of steak. It was juicy and seasoned to perfection. "One of the best steaks I've ever had."

Scott lowered his fork. "One of?"

Madison smiled. "Okay, the best."

One bottle of wine and one delicious steak later, Scott became suddenly serious.

"There's something I want to ask you," he said.

"Go ahead." Madison braced herself for whatever was about to come out of his mouth. Judging from the Heathcliff frown, it was nothing good.

"David." Scott stalled for a few seconds. "How did he know about your feelings for me?"

Madison's face flared with heat. She already was the blushing type, and after several glasses of wine, it got ten times worse. "Good intuition, I guess?"

"Why would you confide in him?"

"I didn't. But when he flat-out asked, I couldn't really deny it."

"So you two talk often?"

Madison shifted in her chair. She was about to reply when Scott spoke again. "Should I open another bottle of wine?"

"Yes, please," Madison said.

More wine was essential if they were having the "David" conversation.

Scott got up and was back in no time with an unopened bottle. Damn, he was sexy as he worked the corkscrew. The cork came out with a loud pop, and Scott refilled both their glasses.

After they'd both taken generous sips, Scott spoke again. "I'm sorry for the third degree," he said, smiling. "But given recent events… I need to understand what the deal is with you and my brother."

"Fair enough…" Madison nodded. "I guess you could say we're friends."

"Friends? You two were dating last year…"

"Yeah, for a couple of months. He was a total douche, though, so no regrets there."

"But if he was a douche, how can you be his friend?"

"I told you he apologized… and he can be pretty convincing." Madison wasn't sure how to make Scott understand. "We sort of bonded over the situation, you know? He was in love with Haley, I was in love with—" Madison stopped talking, aghast at what she'd been about to say.

Scott's emerald green eyes sparkled. "With me?" he asked.

"You can't ask me that on a third date." Madison scoffed.

"If you consider the first unofficial three, it's our sixth…"

"This isn't fair. You already know more than you should! And I can't tell you how I feel after such a short time."

"Why not?"

"Because guys run away from strong feelings, and they don't want to hear how completely obsessed a girl is with them. I'm supposed to play hard to get here…"

"You're so cute when you blush," Scott said. "Did I ever tell you that?"

Madison's cheeks burned. "Oh, you're having fun, aren't you?"

"Yes." He flashed her another grin before turning serious again. "Madison, I spent the last four months of my last relationship like an unwanted guest in my own house. I was with a girl that wasn't just playing hard to get; she *was* hard to get. And it was exhausting. All the doubts, the second-guessing, the jealousy… So, I wish my next girlfriend to tell me exactly how strong her feelings for me are, and how completely obsessed she is with me."

"In short, you want a full confession."

Scott nodded and stared at her. Madison stalled, taking another sip of wine. What he was asking her to do was relationship suicide. He wanted her to lay her heart bare, while he still hadn't even admitted to anything more than liking her. Madison was seriously tempted to keep her mouth shut. But what would that accomplish? Yeah, she'd save face, but then she'd just keep on being miserable. It had been so hard to conceal her feelings this past year, and now she had an opportunity to let it all out. And if Scott laughed in her face… well, then, she knew the drill: *Stay strong and pull through.*

"Okay." Madison dropped her glass on the table and stared up at Scott. "I've had a crush on you since you walked into McDougall's class freshman year."

Scott's lips parted in a goofy smile. "Really?"

"Yeah. You had the full attention of the female population the second you walked in. Let's just say that tall guys of the basketball playing kind are not that common in poetry classes. And then… remember our first assignment?"

"The sonnet?"

"Mm-hmm. You wrote that piece about water…" Madison rehearsed the first few lines. "My cold water, you inspire me to write. How I hate the way you flow, lap and rush."

"Invading my mind day and through the night," Scott recited the next line of the first quatrain with her. "How do you even remember that?"

"I used to annotate all poems, and I liked yours the most… so my crush became certified."

"But you never said more than 'hi' to me."

Madison shrugged. "I'm shy. I don't talk to guys…"

"Okay, go on…"

"Isn't this enough?"

"Nuh-uh." Scott smiled devilishly. "I want the whole story."

Madison took another sip of wine. "Last year, when Alice was dating Peter, we started going to Lavietes to watch the games with her. Watching you play was… did I ever tell you how good you look in a basketball uniform?"

"Just now, I think." He winked.

Madison smiled, but then her brain moved on to the next phase.

"What's with the sad face?"

"Well, the next part of the story starts at Christmas…"

She held Scott's gaze and recognized the shadow passing behind his eyes.

"When Alice asked us to go with her to Hawaii, I wanted to go, but my family is… complicated. My grandparents are big on Christmas, and I couldn't go. But I had this irrational fear that something would happen between you and Haley… and it did."

"Did she know how you…?"

"No, not back then. Alice had guessed it, and she was the only person I could talk to for a long time. And that's also when things got worse…"

Scott frowned.

"Before, you were only a guy in my class I had a silly crush on. But when you started dating Haley, we all started going out together, and I got to know you better… That's also when you started sitting next to me in class, when we started saying something beyond 'hi' to each other, and I fell more and more for you."

"But you were already dating David back then."

"The first night I went home with David was also the first night I saw you and Haley together. I drank more than I should have, and David was there, as broody as I was. He noticed me, and… I knew it wasn't right, but you know when you want to do something specifically because it's the wrong thing?"

Scott nodded.

"That was me that night. But dating David didn't mean I couldn't still think about you."

"And when did Haley find out about… you know?" He gestured between them.

"At the end of the school year. I got into a huge fight with Alice, and since she was mad at me, she spilled the beans to Haley."

"She never said a word."

"Because I asked her not to. And, Scott, it was hard on her. It wasn't fair of me to ask her to keep secrets from you, and she's felt guilty about dating you from the moment she found out about me. She must've hated not being able to tell you why, but she did it anyway because she's my best friend."

They both stood silent for a while.

"I know the period you're talking about," Scott eventually said. "A few things make more sense now. Why did you break up with David?"

"We got into a stupid fight, and he was dating me only to make Haley jealous."

Scott's jaw tensed.

"Don't get mad at him for that. I was dating him to get over you, so I wasn't really any better. And he's already apologized for everything he did."

"Well, not to me."

"No, but when enough time has passed, give him a chance. I know he's impossible, but, Scott, he loves you. The day you got into a fight at Blake's house he was heartbroken over Haley, but the moment it seemed you were about to get yourself involved in a brawl, he was there by your side to back you up. And when they pushed you into the pool… You should've seen him. He dove right in and pulled you out, and…"

"Saved my life."

"Exactly. When it looked like you weren't breathing, he lost it. I've never seen anyone so desperate. That wasn't a lie."

There was another long silence as Madison gathered the courage to ask him to clear the doubts she still had about them. His turn to be honest…

"Are you… are you really sorry about any of what David did? I mean, I know he's not in the running for brother of the year, but if he hadn't lied to you about kissing Haley, you wouldn't have gone to California… and now you would…"

"…still be dating her," Scott finished.

"Is that what you'd prefer? To be with Haley?"

Scott stood up and rounded the table, taking one of Madison's hands and pulling her up. He pushed her hair behind her shoulders and cupped her cheeks. Then, looking her straight into the eyes, he said, "There's nowhere else I'd rather be tonight… with no one else." He kissed her. "You know when was the first time that I realized the world would keep on spinning after Haley and I broke up?"

"No."

Scott ran his hands down her arms and wrapped them behind her back. "That afternoon with you in the library. You made everything better. Being around you felt… right. Since David told me about you having feelings for me, I haven't been able to push you out of my head, and I've never felt more wanted or serene than I do with you. Madison, we've been classmates, then friends, and now… you're my rock. I spent the last month waiting for our Wednesday nights together… You're smart, beautiful, kind…"

Did anyone have a fire extinguisher? Because Madison was sure her face was on fire.

Scott nuzzled the tip of his nose against the tip of hers. He leaned in to kiss her, but Madison pulled back.

"I know I've said a lot of things tonight, and I don't want to rush us, but if you want to run for the hills, this is probably your moment."

Scott pulled her close again. "I'm not going anywhere. So, that's it? You've left nothing out?"

Madison bit her lower lip. "Jack London isn't really my favorite author."

Scott's eyes widened. "But we've discussed all his books. You know them almost by heart!"

Madison smiled shyly. "Well, after I told you I liked him, I had to read them… didn't I?"

"I can live with that," he said with a foxy grin, before killing any further conversation with another kiss.

Scott scooped Madison up in his arms and carried her to his room, where he laid her on the bed. He climbed on top of her and stopped to look at her. "You're so beautiful," he whispered.

And as he leaned his head down to kiss her again, there was nothing or no one holding them back. They'd laid everything out in the open, and even if neither of them had said the three magic words—I love you— they shared a connection so deep it didn't need to be expressed in words.

Making love with Scott overwhelmed Madison in ways she wasn't prepared to handle. Her emotions ran so deep that tears rolled down her cheeks. He didn't mock her about it, or shy away; he kissed her tears and made her feel like the most beautiful and wanted woman in the world. He made her feel loved, he made her feel finally home…

Three Months Later

Ethan

"Can you hold her?" Georgiana dropped a smiling Jane into Ethan's lap and went to join the queue of new graduates.

Ethan stared dubiously into the baby's eyes, not sure he was up to babysitting her for the duration of the graduation ceremony. But then his niece smiled at him, and Ethan found himself cooing over her like a mother hen.

Lifting his gaze, he caught Rose staring at him with an amused smirk.

"Baby looks good on you," she mouthed from across the podium where she was waiting with the other graduates for the ceremony to start.

Ethan stuck out his tongue, which earned him an enthusiastic chuckle from baby Jane. So he bounced the baby on his knees to make her laugh louder.

When he looked back up at the line of grad students waiting to receive their diplomas, his eyes drifted to Rose's left hand, and to the engagement ring he'd given her at Christmas. In three months, she'd be his wife. A proud smile surfaced on his lips. He sure was a lucky bastard.

Next, his eyes wandered to his sister's naked hand. No wedding band there, same as Tyler. Becoming a mom had changed Georgiana so much that Ethan hardly recognized her sometimes. She'd matured and stopped acting like a spoiled princess. In just a few months, she'd grown up enough to face her mistakes. She and Tyler had agreed they were wonderful parents, but terrible at being husband and wife. They'd be divorced by the end of the year.

Ethan stared at his soon to be ex-brother-in-law, wanting to hate the dude for everything he'd done to Georgiana. But he finally had to admit his sister shared a big part of the responsibility, and… If it weren't for Tyler, Ethan would've never met Rose, and now he wouldn't be holding this bundle of joy in his arms.

Ethan stared into Jane's blue eyes—his eyes, Georgiana's eyes. The past two years had been a mess for his sister, but she'd still managed to graduate on time and give birth to the most beautiful baby in the world… and now she could find someone who really loved her, someone who deserved her and who would make her happy.

And, yeah, Tyler, too. Provided he kept away from Rose.

Some things never changed, after all…

A professor walked on stage and grabbed the microphone to kick off the ceremony. Ethan settled back in his chair and whispered in Jane's ear, "Look, your mom, your dad, and your aunt-to-be are all about to graduate."

Baby Jane replied with a satisfied, "Ghe-ghe-gwakh."

David

David adjusted the angle of his phone, orienting the camera to include everyone in the picture. Five people stared back at him through the lenses, all dressed the same in their black regalia and caps.

To the left, Scott kept an arm wrapped around Madison's waist, as did Jack with Alice to the right. And in the middle, one arm around each of her roommates' shoulders, was Haley. The girl who'd stolen his heart almost two years ago on a starry summer night.

"Say 'cheese!'" David yelled, snapping away on the phone's camera. "Hang on, let me change the angle."

He shifted to the left, and the five new graduates rotated their ranks with him to stay in front of the camera.

"Okay." David stopped. "Now say, 'David's so handsome.'" He snapped another shot and grinned as he looked at the picture flashing on his screen.

Scott, wearing a half-exasperated smirk. Madison, rolling her eyes. Jack and Alice, staring into each other's eyes, smiling, and not giving a crap about him. And Haley, her lips pursed to blow him a kiss, her green eyes sparkling with joy in the sun.

The End

Note From The Author

Dear Reader,

I hope you enjoyed *Just Friends*. Thank you so much for following the series to the end! Rose, Tyler, Ethan, Georgiana, Madison, Alice, Haley, Jack, David, and Scott all want to say, "Thank you, and goodbye."

If you loved their story, **please leave a review** on Amazon, Goodreads, or wherever you like to post reviews (your blog, your Facebook wall, your bedroom wall, in a text to your best friend…) Reviews are the best gift you can give to an author, and word of mouth is the most powerful means of book discovery.

If you're craving more romance, you can turn the page for a sneak peek from *Love Connection,* the first book in my romantic comedy series *First Comes Love.*

If you want to keep up to date on my new releases and works in progress you can join my Readers' Group at camillaisley.org

Thank you for your support!

Camilla, x

Sneak Peek: Love Connection

Two Weddings

Saturday, June 10—New York, JFK Airport

"You've been staring at those two plane tickets for almost an hour now. My role as bartender compels me to ask: what's the big dilemma?"

I stare at the guy behind the bar for the first time since I sat on this stool an hour ago. He has a broad smile and a friendly face.

"If you stop pretending to be drying glasses just to peek at my tickets and pour me another drink," I say, "I'll tell you."

"Sambuca, with ice?"

I nod and shift my attention back to my tickets. Maybe if I stare at them hard enough, the letters will magically move and spell out a solution for me. In the background, I can hear ice tinkle as it hits the bottom of a glass, then crack when the bartender pours the Sambuca. These sounds mingle with the general noises of the airport: flight announcements, passengers chatting, and luggage rolling on the floor.

"Here you go." The bartender sets my drink on the glassy surface of the bar in front of me.

"You added coffee beans," I observe. "Nice touch."

"Pleased to please. But isn't 7 a.m. a little too early for double heavy spirits?"

"I'm on U.K. time, and believe me, I need the double heavy spirits."

"Which brings us back to the tickets. I've earned an explanation."

I sip my Sambuca and take a closer look at the guy's face. Young— mid-twenties, I'd say. Short sandy hair, intelligent eyes, and always the big smile. He's back at his occupation of drying glasses that don't need drying. Probably one of those people incapable of standing still with nothing to do.

On the screen behind him, a report about a fire at Miami International Airport is taking over the news. The screen reads that the fire has been contained with no casualties, but the airport will sustain heavy delays throughout the day.

"Looks like they're having troubles in Miami," I say, jerking my chin toward the screen.

"Trying to change the subject, are we? You're not going to make me beg for your story, are you?"

I swirl the ice in my glass. "Is this on the house?"

"On the house, along with the free advice."

"All right. One ticket's for San Francisco, the other one for Chicago. There're two weddings today, and I need to choose which one to go to."

"Two close friends?"

"You could say that."

"Oh, okay. Let's see, do you have a particular role in one of the weddings? I mean, do both your friends expect you to show up? Don't you usually need to RSVP months in advance for this kind of thing?"

"Mmm, this wedding…" I push the Chicago ticket forward. "I'm supposed to be the maid of honor. This wedding…" I slide the San Francisco ticket next to its twin on the countertop. "I'm not invited."

The bartender snorts. "Seems pretty straightforward to me. Why would you want to bail on a friend to go to a wedding you're not invited to?"

I look him in the eyes. "To stop it from happening."

"Woo-oh. And the plot thickens. My morning just got a lot more interesting than I was expecting. Is it about a guy? Is he the one who got away?"

"Yep." I take another swig of Sambuca; it burns my throat as I swallow. "You don't make burgers here, by any chance? I'm starving."

"Burgers at seven in the morning?"

"I told you, I'm on U.K. time. And burgers are my favorite."

"Sorry, but the kitchen's closed. I can give you some tortilla chips." He opens a new bag and pours them into a wooden bowl. "So, what's his name?"

"Jake."

"Jake." The bartender pauses. "The name has appeal."

"Not just the name." I sigh.

"You want to tell me what happened?"

"We first dated in high school. After graduation, he wanted to go to Stanford, and I wanted to go to Harvard."

The bartender whistles. "The war of the Ivy Leagues. What do you guys do?"

"I'm a lawyer. He's a surgeon."

"So what happened? You fought over schools, went your separate ways, and drifted apart during college?" he asks, his tone saying, *"Same old, same old."*

"No. I went to Stanford instead, to be with him. He assured me we'd go to Harvard for grad school."

"Oh. I sense that promise didn't come true. So you stayed together through college as well. And…?"

"Stanford offered him a scholarship for Med School. Everything paid for. No student loans, no living expenses. It was an offer no one could've refused."

"And that's when you broke up?"

"No, not yet. I hadn't applied to Stanford Grad School, so for me, it was either lose one year or move to Boston. Harvard was my dream, Stanford his. It wouldn't have been fair for either of us to have to give up our dream school."

"So you left?"

"Yeah. We spent the summer in California and I moved to Boston at the beginning of the fall term. We thought three years apart would be manageable. That's when we found out why everyone says long distance relationships don't work. School was demanding for both of us and catching a six-hour flight over the weekend became more and more difficult. We settled on leading different lives. We were used to sharing everything. Every day, every moment. Suddenly, we both had this huge chunk of life with different things in it. Things the other couldn't understand or get excited about. It was hard. We started arguing, and…"

"And?"

"Depends who you ask. If you asked Jake, he'd probably tell you it was a miscommunication issue. He'd say I overreacted to him telling me about a job offer he'd received in San Francisco. If you asked me, I'd give you a slightly different version…"

"Was your career really that important?" the bartender asks.

"It wasn't that I valued my career over my relationship with Jake. It was the sensation of always coming in second after *his* career. I'd given up my college dream for him. I'd waited all of graduate school… it was his turn to put me first. To put *us* first."

"If he's still in San Francisco, what's made you change your mind now about being together?"

"I'm not sure I *have* changed my mind."

"So why buy a ticket to San Francisco if you're not even sure you want to try to work things out with him?"

"It was a rash, stupid decision. When I found out Jake was getting married, I panicked. My first thought was that I couldn't let him do it."

"So what's changed?"

"I cooled off and thought about it."

"And?"

"And I realized flying to San Francisco and confronting him was crazy. I mean, what are the odds, really, of us getting back together? I live in London, and he lives in San Francisco. I haven't seen him in forever. I know nothing about his life. We ruined everything once already. How can we possibly make it work this time?"

"And yet here you are, staring at a ticket to San Francisco and contemplating crashing his wedding."

"I can't stop asking myself the 'what if?' question. I'm tired of living in a world of what ifs."

"Meaning?"

"I might've been a tad unreasonable after our break up," I admit.

"As in?"

"As in I moved to the other side of the world and ignored all his calls, emails, and messages. I wanted a fresh start, so I cut him out completely."

The bartender grabs the now-empty wooden bowl and refills it with tortilla chips. "Why?" he asks.

"I was sure he could talk me into moving back to San Francisco if I gave him the chance."

"And you didn't want to quit your job for him?"

"I couldn't. I owed it to myself to make the best choice for *my* career. But the fact remains that moving to the other side of the world didn't help much in forgetting him. I'm still in love with him. He's the only one I ever loved."

"How long ago was this?"

"Three years."

"And you haven't seen him or spoken to him since then?"

"I'm a mess, I know."

"How did you find out he was getting married?"

"Amelia told me—my best friend, the other one getting married today. Amelia, Jake and I are all from a small town near Chicago. She moved to London after getting her bachelor degree and she lives there with her soon-to-be-husband William. But she wanted to get married at home. Anyway, Amelia and Jake had some guests in common, they told Amelia about Jake's wedding as they'd already RSVP'd 'Yes' to him."

"Do you know the girl he's marrying?"

"No." I shake my head decisively. "I don't know anything about her, and I've forced myself not to search Google for intel."

"Aren't you curious?"

"*Yes*. But I can't give her a face. I'd never be able to crash her wedding if I did. She has to stay a ghost."

"When are the weddings?"

"This afternoon."

"Whoa. What's so special about June 10 that everyone wants to get married today? And you're hard-core. Shouldn't you have tried to talk to the guy a little sooner? Are you literally going to barge into the church and yell 'STOP!' in the middle of the ceremony?"

"I'd decided not to go at all."

"But you brought the ticket all the way from London, just in case."

"I did. Having the ticket, even if I knew I wasn't going to use it, made me feel calmer."

"And now you've changed your mind?"

"I don't know. I have no idea what I'm doing."

"When does the plane leave?"

"Which one?"

"Tell me both times."

"San Francisco's eight thirty. Chicago's ten forty-five."

"So you have less than…" He pauses to look at his watch. "Twenty minutes before they start boarding for San Francisco."

"That's correct."

"What's Amelia's take on the situation?"

"She got mad at me at first for even thinking about ditching her wedding. But then again, she's always been a huge fan of Gemma and Jake."

"Gemma?"

"That's me. We all grew up on the same street, and we've been friends forever. Anyway, she's marshaled a back-up maid of honor and she told me to follow my heart."

"And what does your heart say?"

"My heart's telling me it loves Jake. But this is too big. As you said, I can't run into the church and beg him to cancel the wedding."

"What time's the wedding?"

"Six p.m."

"What time does your plane land?"

I look at the ticket. "Noon."

"So you'd have plenty of time to get there before the ceremony starts."

"Mmm, I'm not so sure. The wedding's in some fancy winery in Napa."

"That's barely an hour's drive. You'll still have all the time you need to get there and talk to him before he goes to the altar."

"But what am I going to say?"

"Say that you love him."

"And?"

"Nothing else. If he's in love with you, it'll be enough."

"Say he doesn't laugh in my face and tell me to leave. Say he admits he still loves me. It doesn't change anything. I'm still in London, and he's still in San Francisco."

"You'll figure something."

"I'm not so sure."

"You said it yourself: you don't want to live in a world of what ifs, right? So it seems pretty obvious you have to try."

"But I'm so scared."

"Do you have anything to lose?"

"No, not really."

"Then why not go?"

"What if he doesn't love me anymore?"

"Then he doesn't, and it will suck, but at least you'll have your answer. But if you don't go, and you don't ask, you'll never know, and you'll regret it for the rest of your life. If you love him, go."

My face becomes suddenly hot and an electric prickle spreads from my heart to my fingertips. "Right. What's the worst that could happen?"

"They could arrest you for crashing a private party. Or the bride could sue you for emotional damages. Or…"

"I'm a lawyer; I can take care of myself in the law department. Are you on my side or what?"

"Of course I am. So, what's the next step?"

"A car. I'm going to need a car in San Francisco. I need to rent a car." My pulse is racing. I pick up my phone and tap away frantically. "Uhhuuuhhhu. It's done. I did it. I've booked a car. I'm really doing this. Oh gosh. I'm doing it! Is it too lame if I want to high five you?"

"No, not at all." He raises his palm. "Shoot away."

I slam my hand into his. "I have to tell Amelia so she can get her maid-of-honor-plan-B rolling."

"All passengers. Flight UA 730, with destination San Francisco, is beginning boarding at gate B 25. We're going to start boarding families with small kids and passengers with special needs. Then, we're going to board first and business class passengers. And finally, all other passengers…"

"That's your flight they just announced."

"It's my flight. I'm going." I fumble with my bag and carry-on luggage and almost fall from the stool. "How much do I owe you?"

"It's on the house."

"Everything?"

"Yeah. You go tell your man you love him. Go catch your love connection."

"Thank you. Thank you so much." I hurry toward the gate.

"Hey," the bartender calls after me. "Let me know how it goes! I'm on Facebook."

"What's your name?" I shout back without stopping.

"I'm Mark Cooper. And you?"

"Gemma Dawson."

Acknowledgments

Thank you to all my readers. Without your constant support, I wouldn't keep pushing through the blank pages.

Thank you to my editors and proofreaders, Michelle Proulx, Helen Baggott, Emily Ladouceur, Hayley Stone, and Jennifer Harris for making my writing the best it could be.

And lastly, thank you to my family and friends for your constant encouragement.

Cover and Interior Image Credit: Created by Freepik

www.ingramcontent.com/pod-product-compliance
Lightning Source LLC
Chambersburg PA
CBHW022008300726
48970CB00003B/800